DALIVIA PLAUT

PRESENTS

MIDNIGHT WORLD
THE STORY

DARK PLOT
PUBLISHING

• • •

First Edition, October 2018 - November 2020
Story by Dalivia Plaut
Written by Dalivia Plaut
Edited by Ireland Lelisio

ISBN: 978-1-7344831-3-0
Plaut, Dalivia, 1983—
Midnight World: The Story
I. Title. Fiction. Dark Fantasy/Horror

ISBN: 978-1-7344831-3-0 pbk.

Cover Design by Low Key
Book Design by Dalivia Plaut

Cover photographs by hiphoto40 (istockphoto.com) / Geerati (istockphoto.com) / adogslifephoto (istockphoto.com) / joegolby (istockphoto.com) / weareadventurers (istockphoto.com) / InvisibleNature (istockphoto.com) / DenisTangneyJr (istockphoto.com) / BenAkiba (istockphoto.com) / joebelanger (istockphoto.com) / LaylaBird (istockphoto.com) / AndreyPopov (istockphoto.com) / AMR Image (istockphoto.com) / Yuri_Arcurs (istockphoto.com) / NejroN (istockphoto.com) / chainatp (istockphoto.com) / jacoblund (istockphoto.com) / LightFieldStudios (istockphoto.com) / gremlin (istockphoto.com) / maxiporik (istockphoto.com) / Ljupco (istockphoto.com) / WaffOzzy (istockphoto.com) / Hiraman (istockphoto.com) / brainmaster (istockphoto.com) / Grandfailure (istockphoto.com)

A very special thanks to the artists and photographers listed above!

Published by Dark Plot Publishing

• • •

_CONTENTS

MIDNIGHT WORLD
THE STORY

SYMPATHY FOR THE
MONSTER

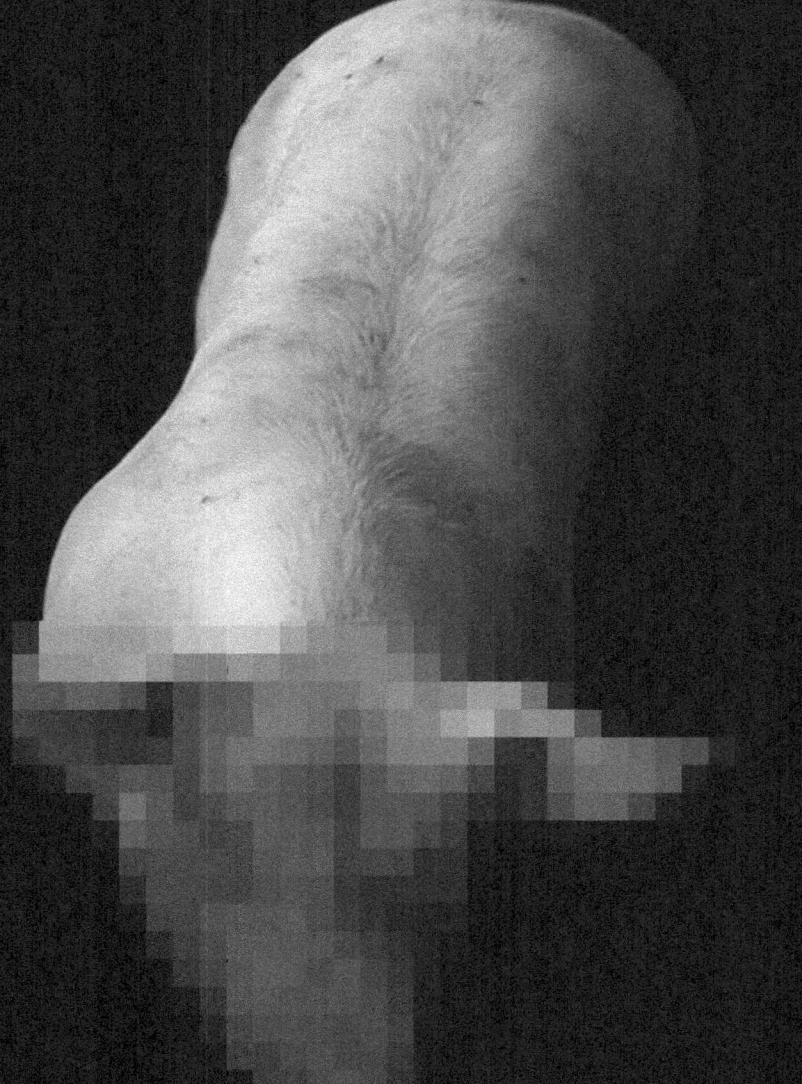

ARE *we so different from them?*

The thought consumed Kid as he stared at the two black widow spiders tangled up in a messy web inside a dark crevice behind the anchored shutter next to the windowsill.

Intrigued by the violent nature of their species, Kid leaned closer to the shutter for a better look. The larger spider—or what Kid discovered, after an extensive research on his tablet device, was a highly venomous female spider that had recently mated with a smaller male spider—started to overpower and dominate the smaller one, forcing it into submission.

For days the larger black widow had been hanging outside his window, spinning its thick durable web that could withstand the brutal autumn winds that slipped past the corners of the shutter.

Every night Kid would poke his head from the window and shine a flashlight on the elusive spider, making sure it was still there. It was. At times he'd tap on the shutter and talk to the spider whenever Runt was too exhausted to play. Of course, the black widow never responded. But the spider did something that nobody on the farm would ever do with Kid—at least no human—it listened.

The other spider's legs twitched before it finally stopped moving.

Kid wasn't sure whether or not the spider was dead when the other larger one started to consume it. He knew that for any spider—either male or female—to hang around in one spot all the time probably had more disadvantages than it did advantages. But then again, he retraced his thoughts back to the female spider and the information he read on his tablet device.

What if she spun her web in order to lure in the other spider?

Kid's attention was drawn to both Unk and The Irishman, who were escorting one of the pigs, a butcher hog, a two hundred pounder, from the barn to the shed. He spotted what looked like a pistol dangling in Unk's left hand.

Dread came over Kid.

He leaned back inside his bedroom and turned toward the closet behind him.

He knew exactly what day it was.

ON these days, the Day of the Slaughter, Kid never left the house.

Kid cracked the window and carefully listened. He didn't hear a sound, not a single squeal from Alberto. They'd normally let out a grating squeal, which was much higher in pitch than any normal one, a last-second utterance of both fear and imminent death. All Kid heard was the sound of a soft *tha-thump* from the safety of his bedroom. Then, moments later, he watched the two lanky shadows of men pacing back and forth inside the grayness of the shed, diligently working with glistening objects gripped in their hands. He never saw Alberto get the bolt to the brain. All he saw of Alberto was a trail of blood slithering from the doorway of the shed. Kid watched the blood run like a red teardrop from a small ramp and drip onto the dirt pathway. The most he observed was the aftermath of a kill, The Irishman hosing away puddles of blood, as well as random red streaks from the floor inside the shed. Then, he'd see whatever was left of the recent kill hoisted upside down, its entire body precisely split in two halves, the hair of its skin scolded away, giving off a slick and remarkably glowing appearance. Unless it was disease-ridden, every part of it never went to waste—even the ears; they, too, were used for consummation. By that final stage of the whole process, it was, as Unk stated to Miranda, "a means of income."

Kid didn't know why—maybe it was a culmination of things or maybe it was the curiosity of a young mind—but Kid wanted a better look.

As Kid stepped outside the house, it was deathly quiet on the farm. Normally he could hear the herd from the inside of the barn or one of the several sties outside, talking among themselves in their own peculiar way, farting or snorting or even squealing, nonetheless, communicating. Kid compared the pigs to dogs, and how they, too, were incredibly sociable animals.

After Alberto's death, they were silent, almost reverent.

Kid made his way to the red shed.

Each step felt long and slow.

Somehow, time slowed.

As he made it to the shed, Unk stepped outside with a red-stained towel in his hand.

The expression on Unk's face was one of great surprise.

"Kid?" said Unk, as he wiped the blood from his hands. "What you doin' out here? You know what day it is."

Quietly, Kid shrugged.

"I know," he mumbled. Then, he said more clearly, "I just was tired of being inside, that's all."

"You okay?"

"Yeah," Kid said and nodded at the barn. "What's wrong with the herd?"

"What you mean?"

"They're quiet."

"Yeah, well," Unk sighed, "they usually is on days like today."

"They're sad," Kid said over the strange silence.

"They don't have feelings, Kid."

"But they do."

Unk turned toward the shed and yelled out at The Irishman who was holding a bloody hacksaw in his hand, "Hey, Paddy, give me a minute, will you?"

The Irishman, who was a short fellow who made Unk look like a mythological giant, didn't respond as quickly as Unk wanted.

Unk once more: "McKellar?"

Finally, The Irishman responded with a wave of his hand.

Unk pointed at the barn and told Kid to follow.

Kid followed.

The tension between the two was awkward; Kid remained, like the pigs, reverent in the recent passing of Alberto while Unk fished around inside his head for something to say to Kid.

"So," Unk started, "where's your little iThingy," Unk said, referring to Kid's tablet device. "I don't see you on it that much anymore."

Kid followed with a shrug, as if it was starting to become an involuntary gesture on the farm.

"I dunno," he said shortly. "I guess I'm not interested in it anymore."

"Well, good," Unk snapped, "those damn things will rot your brain."

"It's not like that," Kid said defensively. "I just, I dunno. I miss home that's all."

Unk stopped walking.

Then, Kid stopped.

"Don't be talking like that, Kid," he said. "You just miss your mamma, don't you?"

"Yeah."

"Your momma's a strong woman, probably the strongest woman I've had the privilege of knowing, but you know she can't raise you on her own, at least not in her current condition. And don't be thinking it has anything to do with you 'cuz it don't. What your momma is going through is her own doing, you hear? She has her demons, Kid, and right now, she's at war with them."

"But demons don't exist."

"Well sure they do, Kid," Unk chirped. "They exist like you and me. You may not be able to see 'em just yet, but they're there, Kid."

"When will I be able to see them?" asked Kid.

"Well," Unk said, "hopefully, you won't."

They approached the barn.

Unk held the door open for Kid. They stepped inside where all the pigs were waiting.

"How about the pigs?" asked Kid. "Do they have demons?"

"No, Kid," he said. "They don't have anything—"

"—But they have each other."

Unk laughed.

"I swear, Kid, you something else."

They walked through the barn, occasionally stopping next to the rails which surrounding the pigs.

Kid posed an unusual question, which caught Unk by surprise: "If we didn't kill the pigs, do you think they'd evolve too?"

"Evolve?"

"Yeah, like us," said Kid. "Humans evolved."

"You talking about evolution?"

"Yeah, you know, like us and the monkeys."

"Kid, you know I won't tolerate that blaspheme in my household," Unk said, his voice louder. "We're here 'cuz the God Almighty put us here—"

"—But according to science, *all* humans evolved from monkeys."

A grin broke free, stretching across Unk's glistening face.

"So, is that what these fools teaching you in school these days?"

"The scientists people even have one of them skeletons from way back when it began to walk upright. Actual physical evidence, Unk—"

"—How you know?"

All seriousness washed over Unk. He glared at Kid.

"I've seen one."

"Where? On that iThingy?"

"Yeah."

Unk leaned in close to Kid.

"If you can't touch it with your own two hands, then it ain't real, you hear?" He stood up and pointed at the herd before him. "You see that, Kid. That's real."

The words suddenly came to Kid, even came so close to reaching his lips, yet they dangled on the tip of his tongue.

What about God?

He thought about those words. He thought about this god-figure whom Unk always talked about whenever he felt His presence. Most importantly, he thought about the backlash in speaking those words, let alone even thinking them.

Unk towered over Kid and pointed his sharp, twisted finger at one of the pigs standing against the railing. "Go on," he urged Kid. "Touch it."

Kid was hesitant, but eventually he touched the backside of the pig.

"You feel that? That's real. Somebody put them here for us. And you know who did?" Unk didn't give Kid a chance to answer. "It was God. He's the One and the Only who put these creatures here on earth for us to survive."

"But, Unk, all I'm saying is *what if* it's true—"

"—Kid, don't you dare start with me."

"But I'm being for real, Unk," said Kid. "Think about it: pigs walking upright. That'd be so cool! What if they learned to talk? That'd be even cooler!"

"Kid, I tell you what," Unk said, shaking his head in amusement, "you're just like your momma, always thinking about wild stuff. But don't look at it as a bad thing; in fact, Kid, don't you ever lose that imagination of yours. You hold onto it as long as you can 'cuz one day it might vanish just like that and you might never get it back. Who knows? That imagination of yours might make you famous one day."

"Famous?" Kid puckered his face. "I don't wanna be famous."

"You don't want to live in a big house with lots of money one day?"

"Not really."

"You could have a house all to yourself. That doesn't sound interesting?"

Once more, Kid shrugged.

"Lemme ask you something, Kid. You like it here?"

"It's a'ight, I guess."

"You know when I was your age, my old man and I didn't get along too well. I admit there were times when I hated him. *But*, Kid, I respected him and what he did for a living. When he died, he handed this place down to me. I didn't own a iWhatever—"

"—My tablet," Kid said.

"I didn't have the opportunity to lose myself in technology. For me, Kid, this is all I really know. It's all I have, you hear?"

"I know."

"No," he said, his tone sharper. "I don't think you do, Kid."

Kid kneeled down and started petting one of the piglets.

Unk grabbed Kid's wrist and removed his hand from the pig.

Kid stood.

The abrupt movement frightened the piglet, causing a strange domino effect among the other pigs.

He said over him, "Miranda's been telling me she thinks you've been wetting the bed."

"What?" Kid blurted out over the squeals. "No!"

Unk backed Kid away from the pen.

"There's no shame in admitting it, Kid."

"But I didn't wet my bed," whined Kid. "I'm too old for that."

"Then, who did?"

"I mean," Kid backtracked, "I might've spelt milk or something."

"I'm not buying it."

"But it's the truth."

"The truth?"

"Yeah."

Kid struggled to look Unk in the eyes.

Unk sighed.

"So who's your Boogeyman?"

"Boogeyman? I don't have no Boogeyman."

"Don't lie, Kid," Unk said.

"I'm not."

"Every kid your age has one, Kid," he said. "I did."

"You did?"

"Sure did," Unk said. "I reckon, for me, it was clowns. My daddy once took me to the circus when I was around your age, maybe a bit younger. I remember being scared half to death by them clowns jumping all around, doing tricks, with their smiling faces and painted white faces. Ain't nobody normal be smiling that big. I remember I couldn't stop thinking about those faces, like they was etched into my brain. For weeks, I dreamt about them ghostly white faces with dark sinister eyes. I imagined them creepy clowns lurking in my closet, sneaking into my bedroom, stalking the dark hallways at night. Then, one night, you know what I did?"

"What?" asked Kid.

"I killed them."

"You killed them?"

"In my dreams, I did," Unk clarified. "They ain't haunt me since."

"I ain't afraid of clowns."

"Then, tell me, Kid, what you afraid of?" asked Unk.

Kid paused and thought about the question. He didn't think about clowns or giant arachnids lurking through the darkest corners of night. All he could think about was Miranda and how she, like them clowns Unk spoke of, had been sneaking into his bedroom to strip the sheets bare from his bed and washing them without his permission.

Would she ever find Runt?

What if, Kid thought, *she looked in my closet?*

As before, Kid shrugged his shoulders and did what he usually did whenever Unk had him under interrogation. He deflected. "I dunno," mumbled Kid. "I ain't afraid of anything."

"Is that so?" Unk asked.

Kid turned his shoulder and looked Unk in his murky eyes.

"Yeah," he said. "I guess so."

"I tell you what, Kid," Unk said as he picked up a candy wrapper sticking out of the hay, "I given you your space. I've respected your space, hadn't I?"

Kid bobbed his head.

"Guess so."

"Well, I think you're getting old enough to start helping out around the farm. You think you're up to it?"

Kid faced Unk.

"Help out like what?"

"Like cleaning the barn, maintaining the barn, feeding the herd," Unk listed.

"I can do that," Kid said cheerfully.

Unk stepped closer and kneeled down until he was face-to-face with Kid.

"If you're gonna help out," Unk said, "there's one rule and one rule only and every person who works here at the farm must abide by it."

Kid asked, "What's that?"

"Don't get close to 'em," said Unk as he nodded at the herd.

"Well, I can do that," Kid said, as he took another step back.

"No, Kid," Unk corrected. "Don't get close to them—emotionally. You best keep your feelings at the same door you come in. And don't you look at them as pets 'cuz they ain't."

Kid didn't respond to Unk's grim remark.

"André, am I making myself clear?" asked Unk.

He waited for Kid to make any type of response.

Eventually, Kid sold Unk a nod.

But Unk wasn't buying it.

"Kid," Unk said and grabbed Kid's chin, "we gonna have a problem?"

"No, sir," Kid said, clearing his throat. "I—I understand."

Unk stood up.

"Good," he said, still not entirely convinced with Kid's response. "I'm glad we have an understanding, Kid." He turned to a massive door at the far end of the barn. "There's somebody I'd like you to meet."

Unk walked Kid over to a dimly lit area. He opened a wide sliding door, revealing yet another pen separate from the other one.

"I thought I wasn't allowed to go in here?"

"You ain't," Unk said. "But if you're going to be working around here you need to know about Boris."

"Boris?"

"That's right," Unk said as he guided Kid into the dark, dusty room. "I don't have any names for the others. You can think of them as Boris's minions. Boris is the leader. And whatever Boris does, they usually follow."

Kid waved his hand in front of his nose.

"He don't smell like the others," said Kid.

"That's 'cuz Boris ain't like the others."

"What is he?" asked Kid.

"He's a monster," said Unk.

Unk walked Kid to a more secure pen where a shadowy figure awaited. Kid saw a pair of eyes glowing in the darkness. Then heard a low guttural noise, like a cross between a wet fart and a belch coming from the smelly darkness. The rickety boards surrounding the pen trembled as Kid stared at the two glossy eyes lift through the dark haze. Other pairs of eyes manifested inside the darkness, smaller in size but equally as terrifying.

Boris finally stepped forward into the dim light, revealing his scarred face. He had tusks nearly the size of Kid's arms. One of the tusks had been chipped during a recent skirmish, part of the tooth broken off, leaving one side of it serrated like a saw blade, making it twice as easy to slice through the toughest hide. Ropes of drool dangled from his fleshy swollen lips and as the monster took another step forward into the light, the drool swayed from side to side like viscous pendulums.

"Meet Boris and The Minions," Unk said, pointing at the boars.

"Sounds like the name of a rock band."

Unk laughed.

"Boris here is a reminder of what we're dealing with."

"Why you keep them separated from the others?" asked Kid.

"If I set Boris loose with the other hogs, there'd be absolutely nothing left of the other hogs."

Curious, Kid asked, "Why would he kill others like him?"

"Why does a man decide to become a politician?" Unk asked Kid.

Kid didn't answer.

"Power," Unk snapped. "Control. Eventually, it all leads to corruption, Kid. And Boris here, he's a master of corruption. A true artist, Boris is." Unk waved Kid in closer. "They ain't our friends, Kid. These here animals were put on this very earth for one reason, Kid, and one reason only. For us," Unk said. "Without them, there'd be no us. They're what keep us alive, you hear?" Kid didn't move his attention away from Boris, even though the sight of Boris sent chills through his body. "As for us, the workers on this farm, the town relies on us to make sure they're fed properly. That's our obligation. That's 'us' doing our part in sustaining human life."

"If animals were put on earth just for their meat, then why don't we eat dogs or cats? I mean, is their meat different from a pig's?"

"I'm sure it is, Kid," Unk said. "They eat dogs or cats in other countries."

"How you know?"

"I just do."

"Then, why don't people eat dogs or cats in this country?"

"People, especially groups of people, have a way of choosing what's wrong and what's right. When it comes down to it and there was no more pigs or cows or chickens or even fish left on this earth, who do you think people would turn to next?"

Again, Kid didn't answer. In a way, he didn't want to know the answer.

"My point exactly." Unk tilted his head as if he was tilting the very thought in his mind. "Then you got another group of people, people like that uppity white bitch we ran into the other day—"

"—Ms. Meghan?"

"Think about Kid," Unk said. "You think someone like that, someone who's living high off the hog, is going to strut her honky ass down here, roll around in the mud with us, and get those silky smooth hands of hers dirty?"

Kid stepped closer to the pen.

In return, Boris let out a sudden snort, the burst of air hitting the ground below and sending a cloud of dust through a ray of sunlight beaming from above.

"You understand the point I'm trying to make, Kid?"

Kid turned to Unk.

"Yes, sir," he said. "I think so."

As Kid turned back around, Boris was standing even closer to Kid. A sudden fear gripped Kid, draining the dark color from his face. His eyes, like his already gaping mouth, widened. Face went long, expression slack.

Kid found himself gradually taking a step away from the pen.

The other boars stepped forward into the light and stood behind Boris. Boris lowered his head, his sharp eyes focusing on Kid.

Unk placed his hand on Kid's shoulder, startling Kid.

"Don't you dare underestimate them," said Unk. "They'll tear you to shreds the second you drop your guard. To them, Kid, you look like food."

The sight of Boris standing so close to Kid spread fear throughout his entire body. Kid imagined if this was what it felt like when Runt first laid eyes on him. Yet, as Kid stood face-to-face with the boar that Unk called the monster, Kid couldn't take his eyes off Boris. The two locked eyes. In a way, he felt hypnotized by the large boar.

⏱

WITH Boris still on his mind, Kid went back to his bedroom. He walked straight to his closet and opened the door. To the right of the closet was a litter box with a couple of turds, which were coated with kitty litter.

"Runt," Kid said, "you in here?"

Kid heard a *rustling* of clothes.

On the other side of the closet, a pile of old clothes moved.

The head of a piglet "Runt" suddenly emerged from the clothes. It was much smaller than the other piglets in the herd, hence why Kid decided to brand it with the name, Runt. It was a white pig, its hair white as well, with black spots scattered over its body. It had a particular black spot around its left eye, which made it stand out among the herd.

Kid pulled Runt from the clothes and held the piglet in his arms.

He couldn't stop thinking about Boris, what Unk said about treating pigs as if they were pets, but mainly, he couldn't stop thinking about how wrong Unk was.

Kid petted the top of Runt's head.

Runt gazed up at Kid, its soft eyes attached to Kid's. It let out a sound close to a purr.

"I'm not going to let anything happen to you, Runt," Kid said. "I promise."

FOR the rest of the day, Kid holed up in his room and hung out with Runt.

They played all kinds of games together, apps, first-person shooters, even chess; and by the time they moved onto something else, the screen's surface on his tablet device was covered with white imprints of Runt's snout from where Runt had used its moist snout to tap on the touch screen. Together, they'd binge-watch a TV series. Whenever the piglet got hungry, he'd feed Runt milk through a baby bottle.

After supper, Kid sneaked Runt into his bookbag and carried the piglet to an open field on the other side of the woods where, together, they played catch; however, Runt never caught the ball. But he was a good kicker. Kid and Runt practically did everything together, and all of it was done in secrecy.

KID couldn't sleep.

He never did on the Day of the Slaughter.

Wrestling through the bed sheets, the images of gore plagued Kid's mind. In the red haze, he witnessed Unk hang a lifeless Alberto upside down on a rail, then he inserted a knife into Alberto's jugular vein. The blood poured from the pig and dripped into a bucket resting below. Once the pig was exsanguinated, it was then placed inside a pig scolder; the scolding hot water removed the hair from its body.

Then, from there, the gore came in hot flashes: the pig was first eviscerated, its bowels stripped from its body, then placed inside trays. Next to go was the pig's head. It was chopped off. Then, its body was cut in half.

Sweating profusely, Kid bolted upright from bed.

He rolled out of bed, walked to the window, and stared at the barn outside.

ONCE Runt was secured in the closet, Kid grabbed a coat and walked to the barn. He ignored the other pigs, as well as the piglets, and checked on Boris. He only made it a couple of steps into the dusty room before he heard Unk call out from behind, "What you think you're doing in here, Kid?"

Startled, Kid turned around.

At the entrance of the barn stood Unk with his arms folded across his chest.

"I—I was just—I wanted to see Boris."

"You have no business in there." Unk waved Kid close. "Come on. Back to bed."

With his head hung downward, Kid walked to Unk.

"You know you ain't supposed to be in here at night," Unk said. "What's a matter with you?"

"I couldn't sleep."

"Again?"

Kid quietly walked with Unk back to the house. Unk walked Kid to the table in the kitchen. He grabbed a pill from a bottle in the top cabinet, then poured Kid a glass of water from the sink's faucet. He held out both the pill and water in his hands and waited for Kid to grab them.

"What is it?" Kid asked hesitantly.

"It'll help you sleep," Unk said, holding out the glass of water as well as the blue mysterious pill. "There's absolutely no reason why a boy your age shouldn't be getting his rest. Now go on. Take it."

He grabbed the glass of water as well as the pill from Unk's hands. He didn't think twice about it. He popped the pill into his mouth and washed it down with a sip of water.

"That'll help you sleep," Unk said as he escorted Kid to the staircase. As Kid walked upstairs, Unk stopped him and said, "Sleep tight."

🕐

KID slept heavy.

By the time Kid surged from the blackness of his dreams, the sun was already high in the sky.

Feeling more energetic, Kid bounced from the bed and stretched his arms to the ceiling.

First, he checked on the black widow next to the windowsill.

The sturdy catacomb-like web with dozens of carcasses of dried flies and curled-up bugs was still tucked away in the cozy nook of the shutter, but the spider was gone.

Kid's attention was drawn to a commotion outside the house.

Below, Unk was marching toward the shed as if he was on a mission. In his hand he was holding a piglet—perhaps a suckling pig—by the legs. He didn't see any dark spots on the piglet; however, it was seldom for Unk to slaughter suckling pigs for their tender meat.

The piglet was squirming all around, kicking its front legs.

Kid should've been relieved, knowing the piglet wasn't Runt.

But he wasn't.

Glum shrouded Kid.

All of a sudden, Kid thought about last night. A distant image surfaced in his mind, one of Unk studying Kid trudge back to his bedroom as he stood in the dark shadows at the base of the staircase. For a moment, Kid wondered whether or not it was a dream. He recalled rolling out of bed in the dead of night to check on Boris. He never made it to Boris nor did he see Boris, only the thought of the boar which he held inside his mind ever since he saw Boris. Then, in the blackness of night, he saw the shifting eyes of the great monster.

12

Enraged, Kid rushed to the closet and swung open the doors but found Runt nowhere around. He grabbed clothes and newspapers and started throwing them back into the room. He checked underneath his bed but Runt wasn't there either.

AFTER combing his entire bedroom for Runt but coming up empty, Kid ran past Miranda, who appeared concerned by Kid's frantic state. She asked if everything was all right, but Kid ignored her and ran outside where Unk was carrying yet another piglet to the red shed.

"There he is," Unk said, as he spotted Kid in the corner of his eye, "you sleep well—"

"—What you doing?" asked Kid.

Unk furrowed his brow in confusion.

"My job, Kid," he said. "What does it look like I'm doing?"

"They're just piglets," said Kid.

"What's your point, Kid?" Unk said shortly.

"Can't you just kill Boris?"

Unk laughed as he handed off the piglet to the smiling Irishman whose apron was covered in random smears of blood. Kid peeked inside and spotted a mound of piglets, dead, at least thirty of them, all stacked in a dark corner of the shed as if they were about to be bulldozed into a massive grave.

Kid frantically scanned the pile for black spots but didn't see any among the other dead piglets. Unk nodded toward the barn. "I'm actually glad you're up. There's something I need to show you."

Unk walked Kid over to the barn.

Kid heard a thumping sound followed by a squeal behind him. He turned his shoulder and saw The Irishman whacking the piglet's head against the side of the cutting table. He flung the piglet on the ground where the piglet started convulsing, all four of its legs kicking as if it was trying to flee from the inevitable death that awaited it. The images of The Irishman slowly killing the piglet without displaying an iota of remorse enraged Kid to the point where he was tempted to snap at Unk and his willingness to stand by and let a massacre happen. For some reason, he thought about the spider consuming the other spider outside his window.

The walk wasn't that far, only a good fifty yards or so, but to Kid, it felt as if he was walking to the ultimate doom.

Time slowed.

His legs started to buckle. He could feel each step getting harder and harder. Muscles tightened.

"Where you taking me?" Kid asked, his voice, like his body, trembling.

"Did you not listen to a word I told you yesterday?" asked Unk. "I gave you a chance, Kid. Didn't I?"

They arrived at the barn. Kid could hear all of the *squealing* inside with that one particular squeal being the most prominent among the other squeals, the death squeal. Unk walked Kid into the barn. Kid frantically searched for Runt. He saw Runt inside a pen all by himself. There were many other piglets in a pen next to Runt and they, too, appeared mortified by the sudden commotion.

Kid ran to Runt.

Unk grabbed Kid by the arm and yanked him close.

"Not so fast, Kid," he said as he grabbed a knife from the table. "This is for your own good, André." Unk dragged Kid toward the pen. "If there is one thing you never—I mean, *never*—do, Kid, you never mess with another man's livelihood, you got that?"

"Don't hurt him," Kid whined. "Please. . . "

"What did I tell you, Kid?" Unk said, jerking Kid around. "These ain't pets! These things ain't to be played with, you hear! They're what puts food on the table! Do you understand me, Kid?"

Unk opened the pen and held the knife with an open palm in front of Kid.

"Go on," Unk urged, "kill it or I will. . . "

"I ain't gonna kill it," Kid cried. "Runt's the only thing I got here."

"I don't care," Unk said. "You went behind my back and you disobeyed me. Did you think there wouldn't be consequences for you actions? If I let you off, then how do I know you ain't gonna go behind my back and do it again?"

"I won't! Trust me!"

"No, Kid," said Unk. "That trust was broken the second you defied me."

"But it's just one pig, Unk," Kid begged. "I'll pay you for it!"

"This ain't about money, Kid. Don't you get it? You need to learn a lesson."

"It'll never happen again," Kid begged. He made his body go limp and fell to the ground. "Please, Unk! Don't make me do it. Please. . . "

"You ain't gonna do it?" Unk asked, as he waved the knife in front of Kid.

Kid shook his head.

"Fine," Unk said and walked into the pen.

Runt tried to flee, but Unk cornered Runt and snatched the piglet by the legs.

Kid yelled, "Don't!"

As Unk raised Runt in the air, Kid dropped his head and cried.

"I want you watch, boy!"

Kid didn't, wouldn't. He'd never watch. Kid knew that, if he did, then he'd never forget. He'd carry the image to his grave.

Unk screamed, "I said 'WATCH!'"

As soon as Kid barely raised his head upward, Unk suddenly drove the knife into Runt's chest.

Kid turned away, crying.

"No," he bawled into his hands.

All of a sudden, the rage was back. Kid balled his hands into fists; his body started to shake. With his teeth bared, Kid charged at Unk. But Unk was a rather sturdy man who stood over six feet tall. He was slender but he had what the folks around town called the "country-strength" of a black man.

Unk threw Runt's body to the ground and grabbed Kid by the collar. He was punching at Unk's legs. Unk tossed the knife aside and put Kid into submission with a headlock.

14

"You gonna stop!" shouted Unk.

"I hate you!" Kid shouted back. "I hope you die!"

"Oh yeah?"

Angered, Unk dragged Kid to Boris's pen.

"Lemme go!"

"You hate me? I'm gonna show you what hate looks like, boy!"

Unk held Kid close to Boris's pen and started banging on the side of the pen.

"Wake up!" he shouted out.

All of a sudden, Kid heard a low grunt.

Out of the darkness Boris charged directly at Kid and rammed his tusks into the side of the fence.

Kid screamed with terror as he tried to duck for cover but Unk grabbed Kid by his wrists and forced Kid to watch the rage that drove Boris.

"You hate me?" said Unk. "Well, too bad 'cuz they hate you!" Boris continued to ram the fence. Kid tried to jerk his hands away to shield not only his body, but also his mind from the primordial hunger before him. He thought about God, Unk's god, and asked himself what kind of God would bring such a beast into this world. Somehow, Kid managed to slip one of his wrists free from Unk's slippery grip. "Look at them eyes of his! Look at 'em! He's ready to eat you up!" Unk reinforced his grip around Kid. "You think he cares about your black ass?"

Trembling, Kid covered his eyes with his hand as he pleaded for the comfort of his momma.

Unk jerked Kid's hand away from his face and forced Kid to watch Boris.

"Boy," Unk seethed, "I said 'Look!'"

He pinned Kid's arms behind his back and with his free hand, steadied Kid's head upright and told him once more to look.

Kid couldn't—wouldn't—as he tightly shut his eyes.

In the red darkness behind his eyelids, he heard the sounds of rage, savagery, and hunger. Kid couldn't understand why Boris was so desperate to rip his body to shreds. A part of Kid didn't want to understand. A part of Kid didn't care.

Unk squeezed his hand tighter around the top of Kid's throat, his fingers curling around Kid's jaw like a vise.

Kid resisted, squirmed, tried to break through the chapped, callused flesh that smothered him, but Unk overpowered him. Kid fought through his restraints, but Unk fought too and he was ten times stronger. Kid suddenly hurled his body into the air and attempted to kick Unk with the backside of his heels but Unk drove his boots into Kid's feet like coffin nails. Eventually, Kid tired himself out as Unk curled both his arms as well as his legs around Kid's body.

Weakened, Kid cracked open his eyes.

"You gonna stop? Huh?" asked Unk.

Kid didn't respond, too weak.

"I don't want to do this to you, Kid," said Unk. "I don't. But you must realize that these things ain't our friends." Boris ran back to the shadows, kicked the dirt below him with its hooves, and once more, charged at Kid. He battered the fence, loosening several boards. "When we're at our most vulnerable, Kid," Kid turned his head away but Unk straightened it for him, "Don't just look at it, Kid! Look through it! Do you see it? The evil inside it! *This* here is what your precious animals really look like." Boris backed off for a moment and as it paced around the halo of light inside the pen, he stared down Kid from the center of the pen while the other boars waited in the shadows outside the light. "They're animals, Kid, and the laws of nature forbid us to coexist with them."

"But Runt's different," Kid cried. "He's not like the others."

"He may be, for now, but sooner or later, this is what they turn into."

"No."

"Yes."

"I don't believe you," cried Kid, his body going limp. "You're wrong. . . "

Unk loosened his grip around Kid.

"If they're so evil, then why do you keep them separated? Why do you keep Boris back here, away from the others?"

"You can't be that naive, Kid," said Unk. "I thought your momma raise you better, but I was wrong."

Unk removed his grip from Kid, who, in return, fell to the ground. The very moment he found himself free from Unk, he stumbled to his feet in a blast of reserved energy and darted from the barn.

"Go on!" yelled Unk. "Run off to your video games! Reality can be a hard thing to deal with, Kid. The sooner you understand it, the better off you'll be!"

Kid ran and didn't look back.

Unk kept yelling at him from behind.

But all Kid heard was the beat of a pulse throbbing in his ears.

Miranda stepped in front of Kid as soon as he scurried from the barn.

She called out to him, but like before, all Kid could hear was his pulse.

His song.

The drumbeat of war.

🕐

EVENTUALLY, the beat could only carry Kid so far.

He was out of breath and struggling to stand once he reached the edge of the woods. He rested for a moment behind an oak tree while he caught his breath.

From a distance, Miranda was calling out to Kid.

The closer her voice grew, the more he thought about Runt.

The thought alone gave Kid the drive he so desperately needed to survive.

He gathered himself and told himself to stand.

He stood.

Then, when the moment came, he told himself to run.

He did exactly that.

He ran.

KID spent the rest of the day hanging out by a creek in the woods. He shed all the tears he had for Runt and when he thought he had no more tears left to cry, he reached deep down inside, throughout the gore and violence, and out came more. He thought about what he could've done differently—*if I hadn't been so scared*, Kid murmured to himself as he slammed the ball of his fist against the top of his thigh. *It's all my fault.* His thoughts were mostly consumed with his uncle, what he had done to Runt, how he drove a knife into Runt as if Runt was nothing more than a stuffed animal filled with wads of crumbled up dollar bills; and when his blade pierced Runt's carotid artery, the only blood that Unk saw pouring from the piglet's body wasn't blood at all but a glimmering flow of quarters, dimes, nickels, and pennies.

IT was getting dark outside when Kid returned to the farm.

From beside the porch, Kid watched Unk devouring a piece of meat over the kitchen sink as Miranda scraped away the leftover food on her plate into a trashcan, which would probably be used to help feed the herd. Kid thought it was ham maybe, but whatever it was, like most of the meat served around here, it came from a pig. Normally, Kid would just dismiss it and wouldn't think too much about it, as he pushed food around his plate as if playing hockey with his peas. The sight alone of Unk chewing through succulent meat sickened Kid to the point where he felt nauseous. Each bite his uncle took reminded him of a great white shark chomping through a hunk of rare chuck roast attached to a fisherman's hook.

In the cool darkness, Kid waited for Unk to leave the kitchen before he made his run to the front door. He crept inside, carefully shut the door behind him, and tiptoed his way upstairs. The hardwood floors creaked below him, forcing him to slow down his creep to a near cat's prowl.

As Kid finally reached the top of the landing, Miranda appeared at the bottom of the staircase.

Moments later, Kid heard the sound of footsteps thumping against the stairs. He could tell from the quickness of each step that it was Miranda. She had a distinct walk, opposed to his uncle, who was a man who moved slowly and often had others move for him. Miranda appeared at Kid's doorway with a plate of food in her hand. She tapped on the door, which was cracked open but not entirely shut, and glided into the bedroom.

"Leave me alone," Kid said, his face pressed against a pillow.

"I brought you some food, André."

"I ain't hungry," said Kid.

"You have to eat, André."

"I'm done eating."

"So, what? You going to starve to death? Is that it?"

"Yeah."

Miranda placed the plate of food on the nightstand. She couldn't help but notice the mud on Kid's feet and how he was getting mud all over the bed sheets that she recently washed. She turned to the plush toys on the ground, some of which were slick with slobber while others appeared as if they had been chewed through. She turned her attention back to Kid, his fragile state. Miranda leaned over the edge of the bed and touched the backside of Kid's shoulder. With his face buried in the pillow, Kid shrugged away her hand.

"Tomorrow is a new day, André," Miranda said, leaning away.

"I don't care."

"I'll talk to Cordell," she said. "Maybe we can work something out and find a new one for you."

"Runt can't be replaced," said Kid.

"Sure he can, André—"

"—Just leave me alone already."

"Okay," Miranda said and eased from the bedroom.

Once Miranda had gone back downstairs, he rolled over and found a plate of food, as well as a glass of milk, on the nightstand. On the plate were two slices of ham, a scoop of mashed potatoes and green beans, a corncob with a square of butter, and a wedge of homemade cornbread, which, unlike everything else, was still fairly warm. He could hear his empty stomach rumbling. His mouth even moistened from the sight of Miranda's homemade cornbread.

Kid reached over and grabbed the plate.

After taking two bites of cornbread, his eyes trailed downward onto a couple of strange-looking crumbs next to the green beans.

As he held a ball of cornbread in the side of his mouth like a mouthful of Big League Chew, he pressed the greasy tip of his index finger against the crumbs and held them up to his face for further inspection. The crumbs were the color blue. Kid thought about that particular color and only one thing came to his mind.

All of a sudden, Kid spat out the cornbread from his mouth!

He dashed into the bathroom where he thoroughly rinsed out his mouth with water. He noticed a couple of blue dots, no larger than the size of a speck of dirt, in his spit as well. He hadn't swallowed any of the cornbread. But he didn't take any chances.

IN the middle of night, Kid snuck out of the window.

Carefully, he tiptoed over the roof above the porch and used one of the pillars to climb down. He didn't know exactly how he was going to sneak back into the house. The climb was much tougher up than it was down. He told himself he'd cross that bridge when the time came.

Once Kid reached the ground, he pulled around his bookbag and checked the plate of food, which was sealed in clear clingwrap. The food on one side of the plate had shifted to the other side a bit but was still encased inside the clingwrap.

With his bookbag worn over his shoulder, Kid entered the barn. First, he decided to visit the herd. He placed the bookbag against a post and closed the door behind him. The herd woke from their sleep and they all circled around Kid. Kid dropped to his knees and strangely enough, the pigs dropped as well.

He spoke to them and strangely enough, they all listened to him. Kid told them how sorry he was for Runt and how he felt responsible for Runt's death.

"I came here to make a deal," Kid said to the herd. "I have a plan, but in order to make it work, I need your help." Kid looked at each one of the pigs. "Will you help me?" asked Kid.

All of a sudden, Kid saw something moving underneath the pigs' legs. One of the piglets emerged from the herd, walked up to Kid, and rubbed the side of its head against Kid's leg.

In a way, they knew exactly what Kid wanted from them.

Kid turned to his right, to the dark room at the other side of the barn. There, he witnessed Boris, as well as the other boars, standing at the front of the pen.

They, too, knew why Kid came to visit them.

KID carried the bookbag to Boris's pen.

Boris's snort was much more phlegmy and deeper than the other boars; and to Kid, it sounded as if Boris was warning him to keep his distance or else. Kid had no interest in knowing what the "or else" part involved. He hoped not to put himself in a dangerous position where he teetered along a tightrope of life and death. But, Kid thought, *what other choice do I have?* Good thing for Kid, Boris was a predictable monster.

Using the same slow, almost sneaky movements Kid practiced with the other pigs, he pulled out the plate of cold food from the bookbag and inched closer to the pen. Kid was well aware that Boris's kind didn't like quick or sudden movements. So, he was slow in everything he did. Slow and strategic. With the tips of his fingers, he removed the clingwrap from the plate. Boris salivated. He looked up at Kid with dog-like mannerisms. His snout twitched as he sniffed the aromas of Miranda's home cooked meal. Kid brought the plate to the pen and found himself a couple of feet away from Boris.

Once Kid found himself face-to-face with Boris, he set the plate underneath the door and used the handle end of a shovel to slide it into the pen.

Kid backed away while Boris pounced on the plate and fiendishly swallowed the food quicker than he could chew.

"There's more where that came from big boy," said Kid, as he watched Boris eat in queer fascination.

Boris licked the plate clean and once more, looked up at Kid. For a moment, Kid actually witnessed Boris's tiny stub of a tail wiggle.

"You like that, don't you?"

Boris replied with a snort.

Kid inched closer to the pen.

"So," he said to Boris, "let's talk."

THE next morning, Kid beat Unk to the cereal. By the time Unk was awake, Kid had already finished his breakfast and he was ready to help out on the farm. Half asleep, Unk was surprised by Kid's complete one-eighty. He didn't put too much stock into his nephew's abrupt change in attitude. Kid was still too old to be considered a boy, even though he'd often be addressed as "Boy," whenever he goofed up, spoke out of turn, or made a mess; yet, at the same time, he was too young to be a man who carried the weight of responsibility on his shoulders. Decades ago, Unk was young, too, and every now and then, when he sat alone on the porch and relished the dying lights of twilight, he'd reminisce on his days as a young man, the warmness in his blood, the inexhaustible appetite to emerge unscathed from a word, like *boy*, a word that held so little influence yet the power of its unseen bite stung twice as hard and lasted equally as long as the many years it was thrown at him. He witnessed that same look he once had in his eye in Kid's eye. They both sat at the table in silence, Unk sipping on coffee Miranda had made while Kid gulping down a glass of orange juice. For the first time ever since Kid arrived at the farm, Unk felt a warm sense of optimism. . . and fear of the unknown.

🕐

WORK began after breakfast.

Kid was tasked with a new role on the farm, which was to feed the herd. The task was normally designated to The Irishman. Instead, The Irishman trained Kid and showed him Pig Feeding 101. Kid caught on fast. The Irishman ghosted Kid for the majority of the morning. Then, once he felt comfortable enough to leave Kid alone to his task, he left the barn and tended to the shed.

Everything was running smoothly until Unk and The Irishman heard a shriek coming from the inside of the barn.

Both Unk and The Irishman rushed into the barn where they found Kid lying on the ground next to Boris's pen. Kid's arm was drenched in blood. He had two deep lacerations from where he said Boris bit him. Kid could hardly control himself for the pain was too great. Unk attempted to pick up Kid but Kid hollered out in great agony.

Unk specifically told The Irishman to watch over Kid while he grabbed the first aid kit from inside the house.

"No!" Kid cried out in desperation as he grabbed a hold of Unk with his good hand. "Don't leave me, Unk!"

Unk paused. He stood over Kid and they made eye contact. Unk witnessed a pain in Kid's eyes, a deep pain, not topical or one that belonged to the flesh, but a pain that ran much deeper than blood. Unk let out a noisy sigh. He turned to The Irishman. "Go grab Miranda," he said. "Tell her what happened—"

"—But Cordell," The Irishman started.

"Just do it," said Unk.

As The Irishman ran from the barn, Unk kneeled down and tended to Kid's injuries.

"I need to stop the bleeding," he said, as he pressed his hand against the lacerations.

Unk furrowed his brow from the shape of the cuts.

While Unk was inspecting the cuts, Kid's free hand slipped behind his back.

20

"These ain't bite marks," Unk said, a sudden coldness washing over his face.

Unk's eyes were drawn to a trail of blood. He left Kid and followed the trail of blood to the knife that rested in the hay.

"What's going on?" asked Unk, as he reached for the knife.

All of a sudden, Kid yanked on the end of a piece of string that was attached to the door of Boris's pen.

The door violently swung open, knocking Unk on his side.

Kid bounced to his feet, shoved Unk into the pen, and closed the door behind him.

Before Unk could open the door, Kid locked it shut and banged on the side of the pen. Boris, as well as the other boars, exited from the shadows. Unk rotated around and saw Boris closing in. He turned back around to Kid.

"Kid," he said, "André, open the door, you hear?"

Kid didn't budge. He stared Unk in the eyes. He watched the fear creep into them. Then, that old rage.

Unk bared his teeth. He suddenly reached his arm out between the openings of the fence and tried to grab hold of Kid.

Somehow, Kid must've known exactly how long Unk's reach was. Like before, Kid didn't budge, didn't even flinch.

As Unk hollered for help, the herd drowned out his voice, making it unrecognizable, a soft murmur among a symphony of harsh squeals.

Unk turned around once more and Boris was on top of him. As he grabbed Unk by the ankle and dragged his body deeper into the pen, Unk tried to fight off Boris and the other boars. But they had numbers. Kid grabbed the piece of string from the fence, as well as the knife from the ground and snuck them both in his pocket as The Irishman and Miranda rushed into the barn. Unk's screams turned wet. In a streak of sunlight beaming down from a hole in the roof, Kid witnessed Boris sink his tusk into Unk's side while another boar grabbed him by the jaw and tore it completely from his face.

The Irishman pushed Kid aside, Miranda not too far behind.

Once The Irishman saw the horror inside the pen, he quickly grabbed a pitchfork from the wall and climbed into the pen. He shooed away the other boars. He ended up stabbing one of them. The other boars backpedaled into the shadows. Boris, on the other hand, stood his ground. He even placed one of his hooves on Unk's chest as if he was claiming Unk as his prize.

The Irishman displayed dominance by screaming and banging the pitchfork against the ground.

Boris backed off but now had The Irishman in his crosshairs.

He was ready to claim yet another prize.

The Irishman managed to grab hold of Unk's foot while Boris paced around, kicking his hooves into the dirt as if he was about to make a deadly charge. The Irishman pulled Unk's lifeless body close enough to the fence for Miranda to get a hand around Unk. Kid stepped in to help as well.

As they pulled Unk from the pen, Boris stomped his hooves into the ground.

Considering the weapon in The Irishman's hand, he'd more than likely win in a fight with Boris.

21

But Boris had his minions and each one of them was creeping closer to The Irishman.

As Boris charged at The Irishman, The Irishman darted toward the fence and leaped over in the nick of time. Except for a couple of scraps and bruises, he was unharmed. Unk was a different story.

🕐

MIRANDA rode inside the back of the ambulance as Unk was being transported to the nearest hospital, Saving Grace, which was located roughly thirty minutes from the farm, but with the siren blaring, they made it in twenty-five. Kid rode inside The Irishman's truck with his head pressed against the window and his body hugging the side of the passenger door as if The Irishman was infected with a contagious disease. Kid asked The Irishman what he was going to do with Boris, if he was going to put him down. The Irishman said he was going to do what was necessary. From that point forward, neither one of them uttered a single word to each other.

🕐

IT was late in the night. Doctors spent hours working on Unk, stitching up his open wounds, realigning and setting bones. The doctors wanted to know exactly what happened to Unk, what kind of animal attacked him, what triggered the attack. Kid, being the only one who was at the scene when Unk was attacked, had told Miranda, who then relayed to the doctor, that Boris, the boar, kicked open the door and dragged Unk inside the pen where he was ganged up on by the other boars. And the reason why the door was shut when she arrived in the barn was that Kid feared for his own safety.

Once Unk was stable, the nurse allowed those who were closest to him to pay a visit, Miranda being Unk's first visitor, then, Kid, second. After spending a few minutes inside the hospital room, Miranda stepped into the hallway and told Kid that Unk wanted to see him. Kid clung to his fidgety momma, Shakira, who had driven three hours from the city to visit her brother. He didn't want to see his uncle, nor did he have anything to say to him. He had a general idea of the extent of Unk's injuries based on all the questions the doctor was asking Miranda. Kid remained close to his momma's hip. She held Kid by the shoulders, nearly made a scene in front of everybody, and urged him to grow up and visit his uncle out of respect.

So, he did.

When he entered the hospital room, an overwhelming sense of dread washed over him. He was tempted to turn around several times. He wanted to run out of the room, ride home with his momma, and never *ever* think about what happened in that barn. In a way, he wanted Unk to be dead.

But he wasn't.

Unk was alive.

Miranda told Kid that he was able to communicate to her through hand gestures as well as blinking, one blink being *yes*, two blinks being *no*.

But he couldn't speak. His jaw was no longer there.

Kid walked to the edge of the hospital bed. He couldn't recognize Unk, but he could recognize the severe pain he was in. Miranda stepped outside while Kid walked closer to Unk. He sat by his bedside and looked over his injuries. His left hand had been bitten off. His stub was dressed in white bandages. He had various cuts all over his face, neck, chest, as well as his legs. Kid showed no emotion as he stared at the torn flesh, the broken bones, the cuts. He didn't feel anything, didn't shed a tear, didn't want to make a scene for that matter. He just wanted to go home. Kid moved his attention away from the injuries. He struggled to look Unk in the eyes. A part of him was just too ashamed. He finally gathered enough courage to look Unk in his soft brown eyes. In return, Unk opened his right hand, his eyes flicked downward. Unk's hand opened wider, revealing his palm to Kid. Kid thought about a lot of things, sleeping in his own bed again, playing basketball and video games with his neighborhood friends. Mostly, Kid thought about the offer before him, his uncle's offer. Kid reached down below and sat his open hand inside Unk's hand. Kid didn't lift his hand away. A part of him just didn't want to. So, he squeezed, not too hard but not too soft, but strong enough for his uncle to feel his presence pressed up against his. Unk squeezed back, and Kid felt the subtle beat of life inside Unk. A gesture, like the squeeze of a hand, was an action he never understood for he only saw the adults do it from time to time whenever they shook hands. To Kid, the idea of one person grabbing hold of the hand of another person seemed so insignificant and, at times, so silly. Yet, at that moment in time, Kid realized for the first time what it truly meant.

CUT AND PASTE

JANE often thought about what it'd be like to be hunted.

Stalked.

Then, *finally*, killed.

Or, as Chandler coined, the "Big Sleep."

Jane carried around these macabre thoughts ever since she became a collector of all things creepy. Her fascination began with the more vulnerable bugs. Black ants. Carpenter ants. Sugar ants. Caterpillars. Earthworms. Silverfish. Various types of beetles, including the ladybird beetle—the "ladybug"—longhorn beetles, the American carrion beetle, oil beetles, acorn weevils, fireflies, click beetles, tiger beetles, rhinoceros beetles, stag beetles. Earwigs. Phasmids. Then, various types of crickets—Jane was dumbfounded by the many different types of crickets. She kept all of these tiny beautiful critters in a Mason jar that once belonged to her grandma before it was handed down to her mother. Eventually, as Jane's diverse collection grew, so too did her "bug hotel." Jane replaced that old Mason jar with a shoebox and as with the Mason jar, poked holes through the top of the lid. Parts of the shoebox eventually became heavily saturated from the dampness of soil and other loose vegetation inside and started to break down and eventually, collapse. Jane upgraded to an aquarium that she bought with a brick-sized Ziploc bag of change she earned by secretly pawning away clothes that she outgrew on eBay.

As Jane's hotel grew, so did her fascination with bugs. Jane sought out those that didn't want to be sought out. The creepiest of crawlers. Spiders. Centipedes. Even reptiles like baby garden snakes and lizards.

She was a collector of God's banished children.

After awhile, the grasshoppers, the ants, and the worms—the smaller, more vulnerable ones—were looked at as more of a food supply rather than a friend or fancy she'd say, a "guest" at Bug Inn. Jane thought it was an incredibly bizarre idea for a living thing to consume another living thing in order to survive.

What savagery, she thought.

One girl's bug collection was another one's dinner.

On the contrary, the savagery of survival made Jane even more curious to seek out more bugs, as if the savagery in itself was her own little gateway drug.

Either way, she collected these creatures as if they were a part of one big dysfunctional family inside a fish tank which was layered with sand, rocks, and grass, as well as spruced up shrubbery and tree branches that she gathered from the woods behind her cozy yet, often times, obscurely deceiving peach colored Victorian-style house. She resided in a predominantly white neighborhood where the only crimes committed were soft dialogue, subtle prodding, invasive moments, and occasionally, a late night egging and rolling by the royally privileged high schoolers or a sexually frustrated spouse privately scratching an seven year itch.

Jane was an only child. Both her parents had decent jobs, content, itch-free. Both had comfortable six-figure salaries with 401ks, health insurance, including dental, and a weird and wonderful daughter who found companionship with those who dwelled in the most unlikely, yet dirtiest of places.

Jane didn't have many human friends whom she could call her besties. But she had her bugs.

Eventually, Jane looked upon her vast collection of insects and reptiles on a much grander scale and changed the name of her hotel from Bug Inn to Jane Cutter's "Brave New World" because she didn't want to offend the reptile or arachnid community. She even handcrafted a marquee-style sign speckled with glitter and plastic emeralds. Hung it up above the fish tank for all her imaginary friends to see.

But nature started to run its wicked course.

Through Jane's rougher side of adolescence—or what she branded her "mutant years"—she graduated to the ever so elusive praying mantis, which she kept in a special jar and would only let it play with the others during dinnertime. That was when those dark thoughts took shape, the stalking, the killings. The praying mantis was, in a way, the "King" of all stalkers, a natural born hunter who put any cockroach to shame. Even though the mantis was related to the cockroach, it was anything but. Jane knew it as the bug's predator. Graceful yet deadly, unlike its ugly cousin. Blended into its surroundings as it stalked its prey. Most of the time its prey would ease right next to the praying mantis and not even realize it was about to become dinner until the predator was right on top of it.

Then, as Jane started to develop into a woman, her bugs got bigger and more deadly. Tarantulas. Scorpions. She'd go well out of her way to locate these tiny monsters.

By the time her junior year rolled around, Jane was spending most afternoons combing the deserts with a backpack full of jars, rather than studying. Jane wasn't the type of student who excelled in one particular subject. She was your average student who put in an average effort. Pre-calculus, world history, English literature: none of these subjects appealed to Jane.

Every now and then, she'd even skip second period to search for tarantulas at an old desolate quarry, which, over time, had eventually turned into a lake known as Quarry's Lake. But the kids called it "Devil's Throat." Over the years, Devil's Throat had become a go-to spot for kids to cool off the hot boredom of summer. However, after one of the kids from Jane's class died from hitting his head on a rock in the shallow end, Devil's Throat had become more of a safety hazard than a fun hangout spot, which meant the quarry attracted fewer humans and more animals.

Even the highly evolved kind. . .

Throughout most of Jane's senior year, Devil's Throat was Jane's own personal paradise. She had a world of creatures at her disposal.

The tarantula was one of her greatest discoveries. During the day, she'd keep it famished. Same with the scorpion. She'd place it a separated jar and have it facing the tarantula. Only at night would Jane put them in the same arena and let them spar in a battle royal to a bitter death.

Night was a cruel child which brought out its most strange mysteries.

On some mornings when the air in her bedroom felt slightly dense, her collection would be disturbed. Several bugs—sometimes, a lot of bugs—would be missing from the fish tank. Later, she'd find them throughout the house: cowering under the fridge, chilling on the kitchen countertop, or making a desperate flee to an open window. Other times, she'd listen for an inevitable scream from her mother.

"Spider!" she'd shriek from the downstairs.

Then, Jane would sweep in before her mother would splatter the spider's guts all over the floor with a broom.

Jane was left baffled as to how—and why—her bugs were escaping from her "Brave New World."

Determined to catch the miscreant red-handed, Jane decided to hide a camcorder in front of the fish tank before she went to bed.

When Jane woke the next morning, the fish tank had been tampered with, as predicted. She noticed some of them were dead. She rewound the footage on the camcorder. That was when she soon realized the bugs weren't escaping.

She was setting them free.

Back to the very world that she scorned.

Or, as the film showed, smashed with a rock.

Jane's mother took her daughter to the doctor where they ran extensive tests on her. But the doctors couldn't find anything wrong with Jane. After bouncing around from one specialist to another, Jane was diagnosed with a sleeping disorder. They gave it a name for it: *somnambulism*. But she knew it best as "sleepwalking."

A once diplomat of the insect world who waged wars or brought adversaries together in unity by constantly welcoming new members to her secret society of creepiness, Jane was no longer allowed to collect any insects or reptiles—parents' orders. Her "Brave New World" was no more. All of the insects that Jane kept inside the fish tank were liberated back to the woods—or as she hopelessly put it, exiled. The fish tank was left on the side of the road for the local garbage man to collect. One girl's world had become another man's trash.

By the time Jane reached her roaring twenties, she finally got a handle on her sleepwalking. The insect world started to fade like a fad. During her first couple of years at Western University, she'd often go on bug hunts between classes. But it wasn't the same. Jane met another friend, a human one, whom she could genuinely call a friend: Ruby, a brazen tattooed chain smoker from Wensburg, Virginia. She, too, could relate to Jane, not because they both had more love for the animal kingdom than the human race, but because she, too, was a victim of the harshness of scrutiny. The boys hated Jane because she was too much like *them* in certain aspects. The girls hated Jane because she was nothing like *them*.

"Them."

Two different sexes used in the same naming: them, *they*, you people.

But Jane wasn't the only person who called her relentless oppressors, as well as her abusers, by the same pronoun.

Ruby had an eating problem. Like all doctors, they gave it a name just like they had given Jane's sleeping disorder. Bulimia nervosa. Which kids often mistook for anorexia.

When Ruby was sixteen, the "popular years," as she called her peak of fame, she started to shed weight so fast that those who often ignored her in class started to pay attention. "Popular years," as in the worst years ever. But at that age, what was the difference?

By the end of the year, Ruby was a stick figure. She'd binge-eat in private, in the bathroom, in her car, at the park; then, she'd find a bathroom and purge it all away. She always kept a bag handy wherever she went out in public just in case there wasn't a bathroom in the vicinity. Ruby pulled this shady act for the entire year. She'd binge and purge. Purge and binge. The vicious cycle had drawn the kind of eyes that Ruby had feared. At the rate she was going, she was going to be dead by the age of twenty-five. Finally, Ruby got the help she so desperately needed and gradually put the weight back on.

By the age of seventeen, she was a brand new person. Ruby no longer cared about "them"; in fact, she wanted absolutely nothing to do with them—and whenever the topic of "them" came up, she'd often speak of *them* as if she was speaking of something less than human, less than a bug. Like something as primordial as evil itself. Like something that couldn't be seen with a trained eye, only sensed through human intuition.

Before Ruby enrolled at Western, she got herself a dog.

Jane wasn't into dogs, at least not enough to look at their kind as a friend because she always carried around this image of dogs being ushered down sidewalks by humans, but she fell in love with Gorgomite. He was a wild dog, free spirited, unleashable. Gorgomite was a Great Dane named after a ballsy sorcerer from one of Ruby's underground fantasy books and he was about the size of a small horse.

Gorgomite—or "Gorgo," for short—had unequivocally erased the image Jane once had of dogs: these small yappy battery operated things wearing cute tailored sweaters and colorful hair ribbons and scuttling around on leashes while scouting out a good piece of Bermuda or a lovely flowerbed to squat over to do their business and then afterwards, their owners picking up their smelly prize with one of those black poop bags and disposing it in the proper doggie waste bin as if ironically the roles had been somehow reversed and it was the humans who were loyal servants and the dogs were their pampered masters. That, of course, and sniffing or humping assholes *was all dogs were good for*, Jane once thought. However, Gorgo was neither small—obviously—or yappy or a nuisance; in fact, he was Ruby's most loyal companion. He was the love of her life.

Jane had her bugs.

Ruby had Gorgo.

Eventually, Jane stopped collecting bugs altogether, stopped looking for them throughout the slower parts of her day, stopped tending to them, stopped talking to them. She found a bond with a beast of a dog named after a fictitious character and developed an appreciation for its fellow canine pals.

After Jane graduated from Western, she spent the following year hopscotching from one shithole job to another. A part-time bartending job where the drinks were dirty and the men whom she served were even dirtier. A job as a waitress at a trendy restaurant in a newly gentrified area where ninety-nine percent of the clientele were either pretentious Silicon Valley wannabes, overeducated and underpaid hipsters, or shaggy-haired freeloaders; then the other one percent were manboys who still held a grudge against George Lucas.

If there was one thing Jane learned during her brief stint in the food industry, most of the guests were no different than the bugs she used to keep imprisoned in her jars, waiting to be feed.

All in all, the food industry wasn't for Jane.

She tried several other jobs. Retail jobs. Cashier. Sales associate. But they were no different than those food industry jobs. Catering to giant bugs.

Since Jane had a new appreciation for dogs, she started to walk dogs for other people. She'd take them to parks or open fields and let them frolic around as if they were in paradise.

Surprisingly, Jane earned enough cash from "walking dogs" to pay a month's rent, but it wasn't enough to pay the bills.

As the bills started to pile up, Jane stopped walking dogs. But she still loved them. And cats, too. She got into them after the whole Internet craze. Had two. Named them after the two characters in her favorite book, *Fight Club*. Tyler Durden was a Russian blue. Marla Singer, a sweet tortoiseshell. They, too, had fallen witness to Jane's mounting frustration with the workforce.

She had a major in political science, which was like accidentally dropping a hot french fry on her résumé and all that remained under college education was a smudge of grease forever stained into the paper. Since Jane's parents had paid for most of their daughter's college—Jane promising her parents to pay back her debt as soon as she found a decent job—Jane wasn't too concerned about the money. She was more concerned by all the time she had wasted. Time she could've spent finding a job. Time she could've spent finding her own unique voice without it being stifled by college mobs who chased after trends.

After weeks of searching for jobs related to her major, Jane simply gave up. She started to feel as if the last four years of her life was all for nothing, as if the four years weren't a part of a "growing up" phase. Instead, they were taken from her, stolen. All the money that her parents spent on her for college could've been loaned to her for an investment or a business venture or opportunity. Jane started to question whether the experience of something, like college, was worth the price.

Was it any different than trying to buy friends?

It wasn't until a couple of days after Jane returned home from visiting Ruby, who was visiting her parents for the weekend in Virginia before heading back to New York where she was doing a six-month long internship at a highly respected magazine, when she got the idea to work at an animal hospital. She was motivated by the horrid thought of moving back home with her parents. Jane could visualize herself sunken into the couch, hugged by it as if she only received hugs by her parent's criminally expensive furniture, then her body prematurely wilting like a recently bloomed flower after spring's last freeze, as she lost herself in reruns of *The Real Housewives of Atlanta* while her passive-aggressive parents, too timid to confront their own daughter whom they had spent their life's savings on for college, routinely shot her age-old glares from the other side of the living room; whereas on other days, which seemed longer and less bright, her mother would accompany her patent glare with stingy spoken criticism, yet not entirely directed, at her daughter. The remarks stayed with Jane well after they were spoken. Often times, she'd fall into a trapdoor of the worst scrutiny a young woman could ever endure whenever Jane didn't respond to her mother in a timely fashion, which, consequently, was met by disguised lingual assaults, such as "our daughter is so friendly, isn't she?" Jane's mother would sarcastically say these words to her husband as if their clueless yet fragile daughter was in another room pounding her head against the wall. Jane's mother would randomly spit out playful yet internally damaging lines such as, "you're never going to get married" or "it's no wonder you don't have a job," whenever the two had a trivial disagreement about a dinner arrangement or with very little disregard of her daughter's attempt at building confidence, speak for Jane whenever she was in the company of strangers or distant relatives, as if her daughter was a closemouthed mute who didn't possess what humans referred to as a tongue; these incredibly strategic yet manipulative remarks lived with Jane throughout the pauses of the day, constantly plaguing the rest of her day, ruining her day, destroying her day. Ever since Jane was a girl, she displayed, from the trials of ridicule, a natural, altruistic ability—one that Jane harvested at an early age from her grandma who had been shunned from the family as a Bohemian recluse who lived deep in the woods—to use whatever was spoken to her as a shield to protect her from the outside world. The last time Jane visited her parents, Jane was only half-there. Her body was present, but her mind was off somewhere else. For Jane, it was better this way. The sly remarks would only ricochet off her. In the past, though, it'd only take one *word*, one remark, to send Jane into an internal war of suffering, then the words taking shape into other mysterious forms, battering against the corners of her skull until she felt as if her mind had been reduced to atom particles. The words would *still* be there, though, even after her parents were gone. The words living inside her, lingering like a cool villain in the back of a dark, smoky lounge.

But her mother was running out of insults, and Jane knew every single one of them before they were flung her way.

The last thing Jane wanted to become was a cliché.

While Jane and Ruby were visiting Bush Gardens, Ruby was actually the one who made the suggestion of Jane working at an animal hospital. From there, the wheels started to turn. She found a vet not too far from her apartment. There was an opening for a veterinarian technician. Without even knowing what the job involved, Jane applied for the job. Easily got the job. Lived happily ever after.

End of story, right?

Wrong.

Jane spent just shy of a month as a veterinarian technician before the strange events started to happen. Jane didn't exactly know when it really began. But she knew things started to change for her after she heard the story about a Rottweiler not only killing a baby, but also attempting to eat a baby after the baby died from its injuries. Having spent time around dogs, Jane was well aware of the power of a canine, its bark often being louder than its bite but when provoked its bite could make its bark sound like a murmur underneath the average scream of any individual and would pale in comparison to a human's bite. That was the one thing Dog had over Man: its bite. Even the bugs Jane used to collect could pack a real punch. A tick spreading Lyme disease; a snake injecting lethal amounts of poison into a human body, making it extremely deadly if untreated; even mosquitoes carrying a range of diseases such as malaria or encephalitis. There had been cases of hairy scorpions killing humans. Jane read online about a baby boy dying from a hairy scorpion's poisonous sting in the middle of the night when he was sleeping. She also heard on the news about an elderly woman who got stung but didn't even know about until it was already too late. But a dog, a Rottweiler, not only killing a human being, but also eating one: for Jane, this was like uncovering another side of life. A darker side.

The macabre thoughts returned, slowly at first.

Scattered deeply in a lost dream.

Jane warded off these violent thoughts by experimenting with the one thing she had always wanted to do but never had the courage to do.

Dating.

Again, Ruby's idea.

"Start off small," she'd say. "Coffee. Drinks. Work your way up to 'Dinner and a Movie.' The ultimate test for a young bachelorette like Jane was the 'Day Date.' Go on dates that involve outdoor activities, like bike riding, hiking, even camping. Let him show you that he's a man who has blood pumping through his veins. If you can stand sharing each other's company when you're both as sober as monks, then you might just have a chance at being somebody's girlfriend."

Jane took Ruby's advice and played the field. She had never been on a date before. Never even had a drink with a person of the opposite sex. Growing up, Jane had never been comfortable around boys. Jane had never been comfortable around girls, either. Except for Ruby. Jane was "physically" attracted to Ruby. After Ruby's health crisis, she did a complete one-eighty and turned into what the boys called a "gym rat." Twice a year, she ran a 5K. She cut bread from her diet and only ate meat, veggies, and fruit. Never once indulged, not even a crumb of a cookie. She was a walking cliché of a full-time health nut. However, Ruby was clueless when it came to Jane's feelings toward her. Sometimes she'd often appear unclothed in Jane's mind. Jane and Ruby once shared an intimate kiss on the way home from a Pi Kappa Alpha party, which ended up getting busted by the campus security after one of the Pikes set a sacred tree on fire. That night, Jane and Ruby were both wasted from slurping body shots of bourbon and pounding down skunky keg beer. Ruby hardly remembered it the next morning—in fact, she spent the most active parts of the morning with her head buried in the toilet—while Jane, on the other hand, couldn't get it out of her head even if she tried. The kiss. *That kiss.* Their relationship was strictly platonic, no chaser, no regrets. That, they both understood, especially Ruby. After Western, Jane looked at their relationship, more or less, as a "fantasy friendship," as if there would soon come a day when all Jane had left of Ruby were fond yet distant memories, only touchable via mindscape. In a way, Jane always looked at what she and Ruby had as "too good to be true." Something only discovered in a timeless fairy tale patiently sitting on the back of a dusty shelf somewhere in some dusty library, waiting to be digested. Even when Jane was attending Western, she had a feeling in her gut that she and Ruby's relationship, like all beautiful things, wouldn't last. A part inside Jane—a darker part—wouldn't let it. The time being separated from Ruby eventually turned Ruby into a voice on the other end of her phone, nothing more than a voice to listen to whenever Jane was lonely or needed pointers. Jane wanted more from Ruby, more than her voice, but she knew the closest she'd ever have with Ruby was exactly that, just a sound.

The first date Jane went on was a disaster. Drinks with a guy named Jeffery Maiden—or "Just Jeff," as he introduced himself. She met him online through a dating app called MINGLE. The guy was a real jerk, Jane thought, had the wrong kind of arrogance that made his perfectly carved jaw and cheek structure look annoying, as if she was tempted to punch him in the face during his hour-long bragfest about his job in advertising. Throughout the entire night, he didn't ask Jane one question about herself; and whenever Jane did talk or strategically divert the conversation away from Just Jeff, he never followed up with interest. Instead, he went back to kneading his own ego with a cat-like satisfaction. He looked at her merely as an object with two holes for releasing himself—three, if Jane was into the kinkier recreations, but he'd never bring up the subject on a first date.

By the end of the night, he only got to first base with Jane after he "purposefully" fed her shots of Jägermeister. His goal for the night was to round first base and do an inside-the-park homerun, but Jane wasn't at all waving him to home plate. And that was all that remained of "Just Jeff," a self-absorbed man who hit a routine single up the middle but got way too cocky by squeezing that single into a double and getting thrown out at second base.

Jane's second date was equally as poor as the first; however, she was starting to master her curveball. The guy made a half-ass attempt at bunting: a small peck of a kiss on her lips. Jane turned her head at the last second and received a dry, thorny kiss on her cheek instead. To Jane, a dog could kiss better.

Some of these guys—and girls—hung around for a couple of days, shooting her text messages laced with selfies, insincere compliments, and innuendos of sex or copulation. One woman she met on Mingle talked about how much she wanted to adopt a kid. Even said Jane make the ideal partner. Jane had only spent a couple of hours with her at a local coffee shop and by the time she was done with her caramel macchiato, the woman was already talking about touchy subjects normal couples didn't even bring up until they moved in together or mutually committed to raising an animal by rescuing an old Golden Retriever named Waggles from the pound before they decided to raise a human life. Even the good guys, preppy or non-preppy, who acted decent enough to keep their minds from the gutter folded after a week; however, they couldn't hit Jane's wicked curve, which usually came barreling by with first, a cordial hug then followed by a swift "good night' as soon as her date was about to lean in for a kiss. Most of the dates on Mingle, Jane realized, turned out to be disguised booty calls or foreplay into much carnal activities cloaked with a phony interest as to what Jane was getting herself into that day, as if it was reverse psychology 101. These deviants certainly weren't going to "get inside" Jane anytime soon. She made sure of it—or at least, tried to.

Despite dozens of dud-dates that turned out being a bust, Jane ended up getting lucky a handful of times. The relationship only lasted for two weeks until the fire was put out, but it was Jane who did most of the extinguishing. Again, it was that darker side of her, a vengeful, ruthless darkness that had been living with her ever since high school, her "mutant years." Two weeks of putting up with Jane's resilient optimism was all it could endure before it killed any desire she felt about sharing a life with another individual. Several guys—and girls— had come along and showed prospects of being that person her fantasy-friend, Ruby, could *not* be. After two weeks, the light changed. All of a sudden, Jane started to see her prospects in a much darker, less attractive light. Like the Darkness wanted Jane all to itself and it was deceiving her by showing her what "these people" appeared like underneath poor lighting. She'd pick out a flaw on their face or in their personality or whatever, highlight and then exaggerate it to the fullest, so much that, after those two weeks, it was all she saw. Eventually, she gave up on the dating scene, dropped the whole online dating thing, dropped "seeing" other people in general, and just "got around." *But* there was only so much of "sleeping with strangers" she could condone until she wanted something more.

Something real and right.

But her dreams started to turn on her.

The thoughts became more vivid.

Red and deadly.

This time around, those curious thoughts had become a reality.

Later, Jane would go on to call him by the name, Mr. Moonlight, because his eyes looked like tiny moons, at times full and bright while other times, keen and sickle-esque, like a waxing crescent. She had once heard the name on the night of a rare lunar eclipse when both her drunken parents were singing the hazy lyrics to The Beatles song, *Mr. Moonlight*, on their fuzzy-sounding antique vinyl record player. Jane remembered stretching her seven-year-old body over the banister along the staircase and gawking at the tall, wavy shadows of her parents swaying back and forth like buoys over the glossy hardwood floor in the kitchen as they repeatedly howled that one name, "Mr. Moonlight," in the candlelight, occasionally laughing while doing so, as if they were performing some kind of ritual downstairs—*a sacrifice*, Jane would later consider, maybe even satanic—as she was strangled by the sweaty teeth of night. Cowered between her covers, she visualized the shadow of a disproportionate arm of her father striking down with a strange, twisted blade of some kind on a much smaller shadow strapped to the kitchen table. Followed by the stabbing motion was the deafening yelp of an animal. Then the Shiraz that her mother had been supposedly drinking spilled over the hardwood floor. But was it red wine that had been spilt? Or, Jane thought, was it something else?

Maybe that was where the name came from, a young girl running away with an imagination so rich and wild that would make other girls her age jealous.

Maybe she just liked the name when it rolled off her tongue.

Mr. Moonlight.

Jane never actually saw him, Mr. Moonlight, well enough to identify him to a sketch artist. For one, Jane had seen him only at night; and two, Jane didn't even know what race he was because he looked no darker than a silhouette.

A dark, faceless figure.

Watching her.

After the second time Jane saw him outside her apartment window, she called Ruby long distance and told her about the stalker. Ruby told Jane to call the cops. But the guy had committed no crime.

Another month passed.

Jane was starting to hit her snooze button more often.

Each and every day, her passion for animals started to diminish, like the bugs she once collected. Going to work everyday seemed as if it was becoming an unwanted choir, something to be put off, inevitably neglected. She even started to change the way she felt about her cats, Tyler and Marla, once thought of as two lifelong pals; but after awhile, they became these burdens as if she was taking care of two upset babies that forever remained upset babies, never at all cute and cuddly, just ugly and upset. Even the sounds of their meows started to have a piercing wail of a baby.

The thought that kept nagging at Jane: When would her violent thoughts turn to action?

Then, one day before work, it happened.

Jane was scrambling around her apartment, racing from the dryer to fetch her clothes and then back into the kitchen to grab a breakfast snack to go, when all of a sudden Tyler snuck up behind her and gently pawed at her ankle.

Not thinking, Jane reacted.

To Jane, it felt more like a shove than a kick, a way to keep Tyler in check by showing him who was boss. Tyler didn't see it that way at all.

Tyler's eyes swelled with blackness. His pointy ears folded over the sides of his head. Everything about Tyler folded, his body and soul, as if he was winding himself up to spring himself into an attack. Jane saw these defensive gestures and yet, she did it anyway. She "shoved" Tyler once more. Tyler let out a high-pitch hiss and scratched Jane across the shin, drawing blood.

Jane snapped from her red haze and ran to the bathroom, crying.

Soon after, Tyler poked his head into the bathroom. Jane welcomed Tyler; in return, he rubbed on her leg in the most deliberate act of forgiveness.

Jane couldn't apologize enough to Tyler. She didn't know what happened or even *how* it happened. She was beginning to feel as if these behaviors alone had come straight from the deleted scenes cut from another movie where she, the star of the movie, was no longer a relatable character.

Later that night, when Jane was driving home from work, a deer suddenly ran out in front of her car.

With no time to react—no time to even blink—the deer struck the side of her car. The side airbags deployed, forcing Jane to swerve the car off the side of the road. She managed to slam on the brakes before driving into a ditch. It was dark out, late. The accident happened on an empty two-lane road in the middle of the woods where the only life forms came from Jane's imagination. She switched on the caution lights and pushed open the door, which had a massive dent. She saw the blood on the door, a chunk of hair wedged between the hinges. She found the deer sprawled out on the side of the road. But it wasn't dead. She, Jane realized, was still alive. But barely.

With no car in sight, Jane looked around and realized that she only had two options: *Let the deer suffer to death and eventually, die alone out here on the road and hope that possibly someone will come along to "finish" off the deer or do the one thing that she most feared, put the deer out of her misery?*

Jane didn't think twice.

She chose option number two.

However, it was the way she killed the deer that disturbed her the most.

This wasn't a deleted scene, Jane soon realized once she made it back home and tossed her bloody shoes into the trashcan.

This was the moment in *her story* where everything changed.

After Jane had confessed as to what she had done, Ruby made a suggestion that Jane join a club or even go out more during the day, do anything to keep her mind away from what took place that night.

Jane decided to give love a second chance.

"No more hooking up," Jane told herself in the mirror. "Find someone who sees you for who you are."

Jane tried one of the easiest places on earth for human interaction. The bar. Literally, the placed was named, "The Bar;" however, the word *the* was replaced with the slang word 'Da. The bar read: 'Da Bar. Kind of the stereotype of a Chicagoan saying 'Da Bears. So, 'Da Bar. A sketchy lit joint, which was located not too far from her apartment. Everyday, Jane passed by the place on her way home from work. Every Saturday night, a local band played at 'Da Bar. However, 'Da Bar received most of its business on Thirsty Thursday nights and Sunday Funday afternoons, Thursday nights typically drawing the rowdy football crowd and Sunday afternoons pretty much drawing the same crowd, only younger. Jane decided to rid any stereotypes that she had about 'Da Bar's regulars and try Thursday night.

For the first twenty minutes or so, Jane wasted away the time hidden at the end of the bar while randomly looking over parts of her body as if she was giving herself a self-examination or making minor clothing adjustments or primping herself. Jane did all these tiny movements as if it was a nervous tick. At times, she acted as if she wanted to leap out of her own skin, like some junkie falling into a wicked pattern of fidgety movements. She'd take a bird-like sip of her bitter gin and tonic; then she'd sweeten it up with a squeeze of lime; then she'd take another bird-like sip; then she'd watch a couple of minutes of some game that she wasn't the least interested in on the idiot box; then she'd check her wristwatch that she only wore on special occasions; then she'd check the time on her phone to make sure it matched the time on her watch; then she'd take another bird-like sip of her drink; then she'd dizzily swim back into her phone and act as if she was texting somebody, like her bestie or business associate, when she was only pretending to text another human being to make it look as if she was normal and that she wasn't alone but instead anxiously waiting on her bestie or business associate whom she was meeting up with for drinks (depending on the sex of the party involved, bestie if it was a man and business associate if it was a woman) when, in fact, she'd use the common excuse of being "stood up" if she was ever asked why she was drinking by herself.

By Jane's second drink, she finally mustered the nerve to talk to an older man who sat down next to her. The conversation started out like any other small talk. Weather analysis. Unseasonably cold conditions, cold fronts, and whatnot. Then, he acted like a broadcaster on TV and gave his own one-sided commentary on the overpaid football players on TV.

Then, after he plowed through his third drink—Jane still working on her second—he started to get political by bashing the specific players who kneeled during the National Anthem, comparing the sport to a job, and how his ass would get fired in a heartbeat if he brought his politics to the job and started kneeling during the Monday morning staff meeting. The old man had what Jane thought was the attention span of a goldfish. He even forgot her name twice; and by the third time she told the old man her name, he misheard it— probably not—because he started calling Jane Lorraine.

Riding on her smooth buzz train, Jane wasn't the least interested in anything the drunken man had to say to her, but it felt good just to talk to somebody even if the old man was incredibly mouthy and full of shit and most of the conversation felt like Déjà vu.

It wasn't until a couple of minutes into his rant when Jane wished she hadn't opened her mouth to say hi in the first place.

Jane excused herself, shouldered her way to the bathroom, didn't relieve herself yet hung around in front of the mirror for a moment and gathered herself; then when she made her way back to the bar, she found another seat far away from the local drunk. The night barreled along like a hurricane along the Gulf Coast.

Waves of people flowed into 'Da Bar in intervals, at times, overflowing.

Jane ended up talking to several other people among the crowd, but they, too, had nothing interesting to say to her. Most of what they had to say was the same stuff the other guy was saying, as if their conversations were being controlled by what they heard on TV or read on social media and that they, too, all watched or read the same stuff. More stuff about stuff. Stuff on stuff. Weather stuff. Sports stuff. Hollywood stuff. Then, the stuff did a full circle and wound up back at political stuff like a vicious feedback loop. The night gained momentum, more stuff upon stuff, loops upon loops. For some reason, Jane thought more about goldfish, the internal design of a goldfish and that *old myth* about them being masterminds of their own brutal short-term memory and being able to forget just like that, for instance, like being trapped inside a glass fishbowl and tediously swimming circles into what Jane could imagine was an endless ocean where the only predators came in the wicked shape of warped eyeballs and fingertips.

At one point in the night, Jane unfocused her eyes as if she was staring at one of those stereogram posters where, inside the image, there was a visual illusion of a three-dimensional picture. She'd blur out each pale face and in that white blur, she'd witness puckered lips forming into black dots.

They—the people—actually looked like goldfish.

The talk became looser, so did the crowd—or in Jane's eye, the school.

A couple of men complimented Jane on her ass and how nice it was. She was tempted to slap one man; but after Jane decided to cool off with a stiff drink, she rid any notion of doing so.

Another man smelled her hair and started talking about lions and how the male lion would smell the scent of a lioness right before he was about to mate with her. Jane laughed off the man. She needed another drink, a stiffer one.

Another man came along and bought Jane a whole bunch of shots. He acted as if it was his sole mission to make sure Jane wasn't taken advantage of by any of the other men. Yet, the man bought her shots without any regard for her personal safety, as if his whole angle of being the "only gentlemen" at the bar who made enough money at whatever make-believe job to afford expensive shots of extra rare Crown Royal—the top shelf stuff—was his stealthy scheme to convince Jane to come home with him before the last call. On several occasions, Jane attempted to brush off the guy like a pesky fruit fly. He kept lingering around her, either eye-flirting with her from across the bar or "mistakenly" bumping into her as soon as she turned a corner. Jane wasn't at all interested in the guy getting in her pants by the end of the night nor was she remotely interested in his issues and his overly sentimental behavior towards her; in fact, Jane wished the man would disappear—or better yet, Jane thought, wished the man would shrink in size, like an action-figure. Then, she'd pick him up by the back of his collar, his tiny, stiff action-figure arms and legs aerobically winding all around, and then she'd flush him down the toilet and watch him go 'round and 'round.

Her eyes still remained unfocused.

Her body swayed.

At that point, Jane felt it was best to call it a night.

But when Jane left 'Da Bar, she wasn't alone.

As she stumbled to her car, she witnessed him, her avid follower, her stalker, "Mr. Moonlight." She didn't know if it was him or not for the lighting was poor outside 'Da Bar and the moon was nearly full, too, with its pale light casting over parked cars, causing certain metallic areas to faintly glint and deceive. Her head was also heavy from the house gin that she had consumed in short time. Her eyes red and burning. Her thoughts extra swampy.

She strangely extended her head forward and looked twice at the dark figure. Did the one eye trick and steadied her Cyclops-gaze.

It was him . . .

Mr. Moonlight.

It was on this particular night Jane had officially branded him with that name, *Mr. Moonlight*. Maybe it was the alcohol distorting her vision. Maybe it was all of the bar-folks who wore down her spirits into an old, cracked nub with all their crassness, rude ambiguity, and flaming contradictions. Maybe all of those nasty things they said to her directly and indirectly had come straight from alcohol, as if the alcohol itself had the power to make people extremely mouthy. Jane considered herself a social drinker, the ever-so elusive "When in Rome" type drinker, a featherweight who easily got knocked out when it came to throwing back shots of hard liquor. Besides attending a few parties in college, she hadn't been around enough drunk people to fully understand the power of influence that the bottle had on weaker saps who were bewitched by its liquid spell. Maybe Jane was only listening to things *they* had secretly kept locked away inside their skulls throughout the sober hours of the day; and alcohol—for some—was that key to unlocking that dark, foul chamber of demons.

Maybe it was just a whole bunch of things.

Maybe it was what went down on the road the night before.

The dead deer. The crushed skull. The eyeballs. The leaking brain matter.

Maybe it was nothing.

One thing was certain: Jane didn't see these people as people, but rather saw *them* as another "them."

Throughout college, she saw people, other walks of life, other figures open to the world, like Ruby, who shared a kinship with Jane, a person who lived in the moment. After they shared their first kiss, Jane questioned if she overstepped her bounds, if her being human was too much to ask from Ruby. She felt something for Ruby, that, she was certain of. Whether it was the flesh or not, Jane longed to feel what she had felt when she was with Ruby, to see life. She used to study the other students whenever she wasn't preoccupied with her tiny fellowship; and despite all of their differences, Jane saw these other walks of life for everything they were so ready to be and nothing they were trying to be in order to fit into the societal contract of normalcy. Throughout the day, she observed all of their unique quirks, mannerisms, and independence charging through as she overheard native tongues slip through group conversations. She observed clingy high school bullshit being removed from their shoulders like hooks; and at night, sitting alone in her dorm room, she heard sounds of life roaring in the night darkness. Her skin pulsed. Pulsed hard. In a way, Jane envied them, not as docked vessels eager to embark to a new world without rules, but rather ones charting a path feared by their ancestors.

Being back in her small town, she started to feel small again, irrelevant. She didn't see people anymore, only "them."

When Jane looked at herself in the mirror, she saw a young woman without any color. Her skin translucent like a jellyfish, revealing a complex nervous system, as well as a skeletal structure and the organs she kept inside. Everything was starting to blacken, shrivel, and warp. She was dying, but regardless of the factual evidence of her slow decay, she was still working overtime behind the scenes and doing everything solely in her power to escape death by reaching for something that seemed unreachable.

Mr. Moonlight was *that* something who saw Jane.

She saw him too.

In a perverse way, Jane longed for him and his tireless observations.

At first glance, her head lowered, shoulders hunched, eyes honed. Her upper body went hanging, like her left wrist whenever she buckled the strap of a watch. Jane's body, like her wrist in some way or another, was loose and limp, as if she was waiting to be secured by time.

Jane peered closer.

The sight of Mr. Moonlight made her skin pulse and throb, despite the inability to act upon its very urges.

She was the girl who used to stick her hand into a sketchy burrow in the desert and pull out whatever creatures resided inside it. At times, she was stung in the arm or hand, her body filled with poison. She'd ride out the rush of poison, at times sweating it out throughout the day like a cruel fever, while, other times, feeling great arousal from it. Over the years of collecting, Jane had become immune to the creature's poison, never at all frightened by its sting or bite.

But when it came to being in the presence of Mr. Moonlight, Jane's body was left in a state of paralysis. Not once did Jane ever approach him nor think about doing so. Even the liquid courage had no effect on her. She was too mortified by his ghostly aura.

As Jane fumbled for her car keys, Mr. Moonlight stood behind the bed of a truck parked at the other end of the gravel parking lot.

With her eyes never leaving his, she managed to get a grip on the keys while Mr. Moonlight remained in the shadows outside a flickering halo of an amber colored floodlight. Not doing much, just staring down Jane with those glossy moonlit eyes. Dressed in all black. Faceless. A rather lanky man with arms as knobby as tree branches. *Around six feet tall*, she guessed, maybe even a couple of inches taller.

Trying not to make a sound, she carefully opened the door and eased into the car as if she was stepping into a tub of ice-cold water. Jane inserted the key into the ignition the same way she opened the door.

Once she started the car, Mr. Moonlight was gone.

She checked all around her, checked her blind spots. Lastly, she checked the rear view mirror, thinking maybe he might've slipped into the backseat of the car without her knowing and she'd find him seated directly behind her, not saying a word, not doing much, just staring in the rear view mirror with those empty white eyes of his. She felt almost feverish by the thought.

This time, she turned fully around and checked the seat behind her.

Then, as Jane faced forward, the sudden thought of Mr. Moonlight standing directly in front of the grill of the car flashed through her mind.

But he was not there.

He was nowhere.

He was gone.

Mr. Moonlight didn't show up until a week later when Jane decided to join a tennis league. The morning after her run in with Mr. Moonlight, she determined that the bar life wasn't for her anymore not because of the cold dis or the political spats and camouflaged racist rhetoric or the lewd behavior or the other countless insults she received throughout the night, but because of the hangover she experienced the morning after. The worse part: there wasn't a magical pill to cure a bad hangover. A hangover was no different than a virus. It just had to run its course. Even worse: the hangover could've been avoided.

But if she hadn't gone to 'Da Bar that night, would she have seen him?

All Jane knew was that he wasn't a hallucination brought on by alcohol.

He was real.

Mr. Moonlight.

Doing that thing he does.

Just staring at Jane.

He was standing behind a picnic bench underneath a canopy not too far away from a playground.

His body was hard to make out for the night darkness.

But his eyes, though, were like distant headlights burning in the dark.

Several times Jane found herself distracted during the match. Every now and then, she'd take her eyes off the ball or remain in a trance-like stare during breaks or catch him in the corner of her eye while chasing down the ball. She was playing doubles and her teammate, a retired lady who spent her entire week preparing for these Thursday night gatherings, grew irritated by Jane's lack of interest.

Once, between games, she pulled Jane aside and asked her if everything was all right. Jane mentioned the strange man watching her. Even asked her teammate if she saw him standing underneath the canopy. Her teammate couldn't see him. But Jane figured the lady had glaucoma or something. That was her excuse.

The following week, Mr. Moonlight was back.

Jane made quite a scene. She spotted him during her serve. Distracted, Jane took her eyes off the ball as she was about to swing. The ball struck the corner of her racket, darted off to the right, and plunked her doubles-teammate in the back.

Her teammate went down hard, wincing and grabbing her back as if she had broken it.

Jane didn't care about her, about what she had done.

She had her eyes on Mr. Moonlight.

Without apologizing, Jane hurried off the court and did the one thing that she said she was going to do all week.

She approached Mr. Moonlight!

Her adrenaline had taken over and she was jacked up. A couple of the tennis players tended to Jane's teammate, Ms. Walsh, while the others stood in awe and watched Jane storm directly to the canopy.

Jane suddenly flung the tennis racket to the ground and curled her hands into fists. Both of her eyes were wide and mad. Her jaw clenched so tight she could crack a filling.

Jane yelled to the top of her voice: *"For crying out loud, what the hell do you want from me? Why are FOLLOWING me? Why can't you just leave me alone? WHAT DO YOU—"*

Once she reached the canopy, the fire she had burning brightly in her belly turned all to smoke. Everything about Jane had fizzled out, as if the sight alone of the dangling canned light fixture underneath the canopy had burst her balloon.

She pushed the fixture once, then it responded by swinging back at her. She stepped closer to the canned fixture and touched the light bulb inside. The bulb was as hot as fire. Yet, the bulb was dark and dead inside.

Jane quickly recoiled from the flash of pain.

Even when she tapped on the bulb, the spring inside rattled like a maraca.

More intrigued, she removed the scrunchie from her ponytail and used it as a glove to twist the loose bulb clockwise.

Surprisingly, the light bulb turned on!

She suddenly flinched.

The light nearly blinded Jane.

Once she knew it was safe, she leaned closer to the light and stood there more surprised not by the sight of the light but by the other players staring at her from the tennis courts.

Like the bars, Jane's tennis days were over. Even though she enjoyed playing tennis more so than drinking and at least trying to socialize at bars, Jane knew she couldn't go back to the tennis league. She was the one who hurt Ms. Walsh—or as Jane saw it, the Mother Theresa wannabe who bent over backwards to make sure everybody was hunky-dory by lending spare rackets to those who didn't have one or bringing extra Gatorade and granola bars for everybody. Jane was the one who went on a psychotic fit after "accidentally" hitting Ms. Walsh with a ball.

In Jane's mind, she was the one who just didn't belong. The elephant on the court. Jane did her research on the Internet and found another league that met on Tuesdays. But they played all the way in Bentwood, which was on the other side of town. Jane wasn't about to drive out of her way just to smack around a tennis ball for an hour or two.

She went back to her daily life, to movies, to her cats.

The one perk about tennis was that, like dating, it helped ward off the nightmares.

But now, with no tennis, no more dating, those nightmares were back with a vengeance.

The nightmares started to bleed into Jane's job. At times, she'd drift off into the reddest daydreams and fantasize about killing animals. Strangely, something darker had manifested itself inside her nightmares.

Somehow, Jane was no longer a prey, but rather the opposite.

The darkness spread into her day. Jane found herself in serious trouble while she was clipping the nails of Mrs. Keddlemen's boxer, Ali. All of a sudden, Jane fell into one of her violent daydreams—sunk, really. Her hand felt as if her hand no longer belonged to her body, not even loose or limp, but vanished; yet, she felt as if it was being controlled by something else, as if the nerves themselves were stuck on a GIF-loop. The violence swelled inside her and all of that red fury had somehow. . . moved. She tried to speak but all that came out were noises, barks? For a moment—and just a moment—it felt as if her soul had been cut, copied, and pasted into Ali. Jane wasn't aware of what she had done until she heard poor Ali howl out in great pain. A part of Jane had embraced that pain as it rippled across her body like a shockwave. Jane snapped from her red thoughts of chopping and looked down at Ali's paw and its fur drenched in blood. One of its toes was partially severed and hanging on like a baby tooth.

Baffled, Jane couldn't figure out whether or not it was an accident.

Ali, being a dog who was adored by the entire staff for his charming personality, ended up losing its toe.

Mrs. Keddlemen came from old money and white privilege. She was a sassy lady who'd make the most villains on soap operas look like kindergarten teachers. For Mrs. Keddlemen, her happy hour began at one o'clock with Pinto Grigio and smoked salmon and cream cheese on gluten-free crackers.

She obsessively dolled herself up everywhere she paraded, including the animal hospital. As if a gust of wind followed her everywhere, the doors would swing open for her. She'd roll up in there as snobby as a horse with her pencil-point chin raised high in the air as one of her obedient assistants—usually a handsome boy toy who got paid in game tokens—carried a personally tailored Gucci bag. Ali's head would be poking out of the bag licking the pungent aroma her proud "master" Mrs. Keddlemen left behind. She was the type of benefactor who was not to be messed with, Jane knew. After the incident, Jane pleaded with Mrs. Keddlemen, couldn't say sorry enough. But on that day, Mrs. Keddlemen was in a rare mood.

Jane kept her job.

But after the whole incident, everybody at work was watching Jane.

It seemed like everywhere Jane went, everybody was watching her, studying her, waiting for her to snap or lose control.

Jane had to act fast; otherwise, she'd be out of a job. She started looking for nightly activities, something—anything—to keep her mind off violence. Jane hit the streets, scouted out flyers hanging on street posts, and then, when she didn't have much luck, she got lost in the good ole Internet. She went on Facebook and found a page for a cooking class. *Looked fun*, she thought. In the photos, the students were smiling from ear-to-ear while preparing gourmet food that you'd see on the cover of *Bon Appétit!* The students looked so care-free, as if through their warm hospitality, they were welcoming Jane to join them and show her what she had been missing. The class was called "Be a Chef."

Jane was in.

Be a Chef started at seven o 'clock, which gave many of the students time to get loosey-goosey. The class was located in the historic district, which, like most American towns, had been revitalized to appeal to a needy generation. The night started out optimistic. Jane was looking forward to cooking. However, when she arrived, her spirits were surprisingly dampened from the sight of the students in her class. Most of the people were either newly wed couples or retirees or cliquish Soccer moms trying to spice up their lives with fancy dishes that most of them could hardly even spell or even pronounce. In a way, Jane was desperate to find human connection with "them," but they ended up shunning Jane as if she was a damaged product. It was there, at Be a Chef, when Jane started to feel like one of those old, smelly dogs rescuers took in off the streets.

When she'd scrub away the street grime and pull off the dingle berries hanging from their rears, she couldn't help but think about the dogs' former owners. What kind of person would agree to take on the sole responsibility of caring for another life, then reject it or cast it aside as soon as it showed the first signs of trouble.

Through the mistreatment of these dogs and even cats and other animals, Jane saw firsthand the sheer laziness of society. Yet, she felt as if she was no different than these people whom she started to detest. Like with Mrs. Keddlemen's dog or even the neglect she had shown Tyler and Marla, Jane wondered if it was she who was behaving so out of character.

Was it I, *Jane*, who accidentally kicked Tyler after he scratched me? Was it I who accidentally cut off Ali's toe?

Or, she thought, was it someone else?

Someone—or something—*inside me?*

That was when Jane thought about him.

Sure enough, he showed up as if he was there all along.

Her own personal phantom.

Outside the window of the kitchen, he was standing behind a street post and watching Jane as she learned how to make the popular autumn dish, squash soup.

Jane went about her business, gutting the squash, going by whatever the instructor told her to do. Then, Jane switched stations. Her next task was "How to properly cut an onion," which didn't seem so difficult; however, there was an art involved in thinly slicing an onion, which would be used for the classical French-inspired side dish, potatoes au gratin.

As the instructor guided Jane to curl her knuckles into the center of her palm like a fist and press down on the onion using the same hand, she sliced the onion as thin as a sheet of copy paper. The whole goal was to prevent Jane from making an amateur move by chopping off her fingers—hence curling them into her palm and keeping them from exposure. She did the same for the potato, held the potato down with her hand shaped in a fist-like position, and sliced it as thin as a potato chip with her other hand. While she was working through yet another potato, she looked up and took a glance through the window. She'd make yet another slice, look up, and see him watching her. Jane didn't ignore him, though, Mr. Moonlight. She didn't let him entirely distract her, either.

She, more or less, accepted him for who he was.

Her stalker.

The very next morning, Jane woke up seconds before her alarm clock sounded off.

Energized, she struck the snooze button with authority and rolled out of bed.

The red light cast from a new dawn was burning bright through the windows, causing the blinds to glow. She felt drawn to that red light. She cracked open the blinds, peeked out her window, and fell witness to a red autumn sky. The clouds around the sun lit up with shades of reds and soft pinks and purples; the closer to the sun, the brighter the color red. She felt as if a small part of her was at peace with the world, as if the red light was telling her to be patient, that her *final* peace was ahead of her.

Riding the early morning high, Jane glided into the kitchen, no rush or panic. Most mornings usually consisted of Jane frantically scrambling around the apartment, making last minute wardrobe adjustments before grabbing a biscuit and coffee from one of those eat-at-your-risk fast food joints on the way to work because she didn't have time to prepare herself a decent breakfast. Unburdened, Jane decided to cook one of her most frustrating dishes: the omelet.

For eight years Jane had been a vegan and except for maybe being tempted to eat a slice of bacon that her mother deliberately cooked every Saturday morning as if it was a tradition, not once during those eight good years had Jane ever felt persuaded to hop back on the meat wagon. When she originally gave up on all things meat at the age of sixteen and converted to a life of veganhood, Jane told herself that she was in it all the way. Her parents went out of their way to cater to Jane's new lifestyle. She substituted the meat with protein shakes and supplements. She tweaked her diet accordingly, did it for the little ones, maybe to prove to them that not all humans were the cold-blooded killers like they played out to be. When she *finally* got a place of her own after she graduated from Western, she bought a carton of eggs every week. Every week, Jane kept her fridge stocked with eggs; and every week, she ended up throwing away the eggs. Her only explanation was that she bought the eggs "just in case" she went hungry, as if the eggs were some kind of life raft, an easy "go-to" meal when fruit, salad, tofu, or veggies weren't cutting it for her. Jane was ready to let those eight years slip away. In a way, she felt no different than a recovering alcoholic who feared, yet worshipped, the number zero.

"Just two eggs," she told herself.

After all, it was *only* two eggs.

Jane was no Julia Child when it came to cooking the perfect omelet; in fact, every time she tried to make one when she was younger, she'd end up overcooking the outside or undercooking the inside or, the most common mistake, ruining the physical structure of the omelet after the first flip and then, in most attempts, the final product turning out like roadkill. For as long as she could remember, she looked at the finished result of her infamous omelet like that half-eaten Big Mac, only it'd look twice as messy and falling apart before she'd even take a single bite of it. It would always break down midway through eating it, she recalled her days from her youth.

When cooking an omelet, the onions or bell peppers or mushrooms or spinach would somehow, like the middle bun, lettuce, pickles of a Big Mac with that special sauce acting like lube, wiggle its way out midway through cooking it.

After Be a Chef, Jane realized she was doing everything right, except for one minor yet crucial part. The temperature of the stovetop was too hot. The whole time, she realized, all I had to do was turn down the heat of the burner to its lowest setting. Just a slight twenty-degree turn of a knob separating a sloppy, uneatable omelet to something of great beauty.

While she was gliding around the kitchen and gathering last-second ingredients she needed to finish the perfectly cooked omelet—not too brown on the outside, not too yolky on the inside, but just right, Jane could hear the foodies say—Jane caught a familiar face in the corner of her eye.

She stopped dead in her tracks and turned toward the TV in the living room.

For some reason, she thought about *him*.

A sudden hopelessness washed over her.

On the TV, there was a news report about a man whose body was discovered last night in a car parked in the parking lot of an abandoned strip mall. His wife, Heidi, had reported her husband missing when he didn't come home from his recent book tour. His name was Mark Sakowski, a former executive director of the nonprofit, Green, which promoted sustainable farming, turned bestselling author and controversial filmmaker behind the book, *The Takeover*, which pulled back the curtain on an outdated conspiracy that the food agencies inside the federal government were carrying out covert operations known as "Population Control" linking cancer to many food additives, as well as certain preservatives used for processed foods and other food products. His earth-shocking documentary, *A Side of Arsenic*, focused on pesticides and the dangerous levels of arsenic and carcinogens and banned drugs, such antibiotics, antifungal medications, anti-inflammatory drugs, and even drugs, like the hallucinogenic party drug, ketamine, which were discovered in contaminated meat such as beef, poultry, and pork, and showed levels well beyond the cutoff of the Food Safety and Inspection Service (FSIS). Sakowski was widely known for calling out big corporations and how they were making the public sick in order to take advantage of them. "First, they poison us with their food," Sakowski wrote, referring to CEO, Luther Sims, of *Feature*, a well-known pharmaceutical company, as well as one of the largest beef producers in the world, "then, they heal us. It's a win-win for all parties." In *The Takeover*, Sakowski compared America's corporations as "chiefs who cook high-cholesterol foods for a living, then sale cholesterol drugs as their side hustle." Sakowski left behind a wife and two children. The police were notified after a street sweeper found the body slumped over the steering wheel of a luxury Mercedes Benz. Sakowski had been stabbed to death; in fact, the reporter said he was stabbed over sixty-four times. Police were officially calling it a crime of passion.

"Personal," one investigator stated in an interview.

Jane didn't exactly know where she had seen this man, Mark Sakowski, before, but she had *seen* him somewhere.

As Jane directed attention back to her omelet, the stovetop was smoking. She removed the scolding hot pan from the stovetop with an oven mitt, tossed the pan into the sink, and ran cold water over the pan. Steam rose from the sizzling pan. Jane picked at the omelet, trimmed over the dark spots, and tried her best to salvage what was left of it, but one side of it was black and inedible.

Throughout most of the workday, Mr. Sakowski's face was seared in Jane's mind, as if it was surrounded by so much darkness. It wasn't until a similarly profiled middle-aged man strolled into the animal hospital with his gray Scottish terrier that Jane remembered where she had seen Mr. Sakowski. She was immediately dumfounded when the notion struck her.

But *how?*

Jane had a stark image in her mind of a slender dark skinned man with blue eyes and shoulder-length purple hair pulled back tightly in a ponytail stabbing Mr. Sakowski in the chest with a pair of scissors. Even the windows surrounding the two men were foggy from the hotness that radiated from the killer's body.

A *crime of passion*: those were the words that came to Jane.

Another detail that stood out inside the car: Mr. Sakowski's pants, as well as his underwear, had been pulled down to his ankles, exposing himself.

Rather trying to defend himself from the attack, Mr. Sakowski was too occupied shielding his manhood. The news report didn't mention anything about sex or any kind of sexual transaction between both the victim or suspect, only that it was "personal." They did say, however, that most of the victim's wounds were located around the chest, as well as the neck and shoulder region, not on his arms, which, Jane assumed, would make sense if a man was leaning forward trying to pull up his pants instead of using his arms to block the scissors from severing any major arteries or striking any vital organs.

Jane had indeed seen these graphic images before.

But she was more intrigued by the notion of seeing these images in a dream. But how?

Throughout the remainder of the day, the thought alone of Sakowski's final moments were followed by two words that remained hovering in the dense air like a cloud of smog.

But how.

Later, the police would reveal to the media that a witness had come forward, a homeless man who saw a woman in the vicinity of Sakowski's vehicle and possibly interrupted the killer from disposing the body. He claimed she stepped into his car and then exited with a knife. "Ran away once she made eye contact" with the homeless man. These were his words used to describe the situation. He also described the young woman as short and sickly thin, had long hair worn in a *ponytail*. Jane remembered the ponytail from her dream. However, the witness said it was a she, *not* a he, and her hair was blue, *not* purple.

Jane didn't know whom to believe: her dreams or the witness.

An entire week passed with no leads into the death of Mark Sakowski. Each day of the week went by like the day before, with Jane spending most of the day trying to recall a dream from the night before. She'd occasionally drift off at work, as if, at times, she was trapped in the cell of her own mind.

Each night, Jane's dreams became redder, darker.

Each dream, she saw a new face.

Each face, she saw a new death.

Each one of the victims' faces from her dreams was filled with more detail, each feature attached to scrambled fantasies and haunted house-style flashes of horror.

The killer, however, remained as elusive as a leopard.

Throughout the latter part of the week, Jane found two of the same faces from her dream reported "MISSING" on TV by loved ones, both friends and family.

One of them being Jake Durbin, a police officer. Like Sakowski, he, too, had two children.

Then, the other one, Mary-Anne Simmons, married to Jonas Simmons, made her own jewelry at home, lived in a wealthy neighborhood.

Having grown up in a small town where everybody knew each other's business, Jane immediately recognized both their faces from high school. But she wasn't friends with either of them. The two were part of the whole "in-crowd." The sight of Jake and Mary-Anne's face on TV resurrected a lost memory. Mark Sakowski. Jane knew him, and not only from her dream. He was her eleventh grade horticulture teacher. He was creepy-quiet, Jane recalled, socially awkward. Every time she tried to dig deeper into the memory of Mark Sakowski, the darker the memory of him became. He was a man shrouded in darkness.

Which made her wonder if he had any connection to Mr. Moonlight.

Did they know each other?

The next time Jane saw Mr. Moonlight was at a family owned café called Hot Java. Like 'Da Bar, Hot Java was an older establishment that recently overhauled its interior decor, which used to be as bland as a doctor's office, as well as its entire brand in order to appease its more vocal fan base while, at the same time, trying to bring in the younger generation of coffee drinkers by sprucing up the café with the whole island theme inspired by Java, the island in Indonesia, in particularly the active volcano, Mount Bromo, and making it safer and more inviting and adding free wi-fi connection for its customers, which would come in handy whenever a customer ordered a cup of coffee through Hot Java's own personal app—this particular feature allowed its customers to place an order through their phone without having to go through the trouble or inconvenience of looking another person directly in the face. Hot Java was way more laidback than 'Da Bar, drew more of a diverse crowd, more PC but less cliquish, and moved more at Jane's pace.

After a long day of work and mind games, Jane wanted to treat herself. She arrived at Hot Java during a post-dinner rush and ordered a caramel macchiato the old fashion way by opening her mouth and speaking her order.

While Jane waited on the barista to concoct her drink, she grabbed a seat near a cozy fireplace and researched other activities to do on her laptop.

When she looked away from the laptop and rested her eyes for a moment, she smelled something burning in the kitchen.

Suddenly, she heard the sound of a cooking sheet crashing to the floor. The sheet danced around for a while until it finally came to rest like a spun coin.

A young baker darted out of the kitchen, a cloud of dense smoke trailing behind him like the one in a Wile E. Coyote cartoon. The baker was coughing and fanning away smoke.

Jane overheard the baker saying something about burning a batch of brownies. She couldn't quite make out the rest of what the baker was mumbling for she was paying more attention to the customers around her. Some of them were filming the baker with their phones and posting their recently shot videos online and then constantly wiping their thumbs down their screens of their phones, refreshing their pages for new LIKES or comments. Jane wondered if they were receiving gratification out of exposing another man's humiliation—*in this day in age,* the Age of Narcissism, *of course they did*. His cheeks were red and cloudy and he was hanging his head downward like one of those same dogs that had been brought in from the streets. Jane looked around in both amusement, yet confusion, and thought if these people's lives were so bankrupt that they went back home, sat in the comfort of their Lazy Boys, and watched these videos they recently recorded instead of capturing the moment with their own HD eyes. Jane knew that, unlike a video, a memory could *never* been deleted.

The more Jane wondered about these things, the deeper she started to delve into her laptop.

Before she lost herself in the Internet, the baker swung open the back door in order to air out the bitter smell.

Jane saw a tiny orange glow coming from the doorway and thought it was a floater in her eye, but it was only the glow of a cigarette the baker was smoking behind the café.

As the white cloud of cigarette smoke faded into the air, Mr. Moonlight revealed himself standing still in a dark alleyway outside Hot Java's.

Jane's head gradually rose from behind the laptop, her keen red eyes cutting through the pale blue haze of the screen.

She locked eyes with him.

Like before, he was watching Jane. And like before, his pale eyes never left Jane.

To Jane, the baker looked as if he wasn't aware of Mr. Moonlight's presence as he continued to puff away, probably replaying the recent goof in his head. Jane thought it was strange, though, how the baker didn't pay any attention to Mr. Moonlight. *Was it because he didn't see him?* He was only standing a couple of feet away from him. *Or was Mr. Moonlight that good at disguise?* Jane only caught a glimpse of his face, but in that brief glimpse, she saw more detail on her stalker's face.

Mr. Moonlight was, in fact, a man. She only had two choices to choose from; and all along, she had been leaning toward male. He was young too, but feminine in the way he posed for Jane. She thought that he could pass as one of those models on the front cover of a glossy magazine, stern and striking face, chiseled body. He was sneaky, thin, yet cut, his shoulders broad like a farmer; he appeared fragile, yet strong. He stood out, yet he blended into the night like a shadow.

He had the perfect color, Jane thought, *black.*

He had the perfect cover: night.

Jane guessed he was around twenty years old, but maybe younger than that, maybe even Jane's age or older. She couldn't put a number on his age because of the clear-rimmed glasses he was wearing. The man was dark skinned, as Sakowski's killer in her dreams, his hair was long, purple, and silky; and it hung over his shoulders like a horse's mane. He was also wearing a silver looped earring that glinted whenever it moved around the oversized collar of a sequined turtleneck he wore underneath a sleek-looking black duster.

Later that night when Jane fell into her dark slumber, she dreamt of death.

Murder.

A woman's murder.

She didn't know her name, yet, beyond the blackness of her thoughts, she felt as if she knew her from somewhere, maybe a run-in at a store or a place opened to the public, like a movie theatre or a park. Her face was so clear to Jane it seemed as if Jane was right there with the killer. She could even smell the faint aroma of shea butter under the killer's pungent funk. Jane picked up more detail than any other dream, especially the woman's face, as well as the horror etched on it. The face had been imprinted on her, as if she could easily point it out in a lineup. The woman was black-black. Everything about her was bold and voluptuous, even her personality; she also wore her hair was like one of those rockers from a hair metal band. Jane remembered seeing the hairdo in an old music video on *VH1*. She was also wearing a jeans jacket underneath a zebra-spotted shirt. Jane didn't know why these details had popped the most, but the clothing attire didn't reflect the fashion style of the current decade.

Both of the woman's shoulders were being pinned down by two pointy knees. The last detail was the pair of holey jeans that her killer was wearing. The kind of deliberate holes that were considered fashionable or dare Jane say, chic.

Then, the killer hushed the woman with a black-gloved hand while brandishing the pair of scissors with the other hand. Strangely, Jane could feel the grip of scissors in her own hands, *not* the killer's, as he playfully ran the tip of the blade down the sweaty woman's face.

Snip, snip!

Made the sound of the scissors as he opened, then closed the scissors in front of the woman's face.

Panicked, the woman's eyes swelled and stilled on the killer towering above her. The tears were like shrink-wrap covering her murky brown eyes.

As the killer struck, Jane's eyes snapped open! She never fully witnessed the violent parts, only the highlights of the moments leading up to the woman's death.

Jane gathered herself. She was sweating profusely, the bed sheets around her were as wet and wrinkled as an old dishrag.

Sitting against the headboard of her bed, she wondered where such violence had come from.

A couple of hours later, when the morning sun cut through Jane's windows and lit up the apartment in an eerie reddish haze, Jane finally rolled out of bed and grabbed the TV remote wedged between the cushions of the couch.

At first, Jane stared at the remote, tempted to put it away, even hide it.

After second thought, she turned on the TV.

She cycled through several news channels until she found one that caught her eye.

Her name was Shanique Willis, Jane had later learned.

Hours after Shanique's mother reported her missing, a pair of brown eyes was discovered at Hot Java.

One of the baristas was reaching for a blueberry scone when all of a sudden a customer screamed out, causing several other customers to dash in a frenzy to the door. Somehow, the word *gun* was shouted out and moments later, it was all pandemonium inside Hot Java. The word traveled from one customer to another and by the time the word reached the back of the line, the customers thought there was an "active shooter" inside Hot Java. More customers sprinted out of the café while others cowered under tables, earthquake drill-style, and started praying to the god of their choice. There wasn't an active shooter inside the café, people would soon realize after the barista called the cops and told them about the eyes sitting next to the cinnamon coffee cakes.

Once the excitement fizzled out, the brave barista picked up one of the eyes with his gloved hand, the eye as slick as the stone of an avocado. Still bloody. At first, the barista thought it was a gag or something, an immature employee pulling a gag or a disgruntled employee's prankish way of quitting the job, the big middle finger to the boss man.

Then, he held it underneath his nose and took a whiff of it.

He suddenly recoiled from the smell and dropped the eye to the floor.

The barista looked at the other customers standing around and they, too, were equally as repulsed.

Later that very same morning, a dumpster had been lit on fire directly behind a nail salon, which shared the same alleyway as Hot Java's. Before the firefighters arrived at the scene, workers from other nearby stores managed to put out the flames with buckets of water that had been circulated through a human chain.

Once the smoke *finally* cleared, the workers discovered a dead woman without eyes buried underneath piles of trash. The next of kin later identified the body as Shanique Willis, the same woman missing earlier that very same day. According to the autopsy report, Shanique's eyes had been cut out postmortem (meaning they were removed after she died).

Like the other victim, Mark Sakowski, Shanique was stabbed multiple times with a pair of scissors.

Based on the report, the coroner determined that Shanique died from a massive hemorrhage. She bled out.

Investigators interviewed those close to Shanique; and according to her closest friends, she was a regular who frequented the café.

The motive would be later speculated through the gossip queens and the true crime enthusiasts of social media that the serial killer—or "copycat," investigators weren't still convinced it was the same killer—was trying to make a bold statement for his or her audience. The exact position of the eyes was clue number one. The eyes were positioned at an angle inside the pastry case, pointed directly at the same seat Shanique always sat in, as if the seat itself had her name on the back of it. Shanique's murder was the first of many other murders to raise eyebrows. The criminal analysts on TV would say, "The killer is evolving."

The next victim resulted in the local newspaper, *The Messenger*, branding the killer with the name, "The Snipper," because of the killer's modus operandi—its method. Gary Worthington was discovered by an elderly woman who was out on one of her routine walks at the crack of dawn. Sugar, her cocker spaniel, was first to notice Gary, initially barking for the entire block to hear, then attempting to run over to Gary for a quick hump or lick. Sugar's owner stepped closer for a better look. Gary's injuries—or injury was brought out in vivid detail underneath the streetlight. Gary's ankle was shackled to the fire hydrant. The galvanized chain wrapped around his ankle had left it black and blue. He was exhausted, famished, his face as pallid as a ghost, his lips dry and crusty from extreme dehydration; and from all the head-bobbing he was doing, he appeared to be drugged.

(Later in the investigation, it would known that Gary Worthington had been, in fact, drugged; and after blood tests, it was revealed that Gary, as well as several other victims, had traces of a common animal tranquilizer in their systems, which made the investigators believe that the killer was drugging his victims before the final *snip, snip*)

Gary's other injury, the most noticeable one, came from his mouth. His chin was caked with blood as dark as tar from where the oxygen had hit it.

As soon as she realized he was still alive from his sloth-like movements, she tended to Gary. That was when he cracked open his mouth and revealed his injury to her.

A rope of blood gushed from the corner of his parched mouth and dribbled down the side of his chin.

Gary tried to speak but couldn't.

All Gary spoke were vowels for his tongue had been cut out—snipped away with scissors by a new threat on the block known as The Snipper. But Jane had a different name for him. Jane didn't exactly know why Mr. Moonlight had spared Gary Worthington's life. No words were exchanged in her dream; in fact, during each dream, Mr. Moonlight's voice, like his identity, remained a mystery. A part of her thought maybe he kept Gary alive to tell the world about his tormenter—or punisher; Jane was still on the fence about the killer's motives. But Gary couldn't speak; however, he could still paint. Gary was this famous artist from New York. Had a lifetime of success throughout the more productive side of his twenties but that premature fame dimmed significantly when Gary reached the wrong side of thirty.

Of all the victims, Gary had stayed with Jane the most. She couldn't help but wonder why Mr. Moonlight didn't cut off Gary's fingers or hands since he was an artist. If Mr. Moonlight was trying to punish Gary, then wouldn't the ultimate payback be to take away the very tools that he held most dearly. She wondered if he was shining the spotlight on Gary for all the wrong things, carry out Mr. Moonlight's bidding or legacy, provide Gary with his own inspiration to paint again, act solely as one, the great muse.

Then, perhaps later, a pivotal curator.

The next day after Gary was targeted—according to police, the word *targeted* was purposefully used during a press conference because Gary confirmed through a series of head nods and written statements that he had been followed prior to his abduction, which made investigators believe the killer knew Gary—Gary's partner received a blank package in the mail: Gary's tongue.

When Jane had dreamt about Gary the next night, she felt as if she knew him, like the killer, but only the façade the two hid behind. Oddly, Jane didn't feel the least amount of pain for Gary despite how the media had treated him as this kind of sympathetic figure. She didn't even know if it was her feelings that she was feeling or someone else's. Like Shanique's face, Gary's muffled voice was imprinted on her mind, as if Jane could access it at any time of the day; however, she could only hear the low end of his voice which sounded like the trailing resonance of a cave echo, like an overlapping mumble. She pinpointed certain *words* among the noise, heard nothing but bigotry and menace behind it. He sounded jealous of Jane or Mr. Moonlight. She couldn't quite tell if Gary was speaking to her or Mr. Moonlight.

But why, Jane wondered.

Gary was an artist struggling to rediscover stardom.

Was Gary jealous that Mr. Moonlight (?) was soaking up all the limelight?

Either way, Jane sort of liked the way it made her feel after she woke up from a dream. A feeling of power that she had only felt when she was a little girl carrying around a jar and collecting whatever creatures she could find in the desert. If Mr. Moonlight was punishing his victims, Jane thought that he could've been a vigilante. In her eyes, though, her Day-eyes, Mr. Moonlight was a monster. Like all monsters, they did their best work in the dark.

After Mr. Moonlight's next victim, Jane realized Mr. Moonlight was becoming even more complex.

Dylan Canto ran a podcast about true crime stories called *The 187*. Each episode involved old, unsolved murder cases, as well as kidnappings; and every now and then, Dylan would stray away from old cases and focus on new, more trendier ones, or as for "The Snipper," an ongoing case. Dylan didn't do much investigation per se, like the widely known stereotypes displayed in Hollywood movies as self-loathing men—or women but mostly men—adhered to the drink while obsessively tracking the movements of a killer at large. Dylan called up former detectives or journalists who once worked on old cases—solved or unsolved—over the phone and incorporated their conversations into a weekly podcast where he'd profit from it by spreading it all over the Internet for entitled, gullible kids to devour. He was, simply put, like many who thrived in the Internet world, an opportunist. And once Dylan heard about The Snipper, he couldn't help but jump all over the story.

When Dylan's sidekick, Gumshoe, found Dylan's body in a makeshift studio inside an older rented out building downtown, which used to be home for an insurance company before it went bankrupt, Gumshoe thought Dylan was pulling a twisted prank.

After all, Halloween was right around the corner and like they all say, everybody was entitled to at least one good scare.

Dylan wasn't moving, wasn't breathing.

By the time the paramedics arrived, Dylan was dead; in fact, Dylan had been dead for over twelve hours. The initial cause of death was mysterious; however, Dylan was missing a part of his body. The details of the autopsy report were left for the late night shows, past nine o'clock, when the children went to bed. Apparently, The Snipper had snipped off Dylan's genitals, the whole works. However, the genitals weren't mailed to anybody close to Dylan or lying around somewhere for some poor schmuck to find. After a surprising discovery while examining the contents inside Dylan Canto's stomach cavity, the coroner determined the victim had choked on them. The medical term was asphyxiation.

Through a rigorous investigation, investigators unearthed Dylan's latest podcast where he designated an entire episode to The Snipper and his recent killings or no-killings. On his podcast, Dylan blasted the killer with false information and bogus allegations. Ridiculed The Snipper. Even provoked The Snipper by filling in the gaping holes of The Snipper's background and suggested he was a toothless backwoods inbreed who burned too many ants with a magnifying glass as a child. The investigators determined that Dylan's podcast would come in handy and used it solely for their benefit. The Snipper had a glaring weak spot, so they thought, and maybe they could use what they learned from the podcast to their advantage. The investigators tried a couple of days later with Dylan's trusty sidekick, Gumshoe, not to draw any suspicion. Had Gumshoe record a new podcast to lure out Dylan's cold-blooded killer. Had Gumshoe rail against The Snipper. Had him read off from a shit blender of insults, as if he was hosting a roast and The Snipper was his roastee. He even went so far as to pull out a hefty supply of "Your momma so fat" jokes from his back pocket and slung them all over the stream-waves as if it was a national hashtag day. Gumshoe's tirade was so derogatory that it was even trending across every digital corner of the Internet.

For weeks, Gumshoe had a security detail covering his every move, a team of rough and tough bodyguards following him around everywhere he went. Watching him. Waiting for The Snipper to make a move.

For weeks, though, no sight of The Snipper.

The Snipper had moved onto other victims: a mother of two daughters named Camilla Hayes. Camilla's dead body was found underneath the blenchers behind Clover High. Her nose was missing.

Investigators believed The Snipper lured Camilla to the high school where he killed her.

Another clue: investigators found a half-pound of Oxycodone on her person.

After Camilla, it was Travis Pierre.

Then, Relene Applegate.

Sandra Cotes.

The list went on and on. Each one murdered by the same exact modus operandi: a body part removed before or after they were stabbed to death—or what the investigators refereed to as the most exaggerated yet vaguest statement that would literally and often times, metaphorically highlight a stigma of each victim.

For instance, a detective had a theory that Camilla's nose was cut off because she was prying into The Snipper's business—being "nosy." The only evidence he had to back up the wild theory was a ghostly photo posted on her Instagram page. In the shaky photo a dark blurry-faced man had one hand in front of his face while the other one was trying to shield the dotted lens on the top right-hand corner of Camilla's phone. The photo appeared to be taken at a nightclub due to the various colored lasers and mega-screen graphics slicing through the photo like distorted street glares and what appeared to be fog-like smoke hovering over a wavy crowd of intoxicated people standing shoulder-to-shoulder around the strange man.

Of all the victims, perhaps Camilla knew the identity of The Snipper.

Or, as the detective pointed out, was "onto" The Snipper.

Or, the man could've been a drunk who was giving Camilla a hard time at a nightclub—who knows?

For weeks, the nightmares had become exceptionally vivid for Jane.

In the darkness of her bedroom, she'd hear the distant sounds from her nightmares echoing through reality.

Snip, snip.

She'd hear those very sounds—*snip, snip, snip, snip*—from another room or, even at times, inches away from her ear at the most random times of the day; and every time, they'd cause the hair on her bumpy skin to rise.

She'd hear, as well as smell, such noises accompanied by the sudden squeals of a businessman sporting the smelly head of a dead pig. She could see and smell the man as if he was sitting directly in front of her. He wore a loose blue tie like a noose around his neck. Scratch that. The outfit changed. All of a sudden, he was wearing a cliché black hacker's hoody. With the fuzzy glow of the screen highlighting the shadows of his pig-face underneath the hood, he was hunkered behind a laptop, typing and squealing.

Whenever Jane closed her eyes to go sleep, she murdered inside the confines of a dream and yet, it felt as if she was the one being murdered in a way, as if she could feel each stab, hear each *snip*; then, the next morning, she was awakened to an unearthly creation, reborn for the masses. During each wake— each revival— Jane brought a piece of Mr. Moonlight with her, as if she had somehow stolen a memory from him.

At night, Mr. Moonlight would still visit Jane. During whatever activity, if it was grabbing a nightcap with a pity-friend from her work or catching a late night movie by herself, she'd find him standing at a distance, like always, staring at her, as if she possessed something that belonged to him; but he'd never ask for it. Either standing on a desolate street corner or sitting in an upper seat of a theater, Mr. Moonlight was the one constant in Jane's life.

Twenty-four days after The Snipper first struck, The Snipper made it to number one on the FBI's Most Wanted List.

But it didn't stop The Snipper from spreading terror all over the town.

The day after the lead investigator pulled Gumshoe's surveillance, The Snipper struck yet again.

The Snipper's next victim: Othello Brown, also known as "Gumshoe."

Gumshoe's severed head was found by a groundskeeper on the fifty-yard line Viper's logo in the center of Blight National's football field. The rest of his body was eventually found at a construction site, which led investigators to believe the body was meant to be found. What other reason would a serial killer dump one of his victims' bodies at a well-trafficked sight? Or, one investigator theorized, The Snipper was toying with them. Stretching the limits. Seeing how far he could go.

After extensive research into Gumshoe's social media pages, the investigators learned that Gumshoe was an avid Viper's fan. Went to games. Sported the Viper's logo, decals, and clothing. Trolled opposing teams and frequently started twitterwars with fans from rival teams.

The grisly details of both podcasters' murders were nearly too much for Jane to stomach.

"The final straw," she'd say.

The more Mr. Moonlight killed, the less she started to know him.

Which was strange, to say the least.

Jane became more paranoid and thought maybe she was The Snipper's next victim. Maybe the other victims had experienced Mr. Moonlight prior to the big *snip, snip*, but they didn't say a single word about it to friends or family members. Maybe Mr. Moonlight was the harbinger of death. There were a lot of maybes to throw around. One *maybe* Jane overheard while at work— another ridiculous theory—was that The Snipper was making his own personal Frankenstein's monster, constructing other body parts to form a singular body. Of course, the theory then evolved with more absurdity; and after Jimbo, one of the part-time techs, joined in the conversation and started brainstorming through that head of his, he proposed that The Snipper was making himself a skin suit, like Leatherface, only the whole body. As ridiculous as it sounded, it made perfect sense the more she had thought about it—the Frankenstein part. Jane wasn't certain if she had teamed up with the rest and bought herself a one-way ticket to crazy town. But Jane was certain that, if anything, something— maybe something positive—was going to come out of all of this. She didn't exactly know what, but she knew deep in her bones that somehow she was connected to Mr. Moonlight.

The morning Jane decided to drive to the police station to inform the detectives who were working The Snipper case about her "official" stalker, Mr. Moonlight and his possible connection to The Snipper, The Snipper struck yet again.

He was no longer killing his victims.

He was removing their eyes.

Each statement victims had given to the police was a near carbon copy of one another. At first, the investigators couldn't help but notice the oddity of it all. The Snipper was a killer who didn't show any mercy for his victims. At first, they thought it might've been a copycat—for real this time—who was inspired by what happened to Shanique Willis. However, as with the case of Gary Worthington, The Snipper was known to make statements and what better way to make a bold statement than to have the victims live through probably one of the worst moments of their lives. As the victims retold each one of their stories, the details remained the same: The Snipper snuck up behind them whether it be leaving work or walking to a car or running errands; then, each one was blindsided by a sudden dizzy spell, and then blackness. Each one woke up in a strange and dark place.

The black world.

For weeks, The Snipper and FBI played this cat and mouse-type game. The closer they'd get to catching The Snipper, the more he'd evolve. He was one step ahead of them; and to the FBI, it was as if The Snipper was one of their own.

Soon, the FBI started looking inward, doing internal investigations, but all of the witch hunts led them nowhere, only back to square one.

Forty-nine victims later, the detectives received a break in the case.

Hykem Thistle.

"Internet Troll."

Thistle spent his entire day trying to make himself a name on the Internet by trolling users and making up lies to feed, as well as distort the public's perception. It wasn't just the name-calling that set him apart from other trolls. He'd post false accusations backed up by professionally photoshopped photographs. He had multiple accounts and usernames, created all kinds of memes that went viral in hours, reeked havoc across social media. Each victim shared the same pattern as Thistle. The ages of each one of the victims ranged from twenty-one and up. The Snipper wasn't gender bias, either. He targeted males, as well as females. Allen Starnes, who was a failed YouTuber turned so-called "journalist," reported bogus stories on celebrities, headliners, or whoever was currently (hashtag) trending in order to whet his own farfetched agenda of rallying up mobs to publicly shame those considered "hot" at the moment.

The news broke that The Snipper was targeting trolls on the Internet, specifically "bullies," those who were inclined to promote or push their agenda of toxic masculinity, lowlifes, even the office rats who exhausted every hour of their days as a Clark Kent-type figurine around the office, only to become Trollman behind the confines of their cubicles. One of The Snipper's latest victims, a woman, not a man, Kirsten Maiden, turned out not being a "victim" after all. She served eight years in jail after she was charged as an "accessory" to the death of her classmate who died after she was bullied into committing suicide. Three years after Maiden was released on good behavior, The Snipper paid her a visit. With Maiden's background at the forefront of the investigation, FBI combed all of her twisted social media pages and found suggestive language broadly used at other individuals and groups. FBI profilers concluded that The Snipper was removing the eyes of his victims as if it was his subtle way of branding them with his own "scarlet letter." These sudden revelations had made it easier for FBI to narrow down their search for the killer—or, as in The Snipper's eye, vigilante.

Eventually, the public created a persona behind The Snipper and he became a myth, this imaginary figure like the Tooth Fairy or Santa Claus, only he was very much real.

"If you wrote something bad about somebody or if you did everything in your power to make somebody feel awful or unworthy of life or hinder their pursuit of happiness, The Snipper was going to track you down and send you straight to the *black world*."

Whenever Jane grabbed a caramel macchiato from Hot Java or ran errands or picked up groceries, she couldn't help but notice the "change" in people's behaviors. People were way more observant of their surroundings. Instead of having their head buried in their phones while waiting in checkout or pumping gas at the gas station, people were looking over their shoulders. People were awake.

Jane thought about Lady Justice, the blindfold she wore over face.

The Snipper was preaching.

About what?

For Jane, the young introvert who, in her dreams, often found herself trapped inside the mind of a killer, the answer couldn't have been more obvious.

Jane *finally* decided enough was enough.

She had to track down and *finally* face the man from her murderous dreams.

Her stalker, Mr. Moonlight.

Jane thought the real reason as to why she couldn't confront Mr. Moonlight whenever she saw him stalking her in public was that he wouldn't let her confront him. There was an invisible line wedged between the two, separating them from two completely different realms or dimensions. Even when Jane first *tried* to confront Mr. Moonlight at the tennis courts, Mr. Moonlight was no longer standing there and it was as if he *never* was standing there. Somehow, Mr. Moonlight disappeared in the nick of time. However, to Jane, she sensed that he was *still* there even though she couldn't actually see him with her own eyes. Like a feeling deep inside—a gut feeling—she felt as if it was the *feel* of the air all around her, another world in that very air she breathed;

even the way the cool air pressed against her body, it was as if she was wearing the air like a heavy fur coat. Jane was certain that she wasn't his next victim. Jane wasn't part of social media—at least not enough to draw attention—wasn't a member of Twitterverse, the Facebook scene, Snapchat, or any of the mind-manipulative outlets to alternate realties controlled by The Silicon Valley Overlords. She was hardly plugged in, except for the entire month of September when she quit her job at the animal hospital. She spent the late night hours researching past murders and violent crimes in and around, of all places, the West Virginia area. Jane scrolled through hundreds and thousands of mug shots available to the public, scouring the pits of the criminal database. The entire month of September was dedicated to research; however, Jane didn't know who she was looking for. She was just doing exactly that, *looking*. Maybe a part of her was consumed by the idea of wanting answers as to why she was so special. Jane certainly didn't fit the description of The Snipper's victims, didn't have a mean bone in her body—at least, not advertised. Yet, Mr. Moonlight habitually followed her around like clockwork.

Jane brainstormed an "old idea" the Feds tried with the late podcaster, Gumshoe. She had no other choice than to be a victim. She was going to be the bait.

Unlike Gumshoe's plan, which had backfired in his face, she wasn't going to lure out Mr. Moonlight by insulting him or trying to belittle him. Jane didn't have her own personal bag of insults lying around somewhere. No good punchlines or zingers or jabs or cheap shots to fling at the one whom she apprehensively called Mr. Moonlight. Wasn't her style. However, Jane was in a particular position that set her far apart from all the others. What made her so unique—and qualified—to carry out her mission successfully was that she had boatloads of material from her dreams. After all, she had been *inside* his head. She used it.

The day before her big plan, Jane went into the city and bought herself a gun. Something lightweight. Easy to carry. Only ten ounces. Like the ones the prostitute carries in his or her purse or the ones a well-endowed agent straps to his ankle. She liked the name of it too. Ruger. It sounded like a man's gun. Carried six rounds. Which meant, if he made a move on her, she had six attempts to put him down. But Jane was hoping for it *not* to go down like that. She took the Ruger for a spin the same day she purchased it with the money from her last paycheck. Used the shooting range below the ammunition shop to pop off round after round. During that time, an instructor shadowed Jane. Showed her the ropes. The do's and don'ts while handling a loaded gun. Jane caught on pretty quickly, though; in fact, she was a good shot.

"A real deadeye," the instructor told her.

The remark stayed with Jane for the rest of the day.

Deadeye.

Jane liked the name.

With her newly licensed weapon in possession, Jane spent her days glued to her laptop. She created a blog, which was sort of like her own journal, only every word was written for the entire world to read. She signed up and logged onto various social media pages in order to spread the word.

Mr. Moonlight was out there and it was only a matter of time before he found Jane.

On her blog, Jane recounted every little thing she knew about Mr. Moonlight, starting from the moment she first saw him hanging around outside her apartment to the time she encountered him at 'Da Bar. She was viciously candid in her blog. She wrote about how she could relate to him. The solitude she felt whenever she fell asleep and put herself into his mind. The loneliness. How awful it felt to live in such a ghastly place where its only inhabitants constantly went out of their way to stroke their own prerogative by picking apart, ridiculing, and trying to destroy anything that didn't belong to the starry-eyed world *they* observed behind their eyes. Jane didn't know whether or not the parts about loneliness or the feelings of being completely miserable in a world that she could no longer recognize anymore were totally true. In a way, the words came out like a hiccup. But she ran with them. She also wrote about the candid memories that had surfaced deep inside her dreams. Dreams within dreams. Deep slumbers, REM sleep. Sinking past the black place and experiencing the kinds of memories that made Jane question whether or not these memories were her own or somebody else's. She wrote in full detail about an "Uncle Cordell," or *Unk*, as she recalled. Certain traits and smells had come to Jane while she slept: the metallic smell of his ulcerous-laced breath, a tall and lanky man whose knobby fingers were always sticky with butterscotch, and the noises he'd make with his mouth as hard candy knocked against his teeth like a hockey puck. She carried all of these *little* things locked away inside her mind. However, Jane had never "physically" met Uncle Cordell before. But Jane *knew* him. *Knew* that he used to take her to the aquarium when she was a girl. Jane had these stark images inside her head and even though she wasn't a hundred percent sure if these images were hers or somebody else's, she knew they had come from a real place, not a black place. She also recalled the horror of the one-day she was bombarded by a horde of pigs. She remembered being smothered by them. She remembered hearing all those high-pitch squeals stinging her ears as they battered her body to the ground, their coarse hooves pushing her face into cold mud.

Jane hashtagged it—her memories or fantasies, whatever they were—for everybody to see.

After a full week of putting her thoughts out there, Mr. Moonlight started to take on a life of its own. Like The Snipper, Mr. Moonlight became a myth. Like all myths, they start out with a single buzz. Unlike The Snipper, Mr. Moonlight appealed to the underground scene, the cultists and theorists. He wasn't nearly as "mainstream" as The Snipper. But his name was out there. In a strange way, Mr. Moonlight's followers felt as if they could relate to Jane, her story. Some of the commenters mentioned that they, too, had encountered Mr. Moonlight at night.

The week after Mr. Moonlight became a new "thing" to talk about, Jane received a strange email in her inbox.

As soon as she read the email, she knew it was him, Mr. Moonlight.

First, the name of the email read:

POOCHYQUEEN@PAPURREMAIL.COM

Poochy, spelled with a *y*, not *ie*; however, she once saw it spelled *i* dot *e* dot.

She had also heard the name, *Poochy*, before, twice in her dreams, once when she had a dream about watching a YouTube video on "How to Make the *Purrfect* Cosplay Costume," and then, once again, when she dreamt of Camilla, one of Mr. Moonlight's victims, murmuring the name right before she received the *snip, snip*; then, another time, she overheard it being spoken when she was waiting on an airplane inside LAX. Once the plane touched down in Charleston, she was going to take another flight from Charleston to a smaller airport just outside Wensburg, Virginia, where Ruby would be waiting to pick her up. However, the airplane experienced engine failure, resulting in the plane having to make an emergency landing at the O'Hare airport in Chicago. Eventually, Jane made it to her destination, visited her friend for the weekend, and then flew back home. Jane suddenly realized that *he* was on that flight to Charleston. *He was!* She recalled this young yet extremely confident man, a similar profile as Mr. Moonlight, strutting down the center aisle of the airplane as if it was his own personal catwalk. Another passenger stood up from his seat two rows in front of Jane to stow a personal item into the overhead storage bin, the passenger not only temporarily blocking the aisle, but also blocking the young man's path. He had a silver Bluetooth in his ear and he was talking to somebody over the phone; but to Jane, it appeared as if he was talking to himself due the hands-free device. He was wearing lots of jewelry on his ears, hands, and all around his neck. What stood out the most was his pink hair which he wore in pigtails, as well as the light-colored cutoff jeans jacket worn underneath a holey top that matched his pink bubblegum-pop sunglasses.

The young man not only grabbed Jane's attention, but also other passengers' attention, not by the way he looked, but by the way he was acting.

Displaying an attitude for everyone to see, the young man stopped dead in his strut and deliberately shifted his weight to one side of his body as he waited in the most obvious exaggerated annoyance.

Once the passenger sat back down in his seat, he continued to strut toward his seat a few rows behind Jane. She couldn't forget the particular name that he said to himself—or at least, it had sounded that way.

Poochy.

Secondly, the email service.

Pa-per-email, the word per replaced with *purr*. Their logo was a cat dressed in a saddle with an emoji of an email riding on the back of the cat as it delivered an email. She reckoned the email service appealed to "cat lovers." She used to be a cat lover herself, back when she saw them as mutual friends instead of whining burdens. Mr. Moonlight had a thing for cats, she remembered. When Mr. Moonlight chained Gary's ankle to a fire hydrant and left him there to be found, he was rocking a lime green shirt with a flamboyant Siamese cat dressed in a sparkling gold dress and high heels. Above the Siamese was a cartoon bubble, the dialogue inside it reading something like "How you like *meow?*" She wasn't entirely sure, but she remembered the word *meow*. The image was distorted from the reflection of Mr. Moonlight in the tinted window of his car.

Thirdly, the contents of the email itself.

The email read:

I no wutt u doin. STOP it. Or elles.

Jane had only heard him speak several times in her dreams and she knew he wasn't the type of person who often used longhand or proper grammar. He was a visual monster who was *keen* on fashion.

For a moment, she pulled herself from the laptop and paced around the room.

Poochy.

Jane marched back to the laptop and googled the name, *Poochy*.

She came across the YouTube page of Drenelle St. Croix, the name *Drenelle* a combination of his birth name, André, and his "coming out" name, Shenelle; but most of his avid followers knew Drenelle as a famous Cosplayer who went by the persona, "Poochy Queen." Drenelle was a clothing designer who owned his own clothing line called, Cut and Paste. He was also known for designing his own extravagant costumes, which he showed off at Cosplay events. Drenelle was a celebrity among the tweens and teenyboppers, as well as the trans community, a role model who was an inspiration to our curious youth. But from recent comments Jane read in the comment board, Drenelle was also a subject of sharp criticism.

Once more, Jane pulled herself from the laptop and paused for a moment.

Was it really a dream?

Or, had Jane really been on Drenelle's page before?

Jane looked up Drenelle's profile, looked up his recent Cosplay events.

The last Cosplay event was at Hexacon in Huntington, West Virginia.

Drenelle went as Kilobit, a dark warlock/hacker from the *dΛ®κ Night* series.

Jane researched the date Hexacon was held.

The convention took place the same weekend she visited Ruby.

Without hesitation, Jane replied to the email.

Be at The Bullring tonight. Eleven o'clock sharp.

The Bullring was the nickname of Forsyth High School's football stadium. If "Poochy Queen" was the real Mr. Moonlight, then he'd know exactly what Jane was referring to when she used the word *bullring*.

Forsyth's mascot wasn't a bull, as most expected.

It was home of the Matadors.

The Forsyth Matadors.

🕐

WHEN Jane arrived at Forsyth High ten minutes earlier than the time she arranged in the email, Mr. Moonlight was already waiting for her. Jane couldn't see him, though, but she could definitely sense him.

She parked her car close by. Just in case something happened. Like her gun jamming or whatever. If so she'd beat Mr. Moonlight in a foot chase, although she hoped it didn't come down to that.

With her gun concealed behind her back, Jane stepped onto the football field. A distance floodlight shone its light on a dark lanky figure standing at the opposing team's end zone. Jane stopped in the end zone as well, her eyes slowly adjusting to the darkness. She spotted the eyes—or at least thought she did.

As she started to walk to the five-yard line, she noticed the dark figure getting closer to her.

Once she reached the twenty-yard line, she realized it was Mr. Moonlight and he, too, was walking forward. She made sure to keep her hands down by her side, inches away from her gun. Again, just in case the meeting turned hostile.

By the time Jane reached the forty-yard line, she didn't really know what she hoped to get out of the meeting.

Once, during her slow walk, she actually hesitated for a moment with a stutter-step and questioned her reason for being here.

She didn't have a reason—or did she?

In a way, she just wanted to talk to him.

Face-to-face.

Jane stopped in her tracks as she reached the fifty-yard line.

Mr. Moonlight stopped as well; in fact, to Jane, it looked as if he was mimicking her every move. His face was shielded by the night darkness. However, his profile remained the same from her dreams. He was wearing hippie-style sunglasses with small circular lens, which barely covered his pale eyes. The lenses made his eyes appear like lunar eclipses behind the wiry frame of his vintage sunglasses. Jane was also baffled as to why he was wearing sunglasses at night. She didn't bring up his taste in clothing attire or his need to accessorize. She started to focus on the *real* reason as to why she wanted to meet Mr. Moonlight.

Once she found herself in Mr. Moonlight's presence, the reason was simpler than she thought, as if the reason was there the whole time, dangling right underneath her nose.

The memory that she had been running from for so many years flooded over her thoughts. She turned her shoulder toward the field goal post in the end zone.

Jane nodded at the post and said, "That's where they tied me up. Right there. That's where they *killed* me."

She turned back around and faced Mr. Moonlight.

"The part that really counts, that is."

Strangely, Jane didn't expect him to answer her.

A part of her—a dark part—knew he wouldn't.

"I was only a sophomore in high school," she said as she started to tear up. All of a sudden, she found herself in deep thought. Reliving the moments from her teenage years, the mutant years, the awful years. "I had my entire life ahead of me," she said. "*They*, they took it all away from me." Jane paused for a moment to catch her breath. "When I saw that man's face on TV, I didn't recognize him at first. I suppose he put on all that 'daddy' fat. But his eyes, those reptilian eyes, those I recognized. The students used to call him Mr. Sakowski, aka Dr. Greenthumb. But I called him Mark. At the beginning, Mark was nice. *Socially awkward.* He once said that he was like me when he was my age. He didn't have many friends at school. Most of the students looked up at him. He was the 'cool teacher,' although misunderstood. Some of the students poked fun at him because of his nervous ticks and oddball analogies. He went out of his way, pulled strings to get me in his horticulture class with the juniors. There were like this 'exclusive group' untouchable by the rest of the school. I guess, at the time, I wanted to be a part of their group. To fit in, I guess. I used to hang out around the quarry not too far from school. At times, I'd skip school to hang out at the quarry. Once, I saw them there. They seemed so. . . alive, so untouchable. Mr. Sakowski brought me into his class, introduced me to them. And for a couple of weeks, they acted as if they truly cared about me. They all took me under their wing. We hung out at the quarry together, went swimming. Partied the nights away. Little did I know they were all using me, included *him*." Jane pulled herself away from the tragedy that consumed her for so many years and focused on the one good memory she shared with her horticulture teacher, the moment when Mr. Sakowski was no longer Mr. Sakowski, but Mark, the guy who talked a good game but was equally as cruel and wicked as the rest of them. There was only so much light and kindness in Jane's memory before it all turned to darkness.

Jane remembered staying after class to learn more about the plants inside the greenhouse. It started out as a harmless touch on Jane's shoulder. But to Jane, it was more than a touch. To Jane, Mark acted as if he was the only person on the planet who not only saw Jane, but also listened to Jane.

"On the night they brought me here to hang out or better yet, *lured* me here, I saw him standing across the field. I wasn't sure whether or not it was my mind playing tricks on me. But I saw those eyes of his in the dark," she pointed beyond the blenchers, "hiding in those shadows past the light, receiving some kind of sick pleasure from watching me in pain, not doing a goddamn thing to help me while they. . . *defiled* me. They knew about Mark and I—our relationship—and yet they acted as if they knew he wouldn't do anything about it. The next Monday, I saw him talking to them in the hallway, slapping hands with him, joking with him, acting like it was just another day, like what they did to me was okay, like it was a 'normal' thing to do to a girl. Even if Mark wasn't here that night, he knew what those people did to me. *He knew*."

The tears streamed from Jane's eyes.

She never wiped them away.

"When it came down to having my back when I needed it the most, he chose to protect himself by denying any relationship we had rather than facing the consequences of what he had done to me. I was partly to blame, I know. But I was young, vulnerable. He was an adult. He had a choice to do the right thing. But he didn't. He chose to be *silent*."

Jane sharpened her red-eyed gaze on Mr. Moonlight.

"All this time I was searching for the answers as to why I could never get a handle on my life, why every road I took—or every relationship I've ever had—ended up at a dead end. My road leads here and it'd always lead right back here if I didn't *finally* do something to stop it. It was 'them,' you see. *They* did this to me. *They* did this to *you. They* did this to *us.*"

Mr. Moonlight started to tremble as if he was feverish.

"I know," Jane said sympathetically as she studied Mr. Moonlight's weakening condition.

She took a closer step toward Mr. Moonlight.

In return, he mimicked Jane and took a step forward as well, only this time he looked as if he was strutting through a gale of wind, his knees about to cave in.

"I know how it feels to have your voice stripped away from you—from your soul—only to be made into a mockery." Jane stepped closer. Mr. Moonlight attempted to step forward but couldn't, for he was too weak. "I know *exactly* how it feels to have ev-ery-thing that makes you who you are reduced to something not even worth being picked apart and it feels as if you're nothing, less than nothing—"

Mr. Moonlight tightened his jaw, the muscles along his face stretched into his neck, and he finally uttered the words *release me.*

"I'm sorry," Jane said flatly. "I can't. Not now. But soon, maybe."

She reached behind her back and pulled out the gun from behind her back.

Hesitant, she felt the weight of the gun in her hand and readjusted her grip.

She looked up at Mr. Moonlight and said to him, "Do you believe two people can share the same conscience?"

Mr. Moonlight didn't answer, couldn't. His jaw was starting to tremble as if he was standing half-frozen in a meat locker, and he was too feverish to speak.

"Right," Jane said with utter deflation and once more, looked down at the gun loosely gripped in her hand. "*Crazy world*, huh?" She took her eyes off the gun and looked at the empty stadium around her. "I remember when I was a little girl my father used to say this ridiculous expression all the time. 'Here goes nothing,' he'd use to say. He used to say it whenever he was about to do something that he knew would result in failure. Like the time the lawnmower broke down on him. He tried everything to fix the damn thing, checked every part. Finally, he thought it needed a new spark plug. So he drove to the hardware store and bought a brand new spark plug. Came back home. He changed out the spark plug. I remember I was like his little helper that day, doing everything he asked me to do. I watched the frustration slowly mount inside him, as if it was starting to take over his body. I watched him waste away an entire day toiling away at that piece of shit lawnmower when the easy fix would've been to buy a brand new lawnmower instead of a spark plug because the lawnmower he had was old and falling apart. Just as he pulled on the cord, he turned to me." Jane drifted in thought, her face slackened. "He had this light twinkling in his eyes—I'll never forget that look." Jane paused for a moment and readjusted the gun in her hand. "Then, he spoke those words to me, '*Here goes nothing,*'" she said to Mr. Moonlight. "I wondered why someone, like my father, a person I looked up to for so many years, would say or do something when he knew it would result in failure. He did it anyway. Why? I guess it's because he believed."

She suddenly pressed the barrel of the gun directly to the side of her temple.

With her eyes open, Jane said to Mr. Moonlight, "Here goes nothing—"

And then she squeezed the trigger. . .

As Jane fell to the ground, Mr. Moonlight gradually stopped trembling. His posture changed as well, going from weak and badly hunched to tall and straight. Everything about him had changed.

Cool and collected, Mr. Moonlight removed the sunglasses from his face and looked over his arms and hands and then checked the rest of his body in awe. He moved his eyes to the body lying before him. Jane's body.

Mr. Moonlight kneeled over her and studied the gunshot wound and what it had done to the side of her head.

Throughout the gore, Jane's left eye was still fully intact.

The eye was pinned open and staring directly up at him.

The pale light gradually went out in his eyes, softening like a dimmer.

He turned around and walked back to where he had come from, to a cool and dark place where he'd always be welcomed, never neglected.

IN the autopsy's report, which was conducted immediately after the body was discovered, Jane Cutter's death was ruled a suicide. The townspeople had their own little stories as to what really happened to Jane, why she killed herself. Most of them blamed her suicide solely on her type of character. "A troubled young girl who couldn't cope with reality," they said. "A loner. Didn't have many friends." These comments mostly came from those who didn't have the privilege to speak to Jane. Words like *quiet* or *nice* or *different* were thrown around a lot to describe Jane—the word *"different"* usually met with slight hesitation in respect to Jane's family. For the most part, Jane was a quiet character, strangely quiet, different as most had spoken; however, Jane was loud inside, bold, roaring.

Her parents tried to honor Jane's wishes the best they could. Jane once mentioned to her mother that, if she died before her parents, she wanted her body not to go wasted. Jane claimed it was her way of giving back to the land. After all, she said it was the earth that created her. It was the very least she could do. Jane didn't own a will or anything, never had any plans to instruct those who survived her on what to do with her remains or possessions. She had nothing written down in contract, only the sacred words she left behind to a mother whose memory and temperament was drastically failing her by the day. Jane's mother thought maybe her daughter was saying all of those absurd things about death because she played around in the dirt too much or hung around too many bugs as a child or wasn't as social with her own kind and maybe didn't understand that no human being wanted their body eaten by worms. Jane's parents decided to cremate Jane instead and have her ashes scattered over Mount Newman. They had a small but polite gathering at the house, nothing pretentious. Jane's mother, a devout Christian woman, corrected herself on several occasions that it wasn't exactly a wake, considering Jane's beliefs in religion or lack thereof, but it was exactly that, just a gathering of those who knew her daughter, Jane.

The turnout reflected the way Jane Cutter lived her life, surrounded by people—strangers, really—who, other than her name or a faint glimpse of what Jane looked like, hardly even knew anything about Jane. Most of the guests were distant relatives from Upstate, second cousins and whatnot, mostly her mother's bookclub buddies, basically "strangers" who had used the rare opportunity as an excuse to either get wasted off free booze and eat fancy hors d'oeuvres or try to buy a ticket into Heaven by using Jane's name to startup scholarships or charities.

Only a handful of people from Western showed up at the gathering. The only close friend was Ruby, who took the loss the worst. One person in particular caught the attention of Jane's mother. Not once had she ever seen the queer man before, but, in a strange way, she felt as if she had. He stood out among the crowd of guests with his bright red hair. Yet, he reminded her of Jane in the way that he, too, looked out of place.

🕐

THREE days after Jane's ashes were scattered over Mount Newman, detectives, who were tirelessly working on the missing person's case involving Jane's former classmate Mary-Anne Simmons, received an anonymous tip about Mary-Anne or, someone who looked like Mary-Anne, being spotted at Devil's Throat.

When detectives arrived at Devil's Throat, they saw no sign of Mary-Anne. It wasn't until they got an overhead look of the quarry that they realized "something was in the water." *Something* not right. It was Detective Sharpe who found suspicious-looking tire tracks along the edge of a bluff. He put the two clues together, the tire tracks painting a stark image of a car driving off the ledge and then a murky shadow of a vehicle in the bottom of the lake.

Divers ended up finding not only Mary-Anne's car at the bottom of Devil's Throat, but also "other" cars. Six cars in total. Inside each car was a corpse. The marks on each one had varied. One victim, an attorney named Stephan Brodrickheimer, had been stabbed multiple times in the chest. All of the other bodies had less injuries. "There was a pattern," detectives learned from the condition of the bodies. Brodrickheimer's injuries had matched those of Sakowski's, most of the wounds being consistent around the upper torso region. However, some of the other victims' wrists had been zip tied to the steering wheel. One of the victims, Jay Carter, like the others, also Jane's former classmate, was strapped down to the driver's seat with a belt tied around his neck and secured around the headrest. The way they were murdered matched The Snipper's slow evolution. Detectives believed Sakowski and Brodrickheimer were The Snipper's first two victims; and then after that, it was Jake Durbin, Audrey Knox, Mary-Anne Simmons, Edward Lee, and, *finally*, Jay Carter. The victims' connection was obvious to the detectives. They all went to Forsythe High School. Four of the victims were on the high school football team, two were cheerleaders. They all knew each other. They were good friends. But it turns out the detectives were chasing a ghost. All fingers pointed to Jane Cutter, the recent suicide who shot herself in the head on the same football field where their recent victims played every Friday night.

However, there was one major **hole** in the story. . .
The Snipper was *still* out there.
Snipping away.

🕐

THE next morning the remainder of the missing persons' bodies were pulled from Devil's Throat. Drenelle, as he did most mornings, was doing his ritualistic pass through one news outlet to another. He reveled in the way each news outlet provided their own unique narrative to Jane's story when, in fact, there was only one story. There wasn't two, three, or four. There was one story. *His* story.

Drenelle left his studio, which was located in the basement below his auntie's townhouse, and met up with his friend, Latona.

"About time, Diva," she said, all sassy.

"That's 'supreme' diva to you—"

"Well, *Supreme Diva*, I've been waiting on you for a minute."

"You know me," Drenelle said, laidback.

"Yeah," said Latona. "I know you. Always taking your good easy time, like you always gotta look like you trying to impress everybody."

"So what you think, gurl?"

Drenelle opened the flaps of his bright orange blazer, did a twirl for Latona, and showed off the yellow meshed tank top, which matched his bleached blonde hair, as well as his green contact lenses.

Latona snapped her fingers.

"Flawless and fabulous, as always."

"Peaches and cream, baby gurl."

"Hey, ain't nothing wrong with dressing with the colors of the season."

Drenelle tapped Latona on the tip of her nose.

"Whoever said there *was* anything wrong?"

Latona shrugged her shoulders.

"I dunno."

"Hey, lemme ask you something."

"Yeah."

Drenelle and Latona started to walk toward the café.

"What you think of the name Mr. Moonlight?"

"Mr. What?"

"Moonlight?" Drenelle pointed to the sky. "You know, *moon*light."

"*Mister* Moonlight? You and I both know, Drenelle, you ain't no mister. Far from one. As a matter of fact, you said it yourself you against labels."

"I said that?"

Latona furrowed her brow until her forehead wrinkled and looked at Drenelle through the corner of her eye.

"You feeling a'ight—"

"—So, Mr. Moonlight. What you think?"

"You want to know what I think about Mr. Moonlight?"

"Yeah."

"Well, sounds like the name of an old Sinatra song."

"Sinatra?"

"Yeah," Latona drawled. "Frank Sinatra."

"How you know Frank Sinatra?"

"Drenelle, quit treating me like I'm dumb."

"I didn't say you was. You just did."

Latona smacked her gums.

"Anyway, you be thinkin' of that *Fly Me to the Moon* jam on TV."

"TV? Who 'da hell watches TV anymore? I get my shit from my phone."

"And where you think your phone gets its shit?"

"Whatever. It sounds 'old fashioned,' you think. Why you be askin'? You ain't thinkin' about retirin' Poochy Queen, is you?"

"Poochy Queen be *Poochy Queen*," Drenelle said, "and there will always be 'one' Poochy Queen. But I be thinkin' about another name, like something on the side, you feel me?"

"Nah," Latona said, shifting her weight to the side. "I don't really."

"All the great artists be changin' their names all the time. Look at Tupac. He did it. Prince did it—

"—Prince changed his name into a symbol."

"Yeah. So?"

"So, what 'da hell people gonna be callin' you if you change your name into a symbol?"

"Whoever said I was gonna change my name into a symbol?"

"You just did."

"No. I didn't," Drenelle said. "I'm just sayin'."

"What is you saying, Drenelle?"

"All I'm saying is I'm ready to—I dunno—expand."

"Expand? Like in doin' commercials and advertisements and goin' all mainstream like some sellout? Like that kind of 'expand?'"

"Not sellout," Drenelle said. "Just doin' something different."

"Drenelle, sweetie, you be makin' bank from all them subscriptions on your YouTube channel. You got the kind of fan base that most people your age would kill to have. They be showing up at all your shows. They be buying your clothes. You got it made, really. I'm jealous myself. Seriously."

Drenelle stopped underneath one of the many red maple trees along the sidewalk. Latona followed suit and stopped as well.

"You serious about this?"

Drenelle tilted his head in heavy thought.

"What about the name Moonbeam?"

Latona didn't respond as quickly as Drenelle liked.

"A'ight then," he said. "How about Moonstone."

"What's up with you and moons?"

"Moonbreaker."

Latona suddenly giggled at the name.

Once she realized the seriousness in Drenelle, she concealed her laugh.

"Moonbreaker? Seriously? Sounds like very *MCU*, don't you think?"

"Shear Solider."

"Shear—ah, no."

"Black Dragon."

69

"You ain't no dragon."

"Firechild."

"Child, please."

"Nightstar?"

"Drenelle—"

"—Black Night."

"Okay, Batman. We done here? Can we please grab something to eat already?"

"No," Drenelle said.

"No?" snapped Latona.

"That's Dark Knight. Knight spelled with a k. I'm talking about night as in the time of day."

Latona rolled her eyes.

"I get it."

"You ain't being helpful, you know?"

"Well, all of these names you keep spouting off sound like ridiculous superhero names, Drenelle, like. . . RE-DICK-U-LOUS," Latona emphasized for Drenelle. "You ain't no superhero, is you? Besides, what you planning on doing with this new side hustle?"

Drenelle noticed something hanging over Latona's shoulder.

"Don't move," he said abruptly.

"Don't move? Now, that's kind of catchy. 'Don't Move.' Like I'm 'Don't Move.' Which could act like some kind of reverse psychology shit. Your name's 'Don't Move' and all, yet the people who follow you would be the ones not moving 'cuz they too busy checking your fine-ass out. Sort of like the effect that lame band you be bumpin' to the other day. What'd you call them?" She paused for a moment and thought of the name of the 80's band Drenelle played for her yesterday while a spider started to crawl over her shoulder. "Oh yeah, *A-ha*! Like those fools who listen to them be like 'A-ha!' This is like some great music, dude!"

"Don't you dare talk about A-ha like that or else—"

"—Or else, what?"

The spider inched closer to Latona's neck.

"Don't move."

"You messin' with me, ain't you? What? You got you another one of them stalkers following you? I be tellin' you, Drenelle, you just you be paranoid from all that Internet fame. It's gonna straight to your head—"

"—No, Latona," Drenelle said clearly, his eyes attached to Latona's shoulder. "I mean, DON'T. . . MOVE. . . "

Without moving her head, Latona's eyes slowly moved to her left shoulder.

Next to move was her head, slowly at first, then, once her eyes met the brown spider sitting on her shoulder, her chin recoiled into her head and she leaped backwards. She flicked the spider to the sidewalk, dancing around on her tippy-toes as if not just one spider was still attached to her, but many. In fact, she combed her entire body, making sure the spider was nowhere on her body.

Drenelle couldn't help but laugh at Latona, her phobia in spiders.

As Latona nearly had a panic attack, Drenelle located the spider.

"What you doing?" Latona yelled out.

"Chill, would you?"

"Chill? Don't tell me to chill! You chill!"

Drenelle ignored Latona, blocked out all of the yelling she was firing away at him, and pulled out a can of Altoids from his coat inner pocket. He emptied out the mints and placed them inside both of Latona's cupped hands.

With hands full of mints, she asked Drenelle, "What in 'da hell you want me to do with this?"

"I dunno," Drenelle said, shrugging off Latona's bickering. "Put 'em in your pocket or something."

While Latona did as Drenelle asked and stuffed as many mints into her pockets as her blue jeans could handle before bursting at the seams, Drenelle reached down and picked up the spider with his bare hand.

"See, Latona," he said. "He's cool—"

"Drenelle! What you doing?"

"It's all good, Latona," Drenelle said as he carefully placed the spider inside the empty Altoids can.

"You've lost your damn mind, that's what it is."

"It's just a spider, Latona."

"Just a spider? That thing almost killed me."

"Nah," he said. "He ain't no killer. He just hanging out. That's all."

"Besides, I thought you hated spiders," Latona said clearly. "In fact, last time I remembered you were terrified of 'em. So what changed, Drenelle?"

Drenelle looked Latona in the eye. She was still terrified, still shaking a little from the minor scare.

"I guess I just look at 'em in a different light," he said to Latona.

"But you used to be—"

"—Used to be. But I think when I was little I used to like 'em."

"You liked spiders as a child?"

"Yeah," Drenelle said. "I think so."

"So, what? You regressin' now like my Aunt Miranda?"

Drenelle didn't respond to Latona's assumptions about his mental health.

Instead, he closed the lid and placed the can in his coat pocket.

Latona smirked.

"New pet, huh?"

Drenelle shrugged and stood to his feet.

"Old habits never die, I guess."

"Old habits, as in collectin' little ole spiders?"

"Yeah, so? Gotta problem?"

"To each his own," Latona said under her breath and then nodded toward the intersection ahead of them. "Let's go already," she said, louder.

"A'ight, a'ight," Drenelle said and followed Latona to the intersection.

"So, don't you need to poke holes in that or something? Won't it suffocate?"

"He'll be good for the time being until I can find him a better home."

"*Better* home? You should listen to yourself, Drenelle."

Again, Drenelle didn't respond.

He'd rather listen to Latona.

🕐

WHEN Drenelle and Latona made it by foot to one of their favorite spots in Chinatown called The Tea House, Inc., Latona couldn't shut up about how starved she was, but mostly she couldn't keep her mind off waffles with green tea ice cream, which was like a staple dish for anybody who visited the famous tea house.

Drenelle came for the *oolong* tea; however, by the way his interest was more focused on the three young men hanging out a few tables away, it appeared to Latona that Drenelle had another agenda in mind.

Latona took her eyes off the waffles and asked, "What you keep looking at?"

"Nuttin'."

"Drenelle," Latona said, "you hadn't spoken a word since we got here."

"I just like watchin' you eat. That's all."

"From what I can tell," Latona turned her shoulder and glanced at the group of young men at the other end of the tea house, "you ain't just watchin' me."

"Who? Them?"

"Yep."

"I don't know them."

"You act like you do—"

"—But I don't."

"Whatever," Latona said dismissively and noticed Drenelle glancing down at his phone. "Any word from Corey?"

Drenelle puckered his face in disgust from the sound of his name and let out a loud and exaggerated sigh.

"You still talkin' to him, ain't you?"

"Nope," Drenelle said, *popping* his lips from the letter p. "I'm done with that nigga. Corey Grugier. Nigga need to change his name. He ain't even French."

"You still got me, Drenelle," Latona said.

Smiling from ear to ear, both cheeks ballooned outward like a puffer fish from the food still balling in her mouth.

"You will always have me, gurl."

Latona continued to eat the waffles, savoring each bite.

Meanwhile, Drenelle moved his eyes back to the three men huddling over the table, whispering to one another in secret.

One man, who was wearing a raggedy Western tee shirt, broke away from the other two and stood behind a quiet homely woman in line.

Without her knowing, the man extended his arm behind her back, positioned his phone flat, camera-side up underneath her skirt, and took a picture.

The young woman suddenly rotated around and asked what the man was doing.

He shrugged innocently and said, "Nothing. Just drop something."

She wasn't fully aware of what the stranger behind her had just done; however, from the way she retreated back into herself in a restless state of anxiety, it appeared to Drenelle that she knew *exactly* what happened but she was too afraid to say something. Both her legs inched closer together, so close that the heels of her shoes were nearly touching one another. She moved her pocket book in front of her shaky body and folded both her arms tightly across her chest, as if she was wearing her arms, as well as the pocket book, as some sort of protective shield.

The young man didn't bother ordering anything, which was another red flag.

Instead, he walked back to the table he came from, huddled close to his other buddies, and showed them the recent photo he had just taken on his phone.

With a wide grin on his face, the man started texting or writing something on his phone while the other two couldn't keep themselves from laughing.

"You know," Drenelle said to Latona, as he removed his eyes from the three men and sipped from his oolong tea, "it's supposed to be a full moon tonight."

"So, what?" Latona mumbled, chewing her food from one side of her mouth. "You gonna turn into a werewolf?"

"I dunno," Drenelle said. "Maybe."

"So, you have any plans tonight?" Latona asked, as she looked back down at the plate of waffles.

Without Latona looking, Drenelle glanced at the young woman grabbing her tea from the server and taking it to a booth in the very back of the tea house.

"As a matter of fact, I do."

"Oh yeah? Like what?"

Once more, Drenelle moved his eyes toward the young woman.

"Just a few things."

"Like what, *Mister* Mysterious?"

"Mr. Mysterious, huh?"

"No," Latona said suddenly and stopped chewing. "Lame. *Super*-lame."

"Yeah," Drenelle said, deflated. "You're right. Cheesy."

"Cheesy? What you mean cheesy?"

"You know, like corny?"

"Corny?"

"Like, I dunno, like something that's overused."

"What didn't you just say 'overused' then?"

"You know, at times, you can be real finicky."

"Me? Finicky? *Guuurl*, like you one to talk."

"Ain't like being finicky is a negative description of one's character. In fact, I wouldn't even call it a flaw. I wish there was more finicky people out there like you," Latona pointed to herself, "*and me*, too. Like just the other day, my cousin was telling me how finicky I was."

"Gurl, your cousin don't know shit from sand."

"Technically, most sand is shit. Fish shit," Latona said as she wrinkled in her nose. "Saw it on one of them nature channels."

"Is that so?"

"Finicky people pay attention to details," Latona said with a shrug. "Without them details, it's like trying to make a batch of waffles without cracking an egg. Sure, you can use that powder mix shit, but you and I know a waffle ain't a waffle without eggs."

"And that's what I love about you, Latona," said Drenelle, raising his cup of oolong tea in a toast. "You *see* the details even when you can't."

The woman, who was sitting in the back of the tea house, suddenly stood up from her seat. Both of her eyes were red from where she had been rubbing away tears. She glared at the three men from across the tea house, grabbed her belongings, and stormed out without trying to make a scene.

Drenelle turned his narrowing green eyes to the three obnoxious men laughing it up a couple of tables down. He already knew what had to be done to them.

For Drenelle, it was already done.

UNDER the harvest moon twelve-two pulsated like a lazy virescent phantom in the corner of Star's eye.

She moved her eyes from the radiant moon and trained herself to focus on the numbers, four numbers, *not* three.

Twelve *o' two.*

Myko is late, Star thought to herself.

Two minutes late.

To Star, it felt like twice an eternity.

But it wasn't the matter of time that disturbed her the most.

I was going to murder somebody.

A real-life person.

The notion alone of plotting away inside her parked car in a seedy alleyway in one of the seediest, most detestable areas of town and doing exactly what her sagacious father warned her *not* to do caused her jaw to tighten with the tamed rage of a tigress.

Star questioned herself, her motives behind the madness: *Is this what it takes to find happiness?*

In that moment of great uncertainty, all Star could think about was time and where the hell it had gone and how, such a precious commodity, like time, was no longer her ally. Mostly, Star thought about her ole dada, Carlos, as if he was an oblique depiction of time and the callousness of its seemingly harsh nature. Star realized how disappointed her dada would've been to know his daughter, his little "Starlight," had jeopardized her own well being by putting herself in a position of eminent danger, even worse thinking, the very idea of taking another person's life. Carlos Walker was dead, been dead for over three years—or three "long" years to his only daughter, Star. Carlos died unexpectedly after his battle with stage-four lung cancer, which had caught Star, as well as her mother and her family, by complete surprise. Carlos wasn't a smoker. Except for taking a toke when he was at a curious-age, he never smoked a cigarette in his life. He had a distant-distant relative who had died from cancer of the brain. Other than that, he didn't have any family members who died from the big c-word. Star always thought it was either the secondhand smoke that killed him or the pollution in the air. He was always hanging around smokers. *They killed him*, she once thought. They were the ones who murdered my father, *the smokers*, and so, too, did the world around him. Eventually, the thought passed. But it didn't change the way Star felt about them. Carlos had better than good genes. Had the kind of genes that most would kill for. Had a greater grasp on maintaining a healthy diet with a balance of work and exercise. Every morning he jogged four miles around The Harbor. Ate right eve-ryday, hardly indulged. However, he seemed prehistoric by the time Star was in grade school. He had Star when he was an older yet relatively fit man strong enough to give Star a queen-esque piggybank whenever their family visited Fantasy World every summer. Carlos's father, Star's grandfather, was one of the first black cartoonists to have his cartoons published in the daily *Bystander*. Which, having survived the Civil Rights Movement, was a big deal for the Walker family. Carlos Senior was a pillar of the community. Some would say, a man who had rightfully earned the title as "legendary." His son made sure to carry on his father's legacy through his own artwork and creations, as well as a foundation dedicated to his late father. Even though these men were long gone, a piece of their presence was very much alive in Star.

Pulling herself from the thought of her dada, Star glanced at the time on the dashboard and thought that maybe she forgot to change it after the end of day-light savings time. She grabbed the phone from the cup holder and checked the time on her phone.

Same.

Two minutes past midnight.

As Star unlocked her phone, a car pulled up behind Star.

"*Finally*," she said under her breath.

One of the headlights of the car was burned out while the other one, the glaring one, shone through the rear view mirror and forced Star to squint.

Once her eyes adjusted to the bright light, Star could hardly recognize her-self in the mirror.

Again, she thought about her dada, his disappointment.

"I can't believe I'm doing this," Star whispered as she shut off the engine.

As she held in a deep breath through her nose, she turned her shoulder to the cat carrier in the backseat.

The glow of its eyes materialized in the darkness inside the carrier.

The sight of the creature alone nearly stole her breath; and for a moment, Star forgot to breathe.

As she leaned in closer to the carrier, it released a low-pitch *growl*.

Startled, Star leaned away and took a moment to gather herself.

She reminded herself to breathe. She breathed. Then reached for her purse in the passenger seat and pulled out a pair of purple gloves. First of all, she slipped the glove over her right hand. By the time Star reached her left hand, she paused and thought it over again. Mainly, Star thought about all of those articles she had spent hours skimming through on the Internet before she ar-ranged this very meeting. Mainly, Star thought about her own health risk.

On second thought, she decided to put on an extra pair of gloves over the pair she was already wearing.

With her hands protected, Star cut the engine of her car.

She was first to step out.

Then, Myko.

Star wasn't sure whether or not that was his real name.

She didn't care.

As Myko stood by his car, Star opened the backdoor and carefully pulled out the cat carrier.

Confused, Myko pointed at the carrier.

"Hold up," he said suddenly. "What the hell is this?"

"What you mean?"

"Is that thing alive?"

"Of course, it's alive."

"I thought we agreed that y'all kill it."

"Like hell we are," Star said, disgusted. "That wasn't part of the agreement, Myko."

"Have you ever killed and skinned a dead animal?"

"No."

"It's a pain in the fucking ass."

"Then, deal with it," Star said coldly. "Besides, I thought this kind of stuff was your expertise?"

"It is, but—"

"—*But*," Star said over Myko.

"Whatever," Myko said in deflation. He nodded at Star's hands. "What's up with the gloves?"

"I'm just being precautious," Star replied, making sure to keep the cat carrier away from her body.

"Is it contagious?"

"No," Star said. "Of course not."

"Then, why wear the gloves?"

"I *just* am."

"This thing ain't gonna scratch me, is it?"

"Could," Star said, "if you do some dumb shit like poke at it."

Star handed the cat carrier to Myko.

In return, Myko was hesitant about touching the carrier.

"It's not going to scratch you."

"Well, how you know it ain't gonna bite me?"

Star clenched her teeth and inhaled deeply through her nose.

Deep breaths, she thought.

"Don't mess with it and you'll be fine, all right?"

"You sure?"

"No," Star said bluntly.

Myko finally grabbed the handle on the cat carrier.

During the exchange, the cat carrier shook violently.

Myko suddenly flinched.

Star readjusted her grip over the handle and rolled her eyes at Myko.

"Are you gonna take it or not?" asked Star.

"Yeah," he said sharply, like a boy answering a smothering mother's question.

This time, he grabbed the handle and a sudden odor caused his nose to wrinkle. First, he smelled himself. Then, the cat carrier. His head jolted backward.

In disgust, he said, "This fucking thing's gonna stink up my car."

"Roll down a window or something."

"Where the hell did you get this thing?"

"Does it matter?"

"Forget I asked."

Myko lugged the wobbly carrier to his car. He placed the carrier in the backseat of his car and shut the door behind him.

"How long will it take for her to feel the effects?"

"According to my sources, it should take at least forty-eight hours—"

"—Your sources?" Myko giggled. "What? You like friends with someone who works at the CDC or something?"

Star flexed her jaw, her rage lukewarm but tame.

Myko asked, "How sure are you that this is gonna work?"

"Once it's done, my partner will wire the money into your new banking account," Star said, her tone stern like a businesswoman. "You just make sure you follow all of the details he gave you and everything should run smoothly."

"You don't sound too confident."

"It *will* work. Just do your part. Got it?"

"Yeah," Myko said with a stutter. "Got it."

"Are you sure?"

"Yeah," Myko said, more sharply. "*Got it.*" As Star started to walk back to her car, Myko asked Star from behind, "Tell me. What did this woman do to you to deserve to go out like this?"

Star stopped just before she opened the car door.

"It's only a matter of time before she destroys me. If she was in my position, she'd probably do the same thing." Star shrugged her shoulders. "Of all people, you should know what it's like to lose everything—the ones you love—to wonder whether or not you're going to survive the night, spending your waking hours suffering like a wounded animal desperate to be put out of its misery. I'm trying to salvage whatever life I still have left and the only way I can achieve that, Myko, is with her out of the picture."

"You know there are other ways. Simpler ways—"

"No," she said, unwavering. "I know your other 'simpler' ways and they will draw *way* too much suspicion. This right here. This is the *only* way."

"Whatever," Myko said callously. "Y'all just make sure y'all follow up on your end of the deal."

"You don't have to worry about us."

Star didn't even wait for Myko to reply. She got back into her car.

As Myko drove away, Star hit the ceiling of the car.

"Pop-eye," she murmured.

For good luck.

🕐

STAR spent the early hours of the morning disinfecting the entire backseat of her car. She scrubbed and scrubbed until her fingers blistered. Spent at least an hour on the area where she had set the carrier. Once she was done cleaning the seats as well as the floors, she cleaned them again.

🕐

DURING the drive to Chop Soy, Star received a text message from Carmen:

I'm going to be running a little late.

Star patiently waited until she stopped at a red light to shoot Carmen a text back; however, her phone was acting up. For some bizarre reason—Star thought it might've been a service issue maybe or something to do with cell phone towers or even the new upgrade, which apparently included the so-called "bug fix"—she didn't receive a decent signal whenever she left China-town and entered Little Tokyo. Star started to lose her patience with her phone as she waited until that little white bar moved across the screen in turtle-pace speed.

By the time the text went through, Star was pulling into the restaurant's parking lot.

No worries. I'm almost here.

Eventually, Carmen received the painfully slow text.
Then, texted back:

Okay, Early Bird.

Star didn't want to be rude. She had a diplomatic response for Carmen:

I'll grab a table in the back.

Then, Carmen:

Sounds nice. See you soon.

🕐

WHEN Star stepped inside Chop Soy, Fay had already grabbed a table located near the back of the restaurant.

Fay spotted Star at the entrance and waved her over.

Star told the giddy hostess that she was meeting a group of friends.

The hostess grabbed a menu and escorted Star to the table.

"If it isn't Lady Justice standing right before my eyes," Fay said, opening her arms.

Star forced a smile upon her face and hugged Fay.

"Hey, girl," she said, her voice climbing in forced excitement as well. "How are you?"

Surprised by Star's glow, Fay said, "Can't complain." She stepped back, her eyes did an once-over Star's toned body, her getup, her hair, then she redirected the question back at Star. "Look at you. Looking all spiffy. You wear the look of a woman who spent a month in Love Town. So, tell me, who's the lucky winner?"

Star paused, her face somewhat recoiling from the remark.

"Please, Star," Fay begged. "I want details now."

With her chin pressed against her neck, Star said, "I don't know what you're talking about?"

"You know you haven't changed one bit, Star. Still as modest as a mouse."

Star sighed away what she took as a harmless insult.

Fay always carried a pocketful of them, she thought to herself.

"So," Star said, cutting through nervous tension, "you've been here long?"

"Just got here," Fay said. "I figured I'd go ahead, grab us a table before this place gets swamped. I read somewhere that there was some Cosplay thingy at the CP Convention Center this weekend. So, you know it's probably gonna be, as the kids say, 'popping' around here."

"A Cosplay thing, huh?" Star nodded at Fay. "That's right up your alley."

"Not really," Fay said, her brow curling with what Star considered as embarrassment. "Haven't been to one in like years."

Star looked around the restaurant, which was half-full. Strangely, the sight of people being in the vicinity of Star felt comforting. From a legal standpoint, Star looked at them as, more or less, witnesses.

Fay pointed at her seat.

"Take a seat."

Star took a seat as the waitress stopped by the table and poured Star a glass of water and asked Star what she'd like to drink.

"Just water," Star said and pointed at the glass of water.

"Just water? Come on. Really, Star?" Star noticed Fay do that slight move with her brow again. "We haven't seen each other in months. Please, don't make these lunches out as if they're chores, Star."

Fay held up her gin and tonic, tempting Star.

"I would, but I have to go back to work."

"So? One drink ain't gonna kill you, girl."

"Yeah, but it can get me fired."

"You're telling me all your lawyer buddies don't have a cocktail for lunch. Thought it was like a requirement for your profession."

"Fine," Star said annoyingly. "One gin and tonic."

The waitress listened, waited.

Star turned to the waitress, who repeated the order and then walked to the bar area.

"That's more like it."

"So, how've you been?" asked Star.

"Same thing, different—"

"—Different day, right?" Star removed her sport coat and placed it over the chair. "So, any new clients?"

"As a matter of fact, I'm working with a new client right now. A comic book artist."

"Really?"

"Strange fella."

Star's cheeks darkened.

"Strange is good, right?"

"The guy's borderline psychotic. I'm talking grade-a perfectionist, like the *autocrat*-type."

Star laughed at the comment.

"One of them, huh? He sounds committed."

"Anyway, he wants me to do an entire facelift on this new book. Fonts, design, everything."

"What's the name of the comic book?"

"Technically, graphic novel."

"I see."

"So, what's this 'graphic novel' called?"

"*Slow Motion.*"

Star paused.

"Interesting."

"I know," Fay said. "I don't care much for the title—"

"—Nah. It's good."

"The story is really incredible, though. It's about a gifted girl who can slow down time. People of power—in particular, *men* of power—want what she has so they try to take it from her."

"Slow down time, huh?" Star thought aloud. "Relatable. I think everybody would love to slow down time, especially living in a time that's moving at a thousand miles per hour, you know, with technology and all."

"I know, right? Anyway," Fay said, "this girl ends up using this gift she has for the greater good."

The waitress arrived with Star's drink.

Star made sure to thank the waitress.

In return, the waitress asked if the two wanted to start off with appetizers, but Star insisted on waiting for the others to show up before placing any other orders except drinks.

Which didn't sit too well for Fay.

She was hungry, already half-buzzed. She ordered yet another gin and tonic to keep her busy. Then raised her partially full glass in a toast.

"Well," Fay said to Star, "to the High. . . " Fay looked around at the empty seats around her, ". . . Five."

"Right," Star said flatly. "More like High Two."

"More like the Trusty Two," Fay said. "First to show and last to leave."

"Salut." Star paused before tapping her glass against Fay's. "And, to *Slow Motion.*"

"Cheers."

Star sipped from the gin and tonic.

Then scrolled through the messages on her phone.

"Okay, Ms. Modest," Fay said. "Out with it. I want details. Who is he?"

Star put her phone aside.

"I assure you, Fay, there's no 'he,' only me."

Fay tilted her head to the side and stared at Star, as if she wasn't going to say anything for the remainder of the lunch until Star was completely honest with her.

"Okay, geez. You're worse than my mother. There is one guy."

"Now we're talking." Fay leaned forward, rubbing her palms together. "So, what's this one guy's name?"

Star hesitated.

"John."

"John, okay. And what does John do for a living?"

Star thought of the first word that came to mind.

"Nothing."

"Nothing? He's gotta do something."

Star shook her head.

"Nope," she said, more confidently. "He does nothing. Absolutely nothing."

"Very ambitious, this John guy sounds."

"Well, you asked, Fay. I told."

"So, you mean, he sits around the house all day and does nothing."

"Yep," Star backtracked her immediate answer, "well, he doesn't exactly sit around the house all day. Every now and then, he'll get up off the couch and help me out whenever I'm tied up."

Fay furrowed her brow.

"You talking about what I think you're talking about?"

"What you mean?"

"You know?"

"What? You mean sex?"

"Star Walker, you *are* a freak," Fay said as she could hardly contain herself. "I knew it. You have a sex slave and his name is John. You never cease to amaze me, Star."

"Careful now with the slave talk, Fay. You are talking to a woman of color."

"Wow, Typical-Star," Fay replied, the tops of cheeks reddening. "You went straight to the race card."

"Well, you did use the word *slave* in front of a black woman."

"Yeah, all right," Fay said. "We get it. I forgot you were so sensitive about the subject, Star." Fay pointed at herself. "I'm a woman of color." She pointed to a dark skinned woman sitting at the other end of the restaurant. "She's a woman of color. We're all people of color. I'm sure, somewhere in the *distant* past, we all had ancestors who were slaves. I'm pretty sure I had relatives who were slaves, having, like, one percent Egyptian in me. You don't see me getting all offended by the word."

"You're a woman of color? You white?"

"Last time I checked white was a color. I mean, if you wanted to get technical, I'm more of an oatmeal-brown."

"Oatmeal-brown?"

Star tried not to laugh.

"As you know, Star, my dad is white. Mother, Asian. Besides, if you look at it from the bigger picture, we're all slaves. Every single one of us," Fay reached into her pocket and pulled out her phone, "only our master isn't a man. It's a machine."

Star took a sip of her drink, her face expressionless.

"You know, I'm just messing with you, right?"

A laugh broke through Star's stern exterior. Fay started to laugh as well.

"For a second, I thought you turned into a snowflake."

"Snowflake? What?" Star said, "Nuh-uh. Not me. But you, damn, girl, you really get worked up about this race shit." Star took yet another sip of her drink. "But that's what I like about you, Fay," she lied. "You get really funny, like hysterical, when you're mad."

"I'm not mad."

The waitress arrived with Fay's drink.

"I think you need another drink, my sister from another mister." Star waited for the waitress to leave. Then said from the corner of her mouth, "By the way, I have a sex slave named John. Yep. He's my bitch."

"*Freak*," Fay said under her breath.

She removed the lime from the glass, squeezed what little juice it had into the drink, and used the handle-part of a fork to stir the drink.

"Too bad they joined the trend and stopped using straws," Fay said. "It's like they're promoting the erosion of tooth enamel and early gum disease. #Fuckyou. I was going to say something earlier, but the waitress is kind of cute and I didn't want to make her feel uncomfortable."

"It's all to save the planet, you know?"

"From what? Plastic?"

"Centuries from now when highly intelligent aliens take over the planet Earth and obliterate all mankind, forcing our entire race into extinction, they'll comb what's left of the earth for artifacts we left behind—traces of our accomplishments and failures—and the only thing they'll discover is, you guessed it, plastic. That's all we'll ever be known for." Fay's eyes widened. "Hey, Earth. What was it that you really needed from those pesky humans? Earth's response: Plastic."

"Cynical-much."

Fay shrugged.

"So, tell me more about John the Sex Slave. Is he a good kisser?"

"If I had to rate him like a movie on Rotten Tomatoes, I'd probably give him around a seventy-six percent—on the lips, that is. However, whenever he's, you know, kissing other places of my body, I'd give him ninety-eight percent because a hundred percent would raise way, *way* too many eyebrows and make it look like the producers 'paid me off' all for the sake of a good score."

"John sounds 'Certified Fresh.'"

"Oh," Star said, "he's got a Oscar-worthy tongue, baby."

"Does John have a sister?"

"No," Star said. "But he has a brother."

"Not interested."

"Speaking of bitches, you still seeing that one bitch?"

"Which one?"

"You slut." Star said to Fay, "I see you still approach your sex life the same way you vote."

"Which is?"

"Undecided."

"You know I'm not all into labels."

"What's so wrong about a woman being with a man? Being a hetero or lesbo or whatever your sexual preference is, none of those things are really considered a 'label.' It's a part of the human condition."

"Really, Star?" she said bitterly. "Why don't you try walking down Jefferson Street holding another woman's hand and you wait and see how many ugly stares you get—"

"—Did you ever think that they're staring because they're probably checking you out," Star said. "What other reason would they be staring at you?"

"Some of them—*some*—have the balls to actually say whatever it is they're thinking. But, for most of them, I already know what they're thinking."

"So, you can read minds now?"

"Good idea for a new comic book: A girl who can read minds."

Star ignored the idea, ignored the triteness behind it.

"Forget about 'em. That shows a lot about their character and how simple-minded they are."

"Well, it happens way more often than it should."

"People will come around. Eventually. They always do."

"Easy for you to say." Fay shrugged. "Ever since I broke up with Steph, I've been O for six on the other team. I'm not hating on your team at all. But, I swear, some guys act as if they're entitled to be with us, like they shouldn't have to put in any actual work to earn our affection."

"Not all guys are dogs, Fay." Star found herself thinking about the comments that she said earlier. "Well," she corrected, "most of them are. You just haven't found yourself the right one, you know, the overly sensitive type who makes you a better person."

Star was eating her words.

Better person, she thought. *Is that what am I?*

She washed down the thought with another sip of her gin and tonic.

"Well," Fay brought Star back into the conversation, "the last two I've been with have ended up in total disaster. It's like I have a magnet that attracts losers."

"When it comes to choosing a man, you're about as picky as a Forty-Year-Old Virgin."

"Men have enough flaws as it is."

"Women have flaws too, Fay. Sorry, Beyoncé. We ain't 'flawless.'"

"The last guy I was with was named Kelly—and by the way, what kind of a man's name is Kelly? Rhymes with belly, as in bellyache. Which makes perfect sense because every time we made out he gave me heartburn. Not only that, his penis was bent like a question mark and half the time, the guy acted as if he didn't even know how to use the damn thing. It's not rocket science!"

"I once read in *Women's* magazine that a curved shaft heightens the pleasure for a woman during intercourse."

As Fay sipped from her drink, her throat clenched in a burst of a laugh, which caused her drink to spill a little bit over the rim.

She cleared her throat and said to Star, "I would have to go on the record here and respectfully disagree with you, Star. I mean. . . have you like seen one?"

"What you mean? Like for real or on the Internet?"

"No," Fay said. "I mean, like 'seen' one, like close enough you could shake its hand." Fay waved her hand in the air. "Hello, nice to meet you!"

"No," Star said, sipping from her drink. "I can't say that I have, but I once dated a guy who hung thirty degrees to the right. At times, it acted like it had a mind of its own. I wanted to anchor it down like a newly planted tree."

"He could've broken it, you know."

Star shook her head.

"That's like an urban legend," she said. "It's not like it's a bone. It's mostly tissue and veins. And we all know you can't break tissue."

"But you can tear it, can't you?"

"I don't know, can you?"

"I think we'll leave that up for Mandy to decide."

"Yeah," Star murmured. "I'm sure she'd know a thing or two about the male anatomy."

"She's a doctor—"

"—A pediatrician. Much different."

"How so? It's no different than a veterinarian. You got to treat a cat, a dog, a lizard, a snake."

While Star glanced down at her phone, Fay studied Star's change in mannerism soon after the name Mandy was brought up into the conversation. She didn't think much of the change—at least, not yet.

"You know," Fay said, thinking, "another thing about Kelly that I couldn't stand—I mean, it drove me crazy whenever we'd go out in public. The clothes he wore. For fuck's sake, he's a grown ass man dressing like he's an eight year old boy. A fucking manboy is what he is. He's always wearing these superhero T-shirts two sizes too small. It's absurd what some men have turned into."

"Was he in shape?"

"Does it matter?"

Star was leaning toward yes, but she said no.

"He's ripped," Fay said. "You know, typical gym-body. The ego matched the size of his muscles. More than likely, he's probably standing in front of a mirror somewhere staring at himself. I swear, put him in a nice suit and tie and he'd make a good news reporter."

"That type, huh?"

"The *Narcissistic Asshole*," both Star and Fay said together in synchronized harmony.

"Well, to me, sounds like you're not over Kelly. You've mentioned his name two times thus far, once in the present tense. One more time and you're potentially looking at regret. Then, from there, I can't help you. We're talking full-on cyber stalking. Checking his Facebook updates. Monitoring his current status—"

"—You're crazy."

Once more, Star looked down at her phone in a strangely tense silence.

Again, Fay noticed the sudden change in Star, her aura.

She didn't know what to think of the expression—or lack of one.

Star looked up at Fay, saw her eyes shift.

"Look who I bumped into on the way over here," said the voice behind Star's shoulder.

In perfect timing, the next two members of the High Five arrived.

Rhonda and Carmen.

Fay was first to acknowledge Rhonda. Then, Star turned around in her seat and saw Rhonda standing behind her. Carmen wasn't too far behind.

Star stood from her seat and greeted Rhonda with the common, "Hey, how are you?" along with an awkward hug, which came across as a full body heave. Carmen was next to hug Star. Other than a drawn out "Hey, gurl," they didn't say much to one another. Fay remained in her chair and greeted Rhonda with an animated wave.

Rhonda sat down to the right of Star while Carmen sat down right next to Fay and reached over to Fay in a half-hug.

Once they were all settled into their seats, Rhonda had some shocking news for the rest of the gang.

"So, did y'all hear about Mandy?"

At a loss of words, Star tilted her head in utter surprise. She embraced for the worse.

Fay and Carmen shook their heads.

Slack-faced, Star said before Rhonda could follow up, "What happened? Is she okay?"

"Yeah," Rhonda said, laidback. "Of course. She's fine. She had to cancel. She said she had a thing."

Both Fay and Carmen let out a sympathetic *awh* while Star was more interested in why Mandy had canceled.

"A thing?" she said. "What thing?"

"A new patient probably. She didn't exactly say. You know how she's always saving lives."

"Yes," Star hesitated, trying not to draw anymore unwanted suspicion to herself. "Well, that's unfortunate, I guess."

"It's not the High Five without Mandy," Carmen whined.

While Carmen turned to Fay and felt her material and complimented her on her fashion taste, Rhonda leaned closer to Star and asked about her life as a paralegal.

"Busy" was the first word that came to Star's mind.

That, and "demanding."

"Still locking up big, bad wolves."

"That's not exactly my job," Star said. "But I've been preparing myself for The Bar. Hopefully, by the end of next year, I'll be on my way to becoming a lawyer."

"Criminal or civil."

"Criminal."

"A friend of mine's husband has already taken The Bar, like, twice. From what she told me, he basically said it's hard to pass."

"Not if you study, it's not."

Star took a sip of her drink.

"You still teaching at Red Valley?"

"They moved me up from ninth grade to eleventh. If I knew I was going to have to work twice as hard, I would've stayed in ninth grade. Eleventh graders treat reading as if it's a chore. Sometimes, I feel so—I dunno—old around them. The worst is when they call me Ms. Abbott."

"What's wrong with going by a miss?"

"It's makes me feel so old."

"You are old, Rhonda."

Rhonda dropped her jaw and leaned back in repulsion.

"You serious? I'm only a few months older than you."

"I'm not saying I'm not old. I am old—"

"—I ain't old," Fay chimed in.

Star received a text from Carmen:

She's going to kill you.

Rhonda couldn't help but notice Star reading the secret text.

Star subtly put the phone away without drawing more suspicion.

"You know I didn't mean it like *that*, Rhonda," she said, trying to put out the fire, which was slowly building inside Rhonda. "Once you step out into the real world, they, the kids, tend to look at you differently. You're no longer considered cool or whatever word they use these days—"

"—They still use the word *cool*."

"My brother still uses the word *phat* to describe things."

"Fat? You mean like fat-shaming?"

"No," Fay said. "*Phat*. Ph-fat."

"I've never heard of that one."

"You're telling me you've never heard of *phat*—"

"—All I'm saying, Rhonda: You're one of 'them' now. The uncool people. Don't take offense to it. I'm uncool." Star pointed at Fay. "You're uncool. Face it. We're all uncool."

"Hey," Fay interrupted, "I don't care what you say. I'm cool."

A chirp of a laugh slipped from Carmen.

"What?"

Rhonda was still caught up—in fact, obsessed—by what Star referred to her as "them."

"Them?"

"You know," Star shrugged, "an adult."

Holding up her glass, Fay said to Star, "Thanks for stating the obvious, Killa of Cool."

"You know what I mean, Fay."

"In a way, they do make me feel old," Rhonda said carefully. "I used to text all the time in high school. Now, it's like texting is their only form of communication." Rhonda sighed. "God, just listen to me. I *am* starting to sound like my mother."

The comment drew a couple of laughs.

Right on cue, the waitress stopped by the table and asked for orders. Rhonda stuck with water while Carmen spent every bit of five minutes grilling the waitress about Chop Soy's tea by throwing random yet legitimate questions at her in which most waitresses wouldn't know, like where the tea came from or what kind of soil was used in the process. The waitress surprisingly answered each question as if she was throwing them at Carmen in vain for attempting to undermine the integrity of Chop Soy and their dedication to their message of being a green company. Carmen swallowed each answer that came her way. Not once did Fay interject her feelings about Star and herself being the only ones drinking alcohol for lunch. She was too preoccupied by listening to the proficient waitress one-up on Carmen as she dropped some knowledge on the process of making tea. Star finished the rest of her drink and ordered another one without second thought.

Star felt as if she needed the drink, as if it had become a necessity for getting her through the next hour.

Once Carmen was done interrogating the waitress, she made her best attempt to draw more attention to the straying topic in the conversation.

"I know exactly what you mean, Star," Carmen said directly to Star. "Everything changed for me after I had Charlie. I feel like a better person. I no longer feel like I have to prove to anybody that I'm not a responsible person. Trust me. I am perfectly happy with being 'uncool.'"

Rhonda cut in, "I was meaning to ask you, Carmen. How was you momcation?"

"Did I miss something here?" Star asked. "What the hell is a 'momcation?'"

"It's basically where you take a vacation from being a mom. Hence mom-*cation*."

"So, what? You went on vacation by herself?"

"That's the whole point, right? Get away from being a mom for a few days."

"Where'd you go?"

"I went to the Cayman Islands. Did the whole works. The full body treatment. Spa. Facial. Massage. After about a week, I felt like a brand new me. If you ever have a child, I totally recommend taking a momcation. It will *literally* change your life."

"I don't have any plans in spitting out a rug rat anytime soon," Fay said from the corner of her mouth. "So, no, I'm good—and forget about this whole 'on-the-clock' bullshit. A woman can have a child at any age. I mean, nowadays, women are giving birth in their fifties."

"Fifties is like the new thirties."

"You are aware that there are many risk factors, including—"

"—So who watched Charlie?" Star interrupted Rhonda.

"Max," Carmen said, shooting a glance toward Rhonda. "Why?"

"He didn't mind?"

"Max?" Carmen repeated. "Not at all; in fact, he's really good with kids. He and Charlie get along very well. Did you not check out the photos I posted on my Facebook page?"

Star shook her head.

"No."

Carmen then turned to Rhonda, waited.

"I didn't get around to it," Rhonda said. "I've been literally swamped with school."

"You got to see these photos," Carmen said, pulled her phone from her purse, and showed the photos to Rhonda. She made sure to describe each photo, where it was taken, what she was doing at the time. She handed off the phone to Star, who only looked at one photo, which was a photo of Carmen sitting on the beach while she was holding a brightly colored drink shaded with a miniature umbrella in one hand and a black pole of some kind in the other hand. Star couldn't quite tell what it was.

"How'd you take the photo?" she asked.

"I brought my selfie-stick, of course."

Fay said in a lowered tone, "You own a selfie-stick?"

"Yeah," Carmen snapped. "Don't judge."

Fay raised her hands, as if she didn't want to fight.

"Next month, I leave for Haiti."

Carmen asked, "Is Mandy going with you this year?"

"No," she said. "Unfortunately, another 'thing' came up. I know, right?"

"That's Mandy," Carmen said. "Always saving lives."

Always saving lives, Star thought as soon as the words spilled from Carmen's lips.

"This year's going to be extra special because of all the destruction left behind by Claudia. Armey, who's head of Mount Zion, is bringing in tons of worshipers from other churches around the country to lend a hand. I talked to Rachel Merger—"

"—Who's Rachel Merger?"

"She's one of my teacher friends from school. I talked her into coming with me. She's looking forward to it. It's going to be a *huge* event."

The waitress returned to the table with Carmen's green iced tea and asked if they were ready to order.

Two out of the four were still undecided.

The waitress said she'd give them a couple of extra minutes to look over the menu; and then, once more, she left the table.

Over the pause, Star asked, "What about your job?"

"The trip takes place right before Fall Break. So, I'll only miss a couple of days of school. I've already got a sub and everything."

"How about starting off with an appetizer?" Fay suggested while skimming through the menu.

"How about lettuce wraps?" Rhonda suggested. "I haven't tried them yet."

"I'm down," Fay said.

"Fay, you're down for everything."

Fay's brow curled.

"What's that supposed to mean, Carmen?"

"You're like a garbage disposal."

"I am not."

"Are too." Carmen put the menu aside and leaned closer to Fay. "Hey, Fay Baby, I'd kill to have your metabolism. You can eat whatever you want and not worry about gaining weight. Me, on the other hand, I eat a bite of ice cream and I can feel my ass getting fatter."

"I'm sure you dread this time of the year."

"Tell me about it."

"I hate Thanksgiving."

"I actually like Thanksgiving, but not because of the food."

"Then, why do you like Thanksgiving?"

91

"*Duh*," Fay said. "Family, of course. Except for maybe my birthday or a random pop in, it's like the one time of the year I get to spend more time with them."

Carmen said, "Max and I are thinking about getting away after Thanksgiving. We haven't had any 'alone' time ever since Charlie. We've been currently in a jam with the whole 'babysitter' situation. Like this morning, right, it literally took me forever trying to find a babysitter."

Rhonda asked, "What happened to that new girl, Angela?"

"She quit."

Fay narrowed her eyes in a manner that would suggest deviance.

"Let me guess," she leaned closer to Carmen, "Angela was snooping around your house and she found a little 'something-something' that she wasn't supposed to find. Am I getting warmer?"

Carmen shouldered Fay.

"Cut it out."

"Come on, Carmen San Diego. Am I getting warmer?"

Carmen paused, then smirked.

"Warm," she said.

"Okay," Fay said, sitting more upright. "So, Babysitter Angela found something, something that either made her quit or something that forced her to quit *or*," Fay exclaimed, "you," referencing Carmen, "were looking for some excuse to fire her because you didn't like her *or*, even better, you fired Babysitter Angela based on what she found, *but*, instead of telling us you fired her, you decided to say she quit so you wouldn't draw any suspicion to the matter."

"Too late," Star chirped.

"She found Max's secret stash of pot that he keeps hidden in the flower vase in the foyer."

Carmen rolled her eyes.

"Cold."

"Of course," Fay said, "what kind of teenager looks through, of all places, a vase?"

"One who was desperate to dig up some dirt on you. No pun intended."

"No," Fay said, squinting her eyes. "Angela was a curious girl who spent her weekends babysitting when she should've been spending them with her new stud of a boyfriend who was still trying to get some action but hadn't rallied up enough confidence to make a move. After Charlie was put to bed, she was all by herself. Her new boyfriend was out probably partying with the other football players or even hooking up with a girl who showed him the attention. So, Babysitter Angela turned into what most girls her age turned into: Curious. She went through your jewelry and potential items she could pawn off for that boob job she so desperately wanted for Christmas, but—"

"—Cold," Carmen said. "Ice cold."

"*But* Angela's no thief. So, feeling like the curious one she was, Babysitter Angela decided to go through your more 'personal' items, ones that you keep tucked away in the cozy confines of a drawer."

Carmen smirked.

"Warm."

"Oh," Fay said, "I'm boiling, Ms. San Diego. Babysitter Angela started with Max's stuff. Maybe tried on a couple of his things. Maybe she wanted to know what it felt like to be inside the clothes of a man. No. That's not Angela's style. She's crafty, you see. She's like some young Nancy Drew, only way smarter and more bitchin' and has a keen eye for the perverse nature of the human race—"

"—All right," Carmen blurted out. "She found Craig."

"Craig?"

"That's her big black dildo," Fay said with a grin on her face.

Star said, "You have a big black dildo named Craig?"

"That's not all she found," she confessed. "She found all of Craig's buddies, too. She found the whole gang. Believe it or not, it was my idea. I mentioned it to Max out of the blue. He was into it. The next day, he comes after work with bags full of sex toys, gags, and bondage junk."

"Okay, *Fifty Shades of Grey*."

"And what exactly spawned this salacious idea, Carmen?"

Carmen pointed at Fay.

"What she just said?"

"A movie?"

"The book, actually. You've read it?"

"You think I'm the kind of person who would read that smut?"

Star said, "I'd rather watch a porno."

"I thought it would spice up our marriage."

"Let me guess," Fay said. "He's gotta bent dick?"

"Fay!" Rhonda said, repulsed but not entirely surprised by her candor.

"My husband's penis is just fine, and, for your information, perfectly shaped. But I appreciate your concern."

"Well," Star asked, "did it work?"

"Did what work?"

"These, you know, toys."

"What you think?"

Fay said, "And I thought Star was the freaky one of the group. Man, was I wrong?"

"Fay, really?" Rhonda retorted. "Is that necessary? During this current climate of inequality and toxic masculinity, don't you think comments like those have further divided us women when we—collectively—should be uniting around all females regardless of their sexual preference? The woman's image has already suffered enough damage as it is. One side calls us brave for finally standing up for ourselves once and for all; while, at the same time, we're frowned upon by the other side and treated like a bunch of prudes who've never gotten laid before. Let's not dig the hole any deeper, shall we?"

"Not only is she starting to sound like her mother, but she also sounds like your typical Millennial who practices hypocrisy," Fay said as she reached in her pocket and pulled out an Altoid. "Wanna mint to help you feel better? Or," she said, "how about tissue?"

Carmen leaned closer to Fay and mumbled, "Watch it, Fay."

"Guys," Fay said innocently, "I'm teasing."

"Sure you are."

Star asked Fay, "Aren't you a Millennial, Fay? Oh, that's right. I forgot you weren't into any labels."

"Hardy-har-har."

"I think *Millennials*—our age group—gets a bad rap," Star said to the other three, "like the Hippies or Yuppies or Whoever."

"Don't forget about the ever-so precious Baby boomers," Fay seethed from what sounded like across the room. "They use innocence as an excuse for intolerance. By any means, they certainly don't get a free pass in, as Rhonda said, the current climate. All you have to do is pick up a history book. I mean, just look at all the shit your grandparents went through."

"I don't have to look, Fay," Star said, trying to hold back her anger. "I already know."

"I know you do, but still."

"It's hard to compare the two because it was such a different time back then," Rhonda said to Fay. "It's like trying to compare an athlete from thirty years ago to an athlete in today's world. I hear my students do it all the time, like they lived during that time period when, in fact, they weren't even born. Athletes have gotten stronger. Back then, it was just a game. Now, for some, it's like a way of life. So, you can't say one athlete is better than the other. That conversation is a bust. The only way you can justify your argument is by creating a time machine. Last I checked it hadn't been built yet. But until someone does create a time machine, what's the point arguing about it? The world has changed. If anything, the Baby boomers have showed us, by their mistakes, who we should be and who we shouldn't be. That's a good thing, right?"

"I agree, but what does that makes us?" Star questioned.

Rhonda shrugged.

"Opportunists."

"But don't you agree that, as soon as a generation is defined or pigeonholed into a category, it creates a whole new entity completely separate from reality?"

"Yeah," Rhonda said. "Could. But people see what they want to see. Most people just see things to justify their means, as if they're ignoring what makes us unique and only looking at the certain things that give us, as you said, a bad rap."

"Like we're 'entitled,' they'll say. Or, 'spoiled rotten.'"

"'Indecisive.'"

"'Too distracted.'"

"'Too soft or hypersensitive.'"

"'*Easily* offended—'"

"—By the way, Star, who exactly is 'they?'"

"You know," she said, looking around the table, "The Internet."

Baffled, Rhonda said, "You don't really take the Internet seriously, do you?"

"Don't get me started on The 'Internet People,'" Fay said, chewing on a piece of ice.

"That reminds me," Star cut in, her seriousness gathering everybody's attention. "I have an announcement to make. I was going to tell you guys earlier, but I guess, I was waiting for the right moment."

"You're not pregnant, are you?"

"No, Fay," Star said with annoyance. "I'm not pregnant."

Carmen asked, "Is everything all right, Star?"

"Yeah," Star said, looking down for a moment. "It's fine."

"What is it?"

Star paused.

The other members of High Five leaned forward in anticipation.

"Star, what is it?"

"I'm *finally*. . . "

"Finally?"

"I'm finally quitting Facebook."

Carmen gasped.

"What? Why?"

"You've been saying that for months."

"No," Star said seriously. "I quit Facebook."

"Quit? Like done—"

"—Quit, as in I deleted my account this morning."

Fay raised her glass.

"Congratulations, my friend."

Carmen leaned closer toward Star.

"Why'd you quit Facebook?"

"I dunno." Star corrected herself, "I guess I'm just tired of it trying to control my life." She pointed at Fay. "Like what Fay was telling me earlier, before you guys showed up, about machines taking over."

"Really, Fay," Carmen said to Fay. "You brainwashing Star now?"

"But it's true—"

"—I just don't understand the whole 'wanting to share my entire life with the world' thing anymore," Star said. "It's my life, not theirs. I don't want to be *that* person who gets criticized or ridiculed by some troll for a post I made on the Internet. I'm sick and tired of *all* of it. I'm sick and tired of all the fake news, the one-sided point of view. I'm sick and tired of *all* the anger comments showing up in my news feed, starting fights, provoking me to be someone I'm not—articles about 'people' being upset about 'whatever,' some trivial bullshit when, in reality, only a small group of angry people who have nothing better to do with their lives than to be angry about whatever, make a couple of tweets and all of a sudden, its considered headline 'news.' Comments from people I don't even follow, as if it's Facebook or Twitter's way of trying to make me angry all to benefit their companies' profits. The longer I'm plugged in, the more money they make. The more money they make, the more control they have over me. No way. I'm not going to let these people hijack my brain. Then, you have all these advertisers eavesdropping and tracking your every move. I'm sick and tired."

"Over half the Internet is fucking click bait," Fay said. "Like yesterday, I got some web-cam chick following me on Twitter. I checked out her page and it was clearly a spambot."

"Or some Russian dude posing as a web-cam chick?"

"Or that," Fay said. "Whoever it was, they were trying to entice me to click on a link to a naked pic."

"And did you?"

"Hell no!" Fay paused. "But that's not to say I didn't check out the rest of her Twitter page."

Rhonda said, "I once knew a teacher friend of mine whose phone got hacked. A week later after the hack, she found these bogus accounts on the Internet with her picture in the profile."

"Don't be so negative," Carmen said over Rhonda.

"Like you're one to talk, Carmen," Rhonda said. "The other day, you were talking about changing your name on Facebook."

"That's totally different."

"Change your name?"

"Just my middle name."

"You know, I didn't even realize the initials until this jerk, who's been stalking me, pointed it out. Which I'm kind of glad he did."

"What's your middle name?"

"Úrsula."

"Úrsula, huh?"

"I know what you're going to say, Fay." Carmen shot a glare at Fay. "Don't even go there."

"Carmen Úrsula Navarro Treviani."

Fay repeated the full name to herself.

Then, spoke the letters out loud.

"C, U, N—*Cunt*!"

The others couldn't help but laugh.

"Of *ALL* the men out there, you just so happened to pick the one man with a last name that starts with the letter T."

"Now, I see why you want to change your name."

"Well, drop the middle name."

"Besides, Carmen, most women I know drop their middle name after they get married."

"It's *my* name, not yours."

"Then, don't let some loser on the Internet tell you otherwise."

"No," Carmen said, looking down. "It's probably better that I do. I'm saving myself from future humiliation."

"Lately, it seems like it's getting harder to go on there."

"I don't think so," Carmen said. "I personally don't know what I'd do without the Internet. Where do you think I met Max? All the single women I know don't even go out to bars anymore. They're all on some dating site."

Star said, "You can't buy love or a follower. You have to work for it."

"Star's right," Fay said. "*But* I can't quit Facebook. So, what if it's for like old people. I need it to help promote my business."

"I go back and forth from Instagram to Facebook. But I like Facebook better."

"I still use Facebook," Rhonda said. "I probably use Facebook more than the other social media pages."

"Yeah," Fay said. "You're old, remember?"

"You're hilarious, Fay."

"Why thank you," Fay said politely and then nodded at Star. "I think eventually I'll quit Facebook."

"Eventually is another word for never."

"Facebook has complicated my sex life," Fay said. "For instance, last week I wanted to share a gorgeous photo I took while I was kayaking at Devil's Throat, but I was like, 'Oh, shit!' I totally realized I told a 'certain someone' that I didn't want to go out with her because I was too busy working with a new client."

"Why didn't you just tell this 'certain someone' the truth?"

"You mean you haven't lied to someone because you didn't want to hang out with them at that moment in time."

"Yeah, but why not just tell this person you didn't want to hang out?"

"I just met the chick," Fay said. "That's probably the last thing you want to say to someone you just met. I ended up posting the photo and then deleting the photo like a day later, but it was already too late. It was already 'out' there."

"Did she see the photo?"

"She hasn't returned my texts. So, yeah, more than likely, she did."

"Wasn't Devil's Throat the place where the police found all those bodies?"

"That's right," Carmen followed. "I remember hearing about that in the news last week."

"Technically," Fay said, "they didn't find the bodies until like a month or so ago. So, the lake is perfectly safe. Besides, a couple of dead bodies ain't gonna stop me from kayaking—"

"—Have you seen a dead body before, Fay?"

"I heard it was more than a couple."

The waitress was back at the table, anxiously waiting to take orders.

The morbid conversation came to a sudden halt.

Rhonda took charge and spoke for the rest of the group.

"First, we're going to start off with some appetizers," Rhonda said. "The lettuce wraps—"

"—A cup of miso soup," Carmen ordered.

"And some spring rolls," Fay said abruptly. "Don't forget spring rolls?"

"And the spring rolls," Rhonda said and looked around the table. "Anything else?"

Star shook her head.

"That's just about does it," Rhonda concluded.

With a smile on her face, the waitress jotted down the orders on a notepad in one swift stroke of her pen and once more, glided away.

"Doesn't it freak you out, though?" Carmen asked, watching the waitress as she walked back into the kitchen. "Just the thought of kayaking so close to where something awful happened?"

Resilient, Fay shook her head.

"Not really," she said and tapped her finger against the table. "People die all the time, Carmen; *in fact*, I bet ya someone died right here at this very table while eating their lunch. He—*or she*—was probably enjoying their miso soup when all of a sudden he—*or she*—felt a sudden tightness in his or her chest and then, all of a sudden, he—*or she*—had trouble breathing and then—"

Star laughed off the awkwardness of the joke.

"Really, Fay?" Rhonda said contemptuously. "Enough already."

"I'm just saying 'death' happens all around us," Fay said in defense. "It's the only one thing we *all* have in common. Can't we at least embrace what unites us instead of what divides us?"

"Really, Fay?"

"They should give that maniac the death penalty," Carmen said as she tried to break up the soon-to-be scuffle between Rhonda and Fay.

"You know, I actually heard somewhere that The Snipper wasn't the only one who committed all of those crimes. Instead, he had a crazy cult do all his killings for him. Like that one guy—"

"You mean Charles Manson?"

"Him."

"Yeah," Star said with slight hesitation, "but the people he killed weren't exactly saints either."

With exaggerated disgust, Rhonda said, "You actually agree with what happened to all those poor people?"

"No," Star replied. "Not really. But people should take a hard look at themselves before they start throwing around judgments."

"Typical Star," Rhonda said over Star. "You haven't changed a bit. You're just like you were in high school. Always sticking your neck out for the little man who blames society for all of the world's problems." Rhonda said to the others at the table as if Star was no longer sitting right next to her, "Remember when Star went out with that mumbling little pimple-popper, Justin Blaylock, in order to lift up his self-esteem—"

"—Justin, the Zit Machine? If a zit could talk, it'd sound just like Justin."

"I so did not go out with him," Star said louder. "Even if I did, who cares? It was high school."

"He was a creep."

"He was nice."

"Yeah," Carmen said. "And he had a face that would be perfect for a creepy stalker in a horror movie."

"Star, the psychopath was a 'se-ri-al kill-er' who butchered its victims with a pair of scissors and justified it by claiming these people were awful people—"

"—Bullies."

"Whatever," Rhonda dismissed Fay's side remark and then faced Star. "That still doesn't give a person—"

"—A monster."

"It doesn't give him a right to kill people. How can you defend some 'thing' like that?"

"I'm not defending him."

"More like *It*," Rhonda clarified, her tone more bitter. "Not defending *It*."

"I heard somewhere that he killed his victims with the same scissors he used to make his outfits with. Reminds me of that one dude from *Silence of the Lambs*. Buffalo Bob. What a creepo!"

"Buffalo Bill."

"No," Carmen said. "I'm pretty sure it's Buffalo Bob."

"Carmen," Star said, "that's just a movie, you know?"

"Wasn't it based on a true story?"

"I don't think so."

Star checked her phone, googled the movie, *Silence of the Lambs*, and in the matter of seconds, she had the answer for Carmen.

"Nope," Star said, flaunting her phone in front of Carmen. "Fictional. Based on a book written by Thomas Harris. And by the way, it's Buffalo Bill, not Bob."

Rhonda said over a tense silence, "I think what's so disturbing is that it happened so close to home? I actually contemplated moving to another city—"

"What about your job?"

"There will always be other teaching jobs."

"There are psychopaths in every city," Fay said while making a figurine with her napkin. "Just the other night, somebody got shot not too far away from where I live. Like hell I'm going to move. It's the world we live in. There are clinically insane people out there. Probably some right here in this very restaurant."

"Yeah," Carmen said. "One's talking right now."

"Hilarious."

The other members of High Five laughed, except Rhonda.

"You're serious about moving?"

"Not really," Rhonda said, shrugging. "But I'd be lying if it didn't cross my mind. Mandy told me that she swore she saw St. Croix at the House of Tea a few months back in Chinatown. She mentioned something about a weird-looking guy with bleached blonde hair staring at her from across the restaurant. She said there was something 'off' about him."

"He could've been scouting out his next victim?"

"Who knows?"

Fay asked, "Did you guys hear about how he was captured?"

"All I know is that the cops found like blood or something that matched one of the victims."

"Yeah, but do you know how they found that blood?"

The others didn't respond, which Fay took as a no to her question.

"The aunt borrowed the scissors The Snipper used to kill his victims with and loaned them to *her* sister, The Snipper's other aunt, who was going to make one of those human chain decorations to display at a birthday party for her son, The Snipper's nephew. Somehow, The Snipper's nephew got a hold of the pair of scissors while his mother wasn't looking and while he was running around the house with the scissors, he accidentally tripped and fell onto the scissors; ended up stabbing himself."

Star asked, "You're shitting me?"

"I shit you not, Star," she said bluntly. "Tragically, the kid died. Apparently, there was an investigation into his death, even though his death was later ruled an 'accident.' Cops seized the scissors, 'The Snipper's weapon of choice.' Found a trace of dry blood on the pair of scissors. The investigators matched it with The Snipper's latest victim. The cops put the two pieces together. Arrested Drenelle St. Croix, aka The Snipper."

"Talk about karma."

"When police raided his aunt's house and found all those eyes he kept in jars in his studio, one of the reporters said the eyes were positioned in a way that faced his workspace, as if, in a bizarre way, all these eyes were watching him while he worked. They were like his own trophies or his audience—"

"—Can we talk about something else, please," Rhonda said, extremely irked by Fay's morbid interest. "That's all you ever hear about in the news nowadays. It's like everyday they're reporting something awful that's happened. A stabbing. An active shooter. A protest. A riot. A maniac on the loose. Someone murdering someone because of *this* or *that* or because no reason at all."

"You call it news," Fay said blandly. "I call it entertainment."

Rhonda ignored Fay.

"Like a couple of weeks ago, I heard that somebody somewhere in Chicago, I think, was standing in line, waiting to order food, when out of the blue he pulled out a gun and shot somebody in broad daylight because he didn't—how do I say—he didn't 'agree with' the clothes he was wearing."

"Now that you mentioned it," Fay said, thinking, "I remember hearing about that story. The guy was from West Virginia; in fact, it was odd because there was another similar incident not too far from the shooting. Guy and woman arguing. I remember the woman was from West Virginia too. She was visiting Chicago or something. She went all psycho and killed the guy. Stabbed him to death or something like that. What was even more odd was that the two murder-suspects went out the same exact way. Both ran out in front of a car. *But* that wasn't the strange part. The strange part was they had third-degree burns on random parts of their bodies. Yet, there wasn't any indication that there had been a fire or anything of that nature."

"Talk about strange."

"Very."

"There's one theory circulating that it was some kind of botched government experiment, an outbreak of a 'new' disease."

"Here we go," Carmen said and dismissed Fay by getting lost in her phone.

"Fay," Star said, "don't be *that* girl, dear."

"Don't you guys question these certain types of things?"

"Unexplainable things happen, Fay. When it comes to all these theorists, why is it always the government's wrongdoing?"

Nobody was paying attention to Star.

Everybody was looking directly behind Star.

"Mr. Klopper!"

Star heard an old yet familiar voice behind her.

"If it isn't the *Young Professionals*!"

Surprised by the resonant voice, Star turned her shoulder.

Standing directly behind Star was a hunched over man in his early sixties but looked much older from the frailness of his body, as if he had been through several bouts of major heart surgeries. He was Star's twelfth grade English teacher, Mr. Eugene Klopper. Standing not too far away was Mr. Klopper's wife, Remy.

"The lawyer," he said, touching Star's shoulder.

"Not yet," Star said, forcing a smile. "Still a paralegal."

Mr. Klopper pointed at Rhonda.

"Teacher."

Then, pointed at Fay.

"The artist—"

"—Technically, Graphic Designer."

Then, Carmen.

"The Violinist."

"Ex-violinist," Carmen corrected Mr. Klopper. "Now, full-time mother."

"How many?"

"One, for now at least."

"How old?"

"Just turned three."

"Boy or girl?"

"Boy," Carmen said. "It took me forever trying to find a babysitter to look after him."

"I love 'em when they're that age. Enjoy every second. Before you know it, they'll be all grown up and hating your guts."

"Well, I'm just glad the terrible two's are over. I've heard its all downhill from here—"

"—You mean uphill," Fay interrupted.

"Is that what I said?"

"You said 'downhill.'"

Mr. Klopper said over the two, "Uphill. Downhill. Either way, you'll be just fine." He looked around the table. "So how you doing ladies?" Before the others had a chance to answer, Mr. Klopper threw his finger in the air as if a thought had just come to him. "Wait a second," he blurted out. "I believe we're missing one, aren't we? Where's the doctor?"

A smooth, silky voice crept up behind Mr. Klopper.

"*Standing right behind you,*" the voice said.

Each member of the High Five remained in a state of shock, except for one. Star.

Who appeared reserved from the sound of the voice.

Mr. Klopper rotated around and said, "Mandy? How are you?"

Mandy hugged Mr. Klopper.

"I'm good," she said. "And you?"

"I can't complain."

"I thought you weren't going to make it?" asked Rhonda.

"Well," Mandy said, "here I am."

"The last time I saw you ladies was a few months back."

"Every four months, we have our quarterly lunch."

Fay said, "It's like 'our thing.'"

"I think that's swell," Mr. Klopper said kindly, "keeping in touch like that. I remember the last time I went to my high school reunion, except for a couple of old buddies, I couldn't recognize a single person there."

Quarterly Lunch, Star thought.

Even the term, quarterly, sounded like it was a word used by an anal-retentive teacher. Star figured it was Rhonda's only way of keeping tabs on each member of the High Five. *But really*, why did she need to *keep tabs on us? What was she really up to?*

Star didn't think too long about Mr. Klopper's presence.

She had another scheme on her mind.

For Star, it was game time.

Mandy sat down in her seat next to Rhonda.

She said hello to the other three. Finally, once she reached Star, she said with a serious expression, "Star."

Then, Star returned, "Mandy."

"Well, I better let you ladies go so you can play catch up," Mr. Klopper said to everybody. Then, he specifically pointed at Carmen. "If you ever need anyone to watch over the little one, ask Rhonda here and she'll give you my number."

"I couldn't—"

"—I don't mind at all; as a matter of fact, I'd be more than happy to baby-sit. With all this free time now, I'm always looking for something to do."

"I will."

"Till next time, ladies."

"Bye, Mr. Klopper.

"Bye, Eugene.

"Eugene?"

Rhonda shrugged.

"We still keep in contact."

"You still talk to your old English teacher."

"I'm a teacher, duh," Rhonda said to Carmen. "When I was starting out, he was the first person I contacted. Eugene gave me a lot of pointers."

"Who the hell uses the expression 'more than happy?' Nobody's ever more than happy."

"It's just an expression, Fay," Star said.

"Well, it's insane."

"So," Mandy said over a sigh, "who's hungry?"

"Thanks to Fay here," Rhonda teased. "I think I lost my appetite."

"What I do?"

Star said, "It was actually Carmen who brought up The Snipper."

"The Snipper?" Mandy said in a superior manner. "And how exactly did that creature get thrown into the conversation?"

"We were talking about Devil's Throat."

"I see," Mandy said. "Are you still kayaking?"

"Twice a week."

"So, you girls order yet?"

Right on cue, the waitress returned to the table with appetizers.

Lettuce wraps, miso soup, and hot spring rolls with house made duck sauce.

"Here are your appetizers," she said and placed the appetizers on the table.

"I see we have a new one," the waitress said, turning to Mandy. "Shall I give you some time to decide on your order?"

"No," Mandy said, not even looking at the menu. She couldn't help but look at Star in the corner of her eye. "I already know what I want. I'll take the Udon."

The waitress asked, "Your choice of meat?"

"Beef, please."

"I swear you order that same exact dish every time we come here, Mandy?" Fay asked. "Why don't you try something different? You know, experiment. Be a food taster."

Mandy said to Fay, "Whoever said I *wasn't* a food taster? Besides, Fay, I've been waiting all week for Beef Udon."

"And what would you like to drink?"

"Saki," Mandy said to the waitress. "Lots and lots of saki."

The waitress went around the rest of the table and gathered orders.

Fay ordered Vegetable Tempura as well as a California roll; Carmen, Yakitori, which was skewered chicken; Rhonda, Chicken Teriyaki; then, finally, Star, who wasn't at all hungry, soba noodles, which, now that she started to think more about it, was probably a bad choice but she had to order something and soba noodles was the first—*and only*—thing that came to her mind.

Once the orders were placed, the appetizers were passed around the table.

Fay went on an alcohol-induced rant about sushi and how she had been on a sushi-craze for the past month.

Star grabbed a hot vegetable spring roll from the plate and nibbled on it like a bird; and when the lettuce wraps were handed to her, she immediately declined.

Carmen nodded at Mandy.

"Saki, huh? One of those days?"

Mandy sipped from the glass of water.

"It's been a day, all right," she said, unfolding the table napkin and placing it over her lap.

Rhonda asked, "How'd everything go with work?"

Mandy paused.

"I wasn't at work," she said quietly. "The truth is. . . "

Once more, a pause of silence swelled over the conversation. The pause was long enough to draw concern around the table.

Carmen asked, "Is everything all right, Mandy?"

"It's Jack," she said finally. "Jack and I had a fight." Then she said to herself. "It was—how do I say?" She paused. "I'd say *epic* is probably the word I'm looking for. Like one for the record books."

"That bad, huh?"

"Worse."

She hung her head in solemn.

"I've never seen Jack so upset," said Mandy.

Rhonda asked, "What were you two fighting about?"

Mandy faced Rhonda, who was sitting to the left of her.

"He wants to have another child," Mandy said, turning her eyes to Star.

Surprised, Star said to Mandy, "Child?" She quietly cleared her throat. "But I thought you said you wanted another child."

"I did," Mandy said. "I mean I do want a child. Having a child right now is not a good time, though."

"You go, girl," Fay said. "Never ever let a man force a child on you. After all, it's your body. *Not* his."

"But it's not like that, Fay."

"To me, it sounds like he's only thinking of himself."

"Jack's a good man," Mandy said.

Without even knowing, Star's jaw began to tighten with hot anger. It wasn't until she stepped back inside herself that she realized how she might've looked to the others. Nobody was looking, though, except for maybe Mandy, who kept Star in the corner of her eye. Star unclenched her teeth and took another sip of her gin and tonic to help loosen the nerves.

As soon as Star placed the drink on the table, she received a text message on her phone:

She knows.

Carefully, Star removed the phone from the table and held it down in her lap.

She slid open her phone and read the text once more.

The sender was Jack Leland.

"She knows," read the text.

Star took her eyes from the phone below and looked up, specifically toward Mandy's general direction.

Mandy was still talking about Jack. She went from describing him as good to great. All of a sudden, Jack was an extraordinary man who was one of the smartest, most handsome men Mandy had ever had the privilege of knowing.

Star read the text message again.

She knows.

Another text suddenly appeared right below the "she knows" text:

Heads up.

Star quickly responded by sending a text to Jack:

How much does she know?

Then, Jack returned with a reply text:

Everything.

Then, Star:

What do you mean 'everything'?!?

Star pulled her eyes from the phone.

Mandy asked, "Is everything okay, Star?"

"Yeah," Star hesitated. "Why wouldn't it be?"

"You just look like you're not with us?"

"No," Star said. "I am. It's just a new client. He's been giving Frank and I a real headache."

"Frank's probably one of the best lawyers in the city," she said. "I'm sure there's nothing he can't deal with."

"Right."

Star's phone beeped.

Jack texted:

EVERYTHING.

Star texted back.

I'm going to tell her the truth.

As soon as she sent the text, Star's phone suddenly rang.

She answered the phone before it could ring a second time and secured the receiver of the phone against her chest and said, "Excuse me for a second."

"Ms. Worker Bee," Fay said, "always working."

"I got to take this," Star said to the others but was really speaking directly to Mandy.

Star walked outside.

As soon as she was in the clear, she said into the phone, "Are you *trying* to draw more suspicion than there already is, Jack—"

"—Don't use my name."

"How much does she know?"

"Lower your voice, Star."

"She can't hear me," Star said to Jack. "I'm outside."

"So, did she say anything to you?"

"No," Star said, peering back into the restaurant through the window. "But I need to tell her the truth. About us. About everything."

"She already knows, Star—"

"—How?"

"She found an article of clothing you left behind."

"How could you be so careless, Jack?" Star immediately retracted the blame as soon as it reached her lips. "I'm sorry. It's my fault."

"No," Jack said. "Don't do that, Star. If anybody's to be sorry, it's all me."

"Well, there's absolutely no way I can go back in there now."

"You have to, Star," said Jack. "Just act like everything's normal and please, whatever you do, please do not make a scene—"

"I'm not going to make a scene, Jack."

"Just act normal, okay?"

"How can I act normal, knowing that one of my good friends knows that I'm screwing her husband?"

"Listen," Jack said urgently. "I gotta run. I think it's best that we lay low for a while. Just until things calm down a bit."

"Jack, does she know about our plan?"

Jack's phone started to break up.

"Jack?

The other end of the phone went silent.

"Jack, you there?"

Star noticed the call had been dropped.

"Shitty-ass service," she seethed.

Once Star cooled off, she leaned close to the window and checked her face in the reflection and then stepped back inside Flying Lotus.

Mandy was missing from the table.

Star interrupted Rhonda and Carmen, who were gossiping about some recent news report about airlines adding extra leg room inside their airplanes, "Where's Mandy?"

"She had use the restroom, I think."

Star started to walk toward the restroom; however, she stopped after taking three steps, paused, turned around, walked back to the table, and sat back down in her seat.

Fay asked, "Who was on the phone? Boyfriend? Ex-boyfriend? Or, better yet, your sex slave?"

"Fay!" Rhonda called out.

"I'm sorry," Fay corrected. "Boy toy?"

"For your information, it was Frank."

"Sure, it was."

"You know, Fay, I don't think you've had enough to drink."

"Are you being sarcastic? Because, if you are, then you're terrible at it."

"Yes," Star said with frustration. "I was being sarcastic."

Trying to keep the peace, Rhonda asked, "So, what did Frank want?"

"He wanted to talk about a case. Boring legal stuff."

"Doesn't sound boring."

"Trust me," Star said to Rhonda. "It's a snooze fest. Five minutes of Frank talking starts to feel like you just took an Ambien."

Fay asked, "So, what did you two talk about?"

"You know I'm not supposed to talk about that kind of stuff. It's confidential. Plus, I could lose my job."

"Yeah, but I'm sure you talk about cases all the time with your lawyer buddies."

"Enough, Fay, please," Star said seriously.

Silence hovered over the table like a bad stench.

Rhonda tried to break up the sudden awkwardness by asking Fay about her work even though Rhonda didn't have any interest whatsoever in Fay's work— or at least, tried not to show it even though her voice had a particular way of indicating the truth even if her voice wasn't telling the truth. Star was clearly aware of Rhonda's feelings about Fay's profession of choice and how, not too long ago, in fact, the last time she saw Star, she called it in sharp criticism, not a job, but a hobby behind Fay's back. For someone who decorated the walls of her classroom with literary posters, which were designed by graphic designers, like Fay, the jealousy in Rhonda's voice couldn't sound more palpable. Star had a nose for these kinds of things. She'd say she got it from her dada.

FIVE AWKWARD MINUTES LATER

MANDY returned from the restroom in a state of obvious yet seemingly exaggerated disgust.

"We were starting to wonder if you fell in," Fay said to Mandy.

With a sigh shooting from her mouth like a bullet, Mandy sat down in her seat with a heavy thump.

"There was a line," she said. "Can you believe that?"

Star thought it was strange. She didn't see any line when she poked her head toward the restrooms.

"*And*," Mandy emphasized, "some asshole peed all over the seats."

"I hate when they do that," Rhonda said, shaking her head.

"You know," Fay said, "you never saw that before these restaurants started converting their restrooms to gender-neutral restrooms. Honestly, I think men do it deliberately. To rub it in our faces. To show us who's in charge—"

"—I thought you were all for gender-neutral restrooms. So, why the change in heart?"

"No," Fay said. "I am, but still. I think, if you're a man, you should be conscious of the fact that a woman might use the bathroom after you."

"Maybe they're not thinking of that, Fay," Carmen argued. "Maybe some men just pee on the seat. It's like science—"

"—It's like common courtesy."

"Unless you're sitting down to pee—which, I'm pretty sure, most men ain't doing—pee splashes when it hits toilet water. Take Max for instance. Every time he uses the toilet, I have to clean up after him."

"Yeah, Carmen, but he's decent enough to raise the toilet seat before he takes a piss."

"He raises the seat. But, like I said, Fay, the pee still splashes. I once found pee on one of the paintings I have hung up on the wall."

"The man must have one helluva prostate."

The comment drew a couple of laughs around the table.

Star forced a laugh. She couldn't help but draw her attention toward Mandy, who, in return, caught Star in the corner of her eye.

As the tension started to mount, the waitress stepped in between the two and set the tray of steamy food against the edge of the table. The waitress handed out each dish, except for Mandy's Beef Udon. She told her that the Udon was just about ready, and then she went back to the kitchen.

The chatter was tame but steady. The quiet commotion inside Star pulled her away from the topic of discussion, which morphed from gender-neutral restrooms to sexual harassment in the workplace and the stark differences between compliments and flirtation. Star zoned out completely, as if all of the chatter around her had been reduced to nothing more than faint murmurings, like bees buzzing, background noise. She mindlessly made it through a few decent bites of her soba noodles. Occasionally, Mandy would move her eyes toward Star and strangely watch her eat without actually watching her eat.

Before Star could acknowledge Mandy's interest in Star's lack of involvement in the conversation, her Beef Udon finally arrived.

All of a sudden, Star plowed through all of the noise, pushed past the quiet storm inside her, and paid close attention to Mandy as she "dug in."

Mandy removed the sleeve of paper from the pair of chopsticks and rubbed the two chopsticks together as if she was honing a blade with a whetstone.

As Mandy did with Star, Star watched Mandy take her first bite without actually watching her.

Mandy made sure to capture all of the flavors into one single bite, grabbing each ingredient with the grip of the chopsticks. A little bit of the Udon noodle. A little bit of succulent Hida beef. A little bit of the fish cake called Narutomaki, which, to the average guest, looked like a piece of candy with its white star-like shape and a red-pinkish swirl in the center. Then, for garnish, Mitsuba and green onion. She lifted it all to her mouth before it could fall from the tip of the chopsticks and opened wide. Mandy took a bite, chewed twice, savoring each flavor. She closed her eyes, closed off the world. In her closed-off state, Mandy did what only came natural. She reacted with sound, her sound, her own designated noise.

A moan of great pleasure rolled from her tongue and ricocheted off the interior of her closed mouth.

The sound drew eyes toward Mandy.

Star was first to ask, "How is it?"

"*Dee*-licious," Mandy said, holding the food in one side of her mouth.

She swallowed.

Took another bite.

Savored it.

Then, took another.

Savored.

"They make their own dashi broth in house," Mandy said as if she was promoting her dish to her own crowd of curious buyers. "That's what makes the beef so tender."

"What's dashi?"

"It's similar to a vegetable or beef stock."

"What kind of beef is it?"

"I'm not entirely sure," she said. "Maybe prime rib? Whatever it is, it's out of this world."

"Everything they make here is so fresh."

Fay asked Mandy, "Can I have a bite?"

"Only if you give me a taste of your vegetable tempura."

"You got yourself a deal, young lady."

Star said suddenly, "Fay, I don't think you'll like it."

"How you know what I like?"

"But Fay," Star urged Fay, "I've heard the cows they get their meat from are loaded with antibiotics."

"Nice try, Star," Mandy said. "They're grass fed."

"Okay, Fake News."

"You sure?"

"Positive."

Rhonda said, "Not like it's going to kill you, Fay."

Fay forked out a bite of vegetable tempura while Mandy pinched out a bite of Beef Udon with chopsticks. She held her hand underneath the chopsticks, making sure no broth and beef juice spilled onto the white tablecloth. They traded bites.

First, Mandy took a bite of vegetable tempura, savored it, then swallowed it. She nodded her head in agreement.

Next, Fay took a bite of the Beef Udon.

"Wow!" Fay said while chewing. "Delish!"

Mandy turned to Carmen.

"Want a bite?" she asked.

Carmen broke off a piece of chicken, passed it over, and, in return, tasted the Beef Udon. Carmen wasn't exactly a beef-girl. She considered herself a vegetarian, even though, from time to time, she would eat chicken or fish.

"Not bad," Carmen said after she finished swallowing the Beef Udon. "Very hearty. It'd be the perfect dish during the wintertime."

"Oh! I can eat it anytime," said Mandy.

"How about you, Rhonda? Want a taste?"

As Carmen did, Rhonda traded a bite for a bite.

She acted as if she really enjoyed the Beef Udon. She wasn't a good faker.

"It's okay."

"Just okay."

"It's good," Rhonda corrected.

"Star?"

Star immediately held up her hand.

"No thanks," she said.

"But you haven't even tried it before."

"I have," Star said defensively. "I didn't care much for it."

"It's really good, Star," Fay said. "And you know I don't even like beef."

"Come on, Star," Carmen nodded. "Try it."

Then, Rhonda: "You'll like it."

"Okay," Star said.

Mandy broke off a piece of Hida beef, handed the chopsticks over to Rhonda, who, in return, placed the Hida beef on the edge of Star's plate.

Before Star tasted the Hida beef, she looked around the table and it was as if the four members of High Five were encouraging her to take the bite.

She finally did.

Mandy asked, "What you think?"

"It's good," Star said as she carefully chewed the piece of meat. "Better than I thought it'd be."

"Told you," Fay said and went back to her vegetable tempura.

Without the others noticing, Star discreetly spit out the Hida beef into a napkin and waited for the right moment to excuse herself to the restroom.

As soon as Star was away from the others' view, she rushed to the restroom. She didn't have to wait. She went right into the restroom and locked the door behind her. She hurried to the sink where she rinsed out her mouth with water. She even grabbed several squares of toilet paper from a damp roll and used the toilet paper like a toothbrush by scrubbing her teeth, as well as her tongue. Then, she'd rinse her mouth with water. Gargled. Then, she'd grab another couple squares of toilet paper. Scrubbed. Gargled. Then, rinsed. Rinsed and scrubbed. Scrubbed and rinsed.

Lastly, she leaned closely to the mirror and opened her mouth wide, really wide, wide enough to stick her fist into her mouth.

Using the flashlight on her phone for light, Star peered into the depths of her mouth, checking for anything out of the ordinary. Which meant anything "moving." She didn't see anything moving around in there. Everything looked fine.

Once Star felt safe enough to proceed with lunch, she exited the restroom and walked back to the table.

Halfway toward the table, she noticed somebody—one of the staff members, a cook maybe—standing above Mandy. He was dressed in a white chef's attire.

As soon as Star realized who the man was and possibly *why* he was standing there, her heart started to beat faster. Her eyes swelled. Her face went slack. Her chest tightened. Breath swallowed. Her legs heavy. Her walk was unsteady, and she moved toward the table as if she didn't know whether or not to turn the other direction and run for the back exit.

Only a couple of feet away from the table, Star suddenly turned around and started to walk the other way.

Mandy called out from behind, "There she is!"

Star stopped and slowly turned around.

"Where you going, Star?" she said foolishly and waved Star over. "Get over here."

Timidly, Star inched back to the table and sat down in her seat.

She asked, "What's going on?"

"Star, this here is Myko," Mandy said excitedly as she showcased Myko as if he was an exquisite work of art. "I ran into Myko on the way to the restroom."

Star turned to Myko, who acted as if he didn't even know Star.

"Myko and I go *waaay* back," Mandy said as if she had come from an ancient time period where radio was still a custom of quality family entertainment.

"That's right," Myko said and looked down at Mandy. "I hardly even recognized you." Then, turned to Star's direction. "I was complimenting Amanda on how great she looked. Doesn't she look great?"

"Yeah," Star said and forced a smile on her face. "She does."

"Stop, Myko," Mandy said and playfully hit Myko on the arm.

"She's like a ten." Myko corrected himself, "I mean, for real, you were always a ten on my scale. Even back then. But now, you're like a legitimate ten. Like a ten-plus. No joke. It's just too bad you're still married."

Star couldn't quite tell if Myko was being sincere or not.

Or, she wondered, was there *something else* going on.

"Not only is she married, but she's also married to a man who cuts up people for a living," Fay said.

"You're on a roll, Fay," Rhonda said, as if she was talking to a disobedient adolescent. "I mean, really? Why would you even say that? Is that necessary?" Rhonda turned to Myko, who was rather smitten by the complimentary male presence. "Forget all about what you read on the Internet. He's one of the best heart surgeons in town. And he's quite handsome. Dapper, one might say. *And*," she continued, "not only that, he's an exceptional painter, too; in fact, I bought one of his paintings."

"You make him sound like the complete package."

"Excuse me, Rhonda," Mandy said playfully, "that's my husband you're talking about."

The others laughed, except Star.

"Well," Myko smiled and turned to Star, "he's a lucky man."

"Lipo, a couple of facelifts, and don't mention, a heavy dose of Botox will do that to a woman," Fay said indirectly.

"Lately, I've been thinking about getting the 'Mandy Treatment' myself, but Max says he likes me just the way I am."

"You've met Jack before, haven't you?" Mandy asked Myko.

Once more, Myko turned to Star, then to Mandy, then shook his head.

"No," he said unsurely. "Don't think so."

Nodding in Myko's direction, Star said, "So, where was it you said you two met?"

Mandy looked up at Myko.

"It was right outside that pawn shop, wasn't it?"

"Sigmund's," said Myko. "Yes."

"That's it," Mandy said.

"Believe it or not, Amanda saved my life."

"And you saved mine," Mandy said, glancing up at Myko with tears in her eyes.

"He did?"

"If it wasn't for you, I'd probably be dead."

"You were in a bad state of mind," Mandy said to Myko. Then, turned to the others. "We *both* were in a terrible place, mentally and physically. At the time, I was a resident at Pointe Medical. I was going through a lot of issues, depression, anxiety. I'd lose weight. Then, put on weight."

"You never told us this, Mandy," Carmen cut in.

Then, Rhonda.

Then, surprisingly, Fay.

"I was too embarrassed, I suppose," Mandy said, rounding up sympathy from everyone at the table—except Star. "After awhile, it felt as if my world was starting to cave in all around me. Then, on one rainy night, I came across this young man—"

"—Boy," Myko corrected.

Mandy held Myko's hand.

"He was about to do something terrible," Mandy said. "We talked for what felt like hours. We talked about a lot of things—very *personal* things. Eventually, Myko changed his mind. I brought him back home with me and gave him a place to stay for the night. I helped him get sober. He helped me sort through a lot of my issues. We both helped out each other as if we were going through the same thing, only we weren't. I found Myko here a temporary part time at Pointe Medical to get him back on his feet." Mandy looked up at Myko. "You redefined a sense of meaning as to why I wanted to become a doctor." Then, she turned to the others. "He gave me purpose. I suppose, you can say it was one of those gifts life miraculously hands you every now and then."

Star asked Myko, "So what was this terrible thing you were about to do?"

The others appeared shocked by Star's question as if Star wasn't at all in a position to inquire more detail into Mandy's heart-warming story.

"He was going to rob the owner of the pawn shop," Mandy said bluntly.

"It's true," Myko said. "I was."

"But you didn't?"

"Obviously."

"A week later after I found Myko—or better yet, when Myko found me—I heard about a story in the news: a robbery attempt at that very same pawn shop. A man pulled a gun on the owner. The owner shot the robber. Killed him."

"That's some story," Rhonda said in disbelief. Then, she asked Myko, "Have you ever thought about writing a book about it?"

"Me?" Myko pointed at himself. "No. I'm not the Shakespeare type."

"You can always hire one of those—what you called them?"

"Ghostwriters."

"Them."

Myko waved off Rhonda's offer and turned to the kitchen.

"I think I've found my calling right here," Myko said.

"Well, the food is probably the best I've ever eaten and I'm not just saying that to be nice or anything. If you don't believe me, check my Yelp page."

"We all saw your Yelp page, Carmen. *Everybody* in Newbay has seen you Yelp page."

"What can I say? I'm Yelp-Fabulous."

Fay and Rhonda ignored Carmen and all of her braggadocio and then complimented Myko on the food.

"Thank you," Myko said and turned to Star last. "And how you like the food, Star?" he asked with a ghost of a smirk creeping through the corner of his face. "Is it everything you *expected* it to be?"

The question stabbed at Star, sending thousands of pinpricks throughout her entire body.

All of a sudden, she began to feel lightheaded. Myko's face started to double, then triple; then it was as if she had taken a freeze frame of his ugly face and pinned and mounted it to the forefront of her mind.

To Star, Myko made a face. It might've not been the sportive smirk on his face or the distant twinkle in his eye. Nonetheless, it was a "face." The others couldn't see it nor could they sense it. But Star saw and sensed it clear enough to have its own Instagram page.

The only thought that ran through Star's mind. . .

I have been duped.

Star suddenly stood up from her seat and staggered for a moment. She drew her eyes downward at the bowl of soba noodles. Like Myko's face, the noodles doubled, then tripled, then shifted in and out of focus. For a moment, she actually saw the noodles moving.

As her legs started to buckle, she flung her hand outward and grabbed a hold of the edge of the table as if it was a crutch.

"If you would excuse," Star murmured, her words faint and choppy as if she had recently run a marathon.

While the others remained wordless, Star rushed to the restroom.

She used the closest objects that she could touch for support, the very back of a guest's chair, even another guest's shoulder, then, finally, the wall. She stayed close to the wall, using it whenever she felt as if she was about to fall over like a drunken sorority girl. She hadn't drunk much, only enough to ride a buzz, but she felt as if she was beyond wasted, like college-drunk wasted. She questioned herself, questioned her drunkenness. She tried to tell herself that her current wobbly state was from drinking hard alcohol on an empty stomach. But there was a voice inside her head. *That brain noise.* And it was telling her another story.

Star made it to the restroom without passing out. She reached for the greasy door handle. Her hand slipped from it. She reached once more, strengthened her grip, and tugged on it like a loose tooth.

The door was locked.

She tried once more, this time twisting her wrist.

The door still remained locked.

She resorted to *knocking* on the door but didn't hear a sound behind the door. Then, she balled her hand into a fist and banged hard enough to shake the hinges. On the third pound, Star heard a sound behind the door. A voice.

"Just a second," the soft, drawn-out voice said with a ring of vexation.

Following the voice, she heard the sound of water running and then the grating *schrrpt* noise of paper being torn from the dispenser.

The door opened.

The woman was slow to exit.

Not wasting anytime, Star pushed her way inside, nudging shoulders with the woman.

"Excuse me," the woman barked.

Star slammed the door in the woman's face and darted toward the toilet.

Halfway there, the vomit started to climb up her throat. She caught some of it in her mouth but some of it projected from lips and hit the side of the toilet.

In a second hurl, Star hunched over the toilet and violently pushed as hard as her body would let her. For the next thirty seconds or so, her stomach did push-ups against her chest. Each time, less vomit came out and whatever managed to escape was as acidic as stomach bile. Then came the dry heaving. That lasted for about another thirty seconds or so. Eventually, Star wore herself out and used the toilet seat to push herself upright from her squatted position.

As Star was about to flush the toilet, she noticed a slight movement below her eyes. She peered closer at the murky toilet water and once more, saw something moving under the soba noodles, something red in color and as thin as a wire. Star scrambled through her thoughts and retraced everything she had eaten. She ate a protein bar for breakfast. But *it wouldn't be that,* she thought. *That* would've already been digested. Then, she had a glass of orange juice to wash down the protein bar—maybe it could've been an extra long piece of pulp. *No*, she thought, it, like the protein bar, would've already been digested. Or, *maybe* it could've been the cabbage from the spring roll. With the edge of her knuckles, Star rubbed the backside of her eyelids in clichéd fashion and looked yet again. The soba noodles weren't moving. Only one was, that reddish gray one. Star soon learned it wasn't a soba noodle. It was something else.

More intrigued, Star pulled out a tablet pen from her phone, reached down, and picked up the rare toxioplexus, a worm-like parasitic creature that was better known for its nickname "snake worm," from the clumpy toilet water.

Star held the snake worm up to her face. She realized it looked much different than what she researched on the Internet. For one, the snake worm was much more longer and scalier than she expected. Two, she could actually see that it had a face with two beady black eyes and a mouth filled with jagged, razor sharp teeth as small as the tip of a thread.

Star suddenly recoiled and flung the dangerous snake worm back into the toilet. She stuck her index finger down her throat and once more, tried to rid whatever thing it was that she ingested. She had hardly anything left in her stomach. She dry-heaved until all that came out was the spit that remoistened her mouth.

What the fuck did you do to me, Myko, *you son of a bitch*?

Crying, she called Jack who answered after the second ring.

The best she could, Star explained to Jack what happened to her; however, he couldn't understand a word Star was saying.

She emphasized *Myko*'s name and how he *tricked* her.

Jack gave Star specific instructions to drive herself to the nearest emergency room ASAP.

Star didn't want to hear anything Jack had to say.

Not anymore.

Her own well being was the very least of her worries.

She was out for blood.

As before, Jack's phone started to break up.

The last words Jack said to Star before the phone went dead were "*Don't do anything stupid.*"

Star flung her phone against the wall, fracturing the touch screen.

Parts of the phone ricocheted against the toilet and slid underneath harder-to-reach areas.

But like her own well being, the phone was the least of her concerns.

She was *out for blood.*

It wasn't until Star felt her skin crawl, specifically a twitch in the corner of her eye, that she realized Jack had every reason to be serious in instructing her to go to the emergency room.

Hoping the quick remedy which she had used ever since she was a girl would save her from all her troubles, she hurried to the sink and splashed her face with cold water. She removed her hands from her face and looked into the mirror. Her left eye twitched similar to a muscle spasm.

Mindful of the creature in the toilet, Star punched the corner of the mirror. A perfectly triangular piece of glass fell into the sink. Star grabbed the piece that closely resembled a knife and held it close.

With her left hand, Star pulled down on her lower eyelid while keeping the shard of glass close to her face.

She didn't see anything at first glance.

Star pulled her eyelid down until it stretched across her upper cheekbone.

Again, she saw something moving below her eyelid.

Not a muscle spasm.

Not an eyelash or grain of dirt or sand that got caught in her eye.

Whatever it was, it was moving.

It was *alive*.

Star wanted it dead.

WHEN Star returned to the table, her face was all cut up and strings of blood were running down the side of her face like ruined mascara. In her right hand, she held onto that shard of glass, which was covered in her own blood. She was shivering too. And struggling to stand upright.

As soon as Star rounded the hallway, she set her bloodstained eyes on High Five, who were all laughing it up and having a "good ole time," an expression Fay picked up from her firecracker of a mother *who* spent her days riding the tequila train to Margaritaville and bathing in the artificial sun three out of the four seasons of the year to match Star's blackness, wearing it like a cool costume opposed to actually living in it, *who* took overly wide turns opposed to cautiously hugging the curb and being mindfully aware of other drivers on the road, *who* spitballed the first glint of a thought that manifested inside her mind which, at times, seemed like the size of the universe. All of it made perfect sense—now that Star thought about it—as to why it was Fay who branded their so-called gang as High Five, not High as in being recreational drug users who often got high, but *high*, as in higher than everybody else. Privileged cloud surfers.

Star noticed one person was absent. Myko. A man who was neither high nor low but landing somewhere in a tedious gray area where the crimes being committed were questionable and assured dissension. He was no longer standing next to Mandy. He was off somewhere being gray in the kitchen. Star told herself that she'd deal with that assclown later.

As Star returned to the table, Mandy directed her attention toward Star, who had become the sole oddball of the gang. Neither belonging or accepted. "Just" there. Just was a word she commonly used to describe herself to others who questioned her loyalty to High Five. She was "just" a friend. Or, simply "just" there.

"You don't look so hot," Fay said, noticing Star's fragile state.

Of all the members of High Five, Fay was the only one to notice Star's unusual behavior. Mandy, Carmen, or Rhonda didn't even pay attention or at least act the least concerned for Star's fragile mental state or how she appeared to be bleeding all over the freaking place.

Star ignored Fay and sat back down in her seat while Mandy raised her teacup of warm saki. She insisted the members of High Five raise their own glasses in what appeared to be a toast.

"That includes you, Star," Mandy said, urging Star to raise her glass. "Come on. Raise it up."

Star placed the shard of glass on the table and with her bloody hand, raised the glass of gin and tonic.

"I want to thank all of you for coming here today," Mandy said as she looked at the others seated around her. "All of you are my friends and I am truly grateful to call you friends. Of all of you, there is one who rose to the occasion and became more than a friend. She became my very own special friend. All this time, she was right under my nose. Her name is Star," she said directly to Star. "You showed me the person who I am and who I could be. I want to be that better person. I will be that better person, Star, that better doctor, that better wife, that *better* lover. I'm deeply sorry for my actions, which have resulted in my own husband to find connection with another woman. However, if it weren't for what happened between us, *Star*, I never would've fully understood your devotion to our kinship. Now, I do." She raised her glass higher. "To High Five. Most importantly, to my *new* bestie, Star Walker."

As Mandy sipped from her drink, Star stood up and flung the rest of her gin and tonic in Mandy's face.

"Tell that to Jack, you bitch," Star seethed.

"Star," Carmen blurted out, "what has gotten into you?"

"Shut up, you fake bitch."

"Star?"

"You texted me about how much you hate coming to these 'lunches,' yet here you are," Star said, towering over Carmen. "Why are you really here, Carmen? To play catch up?"

Carmen asked, "What other reason would I be here, Star?"

"You and I hardly even talked to one another in high school," Star said. "So, why, all of a sudden, do you want to rekindle a relationship with me? I tell you. *Because* you're a fucking lonely, pathetic person who hates herself so much that she has to cling to others. *Because* you sit at home all day long, caring for a child whom you regret having. No," Star said, her red eyes widening in madness. "I know what it is! You figured motherhood was going to be a piece of cake. Then, once you became a mother, you found out pretty quickly that it's a lot harder than it looks on TV. I admit. You put on a good show. Always posting photos of that ugly-looking thing you call a child on the Internet, showing him off, trying to impress everybody, trying to prove to them that you're not that same phony-ass bitch you were in high school when, deep down inside, you're still that same fake, PC, wannabe, *phony*-ass bitch always following the crowd and wanting acceptance by rubbing that shit-stain of a child in everybody's face. Did you ever stop and think what your kid's going to think of you when he's older? When he has to explain to all his friends why some kid in his class is ridiculing him in class because of some ridiculous photo his mother posted of him when he was a child without his permission? What the hell do you think it will do to his self-esteem? What's he going to do when he steps out into the real world and realizes that he's not special? Did you ever stop and think for a second of the repercussions for sharing every single *iota* of information that pops into that empty hole of a head of yours? No.

116

You know why. Because you don't give a *shit* about that fucking kid. Fake bitch. That's all you are. That's all you'll ever be. A plastic bitch. I mean, do you have any dignity? Any shame? Do you hold nothing sacred anymore? Or. . . " Star looked over Carmen and sneered at her as if she was way down there, ". . . has *this* what you've reduced yourself to? This insecure, *little* thing who posts pictures of her child all for a *like*? Or, a *follower*? Do everybody a favor?" Star leaned in close to Carmen. "Keep it to *your*-fucking-self."

Everybody in the restaurant turned toward Star's direction. Some watched as if they were witnessing some real-life suspense movie unfolding before their very eyes while some went about their business and ate with modest consumption and then there were some who talked among themselves. Most were silent.

Rhonda suddenly cut through—then bludgeoned—that awkward silence with a "Really, Star? Seniors in high school do it all the time. Don't you remember how we used to post baby pictures of ourselves in the back of the yearbook? I don't remember kids making fun of me."

The word *yearbook*—even the whole idea of the yearbook, Star's high school yearbook, and how it had portrayed Star—sent Star into a red glow of unadulterated rage. A flood of red memories washed over her, gripping her so tight that it stole her breath away, images of Star being the "black girl" who was always seen clinging to not only the white girls but also those "cool white girls" who would, over the boredom of summertime, hold their tanned arms next to Star's arm while sitting on the edges of the country club pool and parade a sense of benign audacity to tell Star, their black friend, that their skin matched Star's color. Snapshots of rushed moments printed in the most popular book in school. Snapshots only showing one side of the story without revealing the other side, the truest side. She was the girl who wore a smile that ran a mile across her face, the girl who, at the last second, hurried into a group shot before the school's designated cameraman, who happened to be some goofy foreign exchange student from Germany named Ryan, blurted out, "Fahrvergnügen." She was the girl who was always seen with part of her cropped out next to the school's most popular crew, her so-called gang, her "besties," the girl who was accepted but never belonged, the girl who was visible but wasn't, the just-girl. Books like *The Great Gatsby, Of Mice and Men*, *A Tale of Two Cities,* or Star's favorite, *Anthem*, once monuments representing a time lived decades, even centuries ago, the messages rich and vibrant and left to be digested by a young scrupulous mind, nonetheless, stories only to be cast aside and rejected by the generations to come, paled in comparison to the very moment in time that would inevitably present itself at the end of the school year when the yearbooks were handed out.

"Star," Rhonda shouted, sliding from her chair, "how dare you talk to her like that? How *dare* you!"

"Don't get me started on you," Star pointed at Rhonda. Her finger, sharp and deadly like a shard of glass before her, kept Rhonda frozen in her seat. "Mother-fucking-Teresa. During our senior year, you started a little charity to help raise money for families who were left homeless after the Cayenne Wild Fire. Operation *Getup*. You remember?"

Rhonda didn't answer.

117

Instead, she glared at Star.

"Of course, you remember," Star went on. "Your goal was to clothe all those poor people who lost *everything* in the fire. And what did you do? You took all that money you *stole* from all those gullible people and you kept it all for yourself."

"Star," Rhonda murmured, "Don't you go there. . . "

"Star, you got it all wrong," Mandy interrupted. "Rhonda helped clothe hundreds of people. I was there when she handed out the clothes."

"And where exactly do you think she found those clothes?"

"She bought them with the money she earned."

"She didn't buy shit," Star snapped. "For two weeks straight, she was stealing clothes from the Samaritan's Hand where she volunteered in the afternoons and peddled them as if they were brand new. She even donated her own hand-me-downs. And what exactly did she do with all the money? She used it to buy a new iPhone and told everybody that her father bought it for her because all of her hard work. I was going to expose you, Rhonda, for who you were. A manipulative bitch who thought she was better than everybody else. And now you use your missionary trips as vacations—"

"—That's not true!"

"Don't fuck with me, bitch. I saw your pictures you posted on Facebook last year. You're no different than Carmen. Like peas in a pod. Fake and phony." Star pointed at Fay and Mandy. "*They* might not be able to see you two for who you are. But I do."

The waitress came by the table and respectfully asked Star to calm down; otherwise, she'd be forced to get the manager.

Star wasn't fazed at all by the waitress.

"Go on," she shouted. "Get him! What's he going to do? Call the cops—"

"—Star," Fay interrupted, "I think you've had too much to drink."

"And you," Star seethed, "you fucking flake. You disappear after our senior year and want nothing to do with me. Now, what? You're back in my life like nothing ever happened?"

"Star," Fay said, "you've known all about my situation, my sister—"

"—Don't you dare use her as an excuse for your lack of loyalty."

"I'm sorry."

"Last but not least," Star turned her red eyes toward Mandy, "the ungrateful bitch who doesn't know what a decent man looks like even if he fell out of the fucking sky and landed directly in her lap. You don't deserve Jack."

"What? And you do?"

"Yes," Star said. "More than you."

"What about you, Star? What the hell makes you so perfect? Why don't you find another man who's not already taken?"

Carmen leaned toward Fay.

"What's going on with her?

Fay whispered in Carmen's ear, "I think she's having a meltdown."

Star suddenly roared, "I AM NOT HAVING A FUCKING MELTDOWN!"

The manager finally arrived at the table, the waitress not too far behind. Several others employees were poking their head out from the kitchen and elsewhere. Star had herself an audience.

"I'm afraid I'm going to call the police if you don't calm down," the manager said to Star.

"Don't tell me what to do!"

"All right," the manager said, holding up his hands. "I'm going to have to ask you to leave right now."

"You want me to leave?"

"Yes, ma'am," the manager said, his hands shaking.

Everything about him was shaking, even his voice.

"And what are you going to do if I don't?"

"I'm going to call the police," he said.

"You are?"

"Yes."

"So, you call yourself a man? If you want me to leave, then *make* me leave. Don't just stand there like some coward. If *you* want me to leave, *you* make me. Not the police. You!"

The waitress handed the manager the phone.

With a shaky hand, the manager dialed 9-1-1.

Star waved off the manager.

"Forget you," she said. Then, to the High Five, "Forget all of you!"

Then, Star stormed out of Flying Lotus.

Didn't look back.

The High Five was officially dead to Star.

She'd later say that it was better to thrive among living rather than trying to keep up with the dead.

Her dada was a great man.

The best.

🕒

ONCE all the drama was over, Myko exited through the back door of the kitchen carrying the cat carrier with the glaring sign that read "DO NOT TOUCH." He checked both sides of the alleyway and then, once he realized it was all clear, he carefully set the carrier on the ground.

As he reached for the lock of the carrier's door, the beige paw of what looked like a cat reared back with its claws out and scratched Myko on the backside of his hand.

Myko leaped backward, his hand curling into his body.

"Little shit," he whispered as the scratch on his hand started to bleed.

He grabbed a handkerchief from his back pocket and wrapped it around his hand in order to stop the bleeding.

Then, he grabbed a broom, which was perched against the side of the building, and used it as a distraction by banging the handle against the back end of the carrier while he set the would-be cat free.

Once the door was open, Myko took a couple of steps away from the carrier. He held the broom close to his body, ready to strike or defend himself whenever the moment of acting was upon him.

Eventually, *finally*, the scraggly feline emerged from the hazy darkness of the carrier. It was, in fact, a cat—or at least, the remnants of what was left of

119

an orange tabby. Its body was as thin as a skeleton, its rib cage exposed underneath its scaly skin. Yet, the cat moved ever so gracefully, as if it was being controlled by *something* else.

Something more primitive.

The cat moved its red-stained eyes, which were crawling with maggots, up at Myko. A swarm of flies hovered over the cat as if they were acting as some sort of strange force field. Even the repulsive stench emitting from it, caused him to take a couple of extra steps backward. He did so with the utmost caution, hoping not to disturb the grotesque thing.

The cat suddenly snapped its attention toward Myko, ropes of drool swaying from its rabid mouth like dreadlocks.

It opened its gummy mouth and let out a hiss so sharp and stingy it caused his body to cringe and curl inward. His skin swelled with tiny goosebumps. His hair stood up like the quills on a porcupine.

The cat wound up its foot in a slow step toward Myko.

As soon as its paw touched the ground, its ears shot up and turned to the stirring of damp cardboard sloppily stacked directly behind it.

Its ears flickered and acted like antennas.

Myko swore he heard the faint *squeak* of a rodent as well.

He remained in a statue-like pose and listened closely.

Once more, he heard yet another noise, a squeak so high-pitch that it might as well been outside the range of human hearing.

But, strangely, Myko heard it.

The cat suddenly darted toward the direction of the noise and plunged itself into the pile of cardboard.

A struggle ensued underneath the loose cardboard.

This time, the *squeaking* sounds were more evident.

The cat crept out of the cardboard with a dead rat hanging from its mouth like a bloated sausage. The rat's fur was disheveled-looking. It had several bare spots along its body from infection or battle wounds from former scuffles with competitors. Its tail was red and raw and the tip of it had been severed and it was hanging loosely from the end as if it was a tug away from being torn off.

Myko was safe.

But only for the time being.

While the cat began to nibble away at the rat, Myko inched toward the carrier, which wasn't too far away from the cat. Keeping the cat close in his view, he leaned down and saw something strange moving in the corner of his eye.

With his nose covered by the collar of his chef's jacket, Myko peeked inside the carrier, only to find the insides covered with gray worm-like parasites crawling and wiggling around the carrier.

Snake worms. . .

Myko suddenly flinched!

He picked up the carrier, hurled it into the nearest dumpster, and then rushed back inside the restaurant.

Meanwhile, the cat continued to pick apart the rat for it was completely undisturbed by the commotion Myko was making.

Not so much as a distant holler of a man from the street ambience outside the alleyway seized the cat's attention.

It was devoted and unwavering to its basic needs, which were required for the survival of its species.

THE special report aired on the nine o' clock TV spot as what the people in the TV biz called an "interview in silhouette." You've probably seen it before (more than likely on the couch while channel surfing through an abyss of late-night television shows or, every now and then, on shows like *The Predator Catcher* or other crime related shows like the narco, cartel, or mafia-related crime movies or shows where the victims or witnesses—or as gangsters put it politely, "rats"—chose to remain anonymous in order to protect his or her identity), but you didn't know it actually had a name. But it did.

Interview in silhouette.

The interviewee, whose name had not yet been leaked to the press, was disguised in classic silhouette form in order to protect *her* identity. Face blacked out. Skin. The entire body looking like a dark shadow. The only detail that stood out was her long, wavy hair, which appeared blonde, strands of frizzy hair glowing in the faint overhead light like tethered yarns either caused by too much static in the carpet or, in most cases, an old, overused hairbrush; however, the camera lighting made it hard for the average viewer to distinguish. Most of these specific types of interviews didn't require the interviewee to conceal his or her voice by lowering it—or raising it—depending on the producer. In this instance, the interviewee's voice was disguised as deep as Darth Vader.

Noelle Brice, a respected journalist who had been with the network for eleven years, not in silhouette, conducted the interview with the woman whom she simply addressed simply as "you."

The Accuser, "You," plowed through the first scripted answer to the scripted question that she and Noelle had skimmed through prior to the interview.

During the sudden breaks in the interview, she reminded herself that she was human and humans breathed.

After the opening nerves of the interview faded, Noelle skipped the foreplay and dove straight into the juicy stuff, the "why" in why "you" were here. Noelle asked the Accuser how she came to know Miles Straum, the individual who was being accused of rape twenty-two years ago.

"We knew each other from work," the Accuser said, the nouns in her voice thin and shaky. The broad shoulders of her silhouette swelled and rose slightly as she made a noisy inhale through her nose. "At the time," she said, more patiently and thoughtfully, "Miles was an editor at our local newspaper, *The Courier*."

"What was your job at *The Courier*?"

"At the time, I was working part-time in the mailroom. It was slow work, but it helped pay for college."

The Accuser's breathing slowed.

"Where did you attend college?"

More confidently, she answered, "I attended Darmill University where I was studying to become a journalist."

"How old were you at the time when you started work at *The Courier*?"

"I started when I was twenty," she said. "I just turned twenty-one at the time of the office Christmas party?"

"And how old was Miles?"

"He was around thirty-five, I think, possibly a couple of years older—" she corrected, "—Thirty-six. He was thirty-six, now that I think about it. I remember Miles specifically mentioned the number to me because there had recently been a lottery a few weeks prior to the party. He used the number on his ticket."

"So, did you and Miles know each prior to working at *The Courier*?" Noelle paused. "What I mean is 'Were you two on a first name basis with one another?'"

"No," the Accuser hesitated. "Lansdowne was a small town in Oregon. We were about fifty miles outside Eugene. I grew up in the Holly Springs area, which was about three hours away. I had only seen Miles every now and then in town. But, no, I didn't actually know him until I started working at *The Courier*."

"How well did you know him during your time at *The Courier*?"

"Pretty well, I guess," she said, her dark voice sounding deeper. "I mean, we weren't close, but we talked. Mostly small talk, that is. He'd ask me how I was doing. He'd ask about what I was studying to be. School stuff, work. Small talk. He was nice, but. . . "

The Accuser held her head down, her sniffle sounding like a tear of paper.

"Take your time," said Noelle.

"*But* I always felt like he'd go out of his way to talk for 'other' reasons."

"Were you attracted to Miles?"

The Accuser nodded.

"Yes," she said. "I was. He wasn't like most guys I know. He was, I dunno, really sensitive. Miles acted as if he had a good heart, but I knew something was troubling him. Whenever we would talk, he always had this, I dunno, this *look* in his eye, like he wanted to make an advance towards me but didn't want to in the workplace. Despite what happened between us, he was considerate. A part of me knew he wouldn't make any moves, but another part—a more convincing part— knew I was only kidding myself. There was always that 'what if' in the back of my mind. *What if* I looked at him a certain way? *What if* I said something to him that gave him the wrong impression? *What if* I mistakenly gave him a signal that I was interested in furthering what I considered a civil relationship? I hated that feeling, like it was me who was carrying the burden, not him. I just wanted Miles to stop looking at me that way. After awhile, I started to get uncomfortable talking to him."

Noelle asked, "Did you start to feel this way before or after the party?"

126

"Before," she said. "Then, after the party, it just got worse between us. So much so that I ended up quitting *The Courier*."

"Was Miles aware of how he made you feel?"

"No," she said, backtracking. "I mean, I dunno, really. If Miles did know, he didn't show it."

"Did you ever think about confronting Miles?"

"Yes," the Accuser said. "Many times."

"Why didn't you?"

The Accuser paused for a moment.

"I was scared."

"Scared of Miles or scared of how it would affect the workplace environment?"

"No," she said. "Scared of him, of Miles."

"Why did you go to the party?" asked Noelle.

"I was invited," said the Accuser more aggressively.

"I didn't mean it that way," Noelle corrected. "What I meant was, presuming the way Miles felt about you, did you feel it was necessary to be in the company of Miles, especially at a more relaxed place environment where alcohol was going to be served?"

"Actually, I remember debating on whether or not I was going to attend the party."

"Why?"

"Well, for one, I had class the next day. Two, I wasn't much of a partier. I'd rather stay at home and read a book. I was more of an introvert than an extrovert. And three, I *knew* Miles was going to be there. I *knew* there was going to be alcohol. I knew that, if I didn't go, then he would win. Why should I let a man prevent me from doing what I want to do? That's no way to live life."

"How did you know Miles was going to be at the party?" asked Noelle.

"I specifically remember preparing myself before the party, spending hours trying to decide what to wear. I didn't want to wear anything that would suggest that I was attending the party for 'other' reasons."

"Such as?"

The Accuser paused.

"I didn't want to come off as a slut," she said bluntly.

Noelle asked, "Did you and Miles talk at the party?"

"Yes," said the Accuser as she took another moment to gather herself. "We did. But only for awhile."

"What did you two talk about?"

"I don't remember exactly. I made sure to avoid him throughout the party."

"Then, what prompted you to talk to him?"

"I bumped into him by accident."

"Did you consume any alcohol at the party?"

"Yes," she said. "I had a couple of drinks, but I *wasn't* inebriated."

"Was Miles drinking?"

"He was," she said. "He was pretty drunk."

"Do you remember anything that you might've said or done that would lead him on?"

"No," she said stuttered. "Of course not."

"To the best of your memory, can you describe the moments leading up to the sexual assault?"

"It happened when I was making my way toward the restrooms," the Accuser described. "He jumped me from behind and carried me to one of the offices. The lights were off. I remember it being dark. But I could see Miles's face in a beam of light. Those dark eyes glistening in the light."

"How sure are you that it was Miles?"

"One hundred percent sure."

"When he grabbed you, did you resist?"

"Honestly, I didn't know what to do," the Accuser said. "He threw me on top of a desk and started to remove my clothes. I just wanted it to end."

Noelle asked, "Did you tell him to stop?"

"Yes," said the Accuser. "Many times."

"And did he?"

"No," she said sharply. "He did not."

"After it was over, did you tell anybody in the office what had just happened to you?"

"No," the Accuser said, tearing up. "I felt paralyzed."

🕐

THE night of the interview, Miles dreamt of something moving behind the walls.

A rodent of some kind. Its tiny claws beating against the sides of vent shafts, as well as the backside of walls like a drunken tap dancer.

Miles suddenly bolted upright from his sweaty dream and woke to the sound of *tapping* outside the door.

At first, he thought it might've been the echoes of his dream piercing through his reality.

The tapping continued in intervals of three.

Tap, tap, tap.

Then, a pause.

Then, again, *tap, tap, tap.*

What the hell, Miles said to himself as he rolled out of bed.

Miles checked the door where the tapping was more evident.

With one eye closed, he looked through the peephole and witnessed a young woman standing outside his neighbor's apartment. She was carrying a cup holder with two beverages along the bend of her arm while her other hand, the free one, was tapping on the door with her purple nails. The woman had an orange janitor-sized key chain which looked like a slinky with enough keys to unlock the door of each resident inside The Lofts of Dover loosely worn around her wrist, and that, too, was striking the door.

Miles's neighbor answered the door in an oversized shirt that was barely covering her underwear.

She greeted the woman with a hug and then a peck of a kiss on the lips.

The hardwood floor below Miles suddenly *creaked*!

The woman, neighbor included, turned their attention toward Miles's loft.

Gradually, Miles, feeling the slow burn of their eyes moving through him like a fever, eased away from the peephole.

He waited a few seconds.

When he returned to the peephole, the women were nowhere around.

He heard the *kla-clunk* sound of a door locking.

"Maybe they're European," Miles said exuberantly to himself as if he was his own best audience.

With the warm blood throbbing through his veins, he scuttled into the kitchen and fixed himself a pot of coffee.

Miles couldn't help but direct his attention toward the flat-screen TV hanging from the living room wall.

It was glaring at him.

The blood in his veins turned cold.

Miles told himself that he wouldn't dare turn on the TV. Even if boredom set in throughout the day, which, most likely, it was going to do, he'd remain poised in his protest of no television for at least twenty-four hours—possibly forty-eight, that was how long these things usually blew over.

He walked into the living room, picked up the television remote from the coffee table, and held it in his hand as if it was paraphernalia used for a drug.

"What the hell?" said Miles as he turned on the TV.

The "headline" was on every single channel, every singly network, every single station—even local.

Miles was left stunned by the wall-to-wall coverage. The highlights, clips, as well as sound bites, from last night's "shocking" interview with Miles's Accuser were running on loops while analysts, contributors, and correspondents were strategically yet passionately breaking down each word, each gesture which was used in the interview. On one of the broadcasts, a child psychiatrist was instructing the parents on how their sons should treat and talk to the girls in their classes.

Miles remained glued to the screen, floored by the overwhelming coverage of the story.

Miles's phone rang.

It was *his* parents.

He didn't want to answer, at first. He spoke to them almost everyday. And if he didn't answer, then they might start to worry.

He answered.

It was his mother. She was watching the news, as she ritually did ever morning in her recliner chair with her red and black Minnie Mouse cup of steaming hot coffee in hand. His stepfather was somewhere on the line too, Miles soon realized once he heard Ronnie grousing at the TV set. Surprisingly enough, the story even made it to their "favorite" channel.

"It's not true, Mom," Miles said. "It's all fabricated. Didn't I tell you not to watch that channel? You know how they're well-known for blowing stories out of proportion."

"It's not only *our* channel, Miles," his mother said. "It's everywhere—"

"—Mom, let me talk to Ron."

"You're on speaker."

"Ron," his mother said to Miles's stepfather.

"Yeah," he snapped. "I'm here, Miles."

"It's all bogus, you know that right?"

"It's a smear," Ron said. "That's what it is. A goddamn witch hunt!"

"Ron," his mother called out, "your blood pressure—"

"—All right, all right," he groaned.

Miles could hear his stepfather's coughs becoming less and less blusterous as he stormed out of the room where the two habitually watched daytime television.

"Do you know the woman?" his mother asked, her voice softer.

"No," Miles said. "I've never met her before."

"Why would she disguise her face? It doesn't make any sense, Miles. Even if it did happen, why wouldn't she go to the police after it happened?"

"Mom," Miles yelled out, "it did not happen! Okay?"

Miles still heard the muffled echo of his voice on speakerphone. He removed the phone from his face and gritted his teeth.

"Didn't I raise you right, Miles?"

"I'm not having this discussion right now, Mom. Listen," he said, "I got a lot of things to do today." Which was a lie. "I'll talk to you guys later." Which was yet another life. "*And* don't watch that nonsense. It's not healthy."

Miles hung up the phone before his mother could say goodbye.

He received yet another phone call.

It was a longtime friend, an old female colleague of his at *The Courier*.

Miles was too ashamed to answer. He sent the call to voicemail. Following the call, he received more texts from other colleagues. He received a text from an old buddy named Gus whom he frequently went out with for beers on slow news days. Miles read through the texts.

One caught his eye:

> How does it feel to go from Mr. GQ to the most hated
> man in the world?

Miles decided to text back.

> Not funny, Gus.

Gus texted back:

> Don't sweat it, brohem. Everything will work out. It always does.

Miles texted:

> I don't know, Gus. You know how the story goes. My
> life is ruined now.

Then, Gus:

> Think of it as a blip, brohem.

130

Miles:

> I don't know what I'm going to do around here. I haven't 'not' worked a day in my life.

Gus:

> Think of it as 'me time.' Run some errands. Hitting the gym always works for me. Think of it as an indefinite vacation.

Miles:

> I don't think it'd be wise to leave home right now.

Gus:

> Hang in there, Miles. It'll be all over soon.

Then, finally, Miles:

> Will do.

For the remainder of the day, Miles piddled around his loft: he cleaned; he did laundry; even washed his bed sheets; he dusted, he scrubbed the bathroom; the shower; he emptied his entire refrigerator; threw out whatever was expired or rotten, like week-old Thai food, spotted vegetables, some covered in balls of green and blue fuzz, slick deli meat, sweaty leftover casserole inside containers of Tupperware. Miles even cleaned out the trays inside his refrigerator doors.

After the cleaning spree, he tidied up and rearranged the furniture in different positions, which made the loft looked almost new.

By the time he was finished with everything, it was already dinnertime and he was starved. Miles ordered takeout from The Flying Lotus, which was located only a few blocks away from Miles in Little Tokyo. While he waited on the food, he picked out a book from his impressive library of books. He decided to go with one of the longest ones in his collection: *The Fifth* written by Ellis Kross. It was a monster of a read, nearly a thousand-pager. The story was about a young man in pursuit of the American Dream. In a way, he could relate to the story. He wanted to push the reset button and start over and rediscover the American Dream—the real one, that is.

He only read through a few chapters until he was disrupted by a shrill voice shouting outside his window.

He couldn't quite tell what the person was shouting but one word was clear to him.

The word, *rapist*.

Miles placed the book aside and inched toward the window, only to witness a woman in a brown hoody standing on the street below. Her dark eyes were wide and mad and she was homely-looking with matted greasy hair hanging down her chest like a raggedy mop. She was looking up toward the direction of Miles's loft and shouting out the word, *rapist*, over and over.

As soon as he got a better look at the woman below, Miles suddenly ducked back inside the dim light of his loft.

The woman kept screaming.

"Show you face, you rapist!" she cried out, gathering attention on the streets. She pointed up at Miles's loft and said to a passerby, "A rapist lives in this building! And his name is Miles Straum!"

Miles heard a sudden *clanking* sound coming from the coffee table!

Startled, he snapped toward the noise.

The phone was on vibrate within a silent mode; however, he must've perched it against a metal ashtray whenever he was rearranging the furniture.

Miles picked up the phone and as he had been doing throughout the day, sent the call to voicemail. He inched back toward the window and peeked outside.

Strangely enough, the woman was no longer standing on the sidewalk. However, he could still hear her voice in the distance.

🕐

THAT night, Miles found himself rehashing the same dream from last night.

A remake.

In this new, updated version, he dreamt of a rat infiltrating his loft.

The rat managed to burrow a hole into the space on the wall between an abstract painting which he called *The Squares* and Amish-handbuilt bench that he bought a local thrift shop. The rat fell onto the edge of the rustic bench, then fell onto the ground like a beanbag. The rat rolled to its feet and scurried around his loft, going through Miles's things, like his food, the fruit inside the weaved basket on the kitchen countertop or his tennis shoes resting near the front door.

Then, finally, the rat paid Miles a visit.

Its body was revealed in the amber-colored floodlight, which cast a machete-like beam of light along the base of Miles's queen-sized bed.

The rat was obsessed, scabrous, disease-infested.

Miles woke, sat upright against the leathered headrest, and stared at the rat in his bed.

The two made eye contact.

Across the room, Miles heard that same *tapping* sound, only louder.

Tiny claws beating against drywall.

The sound doubled, tripled. Soon, it was in the hundreds and thousands.

An entire clusterfuck of beating claws.

Soon, the wall started to tremble.

The floor shook.

Miles woke shaking from a dream within a dream. He was covered in a coat of sweat. His breath labored. He reached over and hit the snooze button on top of the alarm clock, which lit up the time. It was a quarter after two o' clock.

132

Disturbed by the sight of the time, Miles let out a sigh and rolled out of bed. He switched on a lamp and lifted up the comforter on his bed. He checked underneath his bed sheets but didn't see any signs of rats or spiders or whatever the hell he dreamt. He wobbled to the window and looked outside at the street below. He heard the sound of giggling coming from the sidewalk. He pinpointed the sound to a suspicious couple drunkenly sashaying hand-in-hand along the sidewalk.

A man and woman, Miles noticed. Nightowls.

The well-dressed man occasionally pulled the woman close and kissed her.

Miles carefully watched the two. They stumbled to a luxury car parked along the curb. The man opened the passenger door for the woman, who, from Miles's point of view, appeared more intoxicated than the man.

Once the two were inside, they made out yet again.

A couple of minutes later, the headlights switched and the car drove away.

"Lucky bastard," Miles mumbled.

As Miles was about to return to sleep, he heard a strange noise coming from the hallway outside. First, he checked the peephole and peered out into the darkness of the hallway. In his mind, he wielded the neighbor's door to open and reveal the source of the sound. He stared, eyes burning and unblinking.

The door cracked open halfway!

Miles witnessed a small creature in the corner of his eye. He looked down at the floor and saw what looked like a rat slipping into the dark loft. He had to inform the neighbor of the soon-to-be nuisance and possibly catch the rat before it scurried away. Or, was that really the reason why Miles decided to check on his neighbor? Was something else going on? Something darker?

Quietly, Miles exited his apartment and walked across the hallway toward his neighbor's loft. He knocked on the opened door, which, in return, opened several inches farther.

Miles was unsure whether or not the neighbor had let the rat inside.

Or, he thought, was it another rat that managed to open the door?

If they could open doors, what else could they open?

Or worse, *what else could they do?*

Miles called out to his neighbor.

He didn't know her name.

"Ma'am," he said even though she didn't look like a ma'am. Miles stuck his head into her loft. "Excuse me," he said. "It's your neighbor, Miles," he remembered the story on TV, the accusation, his once respected name among the media world reduced to mud. He corrected, "Devon Miles."

Miles didn't hear anything in return.

He fully opened his neighbor's door, but it appeared as if nobody was home.

"Ma'am," he said as he cautiously took a step inside the dark loft.

He stepped into the kitchen, which, similar to his own, was located at the front of the loft.

Except for the stairs leading into a sunken living room—Miles soon realized as he stumbled forward—the layout was the same. He grabbed a hold of the wall, preventing him from crashing into an invisible glass table.

He heard another noise, this time coming from the bedroom. He approached the bedroom. He could see two moonlit figures on the bed. One of them was lying on the bed while the other one was position at the base of the bed.

One of them sounded as if she was moaning.

Miles knew what he was doing was wrong. Him being here was not only an invasion of privacy, but also, in most cases, a crime. He mentally told himself to turn around, go back home, use your shirt to close the door behind you, and go to sleep. They'll never know you were here. He started to think about why exactly he would use his shirt to close the door. Of course, because of the fingerprints he had left behind. Miles started to think more about the things he might've touched inside the loft. He remembered touching the wall. But, of course, it'd be nearly impossible to wipe the fingerprints from the wall, especially in the dark.

Miles eyes adjusted to the darkness of the room.

The two dark figures were women, one of them being his neighbor whom he only knew as "ma'am." She appeared as if she was the one lying on her back. As for the other one, she appeared much shorter, almost stubby. He wasn't quite sure if it was the same woman delivering coffee and a kiss for her head was deep between his neighbor's legs and she appeared to be going down on her.

The strange woman raised her head from his neighbor's legs.

Miles first acknowledged that, unless she was wearing a mask, she wasn't human. Its head was covered in scraggly brownish fur. Its eyes were glossy, beady, and black, and when the soft moonlight hit them they gleamed like white marbles. Its nose was long, like a snout with pointy whiskers protruding outward from its face. Its ears were pointed too, bare and veiny. It was that moment when the creature opened its mouth that Miles knew exactly what it was.

Miles's eyes bolted open.

Hit by the light of a red dawn, he gasped for air.

Once he gathered himself, he checked the time on the alarm clock.

6:49 AM.

The dream—or better yet—nightmare was still fresh. The images were vivid and easily accessible.

The teeth.

Those two front woodchip-like teeth chomping up and down, up and down as if it was inaudibly talking to Miles.

Miles shook away the images from his head and went about his daily morning rituals.

First, he checked his phone.

He had fifty-seven text messages and twelve missed calls.

All Miles could think about were those two front teeth.

And coffee.

Plenty of it.

AFTER the accusation, the second day started out the same as the first, with yet another shocking headline.

Apparently, last night more women came forward on late night TV. Three, to be exact. One, a middle-aged woman named Natalie Eisner, was the guest on the late night news program, *Caught in the Midol*, with the notorious whistleblower, James Midol. On Midol's show, the new accuser, Ms. Eisner, claimed that Miles sexual assaulted her six years ago. She even brought a picture of the two standing together with Miles's arm wrapped around her waist as they posed for the camera. Miles had absolutely no idea when or where the photo was taken. She claimed it was taken at a sports bar called Trendy's, but Miles had never been to any place of the name. She claimed that it was later in the night when Miles lured her to his apartment where he "attacked" her.

On the TV, news anchors were talking about the highlights from last night's broadcast. Later in the live broadcast, they were going to have all three of Miles's accusers join the show to shed more light on Miles's past criminal acts.

From inappropriately touching or forcing himself on other women, to sexual harassment among coworkers, to exposing himself, to sexual assault, all of these new accusations made their rounds across airwaves, bouncing from one network to another. It was an all-out smear campaign to defame Miles Straum, a chivalrous man who, overnight, went from one of the most respected, qualified investigative journalists in the business to America's number one sleazebag.

Two days ago, women would gladly bare Miles's offspring.

After the new accusations, women hated Miles.

In fact, some women would gladly watch Miles burn to a crisp over a flaming stake as he screamed out in bloody horror.

Of course, Miles knew these claims or accusations were exactly what his lawyer had described: false allegations, with an emphasis on *false*.

Miles's lawyer, Samuel—"Sam," he called him—wanted to meet up and discuss *all* of the litigations and whatnot. Somebody was going to fork out money to repay Miles for all of the damage that had been done to his good name and it certainly wasn't going to be coming out of the accusers' pockets.

Those who knew Miles well thought it was all a conspiracy, a political stunt; and "fixers" with deep pockets were behind it all. Possibly someone in charge of a competing network, a man in a high castle, a Wizard of Oz, someone powerful who was paying these women—actors—to make allegations against Miles. Women Miles had never even met before, let alone seen in real-life.

An hour into the news, flipping from one channel to another, Miles was done with the TV and all of the garbage spewing from the screen. He switched off the trash TV and in a sudden burst of outrage, slammed the remote to bits against the floor. He turned "off" his phone. He was tempted to break that too, but he took a moment to think about the consequences of not having a phone. Which, as of now, wasn't all that bad. But he was so tired of watching it glow and pulsating in the corner of his eye, as if it was screaming at him in a strange way and reminding him of how much of a loser he was to find himself in such an awkward position. He didn't want to hear or talk or explain anymore about himself or whatever illegal act he most certainly did "not" commit.

Miles didn't bother with the coffee. He needed some fresh air.

Then coffee.

With a black White Sox hat worn low and tight over his scalp, Miles grabbed his textbook-sized book, *The Fifth,* and exited his loft.

Miles stepped into the elevator and as the doors were about to close, a woman yelled out, "Hold that door, please!"

His initial reaction, especially with everything going on, was to flinch, protect himself, then run.

Once he realized she meant no harm, he pressed the button on the side panel but the doors still closed.

At the last second, he threw out his arm between the crack of the doors.

The elevator doors hit his arm, causing the doors to slide back open.

In front of the elevator stood his neighbor.

Miles made brief eye contact with her as she warily stepped inside the elevator.

All Miles could think about was the news and he hoped she wasn't the type to get involved in it. Even if she did watch the news, he prayed that she wasn't the type who was brainwashed by it. For Miles, she didn't look like either type.

A tense silence filled the elevator as soon as the doors closed.

Two levels down, Miles turned to the attractive woman and said, "I'm Miles. I think you're my neighbor."

"Apartment 815?"

"Yes," Miles said, a smile curling over the side of his face. "That's right. I live directly across from you."

Miles reached out his hand.

"Nice to meet you. . . "

"Leelu," she said skittishly as she held her fingers outward and barely shook Miles's hand.

She already knew, he thought.

It was her tone, the slight tremor in her voice.

Either she was socially awkward around new people or she saw my face plastered all over the TV.

Her hand shot back into her body.

Miles saw her take an extra step away from him, her body leaning up against the very corner of the elevator.

"Did you just move in?" asked Miles.

"Two weeks ago," she said shortly.

The woman, Leelu, could hardly make eye contact with Miles. She kept her attention mostly at the doors before her. She pulled out her phone and started to scroll through it, as if it was her way of ending the soon-to-be conversation.

Miles faced forward, his eyes moved down toward Leelu's phone below and he noticed that she had the numbers 9-1-1 dialed and her finger was hovering over the green call button.

All of a sudden, Miles was overcome by a heat flash. He faced turned warm, his palms started to sweat, then armpits. He found himself shrinking.

The elevator arrived at the first floor.

Leelu jetted out the doors as soon as they opened.

"Have a nice day," Miles said, his voice cracking.

The woman returned her head held down with a strained smile on her face.

Miles remained in the elevator in a state of shock. He tried to wrap his mind around the fact that this woman, Leelu, by her actions, was absolutely terrified of him.

Then, again, maybe she wasn't comfortable around strangers.

Miles wanted to believe it was true, that she was only shy, for he, too, was no stranger to the shyness, which consumed most of his adolescent years. When he was a little boy, he had his own internal battles. Eventually, after college, he slew that dragon which was anxiety.

But he could feel it rising again.

From that dark cave, its orange eyes narrowing.

🕐

INSTEAD of driving, Miles decided to walk to a café, The Cup, which was located a couple of blocks from his loft.

About halfway toward the café, Miles saw a woman giving him an icy glare as she stepped into her car parked along the side of the curb. Doubts crept back in. He couldn't help but think of the young woman in the elevator. The look she gave him. The sound of her voice. The fear in her. He tried to put himself in her shoes and wonder as to why an individual would feel such a way in front of someone whom he or she hadn't met before. He thought more directly; maybe she had a *bad* experience with a man who treated her poorly. Maybe she felt threatened or intimidated by men. Or, maybe she was not attracted to men in general. A lot of maybes ran through Miles's head and not a single one of them had any concrete resolution. He tried his best to ignore what happened in the elevator, even though it was at the forefront of his mind.

For the rest of the walk, Miles kept his head down. He passed a rowdy group of teenagers, all male, catcalling at young woman who was dressed in a provocative dress. The young woman turned to the kids and gave them a look of disgust. Miles approached the kids, asked them if that was necessary. They recognized his face from the Internet.

"Like you one to talk, you hypocrite." The kid pulled out his smartphone and blew up Miles's face on his touch screen. "Lookie here, Miles Straum." The kid read a couple of comments on his phone. "Guess what? You're trending and not like the good kind of trending."

"Yeah," another kid said. "Like the dead-kind of trending."

"That's Miles Straum," the other one said. "You're dead, didn't you know?"

"R.I.P.

"Yeah," another chimed in. "Rot In Peace."

"Shouldn't you be in school, getting an education?"

"Well, shouldn't you be like in jail or something?"

Miles shrugged off the group of teenagers and grabbed a newspaper from the dispenser in front of the café. He made the second page. He threw the newspaper in the trash and entered the café.

As Miles waited in line, he could feel wandering eyes pounding down him. He directed his scattered attention to a middle-aged woman with a stony face sitting with another stony-faced woman at a table not too far away. One of the two women pointed at Miles. The other one turned her shoulder and glanced at Miles. They started talking while, at the same time, shooting glares at Miles. He tried to ignore them.

He'd direct his attention elsewhere and find another woman, younger, staring at him.

As Miles turned away, she started texted on her phone, laughing while doing so.

Miles thought one woman took a photo of him from across the dining area.

Miles closed his eyes for a moment.

The chatter around the café increased.

He eavesdropped on several conversations. He heard his name thrown in the mix. *Miles.* Then, *the guy*—no—the *slime on TV.* Then, he heard the word *trash* a few times.

Then, the word *next*.

"Sir?" the young barista said.

Miles looked around the café.

Again, the barista said more clearly, "Next."

A woman standing behind Miles tapped him on the shoulder.

Miles flinched and rotated around.

"Are you going to order or not?" asked the woman.

"Yeah," he said and stepped forward.

The barista wasn't pleased to see Miles.

When she asked for his order, she did so in a manner that suggested that either she didn't want to be here at this miserable job, or she didn't want to serve a customer, like Miles, who treated women as if they were pieces of meat. Miles leaned toward the latter because, just a couple of customers ago, she was laughing and smiling and she told one of the customers to enjoy the rest of her day.

"One tall medium roast," Miles said, struggling to look the barista in the eye.

"Anything else?"

"No, thanks. That's it."

Miles pulled out his wallet, then his debit card.

Before he was about to pay for the coffee, he noticed the price of the coffee was much higher than the last time he was here; in fact, it was three dollars more than what he paid a week ago. He checked the menu above and noticed the price was different, cheaper, three dollars cheaper.

He moved his eyes toward the barista, kept them there on her. Another wave of heat came over his body.

She narrowed her eyes and pointed at the touch screen.

"Slide your card," the barista demanded.

Miles hesitated for a moment, looked at the differentiation of prices on both the menu, as well as the card swiper below, then looked at the barista standing in front of him.

"Slide your card, Sir," she said once more, this time in a hostile tone.

Miles swiped his card.

"Name on the coffee?"

"*Straum*," Miles said confidently as he stared at the barista, "Miles Straum."

As Miles waited in the far corner of the café for his coffee, he saw his face on the TV above the lounge area. Several customers were gathered around on what looked like an inviting sofa and shaking their heads with distaste as they watched the news. The sudden distraction gave the barista enough time to hawk a loogie into Miles's coffee while Miles wasn't paying attention.

The barista called out Miles's name.

She handed him the coffee.

Surprisingly, his name was spelled correctly. Next to his name was a doodle of a smiley face.

"You have a wonderful day, Miles Straum," the barista said with exaggerated glee.

"You too," Miles said modestly.

Miles walked over to the self-serving station adjacent the cash register. He opened the lid of the coffee, first inspecting it for any spit and then smelling it. It seemed fine. He poured cream and sugar into the coffee.

As Miles turned around, a woman suddenly came charging at him with a cup in her hand. She flung hot coffee toward Miles's face and shrieked, "Burn in hell you fucking pig!"

Miles ducked his head.

Hot coffee hit the side of his face, but most of it landed on the self-serving station behind him.

The woman turned to the barista and asked for the manager, "How can you serve this pervert? This man is a rapist!"

Her husband was trying to calm her down.

With the side of his face burning, Miles placed his coffee aside and delicately touched the side of his face.

A young man stepped in and grabbed a handful of napkins and started patting coffee from Miles's shirt.

"Thanks," Miles said to the young man.

Miles grabbed his coffee and hurried to the exit door while customers glared at him and called him all kinds of names behind his back, like "creep," "misogynist," "pig," "bully," "scum-of-the-earth," and even worse, "monster."

Of all the names—or words—*monster* was the one that stayed with Miles the most. Throughout his brief existence, he had been called many names before, but not that one in particular.

As soon as Miles stepped out of the café, the customers cheered in jubilation.

Miles couldn't help but think about the one word and the meaning behind it. Even his once thick skin started to feel strangely thin and brittle.

THE sickness crept in during the latter part of the afternoon when the softening glow of twilight approached and didn't make its presence known until around ten o'clock that night while Miles was plowing through *The Fifth*. His body was hot, feverish. His throat incredibly sore and scratchy; and every time he swallowed, his throat stung. His nose as runny as a dripping faucet. The tip of it red and raw from constantly rubbing it with a tissue. His glands were also swollen and throbbing, a telltale sign he was coming down with something nasty. To make matters even worse, he had a blister on the side of his face the size of his palm. He read somewhere that popping a blister made it harder to heal and would possibly lead to scarring. He left it alone for the time being and figured he'd sleep on the right side of his body, which was opposite of the normal position he slept. The idea of sleep, lying in the confines of his own bed, in that keyed up darkness, closing his eyes, trying to go to sleep, and eventually, dreaming: these were like milestones to Miles. Unwanted choirs. He knew sleep was going to be a challenge and his only temporary remedy was over-the-counter medication until he could schedule a doctor's appointment the next morning. Miles was the holistic-type who preferred to catch a cold before it turned into a flu or pneumonia or let a virus runs its course by treating it with a proper diet, which included leafy greens and fruits, hot soups or broths, hot teas with ginger, lemon, and honey, and loading up on an alphabet of vitamins, particularly vitamin C and D, which were known to ward off ailments and boost an immune system, rather than run straight to the doctor for a quick fix. He went through a phase in college where he experimented with drugs; however, they never wrecked his life or caused any irreparable damage like some he knew. Back then, whenever he got sick or came down with a mild fever, he'd take a pill without thinking twice.

After Miles brushed his teeth and gargled his mouth with warm saltwater, he opened the medicine cabinet and debated whether or not to take anything to aide his face, as well as help him sleep. He came across a bottle of NyQuil, unopened, waiting there like a life raft. For the first time in many years, Miles grabbed the bottle without hesitation and chugged it. He turned off every light in his loft and slept hard in blackness. He slumbered in a deep, dreamless state.

A sudden *BANG* at the door!

Miles jolted upward from his deep, recuperative sleep.

Once more, the door violently rattled from the *bang, bang, bang!*

Miles ripped the covers from his sweaty body as if he was unwrapping a gift and catapulted himself from the bed. The blast of coldness punched his hot body.

He picked up a cardigan close by, threw it on, and stomped toward the closet where he stabbed his feet into a pair of slippers.

Then he stomped toward the front door. He checked the peephole first. Nobody was there.

With a balled-up fist, Miles swung open the door. He looked to his right but didn't see anybody in the hallway. Then looked to his left. Miles saw a shapeless man dressed in black rounding the end of the hallway. Miles chased after him.

The chase continued on the stairs. Miles arched his body over the railing and spotted the dark figure fleeing down a flight of stairs two levels below him. Miles pushed past any reason and pursued. He heard a door swing open then close as he made it to the seventh floor. He wasn't sure if it was the fourth floor or the fifth. He was still riding that bluish-green wave of NyQuil, neither drowsy nor alert but gripped by what felt like a mild hangover.

Panting with exhaustion, he made it to the fifth level.

He walked down a dark hallway that was blocked off. A cardboard sign that read WET PAINT was attached to a piece of caution tape, which had been stretched from one side of the wall to the other. The sign was moving, as if it had recently been disturbed. Miles hunched his body underneath the strip of caution tape and found the man in black anxiously waiting in front of the elevator in the next hallway.

Miles got a better look at him. He was dressed in all black, hoody, jeans, and boots. A walking cliché. The agent provocateur turned to Miles. His face went slack. He was a white young male, he concluded. And scared.

Scared white.

"Hey," Miles called out to him.

The man—or boy, Miles didn't know how old he was—took off in the other direction. He went through a door, possibly one leading to the other staircase.

Miles paused and thought for a second.

He knew exactly where the stairs ended.

It led to only one exit.

With a new plan in mind, the elevator let out a *ding* and the doors opened.

Miles took the elevator to the first floor.

Instead of exiting through the main lobby, he exited through the back exit.

He waited in shadows behind the building until the exit door swung open. He jumped the person from behind, pushed him to the ground, and kneeled over him.

"What the hell do you want from me?" asked Miles, as he grabbed the young man by the collar of his hoody.

"Get the fuck off me!"

Miles picked up the difference in the voice.

It was shriller.

The hoody suddenly flipped backward as Miles shook the young man.

He soon realized it wasn't a man.

It was a woman. Her hair was pulled back in a ponytail. Her cloudy cheeks were trembling with either rage or fear, Miles couldn't quite tell. Her eyes, however, were piercing. He didn't know the woman, hadn't seen her face before, but he knew the look in her eyes. The hatred.

Miles's grip loosened from the collar.

"Why are you doing this to me?" asked Miles. "Huh?"

"You belong in prison!"

"Prison? For what? You're the one who came at me!"

"You're a rapist!"

"What?" Miles backed off. "You're serious? You actually believe that shit you hear about in the news? It's all bogus. Smoke and mirrors."

"Rapist!" she screamed. "RAPIST!"

Eventually, after the sixth shriek of the word *rapist*, she paused to catch her breath.

"You don't even know me, lady—"

"—I know enough."

The woman stood to her feet and thumbed the drop of blood on the corner of her lip.

"Now, I'm gonna sue your ass," she said.

"Listen," Miles said, acknowledging the minor injury. "I didn't know."

"What? That I was a woman?"

The woman puffed out her chest.

"You're gonna pay for what you did," she seethed.

Miles held out his hands and took a step back.

"Whatever," Miles said, making his way to the exit. "Just leave me the fuck alone or else, next time, I will call the cops."

"Go ahead," she said over Miles. "Call them. It still won't stop us."

"Us? Who the fuck is us?"

"The world, Miles," the woman said as Miles opened the door. "Didn't you hear? Your life is finished!"

Miles went back to his loft.

When he finally made it back, the door was wide open. The lights were off inside. He cautiously stepped inside, grabbed a fire extinguisher from the wall, and held it close like a weapon. He flipped on every light switch to every room in the loft. Lastly, he flipped on the lamp in the living room. Hanging from the ceiling fan was a noose.

And it had Miles's name written all over it.

🕐

MILES remained awake for the rest of the night and well into the early morning.

As soon as the doctor's office opened, Miles called to make an appointment. The doctor had an opening at ten-thirty. Miles made the appointment and tried to go back to bed. He managed to doze off for about an hour or so until he heard a commotion on the street outside.

"What the hell is it now?" Miles asked himself as he rolled out of bed.

He staggered to the window and looked outside, only to find an angry mob of people protesting outside his apartment building. Protesters were holding up professionally made black and white signs with words like *rapist* and *criminal* and phrases like "*lock him up.*" Others signs were much more garish, showy and glittery, with the lettering handwritten with Sharpies. Some of the signs were politically based or inspired. Signs with the theme of blame or shame: blaming the current administration for the erosion of our society, blaming the government for the moral decay or lack of civility, but most importantly, signs meant to "shame" not only Miles, but also his fellow sex, as if Miles himself was no longer an individual responsible for his own actions but the sole ambassador of all men.

Most of the crowd consisted of women and extremists who attended the protest for other more sinister reasons. Women were crying and screaming at Miles. To Miles, the scene was surreal to say the least. Miles didn't know whether or not he was still dreaming. He didn't know what was happening, really.

All he knew was that he was here, in the present.

He looked down at his shaky hands and lifted them up to his face. He started to touch his face, feeling each corner and groove.

He was here.

He couldn't say the same about the people below.

Was she right about what she said last night?

The world being after me?

Surely, he thought, the world hadn't become so shallow to rush to judgment.

Who was manipulating these people?

Was there some hidden force, a grand power dwelling underneath the shadows, pulling the strings behind the whole charade?

Was it technology?

Miles looked down at his phone on the nightstand.

Then, he turned to the TV.

Was it people like me? Am I to blame for all of this?

After all, Miles thought to himself as he stared at the people below, *I started all of this.*

An overwhelming sense of glum settled over his body like a thorny coat.

I had to finish it.

The thought alone that he himself was responsible for all of the madness on the streets caused a sharp, thorny pain to knot in his gut.

He rushed to the bathroom and stared at himself in the mirror.

He looked like shit, worst than shit. He looked like the kind of shit that drew flies. The left side of his face was infected. He was wearing dark baggage underneath his eyes, which had made him look twice his normal age.

Miles knew his health was more important.

In time, he knew, the truth would come out—*it will*.

For the first time in a long time, Miles prayed the truth would come out much sooner than later.

🕐

WHILE keeping a low profile, Miles avoided the mob by exiting through the parking deck.

As soon as he pulled out of the parking lot, they were waiting for him. Miles shielded his face with his jacket. Somehow, they knew it was him. If they knew exactly where he lived, then, surely, they knew exactly what make and model of car he drove.

He crept through the crowd, projectiles as well as hands hitting and slapping at the sides of his car.

143

A woman tossed her coffee cup at the windshield.

Creamy-brown coffee spilled over the windshield, forcing him to hit the wipers.

One woman jumped out in front of the hood of the car, flopped like a professional soccer player to the ground, and started wailing and rolling on the ground as if she was badly hurt.

A man tended to her for a moment. Then he came charging at the car. He elbowed the side of the driver's side window, shattering part of it but not entirely breaking it.

Miles feared for his safety.

He gunned the car into traffic, knocking over a couple of protesters onto the street.

He thought for certain he injured one of them, but he kept driving.

🕐

MILES'S condition worsened by the time he pulled into the doctor's office. He met with the nurse first, told her all about his symptoms, the sore throat, the sneezing, the runny nose, the fever, and the most obvious, the burn on his face. Miles was afraid and jumpy at times, knowing, in the back of his mind, she might scold him for what he was accused of doing to a woman. She was professional, though. The issue was never brought up. She treated Miles as if she was unaware of what he was going through. The attention was centered on his well-being, not accusations, false or not.

The nurse left the room.

His doctor, Doctor Delhi, entered soon afterwards.

He went over the chart.

Miles informed the doctor about his symptoms.

The doctor didn't hesitate. He prescribed him medication to help reduce the symptoms. He also prescribed Miles with a strong cream to apply twice a day to his face. Then, lastly, he referred Miles to see another doctor.

Confused, Miles looked over the name on the piece of paper.

"A shrink?"

"Trust me," he said, his hand on Miles's shoulder. "It'll help, Miles. Maybe she'll be able to prescribe medication to help with the anxiety."

"Anxiety?"

"I know what you're going through Miles."

"You do?"

"Everybody does," he said. "It's all over TV. Have you ever tried disguising yourself when you're in public?"

"I shouldn't have to disguise myself," Miles said. "I'm an innocent man."

"What I meant to say is disguise yourself for the time being, you know, until everything cools down. By next week, everybody will forget what happened."

Miles hung his head.

"You know they left a noose inside my loft."

The doctor folded his arms across his chest and shook his head in disgust.

"Did you call the police?"

"No."

"How these individuals break into your home?"

"I must've left the door unlocked," Miles said, unsure. "I don't know."

The doctor leaned in close to Miles and placed his hand over his shoulder.

"You need to take care yourself," he said with concern. "Don't let this get to you." The doctor paused. "My mother, who was a doctor herself, a highly intelligent woman who had an extraordinary gift to identify problems, always told me to 'consider the source.' As a child, I never understood what she meant by those words until later on in high school. 'Consider the source,' she'd always say. Till this day, those words have guided me, not only in life, but also in my practice."

"Right," Miles said emotionlessly.

The good doctor pulled out a notepad from his breast pocket and wrote Miles another prescription.

"I'm going to prescribed you with something that will help you sleep. Make sure you take only *one* pill a night," the doctor emphasized. "It's potent stuff, but it works."

"Thanks, Doctor."

Miles stood from the table and shook the doctor's hand.

"Hang in there, Miles," the doctor said and showed Miles the door.

AFTER Miles left the doctor's office, he killed time by driving around the city for a while until his prescription was ready to be picked up. He wondered about the pharmacist, if it was a woman, and if so, would she slip in a different medication, possibly something that would make his condition even worse. Or, worse, something that would kill him. He started to think about these things, even during trivial times of the day, such as running common errands like picking up medication from a pharmacy. The pharmacist turned out to be a man. Which was a relief to Miles. However, he realized all of that worrying he was doing in the car was all for nothing. And, if he went about his days like this, the constant worrying, then he was going to give himself a stomach ulcer. Or, even worse, Miles was headed straight to Looney Town.

As Miles stepped out of the Med-Mart, he suddenly gagged from the smell of smoke in the air. He covered his nose and mouth with the loose collar of his tee shirt and spotted the smokestack-like column of black smoke spewing into the air. He traced the smoke to his car engulfed in flames. Some people in the parking lot were fleeing from the fire while others were gathering around the fire like a tribe. One face in particular caught Miles's eye. A shaky pale face of a young woman. She crept from the growing crowd, her red eyes moving around the chaotic scene in what Miles recognized as paranoia. She turned her body toward the front entrance of Med-Mart and for a brief moment, locked eyes with Miles. Underneath the stiff collar of her leather jacket, she had a foreign tattoo running up the side of her neck like a serpent. Miles couldn't help but stare at it, that tattoo.

Furious, the strange woman clenched her teeth, the sides of her jaw like tiny bulges.

A man behind her hollered out something like *call the police* to a friend.

The woman flinched from the man's voice. She backpedaled from the crowd and speed-walked to a noisy Honda hatchback across the parking lot and peeled away, her car leaving behind a trail of smoke.

The tattoo, Miles said to himself. *That* tattoo.

He replayed the images in his head. Found himself diagnosing the image. *Durga.*

The name came to him out of the blue.

The tattoo was of a fierce woman—a goddess—a multiple arm-formed goddess from the Hindu scripture. In one of her many arms, she was holding a sword in her hand and slaying an evil demon while riding on top a tiger.

The more he thought about that one name in particular, the name *Durga* with an emphasis on the *Durrr*, the more Miles thought about her, the bearer of the tattoo, the bartender from V Lounge, most commonly known as V to weekend warriors who drank there every festive weekend.

What was her name?

🕐

By the time the firefighters arrived at the scene, the car was all charred and burnt and nothing much remain of it but a blackened shell with a dark melted interior.

The woman's name suddenly came to Miles when he was speaking to the police officer on the scene.

The cop mentioned the word *after* and then *exited*

(*After* you *exited* from Med-Mart. . .)

Strangely enough, those two words were the magic keys to unlock the memory gates.

"*Alexis*!" Miles blurted out as he stood next to the police officer on the sidewalk next to Med-Mart. "Her name is Alexis!"

Strange how the mind works like that, Miles thought, certain words bringing forth trapped memories that remained tiny and unlit, waiting to be wiggled loose into the blazing light of consciousness.

"Girlfriend?" said the police officer.

"No."

"*Ex*-girlfriend?"

An emphasis of the *ex*.

Miles hesitated.

"No."

"She's a bartender at V."

"V?"

"The V Lounge."

"I see," the officer said as he wrote it down on a piece of paper attached to a clipboard.

Miles pulled out his phone and looked this Alexis up on Facebook. He had no luck. He went on V's Facebook page and saw her face in one of the photo albums. He scrolled through the timeline and clicked on the face, which sent him to her profile page. There, he found her full name.

"Alexis Welding," Miles told the officer.

Miles showed the officer a picture of Alexis on his phone.

The officer wrote down the first name.

Then hesitated before writing down the last.

"Welding?"

Miles spelled it out for the officer.

The officer jotted down the last name.

Miles searched through the contacts in his phone.

He completely forgot that he still had her number in his phone.

"So, how do you know this woman, Alexis Welding?" asked the officer.

"We've met before," Miles answered. "She used to serve me drinks at the V Lounge. Plus, we have mutual friends."

"Do you have any kind of relationship with Ms. Welding?"

"We have no relationship, at least not like that."

"But you two do *know* each other?"

"Yes," Miles said. "I guess you can say that."

Miles directed his attention toward the police officer writing. The officer appeared bored with Miles, as if he was going through the motions.

"You're going to catch her, right?" asked Miles.

"One of the detectives will be contacting Ms. Welding," the officer said.

"She's going to say that she didn't do it," Miles said with frustration. "If you don't believe me, then take a look at the footage from the surveillance cameras."

Miles pointed at the camera mounted on the corner of the Med-Mart building.

"Don't tell me how to do my job," the officer said seriously.

Miles backed off.

"I'm just saying."

The officer continued to write.

🕐

MILES ending up taking a UBER back home.

He told the UBER driver to drop him off a block away from his building.

Just to be safe.

If the mob was still there, then he had no protection.

Miles knew he had to be smart about how he'd sneak into his building. The thought alone of "sneaking" in somewhere was ridiculous. Miles felt as if he was sixteen years old again, sneaking into his bedroom window in the middle of night while desperately trying not to wake the sleeping giants.

Miles heard a commotion coming from the street ahead. The closer he came to the commotion, the clearer the words became. He heard screaming, the chants. They were *still* there, still raging. Miles made it to an intersection, poked his head around a corner, and saw the mob outside the front of his building.

Like before, he decided to enter via the back of the building; however, when he arrived in the back alleyway, he saw a crowd gathering around the door. Miles was no *Spiderman*, even though the thought of scaling the build-

147

ing like the web-slinger came to him. *Imagine the possibilities!* But that was all fictional, a world Miles wished was real. Another idea came to Miles, two ideas actually, and both of them he learned from his rogue days in high school.

Bomb threat was clearly off the table.

Bomb threats were taken too seriously, especially given the circumstances of the situation.

However, the other one could work.

He called one of his neighbors, Martiez, his workout partner and the occasion wingman on Saturday nights. Fortunately, Martiez worked from home. He happened to be in the building when he called. Miles asked him for a favor.

A "huge" favor.

🕐

THE building cleared from the fire alarm.

As the residents exited the building, Miles shouldered his way past the crowd and entered the building undetected.

Miles hid inside the last stall of a bathroom while the firefighters were called to the building. One of the clunk-sounding firefighters entered the bathroom but was called upon by one of his colleagues to exit the building once they realized it was the false alarm.

🕐

MILES spent the rest of the day hunkered in his loft. He blasted heavy metal jams through his headphones to drown out the mob outside but could only listen to the music for an hour or two before his ears grew sore. Toward late afternoon, that time in the day when the news was preparing for five o' clock, various news vans showed up at the scene. Right on cue. Cameramen, as well as reporters, some of whom Miles personally knew, were among the mob.

When night *finally* arrived, Miles was tapped out yet still jacked up from the chaos outside. It felt as if he was on a combination of both uppers and downers, as if he just got done slamming five shots of fireball. His body wanted to pass-out, but his mind wouldn't shut off; and at times, he felt as if it was the other way around, like he had a switch inside him and some bratty little shithead kept flipping it on and off, on and off, on and off, singing the words *nana nana boo boo, stick your head in dodo.*

Out of mere curiosity, Miles decided to turn on his phone. His voicemail was overflowing with messages. Same went with text messages. He had hundreds of emails in his inbox. One of the messages stood out the most. It was a voicemail from Noelle, a colleague from the network. She sounded worried about Miles and she wanted to meet up and talk about what was going on— what they were going to do.

Miles hesitated to call her back.

As before, he didn't.

He turned off his phone and took a pill to help him sleep.

THE rats were back.

Hundreds and thousands of them chewing and clawing through the walls and moving like a brown tidal wave through his loft.

Driven by an innate hunger of human flesh, the rats climbed onto his bed.

Miles was stuck inside a dream. He woke but was still asleep. He curled his chin into his neck and peered down his body, only to find a pack of rats crawling up the base of the bed, arching their heads upward as they sniffed Miles's scent, craving his pungent aroma. It was as if they could smell the terror emitting from the pores of his skin, like that mustardy-colored gas in the movies. They crawled up his feet, legs, waist, and settled onto his chest.

With his eyes swelled open, Miles tried to move, tried to wake from the horrible nightmare, but he was completely paralyzed. He was struggling to catch his breath. The weight of the rats made each breath more taxing than the one before.

The rats were smothering Miles.

As the dream started to spin out of control, Miles suddenly woke up from his deep sleep, brushing away the rats from his body. There were no rats, Miles soon realized as he caught his breath and flipped on the lamp.

It was a dream, Miles told himself.

A nightmare.

"It's not real, Miles," he said audibly to himself.

It's not real.

He rolled out of bed and dragged himself to the bathroom. He flipped on the light. In the corner of his eye, he saw something unusual, something darker. He turned to the mirror. Except for his hair, his entire face, as well as his body was as dark as a silhouette. His skin a deep black. He reached up with his black hand and touched his black face. He couldn't feel his hand. He continued to reach farther into the blackness. His hand kept moving farther into his head, going deeper and deeper as if he was reaching into his mind and that, too, was pitch-black. . .

Once more, he suddenly woke up from the dream!

As before, he dragged himself to the bathroom.

As before, he checked his face in the mirror, his eyes, his nose. He reminded himself it was only a dream. He sipped water from the faucet.

With distant images of the strange dream still battering around his mind, he walked to the spot where the rats had emerged from the wall. He turned on a light and noticed a quarter-size piece of drywall on the floor. He picked up the drywall chip and matched it to a bare spot above the electrical outlet.

It's not real, he told himself.

Or was it?

THE next morning, Miles heard a bunch of people talking on the street. The mob had settled down; however, they were still there, loitering around as if Miles's loft and the street that surrounded it had all become an amusement park and they were waiting for the rides to open. Some protesters were gearing themselves up with signs while others were fueling themselves up with coffee.

Miles decided to take up his doctor's advice about wearing a disguise.

He did have a disguise.

A good one.

Miles pulled himself from the window and splashed his face with cold water from the bathroom faucet, which helped relieve the soreness in his face.

Outside, the crowd was starting to get stirred up by a megaphone.

Once more, he checked on the crowd outside.

A handful of protesters, ones that Miles never saw the day before, were fired up and shouting out the word of the week, *rapist*, as if it was a new trend that had graduated into the Hall of Names, which would be used like slander against future political opponents. He thought they looked like out-of-towners. People who had nothing better to do than try to ruin an innocent man's reputation. Miles couldn't understand how these people receive a great deal of satisfaction in bringing added stress to a man's already stressful life. But *maybe that was the whole point*, Miles thought. *To break me down. To drive me out of town.*

As Miles stared at the faces below, he felt nothing but a raw resentment for them and their ability to be easily persuaded.

Miles stormed back into his bedroom and pulled out a shoebox from the top shelf of the closet. He set the box on the floor and removed the lid. Inside was a long blonde wig, as well as various cosmetics, gold tubes of lipstick, a silver stick of mascara, a clamshell-shaped container of powder, a small mirror. He grabbed the wig from the box and held it up before him.

At that moment, Miles knew exactly what had to be done.

Miles was no longer known as Miles Straum when he stepped out of his loft. He was a handsome young blonde named Scarlet, as in the color red. The name, Scarlet, had come to him from the sight of the tall teepee shaped scarlet runner in the botanical garden inside the courtyard of his building. Miles couldn't help but notice the capital A shape of the plant. Plus, Miles liked the name, Scarlet. It was elegant and rolled off the tongue like a wave.

The first person to acknowledge Scarlet was his neighbor, Leelu.

Or, he thought, was it Leila?

She held the door open for the woman in the red dress as she stepped outside. The neighbor stopped in her tracks and gave Scarlet what she thought was a rather flirtatious look.

Miles thought, *Was she checking me out?*

Scarlet pushed the thought aside and thanked her neighbor for being polite.

"You new here?" asked the neighbor.

Scarlet paused and cleared her throat.

"I guess you can say that," Scarlet said, smirking.

She turned and walked away as if she was playing hard to catch. Making just the right impression that would stay with Leelu for the rest of the day. Scarlet had no intentions at all about pursuing any kind of relationship with his neighbor. He liked playing The Game, one where he was the only one who came out on top.

Scarlet pushed her through the small crowd, then walked around a larger one. Nobody looked at Scarlet twice, except for a couple of built fellas who were talking amongst themselves. Scarlet ignored them—or at least tried to. She still received looks, but this time it was mostly coming from men.

They don't know, he thought. *If I've gotten this far, then why not go a little further.*

What the heck?

So Scarlet did. She walked to Miles's once favorite go-to spot for caffeine, the same café where he had hot coffee thrown in his face and heckled out by loyal patrons. She stepped inside the cafe. Surprisingly, Scarlet received similar attention as Miles did the last time he was here. She received glares from men, same from women; however, a couple of women, like Miles's neighbor, appeared as if they were checking out Scarlet.

Not to draw any suspicion, Scarlet ordered the opposite of what Miles would normally order. At first, he thought about tea and how good a cup of hot lemon ginger or chamomile tea would be; however, he was feeling adventurous. He had never tried one of those fancy-schmancy caramel drinks with whipped cream on top and a swirly straw before. Frankly, Miles was too embarrassed to order one in public. What better opportunity to try something different?

The same barista as before greeted Scarlet with a much better jovial attitude, which Scarlet first interpreted as phoniness.

Scarlet waited for the barista to unravel and reveal through her actions, even her words, that she was completely aware of Scarlet's game.

Scarlet vigilantly watched the barista and waited for a sign, the slight lowering of a lip, a dark spot in her eye, a drop in tone, a clearing of her throat, a twitch or sudden fidgetiness of her body, any movement or gesture that indicated that the barista was not only playing the game, but was also battling for the sole rights of dominance.

The barista remained poised and friendly, didn't miss a beat when Scarlet ordered a Caramel Frappucchino.

She smiled at Scarlet. She stayed with character, an extremely cordial barista who had a heart the size of the world, who bent over backwards to make Scarlet's visit the most comforting experience.

The two even started talking about the weather and other things, like the different types of new autumn flavors, which had been recently added to their limited fall collection. The barista talked about what a nice day it was going to be, but strangely enough, she was glad to be right here at the café, working her tail off on a cheap salary shy of minimum wage, and concocting hot as well as cold beverages for thirsty patrons.

Scarlet pushed aside Miles's tongue-in-cheek pessimism.

For the first time all week, Miles felt optimistic about the future. Except for all the preparation involved in the whole transformation process, including all the extra garments worn to make himself plumper in areas that were flat or shaving areas of the body, which weren't meant to be shaved, or the waxing and all the burn and hot pain that followed afterwards or applying more lotions and creams to his skin, or the plucking of rogue or unpleasant hairs or the constant changing of his voice, which, Miles knew, over time and repetition, he'd

151

be able to master, or being able to have an open mind when it came to picking out colors, figure out which ones worked well together, and then dabble in various shades that he normally wouldn't wear or, lastly, possessing a steady hand while applying a new face, he sort of liked being this "new" person.

Despite all of the effort and dedication, Miles didn't understand what the fuss was about.

Besides the looks or maybe a few pounding stares he received every now and then, Miles thought, it wasn't all that bad.

Once Scarlet's Frappucchino was ready for pick up, Scarlet, like the neighbor before, thanked the barista for her politeness.

As Scarlet was about to walk away, the barista asked Scarlet if she liked to run.

Scarlet's face went long.

"Run?"

"Yeah," the barista corrected. "You know, like jogging."

"Oh," Scarlet said and giggled. "Sure. I like to jog."

"This weekend, a few of my girlfriends are getting together for a benefit. If you don't have any plans, feel free to join us. The name's Lou, by the way."

Lou, huh?

Scarlet thought over the invitation.

"That sounds nice. I'll have to check my schedule."

The barista wrote down her phone number on a blank receipt and handed it to Scarlet.

"Give me a call or text me if you're going to come." Lou grinned. "I'll text you the location."

Scarlet looked over the number, smiled back.

"I will," she said. "Thanks."

Scarlet left the cafe and enjoyed her Frappucchino on the patio outside.

She couldn't help but think of how nice the day was going to be.

🕐

AFTER Scarlet left the café, she looked up the nearest car rentals in the area. She found one a few miles away; however, it was beyond walking distance. She decided to grab an UBER.

While she waiting, she spotted a curious man waiting behind a Prius as if he was using it to conceal himself. Scarlet remembered seeing him at the café; now that *she* thought more about it, she remembered his scrunched-up face, his gray eyes wrapped in bitter wrinkles.

She checked her phone.

The UBER driver was seven minutes away.

Seven *long* minutes.

Either the guy knew Miles was pretending to be a woman named Scarlet or the guy had other sinister intentions and was most definitely eyeing Scarlet.

A minute in, Starlet decided to cancel the UBER and lose the guy on foot. She walked down the sidewalk bustling with pedestrians. During her hasty walk, she turned her shoulder. As expected, the guy was following her.

But not just following, stalking.

Scarlet sped up, didn't run; but she sped up her walk into a power walk.

As she rounded a street corner or jaywalked past an intersection, she looked over her shoulder; and the same guy, with his eyes sharp and shriveled, continued to stalk her.

Scarlet was only a block away from her building. She decided to remove the red stilettos from her feet and take off down an alleyway. She stepped on a jagged rock on the concrete; but as with her preparations into making her coming out party official, she pushed through the pain.

Once Scarlet reached the end of the alley, which intersected with yet another alley, she stood on her toes and stretched out her body until she was as thin as a teenager and hid within the frame of doorway alongside the side of the building. She heard footsteps coming closer, then silence, then the footsteps began to travel in the opposite direction. Then, after a couple of minutes, the footsteps faded into street ambience. Scarlet poked her head from the doorway and checked her surroundings. The guy was gone. Scarlet told herself to breathe.

She breathed.

For a moment, the sun came out and sword-like rays pierced the alley below.

Relieved, Scarlet put her stilettos back on and began to walk back toward her building where she'd grab another UBER to the car rental place.

As she exited the alleyway, the same guy from before leaped out behind her, startling her.

The guy paced around Scarlet, eyeing her body from legs-up.

"Hey there, good-looking."

"Please," she said. "I don't want any trouble."

"Too late. Trouble's already found you, sweetie," the guy said with a smirk stretched across his mean face.

Miles was unsure whether or not the guy was making an attempt at foreplay, as if referring to himself as "trouble," as if all women liked men who were nothing but trouble. She expected to hear a pick-up line about his middle name being "maker."

The guy stepped closer to Scarlet and blocked her path.

Scarlet realized the situation was more serious than she originally thought.

"What's a good-looking woman like yourself roaming back alleyways?"

Scarlet took a brief moment to observe her surroundings, her exits, as well as her weapons.

"I'm just taking a shortcut home."

"And where is home?"

"It's none of your business." Scarlet made an attempt to pass the guy. "Now if you don't mind—"

The guy slid to the right and once more, blocked Scarlet's path.

"I said ' I don't want any trouble.'"

"Nothing's wrong with *Trouble*," he said. "Why does *Trouble* get such a bad rap? Maybe you should try getting yourself into trouble. You don't know what you're missing out—"

"—Please," Scarlet said, backing away. "I have cash."

"Cash?" The guy paused for a moment from the word *cash* as if it was holy word, his God. The guy clenched his teeth, shook his head as if he was shaking away thoughts, and said with wide, lustful eyes, "I ain't here for cash, sweetie."

"Please, I'll pay you whatever you want. Just leave me alone—"

"—Leave you alone?" The guy laughed. "You know you want it, baby. It's written all over you, your face, your body, the way you walk. Relax. Don't be so uptight. Think of me as. . . " the guy paused once more, ". . . as one of the good guys."

"Get the fuck away from me—"

"—Easy, sweetie. What's your name?"

"I mean it," Scarlet said, her hands balled into fists. "Back off."

"How rude of me," the guy said, carefully taking a step toward Scarlet, who, in return, took another step back. "I should've introduced myself earlier. Name's Boe, but you can call me *The Chiropractor*. I'm here to straighten you out."

"Please. . ."

Scarlet made an attempt to run around the guy—The Chiropractor.

He snatched her by the arm. Scarlet tried to yank her arm away, but the guy resisted and threw her to the ground.

As the guy crept forward, a bulge formed in his pants. To Scarlet, he showed no sign of backing off; in fact, he started to remove the belt from his pants.

"Wait!" Scarlet screeched.

"Nobody can hear you scream out here, sweetie," the guy said, his bloodshot eyes widening with madness. "I've had my eye on you for awhile. You're mine."

The guy stepped on Scarlet's ankle.

Scarlet hollered out in agony.

Then he proceeded to lift her dress. He fondled her soft breast, which was made out of balls of toilet paper that had been stuffed and compacted inside the D cup of a bra.

Scarlet suddenly removed the blonde wig from her head.

"Wait a second!" Miles shouted out. "Look! I'm a dude!"

The guy—or soon-to-be rapist—backed off in mild disgust.

"Shut the front door," he said, chuckling.

The guy caught his laugh, his face washed over with seriousness.

Witnessing the fury grow inside the guy's eyes, Miles held his hand outward, signaling for the guy to stop.

"I'm a dude, man!"

"Now, you're going to get it. . ."

The guy clearly didn't watch any TV or keep up with current affairs, Miles thought.

He lurched forward, grabbed Miles by the wrist, and pulled him closer to his body. His eyes swelled and darkened. He started to whale on Miles's face with his fist. He got in at least three to four good licks before a nearby pedestrian, who was walking on the sidewalk not too far away, rushed into the alley and stepped in and broke up the fight. The guy—The Chiropractor—took off down the alleyway while the pedestrian tended to Miles.

"You okay?" asked the good Samaritan.

Miles looked down and found a leather wallet on the ground.

As the Samaritan helped Miles to his feet, Miles secretly grabbed the wallet and slipped it inside the fold of his purse without drawing any suspicion.

"Yeah," Miles said, holding the side of his jaw. "I'm straight."

The Samaritan picked up Miles ruined wig from a murky puddle of water and handed it to Miles. The wig was stringy and soaked with brownish water.

The two shared eye contact.

The Samaritan acted as if he didn't care if Miles was dressed up as a woman.

"To each his own," said the Samaritan.

"It's not what it looks like," Miles said depressingly. "My life has become a living hell. I can't go out in public anymore without being recognized."

"What? You famous or something?"

"Or something," Miles said and started to walk from the alleyway. "Anyway, thanks for jumping in."

"No problem," the Samaritan said with a strange look on his face. "We got to look after each other, right?"

Miles looked the guy directly in the eyes and for a split second, he witnessed a crease in the corner of his right eye, a crow's foot, followed by a phantom of a smile creeping somewhere underneath the right side of his face. He realized that the guy knew exactly who Miles was, the unlucky sap on TV whose face had become the greatest meme used for puns and sharp jabs; and yet, the guy wasn't being so forthright with Miles and it was as if he knew something about Miles that Miles didn't know—or least expect.

After a thorough study of the guy's vague facial expression, Miles didn't respond to the guy's comment.

He already said what he needed to say and then he was on his way.

🕑

MILES arrived at his building.

The mob had doubled since the last time he saw it.

One protestor in the middle of the crowd had even blown up Miles's head on a massive cardboard sign and placed it over a piñata. Other protestors were taking turns at beating the piñata with baseball bats, broom handles, and belt buckles.

Miles held up the wig, which looked like roadkill. Then examined the dress, which was partly torn and covered in black scuffmarks and street grime.

Curious, Miles pulled out The Chiropractor's wallet. The man in the driver's license picture wasn't the same man who attacked him in the alleyway. He took a second look at the picture, thinking maybe that the guy had lost a whole bunch of weight or changed his hair color, even eye color. Miles concluded that the man in the picture was *not* the man who attacked him.

Not only was the man a criminal—*a rapist!* Miles thought—but he was also a common thief.

A pick-pocketer?

Miles looked over his phone.

He knew there was only one person whom he could trust.

He had to call her.

Had to.

🕐

NOELLE agreed to meet Miles outside an old laundromat in West District.

Noelle arrived shortly after Miles contacted her, reached over the center console of her car, and pushed open the passenger door.

"Get in," she said to Miles, "hurry up."

Miles skittishly checked his surroundings before getting inside the car.

"Miles?"

Miles stepped inside.

"Just wanted to check to see if you were being followed."

"That bad, huh?"

Miles closed the door.

Noelle sped away.

"Look at me, Noelle!" Miles cried out. "Look what I've been reduced to!"

Noelle reached over Miles's seat and grabbed the gym bag in the back seat.

"Here," she said as she tossed the gym bag in Mile's lap, "brought you some clothes to wear."

Miles's zipped open the gym bag and pulled out a tacky yellowish Hawaiian shirt, which looked two sizes too big for Miles, along with a pair of blue jeans, as well as green Chuck Taylors, a brown bomber jacket, and a red baseball cap with the capital A in bold, yellow Princetown lettering.

"I already standout enough," Miles said, annoyed. "Are you trying to get me killed?"

"It's all I could find," Noelle said.

"What the hell is this? A Halloween costume?"

"They once belonged to my brother. Are you going to wear them or not?"

Miles placed the gym bag on the floor mat beneath him.

"Whatever," he said. "So where we going?"

"I was thinking about we drive to up to Oak Hill," Noelle said. "Lay low for the rest of the afternoon."

"Sounds good," Miles said and sat back in his seat and tried to make himself comfortable. "Anywhere away from here."

"So," Noelle said over the silence, "you want to tell me what happened?"

🕐

MILES and Noelle grabbed a bite to eat in a rural area outside the city.

"I still don't get it," Noelle said as she sat on the hood of her car, which was parked in the back of a Burger Hut parking lot. "This guy—"

"—The Chiropractor," Miles interrupted.

Noelle sighed and glared at Miles.

"Sorry," Miles said.

"If this guy—The Chiropractor—if he was following you after you left The Cup, then he must've been following you before you arrived at The Cup. What if he was one of the protestors on the street?"

"No," Miles said. "You're not listening. Like I said, Noelle, he acted like he didn't know me."

"Well, you were dressed like a woman, Miles."

"Don't recite facts back to me, Noelle," Miles said tensely. "I'm saying *this guy* didn't know me after the wig came off. I want you to look him up."

Noelle sipped from her iced tea as she looked over the stranger's wallet.

"I don't know, Miles," she said, skeptical. "Don't you have more important issues to worry about?"

"The man tried to rape me, Noelle! What if he is a real-life rapist? What if I'm not the only one? What if he's a serial rapist, Noelle? A man like that cannot be out there roaming the streets! People like that need to be locked up! If we can catch this guy—expose him for *what* he is—then maybe it'll change the way people look at me. Maybe this is our opportunity to change the narrative. People like redemption stories. They eat them up like candy. This can be my only chance to salvage whatever's left of my God-given name. Who knows, Noelle? The people might even forgive me for what I did—"

"—But you didn't do anything to her, Miles! For crying out loud, the woman doesn't even exist! Remember? Don't you start cracking on me now, Miles."

"I'm not going to crack."

"Listen, I'm just as much a part of this mess as you are."

"I wish there was something I could do."

"Just leave it be, Miles."

"He has to pay for what he did, Noelle! He must!"

"Then, tell me, Miles, what exactly are you going to do about it? You talking about street justice?"

"Street justice is better than no justice."

"Seriously?"

"If I go to the police," he said, thinking, "I look like a rat. If I don't take care of it myself, I look like a coward."

"Don't say that—

"—*And* if I do take action and somebody gets hurts, I'm more than likely facing a lawsuit. Even worse, thrown in jail. I'm stuck. Unless. . . "

"Unless *what*?"

Miles faced Noelle, his eyes sharpened.

"We catch him in the act," Miles said. "Deal with him ourselves. If he's the real deal, then he'll strike again. He will!"

Noelle paused, rolled her eyes, and placed her drink aside.

"Miles, the network, they want you gone," she said finally. "These new accusations that keep coming forward have put them in an extremely difficult position."

"But we knew this was going to happen, Noelle. It always does, right?"

"Pressure is mounting," she said as she ignored Miles's cynicism. "They've already assembled a team of lawyers. They're expecting you to retaliate, but you and I both know eventually, with all the legal fees, they're going to bleed you dry. You don't have the money to battle them, Miles."

"You act like they're preparing for war."

"Well, they are, Miles," Noelle said. "Their reputation is on the line."

"Their reputation?" Miles couldn't believe what he was hearing. He stepped closer to Noelle and yelled in her face. "What about mine?"

Noelle remained calm, poised.

"They're not going to let you bring them down. They're going to make a decision soon. *And* it doesn't look good."

"So, what happened to the idea that this whole thing was going to blow over once these new accusations came forward? The absurdity of the other accusations alone would be enough to plant skepticism inside the minds of our viewers. Besides, it's not like you don't have to report it. You still have The Snipper's disciples out there, still carrying out his work. Why not just stick with that story."

"That story's played out. People are getting sick and tired of anything related to The Snipper. They want scandal, not murder."

Miles couldn't believe he thought it, but he did—

What if they could get both?

"We didn't think it'd get this out-of-hand, Miles. Times are changing. People want blood, Miles. *They*, they want your blood."

"Well, they can't fucking have it!"

"Face it, Miles," Noelle said soberly as she walked up to Miles. "You underestimated them. You gave them exactly want they wanted. What'd you think was going to happen? You come out scot-free?"

"So, you're saying I'm going to be out of a job?"

Noelle hung her head.

"Yeah," she said quietly. "It looks that way."

"And you? Are you still going to keep your job?"

"Miles, this was *all* you, the whole idea," Noelle said defensively as the anger rose in her voice. "Not me. I just went along with it. I mean look at what this story has done, all of the money it has brought in. The ratings are at an all-time high. They're through the roof! All the other networks are trying to keep up with coverage, but they don't even come nearly as close to what we did. We have the upper hand—"

"—You mean, *you* have the upper hand. My life is hell, Noelle. Ruined!" he screamed out. "I'm not even on trial for God's sake and they're condemning me as if I'm a fucking criminal!"

Noelle seethed, "You want to talk about hell, Miles, huh? A slow day in the news. That's hell." Her face slackened. She shrugged. "Your words, *not* mine."

"Everything's changed—"

"—Nothing has changed."

Miles couldn't believe what he was hearing. He threw out his hands.

"For all I know, they promoted you!"

Noelle paused once more.

"They did, didn't they? I can't believe these sons of bitches!"

"But Miles, I was going to ask you before I said yes to it but you didn't pick up your goddamn phone!"

"So, that's it," Miles said, frantically pacing around the car. "So, you're siding with the network? What in the hell makes you any different? What you did? You're just as guilty as I am—"

"—That's not the way the network sees it."

"Then," he hesitated, "what about our friendship, huh? Does that mean anything to you? No," Miles said before Noelle could answer, "of course not. What am I thinking? All you care about is money. You cherish nothing of great value! You hold nothing sacred anymore, other than the dollar! It has become your god, your only means of getting up in the morning. I thought you were better than this, Noelle. You disgust me!"

"Hey," Noelle said, offended, "I'm not the one playing dress-up."

"Years from now, when you look back on your life, you're going to remember what you did to me, to us, and how it destroyed what goodness you once had, and you're going to have nothing but regret, Noelle. Regret!"

"Maybe," Noelle said thoughtfully. "But now, *I'm* looking forward."

Miles shook his head in utter disgust.

"What happened to you?" Miles asked Noelle.

In return, Noelle said, "I grew up, Miles. What happened to you?"

Miles threw up his hands.

"I'm done," he said and walked away.

"Miles!" Noelle called out. "Where are you going?"

"Far away from you," he said to himself.

Noelle slid from the car and looked down at the wallet in her hand. She kept the driver's license and tossed the wallet in a trashcan.

🕐

THAT night, Miles ended up staying in a shabby hotel just off the main highway. Miles knew that there was no reason to go back home. He was soon going to be out of a job. He didn't have any friends. Except his mother and Ron, he had no other family. He had no place to live. He was stuck. The only thing Miles could think about was the redemption story, *his* story, finding a way to redeem himself from the bogus story that he had manufactured.

At the crack of dawn, Miles received a call from Noelle. Miles was too disgusted to pick up the phone. He listened to the message on his voicemail. In the message, Noelle stated that she decided to research the name on the driver's license. Turns out there actually was a man who was a chiropractor, Timothy Hume, and the name on the driver's license, Abraham Fisher, was a patient of his. Mr. Fisher accidentally left his wallet in Dr. Hume's office yesterday afternoon after receiving spinal treatment and Dr. Hume, The Chiropractor, told Mr. Fisher that he'd return the wallet to him as soon as possible; however, he didn't get around to it. Noelle went on to say The Chiropractor's office was located a few blocks from the spot where Miles was assaulted.

Thanks to Noelle, Miles had everything he needed to catch The Chiropractor. He had a name, an address, and most importantly, a new reason for living.

🕐

WITH new information on his attacker, Miles took an UBER back into city. First, he stopped by a car rental to rent a car because he knew that he couldn't stake out The Chiropractor in an UBER. For one, with the unpredictable nature of a stakeout, it could end up costing a fortune, especially at night, when rates were higher. And two, we all knew it was a solo job—a two-man job, if you got a partner dirty enough to share the company and possible blame. Either way, the job was perilous and required the most hated investigative journalist in America to work in a place where he worked best.

In the shadows.

Everything was all taken care of until Miles paid for the rental. First, the associate swiped Miles CREDIT card and received an "error" message. The associate, like the barista, recognized Miles from TV. Initially, he thought she was just screwing with him, her own subtle way of sticking it to him, hitting him exactly where it hurt: the wallet. She tried once more by inserting card chip-side into the machine.

Again, the card wasn't working.

Miles handed the associate yet another card, the trusty gold one.

Like the one before, it didn't work.

It wasn't maxed out, Miles thought. He habitually checked his bank account everyday, checked his balance, checked for any suspicious activity.

Miles second thought, *How could this be?*

Miles stepped outside the rental shop and called a number on the back of the card. He had charges on his card that he wasn't even aware of. Small charges not drawing any suspicion. Surprisingly, Miles hadn't been keeping up with his account for the past couple of days—considering his unusual predicament. Somehow, an unscrupulous individual had gotten hold of his social security number, as well as his personal information, like phone number and address. He had heard horror stories from other people. He once worked on a story about identity theft and the constant danger that lurks among us. Not once did he ever think he'd find himself in the same position as those poor people he interviewed.

Like them, he was a victim.

🕐

MILES had no other way to get around it. He needed a vehicle. So, he decided to steal one. He searched a parking lot not too far away from the rental place. Most of the cars were push-star—Miles cursed new technology.

With all hope lost, he checked one last car, a silver Frontier truck that used a key ignition. He remembered all those movies he watched when he was younger. He thought "hot-wiring" a car—or truck—was something that only happened in the movies, like an action hero using a gun to shoot a tank of gasoline and causing the tank to explode for added special effects or whatever ridiculous tropes Hollywood used to keep their audiences in their seats.

"What do you know?" Miles said as the truck started.

It works.

As far as his attire, Miles wasn't too concerned about disguising himself. After all, he looked like a tourist.

He camped outside The Chiropractor's office and waited for his last patient to leave the building. Sure enough, it was him, his attacker.

Timothy Hume.

"The Chiropractor."

Miles waited for The Chiropractor to get inside his shoddy Civic before staring up his car. He tailed The Chiropractor to a rundown town home on the outskirts of the city or what most called the "bad part of town."

He waited.

A couple of hours passed before The Chiropractor stepped back outside. He drove off. Miles tailed him, this time making sure to keep his distance. The Chiropractor drove to the nicer side of town. Miles lost him at a stoplight but ended up catching up with him at another. The Chiropractor arrived at his destination, a family-owned Italian restaurant called Luigi's. There, he met up with an attractive woman outside.

"Ole Timmy got himself a date, huh?" Miles said, as he camped outside the restaurant.

She was his next victim, he soon realized.

Tonight was going to be the night, Miles thought. *He tried with Scarlet but failed. The man's a bad wolf, and tonight, he's hungry.*

🕐

TWO and a half hours later, the two finally emerged from Luigi's.

The woman appeared tipsy, Miles witnessed, as The Chiropractor walked her to her car, which was parked around the corner in an unlit area. Miles knew these conditions couldn't be any worse: the woman was intoxicated and she was parked in an area which was dark and without any streetlights.

Miles drove closer to the two for a better view. He parked behind a bus stop. They were both laughing and talking and they appeared to be enjoying each other's company, which, to Miles, was good for the woman—great, actually; she seemed happy, okay with her date—but, as Miles thought more about himself, his dire situation, a feeling of melancholy came over him. He didn't want anything terrible to happen to the innocent woman, but in a dark way, he did.

As the woman arrived at the driver's side of her car, The Chiropractor leaned in for a kiss. He wanted more, though, Miles inspected closer, as she grabbed his hand from grabbing her breast. She pushed away his hand, but he was grabby.

Miles leaned forward.

"Here we go," he said, almost excited.

Suddenly, she pushed him and backed away.

The Chiropractor charged at her.

She quickly reached into her purse for a can of mace and managed to spray him in one eye; however, he struck her in the face.

Dazed, the woman tried to get inside her car.

The Chiropractor snatched the keys from the woman's hand and flung them across the street.

The two struggled.

The Chiropractor was half-blind but he was clearly overpowering the woman.

As he pulled her by the hair and yanked her head in directions it shouldn't be moving, she screeched out, "Help!"

The Chiropractor slammed her head against the side of the car.

She was dazed, but she was fighter.

As The Chiropractor was about to strike her once more, she found an opening and scratched him in the face and then kneed him directly in the groin.

Miles found himself rooting for the woman, but, at the same time, not.

The Chiropractor grabbed his crotch and lurched forward in pain.

This brief pause had given the woman enough time to run away.

Here was the mistake, though.

Instead of running back to Luigi's, a well-lit establishment filled with people, the woman ran into a sketchy, unlit alleyway. Miles didn't understand the intent behind the woman's thinking. Maybe she thought she'd lose him in the alleyway. Maybe she wasn't thinking at all.

Once The Chiropractor recovered, he chased after the woman.

Miles thought about the story.

His story.

Redemption.

If America had given the Jam a second-chance, why couldn't they give me a second-chance?

And if there was one thing Americans loved, it was a real-life hero, like a cop or a firefighter.

Who doesn't like a hero, a savior, a guardian angel?

Each second Miles spent thinking about whether or not he wanted to save the woman reduced her odds at surviving. He got out of the vehicle and chased after The Chiropractor. He heard a muffled scream coming from the end of the alleyway. Cast in a distant floodlight were two silhouettes, the larger one, which Miles suspected was The Chiropractor, straddled on top of the motionless woman who was lying flat on the ground.

Miles yelled out, "Leave her alone!"

The Chiropractor turned to Miles, his devilish eyes glowing in the dark.

As Miles approached, The Chiropractor took off running in the other direction.

Miles rushed over to the woman who was bleeding badly from the face. Her left eye was swollen shut, nose bent to the side, broken. Several teeth were missing from her mouth and Miles didn't know whether she was choking on her blood or her own teeth. He felt as if it'd be a criminal act to examine her body. But he did, briefly. Her blouse was torn open, one leg bent in a ninety-degree angle. Her pants and undergarment had been pulled down to one of her ankles. He saw blots of blood around her inner thighs. He quickly looked away and did all he could do in her final moments.

"Hang in there," Miles told the woman. He reassured her that everything was going to be okay, but he knew it wasn't. It would never be "okay" for her.

Even a word like *okay* would soon carry so little merit in the days to come. Eventually, "okay" would turn into something else entirely, a sacred word, one of great reverence. A word in which she'd desperately strive to touch, even finger. *Just okay.* Even if she managed to survive her injuries, which, Miles knew by listening to her breathing was very slim, the internal damage of what was done to her would remain inside her like a new organ, fatty like a liver and spotted-black and shriveled like a smoker's lung, nonetheless, a thing, vital like an organ but unable to be repaired or even removed. Miles knew that she would carry this unwanted thing, this burden, inside her to her grave.

He cried for her, but only for a moment.

Miles held onto her hand and told her how sorry he was for not warning her. He was sorry for what happened to her. Miles was especially sorry for not doing more to make sure people like Timothy Hume never walked the streets again.

The woman's breath grew more swallow and thinner.

Her face stilled, her eyes froze on Miles's.

Miles checked her pulse and found none.

Once sympathetic, now vengeful, Miles pulled out his phone.

The story, he realized.

My story.

There was still a chance to save my name.

He didn't want to do it, but he had no other choice. He needed proof.

After Miles took a photo of the dead woman, he found a purse lying a couple of feet away. He reached into the purse and pulled out a driver's license.

Her name was Rachael Merger.

While Miles was reading her license, one piece of information caught his eye. She was an organ donor.

🕐

MILES didn't sleep.

He waited until the light of dawn pushed away the shadows of buildings and drove to The Chiropractor's office where he camped out inside his musty truck. He made a phone call to Noelle, told her about last night and how he had proof that Timothy Hume was a rapist. He opened his photo gallery and pulled up the photo of one dead Rachael Merger.

What?

The photo was gone, vanished—or deleted?

Miles swiped through his most recent photos.

The only one Miles could find from last night was a photo of a dead rat in an alleyway. The rat was lying in a puddle. The floodlight cast a light on the rat, as well as Miles's dark reflection in the puddle.

"I must've deleted it or. . . " Miles said to Noelle.

The idea hit him and nearly left him breathless.

Credit card, he thought.

"I was hacked," he said. "Someone must've stolen the photo from my phone. What if they use it against me?"

"*They?*" Noelle said, her voice drawn out. "Miles, who is they?"

163

"The Network," he said.

Noelle asked, "Where are you?"

"I'm parked outside Hume's office."

"What are you planning on doing to him, Miles?"

"I'm doing what needs to be done, Noelle—"

"—Miles," Noelle said patiently. "If what you're saying is true, then this is a police matter. You need to contact the authorities right now."

"The police aren't going to do a goddamn thing—"

"—Miles, whatever you're thinking about doing, don't do it."

Miles witnessed The Chiropractor pull into the parking lot next to the office.

"I got to go—"

"—Miles, think it over!"

"I've thought enough," he said vaguely.

Noelle said slower, "Miles, *don't do it*."

"It's the story, Noelle," Miles said. "It's all that matters."

Miles hung up on Noelle.

Miles waited for The Chiropractor to exit his car, then made his move.

As The Chiropractor was walking to his office, Miles jumped him from behind. He threw him to the ground.

"I know what you did, you piece of shit," Miles said as he started kicking The Chiropractor in the ribs.

The Chiropractor shielded himself by covering his head and curling his body into a fetal position. Miles focused on the ribs, bones that break easily. He broke at least two or three of them. He didn't care. He kept kicking and kicking.

Each time he kicked The Chiropractor in the ribs, the more powerful he felt.

He wasn't going to stop until The Chiropractor was dead.

A couple of pedestrians on the street rushed in behind Miles and tried to pull him off The Chiropractor. Miles pushed them away and continued his assault on The Chiropractor. More people rushed in, but this time they didn't come to The Chiropractor's aide. Instead, they whipped out their phones from their pockets or handbags like weapons and started filming the assault on camera.

Before Miles knew it, he had a whole audience gathered around him filming him as if he was a celebrity.

A woman suddenly shouldered her way through the massive horde surrounding Miles and threw her body in front of him.

"Stop it!" she cried out, as she attempted to push Miles from The Chiropractor.

Through his red haze, Miles glanced at the woman's familiar face.

He couldn't help but look again.

Closer.

She was holding a brown bag lunch in her hair. An apple had fallen from a damp hole in the bottom of the bag and rolled down the sidewalk.

"You?" said Miles.

"Get the hell off him!"

Miles was left in a trance.

The woman's screams, the same ones he heard last night in the alley, snapped him from his trance.

Once more, he studied the woman's face. She was wearing the face of a dead woman.

Rachael's face.

"You're dead," Miles said with confusion.

"What?" The woman furrowed her brow. She placed the brown bag on the ground and waved at several pedestrians who were filming Miles. "Please," she cried, "somebody help my husband—"

"—Your husband?" said Miles.

She tended to The Chiropractor, shielding her body in front of his.

Once she realized the severity of his injuries, she pointed her finger at Miles.

"Get him away from me!" she screamed, her eyes filled with rage.

Miles took a step away.

Another pedestrian called out from the back of the crowd, "That's the pervert all over the news!"

"Miles Straum!"

"Rapist!"

"Pig!"

"Monster!"

Miles rotated around and found himself moving in circles around the crowd. All he could see were the beady black eyes of camera lens aimed directly at him, each one of the pedestrians' faces hidden by the backside of their smartphones. He soon realized he was in the center of the mob. . .

One man stepped forward with his hands curled into fists.

"Miles!" a familiar, more comforting voice shouted out from a distance.

Out of breath, Noelle emerged from the mob. She rushed over to Miles. She first saw The Chiropractor bleeding against the side of the building as he grabbed his abdomen in great agony.

"Miles," she said, "what the hell did you do?"

"You know this man?" one guy yelled out.

Soon, Noelle found herself in the center of the mob, more eyes beating down on her.

Another yelled out: "That's the reporter on TV! She friends with him!"

"Wait!" Noelle said and grabbed Miles by the arm. "He's sick, you see. He needs help—"

"—He needs to pay for what he did."

"This man," Miles said and pointed at The Chiropractor, "he's the rapist. Not me!"

The guy continued to approach the two in a threatening manner.

Others followed suit.

All of a sudden, both Miles and Noelle found themselves surrounded.

Miles leaned in close to Noelle and whispered in her ear, "When I say so, we make a run for it."

"We're outnumbered, Miles."

Miles looked for an opening. He saw one to the right of him. A thin twenty-something woman with a crew cut slouched over with her slick smartphone held directly in front of her face. Miles noticed the satchel she was wearing over her shoulders. From the way it sagged well over her back like a bulky sack of potatoes, it appeared as if the young woman had her entire bedroom stuffed into that satchel. The second observation was the Vans she was wearing. The soles were flat and worn down. One shoe had a penny-size hole near the toe and part of her pink sock was exposed. Which meant she probably didn't get good traction. And not only that, the ground was still slick from last night's rain showers.

When she took her eyes off the smartphone and glanced up for a moment, he witnessed her eyes—or what little eyes she had. Her eyes were beady and black, startling.

She's one of them, Miles thought.

"Just follow my lead," Miles said to Noelle.

"Miles. . . "

"Just follow my lead on the count of three," he said over Noelle.

Miles grabbed Noelle's hand, held it tight.

"Don't you dare do anything stupid—"

"—They're going to tear us a part, Noelle."

"But Miles. . . "

"One," he said.

"Miles!"

"Two," he said over Noelle.

In return, Noelle tightened her grip around Mile's hand.

"Three. . . "

Miles lowered his shoulder and charged at the young woman inching closer to him. She didn't even know what hit her. She fell on her back, which gave him an opening.

Both Miles and Noelle ran through the opening in the mob.

Hands suddenly reached out to them, grabbing them, pulling at them, smacking them like tree branches. Miles and Noelle lowered their bodies and treated it as if they were both plowing through dense shrubbery.

Once they were free, they scurried into an alleyway.

The mob ran after them.

Miles and Noelle managed to lose the mob once they crossed a street that was congested with traffic and cut through an abandoned building in Green Heights.

Noelle lagged behind. She was telling Miles to stop.

"I need. . . to catch. . . my breath," she barely said at one point.

She hunched forward and placed her hands along her knees.

"It's imperative that we keep moving, Noelle," Miles urged. "We're not safe in the city."

Noelle placed her right hand over her chest as if she was trying to calm down her beating heart and embraced slow, deep breaths.

"Where'r you parked?" asked Miles.

Noelle closed her eyes for a moment and then cleared her throat.

"Are you okay?"

"Just give me a minute," she said shortly.

While Noelle was recovering, Miles checked out the internal structure of the building. The entire building had been gutted—looked like an old factory, Miles thought. The walls were stripped bare and holey from unfinished work, paint chipped, peeling, and exposing layers of mold. Support beams were badly rusted. Even the floors had been chewed up and picked apart and covered in a wicked combination of dirt, dust, and debris.

Miles tried his best to keep his mind occupied by closely expecting the integrity of the building; however, the cold fear of imminent danger was lurking like a dark shadow in his thoughts. He heard a sudden *clank* of a metallic object being kicked around at the other side of the building.

"You hear that?" asked Miles.

Noelle finally stood upright.

"Hear what?"

"That noise," Miles said and pointed past a set of stairs spiraling up towards what looked like a raised office on the second floor. "Over there," he said softer.

"What's the plan, Miles?" asked Noelle.

Miles was too concerned with the noise and the thing that was making it.

"Miles?"

"Right," he said and snapped from his trance. "Plan. We need wheels."

"I'm parked next to Hume's office," Noelle said. "If you can somehow make some kind of distraction to draw them away, then it may buy me enough time to make it to my car."

"Sure," Miles said, trembling. "I can do that—"

"—Miles," Noelle said, as she grabbed Miles by the shoulders, "we're going to be okay. Think of it this way. By next week, they'll forget all about us."

Miles nodded.

"Okay," he said. "Let's go."

As the two made their way to the exit, the atmosphere inside the building became much darker. Miles thought it was nothing, clouds blotting out the sun.

What Miles failed to realize was that the mob had found them and they were surrounding the entire building. Their numbers had grown substantially, ten times the size back at Hume's office. Hundreds of bodies slowly came forth, each one standing in front of the cracked, murky industrial-sized windows. Their shadowy hands pressed against the glass, faces too, as they peered through the windows.

Miles and Noelle cautiously stepped outside and as they started to walk from the industrial park, two massive hordes of bodies came rushing in from both sides, flanking them. Miles rotated around and tried to make it back into the building, but one horde blocked his path.

Miles pointed forward and yelled out to Noelle, "Run!"

They didn't make it far. Like on the street, they were quickly surrounded.

The horde grabbed Noelle first. Reaching for Miles, she cried out and desperately tried to free herself from their grips. But there were too many hands and they were all grabbing at her, smothering her. When they grabbed Miles, Miles found a way to slip from their grips. He slid from his bomber jacket like a melted candy bar from a wrapper. He crawled under several pairs of legs, as if he was tunneling through holes of flesh. He managed to get ahead of the mob. He ran. He didn't look back as Noelle screamed out in horror behind him. He was tempted to fight off the mob and rescue Noelle. But like she said earlier, they were outnumbered. Clearly. If he *did* go back for Noelle, he'd be dead as well. But, with him having legs to run, Miles had a fighting chance at survival. And if someone was going to make it out alive, it'd be Miles. He thought about all these awful things while running, the odds, his chances being greater than hers. He needed to tell his story and he damn well couldn't do that if he was rat food. The chase pursued into the same alleyway that he and Noelle first entered. He found a manhole in another alley that led to a dead end. Miles had no other choice. He lifted up the manhole and slipped inside right before the mob could spot him.

As the mob entered the alley, Miles carefully closed the manhole behind him. A circular halo of flickering sunlight cast over his right eye as he watched the sea of flesh moving above him, swaying back and forth, all zombie-like. Miles could hear them through the cracks of the manhole, murmuring among cliques within cliques, lifelessly wandering around like the undead with the craving of human brains, their slick and sophisticated smartphones attached to their hands as if they were ready to film Miles's end game, snap it, tag it, post it, claim it.

After of couple of tense minutes of waiting, the mob eventually moved on.

Miles knew that he, too, had to move as well.

He climbed down the ladder, which lead to the sewers. He followed the narrow passageway, holding his nose from the pungent smell emitting from a stream of shit and piss below. He spent at least an hour trapped in the maze of the sewer system. Each manhole he tried, he heard the mob close by. He kept trying, going from one manhole cover to another. Eventually, he gave up and rested on a piece of cardboard next to the ladder below a sewer grate where a perfectly shape beam of sunlight shone through the opening, making the light interestingly divine.

In his deep trance, he heard what sounded like a footstep. He peeked around the corner and witnessed the stark shadow of a long-limbed man moving gracefully along the round wall. He peered closer, traced the shadow which belonged to a man who was waving him closer. He didn't look like a threat, not like one of them from above. The Phone People. His face was soft and gray; his eyes hidden inside the dark sockets of his skull and glimmering in an overhead beam of sunlight. His posture appeared weak, frail like an elderly man.

"Come closer," the stranger said, his voice thin and raspy.

Despite the imminent danger lurking above him, Miles decided to creep over to the stranger. He was standing in the shadows of a small room, which looked as if it was once a utility room; however, to the stranger, it was home. He had thick sheets of cardboard stacked like a mattress in the corner. Two dead rats were lying next to a hot plate. A rectangular grate along a rather quiet sidewalk on the outskirts of the city was what appeared to be the stranger's only source of light. Miles glanced up at the grate; and occasionally, some pedestrian, clueless of the strange man lurking below, would pass on by.

In the corner of Miles's eye, he was attracted to yet another light, a soft flickering one beating like a pulse. He turned to his right and saw a glowing yellowish light around the corner. He stepped forward, arched his head outward and witnessed a pyramid-shaped shrine of old candles, hundreds of candles; the hot wax that slowly dripped from each one had molded with the other candles resting below, making all the candles appear as if they were one unified candle. In the very center of the wax mound perched what looked like the skull of an animal.

Miles took yet another step closer.

The skull was one of a cat; and its remaining bones were spread out on top of a weathered, slightly skewed table with one uneven leg, which was being propped up by a brick. At the base of the shrine was a Persian rug.

Miles's attention was redirected by a throaty—almost guttural—sound coming from the other side of the room.

The stranger, who was tucked away in the cozy shadows of the room, pointed at a raggedy brown coat draped over a wired rack next to Miles.

"Put it on," the stranger insisted.

Hesitant, Miles put on the smelly coat.

"For disguise," he hissed, his letter s's sounding as if his tongue was as long and split as a snake.

Miles got a closer look at the stranger. He was much younger than he originally thought. Maybe a few years older than Miles himself. But the stranger carried himself as if he was much older, ancient almost, like a rare species undiscovered by man. He was wrapped in rags. His face was skeletal. Miles could see a gray outline of his skeletal structure in the hazy light.

Then, Miles said to the stranger, "Do you know who I am?"

"Ah," the strange man said with fascination, "We know you. My friends here tell me all about you, Mile*sss Sss*traum."

Miles could even smell his breath from where he stood. It was twice as pungent as sewage, deathly. His gums were swollen, and he was clinging onto two or three teeth, which protruded from his gums like fungi.

"Your friends?"

The stranger pointed at the dead rats on the ground.

"Rats?"

"Don't underestimate the rats," the stranger said. "They are the eyes and ears of the city. The unspoken ones. The watchers. 'The silent majority,' if you will. They've been telling me all sorts of things about you. They say you're the chosen one."

Miles soon realized he found himself in even worse danger than the ones that lurked above him. He was in the mouth of the Crazy den. And Crazy had its eyes honed in on him. Miles pointed the other way.

"I'd better get going," he said as he backed away. "Thanks for the coat."

As Miles turned around, the stranger called out from behind, "You can't run away from who you are, Miles Ssstraum."

Miles paused for a moment, turned around, and witnessed the stranger taking a step closer into the light.

The stranger moved robotically.

"How—how do you know my name?"

He opened up the damp rags in which clothed his gaunt body, releasing hundreds of rats from within. Miles flinched and started to back away as rats climbed and crawled over the stranger's body as if they were a part of his body.

The stranger reached into his body, pulled out a rat, and held it in his cupped hands. Miles couldn't help but notice the scaly skin on the stranger's discolored arm and how parts of it appeared infected from where skin had been gnawed away either by the stranger himself or the very rats in which surrounded him.

The stranger petted the top of its head with his bony soot-covered hand.

"We know *everything*," he said, his gray eyes wide and menacing. "They tell me a new king must be crowned."

Shocked, Miles pointed at the rats.

"*They* talk to you?"

"Everything talks, Miles," he said. "The living *and* the dead. All you have to do is listen carefully."

"How did you get here?"

"Like you, I was chosen but," the stranger looked down at his skinny body, "I am not worthy to hold the crown. You see I have what doctors call a bug." Miles couldn't help but look closer at the man's face. He swore he saw his skin move, as if he had a worm or something trapped underneath his skin. "My friends here, they don't get along with Harry."

The stranger's head slowly curled backward, his gums peeled back, revealing not only another set of teeth, but also many sets of teeth, jagged and sawtoothed, like a shark. The stranger suddenly chomped off the rat's head. He chewed, then swallowed it, then tossed the rat's corpse to the ground where the other rats began to pick at it.

"Excuse me," the stranger said with embarrassment as he held his hand over his mouth. "I swear, it had a mind of its own."

"What the hell was that?" asked Miles as he stood defensively.

"Harry."

"Harry?"

"He's my bug."

"Is this a nightmare?"

"Nightmares only exist in the mind, Miles."

"Who the hell are you?"

"I'm Myko," he said. "Or, at least that's what they used to call me."

"What do they call you?"

"They call me all kinds of names. Terrible names." The stranger, this Myko fellow, looked up at the grate above. "I used to have a life up there. Among the humans. A boy with his head in the clouds. Times were innocent back then. Yet, we were blind to the blood on our hands. I used to *be* one of them," the stranger watched a pedestrian stomp by overhead, "optimistic yet unaware of what waits below. If I knew what I know now back then, I don't know what would become of me. Once, you see, I thought the humans were important to the survival of our planet. Then, I peeled back its face and saw its true color." Harry suddenly bared its sharp teeth, briefly showing its hideous face to Miles. The stranger paused and held his head downward, calming

Harry as it sensed the blood pumping in Miles's veins. "I often wonder if it was always like, from the beginning. The greed. The consummation. The innate hunger for flesh. Look at us now." The rats crawled all over the stranger's shoulders, even face. He faced Miles, his eyes glimmering. "Look at what we've become. But you, Miles, you are very, *very* special." The stranger stepped closer, the pack of rats following his every step. "We are at the brink of a *New Age* of Transformation. . . Lead us, Miles! Leads us into the new world!"

Miles backpedaled.

"Like hell I am," he said, repulsed. "You're crazy."

"We're all crazy down here, Miles," the stranger said, grinning.

Miles suddenly ran back the way he came from as the stranger hollered out from behind, "There's nowhere to run, Miles! They'll find you! They'll find you the same way they found me!" He ran as fast as his aching legs would take him. "They're like that, you see!" the stranger yelled, his voice trailing off into an echo along the dark tunnels. *They're smart! They're smarter than you think! In time, you will see, Miles! You will lead them to the New Age! You will! And they will all bow down to you! You'll see, Miles! You'll see. . ."*

🕐

RAINWATER dribbled down the slick ladder leading up to the manhole.

Cautiously, Miles slid open the slippery manhole cover.

Exhausted and dehydrated, Miles emerged from the opening.

Dark clouds parted and for a moment, the sun, like before, crept through and a ray of sunlight hit Miles in the face. He was back in the alleyway, same one as before. The mob was nowhere around, which was a good sign. The ground was soaked from a recent rain shower and somewhere high above, a rainbow was cutting through the gray sky. Miles didn't know how long he had been down in the sewers. Hours? Maybe even an entire day? Two days? Three?

The sight of the sun, as brief as it was, comforted him.

As Miles closed the manhole cover, he looked up and saw what looked like an arm hanging from a nearby dumpster. He was overcome by instant dread. He decided to inspect the dumpster. He pushed away the trash bags and other debris. Once he cleared away the trash, he found Noelle's naked body lying among the garbage. She had bruises all over her face, as well as body. Strings of blood caked onto her mouth and nose. He knew Noelle was dead and that she had been dead for a while now, but he checked her pulse anyway.

"Noelle," Miles said and gave her shake on the shoulder. "Wake up. Please, Noelle. Wake up. . ."

Miles fell down to his knees and started crying. He wept like a baby. Miles couldn't even remember the last time he cried. Despite the little tears he shed for Rachael, in a way, it felt good to cry, to let it all out this time, to release an entire week—or month, whatever—of misery into a liquid form of emotion. He wanted to bottle his tears and save them as a reminder of how precious life was. He had no bottle, though. Except for the smelly scraps of clothes he was wearing, he had absolutely nothing. All Miles had left was his shadow and even it seemed crooked.

As the tears turned warm with anger, Miles frantically searched the dumpster for a weapon, anything sharp to run across his throat or wrist, the ultimate delete button. He wanted to delete himself from this very existence but he couldn't even find a sharp piece of glass to cut himself. He fell to the ground, pressed the side of his face against the wet grit, and closed his eyes. He heard something approaching, something big. . .

When he opened his eyes, he witnessed hundreds and thousands of rats flooding the entire alleyway. The rats surfaced from the openings of the streets, sewer drains and manholes, and moved like a sweeping brown wave from the streets, the sidewalks, and stormed directly toward Miles.

In a matter of seconds, the rats completely engulfed his body. Miles wasn't scared, though. Not the least. He embraced them, the rats, as if they were family.

As the rats swarmed all around Miles and helped lift him from his diminished state, a crown made up of old trash, such as soda can sheets and shavings, scraps of compacted newspaper, pieces of cardboard, and discarded electronics, like torn headphone wires and broken interfaces, was brought forth over the brown wave of rats. The rats passed the crown forward as if they were running an assembly line.

As if they were conducting a sacred ceremony, the rats droned the words over and over in harmony: *He who wears the Crown shall rule the Town.*

Two rats carried the wobbly crown on their backs while another one grabbed it by its sharp teeth and together, they placed the crown on top of Mile's head.

The brown wave chanting: *He who wears the Crown shall rule the Town.*

Next to be passed forward was a small cylinder-shaped object.

Miles couldn't make out the object from the end of the alleyway; however, he was incredibly intrigued. He intensely watched the rats, one-by-one, pass the object toward Miles. The object crowd-surfed along the backs of the rats and when it finally reached Miles, it took at least five or six rats to carry it to Miles. Miles knew exactly what the object was as soon as it reached his feet and he found himself smirking by the sight of it. He was starting to see everything take shape as if he had an inkling of a bigger, much broader picture.

He who wears the Crown *shall rule* the Town, Miles thought to himself.

The rats placed the microphone in Miles's hand and they spoke to him.

And Miles listened.

Indeed, he listened to them.

One rat came forward. The other rats made a hole for it. They circled around this one particular rat that was standing in the space between Miles's legs.

"Miles Straum, you are now crowned 'The *Royal* King of Trash,'" it said, its tiny voice high-pitched like a Chipmunk.

Together, the rats chimed, "All hail the king!"

Next to be brought forth through the river of rats was a camera.

Miles had no cameraman.

No problem.

172

Fortunately for Miles, the rats knew how to operate a camera.

"It's time for you get back to work, Miles," one of the rats said to Miles.

Miles stared at the microphone lying in the palm of his hand and all of a sudden, a wicked smile stretched across his weary, dirty face.

The rats started to pile onto one another, forming a human-size mound. The camera sat on top of the rat mound like a hat.

Miles stood to his feet and cleared his throat. He adjusted the crown with one hand while keeping the microphone gripped in his other. He primped his hair underneath the crown, pushing loose, sticky hair behind his ears.

After he adjusted himself one last time, he nodded his head, motioning to the rats that their king was ready to speak.

The cool red light turned on below the camera.

His listeners around the world were watching.

And waiting.

U NEVER WERE

TRENDING

LUNA'S projected due date was the thirteenth of January, which was a Saturday.

Which meant Luna Salcedo could breathe a little bit easier knowing the *crazy* gene had possibly skipped a generation.

Ever since last June, Luna had the "big day" marked and highlighted on her calendar, had the date memorized like Jörg's nervous tick of cracking his jaw, had spoke often of the date, had considered naming the baby January, if it was a girl, and Cap—short for Capricorn—if it was a boy, had even brought up the subject of babies, particular *her* baby, in conversations with friends and family, even strangers, not to boast or brag but to remind herself of the life developing inside her and that one day, her "big day," she was going to bring new life into the world.

When the baby never arrived on the thirteenth, Luna started to freak, thinking maybe the baby wasn't ready to enter the world or there was possibly something wrong with the baby or maybe its vital organs weren't fully developed or *maybe* there was a chance that her mother would find a way to haunt her from the grave.

The next Friday the thirteenth wasn't until September—another eight months away!

Then, two weeks after Luna's due date, all of her worries were put to rest. It was the last Sunday of January when she felt the life inside her trying to crawl out into the world.

The scene was like she had imagined for last few months when she started to show, except for one piece of the picture: Jörg.

He was nowhere to be found.

He was a ghost.

Horror ran through her mind and all Luna could think about on that Sunday afternoon was the worst possible scenario: Jörg was gone for good, "dipped" on her, ran off to Mexico where he'd assume his new identity under the name George Shilling.

One minute Luna was spending an afternoon at the Baby Emporium picking out onesies, pink for a girl and blue for a boy. The next minute, while placing the different onesies into the shopping cart, she felt contractions coming on. The contractions, however, were much different from before. They were shorter, tighter.

The baby was ready.

But Luna wasn't.

Neither was Jörg, so Luna thought.

As night fell, the scene was upon Luna: legs spread wide open, body sticky with sweat, every inch of her pushing while, at the same time, screaming at one of the nurses to contact Jörg once more on his cellular phone.

The nurse tried his cell—as she had been doing throughout the entire afternoon—even tried his office at work, but nothing. She left urgent messages on his voicemail.

At that moment, Jörg Schäfer had become of the most hated men in the world until he came barreling through the door.

"I'm here," he said, his labored breath helping to disguise his slurred words.

He was pale, had dark circles around his eyes. Luna, as well as everybody in the room, was aware that he was stoned out of his mind not only from his strung-out appearance, but also from the pungent smell he was giving off.

But he was there in one piece.

And it was Jörg's presence that had given Luna that final push to deliver her baby. . .

"*Girl!*" the obstetrician hollered out. "It's a baby girl!"

Jörg remained speechless.

Luna, crying.

Once the umbilical cord was cut and clamped near the navel, nurses cleaned the amniotic fluid from the baby and placed her against Luna's chest. The touch of skin-to-skin contact with her daughter filled Luna with emotion.

As Luna embraced her baby girl for the first time, all she could think about was where Jörg had been when she needed him the most.

HOURS passed.

Baby Girl Renata, now wrapped in a warm blanket, was sleeping soundlessly in Luna's arms. Jörg couldn't sleep a wink; in fact, he couldn't even sit still.

Being a diehard Cowboy's fan, he couldn't resist taking advantage of the opportunity at hand. Hoping—even praying to a merciful God—not to disturb Luna from her rest, he carefully grabbed the TV controller from the side railing, flipped on the TV mounted above, and made sure to keep his finger planted on the volume button in case the volume spiked.

Luna stirred in bed from the change in volume but remained in a rested state.

Once Jörg read the score of the big game, he nearly leaped from his seat. He grabbed the nearest pillow from the windowsill and pressed it over his mouth to muffle his excitement. It was the third quarter of Super Bowl XXX, and the Dallas Cowboys had a 20 to 7 lead over the Pittsburg Steelers.

The broadcast cut to a commercial for *Jimbo's Auto Parts*.

Jörg couldn't help but turn up the volume.

On the TV, "Jumpin'" Jimbo himself was promoting his new auto parts store located a couple of miles away in the town of Monitack. Somehow, in the brief thirty-second TV spot, which had to cost at least a million dollars, Jumpin' Jimbo, who was doing exactly what his nickname suggested and jumping from one department of the store to another in a dizzying SERIES OF quick SHOTS, managed to squeeze in nearly every part of the automobile while, at the same time, going back and forth with a scraggly-looking customer who'd rather save the money by repairing his 1969 Volkswagen van himself than take it to a dealership where he'd pay an "arm and a leg." But "don't fret, Dude! Jumpin' Jimbo was here to save the day!" Jumpin' Jimbo supplied the customer with what he needed, brand new headlight, new radiator cap, new washer fluid—even had "his guy out back" handle the installation "FREE" of charge. The word *FREE* being used throughout the thirty-second TV spot. Once the Volkswagen was looking good as new, the exterior sparkling to a mirror-shine all thanks to a *FREE* car wash, the customer was on his way to explore the New Frontier. Together, they celebrated the newness of the customer's ride with a strange dance routine, which looked more like a refined shimmy, called "Da Whoop."

In the final three seconds of the TV spot, a voice over actor reading at lightning speed promoted a FREE "Monster Gulp" with a single purchase of a car part. And two purchases of car parts would get you a FREE submarine sandwich.

As the commercial ended, Jörg snapped from his trance and heard Luna stirring once more. Jörg rotated around and found Luna staring directly at him as if by him even having the audacity to turn on the television after she had given birth to their child was a mortal sin.

"Sorry," Jörg said, the color coming back to his face.

He immediately switched off the TV.

Through Luna's pounding stare, he could feel his body shrinking with embarrassment.

Trying not to wake Baby Renata, Luna asked, "Who's winning the game?"

Jörg waved his hand.

"It doesn't matter," he said and tended to Luna. "How you feeling?"

"I feel like I've just given birth," she said flatly.

A laugh slipped from Jörg's mouth. He kissed Luna on top of her forehead.

Silence formed between the two of them.

Luna asked the inevitable question: "Where were you?"

Jörg hung his head in shame.

"I'm sorry," he said. "I should've been there for you."

"That's twice you've apologized, Jörg."

"*But*, Luna, I'm here now and I'm not going anywhere."

Jörg sealed his answer with a promise.

As they embraced each other once more as a family, Jörg asked Luna if she was hungry.

"Starved" was her response.

"How about a sub?" Jörg suggested.

Luna smiled and responded, "You read my mind."

🕐

JÖRG found a sports bar called Wings and Things not too far from the hospital.

As Jörg was about to pull into the parking lot, he spotted the same place from the TV commercial—Jimbo's Auto Parts—across the street. He kept driving until he passed the auto store. Noticed it was still open. Which was a surprise because, except for sports bars or anything with the word *bar* in it, most of the businesses around here closed early on Sunday. He slowed down and peered inside. Above the front counter, he saw a TV playing.

On a whim, he pulled into the parking lot in front of Jimbo's Auto Parts. The parking lot was empty, except for a man—possible employee—wandering around inside.

For a minute, he waited in the back of the parking lot, contemplating whether or not to go inside. He thought more about the TV commercial, the *free* Monster Gulp, the *free* subs. After all, Jörg did need a new headlight. One was burned out and he was getting sick and tired of watching other drivers kiss their knuckles and punch the ceiling of their car as they mouthed the name "Popeye" for good luck every time he drove past them. Plus, since Jumpin' Jimbo himself claimed he not only sold auto parts, but also provided basic car maintenance, he thought he could use a new tire rotation.

Three birds, one stone, he thought.

With his mind made up, Jörg parked the car in front of Jimbo's. He checked the store hours on the front door. Then, checked the time on his wristwatch. The store closed in fifteen minutes. He didn't exactly know how much time it took to rotate tires, but he figured it'd take longer than fifteen minutes.

Jörg looked inside the store one last time before he decided it was best to wait till tomorrow.

As he was about to turn around, he saw the same man from earlier in the corner of his eye. Jörg directed his attention toward the man, as suspected, an employee, who was waving Jörg to enter the store.

The employee's aura was strange, Jörg noticed. He looked as if he wanted to help out Jörg with whatever he needed to make his car running "good as new."

Jörg opened the door.

"You opened?" he asked the employee.

"Come on in," the employee said gladly. "Welcome to Jimbo's."

"Yeah," Jörg said, making his way to the counter. "Hey. How's it going?"

"I can't complain. The boys are winning and I'd be ah-grinning."

"Go Cowboys," Jörg replied, the excitement drained from his voice.

He glanced up at the TV above the counter and saw that the game still on. It was halfway through the fourth and the Cowboys still had a commanding lead.

"So," the employee said, drying his hands with a rag that was too white to be found in an auto parts shop, which had a garage "out back."

"I need a new headlight for my car," Jörg said.

The employee pulled out a notepad from his breast pocket as if he was taking Jörg's food order.

"Left or right?"

Jörg paused for a moment and tried to make sense of the vague response.

"Right," he said aloud. "I mean, it's the left," Jörg suddenly clarified before the employee scribbled in his notepad. "The front left headlight."

"No problem," the employee followed before Jörg could finish the rest of his thought. "We got what you need."

"And a tire rotation," Jörg said unsurely, "if that's possible."

"Sure," the employee replied, not missing a beat.

"Is that it?"

"That should about do it," Jörg said.

"If that's it, then I'll get working on the tire rotation and by the time I'm finished, you should be back home before the end of the game."

"Sounds good."

"I just need your keys," the employee said.

"Of course," Jörg said and pulled out his car keys.

During the slow and tedious moments of the transaction, Jörg decided to pass the time by telling the employee about how nice the place was. Which wasn't all bullshit. Jörg was more than impressed by the various departments and how easily accessible they were. The automobile broken down into sections: tires, windshields, steering wheels, headlights, grills and grates, rims, mats, seats, stereo systems, and interfaces.

"Yep," the employee said, gazing around the store, "before James started to spitball names for the place, I told him he should call it 'Crapht,' but spelled with a *ph* instead of a *f.* You know, like ph-phat," he touched his belly, "*not* fat-fat."

"Not bad," Jörg said. "Catchy."

"That's what I thought," the employee said ecstatically. "But you know how it goes. Boss man has the final say-so. He's like a cat, you see—a really big cat with a big head—pissing on everything that belongs to him. But anyway. . ."

The thought came to him as soon as he handed the keys to the employee—Robbie—he said his name was; however, the name on his shirt read "Robert."

"I just remembered," Jörg said while following Robbie to his car parked outside, "I also saw in the commercial about some *free* sandwiches—"

"—Absolutely," Robbie said. "You saw that silly commercial? It was a trip, wasn't it?" He stopped in his tracks and pointed to a room, which looked like a luxurious waiting room, next to the tire department. "We got subs. We got Monster Gulps." He pointed at the TV above. "We got the big game playing. We got basically everything."

Not everything, Jörg thought to himself.

Robbie said jokingly, "All we need now is some women and we'd have ourselves a party. You know what I mean?"

"Yeah," Jörg said, his voice fading. "Sure."

Robbie waited for Jörg to expand on his response, possibly come back with a joke of his own, but when all he received in return was a cold "yeah" followed by a stingy "sure" that trailed off like a snake in the bushes, a darkness swelled over Robbie's face and everything about him was business-like.

"Well," he said, twirling Jörg's keys, "I'll get started on your car. And don't worry about the headlight. It's on the house."

"Really?"

"Just sit back, relax, enjoy the game," he said and pointed at the room next to the tire department, "and help yourself to one of our delicious Monster Gulps."

"Thanks," Jörg said, as Robbie stepped outside. He watched Robbie drive his car around the back of the store.

Impressed by the five-star customer service minus the poor humor, Jörg wandered back to the counter and watched the game from the smaller TV; however, he couldn't resist the food, the game being played on a much "bigger" screen, and he heard the slushy machine calling out his name. Not only that, he had a hungry momma waiting to bring her food.

Three birds, one stone, he remembered. *Two birds down.*

One to go.

As Jörg arrived at the waiting room area next to the tire department, he came across a spread of sandwiches stacked like a pyramid on the marbled countertop, as well as a slushy machine with the decal of the scribbly, cartoonish word *MONSTER*. Jörg noticed yet another TV mounted in the upper corner of the room. Of course, the "big game" was on.

Feeling more at ease by the homey vibe, he grabbed a paper bag from a stack of paper bags that was at least two feet high and stuffed at least four six-inch subs into the bag. He picked from a variety, from turkey to roast beef, decided to give Luna a couple of options to choose from. Surprisingly, the sandwiches appeared remarkably fresh, the lettuce still crispy, tomatoes plump and juicy, meat faintly glistening from the fluorescent lights above.

To be on the safe side, he gave the meat a whiff. The smell alone caused his mouth to salivate and his stomach to rumble, as if it was a natural reaction. Jörg couldn't help but grab a ham sandwich for himself. He stopped at the condiment station and loaded up the sub with yellow mustard.

Next, Jörg paid a visit to the Monster Gulp machine. He grabbed himself a large cup nearly the size of a tub of popcorn. He took a moment to decide which flavor he was craving: Super-Duper Strawberry, Wonderful and Whacky Watermelon, Orange Shock, Electric Blueberry.

After a strenuous debate, he finally went with Electric Blueberry. Which was odd, to say the least, because he didn't care for blueberries. In fact, Jörg couldn't even remember the last time he ate blueberries. Maybe he was drawn to that one particular color, blue.

Jörg placed the Monster Gulp aside and searched for a cap, as well as a plastic straw. He went through the cabinets both above and below, but all he found were stacks of bags and extra large cups.

Eventually, after scanning the room, he found a couple of half-opened boxes stacked along the wall. Sure enough, inside the boxes were hundreds of unopened caps and straws.

🕐

THE game was over.

The Cowboys had claimed victory over the Steelers.

And Jörg, with his belly full, was beaming.

As he slurped down the last bit of his Monster Gulp and was tempted to refill his cup, he completely lost track of the time. For a moment, he almost forgot why he was sitting in a waiting room—the car!

He checked his wristwatch. Over thirty minutes had gone by, and his car still wasn't ready—*How long does it take to rotate tires?* He thought about the other times he got his tires rotated and it only took fifteen to twenty minutes. A strange feeling suddenly came over Jörg. A danger. Stranger danger. The food, all of the enticements, the friendly customer service at a particular time of night when most people wanted to go home and shelter themselves away from the outside world.

Most importantly, he thought about Luna, Renata, his baby girl. He saw himself from the outside. A man who somehow got sucked into a football game only hours after he had welcomed a new life into the world.

In a state of frenzy, Jörg grabbed his bags of sandwiches and tossed the Monster Gulp in the trash. He walked around the desolate store, calling out Robbie's name but only receiving the echo of his own voice.

By the time he made it to the garage toward the back of the store, the Monster Gulp was trying to run right through him. What made it even worse was that his car was still on the lift and Robbie was nowhere in sight.

A flash of anger came over Jörg and all he wanted to do right now was to pay the man for the job—or lack of job—and get back to the hospital where a starved Luna was waiting. The thought alone of the snarling witch Luna transformed into when she was hungry sent Jörg to a more frenzied state.

As Jörg called out to Robbie once more, Robbie appeared right behind him.

"I'm right here," he said casually. "Ain't a need to yell, man."

Startled, Jörg spun around.

"What's going on?" he asked, his tone clearly hostile.

"Sorry for the wait," he said and held up the wrench in his hand. "I couldn't find my wrench."

"Right," Jörg said, backing off. "Well, how much longer will it take?"

"The tire rotation should take no more than ten minutes."

This whole time, Jörg thought, *thirty minutes of looking for a wrench. What a bunch of bull! The man was probably off somewhere watching the game when he should've been working on my car.*

Despite the *free* food, the *free* Monster Gulp, the *free* labor, the thought alone caused Jörg's stomach to turn. The whole situation felt off, weird.

"You know, forget about it," Jörg said. "I can come back tomorrow when I have more time," he lied. "Just take my car down from there and I'll pay you for your trouble."

"Sure," Robbie said, more serious. "Just give me a couple of minutes, will you? And I'll have you back on the road."

With his bladder full, Jörg used his legs and walked in place to help ease the discomfort.

"By the way," he said, "where's your restroom?"

"We don't have one."

More anger flashed over Jörg.

"Serious?"

"Nah," Robbie said loosely. "Just messing with you." He pointed toward a hallway. "Down the hall. Second door on the right."

Jörg was so over Jimbo's Auto Parts, so over Robbie and his untimely sense of humor, ready to take empty his bladder and be done with this place. *The hell with Jumpin' Jimbo! What I'd like to do with that tire iron, you no good piece of shhh...*

Once Jörg entered the men's restroom, he expected to race to one of the urinals along the wall but there weren't any. For a moment, he thought he mistakenly entered the women's restroom. Jörg didn't care, though. He was about to piss his pants!

He rushed to the first stall he could find, entered, then closed the door behind him. He unloaded his bladder, as if he barely got through watching a three hour-long movie without taking any breaks.

Once he was all done and feeling much lighter, he heard a grating sound below him. He ignored the noise and reached over the seat to flush the toilet; however, as he was about to punch the handle, the noise intensified and caused him to freeze.

In a looming suspicion, he cautiously eased away from the toilet. He kneeled down and looked underneath the stall and checked the other stalls but all of them were empty—or at least, appeared to be.

The noise, he realized, which was coming from below his feet, sounded like a bunch of metal gears moving around followed by the *click-clank* cranking sound of what he could only imagine as a rollercoaster moving along a track.

Before he could rush from the stall, the floor suddenly opened up into a dark tunnel below him!

As Jörg fell into the tunnel, he violently smacked his chin on the edge of the toilet bowl. The upper part of his body bounced along the slick tile floor, as well as the sidewalls of the square-shaped tunnel. Somehow, he managed to grab hold of the floor with his right hand; however, the floor was so slick with piss and toilet water that his fingers slipped and his body plummeted into the dark hole.

Jörg screamed out in horror, but even the sound of his voice faded into darkness.

The disguised door along the floor closed, as if it was being controlled automatically.

And just like that...

HAROLD snaps his fingers together.

... Jörg was car parts.

🕐

Keen, glossy EYES brim with flickering waves of fire.

EXT. CRAPHT'S AUTO PARTS - NIGHT - PRESENT DAY

A young black woman, SQUINTS, 19, stands at a safe distance in the parking lot and with a vacant expression on her face, watches the flames devour the entire store.

Squints (V.O): *Ever since I was a little girl, I always found comfort in fire. It always brought me a sense of calm yet, at the same time, a sense of delegation, as if fire was king, the ultimate one, and I was only its hallowed servant. Even on the cool, mundane spring nights whenever I'd stare at the flame of a lighter or watch inanimate objects burn, I felt inferior as soon as the heat pressed against my skin. Fire was life and death, savior and destroyer. And whenever it made its presence known, I was caught under its spell. The way it moved by unapologetically licking across everything it touched. Like a virus: spreading, infecting, consuming, corrupting.*

The flames SLOWLY rise to the ceiling of the store, eating, consuming. A series of explosions rip through the front aisle, causing the windows to shatter. The flames spread to display shelves of tires, turning the black smoke even blacker.

Eventually, the fire ran its course.

The letters HT in the showy sign CRAPHT fall from the facade of the store and crash into the fiery rumble below.

Squints hears the sounds of sirens coming from a distant highway.

> JUSTIN (O.S.)
> Time to split.

A shadowy-faced JUSTIN DEVOID, 28, wearing a hoody, and Squints, who is dressed in black as well, race to the Viper parked in the back of the lot. The two enter the sports car, Squints taking the wheel while Justin riding shotgun, and speed away before fire trucks arrive.

EXT. HIGHWAY, SOMEWHERE IN DESERT - NIGHT

The Viper ZOOMS past a gaudy billboard with the bold words:

WAKE ME TOMORROW

Submitted By
Anonymous

MIDNIGHT WORLD

FADE IN:

EXT. CRAPHT'S AUTO PARTS - NIGHT

As the firefighters work on the raging fire with water hoses, ATHANOR DOWE, aka THE CLEANER, a middle-age man with shoulders as broad as a telephone pole, sporting a black cowboy hat, slips from the crowd of police officers to make a phone call away from all the commotion.

INT. MANHATTAN SUITE 101B, HIGH DISTRICT - SAME

Behind the window stands HAROLD ROMAN, early 50's, who is gazing out at the brilliant cityscape below.

The phone rings on the desk behind Harold. He answers the phone call and puts the caller on speaker.

INTERCUT - TELEPHONE CONVERSATION

                    ATHANOR
          They've taken out another one.

                    HAROLD
               Which one?

                    ATHANOR
          The Monitack location.

                    HAROLD
               Crapht.

                    ATHANOR
They're trying to send you a message. You know we can end
     this right here and right now, if we do it my way—

                    HAROLD
Your way is too messy, too many loose ends. Besides, the
   last thing I need right now is some bigheaded whistleblower, like Cameron Dobbs, breathing down my neck. We
know exactly where they're going next. Find them before
they get there. Bring them to me. Can you handle that?

EXT. EXT. CRAPHT'S AUTO PARTS - CONTINUOUS

The SHERIFF approaches Athanor.

                    ATHANOR
          I'm already on it.

                    HAROLD (V.O.)
          And Dowe, don't do anything stupid.

Athanor hangs up the phone with Harold and nods at the sheriff.

                    ATHANOR
          Put out an APB on a black 2017 Carnelian Viper.

                     SHERIFF
                 On whose authority?

                     ATHANOR
          The United States federal government.

INT. VIPER - NIGHT

Squints takes her eyes off the road and turns to a quiet Justin.

                     SQUINTS
                  Quiet much.

                     JUSTIN
             Just thinking, that's all.

                     SQUINTS
                    About?

                     JUSTIN
                   The future.

                     SQUINTS
     Future is overrated. All that matters is the now. If we
     don't stop Roman, then there won't be any future left to
                    salvage.

Justin lets out a sigh and readjusts himself.

                     JUSTIN
        What are you going to do when this is all over?

                     SQUINTS
                (drifting in thought)
        I guess I really haven't thought about it. You?

                     JUSTIN
                    I dunno.
                 (facing Squints)
          I'm just curious. What's driving you?

Squints smirks and glances down at the speedometer.

                     SQUINTS
                 (sarcastically)
     A Carnelian Viper with a V-10 engine. That's what.

                              JUSTIN
        You know what I mean? This. What we're doing. Why not
        go back to Dover and start a family? Move on? I mean,
        this can't all be just because of one guy you hardly even
                               know.

                              SQUINTS
           Don't tell me who I know or don't know.

                              JUSTIN
            Sorry. I didn't mean it like that—

                              SQUINTS
        And why are you doing this? You could've just stayed in
                     Dover. But you didn't.

A tense silence swells over Squints and Justin.

                              SQUINTS
        When I was five years old, I was terrified of water. Just
           the sight of water made me panic. So, my mom felt the
           only way to curb my phobia was by treating it head-on.

INT. STOP N' SHOP CAR WASH - DAY - FLASHBACK

Squints's mom, TIARA, late 30's, drives the Star Cruz'R
into the car wash and stops the car once the light turns
RED. Squints, 5, frantically looks around at massive
brushers alongside the car.

                              SQUINTS
                           (frightened)
                              Mom?

Tiara grabs her daughter by the hand.

                              TIARA
                            (calmly)
          Listen to me, Candace. Remember what I told you, about
                       the world inside you?

                              SQUINTS
                         (more frightened)
                              Mom?

                              TIARA
         Whenever you feel sad or scared, you can go there.
                            (smiling)
                        Free admission.

The water jets suddenly kick on, showering the car in a
gentle mist. Startled by the chaos around her, Squints
opens the passenger door and slips out of the car.

                    TIARA
               (reaching out)
            Candace! Wait!

BACK TO PRESENT DAY

                    SQUINTS
I watched her fall into that trap underneath the car wash.
The only reason why I wasn't in the car when she went under was because I freaked out. My jacket got caught in
the door. After I freed myself, it was already too late.
            She had fallen in.
          (shaking her head with disgust)
A week later my father died in a car accident. Investigators said he had enough drugs and alcohol in his system to
kill an elephant. Some even said he purposefully ran his
car off the road because he was involved in my mom's dis-
                  appearance.

                    JUSTIN
       What do you think really happened?

                    SQUINTS
I think my father found out about Harold's dark secret.
Threatened to expose him. So, Harold went after those
             closest to my father.

Justin pauses in thought. Looks at Squints with a hard
gaze.

                    JUSTIN
         Did they ever find her body?

                    SQUINTS
   No. Eventually, the case went cold. A part of me went
cold. I guess, when you're that age, you'd do about anything to forget the nightmare. So I shut off, chose to
block it out, like it never happened, like it was all in
my head, like I never had a mother or father. I needed to
remember them. I have to remember in order to make things
                     right.

                    JUSTIN
   That was your mom back there in the caves, wasn't it?

With tears brimming from her eyes, Squints struggles to
nod her head.

                    JUSTIN
I didn't want to say anything earlier. But it makes sense
   now. I'm sorry for your losses, Squints. Serious.

                    SQUINTS
                    (quietly)
                    Thanks.

Squints wipes away the tears.

                    JUSTIN
                    (hesitates)
Why do you think Roman does it? I mean, what does he get
out of capturing people and doing whatever he pleases to
                    their bodies?

                    SQUINTS
                    (sniffling)
            Why do you think he does it?

                    JUSTIN
Sick hobby spawned from a fucked up childhood. I dunno.

                    SQUINTS
I have a theory that he only targets certain age groups
during certain times. The year my mom disappeared, six
other people, both men and women, all around same age,
disappeared as well. I also think he's targeting those
with a strong social media presence, like Damianos...
                    (turning to Justin)
                    ...Like you.

                    JUSTIN
I wouldn't exactly call my presence strong, but I'll admit
            I used to be online a lot.
                    (with air quotes)
                    Used to.

                    SQUINTS
And how's that working out for you, being offline?

                    JUSTIN
                    Well...
                    (more seriously)
            ...I never would've met you.

Squints glances at Justin, they share eye contact. Then,
Squints directs her attention back toward the road.

                    JUSTIN
                    (awkwardly)
            Do you want me to drive?

                    SQUINTS
            No. I'm fine.

EXT. PARADISE MOTEL - NIGHT

Waiting inside the parked Viper underneath the overhang in front of the main lobby, Squints watches Justin from her hunkered position in the driver's seat.

Biddable in manner, the old MOTEL CLERK turns his back on Justin, walks to a shelf behind the counter, and grabs a key from a wall of keys. Behind the clerk's back, Justin turns toward Squints's direction and barely able to control his enthusiasm, gives her a secretive thumbs-up below the check-in counter.

INT. ROOM 36 - NIGHT

Justin holds the door open for Squints, who creeps into the dimly lit room. As she wanders around the room, inspecting its cleanliness, Justin closes the door and switches on a table lamp.

> JUSTIN
> (nodding at the two beds)
> Least I won't have to sleep on the floor anymore.

Justin places the backpack on the bed closest to the door, as if he's already claimed his territory.

> SQUINTS
> Why'd you get two beds? You know we're tight on money.

> JUSTIN
> It's all good. The old man hooked me up, since they were out of single-bed rooms.

> SQUINTS
> (looking over the dresser)
> Whatever.

> JUSTIN
> Is this doable?

> SQUINTS
> (facing Justin)
> Doable.

More at ease, Justin grabs the remote from the nightstand and turns on the TV behind Squints. He flips through a couple of channels before he arrives at the news.

ON THE TV

Squints's face is plastered on the square box to the right of the news anchor's shoulder.

BACK TO SQUINTS

who remains in awe from a two-year old photo of her taken by her Uncle Jojo while she's painting a sea creature in her bedroom.

                    NEWS ANCHOR (O.S.)
          Still no sign of nineteen-year-old Candace Norwood.

                         JUSTIN
            Looks like you're now more popular than me.

                         SQUINTS
                       Not funny.

                         JUSTIN
                   Wasn't trying to be.

With the TV remote, Justin turns up the volume.

                    ANCHOR (on TV)
      The last known footage of Candace was taken at Stop N'
    Shop in Dover, California, where the remains of dozens of
    missing persons were discovered in a dungeon below a car
    wash in what has been dubbed by investigators as a bizarre
                     Car Collection.

                         Squints
                      (overlapping)
              Can you change the channel please?

                         JUSTIN
                   Sorry. Of course.

Justin immediately changes the channel to the show FAMILY
GUY. He places the TV remote on the nightstand, grabs the
toothbrush from the side pocket of the backpack, and
brushes his teeth at the sink.

                         JUSTIN
                (while brushing his teeth)
     I was thinking we'd go grab some better disguises tomor-
            row, now with your face being all over TV.

In the reflection of the mirror, Squints turns off the TV.
She proceeds to remove her shirt, then bra. Bare-chested,
she drops the shirt and bra on the dresser.

Unaware of Squints approaching from behind, Justin spits a
mouthful of foamy toothpaste into the sink.

                         JUSTIN
                    (turning around)
              We can be like a modern day Bonnie and—

Inches away from Justin stands Squints, her breath labored, her face serious, breasts exposed.

> JUSTIN (CONT'D)
> (confused)
> What you doing, Squints?

Squints leans in to kiss Justin. She plants a soft peck
on his lips; however, Justin doesn't attempt to kiss her
back. Yet, he remains frozen.

> JUSTIN (CONT'D)
> Are you sure this is a good idea—

> SQUINTS
> Shut up.

Once more, Squints kisses Justin. This time, Justin
throws his toothbrush aside and returns the kiss.

Stumbling toward the closest bed near the sink, both
Squints and Justin passionately kiss while, at the same
time, remove the remaining articles of clothing from their
bodies.

Once fully undressed, Squints slides both the pants and
boxers from Justin's legs and flings them across the room.
The boxers land on the top of the lamp, dimming the light
in a strange reddish hue throughout ROOM 36.

Concealed inside the SMOKE DETECTOR on the ceiling above
the door a camera privately records Squints and Justin.

INT. SURVEILLANCE ROOM - CONTINUOUS

Standing in front of a row of grainy TV monitors, the motel clerk watches Squints and Justin having sex in bed.
He picks up the phone and makes a call to Harold.

> MOTEL CLERK
> Forgive me for disturbing you, sir. Normally, I wouldn't
> be calling you if it was important—

> HAROLD (V.O.)
> What do you have for me, Mr. Hardy?

> MOTEL CLERK
> Two kids. I've seen one of them on the news not too long
> ago. I think he might be one of yours.

> HAROLD (V.O.)
> Where are they now?

ON THE MONITOR

While kissing Squints's neck, Justin rolls on top of Squints and straddles her in a more dominant position.

BACK TO THE CLERK

who is anxiously biting the edge of his lip.

                    MOTEL CLERK
   They're currently tied up at the moment, but they ain't
 going anywhere for the night. That's for damn sure. What
                   you want me to do?

The motel clerk turns his eyes to another MONITOR displaying a recording coming from yet another hidden camera inside the bathroom.

INT. BATHROOM, ROOM 36 - NIGHT

With her eyes closed and the top of her forehead pressed
against the wall, Squints embraces the warm water against
the back of her head. She lifts her head, allowing water
to run down her face.

Squints turns off the shower faucet, opens the curtain,
and steps out of the bathtub. She grabs a clean towel
from the holder and dries off, starting with her body and
then, lastly, her hair.

Once somewhat dry, Squints grabs a white Tee shirt resting
on top of the toilet seat and throws it on.

As Squints is about to exit the bathroom, she notices an
obvious structural flaw along the very base of the wall --
a two-inch gap separating the baseboard from the vinyl
floor.

Exercising the utmost caution, she kneels down and runs
fingers across the recess. More intrigued, she shifts her
weight by leaning toward the wall. Part of the floor
slightly dips down as if the integrity of the foundation
has been compromised.

Squints exits the bathroom where Justin is lying on the
floor in front of the bed. The sight of Justin's peaceful
state brings warmth to Squint's face. She walks over to
him, slips underneath the wrinkled covers, and tries to
rest without disturbing him.

Justin stirs, then lays on his back, his head turning to
Squints.

                    JUSTIN
              You good?

                   SQUINTS
     I'm great. I'd advise against taking a shower, though.
   The floor looks like it's about to collapse at any moment.

                    JUSTIN
        Really? Well, we'll be out of here by morning.

Squints turns on her side until her body is squared up
against Justin. She runs her hand across Justin's bare
chest, playing with a small patch of hair.

                   SQUINTS
     I never imagined someone like you, who acts like sex is
        the last thing on his mind, having good moves in bed.

                    JUSTIN
          Well, maybe I'm that good at hiding it.

                   SQUINTS
   I was thinking, after this is all over, if we're ever go-
          ing to be able to go back to our lives—

                    JUSTIN
          I thought the future was overrated.

                   SQUINTS
     It is, but sometimes, I think about my future.
              (staring into Justin's eyes)
                   Our future.

                    JUSTIN
        I guess all that matters is the now, right?

Squints barely brings herself to nod. A calming silence
forms between the two, resulting in Squints to rest her
head along the side of Justin's shoulder.

                   SQUINTS
               (over the silence)
        Why'd you move to a small town like Dover?

                    JUSTIN
            School, remember?

                   SQUINTS
        Yeah, but you could've gone anywhere.

                    JUSTIN
     I guess I could. I guess I was—I dunno...

Justin shakes away the thought. More concerned, Squints
lifts up her head from Justin's shoulder and faces him.

                    SQUINTS
It was a girl, wasn't it? She must've been the one—or at
          least what you thought was the one.

                    JUSTIN
How come, of all the people I've ever known, you're the
          only one who can see right through me?

                    SQUINTS
                 (nonchalantly)
          I didn't see you being good in bed.

Justin turns away from Squints's answer. She acknowledges
a sudden change in his manner -- the crinkle in his brow
displaying a cloaked pensiveness.

                SQUINTS (CONT'D)
              So, what was her name?

                    JUSTIN
                    Grace.

                    SQUINTS
That's a lovely name. So, what was it that Grace did that
          made you run away from Seattle to Dover?

                    JUSTIN
                 (somberly)
I wasn't the one who was running. It was Grace. When we
started to get serious, she got cold feet. One day, she
tells me about a new job -- a curating job -- in New York
City. At first, I thought she was just talking. Plus,
she was close to her parents, who lived right outside Seattle. They were getting older, too, and I knew she'd
never leave them to pursue some pipedream in New York
City. But then I found out she wasn't just talking. My
back was up against a wall. I had no other choice. So, I
              gave her an ultimatum.

                    SQUINTS
                  Which was?

                    JUSTIN
Either me or the job in New York. Clearly, she chose the
                     job.

Squints sits upright on both of her elbows.

                    SQUINTS
Could you have gone to New York with her?

JUSTIN
I could, I guess. But I didn't want to be that pathetic
guy who followed his girlfriend across the country.

SQUINTS
Justin, you <u>had</u> a choice. If you really did love her, you
would've followed her wherever she went -- even in hell.
Are you sure it was Grace who was scared? Or, was it you?

Teary-eyed, Justin rolls over on his side, turning his
back to Squints. Ignoring his half-ass attempt at seclu-
sion, Squints cozies up behind Justin and slips her arm
around his side.

EXT. DOVER TOWN SQUARE - NIGHT - SQUINTS'S DREAM

Confused, Squints looks around a crowd of townspeople
holding a vigil for the missing teen, DAMIANOS PIPES, 18,
wavy dark hair, soap opera-handsome. Flickers of candlelight bring forth the sullen, shadowy faces in the night
darkness.

Shouldering through a sea of bodies, Squints makes her way
to the front of the Square. Her walk is forced to a creep
by the sight of a blonde haired WOMAN, who is standing not
too far away from Damianos's PARENTS, DAMIANOS'S MOTHER
holding a framed photograph of her son.

Intrigued by the back of the glowing mane of the woman,
Squints inches closer to her. She touches the strangely
still woman on the shoulder. Holding a candle in her
palms, the woman mechanically rotates around and faces
Squints. The woman is Squints!

Squints backpedals and as she rotates around to an open
space, the crowd is no longer standing there. Instead,
replaced by the crowd are dozens of cars, all circled
around her on a stage-like atmosphere. The headlights are
blazing, shining directly on her like spotlights. Despite
the constant revs of engines, the cars remained without
drivers; however, the only human features of the cars are
the severed heads mounted on the front grill.

Frightened, Squints searches for an escape, but she's completely boxed in. One of the car doors opens. A dark
figure, a MAN, steps out of the driver's seat and then, as
he shuts the car door behind him, Squints opens her eyes.

INT. ROOM 36 - DAY

Squints violently wakes up to the booming THUD of a door
closing behind her...

Startled, Squints throws out her hand across the blanket, only to caress an empty space. The floor CREAKS behind her. She arches her head upward and finds a more upbeat Justin standing at the doorway with a cup holder in his hands. In the cup holder: two cups of coffee, two muffins, and a bottle of orange juice.

> JUSTIN
> (jubilantly)
> Rise and shine.

> SQUINTS
> (rubbing her eyelids)
> What's this? Breakfast in bed?

> JUSTIN
> I know how you like to put in your own sugar, so I just made it black.

Justin sets aside the cup holder on the dresser and pulls out a handful of bags of sugar and mini-cartons of cream from his pockets. He places the sugar and cream on the dresser as well.

> SQUINTS
> I'm that picky, huh?

With her eyes drifting toward the floor, Squints's face melts into a vacant expression.

> JUSTIN
> So, did you sleep well?

Squints snaps from her trance and looks up at Justin.

> SQUINTS
> (hesitating)
> Yeah. I did. You?

> JUSTIN
> Like a newborn baby.

> SQUINTS
> (standing to her feet)
> I'm sure you did.

Squints locates her underwear on the top of the bed, which has been stripped of covers. She dresses. Staggering at first, she eventually makes her way over to Justin, who removes the cup of coffee from the holder and places it on the dresser.

As Squints removes the lid from the cup, Justin holds up two muffins for Squints to pick from.

                         JUSTIN
                   Apple or blueberry?

                         SQUINTS
              (adding sugar into her coffee)
               Doesn't matter. You pick?

                         JUSTIN
                     Apple it is.

Justin sets the apple muffin next to Squints's coffee.
Once Squints stirs the sugar and cream into her coffee,
she takes a bird-like sip. She savors the sweetness.

                         SQUINTS
                       Thanks.

                         JUSTIN
                 You're very welcome.

EXT. ROOM 36 - DAY

Once dressed, Squints and Justin exit the room. As
Squints walks to the parked Viper while cautiously scanning the parking lot, Justin closes the door to the motel
room.

INT. MUSTANG - CONTINUOUS

From across the street, parked in the parking lot of a
rundown strip mall, Athanor stops combing the thin strands
of hair over the metal plate along the side of his head
and pulls his eyes from the rear view mirror. He hones in
on Squints and Justin, who are playfully fighting over a
set of car keys.

Anthanor watches Squints burst out in laughter as Justin
tickles her side. Eventually, she gives in, hands over
the car keys, and lets Justin drive for once.

The Viper drives away, and Athanor follows.

INT. D.J.'S FILL 'UR UP - DAY

Before Squints can open the door, Justin swoops in at the
last second and holds the door for her.

                         SQUINTS
              Such a gentleman today, aren't you?

                         JUSTIN
                       (closely)
Well, maybe we should do what we did last night in the mo-
                    tel more often.

> SQUINTS
> Don't push your luck, buddy boy.

Justin smiles off the remark. Squints walks to the refrigerators in the back of the store while Justin heads
straight to the snack aisle.

> SQUINTS (CONT'D)
> And remember, nothing with peanuts.

> JUSTIN
> Yes, ma'am.

Squints grabs a couple of bottled waters, as well as a
grape and orange soda from the refrigerator.

Carrying a couple of dark chocolate bars in his hand,
Justin meets back up with Squints at the front of the
store where the two wait in a line in front of the checkout counter.

> JUSTIN
> (holding out his hand)
> I'll take those off your hands.

Squints smirks off Justin's niceness. He frees one of her
hands by wedging the two bottles of water underneath his
armpit.

With Justin's right hand free, he drops his hand by his
side, grazing Squints's left hand. Without her knowing,
he slips his hand into hers. Squints doesn't react to the
gesture. Instead, she interlocks her fingers into his.

With only one customer left in front of them, Squints and
Justin shuffle closer to the checkout counter.

While waiting in a comfortable silence, Squints rotates
around and looks over her shoulder where Athanor is standing with a bag of sunflower seeds in his hand. Her eyes
fall from his steely eyes and land on the gun handle protruding from his armpit.

> Athanor
> (nodding hello)
> Ma'am.

Discreetly, Squints faces forward and removes her hand
from Justin's just as the line moves forward. Both
Squints and Justin place their items on the checkout
counter.

> JUSTIN
> Twenty on Pump #7.

Justin pays for the items, as well as the gasoline, while
Squints glances over her shoulder one last time.

After the CLERK hands Justin his change, Squints and
Justin make their way to the exit.

> ATHANOR (O.S.)
> Excuse me, ma'am.
> (holding out a lighter)
> Does this belong to you?

Squints pauses at the doorway, looks over the Zippo
lighter with the blue dragon sticker in Athanor's hand,
and with hesitation, walks toward him.

> ATHANOR (CONT'D)
> I believe you dropped it on the floor.

Athanor hands Squints the Zippo.

> Squints
> (timidly)
> Thank you.

> ATHANOR
> Not a problem at all, ma'am.

EXT. D.J.'S FILL 'UR UP - DAY

Both Squints and Justin walk to the Viper parked next to
Pump #7.

> Justin
> You wanna drive?

Unresponsive to Justin's question, Squints remains in a
trance.

> Justin
> Squints?

> Squints
> No. You can drive.

> Justin
> You sure?

Squints nods her head.

INT. VIPER - CONTINUOUS

Squints plumps herself down into the passenger seat and
places the Zippo lighter in the cup holder. She stares at
the lighter.

EXT. I-30 - NIGHT

The Viper speeds under the bridge where the Texas state line ends and Arkansas begins.

INT. VIPER - CONTINUOUS

Behind the steering wheel, Squints glances in the rear view mirror.

> SQUINTS
> (whispering)
> I sure am glad to be out of Texas.

With his eyes closed, Justin stirs from his sleep in the passenger seat.

> JUSTIN
> (mumbling)
> What'd you say?

> SQUINTS
> Nothing.

> JUSTIN
> Just remember to stay off 30.

Squints passes a sign on the side of the road: "30 EAST." Her sweaty grip tightens over the steering wheel.

All of a sudden, the red and blue flashes of a dashboard-siren appear in the rear view mirror.

> SQUINTS
> Shit.
> (nudging Justin's arm)
> Wake up.

Justin's eyes bolt open. Looking around in confusion, he sits upright in his seat.

> JUSTIN
> (more aware)
> What is it?

> SQUINTS
> Cops. What'd you want me to do?

More concerned for their safety, Justin turns his shoulder and watches the strange car closing in on the Viper.

> JUSTIN
> Were you speeding?

                         SQUINTS (O.S.)
              No. I was going the speed limit.

With his eyes narrowed, Justin hones in on the car as it
quickly approaches.

                            JUSTIN
                 It doesn't look like a cop car.

                           SQUINTS
                            What?

                            JUSTIN
                       (facing forward)
                       It's not a cop.

                           SQUINTS
                       How'd you know?

Justin opens the glove compartment and grabs the PISTOL
from inside. Checks the magazine. Then, the chamber. He
snaps the magazine into the bottom of the pistol.

                      SQUINTS (CONT'D)
                 What in the hell you doing?

                            JUSTIN
                       (more paranoid)
                       It's not a cop—

                           SQUINTS
              —And what makes you so sure that it's not?

                            JUSTIN
        You really think Roman is going to let us anywhere near
        him? We knew this was going to happen at one point or an-
                            other.

Squints glances in the rear view mirror. Red and blue
lights flash over her eyes. The car closes in. Any
closer, it'd ram the back of the Viper.

                      JUSTIN (CONT'D)
                   (flipping off the SAFETY)
                       Pull over.

Once more, Squints turns to the rear view mirror and looks
at the dark shadow behind the steering wheel of the Mustang behind her.

                      JUSTIN (CONT'D)
              Don't worry. I got this, Squints.

After looking straight in Justin's eyes, Squints finally pulls the car over on the side of the road. She puts the gear in park but doesn't shut off the car.

                    SQUINTS
          (staring in the side-view mirror)
          Where's the backup?

                    JUSTIN
          Exactly.

In their tense wait, Squints watches the driver finally exit the Mustang. In the flickering lights, she recognizes the cowboy hat, the brown blazer, the face...

INT. D.J.'S FILL 'UR UP - DAY - FLASHBACK

Squints rotates around toward the stranger calling out to her. Standing in the checkout line, Athanor holds out a Zippo lighter in his hand and waits for Squints to fetch it from his grip.

INT. VIPER - NIGHT - PRESENT DAY

As Athanor cautiously approaches the side of the Viper with his holster unbuttoned, Squints lets out a gasp.

                    SQUINTS
          It's him.

Squints suddenly SLAMS the gear in drive.

                    JUSTIN
          Him who?

                    SQUINTS
          I can take him.

                    JUSTIN
          Wait!

Before Justin can take a shot at Athanor, Squints SLAMS her foot against the gas pedal.

EXT. I-30 - CONTINUOUS

As the Viper skids away, Athanor withdraws the gun from his shoulder holster and fires a couple of rounds at the fleeing vehicle.

INT. VIPER - CONTINUOUS

Both Squints and Justin duck for cover as bullets strike
the back windshield, one bullet cutting the rear view mirror in two.

                    JUSTIN
          Still think it's a cop?

Squints checks the rear view mirror, but she has no view
for the glass is completely shattered.

                    SQUINTS
          What's he doing now?

After the shooting stops, Justin shakes away the shards of
glass from his hair, lifts up his head from behind the
center console, and watches Athanor casually walk back to
his car.

                    JUSTIN
          He's getting back in the car.

EXT. I-30 - CONTINUOUS

The chase intensifies once Athanor catches back up with
Squints and Justin. With Squints accelerating the Viper
past eighty miles per hour, Athanor still manages to keep
up with her.

Athanor BUMPS the back of the Viper's bumper, forcing
Squints to readjust her grip along the steering wheel.

                    SQUINTS
          Fuck! Can't you do something!

Justin rolls down the passenger's side window.

                    JUSTIN
          Just keep it steady.

                    SQUINTS
          I'm trying!

Squints accelerates once more, giving the Viper a little
extra space from the Mustang. Justin leans his upper body
out of the window and fires off a couple of rounds at the
Mustang.

INT. MUSTANG - CONTINUOUS

With steering with his left hand, Athanor pulls out his
gun and sticks the barrel into a bullet hole in the bottom
of the windshield.

> ATHANOR
> Gotcha.

As Justin stops firing and leans back into the Viper,
Athanor takes a shot. He only needs one shot. He's that
good.

INT. VIPER - CONTINUOUS

Justin is shot in his right shoulder, forcing the pistol
from his hand. As Justin hollers out in great agony, the
pistol falls onto the highway and skips away.

> SQUINTS
> Are you hit?

Clutching his shoulder, Justin pulls away a palmful of
blood. He looks over the blood in shock, then shows the
blood to Squints.

> SQUINTS (CONT'D)
> (disappointedly)
> Damn it.

Squints turns her shoulder and watches the Mustang closing
in once more.

> SQUINTS
> Buckle up!

With his left hand, Justin buckles his seat belt. Once
Justin is secured in his seat, Squints SLAMS on the
brakes.

EXT. I-30 - CONTINUOUS

The Mustang suddenly swerves around the Viper, forcing the
Mustang to spin out. Athanor overcorrects. The Mustang
ends up flipping over. Violently, the Mustang barrels off
the highway, kicking up clouds of dust. Eventually, the
Mustang comes to a halt upside down in a ditch.

INT. VIPER - CONTINUOUS

Justin peers out at the overturned Mustang fading off into
the dark, cloudy highway behind them.

> JUSTIN
> Nice move!

INT. MUSTANG - CONTINUOUS

Seated upside down, Athanor smiles off Squints's timely
maneuver to shake him from her tail.

ATHANOR
Bitch wants to play. Let's play.

Grimacing, Athanor pulls out a flip phone from his pocket
and dials a number.

FELIX (V.O.)
Felix here.

ATHANOR
Go to Plan B.

INT. VIPER - CONTINUOUS

Justin faces forward and looks over his gunshot wound.

SQUINTS
How bad is it?

Once the adrenaline wears off, the shock sets in over
Justin. His face goes pale and vacant.

JUSTIN
(nursing his right arm)
I've never been shot before.

SQUINTS
You know you never struck me as the kind of guy who gets
shot at often.

JUSTIN
(jokingly)
Not if you count Playstation.

Squints removes her flannel shirt from her body and hands
it to Justin.

SQUINTS
Here. Use this to wrap around your arm. It should stop
the bleeding.

In a last second decision, Squints takes a right onto an
off-ramp and once she reaches the end, makes a left, then
drives down a two-lane road over 30-East and turns left
into a spit of a town.

JUSTIN
Where you going?

SQUINTS
We have to get off the highway.

JUSTIN
I thought I told you to stay away from the main highways.

Squints looks at Justin with a scowl on her face. Justin backs off and instead of arguing with Squints, wraps the sleeves of the flannel shirt around the wound. Tightens the shirt with a knot.

> JUSTIN
> So, who the fuck was that guy back there?

> SQUINTS
> I saw him back at the gas station when we were passing through Texas. I think he's been following us ever since.

Squints drives past a road sign: "OLD LIBERTY." She makes a right onto AR-195.

> JUSTIN
> Fucking great. You think he's working with Harold?

Squints doesn't respond, doesn't even move for that matter.

> JUSTIN (CONT'D)
> Squints? What is it?

> SQUINTS
> You hear that?

Justin listens closer to the pulsating SOUNDS of a helicopter flying above the Viper. Squints takes her eyes off the road and peeks out the window. Above the Viper, a helicopter is descending closer to the road.

> SQUINTS (CONT'D)
> Shit. I think it's him.

> JUSTIN
> This guy doesn't stop, does he?

> SQUINTS
> He won't stop until we're dead.

INT. HELICOPTER - CONTINUOUS

Athanor leans forward to the pilot, FELIX, 30's, and taps him on the shoulder.

> ATHANOR
> Get me as close as you can.

Felix returns by giving Athanor a thumbs-up. Athanor turns to the person sitting next to him -- a bound ROSCOE DÍAZ, bloody and beaten, his mouth wrapped in duct tape, arms tied behind his back.

ATHANOR
(grinning)
Sit back and enjoy the show, hombre.

EXT. AR-195 - CONTINUOUS

The Viper speeds up and starts swerving from one side of
the road to another.

INT. VIPER - CONTINUOUS

With her hands loosening from the steering wheel, Squints
turns to Justin with a look of defeat on her face.

INT. HELICOPTER - CONTINUOUS

As the helicopter descends just above the power lines running along the side of the road, Athanor aims the gun at
the back left tire of the Viper.

SQUINTS (V.O.)
If you had a chance to go back in the time to the moment
after I found you below that car wash, would you have come
with me?

INT. VIPER - CONTINUOUS

Squints glances over at Justin.

SQUINTS (CONT'D)
Or, would you have stayed back in Dover?

JUSTIN
You're asking me this now?

SQUINTS
Well, would you have come with me or not?

Justin looks into Squints's eyes and as he's about to answer Squints's question, a sudden gunshot from above RINGS
out.

INT. HELICOPTER - CONTINUOUS

Athanor leans back in the passenger cabin and watches the
back left tire of the Viper explode to shreds.

INT. VIPER - CONTINUOUS

Squints loses control of the car and ends up swerving off
the road. The front end of the car strikes a telephone
pole and ends up violently spinning out of control and
onto its side.

INT. HELICOPTER - CONTINUOUS

Once more, Athanor taps Felix on the shoulder and motions downward.

> ATHANOR
> Set us down.

Felix nods his head and lands the helicopter in an open stretch of land next to the road.

EXT. AR-195 - CONTINUOUS

As the Viper starts to catch fire, Athanor steps out of the helicopter and walks toward the flaming Viper. The fire spreads to the engine and erupts in massive flames.

From a safe distance, Athanor inspects the damage. He kneels down for a closer look, where he finds both Squints and Justin dead inside, their bodies burning in the fire.

Once Athanor confirms their deaths, he steps away from the fire and spots a car slowly approaching. He flags down the DRIVER, a middle-aged man, inside the car. The driver, in return, pulls up next to Athanor.

> DRIVER
> You a'ight, mister?

> ATHANOR
> Yeah. Just fine.

Athanor pulls the gun from his holster.

> ATHANOR (CONT'D)
> But I can't say the same about you.

Before the driver can react, Athanor shoots him directly in the head. Then he OPENS the passenger door to make it look like he had a passenger -- or carjacker. He walks back to the helicopter and drags out Roscoe from inside the cabin. He escorts Roscoe over to the flaming car and shoots him in the side of the head.

Lastly, Athanor kneels down and places his gun in Roscoe's hand. Once the scene is staged, Athanor removes the duct tape, as well as the bounds from Roscoe's face and wrists, and walks back to the helicopter.

> ATHANOR (CONT'D)
> Take me back to the wreckage.

> FELIX
> You got it.

With the rotary blades blowing around the thick black
smoke spewing from the Viper, the helicopter flies away
into the night sky. From the cabin, Athanor keenly
watches the flames burn below.

As the fire continues to rage on and burn the Viper to a
crisp, Squints's lifeless arm flops from the window. Fire
chews through the surface layer of her skin -- the epidermis -- resiliently peeling away dark pigmentation, only to
reveal the red tissue underneath.

MATCH CUT:

WITH her chin and neck area caked with dried blood, Renata vacantly stared at
the flames inside the fireplace.

She snapped from her hypnotized state that the fire had left her in for the
past twenty minutes and looked down at her hands, which were spotted with
shades of blood. The notion alone of what she had recently done with her two
hands caused them to tremble, as if it was her own body's reaction, the good
that dwelled inside her informing her of the shit she was in. Her hands still
remained as evidence for cops, detectives, investigators, anyone who would
want to analyze them and want to know what she was wearing—or better yet,
who she was wearing. Even though Renata had run water over both her hands,
the blood was still there: speckles of it wedged underneath worn hangnails;
streaks of it outlined around her fingernails, as well as tucked underneath the
cuticles; red geometrical blotches stained over parts of her skin like old ink.
Her right hand was red and swollen and incredibly sore, especially the knuckles, which were no longer visible. Murder was the only thought on her mind.

Flashes of red murder rose up inside her, as if the fire had somehow tamed
it, if only for a while. Renata urged to move her eyes back to the fire and keep
them there, on its warmth and glow, to remedy the very act that she had committed earlier that night. However, if Renata was going to make it out alive,
she *had* to remember.

Hoping to bring forth anything that she might have forgotten, Renata moved
her eyes back to her shaky hands: *both of them wrapped around Kira's neck
like a ribbon.*

The very last image that Renata remembered before everything went gray
and hazy were Kira's once-soulless eyes and whatever entity that had a command over her finally escaping them. In that moment, Renata witnessed a
glimpse of her old friend and the life thriving inside her being turned off, as if
it was being controlled by a switch.

Renata's chest tightened. She inhaled deeply and stared at the fire, hoping
to drive the images away.

Another wave of panic came over her and choked any attempt she had at
focusing in on anything but murder.

The once comforting warmth of the fire hit her with sudden heat flashes.
The pinprick sensation of sweat poking at her skin flooded her mind with a
collage of red murder.

While scrambling around the kitchen for the closest weapon, Kira grabbed a knife from the cutting board of already chopped herbs and vegetables and stabbed at Renata.

Suddenly, *Renata ducked.*

But *Kira kept attacking at Renata. Her face expressionless, eyes empty. Her tongue, different.*

Trying to rid the memory, Renata leaned forward in agony. She removed her head from her cupped hands and ran two fingers across the backside of both eyelids. The black mascara provocatively spread across the sides of her temples like Nike swooshes.

Choking and clawing, Renata wrestled Kira to the kitchen floor, wrestled the knife from Kira's grip, and while desperately pleading for Kira to stop fighting, accidentally cut her along the forearm deep enough to draw blood.

Pulling her hands from her face, Renata sat back upright and focused back on the fire.

During the struggle, the knife nicked Kira on a main artery on the side of her neck, causing the blood to squirt out.

Renata stood up from her seat and paced laps around the dark living room.

In the corner of her eye, a beam of headlights cut across the living room until the light came to rest along a picture frame of Kira and a group of co-workers who had spent the weekend at the cabin.

With caution, Renata walked to the window and saw Jevon's Beamer parked in the gravel driveway. She could breathe a little easier once she witnessed a tall and lanky, broad shouldered man stepping out of the car. She only knew of one man, who had shoulders like that, shoulders that could be easily mistaken for the shoulders of a highly trained swimmer.

Jevon locked his car with a beeper on his keychain and walked to the cabin where Renata was waiting for him as soon as he stepped onto the front porch.

Not bothering to flip on the light switch, Renata held the door open for Jevon. As soon as she closed the door behind Jevon, Jevon looked over the blood on her clothes, then the blood on her neck and face, as well as arms. He disregarded the blood and embraced Renata.

"I was worried sick about you," Jevon said over her shoulder.

Renata's eyes swelled with tears.

First, he heard the sniffles coming from below. Then, he felt a tiny vibration against his chest of what he realized was Renata crying. He held her tighter.

"Rennie," Jevon said in her ear, "you have absolutely nothing to worry about. We're going to get through this. . . "

The sound of Jevon's voice and the unusual softness in it caused her to break down even harder in his arms.

"I had no other choice, Jevon," Renata cried. "I tried to convince her to leave town, but she wouldn't listen to me. She was going to—"

Renata couldn't even speak the words.

Jevon escorted Renata back into the living room where he sat her down on a sofa across from the fireplace.

Once Renata calmed, Jevon asked Renata: "Where is she?"

Jevon leaned in closer to Renata's range of vision.

Her face was blank, the words not there.

"Rennie?" Jevon asked once more. "Where's the body?"

Renata continued to stare at the fire.

SIX MONTHS AGO

"Is anybody home, Renata?"

Renata snapped from her deep trance and pulled her eyes from a giant flame shooting up from the onion rings, which were arranged accordingly to showcase a flaming volcano on the surface of the teppan grill.

The chef began to juggle the spatula and fork, drawing awe among the guests seated around the grill. Following the trick, the chef tapped the utensils along the grill in a rhythmical fashion while, in between each beat, he spun the spatula between the prongs of the fork. He incorporated a knife, as well as a salt and pepper shaker, striking each one together, from top to bottom, from side to side, as if they were musical instruments used to season the vegetables by sound and rhythm.

Over the hypnotic *clink* of utensils, Kira called out Renata's name once more.

Renata acknowledged Kira, who was seated to the right of her.

"Yes?"

"Paul asked you a question."

To Renata's left was Paul Lauter, who, despite a few banal questions that one would receive by a teacher on the first day of preschool, had remained mostly absent throughout the night.

"I was just asking you where you're from?"

Renata, more or less, rolled her eyes toward Paul's general direction, as if she was forcing herself to look at him. She briefly acknowledged the question; however, most of her attention was focused on yet another flame igniting before her.

"Monitack originally," Renata said, as if she was speaking from the corner of her mouth. "But I was raised in Queens until I moved to Manhattan." More curious, she pointed at the flame and asked the chef, "How'd you do that?"

Paul backed away, his face red, his body shrinking in his seat.

"A little bit of oil and rum," the chef responded, a smile building behind his face. "*But* please," he said strictly to Renata first, then to the others seated around her, "I wouldn't recommend trying it at home."

The comment drew a couple of laughs from the counter.

Besides Renata, Paul, Kira and her date Albert Nnadi, two other couples, one, the owner of the San Jose Marauders, Mory Foochs and his wife, retired fashion model and host of the TV show, *Skin Deep*, Vivian Klein, and the other, clothing designer, Claude Le Font, who were both good friends with Kira's uncle, Kin Nakamura, the owner of yaki, were seated at opposite ends of the counter.

Kira held up the glass of Naughty Empire pilsner and said loosely, "Leave it to the professionals, right?"

The chef acknowledged Kira's remark, forced a rather submissive smile onto his face, and moved onto the egg trick.

Captivated by the chef's skill in the blade and how, with any wrong move or slip-up, it could nick an artery or gauge an eyeball or, regardless, cause some serious damage if handled improperly, Renata was caught off guard by yet another question from her date.

"How about your parents?" asked Paul.

With her tone hovering along a sharp edge, she returned: "What about them?"

"What do they do for a living?"

The question immediately offended Renata; however, she tried her best not to show her resentment.

I've only known the guy for an hour and he wants to know my family history. She figured that Paul, being a data analyst for one of the most popular social media platforms on the Internet, should already know everything about her and then some. He probably even checked out Renata's meticulously "revised" profile before agreeing to go on the date, which had been all orchestrated by Kira.

Renata was tempted to return with a question of her own—in fact, the words were dangling on the edge of her tongue—"Why do you care, Paul From California?" Sorry, Silicon Valley! Renata wanted to wave a flag and say it proud and punctual, as if she was making it abundantly clear to Paul *From Silicon Valley* in her derisive tone that where an individual was "from" had absolutely no basis or bearing as to where an individual was "going" and Renata was destined to be going straight to the bar or, even better, the exit, if her date insisted on getting to the bottom of her origin story.

As the warm emotion rose inside her, the repercussions of any outburst would resonant well past the date.

She took a deep yet subtle breath, remembered to stay positive—*have fun*—and swallowed those ugly words, which were attempting to escape her head.

"*Not* they," Renata said. "Just my mother." Another guardian came to mind, the one who had looked after her for two years when she was between the ages of six and eight. "And my aunt, too," she said distantly, wondering whether or not she was revealing too much about herself to a man whom she met only one hour ago. She shortened her story and focused on her mother. "She worked two jobs, my mother, housecleaner during the day, janitor at night. Whenever I wasn't tagging along with her to work, I was probably spending most of my time with Elmo the Cat. Then, after we moved from Monitack to New York, she decided to finish up college and get a business degree. Now, she runs her own cleaning business."

"How about your father?" Paul asked. "So, what's his story?"

Renata repeated, "What's his story? Well, he has no story—at least, he was never a part of *my* story, if you know what I mean."

"Sorry," Paul stuttered, "I didn't mean—"

"—Mean what exactly," Renata said, her tone sharper.

"You know what I mean."

These techy guys from Asshole Valley are so goddamn boring.

Paul looked over Renata in what she can only imagine resembling a life-size version of a sad emoji face—take that back, a sad face emoji with a tear drop.

Picking up the hostility in Renata's voice, Kira couldn't help but pull herself away from Albert and leaned in closer to Renata, as if she knew that specific tone, especially when the subject of parents—in particularly the father figure—came up in a conversation.

With a half Elvis-like snarl of her lip, Kira nodded across the dining room at the latest pop singer, the nineteen-year-old tween sensation, Mammilla, who, as of lately, had recently been, as Kira rancorously put it, "literally" everywhere: at the top of the Billboard charts; on front covers of *Vogue* and other magazines; all over TV, YouTube, soda and makeup commercials; constantly "trending" on Twitter; doing concerts for sellout crowds; who did *Saturday Night Live* last week.

Kira leaned in closer to Renata and pointed at the pop singer, who was wearing her hair in an upright ponytail. Mammilla was speaking caveman to her "hot" producers and engineers and a PR team, dictating the conversation while, at times, laughing so obnoxiously loud that the guests, who were in town for a film festival, could hear her on the other side of the restaurant—her vocabulary mostly consisting of lots of "OMGs" or "LOLs" or "totallys" or "fucks" and "shits" scattered in her text-heavy dialogue.

Kira whispered in Renata's ear, "I think that ponytail is cutting off the blood to her brain."

The comment drew a snicker from Renata.

Kira said over Renata's laugh, "Care to join me in the ladies room?"

"Hell yes," Renata whispered sourly in Kira's ear.

In return, Kira broadcasted to both Paul and Albert that the two ladies had to "freshen up" and excused themselves from the dining area.

🕐

ON the way the ladies room, both Kira and Renata passed the ever so famous, Instagram-friendly, twenty-foot tall bronze statue of the ferocious-looking, mutative dragon, *ikay*, which was created by Newbay native, Earl Lake. Yaki happened to be one of the hottest locations for every tourist who ever visited New York City, not only for its teppanyaki cuisine or the dazzling performances of each remarkably talented chef who prepared each meal in front of guests, but also for the statue of ikay himself.

Standing on the edge of the tongue of yet another more skeletal, more alien dragon emerging from the other dragon's jaw, which had been stretched open in a gaping yawn as if it was about to shoot out a massive fireball, was a boy holding a flaming torch in one hand while, with his other hand, which appeared skeletal, he was bracing himself against a tooth the size of a street cone. Tourists even had to make reservations way ahead of time—three to four months was the average wait. Some came to yaki to dine while others came for their own personal gratification to snap a selfie of themselves standing in front of the boy, the Great and Powerful ikay, who had, over the years, taken on an open-world lure with comics, movies, and video games, bursting open the door for imaginative minds to decipher each detail of its intricate design.

Having visited the restaurant twice, once with her mother when she was a girl and another with a once-respected boyfriend whom she ended up dumping

215

after she walked in on him making love to his laptop, Renata couldn't help but stop and admire ikay and its mystical, yet theme park-like vibe. Even though she now felt as if the statue was, more or less, an elaborate candle, the sight of it brought back a wave of nostalgia.

As Kira unknowingly proceeded ahead of Renata, walked past the kitchens, and headed toward the restrooms, she bumped into Kin, who nearly spilled a cup of green tea all over his seven thousand dollar blue ombre plaid two-piece suit.

Renata turned to the commotion to the far right of her.

Kin recoiled with exaggerated surprise and removed the white clout goggles, which were once made popular by Kurt Cobain, from his face.

"Kira, my dear," he said, his voice high and gay. "I wasn't expecting you till later this evening."

Renata overhead Kira: "Albert mentioned something about heading over to NoMo afterwards for drinks."

Hesitant to meet Kira's uncle whom Kira had talked so much about—all in the highest honor—Renata walked over and joined Kira and her jovial uncle.

"Kin," Kira said with her arms held outward as if she was showcasing Renata to her uncle, "this is Renata Salcedo. She works with me at CC."

"Is that so?" Kin said, stepping closer to Renata. He folded his sunglasses in his breast pocket and held out a limp hand for Renata. For a moment, she didn't know whether to shake it, as in what most humans do, or kiss the top of it, as if it belonged to royalty. "It's always a pleasure to meet Kira's friends," he said.

Renata bowed slightly as she shook Kin's hand.

"How do you do, Ms. Salcedo?"

"I'm good," Renata said, glancing around at the Japanese decor. "You know, this is a nice place you got here. I can remember the last time I was here like—"

"Why thank you, sweetie," Kin interrupted right before Renata had a chance to share a story about her last visit to yaki—which was actually quite an interesting story about her boyfriend's sleeve getting caught on fire while trying to interfere with the chef's trick. "I would love to chat with you, but apparently, the legendary, Gary Worthington, is in the building and I'm dying to hear what he's been up to."

"Why does that name sound familiar?" Renata asked Kira.

"*The* Gary Worthington," she said. "Artist turned survivor turned *New York Times* #1 Best-Seller. After his best-selling novel, *Unfollowed*, was turned into a major blockbuster, he launched his career in what was known as one of the most epic comebacks of all time."

"I think I remember," Renata said, thinking. "He was a victim of The Snipper, right?"

"Ah-*yeah*," Kira said. "The man had his tongue literally cut off and lived to tell his story."

"So poetic yet so heroic," Kin said to himself, as he drifted off for a moment, as if the thought alone of Gary's touching story always forced himself into a state of deep thought. He pulled his attention back to Kira. "Anyway, gotta jam." He kissed his niece on the cheek, said his see-ya-laters to her, and once more, shook Renata's hand on his way to the main dining room. "Nice meeting you, Ms. Salcedo."

"Nice meeting you, Mr. Nakamura," she said after Kin had already thrown on his shades and sashayed away. Overwhelmed by her uncle's energy, she turned to Kira. "Your uncle sounds like a busy man."

"I don't see how he does it," Kira returned. "Rubbing shoulders with celebrities everyday, running into movie stars like it's no different than catching up with old friends. Me," she said, closer, "I get terrified every time I come here because I know I'm going to see someone famous."

"You know, I was wondering why you looked so ravishing tonight," Renata teased. "Expecting to run into Casa Blacka?"

"You know I don't dig that fool's music?"

"*But* you dig him."

Kira paused.

"Only his body," he said over the gap of silence.

Then, Kira flippantly laughed off her secret crush on the up and coming R&B singer known as Casa Blacka and continued toward to the ladies room.

Renata followed.

☾

WHILE wiping away the smudge of mauve lipstick off her two front teeth with the corner of a paper towel, Renata couldn't help but listen in on Kira in the stall behind her. Just when Renata thought Kira would stop, she kept going and going.

Kira flushed the toilet—finally—slid open the powder-coated glass door, and exited the stall. She looked down and made sure her skirt was "straight," and then moved her eyes to Renata's reflection before her. Renata didn't realize it, but she was staring at Kira.

In return, Kira arched her shoulders upright and said, "What?"

"Nothing," Renata said, turning her attention back to her own reflection.

Kira joined Renata at the white marble vanity.

"I swear beer makes me piss like a racehorse," Kira stated the obvious, as she held her hand next the sensor underneath to the faucet.

"Kira Nakamura," Renata said, her tone drawn out, as if the use of such language in such a fancy place was considered inappropriate.

"What?"

"I can tell," Renata said back and grabbed a paper towel from an arrangement of expensive oils and lotions and handed it to Kira.

"Nosy much," Kira said, grinning.

Renata fell silent not from Kira's remark, but from something else, something that had been on her mind ever since she left the dining area.

"So, what do you think of Paul so far?" Kira asked.

Renata found herself rolling her eyes. Her lack of answer was more than the answer itself.

"Forget I asked," Kira said, tossing the crumbled up paper tower in the trashcan.

Renata followed with a series of questions: "So, what about you and Albert? You think he has potential?"

"Potential for what?"

"Boyfriend."

"Girl, please," Kira said sassily. "It's coming up on two weeks. You know I am incapable of holding a productive relationship longer than three weeks." She paused as she pulled out the tube of lipstick from her purse. "Abiola is a sweet guy and all, but sweet only goes so far."

"If I recall correctly, didn't I hear him mention something about you two going to Barbados for the weekend?"

Kira shrugged.

"Yeah, but I dunno."

"Barbados, Kira," Renata said louder.

"Yeah, so what?"

"Are you serious? I'd kill someone to go to Barbados."

Kira let out a mousy noise from her mouth.

"I'm jealous," Renata said over Kira's sudden quietness. "Me, I wish I could travel around the world one day, explore exotic locations, but Je. . . "

Renata stopped halfway through his name.

"But?"

All of a sudden, her skin flushed. She struggled to look Kira in the eyes. For a moment, she thought her cover was blown.

Renata retracted her thoughts.

"Too busy, I guess," she muttered.

Quietly, Renata directed her attention back to the mirror.

Kira furrowed her brow from Renata's strange behavior and reapplied a layer of scarlet red lipstick. During the smooth stroke, she shot short glances at Renata in the mirror. Then, she moved onto her hair, primped hastily yet strategically, as if she was searching for not a new look but the right look. Once more, she caught Renata in the corner of her eye. Kira stopped primping, stopped making adjustments.

Thoughtfully, Kira faced Renata, who was smoothing out a wrinkle along the top of her silk pale blue halter top.

Renata turned to Kira's reflection, then Kira herself.

She waited in limbo for a reaction from Kira.

"Can I ask you something personal, Renata?" Kira asked heavily.

Renata furrowed her brow.

"Sure," she said hesitantly. "Okay."

Kira asked bluntly, "What happened to him?"

"What happened to *who*?"

"Your father," Kira said. "Was that really true what you said to Paul?"

Renata didn't immediately respond. Yet, she let the question marinate for a moment.

Kira dipped her head downward.

"You know," she said, looking up at Renata, "I lost my father when I was just a young girl."

Kira's words rippled through Renata, drawing her full attention.

"I'm sorry to hear," she said.

"Don't be," Kira said abruptly, as if she already knew Renata's response before it even left her mouth. "It was ages ago."

Another silence fell between them, a deeper silence, as if Kira had given the floor to Renata.

Unsure whether or not to share with Kira, Renata brought herself back to the gray days when she'd accidentally walk in on her mother embracing an old letter written by a man who was shrouded by conflicting stories.

"He left when I was born," Renata finally said, her tone way more subdued, "at least, that's what everybody said, but, I dunno. My mother was—and still is— convinced that he never abandoned us or 'ran away,' which was what everybody was telling her. She was so convinced that something awful had happened to him that she even hired a private investigator to help track him down, but, after years of investigation, nothing panned out. Sometimes," Renata hung her head in similar fashion to Kira and then raised it, "I dunno," she said, looking directly into Kira's eyes, "I think maybe he's still out there, perhaps he has another family, a daughter maybe. I sometimes think about what that conversation would be like if I ever ran into him one day. All those times I needed him when he wasn't there for me. The times I needed the guidance. The times when I felt all alone or cast aside, as if I was the 'thing' that often got talked about whenever I wasn't in the same room, the mistake. Mostly, I think about the times I cursed that man without even knowing him. He was only one man, and yet he was a million different people in my mind. *But*," she paused, her eyes watery, "at least I had Elmo, though. God didn't take him away."

"Must've been some cat," Kira said jokingly. Then, leaned in and followed: "I have good ears. They're only good for one thing."

Renata looked downward at the sink and forced out a tight, unraveling laugh, which helped loosened up the tension that the night had brought her. In that globe of silence, Kira's focus wasn't drawn to the laugh but to the laugher. She soberly studied Renata, who had the profile of a falcon. With her steady eyes, Kira traced the shape of her face and the last bits of laugher trailing out and bringing about a glow in her face that had been dimmed all night by the dullness of Paul's abysmal conversational skills.

"Listen, Renata," Kira said patiently, as she took one step closer to Renata, "I know these past couple of weeks have been tough at Carla and Corvine—I mean, I think everybody at the agency is freaked out about the new launch and you certainly shouldn't be the one to feel the brunt of everybody's frustration. I have this cabin—well, it's not my cabin. My mother looked after the cabin after my father died. Then, when she got sick, she handed it down to me. It's become sort of like this family heirloom. Whenever you feel like it, Renata, the cabin is yours."

Renata tilted her head in confusion.

"What are you saying?"

"I'm saying, whenever you're feeling like you want to *murder* somebody and you're dying to go somewhere for the weekend, even week, or whatever, just let me know and the keys to the cabin are yours."

Renata mulled over Kira's offer.

"Whenever I'm feeling frustrated with work," Kira said, "I go to the cabin for a weekend and then, when I come back, it's as if all that negativity washes away."

Renata hesitated.

"I don't know what to say," she said.

Kira's face formed into a part smile, part frown.

"Just say 'thank you.'"

"Of course," Renata leaned in and hugged Kira, "Thank you."

She couldn't help but turn her gaze toward the mirror behind Kira's shoulder.

PRESENT DAY

WITH her head down, Renata stood in front of the bathroom mirror.

She could barely bring herself to look at herself in the mirror.

With her trembling hand, she turned on the faucet.

She leaned forward and splashed her face with cool water.

Finally, she moved her eyes up at the mirror and in horror, watched the wet, red blood run down her face like a crimson mask.

The sound of two hard *knocks* on the bathroom door pulled Renata's attention away from herself and the horror.

Standing in a loud, humming silence, she listened closely for another knock but instead heard a voice.

"*Rennie*," Jevon said from behind the door, "you good?"

Renata didn't respond. She didn't know how to respond to the question.

"Rennie?"

The doorknob twisted in a clockwise direction.

"Yes, Jevon," she snapped over the running water. "Good."

As she turned off the water, her eyes caught the needle mark on her forearm and the infection starting to spread around it. She poked at the swollen red dot on her arm and recoiled in pain.

She was pulled away from the strange marking by the sound of Jevon's back sliding against the other side of the door. A shadow was plumped underneath that narrow slit of the doorway. Next, she heard the sound of metal jiggling together. In all probability, it was Jevon readjusting the metal band of his wristwatch. But, in that moment, the sound of metal, whether it be a *jingle* or a *clink* or *clank* or the sharp *shing*-sound that a blade made whenever removed from a sheath, triggered a lost memory, like one from a dream or bad nightmare, one that shared the characteristics of reality. She lifted up a worn Tee shirt of the pale face of a silicon creature from the hit manga series, *BLAME!* The shirt was old, the lost remnants cast from Kira's tweens. Renata specifically recalled her mentioning something about keeping the clothes at the cabin for, more or less, sentimental value. But it wasn't the Tee shirt that Renata was most worried about. It was that stab wound underneath the shirt—or *lack* of stab wound. She touched her belly, then ran her hand across her belly, but couldn't find a single mark on her skin, not one!

Renata ignored the infection, ignored the actual thought of being stabbed, and took a seat on the edge of the toilet.

From the other side of the door, Jevon asked Renata, "Did I ever tell you that I, too, lost someone close to me?"

Jevon didn't expect any answer in return and that was exactly what he got, a wall of silence and the subtle movements of a slender shadow moving below him.

"His name was Richard," Jevon said with his back pressed against the bathroom door. "Filthy Rich was what people who knew him well called him because he was born with a silver spoon in his mouth, basically had everything any person could ask for handed down to him. He preferred to go by Ricky better than Filthy Rich; in fact, he hated that name. One night, I met Ricky at a bar, which sat in the shadows of Dunmire Stadium, called The Bucket. He was doing a show at a local theatre outside Tucker's Ridge. He created marionettes and put on these 'grandiose' plays all by himself. I swear he was something else. For years, he had been putting together this entire world of characters, all marionettes, all with a specific trait and background, until one day he finally reached a point in his life where he no longer wanted to look at what he was creating as a mere hobby. So he went on the road, conducted different shows with the marionettes. Ricky didn't make a lot of money, didn't draw much of an audience either, but I believe he was happy at what he was doing. That night, we exchanged phone numbers. I met up with him in Hamshaw, a small town outside Nashville. The more I got to know Ricky, the more I realized Ricky was hiding something from me—*a darkness*. He was the type of person who didn't want people thinking he had money or had come from money. I figured he was embarrassed by the notion of having a much bigger bank account than an average nine-to-fiver who made enough money in a workday than Ricky brought home from a show. He was quite an interesting individual, Ricky was. *But* he had demons. And Ricky battled those demons with drugs and alcohol. I didn't realize—at least, not until much later—he was in pain. He was suffering." Renata could hear the pain in his voice, then a sigh. "The man probably lived eight lives before I even met him. Burning through enough money to build an island. By the time I intervened and got him the help he deserved, it was already too late. The damage he had done to his body was irreparable. His liver was shot. He needed a new one. Doctors were astonished he was still alive. But, being the rich kid he was, he figured he'd just buy himself a new one. He assumed he'd be a high priority. *Nope*. He had to get in line like everybody else."

Silence built behind the door.

Renata was tempted to speak, even open her mouth.

Jevon cleared his throat.

Spoke.

"I think the last few months after he cleaned up—before everything turned to shit—were probably some of the best moments of my life. I started to understand more about Ricky and why he went down the road he did. You see, he never told his parents about his personal life. He told me that they'd disown him if they ever found out about him. Which meant they would cut him off financially, emotionally—"

His words got to Renata. Words that were often spoken to her as a child being raised by a devote Catholic who held the word of God above everything else.

With both hands, she tightly covered her mouth in order to smother the sobbing.

"—But this sort of 'fearful' mindset wasn't only created by his parents alone. It was society, religion. It was everything and everyone who pointed at Ricky and said, '*No. You're not allowed to be that way. You have to be like us. You have to be normal.*' I haven't loathed such a word as I did after I met Ricky. He hid from society because society was told to shun people like Ricky. Society was forced to look at Ricky differently because he was different from everybody else. When he should've been looking at who he was as a good thing—perhaps his greatest quality—Ricky only saw it as a bad thing. 'Evil,' some would even say. Me, having lived in the metropolitans for most of my life, I didn't have it nearly as rough as Ricky. The bullying. The hazing. *The rejection.* There were a few who messed with me when I was younger. But mostly just name-calling. Which I could handle. So, even up until the very end, Ricky continued to live a lie. I saw his parents at the hospital. Whenever I would visit, I'd have to wait until his parents left before I could see him. There was this one time when I showed up in his room. I thought his parents had gone; but surprise, surprise they were downstairs grabbing a bite to eat in the cafeteria. When they saw me in the room with their son, I think they knew who I was to Ricky. I could see the disappointment filling their eyes, *the tragedy.* His parents knew all along about their son and yet, they spent years rejecting the idea like a body trying to naturally rid a virus. If there was one thing they couldn't take away from their son, it was his bond with me. The connection. Together, we ruled the world, showed it how it could be. We created memories, memories that will stay with me till the day I die. . . At the end, when Ricky was all doped up, he wasn't making any sense whatsoever. In a way, he didn't have to say anything at all to me. He didn't have to make sense. Our connection had already been forged by the roads we took in life. Two roads that lead us together. And one that showed us a glimpse of life without *fear* or judgment."

A memory flashed inside Jevon's mind: the moment he first met Ricky at the bar, his head slowly turning toward Jevon while he continued to laugh at a joke he cracked with the bartender. The image of a sickly Ricky lying in the hospital bed crept back in. But it was that other image, the one image with Ricky sitting at the bar and laughing, that painted over Ricky's final moments.

"It's the bond," Jevon said, "that connection, the one that will unite us rather than divide us, that Carla and Corvine is trying to take away from us. Imagine a world without connection, Renata. A cold and dark world constantly plugged in, manipulated by powers beyond our control and those whose greatest profit comes from driving a stake in the heart of civilization. We need that 'connection' in order to survive as a species, otherwise, all will be lost in the darkness."

The bathroom door *finally* cracked open, startling Jevon.

A sword of bright light shone over the right side of his body.

"Renata?"

"Hey," she said flatly.

Standing to his feet, Jevon replied, "Hey."

The two stood in the doorway and stared at each other.

Jevon finally broke through the silence.

"Listen, Rennie—"

"—Forget it," she interrupted. "Let's get this over with, shall we?"

"Of course."

☾

JEVON walked with Renata to her navy blue Ford Taurus, which was located at the side of the cabin.

When they arrived at back of the car, Renata stepped aside and without uttering a single word, maintained a clear understanding as to who was going to open the trunk.

Jevon sighed, snatched the car keys from Renata's hand, and inserted the key into the lock.

Before he opened the trunk, he turned to Renata.

"I'm aware you might've been close to her, Renata," he said. "Possibly even considered her as a friend outside of work. But, Renata, you must understand that she wasn't that person back there; in fact, she wasn't a person at all. *They* got to her, you see. By then, it was all over. Once *they* get to you, *they* own you—your thoughts, your body, even your soul. So, you can forget about everything that you know—or once knew. Once they have you, there's no escaping. And that's what makes what we're doing so important."

"I know," Renata uttered.

Her look was wounded, her words and thoughts tender.

Jevon sighed once more, as if he was sending subtle, unspoken messages to Renata that he was upset with her behavior.

Without any hesitation, he unlocked the trunk.

The trunk *squeaked* open.

THREE DAYS AGO

RENATA grabbed as many bags of groceries as she could fit in two hands from the trunk of her Taurus and closed the door with the bottom of her chin.

While carrying the bags to the front porch of the townhouse, her butt beeped. She placed the groceries on the porch and pulled the phone from her back pocket.

She read the name on the screen of the phone: Kira.

After the third beep-beep, she decided to answer the call.

"Hey, Gurl," Renata said ecstatically.

"Why hello, Renata," Kira replied.

"What's going on?"

"Nothing," she said. "I was just calling to see how the trip went?"

Renata didn't expect to hear the question so soon in the conversation, but the last thing she wanted to do was continue to lie to Kira.

She embraced a deep breath.

223

The only word that came to mind: "*Exhausting.*"

"Really," Kira said, her voice curling with suspicion. "Well, did you at least have a good time?"

"I did actually," Renata said, her voice slightly higher, "but you wouldn't believe the traffic home. Talk about a nightmare."

"That bad, huh?"

"You wouldn't believe."

"I was also going to ask you about the water—"

"—Don't worry," Renata said. "I turned it off just like you asked."

"Just checking because the last time we went up there I totally forgot to cut off the water and you know how that went—"

"—Kira," Renata said shortly. "It's all good."

"Yes," Kira said, more quietly. "Of course it is. I just wish I could've joined you this time around, but the other day I swear I felt as if someone was hammering a nail into my forehead. I haven't felt like shit in years. For a while, I had a nice non-sick streak going on."

"Well, that only means you're human, Kira."

Suspense cut between the break in the conversation.

Renata could sense the *other* question manifesting over the airy silence.

"So, was it just you? Or did you go with anybody?"

Renata leaned against the railing of the porch.

Be honest, she thought to herself.

More casually, she asked, "Remember that one guy, Paul Lauter?"

A noisy silence filled the other end of the phone.

"The name doesn't ring a bell," Kira said finally.

"The guy whom I went on a date with, remember?" Renata said. "We went on a double date with you and Al?"

"Oh yeah," Kira said. "Paul the Sta-Sta-Sta-Stall."

"Yes. Paul the. . . yeah."

"What a total scumbag," Kira said angrily, as her voice trailed off into a dead silence. "Wait a second!" Kira chirped before Renata had any chance of redeeming herself. "You didn't take him to the cabin, did you? Renata—"

"—Yeah," Renata said flatly. "Eww. No. Remember Paul's friend? We ran into him later that night off North Morrison?" Still no response from Kira on the other end. Renata thought of the one thing—or *things*—that would jar her memory. "We had kamikazes?" No response. "The website developer?" Again, dead silence. "You said you liked his jaw."

"Yes," Kira said abruptly. "Ah! What's his name? Trevor?"

"*Trent*," both Renata and Kira said simultaneously.

"Yeah," Renata said over Kira. "That's the one."

"Wasn't he a lot older than you?"

"Forty-three."

"Forty-three?" Kira suddenly repeated, her voice louder and laced with confusion. "He's forty-three?"

"Yeah," Renata said. "So. Why you tripping?"

"He's twenty years older than you."

"Yes," Renata said. "I'm aware of his age. Thanks for stating the obvious."

"I'm just saying—"

"—Well, I'm just saying he doesn't at all act or 'look' like he's forty-three, if you know what I mean." Renata waited for a response from Kira but all she received was more silence. "But," Renata said over the silence, "there weren't even sparks there. You know, all thunder, no lightning."

Finally, Kira put together the clues that Renata had been seeding throughout the conversation.

"You see," she said, her voice sharper, "now, I feel bad."

"Bad? Why?"

Renata caught the glimpse of the front door in the corner of her eye.

"If I knew that you were going to the cabin on some romantic getaway with Trent the forty-three Stud, then I would've at least straightened up the place—"

"—No," she said, her voice facing as she stepped toward the front door. "It's not like that. . . "

More intrigued, Renata looked closer at the front door, as well as the damage around the doorframe. The door was cracked open. The doorknob was loose and hanging from the door like a baby tooth ready to be pulled. The area next to the faceplate looked partially caved in by what might have been from a crowbar.

"This is the part where you give me details—"

"—Listen, Kira, can I call you back?"

"Call me back? Gurl, I want to know what happened between you and what's-his-name—"

"—Kira, I'll call you back."

Renata hung up before Kira could lash out.

Cautiously, she opened the wobbly door and stepped inside the townhouse. "Hello?"

Nobody answered.

Renata grabbed the closest weapon that she could find, which happened to be a small metal pole from a lamp that had been destroyed on the floor. Everything was either destroyed or overturned: lamps, coffee table, furniture. In her bedroom her underwear, shirts, and socks had been removed from the drawers and scattered around the floor. The outfits in her closet had been removed as well and scattered everywhere. Even in the kitchen the food from the pantry, as well as the refrigerator had been emptied onto the floors. Even the walls were covered in various colors of liquid and foods. The inside of the apartment appeared as if a hurricane had blown through each room, throwing and scattering things in the most destructive manner. But nothing was stolen, though.

Which was the first of many red flags.

⊙

RENATA arranged an emergency meeting with Jevon at the abandoned Eastwake Theatre outside Middletown, New Jersey.

She arrived extra early, which had given her more time to think about who or *what* had torn through her townhouse.

After about twenty minutes of waiting around, Jevon was still a no-show; and even though she was expecting Jevon to arrive rather late since the meeting was close to rush hour, she was still a hot mess. She spent the whole time pacing back and forth around the lobby area, which was overgrown with weeds and all sorts of plant vegetation. Surprisingly, the place had power; and every now and then, the lights would flicker along the sunburst lighting, sending Renata into a higher state of alarm.

Renata resorted to biting her nails—which was an old habit that she kicked a year after she graduated from high school. Once she heard the door *squeak* open and witnessed a sword of light cutting through the lobby, she removed her fingers from her mouth and stepped forward for a closer look.

At first, a shadow appeared on the slanted rectangular the sunlit doorway was casting on the floor, then, secondly, a figure emerged from around the corner.

Eventually, after calling out twice to the dark stranger, a worried Jevon appeared before her.

With her brow furrowed in concentration, she stormed straight to Jevon.

Before Renata could unburden herself, Jevon asked her, "Did you remove the battery from your phone?"

"Yes," she said annoyingly. "I removed the battery. I did exactly what you told me to do."

"Good," he said, "because they can track us through the phones."

"I know," Renata returned. "You don't have to talk to me like I'm some goddamn child—"

"—How about your tail? Were you followed?"

"No," she said and swiftly corrected, "I mean, I was followed. Someone was following me. I mean, not here."

"Are you sure—"

"—Yes," Renata snapped. "I'm sure. Were you followed?"

"No."

"Then, we wouldn't be having this meeting if we were followed. Now would we, Jevon?"

Patiently, Jevon held out his hands and tried to calm Renata.

"What's going on?" he asked, holding back his frustration.

"They know about me."

"It could've been anybody, Rennie," Jevon suggested. "Some kid. A neighbor? Have you made any enemies with anyone in the past few days?"

"Gee," Renata thought aloud. "Let me think." Then snapped at Jevon, "Perhaps Carla and Corvine—"

"—What makes you so sure they know about you? You've covered all your tracks. As far as I'm concerned, you haven't raised any red flags. Hypothetically speaking, if they did know about you—which I highly doubt it—I don't think we would be having this conversation. You're still here, aren't you?"

"What the hell is that supposed to mean?"

Trying to keep the civility, Jevon held out his hands.

"Sorry," he uttered. "I shouldn't have said that."

Turned off by Jevon's poor attempt at reassuring her—which, to Renata, felt quite the contrary—Renata gave Jevon the cold shoulder, as if the lack of Jevon's presence would make her think more clearly.

"I dunno," she said quietly to herself. "Who in the hell breaks into a house and doesn't steal anything?" Renata turned around and faced Jevon before he had a chance to answer her question, "I'll tell you who? Some asshole from Carla and Corvine who's trying to send me a message. That's who."

"And what message is that?"

"What do you think, Jevon?" Renata shook her head in disgust. "You know, I thought you were a lot smarter than that—"

"—Well," he said, the frustration rising his voice, "I'd say if they're trying to scare you, then I think they've done a pretty good job at it, don't you think?"

He backed off for a moment.

Then, stepped closer to Renata and touched her on the shoulder: "Listen to me, Renata," he said, his voice tender. "We both knew that something like this was eventually going to happen and it's better that it happened sooner than later."

"Later?" Renata shrugged off Jevon's hand from her shoulder. "Exactly how much longer do you expect me to stay on this story?"

He ignored the question: "Even if you are right, Renata, then it clearly demonstrates that we've tapped into something that they don't want tapping into. We have come way too far to give up now. And you certainly can't keep. . . " Jevon searched for the right words, ". . . *running off* every chance you get."

Renata reacted to the words.

Her face filled with hot rage.

"Running off? Correct me if I'm wrong but it was you who said I needed to find some kind of normalcy in my life. *Cool off*, if I remember correctly. Those were the words you used. No. I'm sorry. *Get away*—"

"—I need you present right now," Jevon said.

The comment prompted Renata to clench her jaw together, as if she was restraining the words in her mouth.

Patiently, Jevon said, "After all of this is over, you can do whatever you want with your life, start a family, travel like you've been talking about, whatever. Just remember, Renata: it's our resiliency that has gotten us where we are today—"

"—And where are we exactly, Jevon?"

"Close."

"Close?" Renata snapped. "I know I'm not in any position to tell you how to run your magazine, but it's time to publish the story. You saw what they did with MindChant and how they're deliberately targeting the vulnerabilities of those who are most vulnerable, tracking people's every keystroke and using subliminal messages in their ads to suck them into whatever product they're promoting. It's no different than a disease, Jevon. And if we don't stop the spread now, then it's going to be too late." Renata paused and gathered herself. She couldn't make herself more clear: "I've brought you more than enough 'sufficient' evidence to expose Roman and Elmahdy."

"You have, Renata, and I'm grateful for all you've done—"

"—So, I say let the people see the facts for what they are and let them decide what to do with Roman and Elmahdy. If we don't have the people's back on this story, you and I know both know that it's the end of us. Like you said, we're talking about people powerful enough to erase us from existence. If they can make Rubin's death look like a suicide, then who knows what they can do to us?"

"The man was unstable," Jevon argued. "You saw his background."

"I did and it was all fabricated, Jevon," Renata said. "Smoke and mirrors."

"Well, maybe you should've dug deeper, Renata."

Renata picked up the hostility in Jevon's voice.

"My own 'vetted' resource," she said, more convincingly, "a man who has no grudges with Carla and Corvine, who has absolutely no reason to talk to me, who arranges a meeting in the middle of nowhere in fear for his own safety, who was paid hush money to keep his damn mouth shut, winds up dead twenty-four hours after he spills his guts to me. *Not* a coincidence." Determined, she stepped closer to Jevon and said clearly, "They haven't erased us just yet. But it's only a matter of time now. Just look at what happened in Dover. All fingers pointed at Harold Roman, yet literally every network runs some heartfelt story about how he lost his second wife to cancer two years after his marriage with Elmahdy was annulled in order to regain sympathy for him and change the public's perception and, just like that, he gets off scot-free, as if he had absolutely no involvement in what was going on with Bernie Shore or Rankin Jericho. How does that even happen? When the hell did 'playing dumb' exempt a man from the very inkling of being charged with murder?"

"And that's why we need to present the strongest case forward, otherwise the story isn't going to stick," Jevon urged. "We still have gaping holes in the story, such as the person responsible for setting these fires or the fact someone out there clearly knows what Roman is up to. And," Jevon emphasized, "what about this doctor character? We still have absolutely no information about him, who he is, or what experiments they're running at this secret facility you speak of. We may have Chione Elmahdy, all of her ties to Roman's crimes, the outrageous donations and contributions to police departments all around the country, but Renata, it's *not* enough. We have to convince the public that 'literally' everything they've been told is a complete fabrication of the truth."

"Why does it matter how much we have," Renata argued. "We have enough to plant doubts in their minds. Most importantly, enough to warrant an investigation!"

"By whom exactly? Corrupted officials? Bought-politicians?" Jevon's cheeks clouded with red heat released from his voice. "What we cannot do at this point is jeopardize the story by presenting it to those who have already been turned!"

"What does it matter? We have a story!"

"It's matters!" Jevon shouted. "We need every single person who's involved, including every single individual who has received so much as a penny from Harold Roman. We haven't even scratched the surface—"

"—That could take God knows how much longer—weeks, months, possibly even years."

Jevon closed his eyes for a moment and took a breath.

"We're talking about bringing down a company that's turned into a monster, a monster that grows stronger while we sleep, a monster that thrives off attention, a monster with an endless appetite feeding off our weaknesses and using them to manipulate us. In order to destroy this monster, we have to do the job that nobody else will do. . . . Renata, we have to tell its story not the way it wants to be told but the way it doesn't. And if we waver now, then all the progress we've made will be for nothing. Our work won't even be an after-thought. I know it sucks, but it's the job."

Jevon stared at Renata and gave her an opportunity to respond. That pissed-off look he once wore on his face like pride melted into an expression of utter disappointment.

The deep sting of defeat suddenly poked at Renata.

She felt speechless, destroyed.

"What do you think you signed up for, Rennie?" asked Jevon.

Holding back the tears, Renata uttered, "I dunno."

SEVEN DAYS AGO

"HEY, *Junior*, you want anything from Café Cloud?" one of the drones from Marketing called out to Renata.

Renata didn't even have to turn around. She could recognize LeBron's voice and the arrogance that emitted from his aura like noxious fumes. Even though the word *junior* was officially part of Renata's new title—after all, it beat names like *newbie* or "noob" or new blood or anything with the word *new* or remotely close to the word *new* in it or even worse, *hey, you*—she never got used to being called Junior.

Biting the words in her mouth, Renata pulled herself from the printer and rotated around where LeBron, the conceited, slack-jawed bastard he was, waited by the doorway for an answer.

"No thank you," she said, remaining professional. "I'm good. . . "

She gave LeBron a professional smile and finished the conversation with a professional acknowledgment by stating LeBron's name back to him. She didn't put any emphasizes on either his name or his title. However, she let it be known to LeBron that he had rightfully earned his name the moment it was given to him. Renata couldn't say the same about his title.

"Suit yourself," LeBron said, his voice and face changing. He appeared as if he was invisibly waving off Renata not with a hand but, more or less, with a slight dip in his facial expression, as well as the rolling of his eyes. Somehow, he took Renata's answer more so as a retaliative response rather than a simple rejection to his kind proposal to the universal link, which was, of course, food.

As LeBron went away, Renata felt a sudden buzz swarming around her. She could feel it in the recycled air—that electricity—while she continued to print out a list of competitive trends, as well as noteworthy news items, that she had found during an intense yet highly productive surf through what she had grown accustomed to calling the "Underworld," including social media and social networking services and other popular platforms, such as the addictive MindChant, which had recently gone "public," as well as the two swiping apps that MindChant, Inc. currently owned, *Men Only* and its counterpart, *Women Only*.

She ignored the strange sensation and watched each page fall into the tray of the printer. While falling into a trance of the mundaneness of watching pa-per fall out of the printer—which was no different than one watching paint dry—Renata came across one page in particular, which piqued her interest. She removed the page from the stack of papers and skimmed it over.

The trend consisted of articles written about other competitors like Zinc Way and Foley and Sons, other marketing companies that targeted a majority of their audiences through online advertising with certain SROs like "Ad-Right," by using various emojis, particularly "food emojis," such as fruits, vegetables, or meat, as innuendos to depict parts of the human anatomy based on their size or shape.

Even though Renata had an idea as to why people—particularly the younger demographic, according to the data, younger males—commonly used an egg-plant emoji to describe one of the most "trendy" organs of the male body, she was still confused as to why people, of all the phallic-shaped foods out there, chose a fruit that often bore the shape of a stumped big toe.

Renata removed the pages from the tray, placed them on top of the scanner in a neat stack, and slid the other page into the stack.

The buzz was back—that electricity.

In a state of frenzy, she looked around the office, through each glass corridor and office where a team of incredibly insightful strategists—whose job description specifically required a knack for telling a story, in other words, a "master storyteller"—was pitching fresh ideas for new projects and advertisements to directors while, in other transparent conference rooms, graphic designers were sketching potential slogans along glass boards, as well as shuffling through a variety of mock-posters displaying multifaceted marketing packages.

One particular slogan stood out the most: the words *Be the Better You* written in bold font on a poster. Other adjectives like "new," "revamped," or other catchy words, were being pitched and often replacing the word *better*.

Renata immediately noticed the head turns, the widened-eyes, and the change in facial expressions or lack of expressions: each strategist, each project manager or director, each assistant or accountant, all directing their attention to a brooding entourage moving like a quiet storm from the elevators to the main offices.

Deeply intrigued—partly mesmerized—Renata dropped what she was doing and peered closer at the entourage. She figured they were "big wigs," "investors," "potential clients perhaps," worse "lawyers"—it wasn't at all uncommon to come across gangs of lawyers gliding throughout the building every now and then like elusive undead armies—even "competitors from competing Ad Agencies." Each expression on each member's face, similar to the ones on each employee scattered around the office, appeared in unison; however, they were darkly grim, war-like in nature, as if the individual at the very center of the wall-like entourage had produced such a contagious vibe.

Renata stepped from the printers and exited the nook where she was working and caught a glimpse of the elusive one rounding the corner along an intersection of hallways, the one in the middle, the boss *wo*-man who had been aggrandized by myths and legends—even as Renata kept a mental snapshot of Chione Elmahdy in her mind, the black and white striped v-neck, those plump shoulder pads tucked underneath a sharp, black blazer that she was sporting like an athlete of the highest caliber strutting into the back of a coliseum, game face on, ready to vanquish the worthiest of opponents, as well as a vacant Michael Myers-type mask which, rumored, had covered her "other face," such lore was being murmured throughout the office, such as the reasons as to why she wore the mask, which was "to cover her disfigurement caused by the overuse of cosmetics that she was marketing, as well as countless botched facial reconstructive surgeries from when she was one of the most sought after fashion models who was later cast aside by the industry when she was a teenager."

Other rumors buzzed throughout a hornet's nest of chatter: Chione Elmahdy was said to "wear that same outfit every single day, not the same way Albert Einstein did, but because the outfit was somehow 'a part' of her," or "Her nickname, *The Redactor*, which she had earned because she was known to figuratively redact anybody who got in her way" or "She sleeps in a hyperbaric oxygen chamber at night" or "She only eats canned tuna fish" and "there's something about the mercury in tuna that her body needs to survive" or "All of her toes were amputated when she was only five years old in order to compete at the highest level of ballet for dictators around the world" or "She has the ability to see in the dark" or "She was once close friends with Saddam Hussein" or "She and Andy Warhol 'supposedly' had a child together when she was eighteen and this child was raised by a family somewhere in Oslo where it was developing the cure to the world's energy problem under several pseudonyms" or "She was able to seize all bodily functions of an individual with the single *snap* of her fingers; however, these unique powers weren't given to her or passed down to her from birth, but rather mastered after spending twelve years tucked far away in the Himalayan Mountains with quasi-Tibetan monks training her how to master the perfect *snap* of her fingers."

Renata even heard a rumor in the midst of the commotion—which she knew wasn't a rumor at all but, more or less, an accurate statement which was closest to the truth—that Chione "murdered Carla and Corvine in cold blood in order to take over the sibling's once failing company."

After the entourage breezed by, Renata found an opportunity to strike.

She left her nook and tracked down the marketing assistant, Selma, who was about to join a meeting with the rest of the marketing team. She handed her report to Selma and insisted on going on a food run.

Selma immediately waved off Renata. "No sweat," she said. "We'll just do it on Munch Run." Renata wasn't aware of Munch Run. Selma explained, "It's a new app."

"I can have the food here quicker," Renata argued.

Someone, Renata thought it was one of the strategists, was complaining how hungry he was. Once more, Renata insisted—nearly begged—to pick up food.

LeBron chimed in: "I thought you were 'good.'"

"*I am good*," she responded swiftly. "But I don't mind picking up the food for everybody; in fact, it would be my pleasure. And not only that, I'll have it here much quicker than Food Run—"

"—Munch Run," someone seated across the conference table corrected.

Selma presented the team with Renata's report, which was the final sell. The team came to an agreement to let Renata go on a food run. They handed her a list of orders. Once Renata acquired the list, she was out of there.

RENATA zoomed through a couple of hallways before she reached the entourage.

She slowed down her pace and eventually, after a couple of swift maneuvers, caught up with the entourage. Without drawing any attention to herself, she crept behind the entourage and blended in as soon as they reached the security desk in front of Chione's office.

The security guard let the entourage through the lobby without even questioning Renata's presence; in fact, she wasn't even sure the security guard had spotted her because her head was kept down and her eyes to the floor the whole time.

Once through the lobby, she followed the entourage to two oak doors—which she assumed led to Chione's office. The closer they approached the doors, the more nervous she became. Her heart pounded in a drum-like resonance throughout her chest. Her palms and other areas of her body, sweaty. She couldn't even believe she had gotten this close to the so-called Redactor; in fact, she couldn't even hold a thought in her head and it was as if she was having some outer body experience and watching herself from the outside.

Chione's secretary acknowledged the entourage and swiftly stood to her feet and opened the doors for everyone.

As the entourage poured into the office, Renata realized she had to make yet another move. With little-to-no options, Renata made a snap decision; and just as the secretary moved her eyes toward one of the members of the entourage, Renata darted behind the vase of a large areca palm plant in the corner of the room.

Renata ducked, her body balled up as tight and tiny as she would allow it.

The door *finally* closed.

Curious, Renata poked her head from the areca palm. The secretary was nowhere in sight. The entourage, gone.

With her heart pounding harder against her chest, Renata tiptoed to the doors.

She eavesdropped over the conversation from within the office. The conversation sounded as if the secretary was taking a possible lunch order. She thought she heard a woman talking about "California rolls." Possibly the secretary. The conversation came to a halt. Over the gap of silence, she heard another woman's voice. The voice was much deeper and pronounced, imperial.

Over the thrumming of her heartbeat, she heard the words "*check on*" a "*Dr. Essen*" and "*update on.*" From there, Renata filled in the blanks. "Go check on Dr. Essen and provide me with the latest update on. . . ?" The last word trailed off and left Renata scrambling through her mind, trying to piece together the remaining word—*or words*—of the sentence.

Renata mistook the sound of footsteps for the sound of her heartbeat. The beating suddenly got louder and louder and she suddenly realized it was footsteps and they were heading directly at her! At the very last second, Renata ducked behind the secretary's desk. From behind the desk, she watched a member from the entourage walking away. Keeping close to the desk, Renata stood upright.

As the door started to close, Renata caught yet another glimpse of Chione as the other members of the entourage began to take their seats around the medieval-sized table.

Renata specifically honed in on the tall woman in the sharp black blazer who was standing at the end of the table—whom Renata assumed was, in fact, the one and only Chione from not only the outfit she was wearing, but also the manners that she exhibited. With her back turned and her head slightly arched upright to a cathedral-like rose window below the high ceiling, she whispered something to the secretary. Her mode was dour and domineering. The secretary submissively nodded her head in return; however, the gesture looked more like a subserviently bow than an act of acknowledgement. Just a couple of inches before the door *finally* swung close, Chione turned her shoulder, her head dipped downward, revealing her unmasked face. Renata's mouth cracked open like a lazy yawn, her insides left gasping from the sight of Chione's face. She froze, as if she had been caught in the eye of Medusa's gaze.

In her statue-like state, Renata heard more footsteps, sharper. The sound reminded her of a horse, only without the *clop*. She soon realized it was a *clip-clip* sound of silhouettes, more importantly, the secretary's silhouettes.

As the door swung open, Renata looked around in a state of utter frenzy. With her mind swirling, she found a trashcan next to the secretary's desk. Then a cup holder inside, as well as two coffee cups.

The secretary called out from behind, "Excuse me!"

Renata snatched the cup holder and coffee cups from the trashcan. Her body erected upright like a freshly watered plant. As she secured the last second coffee cup into the holder, she used way too much vim and vigor in her grip—she possibly had the adrenaline to thank for the sudden burst of energy. The cup caved in but didn't completely crush. Cold coffee spilled from the sides of the white and brown cup and dribbled all over her hand.

Ignoring the coffee, Renata faced the secretary.

"Excuse me," she parroted, trying to rid the surprise from her face.

"You're not allowed up here," the secretary snapped. "Who are you? What department are you from?"

"I truly apologize," Renata said, pretending to be a dumb intern. "I believe I may be lost. I'm looking for marketing. As you can see, I'm running a little late and my boss will kill me if I don't have his coffee on time."

With her painted brows furrowed in several different kinds of emotion, the secretary looked over Renata, the "dumb intern."

"Wrong floor," she said, pointing downward. "It's the floor below."

"Got it," Renata said, more casually. "Thank you."

The secretary looked over Renata once more, her face less busy.

"You're quite welcome."

Renata hurried away.

SOMEHOW, after taking a shortcut downstairs, Renata managed to beat the man in the black suit to the main entrance.

Renata maintained a steady lead over the strange man, lawyer, Chione's assistant, errand boy—whoever; however, he could've been a lawyer from the way he was dressed or the fact that lawyers were always going in and out of Carla and Corvine. Renata was leaning more toward an assistant. Her assumption was mostly based on the man's presence, his look, mainly how she had seen him many times in the building, carrying coffee, bags, purses, or boxes— or what Renata expected to be deliveries—all done in a hasty manner.

Once she reached the parking garage, she jetted to her car and took cover behind the steering wheel.

While Renata was waiting on the assistant, an image of Chione's face flashed through her mind. She could see her vivid face as if it was right in front of her: all the scars along the sides of her face, the chemical burns around her dark eyes, the gaping hole in the side of her cheek, exposing the teeth inside her mouth.

Eventually, the assistant entered the parking lot.

Renata refocused.

From the inside of her car, Renata kept her eyes on him as he walked directly to his car, which was parked at the other side of the parking garage. Once he got inside his car and drove off, she waited for him to do a half lap around the level and eventually pass her car before starting up the ignition.

As he proceeded down the ramp to the next floor, Renata followed.

RENATA was a car behind him at the front gate, which could've worked to her advantage; however, it all depended on the driver in front of her. Once the attendant inside the booth collected the assistant's ticket and waved him through, he exited the parking garage.

All Renata could hold onto was that he took a right out of the parking garage. And that was it. The driver in front did exactly what she dreaded: he was a talker. And he wouldn't shut the hell up! In order to keep the traffic moving, she honked her horn. The loudmouth in front of her turned around and threw up his arm in a typical privileged "how-dare-you" attitude.

Renata honked yet again.

The driver finished his transaction with the attendant and sped off.

Once Renata pulled up to the booth, she handed the attendant her ticket. The attendant, realizing the rush Renata was in, opened the gate for her.

Renata sped off.

EVENTUALLY, after making a last-second guess to make a left on Galvin Avenue, which would take her through the Lincoln Tunnel, instead of staying on West 41st Street, Renata caught up with the assistant's car.

Enormously relieved from the sight of the car, Renata made sure to keep her distance. They stayed on 495 until they crossed over into New Jersey. She ended up following the assistant for about forty minutes to what looked like a business park right outside Caldwell. Renata counted at least four separate buildings; however, each one connected to one another by long enclosed walkways.

As she approached the park, she searched for a sign outside but couldn't find one. Except for a number on the top corner of the buildings, the buildings didn't give much away. A gate with barbwire surrounded the buildings— Renata immediately thought the buildings might've been government, even military, from the cold vibe she was getting. The assistant pulled up to a booth in front of a front gate where a security guard with a gun came out to greet him. He showed the security guard some type of badge. The guard opened the gate and waved him through.

Renata hung back and weighed her options. She clearly couldn't drive up to the main gates and drive right in, considering a possible "badge" was a requirement for entry. She had to look for another way in. She resorted back to her old days, those young and rebellious days where a term like consequences was about as irrelevant as showing a picture of a helping hand to a man suspensefully dangling from the ledge of a high-rise with only three sweaty fingers preventing him from plummeting to his ultimate death.

After the decision was made, Renata moved swiftly. She parked her car at a safe distance and waited until the security guard went back to his cozy hole before she made her next move. Once the guard was distracted by the smartphone in his hand, Renata sprinted toward a chain link fence which surrounded the entire complex and scaled it as quickly as her body would let her.

The climb was easy—maybe too easy—however, when Renata arrived at the top, she was forced into a caution mode.

Using an old jacket to cover up the sharp spikes, she carefully stepped over the barbwire; and on her way down, the jacket snagged on the spikes. She ended up having to tear away the jacket, which had left behind a small square of jacket between two clusters of spikes. The piece wasn't big enough to raise red flags—at least from where the guard's booth was located; however, she didn't have any time to scale back up the fence and fetch the rest of her jacket for there were cameras mounted everywhere around the building.

She *had* to move.

And move, she did.

🕐

RENATA prayed to whatever merciful god out there that the person working in the surveillance room was either on a break or not paying an iota of attention toward the monitors or simply too lazy or slow to witness a twenty-three year old woman darting through a well-manicured lawn and seeking cover behind one of the many evergreen shrubs along the side of the building. Really, all Renata could do was pray for the best and expect the very worse.

As Renata waited to make her next move, she wrinkled her nose and smelled a strange stench lingering in the air. With her head down, she peeked

235

around the shrub and spotted two men, possible employees, one a heavyset man with a heavy beard, and the other a slender man with a rather premature beard. Both men appeared to be on a smoke break. The heavyset one, chiefing on a vapor pen, while the other man, puffing away on what the #Truth kids called an old fashioned cigarette. She immediately took interest in the door and how it wasn't at all guarded like the other main entries in the front of the building. She was more interested in the lock, as well as the door handle, and how it was like a typical door that probably locked from the outside.

Hey, she thought. *Maybe it's my lucky day.*

Maybe it was the *people working in the surveillance room.*

Renata doubted it.

But she still prayed.

She fished around her pocket, pulled out an old receipt form earlier that day, and folded it tightly. She looked down at the piece of paper in her hand and wondered what in the hell she was thinking—really! She knew that she was about to do something incredibly stupid, but she thought to herself: *What other choice do I have?* She had a hard time believing how exactly she got herself in this particular situation—What a situation it was!

She waited until the two men finished smoking—and vaping—and made her move.

The two men opened the door and stepped inside.

Renata sprinted toward the door and wedged the piece of paper into the lock inches away before it closed. She waited a few seconds outside, listening closely to the sound of the two men's voices fading farther and farther away.

In her anxious wait, she couldn't help but look up.

What do you know?

Another camera, this one aimed directly at Renata.

Shit.

Once the two voices faded, Renata gave the door a tug.

What do you know?

Relieved, Renata opened the door and stepped inside the cool building. She immediately noticed the hospital-like staleness. She carefully closed the door behind her; and once her eyes adjusted to the change in light, she spotted those same two men rounding the corner at the end of a hallway.

"What is this place?" she whispered to herself.

Only one way to find out.

Again, with her head down, she moved quickly down the hallway. Once she made it to the end, she had two different routes, the hallway to the left leading to a sketchy set of double doors, which looked like they required a special key, while the other, the hallway to the right, stretching as far as her eyes could see.

Dumbfounded as to which direction to take, Renata's deliberation caused her to draw her eyes upward.

What do you know?

Of course, she found herself standing directly in the crosshairs of yet another surveillance camera. She put aside her thoughts and prayers and said the hell with it and took a right.

She proceeded down the hallway and passed a sign that read: "Zone C." She steadied her walk and made herself look less obvious while, at the same time, trying to make sense as to what organization uses "zones" to identify a level.

Even though the Zone C fellows had vanished, Renata managed to track their scent to "Lab 4." Inside the narrow room were glass vials and test tubes scattered about worktables. On one side of the wall were many rows of animal cages, each one occupied by a furry creature. The "meows" was what gave them away.

"Cats?" Renata mouthed to herself.

She guessed—more or less, assumed—that the cats were used the same way rats were used, which was for testing, but her guess was as good as the next. She could hear the two men talking inside over a harsh symphony of cat meows; however, she couldn't quite tell what they were talking about. Hugging the side of the wall and trying to block out the cats, Renata leaned in closer to the doorway for a closer listen. Suspended on top of a fluorescent table were various prototypes of strange headgear, from helmets to toboggan-like hats with cables hanging downward like octopus tentacles, all smaller in size, smaller than a baby's head, clearly not intended for humans. She was suddenly hit by her own *duh!* Glancing around at the cat cages inside the room and the headgear, which, clearly, matched the size of a cat's head, Renata was left in a deeper state of confusion.

The two men suddenly came back into frame, their appearance different.

Renata ducked back behind the wall before she could be spotted. She noticed the two men were no longer dressed in casual clothes. Yet, they were both wearing white lab coats.

One of the men, the slender one, removed a lifeless cat from one of the cages. The cat appeared sedated by the way the man was carefully handling it.

He gently placed the cat on a metal table while the other man, the heavyset man, was snapping a couple of plugs into the very back of a small cat-size helmet at his workstation, which was covered in various electronic gear.

The two men continued to argue while prepping the cat for "collection."

The heavyset man: *"There's absolutely no question in my mind that Bethany murdered Jon."*

The slender man: *"What!?! You're completely insane, dude! You're telling me that the sneaky witch Fiona didn't play a role in Jon's untimely demise?"*

The heavyset man: *"Hey! She might have. But all evidence points directly at Bethany. You know, if turns out, Bethany is the murderer, a part of me will be somewhat glad, especially after the way she treated Mark. Talk about a heartless bitch."*

The slender man: *"What's your deal with Bethany, dude? You're not one of those Bethany haters, are you?"*

The heavyset man: *"No!"*

"Bethany?" Renata said to herself, leaning back behind the doorway. "Who the hell is Bethany?"

After a heated argument ensued, Renata soon realized the two men were talking about fictional characters on an HBO show and not real-life murderers.

The headgear was placed over the cat's head. Once it was secured, the two men turned their attention toward a computer. All she could see were wavy lines of what looked like maybe vitals on the monitor; however, Renata wasn't entirely sure as to what the lines were indicating—*brainwaves,* if that was such a thing?

As Renata leaned in even closer, she saw more people in other rooms conjoining the laboratory. The room was smaller and appeared to be an operating room. Inside were doctors wearing gloves and masks and protective gear. Renata couldn't see exactly who *or* what was lying on top of the operation table for a pale blue curtain, which covered nearly the entire length of the table, was obstructing her view. Whatever it was, it was quite a large thing that cast a large, round, and most importantly, *still* silhouette behind the curtain. One of the nurses removed a gas mask from the thing's face while the other one handed the doctor a sharp instrument—possibly a scalpel—and readjusted the surgical light above the. . . subject? The change in lighting dissolved the silhouette, making it harder to see what was going on behind the curtain. Renata wasn't sure as to what the doctor had called the strange, sleeping thing, but she swore the word "subject" was used on several occasions—or was it *specimen?*

Leaning dangerously close into the corner of the slender man's range of vision, Renata saw the massive paw of what looked like a Siberian tiger.

🕐

RENATA continued her search toward the end of the hallway where she nearly got spotted by a bundled-up team of casually dressed, multitasking dudes who were—more or less—gliding along like phantoms. If it wasn't for their pin-sharp focus on the electronic tablets in their hands, which, from second glance, appeared to be controlling their every movement, then she would've been spotted for sure. The way each one of these puppet-like dudes quickly tapped and scrolled through the greasy screens of each tablet with their *clicking* centipede-leg moving fingers appeared unnatural, machine-like. With no other alternative, she was forced to seek cover in an ominous-looking staircase.

As sudden terror started to take hold, Renata inched closer to the opening between the two flights of stairs and peeked over the railing along the landing.

There, in the deep swell of darkness, she witnessed flights of stairs traveling down at least twelve more stories—*at least.* Her heart beat faster, chest tightened. Her whole body trembled. The notion alone of being inside some kind of underground facility caused Renata's head to spin. Her breathing gradually increased. Words like *trapped* and *lost* came screeching at her, intensifying the terror.

She ignored the head noise and focused on the story—*It's all about the story!*

After she gained control over her breathing, Renata ended up walking down a flight of stairs. She stopped at the floor below, which was called "Zone D." She couldn't help but wonder what came after "D." She walked to the floor below: "Zone E." She continued to travel down the stairs, spiraling her way into darkness. She reached "Zone Z." Renata thought she reached the end of these "zones," but after she leaned over the railing and peered down into the

238

darkness, she soon realized that she wasn't even close to the bottom—there had to be *at least* ten more stories below her! She had gotten this far, so why not go a little farther.

Poised for the truth, she made her way down to the bottom of the facility.

Outside the stairwell door, a red sign read: "WARNING NO SMOKING."

When she cracked open the door and carefully stepped into a stale hallway as if the floor was covered in glass, she looked to her right, then her left. The floor appeared the exact same as the floor she had recently come from. She duly noted the elevator to the far left, which would possibly come to good use if she was to get spotted—which was strange to Renata, just thinking about it, since she hadn't been spotted once while sneaking around a facility that was littered with surveillance cameras.

About twenty paces from the stairwell door was another warning sign outside a closed door: "DO NOT DISTURB THE SLEEPERS."

Renata pulled away from the sign.

"Sleepers?"

Above the door, a red TV studio-like "recording" light was glowing.

Renata's eyes were drawn to the red light and the way it was begging to her.

She walked to the red light and right before entering the room, she came back to the sign.

Sleepers?

Carefully, she pulled on the door handle, immediately feeling resistance. She managed to barely crack open the door but not far enough to sneak inside.

Renata tried once more, this time using more muscle.

With a stronger pull, she opened the door and when she closed it behind her, the room created a suction effect, causing the door to slam shut. She thought the sound would draw attention; but like before with her presence, it went unnoticed.

More poised, she scanned the dimly lit room, which stretched into darkness. She immediately felt cold by the gunmetal gray walls, the lack of lighting, the atmosphere itself unnerving.

Most of the source of lighting came from a station—a control room of some kind—behind a pair of glass panes. A man was operating a control panel, testing levels, and whatnot. Renata witnessed those same wavy lines on a monitor in the center of the control panel. She honed in on a label directly above a row of surveillance monitors that read "The Cloud Room."

All of a sudden, a scratchy voice came on through a speaker, telling the man, the "operator," to "give us the room."

Us?

The operator gathered his things, his tablet, as well as an empty cup of coffee from his workstation, and stepped out of the control room.

Before the operator glanced up from his electronic tablet, Renata immediately took cover in the dark shadows in the corner of the room.

Once the operator left, Renata crept toward the control room. She took cover behind a wall while two strange men were talking inside another, darker room just outside the control room. She peeked over the side of the wall. What she thought was going to be a simple peek-and-duck turned out to be crippling stare. Renata's jaw fell into a gawking expression.

Before her very eyes were hundreds of bodies—the "sleepers," all positioned in midair with the front of their bodies facing upward, while their arms, their legs, as well as their torsos were being held by wires suspended above them and to Renata—at least, at first thought—the bodies appeared as if they were floating in the air. Each body was separated by a length of five feet on all sides, including the top as well as the bottom. Each column consisted of twelve bodies. Above hung an intricate pulley system, which allowed a nurse to access the body. The suspension of the bodies, Renata could only suspect, was to prevent bedsores.

Each body had what Renata believed to be a feeding tube hooked up to their abdomens like a power cord. The creamy beige-colored liquid—or *food*, Renata suspected—inside a clear thirty-gallon communal bag hanging next to the pulley system appeared as if it was being automatically controlled by a suspended device next to each body. What really caught Renata's attention were the hats with wires on their heads and how each one looked similar—if not, identical—to the strange hat that one cat from earlier was wearing.

Renata ducked back behind the wall, tried to make sense of what she had just witnessed; however, she couldn't make any sense of it. She peeked around the corner once more, followed all the wires past the feeding bag, past the pulley system, past to the dark rafters along the ceiling, until she reached a soft pinkish light radiating in the center of the room.

Renata was pulled away by a disturbance coming from one of the bodies.

Every now and then, a quiet alarm would sound, causing the upper torso of a body to automatically elevate either upward or dip downward in a seesaw motion, depending on a blood pressure regulator.

A blonde-haired nurse entered the room from another door to check on one of the sleeper's—or patient's—body. She also checked the device next to the body, punched a couple of buttons on the control pad. Then stroked the hair of a young male, telling him that he was having a "nightmare."

Once the young man's blood pressure returned to normal, his body was automatically lowered to a straight sleeping position.

The nurse left room, bringing the two men's voices back into the foreground. Renata heard a man talking vaguely about "applicable candidates"—she specifically heard the word, *quota*, several times throughout a heated conversation. She tracked down the voice to the assistant, who was talking to a rough-faced man, who appeared to be the head doctor based on a gold lab coat he was wearing—she figured the color of coats had something to do with certain rank.

"You just make sure to tell your boss that there is no turning back from this," the doctor said, handing the assistant a metal briefcase with the word **FRAGILE** written in bold red lettering on the side. *"Once she puts it on. . . she will have access to an entire generation. I hope she's ready."*

The assistant responded with a tone of defiance, *"My boss? She's your boss too—"*

"—Just be a good boy and relay the message for me. Is that so hard to ask, Merlot? If Chione has a problem, then she doesn't have to send over her errand boy. She knows where to find me—"

"—What about the couple?"

"What couple?"

"You know, the troublemakers. He's created a buzz around the office. As far as the other one, it's only a matter a time before she does something stupid."

"And why does this concern me?"

"Well, what are you going to do with him?"

"I think Roman has plans for him. Frankly, it's none of my business. Neither is it any of yours."

"Whatever you say. We all know who the real doctor around here is."

The air between the two grew tense. Neither one had anything else to say.

After a long pause, the assistant threw his head up in a resentful nod and said, "See you around. . . Doc."

The doctor waved off the assistant.

Renata's skin was drenched with a layer of sweat. Her stomach was churning by the idea that she was possibly this so-called "troublemaker" who the two were speaking of. As for whom the "him" might be, only one "him" came to mind and she had absolutely no clue as to what Roman—more than likely, Harold Roman—was going to do to "him."

As Renata slowly sunk back in her squatted position behind the wall, the doctor turned toward Renata's direction but never made any eye contact with her.

Keeping her gaze on the doctor, Renata caught a glimpse of his face and the old scars from premature acne speckled along the sides of his face like dimples on a golf ball.

The assistant left the room. Then, eventually, after a brief scan of all the bodies suspended throughout the entire room, the doctor was next to leave.

Once the room was finally clear, Renata walked over to the nearest body that was suspended in the air. She stood over the young light skinned man, whom Renata figured to be in his late teens to early twenties. What stood out the most was the contraption on his head. This particular hat, unlike the one that cat was wearing, appeared translucent and covered with even more cables. She cracked open one of his eyelids. His eye was neither fixed nor dilated. Which was a good sign. She checked the other eye and, like the one before, it was rapidly moving. Which clearly indicated activity in the brain.

Out of desperation, she tried to wake the young man; however, he was stuck in some kind of deep, *deep* sleep—REM sleep?

Renata drew her eyes away from the young man and noticed the other young men and women all around, all suspended, all asleep, all plugged up to. . .

A massive glass tank in the middle of all the bodies.

She followed the wires above, which were all connected to the top of the cylindrical glass tank, which was filled with a pink liquidy substance.

All Renata could make out was the shape inside—that's all. Even though the creature was roughly the size of a human, its shape, as well as tentacle-like arms, suggested animal, possibly in the phylum category, mollusks which included octopuses and snails. That, she knew.

She shuffled around the other bodies and as she proceeded toward the tank, a beam of yellow light cut through the darkness to the left of her.

The same nurse casually entered. Good thing for Renata the entire level was dark—except for the artificial light inside the control room, which was on the far side of these sleepers, the only source of decent light was coming from the giant nightlight that was the glass tank—otherwise, Renata would've been immediately spotted. But, no, like before, it was as if she was a ghost. Strangely enough, she managed to remain undetected.

A few rows away, one of the bodies was slightly dipping downward.

By the time the nurse tended to the sleeper, Renata joined the shadows.

PRESENT DAY

INSIDE the trunk, her body was wrapped like a burrito inside a gray comforter spotted with continent-shaped stains of dark blood. Jevon wasted no time in peeling back the upper part of the comforter, revealing Kira's pallid face. The lower part of the corpse's face was caked with blood. Her hazel eyes were still wide open, still staring *straight* at Renata, as if, even after death, Kira's spirit somehow knew exactly what her so-called "friend" had done to her.

Jevon attempted to close Kira's eyelids, as they do in the Hollywood movies, but the eyelids sprung back open like a doll's eyes. He placed the comforter back over Kira's face.

Next to Jevon, Renata suddenly started to backpedal from the trunk.

Baffled by the movement, Jevon rotated around and faced Renata, whose face was riddled with horror.

"*Renata*," Jevon said softly, "it's going to be okay." He held out both hands, as if he was using them to help calm down Renata. "Renata. . . "

Renata continued to backpedal, her head shaking back and forth.

"No, no, no," she cried. "I killed her. . . "

"Renata," Jevon pleaded, as he stepped away from the trunk, "you must understand you had no other choice. If I could swap positions with you right now, believe me, I would in a heartbeat. But—"

"—I don't think you would," Renata said grimly.

Before her eyes, Kira was removing the comforter from her body and climbing out of the back of the trunk. She shouldered directly past Jevon. As soon as Renata witnessed Jevon's reaction—or lack of reaction—the horror intensified.

Renata cried, "You—you can't see her, can you?"

Jevon turned to the open trunk.

"Of course, Renata," he said, pointing at the stained comforter inside. "I see her." Once more, he faced Renata. "Renata," Jevon said, his voice more fatherly, "we're going to get through this, okay?"

Renata backpedaled, and Jevon closed in right behind Kira.

"She's right in front of you!" Renata shouted out.

Jevon returned, "Who's right in front of me?"

Apparently, Kira hadn't bled out entirely. When Kira started to speak, it reopened the wound on her neck, causing the blood to pour out.

"Is this how you treat all your friends, Renata," she said vacantly. "I thought you were my friend—"

"—I was," Renata corrected, "I am!"

"Renata," Jevon said over Kira's voice, "you're acting strange. What's going on with you?"

Kira continued to walk toward Renata while Renata continued to backpedal. Her heel tripped over a rock stuck in the ground and caused her to fall backwards. Jevon caught up with Renata, his body passing straight through Kira's body. Kira stayed with Jevon, her motions nearly mimicking his.

As Jevon leaned over to help up Renata, so did Kira. However, Kira wasn't trying to help Renata at all. Kira's face merged with Jevon's.

As the world started to spin before Renata, one body with two faces appeared in front of her. She didn't know which one to trust; in fact, she didn't even know whether or not either one was real. The blurry faces morphed in and out of one another, Jevon's worried-looking face, then Kira's blank dead face, until the face before her was only one face, Kira's more masculine face. Renata's eyes rolled in the back of her head and her body did what only came natural.

🕐

SECONDS passed.

Renata charged through the blackness.

Her eyes bolted open.

As she sat upright along the gravel driveway, she noticed that Jevon and Kira were gone. The trunk door was still open.

Renata called out to Jevon but didn't receive any response. The firelight inside the cabin was no longer flickering. Renata remembered that the fire was still burning when she and Jevon went outside. Which made her wonder exactly how much time had passed. It felt like seconds, but perhaps it was hours.

In the corner of her eye, she found another light, a soft pinkish light pulsating deep within the woods. She decided to check it out.

🕐

ONCE Renata stepped foot into the dark woods, the environment started to change all around her. The farther she walked into the woods, the more the ground below her started to harden and turn more unnatural. She saw less trees and foliage. Similar bodies to the ones she saw at the unmarked facility—the "sleepers" in the "Cloud"—appeared as if they were part of the woods. She came across one with his head partially sticking out of the ground. Another one a part of a tree trunk. Renata arrived at a control panel, which was covered in tall weeds and dirt. She followed the same pinkish light until she eventually arrived in that same place where the sleepers were suspended in the air, the Cloud Room. All of the sleepers were gone; however, the glass tank still remained. She made her way to the tank where a gray-skinned, emaciated man with a wispy white beard floated inside. He had to be somewhere around seven feet tall in height, eight when fully straight and erect. He was rail-thin, zombie-like, cheeks hollowed, eyes sunken deep inside the sockets of his skull, skeleton exposed, including ribcage; his skin was worn extra-extra loose, hip-

243

bone and elbows showing the most flab, mainly excess skin which appeared as if it was an old suit that didn't fit anymore and was ready to be donated away.

As he lifelessly floated inside the pink liquid inside the tank, Renata pressed her hand against the surface of the glass.

The strange man's white eyes bolted open, startling Renata.

As he stirred with life, he floated down to Renata's eye level. Carefully, she studied the strange man's face, looked well past his dead milky eyes, past the airy white beard, and traced the contours of his skeletal face with her finger.

THREE WEEKS AGO

STILL slightly hungover from last night's romantic entanglement, Renata ran into the couch and nearly tripped over the coffee table in the center of the living room. The noise caused the warm body underneath the bed sheets to stir in bed and readjust sleeping positions.

Renata froze in her tracks, as if she was playing red light-green light and she was given a glaring red light. With her eyes still bloodshot from the lack of sleep, she looked over her shoulder, waiting for her to rise, to *hear* her voice, to *see* her smile. She saw none of that. Instead, that awful symphony resumed. She tried to block out the snoring by putting her mind to work. Last night, she shared a story about her father. She also told Renata the history of this cabin. Renata specifically recalled her walking to the triple dresser and standing in front of it while she told the story, and it was as if she was defensive. Renata picked it up in her body gestures, the way her tone changed, the way she stood, and how she appeared as if she was guarding the dresser.

Careful not to make anymore noise, Renata opened the top drawer.

Inside were overturned picture frames of Kira's mother and father, as well as Kira when she was a young girl: photographs of Kira doing girl-stuff around the cabin like hanging upside down on a tree branch or flying a kite or painting her father's face with her mother's makeup.

Renata opened the next drawer and came across both Japanese and American newspapers of Kira's father, who was a famous basketball player in both Japan and America, where he played four years in the NBA before he retired due to a knee injury, which had followed him throughout his professional career.

After combing through the basketball memorabilia, Renata moved to the next drawer, the third and last drawer. She found a newspaper article on Kira's father. His wife had reported him missing after he disappeared while having drinks with former teammates at a bar. According to the newspaper, the former NBA player was missing for over forty-eight hours. The people he was with that night had the same story: "*One minute, they were hanging out at the bar, catching up while having drinks. He excused himself and went to use the restroom. He never came back.*" The investigators never suspected any foul play. Eventually, the case went cold.

Renata heard the *rustling* of bed sheets behind her. She threw the article back where she found it and closed the drawer.

"Hey, Fire Crotch," Kira said childishly, her bare body leaning over the edge of the bed. "Come back to bed, will you?"

A wide smile stretched across Kira's face.

Still wrapped in her thoughts about Kira's father and his disappearance many years ago, Renata rotated around and saw half of Kira's body poking through the opening of the bedroom doorway.

From the bed, Kira begged, "I need your body heat. I'm fucking *freezing*."

PRESENT DAY

KIRA'S father placed his sticklike hand exactly where Renata had placed hers.

Both of their hands touched through the glass, the frail hand of Kira's father looking like an exaggerated Halloween ornament that was three times the size as Renata's hand. Renata stared into his ghostly eyes, the once dark irises appearing as if they were penciled-in, then erased. She knew what she had to do. She didn't know why, *but she knew*. She searched the area for a blunt object. After combing the room, Renata ended up ripping off a metal handle about the size of a softball bat from the side of the control panel. She ended up using the handle to beat away at the tank. Only after a couple of strikes in, the glass barely even cracked. During each swing, she could feel the impact of metal hitting solid glass vibrating through her entire body and causing her bones to ache. She tried once more, gave everything she had, and ended up chipping away at the glass. Several pebble-sized chunks of glass fell to the ground. Renata's bones hurt like no pain she had ever felt before. Her hands were sore and throbbing as if the blood was trying to rip through her skin. Renata picked up the handle, gripped it tightly, and once more, reared back for a swing.

A voice from the darkness: "*I wouldn't do that if I were you.*"

She abruptly paused right as she was about to unleash her unfettered wrath.

A dark, hellish-faced figure stepped forward into the pinkish glow.

"*You're going to severely* regret doing that. . . "

Renata lowered the handle by her side.

Chione appeared before her. She was dressed in the same clothes she always wore: a dark blazer customized by the notorious fashion designer Toufik 2.0 worn over a black and white striped long sleeve v-neck shirt that was so skintight that it looked painted on her skin; signature bootcut pants in modern stretch to match her blazer; black stilettos that appeared to add at least six inches to her height; a gold Rolex given to her by the syndicate commonly referred to as "The Network," the wristwatch matching gold looped earrings. The only attire missing from her sleek wardrobe was *that* mask.

"Why's that?" Renata finally asked after studying Chione.

In a nonchalant manner, Chione nodded at Kira's father.

"If that thing gets out, then everyone you have ever loved will be gone. The world that you know—or at least you thought you knew—gone."

"That thing has a name," Renata snapped. "His name is Reo Nakamura."

Chione's face slackened, the scars making her frown look wavy and warped.

"Why are you doing this?" Renata asked.

"And why exactly do people of power do what they do?" Promptly, Chione answered her own question before Renata could ponder her own: "More power, of course. *More* control. You come from a 'unique' generation—a 'guinea pig generation'—one raised by televisions, phones, devices with one purpose only, which is to distract you from reality." She stepped forward, revealing more scars on her shadowy face. She turned to the tank and touched the glass with her index finger. "The brain is no different than a computer. Once you *hack* it, the possibilities are endless." Her attention was drawn back to the tank and for a moment, she witnessed Kira inside the tank, *not* her father. She appeared to be in a similar state as her father: gray, cloudy skin, skinny, white hair, whiter eyes, could easily pass as the walking dead. "Everything you do," Chione said to Renata, "every choice you make, every thought that enters your head is controlled by us. You are a generation incapable of any individual thought. You *read* the same books. You *watch* the same movies. *Listen* to the same songs. You all *speak* the same. Even *act* the same. Most importantly, you all *think* the same."

"How's this for thinking the same?" Renata said furiously, as she held up the metal handle.

Without the slightest hesitation, she swung at the glass tank.

As soon as the handle collided with the tank, the glass exploded and all that pink slimy fluid came gushing outward.

Renata was hit by incredible force surging directly at her, causing her to fall and bang her head against the floor. The tank eventually emptied. All that pink slimy stuff pooled around Renata's soaked body.

Dazed, she looked around and tried to find her bearings. By the time she finally came to and wiped away the pink sludge from her eyes and face, it was already on top of her body. The weight alone of it pressed against her chest caused her breathing to shorten. She tried to push whatever it was from her body but she felt paralyzed.

With her senses more heightened, she looked closer. It was nearly half the size of her; however, it had no distinguishable shape. The only shape that came to my mind was the look of a heart with the valves and arteries still intact and hanging outward. The texture of its skin pressed against hers was fuzzy and moss-like, gray-brownish in color. The organs inside it buzzed in spastic-jarring beats, as if each one was working in harmony. Somewhere, underneath that tangled mess of wiry bristles before her, Renata witnessed—or at least, thought she witnessed—dozens of beady black eyes protruding outward like Braille.

Eight phallic-shaped tentacles suddenly stretched from its shelled under-belly, one of which slithered up her neck, as well as chin. The slimy tentacle sensually combed over Renata's lips and mouth. She kept her jaw clenched so tight that she thought she might've broken a tooth.

Other tentacles slithered upward, two of which plugged the two holes in her nose that were her nostrils.

Unable to breathe, Renata held on as long as she could until she couldn't hold on any longer.

Fighting for a breath, she gasped.

As soon as Renata embraced the air, the tentacle entered her mouth and slithered down her throat.

Renata resisted, at first. But after her breath was cut short, her vision turned gray and she started to drift. The last images Renata witnessed before she fell into the blackness were of Chione's "other" self, an alter ego. As her throat started to swell, images started to change in shape and character. In those last few moments before the inevitable blackout, she couldn't help but wonder if she was falling directly through the ground, as if her body and soul were somehow melting into that pink sludge pooled around her. The blazer slipped from Chione's shoulders. The gold looped earrings straightened and projected upward like antennas along the side of her head. The black stripes along the v-neck shirt peeled outward, revealing a set of spider-like legs underneath. The legs were incredibly long, too, and stretched well past her *human* legs. Chione grew taller and taller, more domineering. And that was the very last image Renata carried before a black world washed over her.

TWO DAYS AGO

RENATA woke up sweating bullets on Jevon's couch.

She was hit by a fishy stench in the air. She tracked down the putrid smell to Jevon's tortoiseshell, Freddy, and the what-smelled-like-week-old tuna fish it was eating from its *Hello Kitty* bowl on top of the dresser.

Rubbing the crust wedged between the corners of her eyes, Renata sat upright and peeked through the blinds where, outside, the sun was shining just above the treeline. The time on the nightstand read a quarter past six. Renata contemplated shutting her eyes and trying to grab a couple more hours of sleep—perhaps venture back into the recent nightmare—but she heard someone who was larger than a cat moving around in the kitchen.

Wearing a XXL Grape Rush T-shirt that Jevon loaned her to sleep in for the night, she was slow to stand from the couch. Since the bottom of the shirt extended well past her thighs, she didn't even bother slipping into any pants. Renata dragged herself around the room, first checking her cell phone, which she turned off last night. She had "1" missed call and "1" voicemail. She checked the number of the missed call and immediately recognized Kira's phone number. Renata realized that she completely forgot to call Kira back after she arrived at Jevon's. With everything that had been going on lately, coming home to a vandalized townhouse, the sketchy people following her, those "sleepers," Renata decided to give herself a pass and listen to the voicemail. In the message, she heard muffled voices talking—if it was Kira, she wasn't making any sense. The closer she listened, the more she realized that Kira had more than likely "butt dialed" her number by accident. Halfway through the message, Renata heard Kira screaming out loud. Then, other muffled voices came in and out of focus. Renata specifically heard one particular voice while Kira begged for the man to stop. She heard a rustling sound. Then, a man's voice: "What the fuck is this shit?" It was clear, as if the whole time they had been talking over an obstructed speaker. The obstruction sounded as if it had been removed—possibly from Kira's pocket. She heard Kira's voice: "I swear, I didn't know I had it on me," she said. The "it" that she was referring to was possibly her phone. The last words she heard before the phone crunched into a sharp silence were *you sneaky bitch*.

Left in a state of horror, Renata listened to the message once more, trying to make sense of what they were talking about before one of their voices— clearly, a man's voice—started talking into the phone.

After the message ended, she listened to it again.

Then, again.

All that she could take away from the message was that something had happened to Kira.

And it didn't sound good.

🕐

WITH the sound of Kira's voice etched in her mind, Renata dragged herself from the living room and made her way into a cramped kitchen where Jevon was frying a white egg for himself. She passed the guest bedroom. Stopped. Turned back around. Inside the room were Jevon's ailing mother, Aurora, and Aurora's aide, Ezra. A lift was attached to the ceiling, which was used to transport Aurora in and out of her hospital bed. Next to the bed were a wheelchair, a tray, as well as a shelf of medical supplies.

Renata stopped at the edge of the doorway and took a closer look inside.

While Ezra was stuffing a couple of pillows underneath Aurora's side to prevent Aurora from getting bedsores, she stopped what she was doing and shot Renata an unfriendly glance. Renata's silent nod of hello was accompanied by a soft wave of her hand. Ezra acknowledged her gesture with a slight dip of her head, which wasn't exactly in the ballpark of Renata's nod but, more or less, a motion indicating that she was aware of Renata's presence.

Renata, who was now aware of the "situation" Jevon always chose to deflect whenever it was brought up in a conversation, proceeded into the kitchen.

Jevon was turning the egg.

Renata acknowledged a pot of oatmeal bubbling on the stovetop. Next to the pot were containers of fresh strawberries and blueberries and other fruits laid out on the countertop. Renata felt compelled to grab herself a handful of blueberries; but, after realizing all of the strings Jevon had to pull in order for her to stay here, she remained polite.

The coffee was already made—which brought great comfort to Renata. An avocado had been gutted, the stone removed, and the oily edible flesh was laid out on a paper plate in six decorative slices. The wheat bread was in the toaster. She wasn't at all hungry—at least not hungry enough to enjoy a decent meal—but she knew she had to eat. The way the day was destined to go, Renata knew that she needed her strength.

"Sorry if I woke you," he said, sensing Renata's presence. "Surely, I thought you'd sleep in."

"Well," Renata said and while yawning, "I'm up now." Then, from the corner of her mouth, "All thanks to you."

Renata tried to rid the thought of Kira from her mind, Kira possibly hurt or in danger, but she couldn't shake the violent images.

248

Jevon grinned and said over his shoulder, "Looks like someone woke up on the wrong side of the couch."

"Don't start with me," Renata responded, more grumpily. "So," Renata said sheepishly as she turned toward Aurora's bedroom, "are you sure I'm not getting in the way—"

Jevon waved off Renata before she finished her question. "I'm not going to tell you again, Renata. It's no big deal; in fact, I'm pretty sure my mother enjoys the company."

Renata leaned in closer, as the two slices of toast popped from the toaster.

"Can she talk?" whispered Renata.

"Not yet," Jevon said, surprisingly casual. "But she has a therapist who sees her twice a week. I think she's making progress."

"That's good."

Jevon removed the hot white egg from the pan. He placed the egg, the slices of avocado, and toast on a paper plate in an orderly fashion, and carried it to the table where he placed it next to a glass of orange juice.

"Here," Jevon said and pointed at the plate of food. "Eat some breakfast."

"Thanks," Renata said and sat down.

"You're very welcome," Jevon replied and walked back to the stove. Before he could reach the stove, he was drawn to a news report on TV. He pointed at the TV perched on the end of the countertop, as if he was redirecting a frustration that he had been holding onto all morning—the fallout from his own "Serenity Now" moment. "You see this bullshit? I swear, it's becoming an epidemic and nobody seems to give a rat's fuck about it—"

His rant was put to a sudden halt as soon as he saw Ezra entering the kitchen. He immediately apologized for his language. Business-like, Ezra ignored Jevon's usage of words to describe the "homeless problem" in the city and fixed a bowl of oatmeal for Aurora.

"Thank you, Ezra," Jevon said, as Ezra placed the bowl of oatmeal, as well as the berries on a tray and carried it to Aurora's bedroom.

Jevon walked back to the table, his attention focused on both the TV and Renata. "You know, perhaps that should be our next story—expose these corrupted doctors who are getting their patients hooked on snake's milk."

"Snake's milk?"

"Have you been living under a rock for the past year?"

From the redness in Jevon's face, it was apparent that he wanted to take back the words as soon as they left his mouth.

Turned off by Jevon's comment, Renata responded with a harsh tone laced in her voice, "*Really?*"

"Sorry," he said regretfully. "That was out of line. It just. . ."

Renata felt compelled to argue with Jevon, to tell him about this "rock" that was she had been living under for the past year and it was called "Carla and Corvine;" however, for one, it was too early to fight; and two, she had nowhere else to stay.

"It just pisses me off," Jevon said, as Renata redirected her attention toward the news reporter who was standing outside Tent Square, a Mecca for the homeless, in Lower Manhattan. "Seeing all of these god. . ." he trailed off, as if he was still mindful of Ezra's presence, ". . . damn drug companies profit off people, as if they've been reduced to nothing more than dollar signs, pawns exploited by politicians, sound bites, 'hot takes' for headlines, expendable— 'x'd out, huh?" Jevon pointed at Renata with a partial grin on his face, as if the groundwork of this so-called "new story" was already in development inside his head. "It's not a complicated issue. The doctors over-prescribe drugs to patients, get patients addicted, then the insurance companies cut them off, forcing patients on the streets to buy harder, cheaper drugs, like snake's milk. I mean, we're talking about a drug that can destroy a person's life. The damage is irreparable. If you want proof, all you have to do is walk down North Morrison Street. *They're* everywhere."

"What makes 'snake's milk' so different than crack or heroin or any of these other drugs on the streets?" asked Renata.

"What makes it so different?" he repeated. "Nobody knows where in the hell it came from."

"But surely somebody knows," Renata stuttered. "Nobody?"

"Nobody knows," Jevon said.

"Have researchers run tests?"

Jevon bobbed his head.

"Tried."

"And?"

"They don't know," he said.

"They don't know?"

"Crazy, huh?"

"Yeah," Renata mumbled. "Crazy."

The news cut to a commercial break.

Renata couldn't help but draw her attention toward the commercial.

"*Sometimes athlete's foot can leave you on itchy ground.*" In the TV commercial, a soccer player kicked off his cleats and started scratching his feet moments before the game-winning penalty shot. "*Help fight the itch by asking your health care provider about Damianix. Damianix treats those suffering from athlete's foot. Damianix should not be used. . . *" Renata drifted in a trance from the soothing sound of the voice-over actor's voice, "*. . . Call your doctor about fever. This may be a sign of a life-threatening reaction. Side effects may include. . . *"

Heated by the latest news report, Jevon turned off the TV.

The silence in the kitchen forced Renata inward where violent images of Kira filled her mind.

As Jevon was about to walk to the stove, he noticed Renata's paranoid state. Clearly, food was the last thing on her mind. She was looking around the kitchen, as if she was being watched from a window or a closet.

Jevon reassured her, "You're safe here."

Renata faced Jevon and forced a smile on her face.

🕐

WHILE Jevon was washing the dishes, Renata turned on the shower faucet inside the hallway bathroom and snuck into Jevon's bedroom. Thinking about the best place where he would put it, she snooped around his room. She checked the most obvious place first, which was the nightstand. She had no luck. Next, she looked under the bed and checked under the mattress and pillows. She moved her search to the closet where she found a suspicious-looking box on the top shelf. What she thought might've been it was only a box of cigars with a note attached inside from Barron, who was the senior editor at *X'D*. Lastly, Renata checked the dresser and went through each drawer, including his sock and underwear drawer. Not a damn thing. As Renata pulled her eyes from the dresser, she found a picture frame of a young man on the top of the dresser. She looked over the photo of the man inside and thought about whether or not Jevon had any brothers or cousins. If Jevon did, he never mentioned it to her. She picked up the frame, held it closer to her face, and took a closer look at the young man. She shielded the top of his face with her hand, searching for Jevon's mouth or jaw. Then, did the same with the bottom of his face and searched for Jevon's eyes or nose. She couldn't find any features on his face that resembled Jevon, except for maybe his brow; however, he could've been related to him outside of blood. Renata flipped over the picture frame and opened the back. A key fell out onto Renata's hand. Key found. *Check*. Now all she had to do was find where he was hiding it.

As soon as Renata closed the picture frame and placed it back on the dresser, Jevon was standing at the doorway.

"I thought you were taking a shower," he said, leaning against the doorway.

"I was," Renata stuttered, "I mean, I am. I'm waiting for the water to warm." She immediately changed the subject and nodded at the photo of the young man, who clearly wasn't Jevon. She asked, "Who's the guy?"

"He's nobody," Jevon said flatly.

"Nobody? He has to be somebody; otherwise, what is he doing in your bedroom?"

"Don't you have somewhere to be soon?" Jevon asked, the boss in him coming out in his voice.

"Yeah, *Dad*," Renata said sarcastically.

"I don't mean to—"

"—I know," she said swiftly "I shouldn't have been snooping around."

Jevon turned around and pointed toward the bathroom, which was filling with thick steam.

"Think the water is warm," he said.

"Right," Renata said flippantly. "Thanks."

"Listen. . . Renata. . . " Jevon said through the unexpected tension before Renata could make any sort of move toward the shower, "I'm going to step out for a minute while you take your shower."

"Where you going?" she asked.

"I just have to pick up a few things at the Lion's Den," Jevon said. "I should be back before you head to work." He pulled out a cell phone from his pocket. "Got you a new phone." He stepped into the room and handed the phone to Renata. "I programmed my number in there, like the other one."

"So, this one has a tracking device on it as well?"

"Renata," Jevon sighed, "you know, I can't take any chances, right?"

Renata sighed as well, as if she was mocking Jevon.

"Right."

"Trust me," Jevon said, trying to relief the tension in the air, "I can't tell you how much I miss my old phone. I'm now realizing how much it spoiled me. But it's the sacrifice we have to make, right?"

"What are you going to do with the other phone?"

"I already destroyed it."

"You know I could've done that," Renata said, letting out more emotion than she intended to let out. She retracted the anger before it took hold. "I mean," she said, trying to tone back the anger, "you know, I destroy them every time you get me a new one."

"I know you do," Jevon replied sharply with a strange look on his face. "*But* I thought you were taking a shower. So, I did it for you. So, you're welcome."

"Okay, well," she held up the phone, "thanks anyway."

Jevon left the room.

"I'll be back soon," he said, walking away.

🕐

ONCE Jevon drove away, Renata basically had the whole place to herself. Considering Aurora's aide, Ezra, spent most of the morning taking care of Aurora's in the bedroom opposite Jevon's office, Renata decided to skip a shower and went straight to Jevon's office.

Mounted on the walls in sturdy black frames were the front covers of nearly every issue of *X'D*. There was very little space on the walls for other issues—and those, which couldn't fit on the wall, Jevon had tucked away in a far corner of the closet where they were collecting dust. Renata wandered through the office, looking over each magazine cover as if she was touring an art gallery. She wound up at the poster-sized cover of the once-cultural icon turned shamed actor, Vincent Brentano, who was ousted from Hollywood after he was accused of raping a nineteen-year-old actress, Marina Coyle. Whenever Jevon needed to rally the troops at the Lion's Den, he often talked about the importance of this particular issue, not because it happened to be the very first issue ever published, but because it helped launch an external investigation that ended up clearing Vincent Brentano's name many years later. Despite being acquitted, Brentano's reputation was ruined, reduced to false tabloids and parody TV cameos, and left many people with doubts about whether or not he committed the crime. Brentano was unable to find decent acting jobs—hence the cameos—whereas the young, up and coming actress, Marina Coyle, was featured in two summer blockbusters during the time of the accusations. One of the blockbusters happened to set a box office record for the highest grossed movie in opening weekend; however, two years later, Coyle got involved in drugs and alcohol; her career fizzled out like a popped balloon; and by the time Coyle's twenty-third birthday arrived, she was doing low budget amateur porn and barely scraping by. As for Vincent Brentano, who, by then, had turned into a blacklisted actor, he ended up doing Indie films for about four years until he hung up his acting hat. Sixteen years after Brentano's career tanked itself into a coma, Jevon approached him about making a comeback. After some convincing, Brentano sat down for an "Exclusive Interview" that appeared in the first issue of the controversial magazine, *X'D*. Throughout all of these years, Brentano maintained his innocence and denied the charges filed against him. After the magazine was released, just a few months later Vincent Brentano's career took off again, landing him lead roles in three Oscar-nominated movies—he even received a nod in the Best Supporting Actor category for his tour-de-force performance as a struggling hit man turned drug addict in the film, *Home Free*.

With the key in hand, Renata stepped closer to the first issue of *X'D* hanging on the wall. In a way, the poster was begging for attention, as if it had a huge sign on the front that said, "Pull here."

And Renata did exactly that. She pulled back the poster and on the wall behind the poster was a lockbox. She opened the box with the key. It worked. Inside were stacks of cash—at least six-figures inside—and a Glock 19.

She grabbed the pistol from the lockbox, left the cash. She closed the lockbox, placed the poster back in its rightful position on the wall, and midway toward the door, she paused. For a moment, she contemplated turning around and taking the cash, just enough to get by until the story she was working on ran itself into a dead end. In that moment, she felt free. If only for a moment.

🕐

RENATA spent the whole subway ride thinking about the voicemail on her phone.

Once she arrived at her stop, she sat frozen in her seat. Her workbag, which held Jevon's Glock 19, was gripped tightly in her lap. Other passengers walked past her. A voice on the intercom pulled her from a trance. She came back to reality; and as soon as the doors started to close, she darted off the train. She caught her arm in the two doors but ended up yanking it out just as the train took off.

She walked up the stairs leading to the street. The whole time, she felt as if she was being followed. She looked over her shoulder to see if anyone was following her. When she turned back around, she was hit by the sudden force of another pedestrian. Both Renata's shoulder and the pedestrian's shoulder collided in harmony, forcing them to drop their belongings. Renata couldn't be sorry enough for the accidental bump. The pedestrian, who wasn't displaying the least amount of emotion—and if she was, Renata couldn't see it for her face was hiding behind a dark hoody—kneeled down and with her gloved hand, picked up a Zippo lighter that she had dropped on the sidewalk, while Renata grabbed her workbag, as well as the data research papers that had flown from it. Renata couldn't help but notice the Zippo in the pedestrian's hand and the blue cartoon-like dragon sticker, which was partially peeled away on the side of the lighter.

As the strange pedestrian scurried away as if she had just committed a crime or something, Renata felt a sudden pain in her forearm. She looked down, examined her arm, and saw a tiny red dot just below her elbow. She couldn't help but wonder if she was stabbed by a sharp object on the pedestrian's hoody—perhaps a sharp zipper?

253

Renata stood to her feet and was struck by a sudden dizzy spell. She stopped walking for a moment, grabbed her forehead, and tried to catch her balance while distracted phone addicts shouldered past her in a hasty, rude rat-race manner, texting, MindChanting, Twerkstreaming, or whatever was more important than paying any attention to their surroundings.

Eventually, after the crowds thinned out on the sidewalk, Renata managed to find her bearings. The dizzy spell eased a bit, enough for Renata to make it work without falling over; however, she could still feel it lingering.

THE first clue that something wasn't quite right with Renata all began when she was forced into small talk with Arnold, the friendly security guard who worked on the first floor of the Carla and Corvine building. As she did every morning while passing through the lobby, she went through a series of responses, right on command, as if she was sending quick emails using words from a stockpile of expressions. A thought popped in Arnold's head. Everything about Arnold appeared as if it popped, his eyes, mouth, index finger that erected upward in cartoon fashion. Before Renata could ease her way to the elevators, Arnold pulled out a folded up piece of paper from his pocket.

"What's this?" Renata asked but already had an idea of what it was.

Arnold walked over to Renata. He handed the piece of paper to Renata. She looked down and was slow—in fact, scared—to grab the paper from not Arnold's hand but something else's hand. The color of his skin was sandy brown. The texture, rough and partly covered in scales, like the wrinkly skin along the neck of a hundred year old tortoise. Renata recoiled from the sight of the strange hand.

In a state of shock, she drew her wide eyes up at Arnold, whose facial expression changed slightly.

"It's a recipe for the pineapple upside down cake," he said.

Once more, Renata glanced down. Arnold's hand changed and appeared like any normal hand of a sixty-year-old man.

Arnold extended his head downward toward Renata's falling eyes.

"Remember you asked about it the other day?"

"Yes," Renata said suddenly. "Right. Of course."

She grabbed the piece of paper from Arnold's hand.

"And just remember to butter the inside of the pan before you pour in the batter, otherwise—"

"I know," Renata interrupted, "the cake will stick. Got it."

Arnold smiled and waved goodbye to Renata.

"I don't need to tell you."

"Thanks, Arnold," Renata said, turning toward the elevators.

"You're welcome, Renata. Enjoy your day."

Arnold placed his thumbs around his belt along his hips and watched Renata walk away.

RENATA was printing off the latest trends, in particular one trend which happened to be certain types of dances from one of the most popular video games in the market, *Camp Kill*, which was a long awaited sequel to game developers Finger Warrior's debut smash hit, BΔSEHEΔD, an online video game which offered players an opportunity to play a campaign or a free-to-play *Battle Royale*. All the sales data suggested that players weren't actually buying the game. Instead, they were playing the free *Battle Royale*. However, Finger Warriors made most of the revenue from the in-game loot. Each day, new skins and emotes were available to purchase with game loot—or BΔSEHEΔD coins. Also, the more points you earned the more loot. It was like playing a slot machine. Similar to BΔSEHEΔD, *Camp Kill* was a free online game where players spent money on various loot inside the game. According to recent studies that Renata had found while scouring the Underworld, *Camp Kill* was one of the leading causes of a spike in divorces between the ages of 25 and 50. The popular game also reached children ages 12 through 18 and was said to play a pivotal factor in a sudden surge in high school dropouts. Kids were basically making a living off subscriptions or "views" from their own YouTube channels.

After Renata handed off the latest "dance" trends to LeBron, she walked back to the printer where she left her coffee. She saw that the coffee was gone, only a brown ring where her coffee cup once sat on top of the scanner. She thought that maybe one of the interns tossed the coffee. She looked around, first to the right and then the left toward the other offices. As Renata rotated around, she saw Kira standing only a couple of feet from her. The sight of Kira startled her.

"Kira? Hey."

"Hey," Kira said expressionlessly.

"What are you doing?"

"I'm working," she said, her face still blank and emotionless. "What does it look like I'm doing?"

"Sorry." She hesitated. "I didn't mean it like that."

"What did you mean?"

Even though some kind of anger or frustration would come out from such a comment, Kira said it robotically, as if she was somehow heavily medicated.

"I mean," Renata stuttered, "you know, the message."

"What message?"

"You left a message on my voicemail last night. Don't you remember?"

"No."

"Quit yanking my chain," Renata said loosely, tapping Kira on the shoulder. "You know what I mean?"

Kira looked down at her shoulder, her face still blank.

"Yanking your chain?" Kira repeated. "What chain?"

"You know," Renata said, using laughter to lessen the innocent remark, "it's an *expression*." Trying to hide her concern with a smile, she looked over Kira for any injuries or marks on her body. "You honestly don't remember? That's strange. Maybe someone got a hold of your phone."

"Maybe."

Over the one-way conversation, Renata finally asked the inevitable question, "Are you ok—"

"—Now that I think about it," Kira said before Renata could finish asking the question, "it might've been my cousin."

"I didn't know you had a cousin."

"Dovydas Mazeika," Kira said. "David, for short. He's not my actual cousin. Kin adopted David from Lithuania when he was just a baby. You know how kids can be when they get a hold of a phone."

"Sure," Renata said, more relieved as the conversation started to loosen up a bit. "So, how old is Dovydas—David?"

"He's fourteen. He's actually in town performing at Merkin Hall. The show starts tonight at eight-thirty."

"Merkin Hall? Really?"

"He's sort of a boy wonder, the next prodigy—so they say."

"Sounds like it," Renata said, then asked: "Curious, what instrument?"

"The cello."

LeBron called out Renata's name from outside the printer room. Renata turned toward LeBron and acknowledged his interest in the recent report she had given to him.

"*Listen, Kira. . .* " Renata said, as she turned back around to face Kira.

She had only taken her eyes off Kira for no more than three seconds. Baffled by Kira's disappearance, she looked around the office but couldn't find her anywhere.

WITH the recent conversation with Kira on her mind, Renata excused herself from the meeting with the marketing team and located the nearest computer inside an unoccupied office where she googled the schedule for Merkin Concert Hall. She read through all of the names in the ensemble. She came across the name *Dovydas Mazeika* among the musicians performing tonight at "eight-thirty."

Still not entirely convinced, she decided to type in Dovydas Mazeika's name in the search browser.

While scrolling through a gallery of images—some of which shared no relation to Dovydas Mazeika—Renata scrolled past one particular image that immediately caught her eye: a photo of Kira's uncle, Kin, posing with young Dovydas in front of yaki. Kin's arm was wrapped around Dovydas's shoulder, not at all in any kind of fatherly or guardian-like way but more so like a fan wanting to take a photo with someone whom he admired. They were both smiling and throwing up the two-finger peace sign for the camera. She could tell the photo was taken during the late afternoon due to the setting of the sun and a glare on the sides of both their faces; however, one detail grabbed Renata: the cameraman—or cameramen. In the reflection of the glass doors outside the restaurant, a forty-something year old, blonde haired man, who looked as if he could've passed for Dovydas's father—real one, that is—was holding the camera. Next to him stood a dirty blonde haired woman of the similar age

256

who could've passed as Dovydas's mother. She, too, had a camera in her hand.

Renata read the date the photo was posted on Kin's Instagram page. It was taken last year.

Out of curiosity, she clicked on a link that sent her to Kin's Instagram page. She scrolled through hundreds and hundreds of his personal photographs, most of them taken with other well-known celebrities at his restaurant, fashion designers, authors, movie stars, sharks, artists, musicians, Broadway actors, none of Dovydas, except for the one he posted roughly "one year ago."

Renata pulled her eyes from the computer screen. More confused, she looked around the office, only to find Kira, of all people, standing at the front of a conference room at the other end of the office. She was staring at Renata. As soon as Renata's eyes crossed Kira's, Kira turned away and proceeded with her meeting.

Defeated, she dropped her head in thought, wondering as to why Kira, a person whom she once considered as a good friend—even "one time," much more than a friend—would make up lies about her uncle. In her defeated state, she noticed that strange red dot on her forearm and the red cloudy skin around it, as if a large zit was forming underneath it. She gently ran her finger across the red spot on her arm. The area was incredibly tender to touch and felt the same way a day-old bruise would feel. The hot flash of pain on her arm radiated through her body, causing her to flush with sickness. She was hit by yet another one of those dizzy spells. The insides of her mouth started to moisten, as if it was preparing itself for what was soon going to come. Her stomach lurched forward. A bubble of nausea hit her once, then, in an attempt to fight back the urge to vomit, hit her yet again.

With her face all pale and sweaty, Renata rushed to the bathroom where she sought out the last stall. She quickly shut the door behind her and right when she was about to explode, she fell toward the toilet. The vomit splashed on the side of the rim and bowl. Some even hit the floor. Whenever she felt as if she was about to stop and stand up, Renata was forced back to the toilet where she continued to vomit. She ended up dry heaving until she had nothing left in her stomach. For a moment, her eyes rolled in the back of her head. Her surroundings turned gray. The world, spinning. All of that straining caused Renata to temporarily blackout.

After she pushed through consciousness, she found herself pressed up against the side of the wall. The side of her head was throbbing from where she possibly hit her head during the blackout.

Feeling less dizzy, she wiped her mouth cleaned, flushed the toilet, and while grabbing the forming knot on her forehead, stepped out of the stall. The life was drained from her face and body.

Renata ambled toward the vanity where she inspected the red mark on her head. The knot was raised. Which was a good sign. She continued to primp her hair and readjust her clothing. Renata blew her nose into a paper towel and when she pulled the towel away from her face, a Rorschach test of phlegm was revealed inside. She tossed the damp towel in the trash, leaned over the sink, and used her hand as a cup to take a few bird-like sips of water from the faucet. She pulled her face from the sink below and looked into the mirror before her.

Standing motionlessly in the open stall behind her was Chione.

Renata's heart skipped a bit from the sight of Chione's grim presence. In that moment, Renata was no longer exhausted or sick. Instead, she was fully aware—woke. Poised, she kept her keen eyes on Chione, who, in return, stretched open her mouth in a yawning gape, revealing *not* the normal tongue of a human but a set of dark legs that were curled up like two tightly clenched fists. Hairy spider-like legs slowly uncurled and stretched out the sides of her mouth.

Frightened by Chione, Renata suddenly rotated around, only to find an empty space inside the stall. Renata ran through a series of thoughts, all of which were guided by the idea of hallucinations. Clearly, she didn't feel like herself. And her only rush to judgment was that she had eaten something tainted.

She pushed aside the thoughts and crept toward the stall. Halfway toward the stall, she heard strange noises coming from inside the stall. A *winding* noise followed by a strange *clicking* noise. As she stood at the edge of the stall, contemplating whether or not to further investigate the noise, the bathroom door opened, giving way to a glaring white light.

Sensitive to the bright light, Renata was hit by yet another dizzy spell!

She blinked and squinted, hoping to see more clearly through the light. Her eyes felt no different than they did when staring at the sun. An alien-like figure manifested from the light and its body became fuller as it approached. The bathroom door shut, dampening the brightness in the bathroom doorway. Renata blinked and focused until those red blotches in the corners of her eyes were gone from view. She witnessed a petite woman entering the bathroom. She thought it might have been Kathleen from Human Resources; however, she didn't give off a vibe that she was any kind of threat.

🕐

DEEPLY disturbed by her current condition, Renata left the Carla and Corvine building without telling anyone where she was going.

As she stepped onto the sidewalk outside, she felt the same sense that she was being followed. Renata couldn't explain how or why, but she could, more or less, sense it in her bones. She decided to hail a taxi.

The taxi pulled up beside her. She hopped into the taxi, placed her workbag on the seat, and told the taxi driver to take her to "Madison Square Park."

As the taxi driver drove away, Renata texted Jevon on her flip phone.

Meet me at Madison Square Park ASAP.

Only a few seconds later, her phone rang. She looked down at the number on her phone. Jevon was calling her. She didn't answer the phone. Instead, she texted him back.

Can't talk.

Jevon responded: K.

The return text threw Renata for a loop. Ever since she had known Jevon—which was going on for a year now and certainly long enough to understand his usage in words and stock responses—Renata had never read *or* even heard, for that matter, her boss answer with such an abbreviated response.

As Renata put aside her cell phone, she couldn't help but notice the turn that the taxi driver had missed; in fact, the taxi driver was driving in the opposite direction of Madison Avenue. Dread crept into Renata's thoughts—*stranger danger!* Renata realized he was taking her to Lincoln Tunnel. She looked at the taxi driver in the rear view mirror. In that narrow strip of mirror, the driver didn't appear at all to be the same scruffy-looking Middle Eastern man who picked her up; in fact, he didn't appear to be a man at all. His skin was smooth and glossy like hard candy. Along the sides of his protruding insect-like mouth were two fuzzy-looking palps that one would normally find on an arthropod. Two antennas hung from his navy blue Yankees ball cap and stretched down the sides of his face. His eyes appeared yellowish, almost translucent in nature.

Renata remembered the gun in her bag.

As she took her eyes off the taxi driver for a moment to grab the Glock from her bag, the taxi driver changed appearance. He looked just like he did when he picked up Renata. *But* Renata wasn't fooled.

"You're going the wrong direction," Renata said to the taxi driver.

While occasionally glancing at Renata through the rear view mirror, the taxi driver said casually to Renata, "She just wants to talk with you, that's all."

"Please stop the car."

"I'm afraid I can't do—"

Before the taxi driver could finish his sentence, Renata already had the barrel of the gun pressed firmly against the side of his hairy neck.

"Stop the fucking car," she demanded.

The taxi was slow to stop, but eventually, he eased off the side of the road as other cars came screaming by.

With her eyes not leaving the taxi driver, Renata blindly reached for the door handle. She found it. Tugged on it. The door was locked.

"Open the door. *Now!*"

The taxi driver unlocked the doors from his end.

Renata opened the door.

The traffic ambience was clearer; however, Renata made sure to keep the gun pointed at the taxi driver.

With the gun drawn, Renata grabbed her bag and carefully stepped out of the taxi.

Before Renata stepped onto the sidewalk, the taxi driver said from inside the taxi, "There's nowhere to run, Renata. We have eyes everywhere."

Renata digested the comment, didn't put too much stock in it, then took off.

🕐

PERIODICALLY looking over her shoulder, Renata walked briskly through Koreatown. Somehow, the taxi driver's words had stayed with her throughout her walk. Her paranoia was heightened. She checked her six o'clock once more

259

and spotted a sketchy-looking man closing in on her. She had no other choice than try to lose him. She ended up seeking cover inside a restaurant called Noodle Shop, which was located under the second floor of a sleazy video store that sold amateur oriental sex tapes and DVDs. Renata looked as if she was wearing a huge red hat and a Tee shirt with a "Kick Me" sign on the back of it. The guests inside—mostly Korean—moved their eyes from the steaming bowls of noodles and stared at Renata with blank expressions.

Trying to act as normal as she could, Renata proceeded toward the very back of the restaurant, occasionally nodding *hello* to the other guests who were sitting inside the booths that lined both sides of the restaurant.

Renata glanced down at one of the guests' bowls on the table covered in a red and white checked plastic tablecloth. Inside the bowl were cellophane noodles—or "glass noodles," which were known for their translucent grayish color. At first glance, she thought the noodles were moving around inside the bowl. But, after a second glance, the noodles appeared like noodles. She passed another table, saw yet another bowl with noodles. This time, she watched the noodles moving inside the bowl like live worms. Another guest slurped up the worms inside his mouth, the ends of the worms squirming around on the corners of his chin. Her stomach lurched heavily. Her skin perspired with layers of sweat. That dizzying sensation was back. Her world started to spin. Passing each guest, watching each wiggle of the worm, listening to each and every *slurp* and exaggerated *gulp*, Renata quickened her pace. She stormed into the kitchen where mean-faced cooks hollered at her in a foreign language. The words were slowed down. Even after she charged toward the back door with cooks dumbly shouting out behind her, the world itself felt as if it had slowed down. She knew the only way to combat this slowing effect was to do what only came natural: run. And that, she did.

Before she could find the exit, her foot slipped, causing her to stumble into a shelf of pots and pans.

Infuriated by Renata's presence, one of the cooks suddenly came at her with a bird's beak knife. Renata brandished her gun, but the cook stabbed Renata right in the gut before she could open fire.

Clutching her stomach in great agony, Renata managed to shoulder her way outside. With the cook right on her tail, she grabbed a stack of cardboard boxes and pushed them against the back of the exit door. The boxes avalanched onto the ground, preventing the cook from exiting. Through the narrow crack of the door, the cook reached out to grab Renata by the hair, his hand like a pincer snapping back and forth.

Renata managed to escape. *But the gun*—the gun was gone!

She must've dropped it during the attack.

With her eyes honing in on a red STOP sign on the corner of the street ahead of her, Renata ran through the alleyway behind Noodle Shop. She pulled out her cell phone, gripping it tightly in case she needed to call Jevon. Only a few strides in her daring escape, the "slowing" dramatically worsened. She was sprinting in slow motion.

All of a sudden, her legs grew stiff and heavy. Even the pavement below her started to thicken, as if it was made of quicksand. Each stride became harder for Renata. Each motion, each movement, more rigid. Right then and there, Renata found herself sinking into the soft pavement. Her feet were first to go under, then her shins, knees next.

Once the pavement reached her waist, she held out her hand, flagging out the pedestrian crossing the alleyway. The man ignored her.

Another one came by.

With every fiber of her being, Renata called out for help but received no response.

More came walking by.

All ignored.

The pavement was now up to her chest, crushing each word she could muster. Nobody—not one—was paying any attention to Renata.

Each pedestrian, each phone addict, were too distracted by their phones held in their hands below; their heads were frozen in downward positions, the glow of the phones casting a pale light over each one of their faces.

The cell phone slipped from her sweaty hand and came crashing down on the hard pavement.

She continued to sink farther into the ground below until she was eventually swallowed whole.

PRESENT DAY

FRANTICALLY swinging out her arms, Renata searched through the blackness until she found a glimmer of light. She swam toward the light, but the light kept pulling away from her. She reached and reached and reached, the edges of her fingers clawing at the light. Out of desperation, she surged forward and managed to wrap her hands around the light. She embraced the light, as if it was her own.

Gasping for air, her eyes bolted open.

The cold, damp washcloth, which once rested on her forehead, slid down the side of her face.

Jevon, who was sitting at Renata's feet on the couch, grabbed a glass of water next to the bloody blouse on the coffee table, and rushed to her side. She finally settled and in that moment of peace, she was struck by a coughing spell.

Mindful not to spill any water, Jevon handed her the glass of water. With his help, he nursed the water into Renata's mouth.

"I got it," she said, taking hold of the glass on her own. "Thanks."

"You scared me for a moment," said Jevon, as he felt Renata's forehead with the backside of his hand.

The cough finally subsided, which presented yet another issue: her arm. She tried to scratch at the infection on her forearm. Jevon grabbed Renata's wrist during mid-scratch and specifically told Renata to stop scratching.

"It itches," Renata said and looked around and found herself back in the living room of the cabin. The fire in the fireplace was still burning. The mood was less tense. She directed her attention back to Jevon, who told her, "I think maybe your arm is infected. You remember how you got it?"

Renata thought back as far as the last few moments, in particular, Kira rising from the dead.

Jevon stood from the couch.

261

"I'll look for some Neosporin," he said.

Renata asked Jevon, "What happened?"

Jevon walked back to the couch and stood over Renata.

"You had a panic attack," he said, grabbing the glass from Renata's hand. "If I didn't catch you before you passed out, you probably would've been more worse for wear."

"My hero," she said with a trace of sarcasm and sat upright against the arm of the couch.

"You know, Rennie, this is now twice I've come to your rescue. I tell you," Jevon said undoubtedly, "it's not getting easier."

"Thanks again," she said, more quietly. "I just. . . I don't know what in the hell's going on with me. I feel like I'm losing, you know?"

"You're in shock, Rennie," Jevon said, sitting back down on the couch. "After everything you've just been through, who wouldn't be?"

Renata looked twice at Jevon. The second time, she witnessed the softness in his face. She smiled, but, eventually, after Jevon spoke her name in a darker manner, her face melted into a look of deep concern. He had something on his chest, she realized, something *heavy*, something that he was hiding from her.

As soon as he was about to clear the air, two headlights flashed over the living room walls. Jevon stood, first, then Renata, who followed close behind to the living room window. A car was parked at the end of the driveway, its headlights still blazing. They both stood at opposite sides of the window.

More concerned, Renata asked, "What's really going on, Jevon?"

With a shameful look on his face, Jevon turned to Renata.

"I'm sorry," he said. "It's part of the deal."

"*Deal?*" Renata parroted. "What deal?"

"The other day, after I found you unconscious in that alleyway, they came to my place," Jevon said. "I thought it might have been Mom's physical therapist. I went to answer the door and there they were."

"Where was I?" asked Renata.

"You were resting in my bedroom when they arrived." Jevon shook his head in utter disgust, as if the disgust was directed toward himself. "I didn't even have a chance to react. They were already on top of me. I had no other choice. I cut a deal with them." Jevon stepped closer to Renata. "You must understand, Renata. If I didn't do exactly what they told me to do, they were going to destroy everything—*everything*—including the ones closest to me."

Jevon looked into Renata's eyes and held his eyes on her.

"What did you do?" asked Renata.

"They gave me no other choice," he said shortly. "They bought me."

"Bought you? This isn't about money, Jevon. It never was—"

"—Not money. *My* life." He turned to Renata. "*Your* life. Face it, Renata. They own us now. They've been following us ever since we started tightening up our investigation into Carla and Corvine. We swung for the fences. Came close. *Really close*. But, in the end, we struck out—"

"—We can still expose them for *what* they are. We have the evidence linking them to *multiple* crimes, enough to put them away for good."

That awful look was back on Jevon's face, and he wore it as if it was a mask that weighed twice the weight of his head.

"Jevon," Renata seethed, "we still have the evidence, don't we?"

Jevon raised his head and peered into Renata's eyes as if, for a moment, he'd actually cause her bodily harm in order to protect her.

"Did you not just hear me, Renata?" Jevon asked, his voice louder. "They'll kill us! End of story!"

"So, that's it, huh? We're giving up that easily? The story's over and we're just going to sit back and watch while they fuck the human race into extinction?"

The headlights flashed twice, as if they were blinking at them.

"We can't stay here," Jevon said, as he acknowledged the signal in the corner of his eye. "We have to leave."

Renata didn't budge an inch.

"Come on. Time to leave."

"And go where?"

With clarity, Jevon said, *Home.*

🕐

RENATA left the car keys inside the cup holder of the center console, just as Jevon was told, and got into Jevon's car. Jevon started the ignition and as soon as Renata closed the passenger door behind her, he made sure to lock the doors—even secretly flipped on the child's safety lock without Renata paying any mind. She was too busy checking the contents of the glove compartment. After a quick survey, she saw that, except for several owner's manuals and receipts, it was nearly empty. In a cautious glance, Jevon acknowledged Renata's strange behavior.

With one eye on the driveway and the other one on Renata, he drove toward the mysterious car.

"So who the hell is this guy?" Renata asked, as they approached the car idling at the end of the driveway.

Jevon blew out a heavy sigh, as if the thought alone of "this guy" caused him great stress.

EXT. ALLEYWAY, DOWNTOWN DALLAS - NIGHT

Athanor steps out of the stolen police cruiser, grabs the can of gasoline from the trunk with his gloved hand, and douses the police cruiser -- inside and out -- with gasoline.

JEVON (V.O.)
His name is Athanor Dowe.

Athanor leaves himself a sloppy trail of gasoline along the pavement and strikes a match on the side of the building. He drops a flaming match onto the ground, igniting the trail of gasoline.

Jevon took his eyes off the gravel road for a moment and turned to Renata, who appeared curious to know more about this "Athanor" character.

263

INT. ALLEYWAY, DOWNTOWN DALLAS - SAME

Appearing only as a tall, strikingly handsome silhouette, Athanor struts from the massive fire raging only feet behind him.

                    JEVON (V.O.)
I've only heard stories about him. Ghost stories. People
          say he was born on the run from the cartel.

SERIES OF SHOTS - ATHANOR'S ORIGINS

-- EXT. SAFEHOUSE - NIGHT -- In the midst of heavy gunfire, ATHANOR'S MOTHER plucks Baby Athanor from the makeshift crib, places him inside a cardboard box, and with ninja-like movements, pokes holes in top of box with a blade. With a gun gripped in one hand and a box curled by her side like a football in the other, Athanor's Mother escapes through a bedroom window as bullets plug the walls.

   "People? What people?"
   "I dunno, *people*," Jevon said. "They say he spent most of his childhood in and out of juvenile hall."

-- INT. CANTERBURY ELEMENTARY - DAY -- Boy Athanor rolls up his book report on "To Kill A Mockingbird," his knuckles tight and white, the paper making leathery sounds. He hits a BULLY in the back of his head, stuffs the end of the report down the bully's throat and smothers him to death.

-- INT. PRINCIPAL'S OFFICE, CANTERBURY ELEMENTARY - DAY -- POLICE OFFICERS remove Boy Athanor from the office in handcuffs.

-- INT. JUVY COURT - DAY -- The JUDGE barks and wags her finger at Boy Athanor. Then, she SLAMS down the gavel.

                    JEVON (V.O.)
By the time he turned eighteen, he enlisted in the Ma-
                    rines.

-- EXT. VILLAGE, IRAQ - DAY -- Young Athanor breaks into a small hut, murdering armed members of the al-Qaeda organization.

                    JEVON (V.O.)
When he came back to America, he joined the Force.

-- INT. POLICE ACADEMY GRADUATION - DAY -- On the stage in front of a crowd of friends and family members, Athanor shakes the hand of the SUPERINTENDENT.

OLIVIA PLAUT

JEVON (V.O.)
He used his skills he picked up overseas to hunt down bad
guys.

-- INT. CRACK HOUSE - DAY -- Detective Dowe breaks down
the door and fires at an armed DRUG DEALER, who draws an
Uzi. Detective Dowe kills the drug dealer and uncovers a
stockpile of cocaine and illegal weapons. His PARTNERS
congratulate him.

Jevon drove closer to the mysterious car parked at the end of the driveway.
A shadowy face appeared behind the glare of the headlights.

-- INT. DOWNTOWN - NIGHT -- Athanor chases an armed suspect into a shady building.

JEVON (V.O.)
One night, Athanor's life was almost cut short.

-- INT. PARKING GARAGE - NIGHT -- With a shotgun in his
hands, a CRIMINAL creeps up behind Athanor and shoots him
in side of head, blowing off part of Athanor's skull.

Jevon slowly drove past the car, revealing the side of Athanor's face in the
driver's seat. He dragged from a lit cigarette, which cast an orange glow over
his stern, shadowy mien.

-- INT. OPERATION ROOM, HOSPITAL - NIGHT -- A surgeon in-
stalls a metal plate in the side of Athanor's bloody head.

JEVON (V.O.)
Rumor has it that the gun blast destroyed part of his
brain, the part that felt emotion.

"*They* say a lot of things, don't they? So, does he work for Chione?"
"He works for no one."

-- INT. HELICOPTER - NIGHT -- Athanor mercilessly rains
down gunfire on a Viper speeding down the highway, the
flashes of gunfire flickering over his face like a strobe
light inside a dance club.

BACK TO SCENE

"He doesn't exist in the real world," Jevon said, as he looked at Athanor's
car in the rear view mirror. Athanor flicked the cherry from the end of the
cigarette. The tiny flaming ball of ash settled in the gravel below. "He's a
ghost," he said to Renata. "He only exists to carry out the dirty work so that
people like you and me can stay clean."
"Me? Clean?" Renata laughed hysterically. "Jevon, I just *killed* an innocent person. Some 'cleaner' isn't going to take that away."

265

"He will."

"But I can't, Jevon. I can't take that away."

"Well, Renata," Jevon said, as he pulled out on the main road. "You're going to have to try."

"How?"

"You can start by acknowledging what happened." He took his eyes off the road and glanced at Renata. "You can't block it out. You wouldn't be human, if you could. First off, Renata, you have to *accept* what you did, then *move on* with your life. Understood?"

"It's *not* that easy."

"Nobody ever said it was."

ONE DAY AGO

THE pothole in the road jarred Renata to consciousness.

The sounds all around her intensified: the siren blaring outside the ambulance and then two people talking, one of them a paramedic and the other, Jevon, who was holding Renata's hand.

Wringing wet with sweat, Renata pulled the side of her flushed face from the gurney and straightened her focus upward at the light above.

A paramedic's face entered her field of vision. She was reading a thermometer.

"A hundred and three," she said to herself.

"It's lowering," another more familiar voice said.

As soon as Jevon's face entered Renata's view, she tried to sit upright but the paramedic held her down. Renata looked around the inside of the ambulance with a sense of great urgency.

"What happened?" asked Renata. The fear was evident in her voice. "Where are you taking me?"

"Easy now, Renata. I told you," Jevon said clearly. "We're taking you to the hospital. You're not well."

"I'm fine," she said with a swallow and once more, tried to sit upright. More aggressively, the paramedic held Renata to the gurney. "Just take me back to the cabin. I want to go back to the cabin."

Perplexed, Jevon said, "What cabin, Renata?"

Renata wasn't quick to respond.

"Kira's cabin?"

Renata closed her eyes to block out that "sinking" feeling. The pink darkness behind her eyelids drew an image in her mind: Jevon's frail mother standing behind the crack in the doorway, half of her cryptic face visible, the other half lost in the shadows. Somehow, Renata felt as if she was still back in the bed, still sinking through the mattress, still tangled in heavy bed sheets, still unable to free herself from the horrors that plagued her.

"Renata," Jevon said, pulling Renata from her feverish daze, "I'm not going to just sit back and watch you suffer like this. It's unacceptable, you hear? You need to see a doctor—"

"—You didn't see what I saw," Renata cried out, her hands shaking as if she was trying to hold the words in her hands. "His face changed, Jevon. And

266

if you would just listen to me for once, I'm trying to tell you that this wasn't some kind of expression. His face *wasn't* his face. And. . . and. . . and as for Chione," Renata stammered breathlessly, "you should've seen her. She's *not* human either!"

"Renata," Jevon said, his tone softer, "you're not making any sense."

"Relax, Ms. Salcedo," the paramedic reassured Renata. "Everything is going to be fine."

Renata completely withdrew from the paramedic, as well as Jevon.

The inside of the ambulance became smaller and smaller, so small that it was starting to get crowded.

Renata honed in on a small compartment to the left of her, only inches away from where the paramedic was sitting. She didn't exactly know why, but she was compelled to open the compartment. As she reached for the latch, the paramedic grabbed Renata's wrist and guided her arm back to the gurney. The compartment trembled—which caused Renata to shift to the edge of the gurney. The trembling stopped; then, as Renata attempted to open the compartment once more while the paramedic's attention was concentrated on the *beeping* alarm of a blood pressure monitor, the trembling continued, this time more violently. She recoiled and once the trembling stopped, tried to open the compartment again.

"Ms. Salcedo," the paramedic said, as she grabbed Renata's wrist tighter this time, "you *have* to relax."

In a brisk movement, Renata opened the compartment of bagged syringes. A couple of syringes fell out onto the floor.

"Ms. Salcedo!"

The other paramedic driving the ambulance turned to his partner.

"*Bee*," he said sharply, "*control the patient*."

"What is it, Renata?" Jevon asked, as the ambulance slowed down through a busy intersection.

The paramedic eased back Jevon with her hand.

"Ms. Salcedo," the paramedic said while checking Renata's eyes with a flashlight, "if you don't relax, I'm going to have to restrain you. Do you understand me. . . "

Still withdrawn from Jevon and the paramedic, Renata moved her eyes to the contents of the compartment. Her eyes flicked. She witnessed something moving underneath a couple of bags and oxygen masks in the back of the compartment.

Renata heard two voices whispering to one another: "*Has your friend been taking any drugs?*"

As she kept her hands by her side, as the paramedic demanded, other syringes and medical supplies stirred without Renata even touching them.

From behind the compartment, at least four tentacles stretched outward, slithering along the drawers and cabinetry and around the paramedic's legs and moving up the sides of the gurney.

As the tentacles reached Renata's legs, her body trembled violently.

With a serpentine slither, one tentacle moved up her thigh.

Frantically trying to move to the farthest end of the gurney, Renata attempted to brush off the tentacles; however, another one slithered underneath the gurney, making its way up her shirt. She swatted at it while, at the same time, Jevon and the paramedic were grabbing at her, her head, her arms, and demanding that she lay back down on the gurney, as if, in her mind, they were completely unaware—in fact, oblivious—as to what she was witnessing. The paramedic tried to slip Renata's wrist through a restraint, but Renata resisted.

As soon as it was clear to Renata that she had nowhere else to escape, except for one option, which she didn't have time to ponder over since the tentacles were now wrapping around her body, she suddenly bolted forward through the tentacles and the arms, using the gurney to propel herself to the doors. She kicked open the back door and threw herself from the ambulance!

Jevon reached out to grab her arm—or any part of her body for that matter—but half of her body was already out of the ambulance. Right before she hit the pavement, she curled her legs inward, tucked her shoulder into her chest—like she saw one time in a movie—took the brunt of the fall directly on her shoulder, then rolled several rotations over the street.

Just ahead, the paramedic slammed on the brakes.

With horns blaring, cars swerved around the ambulance and nearly crashed into them. Once it was safe, Jevon stepped outside and ran to Renata as other cars screeched by. An awful dread immediately washed over him as soon as he spotted Renata in the middle of the road.

Zigzagging his way through traffic, he rushed toward Renata, who appeared injured from the way her body was lying in a fetal position. Once she saw Jevon running toward her, she stumbled to her feet and drunkenly ran away. She made it to the sidewalk without getting struck by any cars. She ran a couple of blocks, as if she was powered by adrenaline. She came across a dim alleyway, which—at first—looked like a good place to lose him. She was hesitant to cut through. That awful feeling of sinking was creeping up inside her, not entirely but dully like a bad thought. She took only one step into the alleyway before she froze. The dark pavement rippled, causing Renata to immediately back away. She decided that it was best to keep running and hoping that she could lose him on foot. A couple of blocks down, after dodging a couple of pedestrians shopping for fruit at a local stand outside a food market, Renata glanced over her shoulder and saw that Jevon was too far behind to catch up to her. *But still*, he wasn't giving up.

As Renata rounded the corner of a bagel shop, she found herself staring directly at Central Park. Without a doubt in her mind, she knew that she could *definitely lose* him inside the park. She darted through heavy traffic, juking out several cars and taxicabs. She leaped over a brick wall and entered the park through the south end. She ran past joggers, strollers, and sightseers, rested once against a tree to catch her breath, and then took off running as if Jevon was still on her tail.

Racing around both children and parents as if they were obstacles, she ended up cutting through a playground and finally, after both of her legs were about to buckle from exhaustion, taking cover behind the steepest side of Umpire Rock—or "*Rat Rock*," a name which the popular outcrop had acquired after it was once known for not only being a hangout for those who walked upright, but also those who walked on all fours.

While sucking down gulps of air, she bent over and rested against her knees to help ease the sting in her throat.

Eventually, she caught her breath and was ready to run again; however, right as she was about to take off, her eye caught a strangeness in the bedrock below. One rock in particular appeared to be out of place, as if it had absolutely no business being there, like, somehow, the rock was trying to blend in with the other rocks but failed miserably. *But why couldn't other people see it?* She tapped on the flat rock with the tip of her sole as if she was checking for life and received a hollow *thud* in return. She carefully kneeled down and with her knuckles, knocked on the soft rock; and it was as if she was knocking on a door that was shaped like a rock. She dug around the dirt, searching for a door handle but only finding a glacial striation-like gouge on the right side of the rock. She stuck two fingers into the crack and tugged upward until she heard a *click*! The rock suddenly sprung open like a door. She made sure nobody was watching. Then, she swung the rock open and stepped inside a sewer-like shaft that led to a dark space below.

🕐

AFTER climbing down a ladder, Renata finally reached the bottom of the shaft.

Surrounded by darkness, Renata's eyes adjusted. She found an orangish light coming from the end of the corridor. Cautiously, she walked to the light.

🕐

ONCE Renata reached the end of the corridor, she found herself in a boiler room. Various sized pipes were running along the walls and hard concrete. From a distance, she heard the monstrous *screeches*, the *howls*, the *roars*, raw mayhem getting louder and louder. Following the guttural sounds were noises of metal bars beating against pipes, the *clinking* and *clanking*, as well as a piercing, cringe worthy *ring* of what sounded like sharp talons scrapping against rusted metal. Renata ducked behind a pile of waterlogged boxes and fell witness to giant warped shadows stretching like carnival mirror reflections along the beat of firelight cast along the massive walls: shadows running on two legs, as well as all four legs, shadows jumping, shadows dancing, shadows fighting, shadows morphing from humans to eight-armed creatures.

Terrified as to what was storming her way, Renata curled herself into a ball. She prayed to God—*any* God—to protect her from whatever evil was headed her way. Under the breath of her muffled voice, Renata spoke of forgiveness and made vows to make atonement for all of the wrongdoings in her life.

At that moment in time, she was a pious woman.

A woman who was ready to make a change.

🕐

RENATA went undetected as the inhuman vandals raged on. She forced herself to sleep. And that night, she dreamt of blackness. And in that blackness, various unrecognizable shapes appeared like distant apparitions.

269

She was jolted from sleep by an image of fangs coming forth in the dark.

More aware, more refreshed by the long sleep, Renata scanned the massive boiler room. She couldn't tell whether it was day or night. All she knew was that in such a place neither time existed. She finally found the courage to stand. She exited the boiler room and made her way to a locker room, which looked the same way any locker room would look if suddenly abandoned due to a natural disaster over dozens of presidential campaigns ago. Old, dusty, faded clothes were randomly scattered everywhere. She picked up one shirt in particular that had long slits in the side, as if a wild animal had gotten a hold of it. Some were covered in strange resin; others, a sticky phlegm-like goo.

She walked down yet another corridor, this one narrower than the one before, until she reached an "EXIT" door.

Carefully, she opened the door. The afternoon sunlight temporarily blinded her. Once her eyes adjusted to the change in light, Renata realized that she was standing underneath a railroad bridge on Randalls and Wards Island. She stepped outside and closed the door behind her. She looked up and clarified that it was, in fact, Hell Gate Bridge. But *how in the hell did I get all the way out here?*

During her trip back into Manhattan, she spent the rest of the afternoon trying to figure out how she wound up on Randalls and Wards Island.

But she had no answers to her queries.

SIX HOURS AGO

KIRA was preparing her to-go meal, a sort of throw-it-altogether type of Japanese roman noodle soup that she notoriously branded "Hangover Food," when the buzzard sounded. She stopped chopping the shallots on the cutting board and walked to the door where she answered the call.

"Hello," she said into the intercom.

"Kira," Renata said from the other end, "it's me, Renata. I need to see you."

Kira paused, thought for a moment, and then opened the downstairs door for Renata.

"Come on up," she said and paced around the kitchen while Renata made her way upstairs. She finished the glass of Chardonnay and as she was about to pour herself another glass, Renata was already at her door.

Kira opened the door for Renata. She immediately noticed Renata's posture, her strung-out state, and how she was struggling to stand upright in the hallway. Kira stepped aside and waved Renata inside her apartment.

"What happened?" Kira asked Renata, as Renata awkwardly stood next to a bookshelf.

"I think I'm losing my mind," she said, looking away from Kira.

Kira asked, "What do you mean?"

"I'm seeing things," Renata said, holding back tears.

"What *things*?" asked Kira.

Renata shrugged.

"I don't know," she drawled, the emotion showing through her cracked voice.

Kira wrapped her arm around Renata's shoulder and escorted her to the living room where they both sat down next to each other on the beige leather couch.

Renata could no longer hold back her tears.

"Do you want something to drink?" Kira asked, as she leaned forward to look into Renata's eyes. "I can make you some tea, if you like," she said, studying Renata. "For me, a cup of hot tea always makes me feel better—"

"—Do you have anything stronger?" Renata asked, as she wiped away tears and phlegm with the backside of her hand.

"All I have is wine," Kira suggested.

"Wine is fine."

Kira went back into the kitchen; and once she found herself away from Renata's view, she embraced a deep breath behind the refrigerator. She poured two glasses of wine. In secret, she chugged the glass of wine in only a couple of gulps and then poured herself another glass of wine. She brought the two glasses back to the living room. She handed Renata the glass.

Renata sipped from the wine.

"Thanks," Renata said depressingly. Before Kira had a chance to offer a polite response, Renata said abruptly as if she had an important issue to discuss with Kira, "What was up with you the other day?"

Kira's thin eyebrows curled into a question mark.

"What you mean?"

"You acted like you hardly even knew me, Kira," Renata said more clearly. "Like we weren't friends anymore." Once more, she brushed away the tears. "I needed a friend, someone whom I could trust, and you weren't there for me."

"I'm here now, aren't I?" Kira responded and touched Renata high enough on the thigh to warrant Renata's attention.

They both shared eye contact.

"I'm sorry for whatever's going on with you," Kira said. "If there's anything I can do for you, then. . . " her eyes trailed downward on Renata's thigh and then flicked back up at Renata's eyes, ". . . I'm yours."

As soon as Kira made a move up Renata's thigh, Renata grabbed Kira's hand and tried to stir it away from her belt buckle.

In return, Kira aggressively leaned in to kiss Renata. At the last second, Renata turned her head away. Kira kissed Renata on the cheek.

Renata made it obvious by her gentle recoil that she wasn't at all interested in Kira's affection.

"I can't," Renata said, backing off.

"Just relax," Kira said and leaned in once more. She grabbed Renata's wrist and pushed it aside. Her grip was disturbingly tight and when Renata pushed her hand away yet again, she felt a strong resistance from Kira.

"Stop, Kira," Renata said, as Kira attempted to kiss Renata. "Kira," she said, trying to push off Kira, "I said, 'Stop!'"

Kira ignored Renata's demands and pinned down her shoulders. She ripped through Renata's blouse. Renata managed to kick off Kira from the couch. She made a flee toward the door, but Kira grabbed Renata and pinned her down to the floor. She was kissing, licking, and rubbing herself against Renata, as if she was driven by a primordial lust that went beyond any desire.

With a gaping yawn, Kira opened up her mouth to bite Renata. Her tongue, which was as long as a limb, stretched out from Kira's mouth as if it was unrolling like a red carpet and then licked at the side of Renata's face, leaving behind a gummy trail of saliva along her cheek. The tongue slithered around the bottom of Renata's chin, ran down her cleavage, and proceeded toward her abdomen.

Totally aware of Kira's actions, Renata quickly snatched the tongue before it could penetrate her and used it like a leash to yank Kira off her body.

The fight ensued into the kitchen where Kira tackled Renata into the table.

Renata looked around at anything she could grab, a plate, a vase, a floral picture framed on the wall, and tossed it all at Kira. Like a boxer, Kira ducked and dodged each projectile. She shielded herself from the picture frame; however, the corner of it caught her on the top of her forehead, drawing a string of blood to run down her face.

Panting heavily, Renata pushed the words out from her mouth as if each one was carrying her last breath: *"What's gotten into you, Kira?"*

Kira never responded, couldn't. To Renata, the woman circling her appeared as if she had regressed to her most primordial self and had the look of something inhuman, something pre-human. Her fingers were flexed outward, nails drawn and ready to scratch or rake, her pupils swollen black; and that tongue hanging from her mouth like a loose necktie acted as if it was her most underrated weapon.

The fight intensified farther in the cramped kitchen where sharper projectiles were used for defense, as well as offense. With her back against the refrigerator, Kira whipped her tongue around Renata's neck. Renata had no other choice than to remove her hands from Kira and remove the tongue, which was now choking her to death. She blindly felt for a weapon along the countertop. She fingered for the knife. Slid it closer with her index and middle finger. Once she grabbed the knife, she brought the knife forward and severed Kira's tongue with a clean and swift stroke.

Bloody and bruised and now tongueless, Kira elbowed Renata directly in the nose. The blow temporarily dazed Renata, which gave Kira an opening to wrestle the knife from Renata's hand. She turned the blade on Renata; however, Renata overpowered Kira and redirected the tip of the knife at Kira's throat.

With the blade only inches from Kira's throat, Renata begged Kira to stop.

Kira wildly swung at Renata.

Struggling to watch, Renata had no other choice than to make one final thrust forward with the blade.

She stabbed Kira in the throat and cut through a major artery, causing Kira to bleed out on the kitchen floor.

In a state of shock, Renata looked downward at her palms and they were both drenched with blood.

"HOME sweet home," Jevon said, as he pulled his car in front of his brownstone.

After being caught in a daze of staring at the passing city lights, Renata lifted the side of her face from the headrest and turned to Jevon, who was removing the seat belt from his body. She looked him over with suspicion.

"What?" he said once he noticed Renata staring at him.

"Nothing," she said. "Just tired. That's all."

Jevon responded to Renata with a half-smile and exited the car. He walked to the passenger side of the car and opened the door for Renata. Gentlemanly, Jevon helped Renata from the seat and walked her into the brownstone. He flipped on a lamp in the foyer.

During the slow and tired amble into the living room, Renata passed Aurora's bedroom, which was dark and empty.

"Where's Aurora?" asked Renata.

"I ended up putting her in a home," he said and immediately followed before Renata could question him as to why he put his mother in one of "those" places in which he often spoke about with such rancor, "*but* only for the time being. With everything going on right now, I couldn't put her at risk. Eventually, things will settle down, though. That's the beauty of time."

Jevon disappeared in the darkness as he grabbed two pillows and a folded up blanket from the hallway closet.

Renata stood at the edge of the dark living room and asked Jevon over a tense silence, "Are you saying we're safe here, Jevon?"

"Of course, we are," he said and returned to the living room where he placed the pillows and blanket on top of the couch. Without turning on another light—which Renata didn't think too much about—Jevon walked up to Renata and reassured her, "You don't need a gun to feel safe."

"About that—"

"—It's done," Jevon interrupted, as if he wasn't in any mood to talk about the Glock 19 that she stole from his office. "You're safe here. Trust me."

"Trust is hard to come by these days," she said coldly, as she leaned against the doorway.

"After everything we've been through, you still don't trust me?"

Renata defensively folded her arms across her chest and shifted her weight to one side of her body.

"It's not that I don't trust you," Renata said and hesitated. "It's that—"

"—You don't trust yourself," Jevon finished for her.

Renata nodded her head *yes*.

Jevon stepped closer to Renata. His moonlit eyes trailed away for a moment. Then came back to Renata's eyes.

"You have shown me—" he said thoughtfully, "—proven to me actually, that you are capable of bringing down Chione based on the sacrifices you have made not only for me, but also for those whose voice has been stifled by powers greater than you or me. And now you're in a *unique* position where you can do anything you set your mind to." He touched her on the shoulder in a fatherly way. "*You* have the power, *Renata*. One day, when the time is right,

273

you will use that power to tell your story to the world. And those who don't look like you or speak like you or act like you or even *think* like you, they will cheer for you and parade you into the new world."

Renata had an idea of what Jevon was telling her, but she didn't know exactly where he was going with the "point."

Before Jevon could even arrive at the "point," he touched the side of Renata's chin. "It's been a long day," he said softly. "Get some rest."

Jevon walked into his bedroom, closed the door behind him, and flipped on a lamp inside.

Renata made a bed on the couch and rested for a while.

As soon as she closed her eyes, she heard the *click* of a lamp switch—which she assumed was Jevon switching off his lamp. Renata didn't bother to open her eyes. Yet she remained comfortable on the couch, thinking about what Jevon had said to her moments ago. Only a few seconds into deep thought, her eyes flicked open. Unaware of the dark figure sitting in the recliner chair next to her, Renata walked into the kitchen and paced around. Another dark figure was sitting at the kitchen table; however, she was so deep in thought that she completely ignored her surroundings.

Immediately, Jevon's words—those particular *words*—leaped at her.

She marched back into the living room and as she was about to open Jevon's bedroom door, Renata caught a disfigured-faced figure sitting in the recliner. The blood ran from her face, leaving it pale and ghostly. She swallowed a gulp of air down her parched throat.

Before Renata could make sense as to who was sitting in the recliner, a lamp switched on beside the recliner. Part of Chione's scarred face was revealed in the shaded light. In her lap, she was petting a creature—in fact, the same telepath that Renata had witnessed floating inside that large cylindrical glass tank filled with a pinkish substance. The creature's hissy breath made robust purring sounds whenever Chione stroked the back of its scaly skin. Several tentacles slithered outward from its shell, caressing Chione's belly the same way a cat would knead through soft fabric.

"*You,*" Renata said, her voice trembling, "what did you do with Jevon?"

Chione grabbed the remote from the end table and turned on the TV.

The bold graphic of a BREAKING NEWS REPORT scrolled past the screen. The news anchor appeared shortly after, reading from the teleprompter. In the report, forty-seven year old, Jevon D'Agostino, the creator of the controversial magazine, *X'D*, was found dead in a hotel room at The Villages in NoMo. A video appeared on TV, one which was taken "EARLIER" that night. In the footage, coroners were carrying out a body inside a black bag from a sleazy hotel room. News crews and reporters were stationed around the crime scene. Stringers were trying to get the best angle for the shot while reporters were interviewing witnesses and other hotel guests. For the latest report, the news anchor sent it over to Jessica Varner, who was "live" at Jevon's residence.

There, on the TV, was "LIVE" footage of a brownstone, which looked identical to Jevon's, roped off with caution tape. The police, as well as detectives, were gathered outside the brownstone.

Overwrought with emotion, Renata turned to the front door. She didn't see any cops outside or anybody for that matter. She turned back to the TV. Saw that "LIVE" feed.

Confusion swept beneath her.

How can it be?

She tried to scrape the bottom of her thoughts but came up empty.

More confused, Renata focused on what the reporter was saying.

"Investigators are searching D'Agostino's residence, hoping to find more answers into his death," the reporter said, as activity increased behind her.

"It's been on TV all night long," Chione said over the report.

Renata rushed to Jevon's bedroom, checked inside, and saw an empty bed.

As a warm rage built up inside her, Renata turned to Chione, who was sitting comfortably in the recliner.

"What did you do?" she asked Chione.

"Well," Chione started, as she continued to pet the strange creature in her lap, "if you want to know the truth—I mean—if it makes you feel better, Dowe said he put up quite a fight."

The words coming from the recent report caught Renata's attention.

"Police currently have the twenty-eight year old from Seattle, Justin Devoid, in custody. Just recently, Mr. Devoid was reported missing in the town of Dover where he was currently attending community college. As of now, police are currently going through all of Mr. Devoid's social media pages and searching for any possible motives. According to D'Agostino's phone records, D'Agostino met Mr. Devoid through an online dating app called 'Men Only.' The two arranged a meeting at The Villages where several eyewitnesses claimed they saw the two entering the hotel room together. However, police believe that Mr. Devoid did not act alone. Candace Norwood, a nineteen-year-old from Dover, California, who, like Justin Devoid, was also recently reported missing, is wanted for questioning in the death of Jevon D'Agostino."

"Turn it off," Renata demanded, the rage simmering inside her.

The sound of the reporter's voice was like knives stabbing at Renata.

"I said, 'Turn it off!'"

Chione turned off the TV.

"It's bullshit," Renata seethed, shaking her head in utter disgust. "The whole story, it's all fabricated. *Why?*"

"Why do you think, Renata?" asked Chione.

Renata stopped and did exactly what Chione had asked.

She thought. She thought about the dead body in her trunk, *not Kira's body*, but Jevon's dead body—*take that back. As a matter of fact, there was nobody in the trunk of my car*; then, she thought about the person whom she was talking to the whole time inside Kira's cabin, *not Jevon, but Chione*.

"This whole time. . . " Renata seethed. The tears streamed down the corners of her face, and they burned like acid. "Why pretend to be him? Why lie to me?"

"Not *all* lies, dear," Chione said. "Push past the emotion that blinds you, Renata. You're a smart woman. You already know the answer to those questions."

Renata had another vision, a sharp and stingy one that knocked the wind out of her.

All of these fabricated images—hallucinations—Renata realized, all stemmed from the infection on her arm.

"The woman back there," Renata said, out of breath, "the one who bumped into me on the street—or should I say, who 'deliberately' bumped into me— what the fuck did she put inside me?"

"It's starting to make sense, isn't it?" Chione asked with disdain. "Pieces to form a greater puzzle. I'm sure you can imagine that it wasn't easy for me pinning your boss's murder on those two lovebirds. Somewhere, buried underneath the pile of bodies, the foolish girl in me admires Candace Norwood for what she did after she uncovered her mystery, how, unlike most people, she decided to act not on impulse but, justifiably so, on the fundamental truth of self-righteousness. Most importantly, I admire how Candace Norwood traveled across an entire country to rescue the one person whom she loved—or thought she loved—when, turns out, love, her true love, her 'perfect match,' was right beside her the whole time. *However*, as a result of Candace Norwood's careless actions and the. . . unwanted attention she and Justin were drawing to our operation, *the public* will now see the two not as 'vigilantes' but deviants. When you're madly in love—or, in Candace Norwood's case, one who didn't know she was in love—you'll do about anything to hold onto it, that *feeling*," Chione's eyes honed in on Renata's. She held them there like blades. "Even if it means ruining another person's life."

"What the fuck did she put inside me?" asked Renata, as she carefully took a step away from Chione.

Without drawing any attention, she glanced around the living room. In a second glance, she spotted a pair of scissors on the edge of a table next to the TV.

She backpedaled toward the scissors and stood directly behind them.

Villainously, Chione said to Renata, "I've pulled back your eyelids and given you a glimpse into the other side of midnight, into a dark world gnawing away at the very fringes of your own reality."

Renata's eyes flicked toward the creature squirming in Chione's lap. Chione shushed and calmed the creature by repeatedly petting it.

"Is little Genie Beanie making you uncomfortable?"

"Genie. . . ?"

"Genie Beanie can be whoever you want him to be," Chione said childishly. Her voice was higher in pitch as if she was communicating to the creature through baby talk. She leaned in closer and rubbed the bottom of her chin along its scaly skin. Her voice changed. "Isn't that right, Dr. Love?"

The creature appeared different in Chione's lap; in fact, it didn't look like any creature at all. Renata looked twice and saw Chione holding a newborn baby in her arms, not the same grotesque creature with tentacles.

With her index finger, Chione tickled the baby's stomach, causing him to let out an explosive cackle.

"How's my little Lovie Dovie? You're a good Lovie Dovie, aren't you?"

276

Chione tilted forward and started blowing farts along the baby's stomach; and when she pulled her head away, Renata witnessed a tabby in her arms. She petted the sides of the cat's neck; and in return, the cat purred softly.

"Aren't you, my Love Muffin—"

"—Stop it!"

Chione paused and looked at Renata as if her comment was criminal.

"Stop what?"

"*She still doesn't know*," a manly voice said from the dark kitchen.

Renata turned toward the kitchen, saw the dark figure sitting at the table; and then, as soon as she found an opportunity to act while Chione was distracted by the voice, she reached behind her back and secretly grabbed the pair of scissors from the table.

With her arm tucked against her waist, she curled her hand into her wrist and shielded as much as the scissors as she possibly could without getting caught in the act. Chione glanced at Renata, who, in return, kept a hard gaze on Chione, as well as her eyes, making sure neither one of them moved in the general direction of her right hand. They didn't.

"Know what?" Renata said over the stretch of silence.

"She knows enough," Chione said to the voice inside the kitchen.

Without Chione looking, Renata slipped the scissors in her back pocket and covered the grip with her shirt. She walked into the kitchen and switched on the light. There, at the kitchen table, sat an older man with his back facing Renata. He was eating from a bowl of *Apple Jacks*. Next to the bowl, the box of *Apple Jacks* was overturned on its side, empty. Renata walked to the side of the table for a closer look. In a slight head turn, Harold acknowledged Renata.

"What are you not telling me?" asked Renata. A gap of silence brought about a sharp rage inside her. She barked, "Answer me—"

"—Don't you see, Ms. Salcedo?" he said, holding his head down toward the bowl of Apple Jacks. He scooped up a spoonful of cereal and stuffed the spoon into his mouth. A trail of milk dribbled down the corner of his mouth. With his thumb, Harold wiped away the milk from his face and said after chewing the rest of the crunching cereal, "You remain a vital piece of the puzzle and without your sacrifice, everything else fails—all the dominoes do not fall in the correct order, if you know what I mean."

"No," Renata snapped. "I don't know what you mean."

Harold finished chewing, swallowed.

Clearing his throat, he said, "After MindChant was launched last year, Carla and Corvine was given access to the phones and tablets of every single person in the world who downloaded their app, which enabled us to know your likes, your dislikes. Nothing new, right?" he asked Renata but didn't expect for her to answer. "However, we wanted to go *further*, to push the boundaries, to go beyond the limits, to venture uncharted waters, to go where no man has ever gone in order to create something truly special. Believe it or not, Ms. Salcedo," Harold said, "it was the people like your father who paved the way for the next generation—*your* generation—people who sacrificed themselves for the greater good, people who, essentially, gave us a way in." Harold tapped on the side of his temple with his finger. He drifted off in reflection. Not once did he ever turn toward Renata, to look at her or even acknowledge her. Yet, it was as if he was talking to himself. "The people of your generation don't have the slightest clue as to how *easy* they have it, how much generations before them sacrificed in order for your generation to have the privileges that were once considered unobtainable. You have no clue, Renata, that in an instant," Harold faced Renata, his murky eyes sharpening, "we can take it all away from you. Gone." He snaps his fingers together. "Just like that."

Unable to think properly, Renata felt paralyzed by Harold's words, especially about what he had said about her father.

"For the sake of curiosity," Harold leaned in, "tell me. Where exactly do *you* think *you* are right now?"

She glanced around the kitchen, glanced at Chione, as well as that mindfuck of a thing in her lap, then glanced back at Harold.

"We're at *Jevon's place*," she said but her tone suggested that she making an educated guess to an answer on *Jeopardy*, as if she was better off saying, "What is Jevon's place?"

"Correct," Harold said. "We are at Jevon's place, *but* where are you?"

Renata's heart started to beat faster. Her palms were sticky with sweat. Skin clammy. She tried to calm down that tribal drum of a heart in her chest by taking a deep breath. A sudden flash of heat swelled over her body. The "sinking feeling" was back, pulling from below, enticing Renata to not fight it but embrace it. She blocked out that creeping sensation and focused on Harold, his face, his body, his *words*.

"I guess there's only way to find out," she said, her voice fragile.

Renata's face went vacant, dead-like.

Without any hesitation, she pulled out the scissors from her back pocket and stabbed Harold directly in his temple.

His eyes swelled open in surprise. His face, slack—but only for a moment.

The hair on the backside of Renata's neck suddenly shot like quills on a porcupine. She felt the handle of the scissors softening inside her palm. The scissors melted between her fingers. Warm steel oozed from her balled fist, dripped down the side of her wrist, and artfully veined across her forearm. As gently as possible she pulled back her right hand from Harold's head. Opened her palm. Her entire hand was covered in black and silver goo.

Harold appeared unfazed by her unsuccessful attempt at killing him; in fact, he appeared more frustrated as he wiped the goo from the side of his face. Harold glanced down at his clothing attire and found smudges of goo stained on his sweater.

Pissed off, Harold cried out, "Goddamn it, Gene! Couldn't you have turned the scissors into goddamn cornflakes or something less messy?"

As Harold turned his shoulder, he witnessed a blurry, cryptic figure stretched out and covering the entire length of the wide doorway. Renata couldn't help but notice the horror on Harold's face, as if he was staring at the very incarnation of horror. She heard a sharp *clicking* sound coming from over her shoulder. Before she could turn to witness the great monster looming beyond her, she felt a rough nub, which was about the size of an elbow, prodding against the back of her neck.

From behind, she heard Chione's voice: *"I'm disappointed in you, Renata."*

Renata was hesitant to turn around. When she finally did, she was left frozen in shock. Spread out directly behind her in the most grandiose, insectile posture wasn't Chione, rather another more archaic version of Chione with her eight legs stretched outward, one of which was pressed like the barrel of a gun against the backside of Renata's neck, while the others covered the entire length of the doorway. Her eyes were pitch black, demonic. At the base of her abdomen her belly was protruding outward as well, similar to the womb of a woman who was eight months pregnant, however, the bulge was shaped like the thorax of a spider. Renata had a good idea of what the tiny hole, which used to be her belly button, was designed to do. Gusts of wind came at her in waves. She never questioned where the wind was coming from since they were indoors; however, Renata figured that Chione's metamorphosis had something to do with a change in atmosphere. The living room behind Chione was no longer visible, as well. Yet, all that remained was a void as black as space.

The *screech* of a chair skidding along the hardwood floor startled Renata.

"I'll be waiting in the car," Harold said shortly, as he hurried outside.

With her eyes, Renata followed Harold to the street outside. She peered out the window and witnessed Kira sitting collectively in the driver's seat of a modified black Beamer with Trent's severed head stilled in the most shocking expression glowing on the front grill like a three-pronged headlight.

She thought about running far from Chione, running anywhere but right here, from this nightmare. Even when the thought turned to action and she attempted to move both her legs, Renata felt more paralyzed than before, as if the only part of her body that was working properly was her mouth, and even that part felt as if it was failing.

"All I have to do is wake up, right?" she suggested, her chest getting tighter with each breath. "I'll just climb up a tall building. Jump off a ledge somewhere. The fall will wake me up. . . "

"I wouldn't be so sure."

Chione's voice doubled, as if she was speaking through an electric box fan.

"Then, I'll just buy a gun and blow my brains out—"

"—I'm afraid it's not that *easy*, Renata," Chione said statically. "You're either *with us* or you're *against us*. I'm afraid, dear, you've made your choice."

Numbness crept into Renata's right hand, starting with her fingertips first and then coursing through her hand like a prickly wave.

"Please," Renata begged, "I choose to live. . . "

"Oh," Chione said grimly, as her black eyes lit up diabolically, "you *will* live. Where you're going, you are going to *thrivvve*."

"I just wanna go home," Renata cried, as shadows crept up her fingers. "Just please take me home—"

"—As you wish."

Panicked, Renata held up her right hand to her face, and all that remained of her hand was a shadow of a hand.

The shadowing effect continued throughout Renata's entire body, ridding all physical nature as well as being, until nothing remained of her but only a blacked out version of herself.

THREE YEARS LATER

TWENTY-six year old librarian, Emma Newtral—"Em," as she was often called by her peers throughout the Main Library in the small town of Maynard, Ohio—had spent the first week of November gathering enough courage to take the ultimate way out, her final destination, not "deleted" but, in a sense, "escaped," as in, once pushed, she would transport herself to another place that bore neither memory nor regret. The place where no one returned alive.

The months prior to Emma Newtral's predicament, she found ways to get by, as if "getting by" had become her own theme, a tagline used to promote her sad movie. Everyday, she found ways to escape the mundaneness which her life had become through the power of a story, either fictional and non, whether it be from taking in small excerpts like gulps from a book while placing it back on the shelf or helping track down a book for a Reader or chatting up a storm with other garrulous Readers who looked nothing like her but shared common interests about various characters, their flaws, or the decisions a particular character made, as well as offering renditions or long-winded accounts and analysis or "breakdowns" of the author's private thoughts or even, apart from reading, tracking down the notorious "Book Thief" who had been evading Emma for the past two years. She'd school those who were less schooled during political debates and basic ground coverings of classical literature from Jane Austen's *Pride and Prejudice* to John Steinbeck's *Of Mice and Men*. If there was one thing she knew a computer could—and *never* would—convey, it was the experience, a positive or negative one, a human being received after reading a book, good or bad.

However, after the reading stopped, when visual chaos deteriorated from the page, when transition from wits to wane left translation smoldering in a cold toke, when Emma Newtral closed whatever book she had escaped to, life viciously returned to an upright position. Her brain stopped. Initially, the adventure stopped. Yet, a new one began the day Emma met a man—a "boy," was what she skeptically told her mother on the phone—who went by Phil, whose name was easy to remember because it rhymed with Bill. Phil was three years younger than Emma but, despite his normie status, acted twice his age. After a month of dating, happy hour drinks and awkward dinners, walks in the park and late night movies, their relationship grew into titles: "Boyfriend" and "Girlfriend." Emma didn't pin it to one particular moment, but if she had to guess where their relationship felt as if it could've been an unbreakable alliance, she'd say the moment she decided to buy Phil a toothbrush when she was out grocery shopping, since he had spent the night over at her place several times and went to bed with stinky breath. It was the *little* moments like those which kept piling up until, one day, the thought of marriage and even the imagery of it surfaced inside her head; in fact, it was more plausible than anything she had ever known. Phil Watts could be *the man* who'd take her hand in marriage, Emma once thought. She even thought about kids, two of them, a boy and a girl.

Then, one day, Emma decided to bring up a conversation about having kids when they walked past a young woman with a baby bump. Not once during the six months of seeing each other did Emma and Phil ever talk about kids; in fact, the subject seemed as if it was sacrilegious and avoided at all costs. Unlike trying to pinpoint a moment when the relationship solidified, Emma knew exactly when the bond that she had strengthened with Phil started to disintegrate: the "Kid" talk. *Why,* she thought over sleepless nights, *why did I have to open up my big mouth?* The conversation scared Phil so much that he sabotaged their relationship. He'd list off excuses from left field not to see her. He'd speak out of turn and talk ugly to her—nasty, unmanly. He'd often push her away when she went so far as to bat an eyelash at him. He'd tell her that he had a "headache" or was "too tired" to offer any affection. Eventually, after two weeks of Phil's unruly behavior, Phil decided to end it with Emma. Broke up with her through a best-selling text. Even told her to "keep the darn toothbrush."

A month after the breakup, while Emma was sitting on a patio outside a coffee spot where she and Phil used to hang out and trying to soak up a crisp autumn day, Emma witnessed other couples around her—"cute" couples, "hot" couples, "perfect" and "imperfect" couples—all enjoying the afternoon sun and acting as if the world around them didn't exist. She once had that with Phil. Someone whom she could grow old with. Someone who would accompany her on trips around the world—they often shared dreams and aspirations, places to travel, experiencing new foods to eat, new faces to see, new people to meet, new cultures to embrace. She let it slip right through her fingertips. At that particular moment in her life, a black hole blotted out the sun, as if it was suspended above her all this time. The sky went gray. The mood darkened. Faces changed. November hadn't felt colder. After a week of planning her escape, thinking of different ways to do so, from jumping out in front of a car, to taking dangerous routes to work, to overindulging, Emma went with her last option, a less-brave or daring one. She was going to hit the "escape button" once and for all. Without any thrill or glory. Without any grand exit or her symbolic middle finger to the world. And a piece of her laughed off the humiliation. Some "boy," whom Emma Watts had once referred to, had driven her to this state, some "boy" had ripped out her heart from her chest Temple of Doom-style, tossed it on the ground while it was still beating, and then crushed it with his foot like a soda can, some "boy" was going to be her masked executioner and the last face she'd see in her mind before she fell down that rabbit hole. The thing—because there was always a "thing"—Emma wasn't even in love with Phil. But maybe that was the whole point.

That night, Emma picked up a bottle of Tylenol PM from the drug store. Unlike the moment she was brought into the world, she wanted to go out like a quiet riot, not punching or kicking, not screaming or crying out for the warm bosom of her mother, but rather ride a current and let the liquid remedy sweep her away into the great abyss and drift into a final sleep, her eternal sleep, her greatest escape.

She dumped the entire bottle into her palm up, held the pills in her hand like popcorn and stuffed as many as she could fit into her mouth.

Soon, she thought, she'd hit that escape button. Watch it open up like a cellar door and reveal on the top right corner of the keyboard, a flight of stairs drifting off into a dark world, one that shared neither memory nor regret.

As soon as she washed back the mouthful of pills with a sip of water, she received a message via TV spot, as if it was her own "SOS" reflecting back at her.

Earlier that day, Emma came across the same advertisement twice, one, a ten-second video clip on the right side column of a ".org" website on ingesting "toxic chemicals" and another, an enticing click bait window displaying the same actress from the video clip standing proudly on a white beach promoting a recently FDA approved drug on the market. She ignored the video clip while scrolling through the page of harmful household chemicals on her laptop. She "x'd" out the window attached with a link redirecting her to the drug's website while entering some shady health forum on rat poison on her phone.

In the advertisement, *a young woman who looked identical to Renata but was not Renata was sitting in a slouched, turtle-like posture by a garden window while scrolling through old photographs of a young woman who looked identical to Kira but was not Kira on her phone. The two women, both in the bedroom and on the phone, could've passed as siblings. Similar to the way one viewed the sibling of a celebrity or somebody famous. He or she looked identical to the celebrity or famous person; however, a facial feature, a nose, a jawline, the brow—even the shape of his or her face—felt as if it was somehow out of place, whether it be too small or large or misshapen. The mood of the bedroom was heavy and damp. Outside, it was pouring rain. In the back-*ground the song "Mad World" by Michael Andrews and Gary Jules was softly playing. *As the rain dribbled down the garden window, so did the tears along the young woman's face.*

The next scene cut to *the same young woman sitting on the couch in the living room. She was flipping through the channels on TV. Each channel highlighted her grief, either it be from a commercial on the latest perfume—the super model, who was promoting the perfume, looked identical to the woman on her phone—or live coverage of the Oscars—the dolled up actress, who was strutting the red carpet while, at the same time, posing for photographers, like the commercial before, looked identical to the woman on her phone or an epi-sode from the hit television series—the driven detective, who was escorting a criminal, her White Whale, into the back of a squad car, like the previous channels, looked identical to the woman on her phone.*

The next few scenes followed *the young woman through her daily routine: eating dinner alone, watching a movie alone, sleeping alone, eating breakfast alone, working alone, browsing through the aisles of a bookstore alone.*

At the bookstore, a young handsome man made eye contact with the young woman, made a one-sided conversation with the young woman, made his five-star attempt to lighten up the tense mood with an innocent joke but the young woman could barely bring herself to crack a smile. The young man asked her if she'd like to join him for a cup of coffee, but she shook her head. Said she had things to do.

One-by-one, the sleeping pills slowly spilled from Emma's mouth.

Her eyes were glued to the flat screen.

Back to the advertisement where *the young woman was looking over several brochures: exotic places like India, Belize, Madagascar, the Bay of Kotor* in Montenegro, Gozo, Malta, Greece, Nepal, French Polynesia, Chile, Fiji, Cook Islands, Burma, Australia, Ireland, Scotland.

The next scene showed *the young woman sitting at the kitchen table watching YouTube "travel" videos on her laptop.*

In the next scene, *the young woman was riding a carousel in the park. While riding the back of the stationary horse, she visualized the moment where everything went wrong, where her life turned to one of great solitude and depression, the moment when the other young woman, whose photos were on her phone, decided to walk out that door where the light outside was bright enough to blind her.*

Emma emptied out her mouth completely until her mouth was ridded of pills, leaned forward, and turned up the volume on the TV.

As the young woman exited a coffee shop, a city bus with the bold purple sign drove past her.

The young woman came across a similar sign on the billboard when she was driving home. The first part of the word, **Renata***, caught the corner of her eye. Lastly, the young woman fully acknowledged the poster on the wall inside the exam room. Curious, the young woman looked over the poster*

Renatafill™

When the doctor entered the exam room, the young woman pointed at the poster and asked the doctor about the latest FDA approved drug on the market

Renatafill™

The next scene showed *the young woman and her doctor talking about the new drug in the doctor's office. The young woman nodded carefully as she listened to the advice that her doctor was giving her.*

The following scenes showed *the young woman restarting her life on*

Renatafill™

Smiling from ear to ear, the young woman strolled through an airport with her carry-on luggage; she handed a ticket to the stewardess, laughing while doing so; the young woman, still smiling, boarded the airplane. The young woman arrived at the Bay of Kotor—or "Boka."

Gleefully walking through the town of Perast, the young woman sampled the local cuisine; she met a waiter whom she shared a wonderful conversation with. Later that night, the young woman went out for drinks with the waiter. The two traveled farther inland where they both rode horseback on Shagya Arabians.

Emma stood up from couch, walked to the flat screen TV mounted on the living room wall, and listened closely to the advertisement.

Back to the advertisement: *While the young woman was having a loving dinner at a fancy restaurant, the same young woman from the photo on her phone walked past her table. The young woman didn't even recognize her. Ignoring the other young woman whom she had deleted from ther phone, the young woman continued to drink, eat, and laugh with her new boyfriend.*

In the next scene, *the young woman was in the kitchen preparing a cup of coffee when, all of a sudden, her new tortoiseshell cat jumped up on the countertop, startling the young woman yet, at the same time, causing her to laugh away her frustration. With a smile on her face, she embraced the cat.*

"Look beyond the skin with. . . "

Renatafill™

As the young woman walked on a white beach glistening like diamonds in rays of sunlight stretching over the horizon, Emma carefully placed her hand onto the television screen. With the advertisement drawing to an end, the glare of light bloomed over the screen and caused Emma to squint. The glare was so strong and brilliant that it coursed through Emma's warm hand, her once pink skin now outlined with a red glow. The glare continued to brighten until Emma's hand thinned and whitened and eventually, faded into the white light.

A SOUND
BITE

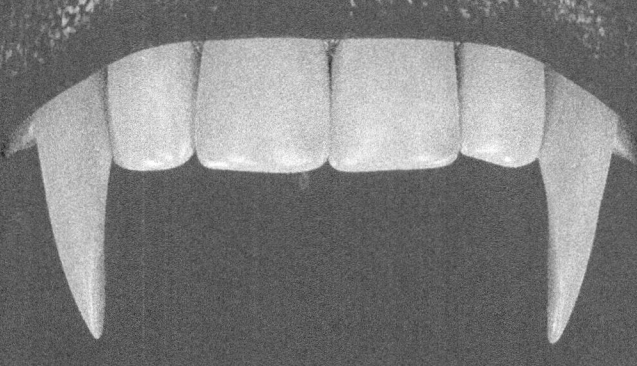
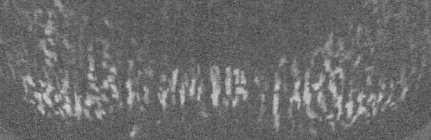

"READY *Governor Washington?*"

The pensive governor stared through the tinted window at a mob of news reporters itching to swarm her once she stepped foot outside the town car parked in front of New Way Academy.

Again, the same voice next to the governor: "*Avanti. . .*"

Finally, Avanti pulled her hard brown eyes from the reporters, in particular, a blonde-haired reporter who had the city buzzing as of late from her fearless reporting and "calling out" politicians, and rotated toward the new aide.

"Yes, Claire," Avanti said under a dark cloud of silence.

The furrow in Avanti's brow ironed out, although both her eyes still remained sharp and snakelike around the beige continent-shaped blotches scattered along her dark cheeks. Once Claire acknowledged that look on Avanti's face—in fact, absorbed the veracity of its raw seduction—Claire immediately backed off.

Sitting in monk-like nimbleness next to Governor Washington: the governor's longtime makeup artist, Violet Odem—or simply "Vye," for short. Vye had been right by Avanti's side well before she ran for mayor of Atlanta; in fact, ever since they met four years before Avanti decided to enter the game of "politricks," the two were pretty much inseparable.

Vye gave one quick eye-turn toward Avanti's gaze; however, like those close to Governor Washington, she knew *that* particular razor-eyed look and definitely knew when not to question such expression.

"Claire," Avanti said again, "What is it?"

"I. . . I have great news," Claire said hesitantly, while skimming through the text messages on her smartphone. "Get this. McCray's ready to come to the table to make a deal."

"Sounds like the lawsuit worked as planned," Avanti said with a half-smirk. "Pawn to e-four."

Inside joke.

"On top of the whole *vamp*-issue," Claire said with a hint of distain, "the media is going to have a field day with us—"

"—I'm well aware, Claire," Avanti said, then trailed off, "Working with ICE to round up thousands of undocumented vamps running around my state fits their narrative. They want to peg me as 'cruel' because that's exactly what their audience wants to hear. It's obvious the media has already chosen their white knight to oust me."

"Don't get me started with Byron," Claire said under her voice. "The woman wants everybody to live in a utopia. 'Save the planet?' That's her solution?" She laughed away the very thought of Bryon. "We can't even save ourselves—"

"—Sure, we've gotten a substantial hit from the movie industry. Companies, like BrainFood and Nikita, are having cold feet about whether or not they should move their headquarters here. The National Basketball League can't make up their goddamn mind about whether or not they want to pull The All Star Tournament out of our state. But, I guarantee you, they'll cave, once they feel the pressure from a party that I do not understand anymore. Which means *no* jobs and no money. But trust me, Claire. Once everything calms down, they'll come running back to us. All of them. They always do. Besides, the *safety*," she emphasized, "of our citizens is more important right now?"

"Of course, it is. *But*—"

"—*But* one thing's for damn sure," Avanti interrupted Claire, "You'll never hear a peep on the news about all the violent crimes these animals committed in the past six months. And I thought wintertime, of all times, was supposed to be the safest time of the year."

The imagery alone of having "untraceable" vamps running loose around her state, from thoroughbreds traveling in packs through late-night hours and devouring anything that had a pulse to lone half-breeds mutilating and committing sexual acts to their victims that'd make wild animals look, dare to say, civil to crossbreeds phantom-flying from one black market blood trader to another in order to whet an endless appetite, caused Avanti to lower head in despair. She ran her palm over the prickly surface of her shaved head, as if she was both stroking for good luck and dissolving any violent thought that manifested in her mind.

"I suggest we propose a strong defensive strategy just in case McCray backs away from the deal," Claire said, her voice distant to Avanti. "If we don't follow through on our end, McCray's going to do everything in his *power* to undermine your campaign for reelection."

One word jumped out at Avanti.

She faced Claire, her eyes narrowing.

"McCray's not the only one with friends in *high* places."

"But don't be fooled," Claire said, not backing away from the governor. "He has a reputation to exploit the weaknesses of those who oppose him. He's sneaky powerful."

"Yeah," Avanti started, "and he'd make a great politician."

Claire's expression—or lack thereof—spoke louder than she could articulate.

Likewise, Avanti acknowledged Claire's change in behavior.

"You have nothing to worry about, Claire," Avanti said, her tone softer. "My constituents know all about my skeletons. Believe it or not, if it weren't for those skeletons, I never would've been voted into office."

"Perhaps you should write a book about them," Claire suggested.

"About who?"

"Your skeletons, ma'am."

The governor ignored Claire and redirected her attention toward the looming storm outside, the chaos-loading. The sight of the mob caused her to take a beat and reflect on the past two weeks, the waves of violence throughout Georgia, bad press, as well as ridiculous conspiracies running wild through the tainted ether.

"Of all the groups out there, no matter what I say or do, I will never win *them* over."

"They can be our friend or our enemy."

"I rightfully disagree, Claire. They're supposed to be neither. Tell me something," the governor said following a heavy sigh. "In this digital age of information where every word that comes out of your mouth is destined to be distorted or taken out of context to merely whet one's own self-glorification, why in the hell do we continue to indulge these people?"

"What people—"

"—Reporters," the governor clarified. "What do they get out of all of this?"

"I guess they're just trying to inform the people."

"Please, Claire," Avanti said sharply, as she held back laughter. "You can't be that naive? Can you?"

"Well, permission to be frank. . . "

"I'd prefer you to be Frank than Dick. That's exactly why I brought you on my team, for your candor."

Claire bashfully cracked a smile.

"The attention," she said, shrugging her shoulders. "There's no surprise here, Governor. Like any Tom, Dick, or Harry who loves being in front of the camera, they're struck on themselves and have been ever since the *Three Stooges* invented the television."

Avanti grinned at Claire's usage of words.

"Yet, there lies the dilemma," the governor said after a slight pause. "People need the media as much as the media needs people. It's all about click bait, *sound bites*, shock-value, likes, and follows. It's one giant circle-jerk, Claire, and everbody's getting off all at once."

Greg the Bodyguard, who was sitting in the front passenger seat, pressed his finger against the earpiece in his ear.

"Ma'am," he said to Avanti, "they're now ready for you."

"Thank you, Greg," Avanti said modestly.

Cue Vye with her fanny pack of cosmetics already out. She zipped open the small pouch, which included a couple of sponges, brushes, puff pads, creams, and powders. She dug through all the cosmetics, sorted through what she needed and what she didn't, for instance, a travel size bottle of sunscreen, as well as foundation, a brownish-beige base to help even out Avanti's skin tone and make her leucoderma—or, best known as "vitiligo," a rare skin disease where the loss of pigmentation created these white-pinkish blotches on the skin—less obvious to the public. Lastly, Vye grabbed two UV cushion compacts, a variety of sunscreen, including sunscreen in powder-form, then, finally, a can of *SunOff* setting mist. Avanti wasn't particularly a "fan" of the sunscreen mist for two reasons: one, the mist provided very little coverage and the only way to get the most bang for your buck was to spray the mist directly into your hand and then reapply the sunscreen onto your skin; and two, if disregarding reason one, reapplying the mist directly to your face, especially those with vitiligo who had extremely sensitive skin, was no different than dowsing your face with Mace, since the inactive ingredient in *SunOff*—and that went for most sunscreen mists—was alcohol and if you weren't careful where you sprayed, even with your eyes closed, then welcome to Burn City.

Since Avanti was already wearing a good base of both sunscreen, which included *Maxfont Coverall* sun protection factor—or "SPF," for short—46 pa+++, as well as foundation, Vye went straight to *Jon Raphael*'s instant mineral broad-spectrum SPF 45 sunscreen, which contained twenty-one percent titanium dioxide and twenty percent zinc oxide powder, which, in essence, was a less expensive yet more effective imitation of the product *SunOff*, and it was also talc-free. Its formula was rich in antioxidants, as well as vitamin A, C, and E; and although it contained silicone, it applied exceptionally well and controlled whatever oiliness was left over from Avanti's base—no cast. Last but not least, Jon Raphael's sunscreen wouldn't show up on darker skin like other sunscreens. The brush was ideal for "on-the-go" reapplication and since Avanti, who normally wore sunglasses while being exposed to the sun, occasionally rubbed off the sunscreen whenever removing the shades from her face, the fine tune-up with Jon Raphael's self-dispensing brush added not only an extra reassurance to get her through the day, but was also gentler on her sensitive skin.

As Vye was just about to make a couple of last-second touch-ups to the governor's face, mainly reapplying more sunscreen to her cheeks, as well as her forehead, she caught the driver—she didn't know his name nor did she care to know his name—staring at her through the rear view mirror.

Vye stared back at the driver until he finally moved his eyes elsewhere.

Once the sunscreen was reapplied to Avanti's skin, she handed her a compact mirror. Strangely enough, Vye ignored the governor's approval and kept her eyes on the driver ahead, as if her poised glare was preventing the driver from moving his eyes in places where they didn't belong.

"I don't know how you do it," Claire said. "I admire your strength."

"I don't look at it as a skin disease, Claire," she said, pulling away the mirror. "I look at it as a gift."

"I never really thought of it that way, I guess—"

"—How do I look?" asked Avanti, as she closed the mirror.

"Beautiful, as always," Claire said.

Avanti glanced over at Vye, flicked her eyebrows, and said, "Showtime."

As Avanti placed the Aviator shades on her face, Claire made one last-second suggestion before she stepped outside.

"And remember to take them off when you look the employees in the eyes," she said. "We need every vote we can get."

Avanti smiled a closed, funeral-like smile.

She didn't say a word to Claire. Didn't need to. Yet, she made a gesture that left her new aide in a thoughtful state of regret.

As assumed, reporters swarmed Governor Washington as soon as she stepped outside the black town car. She immediately recognized one particular face and that face belonged to July August—or better yet, her face belonged to the most watched local network in the greater Atlanta area, WEGT. And yes, the reporter's name shared the same first and last name as two months on the lunar calendar.

With her question locked and loaded, July thrust the microphone inches away from Avanti's face. A plump cameraman, who had a beard that would make Paul Bunyan proud, was standing with a clear shot of Avanti—or what the news industry (and other entertainment industries, for that matter) called the "money shot." Thankfully for Avanti, Greg was there to redirect the microphone from her grill. From behind the mass of flesh, July yelled out exactly what Avanti had expected to hear from Atlanta's "hottest" news reporter on her latest gaffe: "Ms. Washington, do you care to explain what you meant when you said—and I'm quoting—" July read from her notepad, "—'*We should send all of them (illegal immigrants) back to Transylvania*'?"

Considering only twelve hours had elapsed since her "hot mike" incident, she anticipated that her untimely joke to Congressman Weaver would eventually surface but never so suddenly. From any politician's standpoint, especially one who happened to be on the other and essentially, wrong side of the press, it was fair—in fact, it was beyond satisfactory—to compare "news reporters," even the modern day (wannabe) "journalist" for that matter, to a particular kind of bird that fed mainly on carrion and had a known reputation for gathering with other birds of its species in the expectation of inevitable death.

"When there was one of them circling around a carcass in the air, then surely there were others gathering to pick up the scraps."

Other reporters followed July's lead and joined in on the blistering verbal assaults with follow-up questions based on unfounded evidence.

One reporter: *"Is it true you have a bill banning the high-borns from Georgia ready to sign on your desk?"*

Avanti only caught the words *high born,* but she nearly laughed at the reference used to identify yet, at the same time, oblige an ancient race that survived off drinking the blood of its victims. For the most part, it was the "Millennial" vampires who were offended by the slang word *vamp.*

Another reporter: *"Don't you fear your reelection may be at stake after signing a new abortion law that allows women to terminate a fetus past twenty-weeks of pregnancy? Correct me if I'm wrong, Governor, but, to me, is sounds like you just signed your own death certificate as governor of Georgia?"*

Then, another: *"In a speech last week at the Women Work conference, you claimed you're for the rights of all undocumented immigrants from the Old Country, but you continue to round them up like cattle and lock them in cages. How do you explain this hypocrisy?"*

The reporter's words were strategic.

"Cages" sounded better than "jail."

Made them sound like animals.

And, the governor was in the business of "bad policy."

Then, yet another reporter: *"Can you defend the words of some of the members in your party, in particular, Congressman Lumpkin, about considering some radical high borns as hate groups?"*

Then, another: *"What is your response to late-night comedian, Johnny Crumble, calling you a raccoon?"*

The brazen reporter's words, cold and mean-spirited, were not only strategic, but they were also intended to get a rise out of Governor Washington in order to make for "shock" entertainment. Even the word *raccoon* in itself was a poor attempt to get underneath the governor's skin.

Another reporter followed before the governor had a chance to put the privileged reporter in his place: "*So, Governor. Why did you file a lawsuit against one of the wealthiest men in America?*"

Another: "*Are you a racist?*"

Again, a strategic word, one painted with a broad brush, meant to provoke an audience, to bring about divisiveness.

Like "bigot" or "hypocrite" or "flip-flopper."

Of all the words a politician never wanted to hear uttered from anyone's mouth, it was the label "Flip-Flopper."

Then, another: "*Are you working with the big tech companies to implant each illegal alien with tracking devices?*"

Finally, the governor threw up her hand, removed the Aviators from her face, calmly placed the sunglasses in her breast pocket, and said sternly, "I'm not here to talk about myself. I'm here for the grand opening of the school. That's it."

A high-pitched reporter immediately chimed in: "*But Governor Washington, why do you continue to flip-flop on your stance with undocumented—*"

The governor turned to the reporter and looked her directly in the eyes.

"What did you not understand about what I just said?" asked Avanti, her tone as well as her aura dominating. She explained it carefully for the young reporter, as if she was some three-year-old who recently committed a boo-boo. "I told you that I'm not here to talk about myself, yet you persist on asking me questions regarding myself. Now, if you will, please get out of my way, I'm here to show my support to the good folks at New Way Academy." She called out to Greg, who, in return, made a hole for the governor and then Claire, who wasn't too far behind.

Most of the reporters fell silent. Other reporters looked almost deflated from the governor's unwillingness to provide answers to their questions.

Both camera crews and Greg, who was a few pounds overweight or what his doctor referred to as being "borderline obese," tried to keep pace with the two ladies as they power-walked to the front of the brand new state-of-the-art school, New Way Academy, where the ribbon cutting would take place.

From the corner of her mouth, the governor whispered in Claire's ear, "These people," Avanti said in side-thought, "*Actually, I wouldn't even go so far to call them people. Technically, they're dead.* They're given everything for free. Yet, I make one little joke behind closed doors—which, I will admit, was in poor taste, but that's neither here nor there—then some little rat records it behind my back—by the way, how the hell was that rat able to sneak his phone into the meeting?" For a moment, Avanti moved her cold eyes toward a blushing Greg, who appeared as if he was shrinking in size. "Now," she said, redirecting her attention forward, "all of a sudden, I'm made to look like the enemy here. It's like *people*," she emphasized, "that is, the ones still breathing, care more about the undead than their actual *living* human being."

"After the next month's debate, people will forget all about it," Claire said, as she tried to reassure the governor.

Governor Washington put on a smiley face as she approached The New Way Academy staff, including the principal, Marlin Rowe, as well as the private investors who generously donated to the state-funded school. With cameras flashing away, the governor shook the hand of each staff member of the school. Except for a couple of ballsy reporters, who were hanging out past the barricade and shouting out provocative questions during gaps of silence, the photo-op had gone smoothly so far. No gaffes or blips. The skilled governor had a particular way of not showing any kind of "face" when she was in front of the camera. Only "grips and grins," as she called her public appearances.

Lastly, Marlin greeted the governor with a handshake.

"Governor," Marlin said in his thick southern accent, "it's a honor. It's good to see you out and about for a change. For a second," he said, teasing Avanti, "I thought you only did dinners and speeches."

"And I see you haven't lost your sense of humor."

"Thanks for coming, Governor."

"Please, Marlin," she said, smiling. "Avanti."

"How's Ajax?" asked Marlin. "Brent told me that he didn't like these sort of things."

"So sorry he couldn't make it," Avanti responded. "He was feeling under the weather."

"I heard there was a nasty bug going 'round." Marlin leaned in extra close to Avanti and whispered in her ear, "*Wouldn't surprise me if it came from a vamp.*"

Avanti didn't respond to the insensitive remark. Yet, she faced forward and continued to smile for the cameras.

"Anyway," Marlin said, his voice rising. "Sorry to hear about Ajax." Then, he turned toward the front of a crowd where his son was standing with his mother. "Come on over, Brent. Say hi to the governor of Georgia."

Brent bashfully walked over and shook the governor's hand.

"Hello, Brent," Avanti said, remaining professional despite the awkwardness of the conversation. "I swear, you look bigger every time I see you."

"Hey, Ms. Washington."

"Brent's a late bloomer," Marlin said, clapping Brent's shoulder.

"Where's Ajax?"

"Unfortunately, Ajax couldn't make it," Avanti said. "I was telling your father here that he's at home under the weather."

"What's wrong with him?" asked Brent.

Avanti was taken aback by the question. Still wearing a smile on her face, she turned to the cameramen surrounding her and then faced Brent.

"Stomach bug," she said over a pause. "You know, the kind where it comes out of both ends."

Depressed from the recent news, Brent held his head downward.

After acknowledging the sudden change in the young boy's manner, Avanti leaned in close to Brent and told him to stop by the house and pay her son a visit. "He'd really enjoy your company," she said.

"*But,*" Brent returned, "if he sick, I don't wanna be picking up anything."

The governor waved off Brent's concern.

"You'll be fine."

Before he could return with more questions, Marlin shooed him away back to his mother.

"Don't you just love 'em to death at that age?" Marlin said foolishly behind his son's back. "*Question* every single thing you do. I'll give Brent another year or so before he hates my guts."

Trying not to draw too much unwanted attention, Avanti said bluntly, "I think I've already reached that stage with Ajax." With other staff members waiting for the opening ceremony to begin, Marlin escorted Avanti to the pair of giant scissors on the table next to the red ribbon. She eyed the golden scissors and said to Marlin, "He's gotten to the point where he won't even talk to me anymore."

"They just need space at that age," he said. "Hell, I was the same exact way. Didn't even talk to my daddy until he was an old man."

"Is that so?"

"By then, he was already on his death bed."

"Sorry to hear, Marlin."

"Sons are born to hate their fathers," Marlin said and showed Avanti the pair of scissors, "*not* their mothers." Avanti took a brief moment to absorb the comment. "Give him time, Avanti," Marlin said over a thoughtful pause. "He'll talk whenever he's ready."

"And how will I know when he's ready?" asked Avanti.

"You'll know," Marlin said and held up the pair of scissors for Avanti.

Other members of the press, as well as other staff members gathered around Marlin and Avanti, as if they were two actors on stage.

As he was about to hand the scissors to Avanti, his face went long and slack. Everything about his manner turned solemn. "Listen, Avanti," Marlin said seriously to not only Avanti but also to the sudden crowd that had formed around the two, "I know you have your hands full—Lord! I can't even imagine doing what you're—but I just wanted to tell you that Stew would be proud of you, for everything you're doing and what you've done to our community and all the progress we've made. He'd especially be proud of you for raising Ajax by yourself while trying to govern the great state of Georgia. You are truly one *helluva* woman, Ms. Avanti Washington."

Smitten by the words, the governor replied to both Marlin while, at the same time, making her response clear to the crowd, "Why thank you so much, Principal Rowe. *Marlin*. That means a lot to me. It was Stew who actually inspired me to enter politics; in fact, before Stew lost his battle with brain cancer, I told him that I was going to give politics a shot. At first," she said in a punchy way, "he didn't believe me; in fact, Stew thought I was the one with the inoperable tumor. Then, over time, as his condition worsened, he started to come around and accept what I was destined to do; in fact, he often joked about me running for mayor of Atlanta. Encouraged me but, at the same time, threw in a couple of jokes every chance he could. There was one in particular. He once said to me, 'What does a baby's diaper and a politician both have in common?"

Marlin was stumped by the question.

"They're changed regularly," Avanti said, leaning in closer to Marlin. "And, for the same reasons," she added.

Marlin laughed, so did the people gathered around; however, it was a forced laugh, as if it was coming from somewhere else inside them.

"There was truth in Stew's joke," Avanti said, more strongly, "and after Stew passed away, I took a vow to prove him wrong. Even today, he continues to inspire me." She tried to laugh away the glumness by bringing in more lightheartedness to the "broadcasted" conversation. "*But*, I'll tell you this, if it wasn't for Savannah helping me out around the house, I believe this job would've taken me straight to the grave."

Another one of those laughs slipped from Marlin, as if he was now laughing on-demand.

Others in the crowd laughed as well.

It didn't matter what the governor had said from this point forward.

She already had them exactly where she wanted; however, the only problem: she was running out of room on her fingers.

Five Years Later.

"WELCOME to the Big Leagues."

The scene was set.

Present day.

St. Gabriel Hotel.

Manhattan, New York.

The characters were all in their designated places like pieces on a chessboard, except for one: Governor Avanti Washington.

Avanti ignored the tweet from across the room and drifted off while rehearsing her lines for the upcoming speech.

Her eyes glazed over as she stared at the softening glow of the phone's screen and the words on it, which started to blur and brighten.

Eventually, the screen faded into sleep-mode, causing the screen to go black.

So, too, did Avanti's spirits.

The sudden change in mood caused Vye to remove the brown puff pad from her face.

Over her trance, she heard the same voice sounding even more farther away: "Avanti?"

Like a ball player imagined winning the big game and whether it be by shooting a wild buzzer beater to win a basketball game or hitting a walk-off grand slam in the bottom ninth of a baseball game or figuratively—or literally, depending on the mentality of the ball player—knocking an opponent's head off in an important football game, or imagining whatever "moment" in whatever sport that often required the least amount of skill, yet demanded a hundred percent determination to hoist that one word up on his or her pedestal, the two-term governor of Georgia imagined herself giving a *winning* speech. Flashes of grit and grace appeared before her. Her speech was deeply profound, historical. The governor spoke a clear "vision" for her future of America and did so with authentic sincerity and compassion: two traits which screamed "Politician!" Or "Not to be trusted!" "A two-face who says what you want to hear!" Or, best, "*Politicians Suck!*" Which was one the governor heard most often.

Yet, when she delivered the big speech to the audience, Avanti Oluwaseyi Washington came off as one who walked with them but was not one of them. A true leader, not a follower. She left the audience in a state of hypnosis, convincing doubters and silencing haters. She was a mere vessel for the projected path forward; yet, at the same time, she embodied toughness, decisiveness, and most importantly, *practicality*.

Her mouthy campaign manager, Sonny Mims, who had worked for President Townsend during his campaign against Senator Coats eight years ago and with all baggage aside, including his deep affection for Jack Daniels and his outbursts and short tempers, was considered what those in her close circle called the "people's whisperer," snapped his fingers in front of her face and once more, called out her name.

Startled from airy assault, Avanti pulled herself from her trance-like state.

"Yes," Avanti snapped back.

"Where'd you go?" asked Sonny.

Ignoring Sonny's question, Avanti waked the phone by tapping on the screen.

Patiently, she scrolled through the lines on her NOTES app.

"The part where it says," she read the line from her phone, "'After four years of this administration,'" she turned to the other diverse writers who were scrambling to locate the right page, "on page seven, 'it is clear not only to the people of this great country, but also to the entire world that we do *not* need a businessman running our government.' And," she read, "'when I say *our* government, I mean the *people's* government!'" She pulled away the phone. "It's unnecessary, don't you think? I think we should take it out."

The script readers and writers, who had copies of the speech in their hands, flipped to the "diss" section and followed along with Avanti.

"People want to see you take the gloves off, Avanti—"

"—Haven't heard that one before, Sonny," Avanti said under her breath.

Sonny didn't care much for Avanti's disobedience; in fact, he was two ticks away from lashing out at her.

"And," she said suddenly as she scrolled through her phone once more, "on page—where was it—on page nine, the part about Rhodes' track record on deporting illegal vamps. You really think it's wise to bring up illegal immigration, considering my own record in Georgia? You know exactly what Rhodes' people are going to start calling me—the big 'FF.' I mean, do we really want to start rolling in the mud with these people? We're better than this, aren't we?"

Sonny crossed his arms over his chest in defense.

Avanti's partner, Colin Galloway, a highly respected architect born and raised in Harlem but spent most of his adult life studying in Paris, France, was fourteen years older than Avanti; however, his fluffy, snowy white beard that would've made Santa Clause envious made him look much older than his age and often times, whenever accompanying Avanti at nightly fundraisers or high-stakes dinners, he'd receive compliments and sober nods of respect on his storyteller-like beard. He was wearing a black tuxedo that paired nicely with Avanti's sage green lace maxi dress, which was personally designed by a famous French clothing designer named Claudian Bisset. Along a high, halter neckline was an eyelash lace with a sleeveless, darted bodice, and an open back, which complimented Avanti's toned shoulders. Below the fitted waist, weightless georgette cascaded into a riotous maxi skirt.

In most cases, Colin wouldn't dare stick his nose in Avanti's business or even touch it with a ten foot pole; however, while he patiently waited with his earthy brown eyes targeted on the back of Sonny—the look itself was like an unspoken declaration of disapproval for Avanti's campaign manager and his abrasiveness—he couldn't keep his mouth shut any longer.

"*Go with your gut*, honey," Colin said from the corner of the room.

Avanti absorbed Colin's remark, as if she was filing it away under "Note-to-Self."

In return, Sonny gave Colin a look that shouted "Back off!"

"People want to see you take the gloves off, Avanti," Sonny said again, as if he was finishing a thought. "Even if that means poking *Swamp Thing* every now and then," Sonny threw his hands up in the air, "so be it!" Occasionally using his hands to do most of the speaking for him, Sonny paced around Avanti, as if, by doing so, he was displaying dominance—or simply trying to get inside Avanti's headspace. "Think of this as a warm-up. The American people haven't seen this 'side' of you yet. The *fighter*," he emphasized, "who, I know, can throw one helluva nasty left hook. And trust me, when I tell you this, 'People are *dying* to see that side.' They want that side. Otherwise, Rhodes is gonna do what he does best and he has a bottomless appetite. So, believe me when I tell you that Rhodes will eat you alive during the first debate—"

"—Don't get ahead of yourself, Sonny. We haven't even gotten the nominee yet."

"Croom is a goddamn *gaffe machine*," Sonny argued. "Jett is shrinking in the polls by the hour. Turns out Roundtree is a man-whore. And Bullock, she can't save herself from hot water even if someone threw her a life preserver. You have this nomination in the bag. Which means, if you don't strike first, then Rhodes is going to spit you out like he does with everybody who gets in his way." Sonny paused and faced Avanti. "I can't stress this enough, Avanti. America cannot—I will say it again CAN-NOT—afford to have four more years of this clown. Trust me. All I want you to do tonight is STICK-TO-THE-SCRIPT. Can you do that?"

"Sonny, I haven't slung any mud thus far," she returned. "So why start now? I think you're wrong about people—"

"—Of all the elections I've witnessed, not one candidate has ever run a clean campaign. Not ever."

"And that's exactly why this campaign is so special, Sonny," Avanti said, her voice more stern. "I need you on board with this. . . "

Avanti allowed Sonny a chance to respond.

During the break in the conversation, Vye found the right opportunity to apply a light coat of foundation to Avanti's skin.

"Go easy this time," Avanti said to Vye from the corner of her mouth. "The last time, you made me look like a cancer patient."

"Yes, ma'am," Vye said, dabbing foundation on the sides of Avanti's chin.

With a look of disgust, Sonny looked at Avanti and uttered as if he was talking to himself, "*I need a smoke.*"

He pulled out a cigarette from the pack of Mensticks in his pocket, stuck it in his mouth, and as he was about to light up, Avanti wagged her index finger back and forth in the air like a pendulum.

"No smoking," she said softly.

Sonny's shoulder raised upward in a frozen shrug.

"Serious?" he said with a cigarette dangling from his lips.

"It's a non-smoking room, Sonny."

"So?"

Avanti didn't say a word in return.

All she had to do was give Sonny that "look."

More disgusted in Avanti, Sonny shook his head and stormed from the hotel room. Even slammed the door on his way out.

Claire stepped forward from the back of the room and asked Avanti, "Why'd you even hire that asshole?"

"For your information," Avanti said while Vye continued to apply makeup to her face, "that asshole gets people elected."

"It's not like he's carrying a magic wand or anything. He runs his campaigns on shock and awe. He wants you to be someone you're not."

"And who am I, Claire? Since you know everything about me?"

"A woman who doesn't need to roll around in the mud with all the other pigs, that's who?"

"I can get dirty when I need to—"

"—But like you said, you don't have to."

"You're right," Avanti said and shot her eyes toward Claire, "I don't."

⊕

SURROUNDED by her entourage, Avanti made her way from the hotel room.

On the way out, she spotted the bathtub in the corner of her eye. She stopped at the edge of the bathroom and found herself staring at the bathtub— and remembering. Four years had past since his death and every single time she found herself looking at a bathtub—any bathtub whether it be the one in the upstairs hallway or one inside a hotel room—she *always* remembered.

Before she could get lost in the red memory, Claire touched her on the shoulder and asked, "You okay?"

Avanti struggled to smile.

"I want your honesty, Claire," Avanti started with a pensive expression worn heavily on her face. "Am I doing the right thing? I mean do the American people really care what I have to say?"

"Of course, they do," Claire said, more tenderly. "You wouldn't have made it this far based on your looks."

Avanti thought more about Claire's comment.

"Believe it or not," she said, as if, all of a sudden, the temperature in the hotel room dropped twenty degrees, "I'm a little nervous."

"There's no reason to be nervous, Avanti," Claire said. "We got this!"

"There's a lot of money at stake, Claire."

"It's just a bunch of old rich people," Claire said, "donors who are ready and willing to sign you the check. Like Sonny said, just stick to the script."

"Right," Avanti said, losing courage.

More thoughtful, Claire said to Avanti, "I've only given like two speeches in front of a large group of people: once in college and then another time at my sister's wedding. Terrified both times. Even at my sister's wedding, despite the liquid courage. Utterly *terrified*—I'm talking to the point where I wanted to just run away people and never look back. I know it sounds silly and all," she said, grinning. "But the only thing that got me through both those speeches was something my dad taught me."

"What's that, Claire?" said Avanti.

"Speak like I'm speaking to myself."

"Really?"

"I know," she said. "Silly. Juvenile, really. But it worked. I mean, who else knows you better than yourself than your *own* self. What I meant to say is, speak like you're speaking in front of a mirror."

"What would I do without you, Claire?" asked Avanti.

⊕

AFTER Avanti's entourage exited from room 421, three secret service agents gave Avanti and the rest of her team a go ahead to proceed down the hallway. Her two personal bodyguards, Joel and Kobo, who were roughly the size of refrigerators, led the way while her aide, Claire, and her makeup artist, Vye, walked alongside Avanti, whereas Colin followed close behind.

As the team proceeded toward the elevators, Avanti couldn't help but notice the squishiness of the triangular-patterned carpet. The soft feel of the strange carpet pressed against the ball of her foot, as well as that familiar spongy-sound it made while she walked indicated the dampness of the carpet below. Keeping pace with the team, she glanced downward at the carpet. She grabbed a handful of her maxi skirt and below her sage green stiletto the wet carpet bubbled slightly during each step. Since the mass of flesh, Joel and Kobo, were partially blocking the view of the hallway before her, she decided to glance behind her. There, in the opening of several bodies, she witnessed what looked like the wet imprints of a child's feet dotting the entire carpet.

Curious, Avanti paused in her tracks, causing the rest of the team to pause as well. She squeezed through Joel and Kobo, nudged them aside, and inspected the carpet more thoroughly this time. She found more of those dark outlines of soaking wet feet marks trailing toward the elevators.

"Is there something wrong, Ms. Washington?" asked Joel.

Avanti was more focused on the footprints than the question itself.

"*Avanti?*"

As Avanti turned to Claire, she saw what she thought was a young girl sprinting around the corner at the end of the narrow hallway. The EXIT sign merrily flickered, which made Avanti question whether or not it was really the change in light or some girl who had snuck onto the floor.

"I thought you said the hall was clear," Avanti said to one of the agents.

"Did you see something, ma'am?"

299

"I thought. . . " she stuttered and turned around to Joel, ". . . it's nothing. It's just my mind playing tricks on me, I guess—"

"—It's nerves, Avanti," Claire whispered in Avanti's ear. "Remember what I told you and you'll be fine. And also, please remember to breath."

Avanti nodded off the comment, did as Claire said and took in a deep breath while straightening her shoulders. Her posture was taller, prouder. She looked as if she was "ready."

Once her team reached the elevators, Avanti and four other members of her team stepped inside the elevators.

Before entering, Avanti asked about Sonny's whereabouts, if he was off on his "smoke break." However, neither Claire nor the bodyguards had seen him.

Joel hit the number "1" button on the panel.

As the elevator doors began to close, Avanti was drawn to the vacant space in the hallway outside. She continued to stare until her thoughts started to fill in the spaces. The bright colors faded from the memory of her. Before she could visualize that gray, bloated, expressionless face staring back at her through the closing doors, she turned away and embraced yet another deep breath.

"Re-lax, A-van-ti," Claire whispered, more slowly this time as if she was hitting each syllable.

They rode the elevator to the first floor where the ballroom was located. During their descent, Claire pulled out her smartphone and read from an earlier text, "Rhodes is going to unveil his new slogan for 2020 tomorrow night in Michigan. 'Richard Rhodes: Building a *safer* road forward.'"

"He's clearly making it clear for voters," Avanti replied, as she still felt a little off about the upcoming speech. "If there's one thing I do admire about Rhodes, it's his consistency. The man sticks to his message all right."

She took another deep breath and with the back of her hand, patted the top of her forehead, which was glistening with sweat.

Claire tried to lighten up the visual tension inside the elevator by informing Avanti that she had a "quick"—she couldn't emphasize the word *quick* enough— photo-op with a seven-year old girl named Becca Petri. "Friends call her Becky. Becca here," she read from the notes underneath her itinerary, "claims to be one of your biggest fans."

"One of those, huh?"

"Avanti, she's only seven years old."

"What? I can be great with kids."

"Well," Claire said motherly, "just try to be nice. I had to pull a lot of strings to bring her to this private event, considering Adamache basically bought out the entire hotel for the night. Plus, she drove all the way from Locklier, Georgia."

"You know I don't like surprises, Claire," Avanti said, both her face, as well as her tone sharpening. Then, asked: "Was she invited to the dinner?"

"Fifty-thousand dollars a plate?" Claire returned with a hint of sarcasm in her voice. "She'd have to win the lottery to be able to afford to eat here."

"That's not what I asked."

"No," Claire said. "Like I said, it's just a photo-op. Shouldn't take that long. Just be your charming self for the cameras—" Claire paused in mid-sentence, her eyes drifting in a glowing thought. "Why? Do you want me to add the girl as one of your guests? I can do it. It's not too late. I can call Paul from the Financial Committee. Plus, it could leave a good impression on donors."

From the back of the elevator, Vye said coldly, "To me, it sounds like an unnecessary distraction."

Avanti acknowledged Vye's timely yet rare input.

"No," she said over second thoughts. "Just the photo-op," Avanti said, facing Claire. "Besides, I'm not here to win over voters."

"Right," Claire responded and dismissed Avanti's remark. "Apparently, this is Becca's first time in New York. So, be 'extra' nice."

Claire made sure to emphasize the word *extra*.

"You don't think I'm nice?"

"You are. . . " Claire said hesitantly, ". . . when you want to be."

The elevator stopped.

Avanti handed Claire her Bisset rhinestone-covered hand purse.

"Guard it with your life," she said, not referring to the actual hand purse itself but the contents inside the hand purse.

Claire gave Avanti her word, as the elevator doors opened.

As soon as Avanti's team exited the elevator, a horde mostly consisting of the members of the press were ready to pounce on Avanti. Both the body-guards and secret service agents cleared a tight path for Avanti, who answered only a couple of questions about her "change" in the on-going illegal vamp problem and stated, for the record, that she had, in fact, taken a position to give "all" vamps a pathway to citizenship. After all, she needed each and every vote she could find from the vamp community. Initially, her plan was to answer questions after her speech; however, every now and then, the campaign trail offered its own subtle surprises. After Avanti answered in rapid-fire pace, she walked straight over to Becca's camp: a strategically "diverse" group of supposed neighbors, classmates, as well as distant relatives of Becca, all decked out in purple "Washington 2020" getup, including shirts and hats; one of them in particular was waving around a small purple banner with the campaign slogan that read: "*Look out, Washington! Here comes a new Washington!*"

In the middle of the group, Avanti spotted a little girl, who like the others was decked out in a purple "Washington 2020" baseball cap, a wristband with the initials "WWAWD," and an oversized purple shirt that looked as if it was three sizes too big, reading: "*Where my broom at?*" Since the girl was standing ahead of the group, Avanti assumed that she was Becca Petri. That, and she wasn't quite right. Avanti wasn't so sure about the girl's condition until Claire leaned in and pointed out the spotty-faced girl among the other groupies. Apparently, Becca, as well as her aunt, Nay-Nay, who was now Becca's legal guardian, and her relatives, who, not until Becca's story made the six o'clock news, were all but strangers to Becca, had brought members from their local news along with them.

A reporter and a cameraman were standing anxiously next to the group, as if they were primed to wrap a heart-warming story. However, when Avanti and her team approached Becca, Avanti first realized her story wasn't "heart-warming." And, not only that, from the way Becca was standing in a slouched position, she looked extremely ill.

Before the greeting, Claire informed Avanti about Becca and her recent loss.

"Her mother?"

"Joanne Petri was her name," Claire said closely over the chaos and commotion all around them. "Single-parent—"

"—Why does that name ring a bell?" asked Avanti.

"Before Ms. Petri's life spiraled out of control, she was working two jobs and struggling to put food on the table for young Becca. After they were evicted from their apartment, Ms. Petri got hooked up with a rough crowd. The Gist Brothers. She owed them a lot of money. After Ms. Petri was fired from one job, she and Becca wound up on the streets. Ms. Petri then got involved in drugs. Sent Becca away to stay with her aunt. Eventually, she became homeless."

"She was murdered by a thoroughbred," Avanti said clearly, filling in the rest of Becca's story, "same one who I had deported during my first term. I vaguely remember the story. I do remember, however, that it was all over the news."

"You got it," Claire said and then informed Avanti, "After Joanne Petri was murdered, ICE ended up capturing a vampire named Marian Boboc, *a real bloodsucker he was. . .* "

Once more, Avanti found herself drifting from Claire's words. *She was back in the governor's office, screaming over the phone at the health and human resources secretary for more money for the state while, at the same time, giving her piece of mind about how she really felt about the state legislatures. Claire was in the room as well, heard the cheap jabs and low blows being thrown by Avanti, as she pressed the phone's speaker against the side of her shoulder. After the phone call, the two were going back and forth, arguing about whether or not raising the minimum wage would be beneficial to the state.*

"We raise the minimum wage," Avanti argued, "then employers are going to hire less people. Which means more people are going to be out of work. I've said it from the very get-go. We need to push for more schooling. More schooling and practical hands-on training for higher paid jobs. Who the hell wants to make a living off flipping burgers for crying out loud? And I'll tell you this: I don't give a shit what these protestors—who, by the way, have nothing else better to do with their lives—have to say."

"How can you say that, Avanti?" Claire returned. "You're a mother and one day, Robert may want to work at one of those jobs in order to pay for college."

"Ajax can't even lift a finger around the house," Avanti said flippantly.

"Which brings up yet another issue: college," Claire said, pacing around the office. "How can kids afford college on a minimum wage—"

"I'm not raising the minimum wage, Claire."

More voices in the commotion clarified.

One particular voice became clearer: Claire's.

"...*Somehow*," Claire said over a sigh, "Mr. Boboc reentered the states once more and killed another woman who was six-months pregnant. The woman happened to be the wife of an ICE agent. A couple of days after her death, a pile of ash was discovered in a back alleyway. Coroners were able to lift an implant from the remains. It belonged to a one, Mr. Boboc. Investigators never found the person or persons who killed Mr. Boboc."

"If I hadn't taken action sooner," Avanti said, feeling the radiant sting of regret, "then Ms. Petri never would've been murdered."

"Mr. Boboc was quite an evasive criminal, Avanti."

"No," Avanti said, thinking more about her four years as mayor and how she, somehow, won enough votes from the city council to not only relocate a homeless shelter in order to build a new hockey arena, but also gentrify South End. "That's not what I'm talking about," Avanti said, her voice trailing off.

"Then, what are you talking about?" asked Claire.

Avanti finally arrived at Team Becca. In the corner of her eye, she noticed a tiny red dot on the bottom of the camera. After months of being on the campaign trail, no matter where she traveled, she realized the camera was *always* on. Even Becca's relatives had their phones out, fishing for a "like."

Despite Becca's skin condition—"psoriasis," was what the doctors called it— Avanti greeted her with a handshake. The last thing Avanti wanted to do, especially in the middle of a "live" recording, was show the town of Locklier that she was afraid of a red patch, which, by the way, was *not* contagious. After all, during what most would call a pivotal time of the race where it was every candidate for him or herself, every single vote counted, even if it meant reaching out to the seven-year-old who technically couldn't vote for another eleven years or so; however, most of the people standing around Becca were over eighteen, which meant checkmarks for the governor. The sides of Becca's face and neck were also covered with old scars and patches of skin grafts, which had been taken from her legs after Becca developed a serious— near fatal—staph infection that went untreated during that financially uncertain time when she was shelter-hoping and spending a good part of two years of living on the streets with her junkie mother. Her hand was red and scaly; however, Avanti made sure to keep a gentle yet natural grip on it while, at the same time, keep a wide smile on her face for the camera.

"It's nice to finally meet you, Becca," Avanti said ecstatically. "I've heard so much about you."

Star-struck by Avanti's presence, she bashfully rocked back and forth on her heels. She had no words for the two-term governor, only great expectations.

"She's shy," her aunt, Nay Nay, said defensively.

"I was shy when I was your age too, Becca," Avanti said, trying not to look at Becca's scars. "In fact, my parents could hardly squeeze a word from me."

Becca removed her hat, revealing more red blemishes and bare spots around parts of her scalp and forehead. She handed the ball cap to Avanti.

"Can you sign her hat?" asked Nay Nay.

"Why certainly," Avanti said and grabbed the Sharpie from Claire's hand, "It would be my privilege to sign your hat."

As Avanti made out the hat to "her friend, Becca Petri" and signed her John Hancock on the underside of the bill, Becca murmured: "Thank you, Ms. Washington, for all you're doing to help the high-borns. I believe they all have a right to be here just as much as I do."

"I'm so glad you brought that up, Becca," Avanti said to Becca when, in actuality, she was addressing the people who were at home watching her on TV. "I believe, just as you believe, Becca, that high-borns—and *all* walks of life, for that matter—have the God-given right to enter this country whether seeking asylum or education, a job, or even start a new life right here in America."

"*Why the change, Ms. Washington?*" one reporter asked from the back of the crowd. "*Your current position does not reflect your policies in the past.*"

"You're right," Avanti said to Becca, then stood and faced the crowd. "You can call me a flip-flopper, hypocrite, or even your typical politician who tells you exactly what you want to hear. I am all of those things. *But* the truth of the matter is that I have changed. I have 'evolved.' It's only in our nature to *evolve.*"

Avanti made sure to emphasize the word evolve for the cameras.

They were known to use strategic words, sound bites taken out of context, as well as catchy headlines. Why not use a play straight out of their own playbook?

"So, I say, 'So what?'" Avanti said. "Over time, people do evolve, especially when faced with tragedy." She looked down at Becca and softly pinched the edge of her chin. "Like young Becca here, a sweet and innocent girl whose mother was sadly taken away from her two years—"

"*Three*," Claire mumbled in Avanti's ear, as if she was a ventriloquist.

"—Three years ago," she corrected, "by an individual named Marian Boboc, a high-born who committed a terrible crime. Now Becca could've blamed Marian and everybody who looked like Marian for what happened to her mother. But she didn't. And till this day, she still doesn't."

Other members of the press gathered around the two-term governor as if she was giving an impromptu speech. They were holding out microphones and tape recorders. Some of them were jotting down notes on their notepads.

"An 'individual' killed Becca's mother," Avanti said. "Let's remember that, people. An *individual*. Not a group. As long as we are living here in this country, there is only one group—one—and that's American."

Becca's relatives were bobbing their heads to Avanti's every word. Nay Nay applauded Avanti, resulting in other relatives to applaud. By the time Avanti was finished with the photo-op, she had already won over the crowd.

⊕

AVANTI hung out with Becca for a couple of minutes longer, mainly taking selfies with her and signing her signature to other belongings and memorabilia and most importantly, embracing Becca and Nay Nay's appreciation for taking the time out of her robust schedule to meet with young Becca.

Once Avanti said her goodbyes to Becca, as well as her friends and family, she was about to join Colin in a large hallway where she had no more than a minute to catch her breath from the chaos in the lobby before Claire pulled her aside for a moment to question her latest comments, which were more than likely going to be discussed and analyzed all over Shane Lowman's *News Zone*.

"What was that back there?" asked Claire. "Flip-flopper? Hypocrite?"

"The crowd seemed to like it," Avanti said, ignoring Claire's tamed overreaction. "Besides, I feel a lot of better. Less nervous. Your little pep talk worked."

"Just remember the earnings at stake here. Six mill—"

"—I know what's at stake," Avanti interrupted before Claire could even utter the big M word.

Claire glanced at her phone and raised her eyebrows from the latest update on Avanti's online fundraiser.

"We have some good news," she said, flattered. "Looks like your latest tweet helped bring in more money."

"Where's it at now?"

"Just shy of eleven *million*," Claire said.

"Looks like the grassroots donations are working better than you thought."

"But it won't be enough to buy our ticket into Iowa—"

"Enough, Claire," Avanti said. "Go find Sonny or something."

As Claire was about to remind her of the whole "sticking to the script" plan, Avanti met up with Colin and together, the two moved their way toward the ballroom where she was going to give her speech to New York's wealthiest—and elite, including investors, hedge fund types, business magnates, yuppies, Wall Street aficionados, even A-listers, celebrities, TV personalities, as well as athletes, and basically those who had pockets so deep that they could fit a country inside them and, of course, those who had Avanti's ear.

Claire sneaked in a comment by making sure to congratulate her for the bump in the donations but didn't waste any time warning Avanti of the host of the fundraiser who was standing directly at her twelve o'clock.

"Alexandru Adamache," Avanti said, eyeing the older gentlemen in the black tuxedo among a crowd of socialites. Standing next to Alexandru were two other men who looked equally as wealthy, if not wealthier. All three of them looked as if they received monthly "touch-ups" to their faces. Not a single one of them had a single wrinkle on their thirty-year-old skin-tight faces, despite being the age of a man where his wrinkles were considered a symbolic yet honest representation of the many hard roads traveled throughout his life. They were a natural yet inevitable progression; and nothing about the whole vibe seemed natural to Avanti.

Maintaining a presidential composure, Avanti discreetly turned her shoulder and searched for Sonny.

"Did you find Sonny?" Avanti asked Claire.

"I thought I saw him wandering around the bar area," Colin pointed out.

"Frankly," Claire said, "I don't think Alexandru Adamache wants to see his dark horse receiving tips from a man who storms out for smoke breaks."

"Just find him," Avanti said quietly, yet, from the darkness in her eyes, came off loud and forbidding.

Claire tracked down Sonny, who was chatting—but more like flirting—with a cocktail waitress who looked twice as young as him next to the bar. And from the way he was "touching" her material, it looked as if Sonny had other intentions for tonight and none of them involved being here.

"*There*," Claire said exuberantly, as if she just spotted Waldo. She nodded in the general direction of the vague shape that was Sonny Mims. He was wearing a shit-eating grin on his face, his mannerisms loose and questionable.

"Go fetch," Avanti hissed to Claire. "And, remind him why I hired him."

Claire said, "I'll try, but you know how he—"

"—Don't try," Avanti snapped. "Do."

"Yes, ma'am," Claire said and parted ways with Avanti, who, in return, became more composed, as she modeled for Colin.

"How do I look?" asked Avanti.

"Ready," Colin said. "You look ready." He glanced over at the sharks waiting to have Avanti's ear. "You want me to join you?"

Avanti thought over Colin's question. Again, Colin was considerate like that. The last thing Colin wanted to do was get in the way of Avanti's hustle—in other words, he wasn't trying to "distract" her from the prize at hand.

"Can you?" asked Avanti, her face cringing as if it was a burden to ask.

"Absolutely," Colin said, grabbing Avanti's hand. "That's why I'm here."

As they made their way toward Alexandru Adamache and company, Avanti was caught off guard by the mayor of New York City.

Surprised, she turned toward the familiar face.

"Mayor Armitage," Avanti said with an open look of surprise on her face.

Nursing a glass of ice in one hand, the mayor of New York City reached out to shake Avanti's hand with his other free hand.

With a grin on his narrow face, he said, "If it isn't the woman who's going to save this country from the Clown in Command."

"Nice to see you, Mayor Armitage," Avanti said, shaking the mayor's hand.

"Please," he replied. "Call me Marcellus."

"I don't think you've met my partner, Colin—"

"—Colin Galloway," Marcellus said before Colin even had a chance to finish speaking his name. The mayor released his grip from Avanti's hand. Then shook Colin's "money-making" hand. "I've read *a lot* about you."

"Hopefully, only the good," Colin said teasingly in return, as he held firmly onto Marcellus hand before, finally, Marcellus let go.

"You designed the new opera house in Chicago. . . "

"That's right," Colin said. "*Maison de Merveille.*"

"You know, ever since I got back from fighting overseas in Iraq, I've developed a deep fascination with art and architecture—"

"—You were in the service?" asked Colin.

"US Marine Corps," Marcellus said.

"Thank you for your service," Colin said and once more, shook the mayor's hand.

"Thank you, Colin."

As Marcellus shook Colin's hand, Avanti noticed a couple of maggots crawling from underneath the cuff of his sleeve and along his wrist.

"*Your father was a vet as well, wasn't he?*"

Avanti heard the mayor's question, even though it sounded as if it was spoken so far way; however, she was too distracted by the maggots crawling from the mayor's sleeve.

"*Avanti*," the mayor said, leaning into Avanti's range of vision, "your father's a veteran?"

"Yes," Avanti said, pulling her eyes from Marcellus's wrist. "Vietnam. But he doesn't like to talk about it that much."

"Who does?" Marcellus returned, his voice uneasy.

A petite woman in a powder blue off-the-shoulder dress with a cape, which ran down to the floor, emerged from behind the mayor.

Marcellus introduced his wife, Macy. Then, as he was complimenting Colin and his work on the *Maison de*—"Merveille," Colin corrected—Marcellus shifted the subject to Colin's father, "Samuel 'Shoestring' Galloway was an outstanding baseball player—a legend if you ask me—who played in the Negro Leagues. One of the fastest ball players in the League," Marcellus praised. "Correct me if I'm wrong, Colin, but he could barely even afford to buy a pair of shoestrings."

"That's true," Colin said, bobbing his head. "He struggled like many in—"

Marcellus interrupted before Colin had a chance to clarify his response, "—Sammy Shoestring would always tighten his shoestrings whenever he was about to steal a base."

"Wow," Macy said artificially.

Then, Marcellus said to Macy, as if Colin was no longer a part of the conversation, "It was his way of rubbing it in the catcher's face, so the legend says."

Colin adjusted his red-rimmed glasses.

"He was a character all right," he said.

Before Macy had a chance to respond with a follow-up question about Colin and his father, she was sideswiped by one of her colleagues who worked with her at the firm; however, she didn't at all introduce the husband-and-husband couple to Avanti or Colin. Yet, she said, "Pleasure to meet you." Then parted ways with Avanti and Colin.

"Indulge me, Colin," Marcellus said, bringing Colin back into the spotlight. "How does the son of a legendary baseball player become, of all professions, an architect? One would think a man, such as yourself, would follow in his father's footsteps."

Colin turned to Avanti, as if she, too, was waiting for an answer.

"Ever since I was a boy," Colin said over the hot silence, "I've always been fascinated with building things." The silence mounted, hard and heavy. "It's fair to say I was a fiend for Legos."

Laughs broke out among the three.

Once the laughs tapered off, Marcellus directed his attention to Avanti.

"And Avanti," he said, stepping in more closely to Avanti, "I truly admire the work you've done in the state of Georgia and also for taking the initiative, as well as providing your own creativity, to fix our broken illegal immigration system. If it wasn't for your resiliency and your imagination, I honestly don't know where we would be." Once more, he shook Avanti's hand. "I want to personally thank you for paving the way for New York." He reached in his pocket and pulled out his smartphone. "In the past two months, we've cracked down on over two-thousand vamps trying to reenter the state all thanks. . . " He clicked on the black *Untitled* app on the home screen of his smartphone, revealing a GPS grid of the entire city, ". . . to our new app here."

Here, a voice said inside Avanti's head. *"Here," the voice said again. She found herself inside the infirmary. The hospital bed was shielded by curtains. Standing next to her was the Head Doctor of Welkins Correctional Facility.*

With a pair of tweezers, the surgeon picked up a tiny tracking device that was the size of a grain of rice from the tray. "And now," he said, as he loomed over the 'subject' who was lying on the hospital bed, "I'm going to plant the chip into the back of his left shoulder."

"Will he know?" asked Avanti, as she stood at the edge of the bed.

"From the way their skin heals faster than ours," the Head Doctor said, "the incision will be closed by the time he wakes up."

All Avanti could do—all she wanted to do, really—was simply agree with the mayor, even though a part of her was rebelling against everything he was telling her.

Then, the violence came at her in waves.

She was sitting in her office, waiting for a phone call while, at the same time, thinking about all the families that were about to be split apart.

As the phone rang, any notion escaped her head.

Everything about her, both inside and out, went cold and dark.

"A good pal Moonlight here led us directly to a colony at Rainwater Cemetery. Two of my men confirmed they counted at least forty-seven of them hiding inside a mausoleum. Maybe more. Shall we proceed as planned?"

"You have the green light," Avanti said. "And remember, leave no traces."

"Yes, ma'am."

As the gunfire flickered in her mind, Avanti pulled herself from the memory. Her eyes were attached to Mayor Armitage's phone. For a moment, she wanted to grab the phone from his hand and smash it on the floor with the heel of her stiletto.

"You can thank TechRight for that one," she said, putting on a smile in order to shield what she was truly feeling inside.

"Can I get you two something to drink?" asked Marcellus, as if it was his attempt to loosen up the mood.

"No," Avanti said, smiling off the kind gesture. "But thank you. I gave up drinking a long time ago."

Marcellus pointed at a bar across the lobby.

"They have non-alcoholic beverages."

"I'm fine for now. Thank you."

"And you, Colin?"

Colin turned to Avanti. She didn't give him any look of approval; however, it was clear to him that she was "ready" to talk to Alexandru and company.

"Absolutely," he said.

"Do you mind if I borrow Colin here?" Marcellus asked Avanti, even though he was going to steal her partner from her anyway. "I'd like to pick his brain for a minute."

"Please," Avanti said. "By all means."

She refocused her attention on the pale face that looked like a shark's fin protruding from the sea of bodies. The billionaire investor, Alexandru Adamache, acknowledged Avanti from the other end of the hallway. So did the two men who were standing to the right and left of Alexandru.

"Mr. Adamache," Avanti said, approaching Alexandru. As soon as she made her presence known, she held out her hand for Alexandru to shake. "So lovely to see you here tonight," she said.

"Why hello, Avanti," Alexandru said queerly, eyeing her sage green dress. "I must say you look stunning as always."

While Colin was away, Alexandru introduced Avanti to his two friends. The first man was Daniel Pugh, like Alexandru, a business magnate, investor, philanthropist, and humanitarian. He was the principal founder of the multi-billion dollar company, Endolink Corporation, which helped spark what was known today as the app revolution. The other, Gerard Fortune—fitting name—was an investor who often made headlines for his candor, as well as never shying away from any stench of controversy. He was a speaker and philanthropist, as well, and had written checks for millions of dollars to other candidates in the past, including her opponent in the upcoming election, Richard Rhodes. Fortune was the chairman and CEO of Heatherman Brocket Inc., a multinational conglomerate holding company which wholly owned dozens of brand names and restaurants. They pretty much owned half the products consumers not only had inside their households, but also the restaurants they ate at every Friday or Saturday night. Fortune had a net worth of eighty-four billion dollars—billion with a b—and according to *Hughes* magazine, was considered the second wealthiest man in the world.

Avanti expected the two men to be glowing. However, besides the work they had done to their faces, up close, the two men looked like any other two old, rich, *white* men. It didn't matter how much a man was worth or how much money he carried in his wallet. Money couldn't rid the liver spots.

Daniel Pugh wasn't much of a talker. He firmly shook Avanti's hand, smiled his toothy, pearly white smile, and wished her good luck in her speech tonight.

Fortune, however, was sizing up Avanti.

"So this is the rising star of Tomorrow's Politics," Fortune said and shook her hand as well. However, the texture of his hand was smooth, his skin papery. His grip was weak, lady-like. "I was completely blown away by how you pulled off that McCray Deal. That man never comes to the table for anybody, yet somehow you won him over despite all of the 'noise' surrounding offshore drilling and harmful effects it has on the environment. Tell me, Ms. Washington," Fortune said, leaning in closer. "What's your secret?"

"If I told you," Avanti said, staring into Fortune's eyes, "then I'd have to kill you."

Fortune was first to laugh, which, to Avanti, seemed like a cue for Alexandru and Daniel, who, surprisingly, offered the most authentic laughs.

"I like this one," Fortune said, laughing while, at the same time, holding up a tumbler of Scotch that had about as much shelf life as his third wife. He took a gulp of Scotch and then placed his free hand over Avanti's shoulder. "Plays close to the chest." He moved his liver-spotted hand from Avanti's shoulder and tactfully readjusted the eyelash lace along the top of the bodice as if the move was his way of primping his surrogate before she hit the stage. "I like to play close to the chest myself."

Remaining calm, as well as professional, Avanti didn't "react" from the indecent move. From the looks of the other two men, who were both acting as if "adjusting" a woman's clothing in order to suit a man's personal needs or desires, the move came off as more so a gesture than an invitation; however, Avanti looked at it much differently. It was a test.

In an unflappable manner, Avanti smirked at Fortune and said seductively, "It looks like we share something in common after all. See you inside, gentlemen."

Avanti excused herself, leaving the three men speechless.

Once she was out of eavesdropping range, Daniel turned to Fortune and said, "Didn't even bat an eyelash."

Fortune followed, "I like her."

Alexandru sipped from his Scotch and said as if he was closing the conversation, "I told you she was The One. And I've heard she's good at tying up loose ends."

Fortune nodded at Avanti's partner, Colin, who was having a drink with the mayor of New York City at a crowded bar.

"How about him?"

"Who? Uncle Tom." Alexandru smiled a devil's smile. "He's harmless."

"Can you imagine? A black man being the First Man?"

"He's got a good story," Alexandru took another sip from his Scotch, "what I like to call the 'American' story. But don't worry. She has him under control, if that's where you were going."

⊕

WHILE famous actor Tom Mooney, once Academy Award Actor from the 1970's film *Dust* turned notable animal activist, was speaking behind the podium and occasionally peppering the members of the audience with a routine of topical jokes and horror stories about the film industry, a scrawny waiter with a buzz cut placed an appetizer of wild caught Georgia shrimp, which were said to be caught off the coast of Avanti's home state of Georgia, in front of her, as well as the other elite guests at the table. Alexandru Adamache and a handful of wealthy business magnates as well as their wives—and husbands—happened to be sitting at the same table as Avanti and Colin. However, her main focus wasn't on any of the guests, who were, more than likely, watching her every move. It was solely on the young waiter with red hair and that long pink scar he was wearing along the underside of his wrist. The scar was barely visible underneath the white cuff of his sleeve; however, it caught Avanti's eye, if only for a split second, and she never let it go.

310

Following Avanti's eye, the waiter made a gesture with his brow, as if he was aware that she was aware of the scar; and somehow, he was left in a state of disbelief by the sincerity of her gaze.

For a moment, only a moment, she witnessed her son and the raw innocence in his freckled face.

Trying not to stare, Avanti looked away. She couldn't help herself. She took yet another glance at the waiter and saw exactly that, a waiter, *not* her Ajax.

The waiter went away.

Despite the nice presentation of shrimp, Avanti had absolutely no appetite; in fact, the sight of the wild shrimp stacked in a cute pyramid made her queasy.

With the other guests watching and waiting for Avanti to eat, Avanti had no other choice than to force herself to eat.

As she carefully ripped off the tail of the shrimp, a stream of black oil suddenly oozed from the insides.

Startled, Avanti recoiled in her chair. She looked up at the other guests surrounding the table. Then, she looked at their plates and the shrimp on them. Apparently, it was only her shrimp that were leaking oil. At first, Avanti thought it must've been some kind of sick joke, a prank by one of the staff members, maybe a cook from Georgia who didn't agree with her policies as Governor. She leaned in closer and smelled the black oil. She nearly gagged from the potent stench.

"*Is something wrong?*" Colin asked closely.

Avanti directed her attention toward Colin.

"Avanti?" another voice said from the other side of the table.

Avanti followed the voice to Alexandru.

"No," she said strangely. "Will you excuse me for a moment?"

Unsure whether or not abruptly excusing oneself from the table was a sign of weakness, Avanti decided to stand anyway. She regretted the very move as soon as she caught the attention of the other guests at the table.

"I need to have a word with the chef," she said sternly.

Somewhat intimidated by Avanti, Alexandru said quietly, "Very well."

When she left the ballroom, she never went to the kitchen to have a "word" with the chef. Instead, she hooked a right and headed straight to the restrooms at the end of the hallway. One of the bodyguards, Joel, caught up with Avanti and made sure she made it to the restroom okay. Before she was about to enter, Joel insisted on clearing the restroom for her but Avanti reassured Joel that she was fine to enter and that he wait outside in the hallway while she "freshened up."

Joel took his post outside the restroom while Avanti stepped inside the restroom. She went straight to the closest stall she could find, closed the door behind her, and pulled out a small vial filled with a crimson red powder. She poured out a smidgen of powder onto the underside of her pinkie fingernail and snorted it up one nostril, then poured out more powder onto her same fingernail and snorted it up in the other nostril. The leftover powder she rubbed onto her thumb, then between her thumb and index finger, and then ran her red powdery fingers along the top of her gums.

More composed, Avanti found herself not drifting but more so slipping into a daydream, as if, one second, she was in a bathroom stall doing bumps of a mysterious red powder and then, the next, she *was in the back of a town car, riding to a workshop called Teachers Teach for the new website TeachersTeach.Org, which was created in order to get more teachers into the classrooms through higher pay and new ways of teaching young students. No more than twenty-four hours earlier, there had been a shooting in a town outside Nashville, Tennessee, which resulted in the death of twenty-one victims. The shooter tragically ended up taking his own life. Which would've made the grand total of causalities to twenty-two victims; however, the media only reported twenty-one victims.*

"Say what you want, Claire," Avanti argued, "mental health has absolutely nothing to do with the shooting in Sislick. We have to draw a line between being emotional and being crazy. The man was angry. Plain and simple."

"Angry, Avanti," Claire replied, her voice more hostile, "is me screaming or throwing a punch, not killing twenty-one 'innocent' people."

"The man had no history of mental illness," Avanti said, trying to lay out her argument, as if she was presenting a case in front of a jury. "No priors. He was a sixty-three year old man who snapped. And don't tell me about being innocent. In today's world, nobody is innocent. Guns kill people. People kill people. Believe me, I want to be the one to get rid of all the guns on the streets. But a fact of reality: that will not happen. It will never happen, Claire." Her tone sharpened. "You know why? People are good by nature—or at least, they want to be good. But they're also violent. And how do they combat their violence?"

Claire didn't answer.

Avanti didn't expect her to.

"With violence," she said. Then, she shook her head in disgust. "I want to believe that we can live in a society without guns. But it's already engrained in us, Claire. From the movies we watch to the books we read to the music we listen to, it's here. And it's not going away. Not anytime soon. So, what's the solution? Do we get rid of the guns? It's a good start. But where does that leave us? If we take away the guns, then, if people want to do harm to other people, then they'll find other ways. Don't underestimate people. They can get creative when they want to. Will it be cars or trucks? Will they resort to something else, like bombs or knives? Are we going to start banning knives, too? How else are these fat cats going to cut their filet mignons? Let's take away the forks while we're at it and resort to eating with our hands, like the primitive creatures we are." She paused for a moment, but left little-to-no room for Claire to retort. "It starts with the way we treat each other. We are killing each other everyday, if it's the way we talk to one another or don't talk to one another, or the way we deal with our adversaries. The way I look at guns: they're just the cherry on the top. The Big Hush. Do we need them in a civil society? No. We don't. But the only way we're going to get where we need to be starts with taking a good look at ourselves in the mirror and asking ourselves, 'Where does the anger come from and how do we get rid of it without harming those who deserve every right to be here just as the next man?'

When we can find answers to those questions, then it'll be the first step to progress."

Avanti shook herself from the memory—or flashback or whatever you want to call it—and found herself back in the stall, looking over the red smears of powder along her pinkie, thumb, and index finger.

A single drop of blood splashed onto her hand, leaving behind a perfect circle. Before she realized where the blood was coming from, another drop of blood fell onto her open palm. She ran both her index and middle fingers along the bottom of her nostrils and pulled her hand away. Her fingers were covered in blood.

⊕

ONCE Avanti stopped the nosebleed, she exited the restroom where Joel was waiting like a saint next to a water fountain. She caught a small figure darting across the corner of her eye. She turned toward the figure and witnessed the tail end of a girl—possibly the same one as before—rounding the end of the hallway. She instructed Joel to wait at his post. He didn't listen, at first. After all, he had a job to do; however, Avanti told him twice to "stay" put.

She walked toward the end of the hallway, which intersected with yet another long hallway. She heard a strange racket coming from the janitor's closet, which was only a few paces away. The closet door suddenly swung open as she reached for the door handle. Standing before her were Sonny and that same cocktail waitress, both giggling and cackling.

With his face frozen in a gaping stare, Sonny's laugh cut to silence as soon as he laid his eyes on Avanti and her body blocking the doorway.

"Uh. . . " Sonny stuttered, ". . . Avanti? What you doing here?"

"I was gonna ask you the same question, Sonny," Avanti snapped.

"I was showing, uh. . . " Sonny pointed at the waitress and couldn't even remember her name.

"*Novice*," she said for him.

"Right," he corrected. "I was escorting Novice here to the restrooms."

Avanti glanced at a bright red drop of blood on the crease of Sonny's collar. Trying not to draw too much attention toward herself, she turned her eyes upward, back into Sonny's innocent eyes; and in that moment, as soon as Sonny caught a glimpse of Avanti's eyes on his neck, his entire manner changed from imperfect to imperious, as if Avanti was the one, *not* Sonny, who should've been inside the ballroom brownnosing and kissing up to business magnates and filthy-rich investors, *not* wandering around hotel hallways scouting out trouble.

"Why are you not preparing for your speech?" asked Sonny, his tone bolder. "Aren't you about to go on?"

Avanti didn't respond to Sonny's question. She thought long and hard about it. Yet, she glanced him over one last time.

"I hope to see you inside," Avanti said suspiciously, walked off, and met up with Joel, the bodyguard, who hadn't budged an inch from his post.

DEBATING about whether or not to deliver the speech that she was intended to deliver to an audience of potential donors, Avanti eyed over the words on the paper one last time. The words were not hers; in fact, they were far from hers. Yet, except for a couple of lines, they, more or less, belonged to a speechwriter named Bradley Spears, a Harvard grad with a major in political science, who worked as a staffer under Rhodes for two years before his father landed him a job on Avanti's team. Intentionally or not, Bradley borrowed these words from prior speeches, reworded and shuffled the words around and added more emphasis to fashionably tasteful words, which were considered "new," as if, by doing so, he was only rearranging the colors on a palette, instead of changing the final tone of the painting.

With the eyes bearing down on her from all angles, including the beady-eyed audience before her, as well as the wide, nervous gawks of members of her team who were eagerly waiting near the side of the stage, Avanti readjusted her sweaty palms over the podium and peered out into the audience. She could feel the dim spotlight on her face growing hotter and hotter, like a dark cloud gradually drifting from that tiny ball of fire which hung in the sky.

Avanti cleared her throat before speaking *her* words.

"As most of you may already know," she said into the microphone, "I am *not* the right candidate to run this country." From the side of the stage, Claire, as well as other members of Avanti's team, including Sonny, were looking at one another as if they were hearing the same words that they hearing. From their startled reactions, it was clear that the line was *not* in the speech that had been prepared days ahead of the ball. "It's true," Avanti said. "All you have to do is look at my past. *I am not perfect.* But who is anymore? Really?" Avanti looked around the audience, who was equally baffled as Avanti's team. "Who are we to judge people for the mistakes they've made in the past when we live in a society that is constantly changing? If you haven't made mistakes in your life, then I'd say you haven't lived." She shook her head in disgust from the very thought of the mistakes she had made in her life. "No," she said shortly. "We, as a nation, must come to terms that we are *all* a work in progress. *We are not perfect.* I'm aware my past will come up on the trail. Voters are going to want answers to the mistakes that I have made in my past. I'm here tonight to set the record straight once and for all and answer all of those questions, firstly, to dismiss whatever doubts that you may have about electing me for the highest job in office. Like I said, I'm not the right candidate to run this country. But I'm going to prove to you that—of all the candidates who are running against me, including the one who has continually failed to carry out the job that he was elected to do—I am the *only* one who can run this country, even though I am not the right one."

Avanti glanced over at Claire, who was mouthing to Sonny, *What is she doing?* She ignored Claire, as well as Sonny, who looked as if he had an "I told you so"-type of expression on his face, and focused on the words, her words.

"Why?" Avanti asked, not only herself, but also the audience.

Hanging onto Avanti's every word, the audience waited in silence.

"Let's rewind to the beginning," Avanti said. "For those of you who haven't read my book, *Still Intact*—" she said, more casually, as she threw out a blurb from the corner of her mouth for her recent book, "—which is now available at all your major book retailers for twenty-three ninety-nine."

The comment was her attempt at "breaking the ice." The comment was successful by the sound of laughter sprinkled throughout the audience.

"I was born and raised in a small rural town outside Atlanta, Georgia, called Saxmapaw. Growing up, I watched my father come home every night, his hands blistered and bleeding from working long days on the farm, yet, despite how tired or frustrated he was, he still carried not only a sense of great pride for the job he went to everyday, but also a great deal of gratitude for being able to raise a family, regardless of the stress his body had to endure working on the land. We grew up broke, *not* poor. And, there is a difference. One afternoon," she said in reflection, "when me and a couple of friends of mine wanted to go see the movie, *Back to the Future*, which had recently come out in the local movie theatre not too far away from where we lived, I asked my father for some money. I remember looking forward to the movie before its release; but, more so, I couldn't wait to feast my eyes on a young and handsome Michael J. Fox. Whom my friends and I had a crush on. Who could blame us? Who doesn't like Michael J. Fox?"

The comment drew a couple of suppressed laughs from the audience.

"Back then, the movies only cost a couple of dollars," Avanti said. "When he asked me how much I needed for the movie, he could only spare no more than a quarter. I was upset, not only at my father, but also my friends, for their dads had more money than mine. I told him how much I 'hated' being poor and how many friends I had lost over the years for being poor. Like any other father who cared deeply about his son or daughter, my father stopped what he was doing and sat me down at the kitchen table and told me, 'Poor was only a state of mind in which very few people ever recovered from.' He had given me examples of people who were less fortunate than we were, particularly a homeless man, whom my father and I saw almost everyday hanging out on the corner of Fifth and Parker Avenue begging for money to buy himself a bottle of liquor. He emphasized that being broke was considered only a 'financial setback,' a temporary inconvenience, which was fixable, given time. It was what my father said to me that one night in the kitchen that had me thinking more about the homeless man who was always standing on the corner of Fifth and Parker Avenue. One day after school was over, I decided to talk to him. His name was Cameron Limier, but everybody who knew him well called him 'Lemon.' I got to know Lemon, *his story*. Three times a week I paid Lemon a visit. I'd bring him sandwiches, and every now and then, I'd sneak him candy that I pocketed earlier that day. I wouldn't give him money—not a cent— because, even Lemon said so himself, it was money that was enabling his drinking, and worst, keeping him on the streets. So, we just talked. Turns out: all Lemon wanted to do was talk. But was Lemon poor? Yes. He was poor. He was damaged. His family had left him. His children wanted nothing to do with him. Lemon had dug himself a hole that he couldn't get out of. He was stuck in a place, like my father said, where very few ever recovered. One day after school, I went to visit Lemon. It was the week before Thanksgiving and I wanted to invite Lemon to dinner with us. When I made it to Parker Avenue, Lemon wasn't hanging there. Immediately, I knew something had happened. Three days later, I found out what happened to Lemon. A landscaper found him sitting on a bench at a park not too far from Parker Avenue. He was slumped over, dead. Turns out he had been dead for at least 'two days'—that was what the police officer told me. All I could imagine was, for two days, people walked past Lemon as if he didn't even exist. I later found out that he basically drank himself to death because, in a way, that was exactly what society wanted him to do. Society wanted to not deal with him, to ignore him, and, in the end, shut him up by giving him money, "enabling him," as Lemon once told me, instead of getting him the help that he rightfully deserved. But was Cameron Limier to blame for winding up on the streets? Yes—*and* no. The problem wasn't an 'I' problem or a 'you' problem. The problem was an 'us' problem. A 'we' problem. Over thirty years have passed since Lemon's death and 'we' still have the same problems, only 'we' word them differently, soften them up to sound less intimidating. I realized that, in order to fix the problems like Cameron Limier faced—or any person struggling to get by—it started with the way we treated others, by not shunning them but embracing them, despite whatever issues they may be going through,

When my father wasn't toiling away on the farm during those sultry days of Georgia summers, he spent nights working at various jobs in and around Atlanta. It's fair to say my father's drive to provide for us didn't come without its share of sacrifices. It was hard enough for a mother to raise a family of four boys and two girls in the South. It was harder and more difficult for a father, who remained all but a ghost throughout a young girl's childhood,

I lost my only sister, Alicia, to pneumonia at the age of thirteen and witnessed my parents growing farther apart,

Twenty years ago my late husband Stewart and I brought two angels into this world. The first angel we named 'Echo,' and I, like many of the mothers who try to start a family of their own, was grateful to call Echo my daughter. Sadly, Echo was taken away from us at an early age. She was four years old when she died in a drowning accident. I understand why there were so many questions surrounding Echo's death; and if you don't know the story and you haven't read the book, then listen carefully because I'm here tonight to go *beyond* the page,

Before Echo's death, Stewart and I were going through a rough patch as most partners go through. I was thirty-two years old and still, at that age, parenting was 'trial and error.' You can read every book on parenthood, but once you're all the way in it and you are officially a parent, the only real book that can teach you about raising children are the very children you're raising,

I specifically remember the day I laid eyes on Stewart. I had this friend, Lou Myra, who had a friend who knew this guy who was coming up with some weird invention that would allow people to communicate with their pets. I know—odd. But I went with *my gut* and decided to meet with 'this guy' anyway. Despite all the awkward conversations and mixed feelings, the moment I met Stew I knew he was the one. Both of our universes aligned. We were opposites—he was a talker and I was rather shy when it came to the dating scene—yet, after we met, I realized we shared common goals. He was incredibly smart, handsome, compassionate, and most importantly, considerate. He was a gentle spirit, an unselfish man, Stew was, one who'd always put others before himself. But over time, our perfect union started to show its cracks, its blemishes, its imperfections. I can stand here before you and blame Stewart for his infidelity, but such judgment wouldn't at all be fair to neither him nor myself. The fact of the matter: I drove Stew away. My excuse was that Stew was more focused on his work than he was on me. Eventually *that fire*, which brought our universes together, fizzled out; and consequently, when Stewart needed a shoulder to lean on, I was *not* there."

Avanti hung her head in a pause, took a moment to collect her emotions, and pushed on.

Off stage, Claire's eyes widened with bold exclamation marks while mouthing the words *WHAT IS SHE DOING?* to Sonny.

In return, Sonny shrugged his shoulders in exaggeration, then folded his arms across his chest, then shifted his weight to one side of his body, as if he was about to watch the world come crumbling down—and he smiled.

"So," Avanti said, more confidently, "he decided to find affection elsewhere and he did so with a troubled young woman who had her own share of demons. I can remember the day as if it was yesterday. Labor Day weekend. The year was 2003. I was spending an ideal afternoon by the swimming pool with my mother and my two babies, my two angels, Echo and Ajax, who were both four years old at the time, when all of a sudden a troubled young woman named Storm McBride broke into our house and attacked me from behind with a bird's beak knife. I tried desperately to defend myself while Ms. McBride relentlessly swung the blade at me by the poolside. She managed to cut me multiple times, mainly around both my arms, as well as my neck. I didn't realize it at first—I figured it was all the adrenaline rushing through my veins—but during her relentless assault, the blade slipped past my arms and caught me several times in my upper and lower abdomen, penetrating my spleen, as well as perforating my right lung. Meanwhile, my mother Farah was in the water with my four-year-old daughter Echo. Bloody and confused, I struggled to stand to my feet; however, Ms. McBride stomped down on my right knee, causing it to bend in a direction that it normally wasn't meant to bend. During this bloody haze, I witnessed Ms. McBride walking over to Ajax, who was reading one of his comic books only a few feet away from me. The first thing—and only thing—that ran through my mind was, *She is going to harm my son, my angel.* Despite my injuries, my broken leg, the stab wounds, I hobbled to my son and tried to shield him from this deranged woman. I didn't even make it halfway. My injuries overcame me. I couldn't put any pressure on my right leg. Crawling inch-by-inch closer and closer to Ajax, I soon realized that Ms. McBride wasn't going for Ajax. She was going for an umbrella base. She picked up the umbrella base, which had to weigh at least fifty pounds; and she walked back over to me. She raised the umbrella stand over her head and was about to 'finish' me off. As she was moments away from striking down, I witnessed both her vacant eyes turn toward the swimming pool to the right of her. I followed her eyes to the swimming pool and noticed something was wrong with my mother. What I didn't realize at the time was that she was having a heart attack and my four-year-old daughter, Echo, unable to swim on her own, was slipping from my mother's grip. The floaters on her arms loosened and eventually came off while Echo was thrashing her arms through the water. Desperate to save my mother and daughter, I begged and I pleaded with Ms. McBride to think about what she was about to do and let me help them. It was at that moment when I looked into Ms. McBride's eyes that I saw the regret inside them. She dropped the umbrella base and ran off; however, my mother and daughter had already gone under. I tried to stand, but I couldn't. I knew that the only way I could reach them was by crawling to them and hopefully rescuing them in time. Such existence, as time, was running out. As the blood started to pool under my body, I soon realized *my* time was running out. Fighting through my injuries, I used every last bit of strength left in my body to save my mother, Farah, and her granddaughter, *my angel*, Echo. It was already too late. I jumped into the pool; the blood pouring from my body caused the water to cloud with red. By the time I pulled Echo from the bottom of the pool, she wasn't moving. Her body was lifeless. Like a doll. The water had already filled her tiny lungs. By then, I was left with a choice: either resuscitate Echo and hopefully, pump the water from her lungs, or swim back under to pull my mother from the pool and try to revive them both. I chose the latter. And till this day, I wonder, if I hadn't gone back under to rescue my mother, even though a part of me knew she was already gone, would Echo still be alive. Would I have rescued my angel in time? And if so, what kind of life would she have lived? *What* kind of person would she have become? Tragically, I lived to see none of the answers to those questions come to fruition. As for my son, my Ajax, he was left in a traumatized state. And I don't believe he ever recovered from what happened on that day,

Days after the police discovered Ms. McBride's body with a fatal stab wound to her neck inside her apartment, a letter was brought to my attention while I was recovering in the hospital. Apparently, Ms. McBride and Stewart had developed an intense relationship over the past few months, and it was— without doubt—out of jealously, that Ms. McBride deemed it necessary to get 'rid' of me, in essence, remove me from the picture. In no way, shape, or form, was Stewart involved in Ms. McBride's actions; however, for months on end, I questioned myself: *How could I ever forgive Stewart for what he had brought into my mother's life, our children's lives, our lives?* No question there was much blame to go around on all sides. Storm McBride was a human first and foremost, and a woman second; and she, like many women out there suffering from depression, faced 'real issues.' I can stand here and point my finger at Storm McBride for what she had done to my family—after all, it was Storm McBride who 1.) Assaulted me and 2.) Left me to die. But I knew just as much as the next person that pointing your finger at someone wasn't going to get anyone anywhere. So, I decided to place the blame onto my shoulders. Me, *I* was the one who abandoned Stew when he needed me the most. *I* was the one who drove Stew away. *I* was the one who forced his hand. *I* was the one who shut him out. I was the culprit.

Was it selfish of me?

Yes. I believe it was."

Avanti couldn't help but turn her attention toward the two people sitting at a bar in the back of the ballroom. One of them was a salt and pepper haired man in his early fifties; however, he had a tall muscular physique and could've passed as a man in his early thirties. The other, a promiscuous dirty blonde-haired woman who was sporting a red sheath dress with silver bracelets that occasionally flickered whenever the woman turned a shoulder in such a coy manner or, on the contrary, leaned in forward to graze the man's hand or, in a form of dominant femininity, straightened her posture and puffed out her chest to exhibit the exquisite shape of her "modified" breasts below drunken angles of canned lights suspended above the ballroom.

After mildly laughing at a side-bar comment from the lone soldier, who was mentally riffling through the best and most strategic lines that would earn him the golden ticket on Underwear Island, the flirtatious woman rested her reddened elbow against the sweaty bar, her mountainous cleavage exposed to the elements as if it was a landscape painting, and with her white glove gripped in her hand like a handkerchief, flagged down the bartender, who was already waiting for her next command before she could even finish the word *bar*—tender. It was there, in the elements, when the stumpy bartender pivoted toward the woman's direction, that Avanti saw the large 10-gallon glass jar beverage dispenser with a spigot next to a pyramid stack of liquor bottles. Inside were fruit about the size of bananas. She cleared her throat and as she was about to continue her speech for to the audience, she couldn't help but look yet again at the jar and *what* floated inside the murky liquid: over a dozen of dead fetuses, swelled and brined like pickles.

Once given the drink order, the bartender grabbed an unwashed tumbler and poured the woman's drink from the fetus dispenser, causing the murky liquid to bubble slightly, then stir each fetus, moving and bumping into one another, revealing much larger, more developed ones inside the jar. The drink was thick and yellow-brownish in color, syrupy. He grabbed a black straw and a cocktail napkin. Placed the straw in the tumbler. Placed the cocktail napkin on the bar before the woman. Then, finally, placed the drink onto the napkin.

The woman thanked the bartender for the drink, took a sip, and immediately displayed a gesture of approval.

Avanti fell into a trance. *She recalled a protest outside her office while signing the new bill into law. Not too far away, protesters were holding up signs like "Baby Killer" and "Murderer."*

Afterwards, once the chaos ended, she remembered her words: "These people care so much about the unborn than they do about the very same people who are struggling to stay alive. Where's the consistency?"

More *words* came to Avanti, chants, shouts, and rally cries, all surfacing like old words that seemed so familiar yet so distant to her. The same words that she had spoken at the "*Women's Choice*" Rally seven and a half years ago while she was running for governor of Georgia.

"As your candidate for governor," Avanti preached from a makeshift stage to a rowdy crowd of women, "I will make it my duty to provide women with their own healthcare, regardless of their background or economic status. Every single woman in this country has a right, not a privilege, to choose what they want to do with their bodies. And as your new governor, I will make sure that women have access to the services they seek. Even if it means putting a Women's Choice facility on every street corner."

The crowd lit up in applause, random roars and bellows erupting through-
out, including screams of "Hands off our bodies!"

"This isn't just body justice!" Avanti shouted over the lively crowd. "This
is our justice!"

The word *justice* resonated through the close-mouthed audience.

Avanti snapped from her trance and found hundreds of beady eyes staring at
her, the eyes of donors willing and waiting for what she had to say next. Some
of the eyes, however, especially in the front row, were neither round nor beady,
yet, sharp and narrow, repulsed.

"*Selfishness*," Avanti said thoughtfully over the long yet heavy pause, "I
was consumed by own pleasure to keep Stew in the dark, hoping that my silence—my distance—would make Stew understand the pain he had put me
through. After I lost Echo, close friends of mine would ask me why I didn't
leave him. The fact is I was still in love with Stew, despite what had happened.
As much as I wanted to punish him, I simply could not. If you've ever been
fortunate enough to find *true* love, you already know that it is chain unbroken;
however, it comes with a price and in order to keep the chain from breaking, it
takes time and effort. That's why I felt somehow responsible, because I got
lazy. I no longer put in the *time* and the *effort*; and by not doing so, that chain
started to rust, the links deteriorating, loosening,

After Stewart and I worked through our issues, surprisingly, we became
closer; in essence, we did what very few ever had the opportunity of doing: we
rekindled the *flame* that had brought our worlds together. Then, when Stew
was diagnosed with cancer after doctors found a tumor the size of a kiwi, we
became even closer. I know a lot of people—friends, family—thought I only
stayed with Stewart because he was ill. They were right—somewhat. A part
of me thought about leaving, abandoning the warmth of that flame, my one and
only true love. A part of me didn't want to deal with the sickness and all the
mess that came with it. A part of me wanted to 'move on,' start a new life
somewhere else, say my peace with Stew, and be 'done' with it. However,
they were thoughts. And thoughts never defined us. It's our actions that define us and our innate ability to act when called upon. Stewart was calling me.
And the more I started to think about what friends and family members were
telling me, the more I realized how *wrong* they were. I understood why they
might've looked at it like that, but me staying with Stew out of sympathy was
simply *not* true. I stayed with Stewart because, not only did I love him, but I
also saw a side of him that in all my years of knowing him I had never seen.
Despite the grim news the doctors had given Stew and how he only had so
many months to live, Stew remained resilient and determined to defeat cancer,
as if it was his greatest adversary. In those final years, Stewart was a true warrior. Like all warriors, they eventually die. But their fighting spirit lasts forever, living inside each and every one it touches. We must keep that spirit
alive in all of us!"

Avanti paused for a warm applause from the audience.

Seated at a table in the middle of the ballroom was her late husband, Stewart Pettaway himself—or so Avanti thought. Stewart had been dead for over a
decade; yet, there he was, sitting among a group of investors who were decked
out in their Tuesday's best. Among the investors was Jonah Greenberg, a for-

320

mer stockbroker turned celebrity "shark," who contributed most of the funding to Stewart's latest invention called *DogSpeak*^{TM}, a state-of-the-art eTablet that allowed man's best friend to communicate with its human companion through what was known as a "paw-sensitive" screen. The project ended up not being scraped but, more or less, put on hold after the diagnosis; however, a couple of months after buzz surfaced about Stewart's latest invention, other inventors came out of the woodwork, including hardware and software developers who strived to come up with devices and new flavorful apps that shared similarities to *DogSpeak*^{TM}; however, most of the knockoffs were met by one disaster after another: PR nightmares, glitches and virus-resistant bugs, recalls, financial roadblocks, termination.

Jonah and the other investors clapped politely, but *not* Stew. He was clapping hard and slow, elaborate, as if he rubbing it in Avanti's face. Except for the way Stewart was clapping, what stood out the most was his appearance. He was bald and his appearance was much worse than when he later died. On the side of his head was a jagged incision that was sealed close with staples. Stewart was nothing but a skeleton in a leotard of tired flesh, his face pale and haggard with each contour and outline of his skull visible to the eye; and buried deep within the dark eye sockets, two moonlit eyes were pinned on Avanti like thumbtacks.

She looked around the ballroom and saw others—at least a dozen or so, possibly more in the very back—clapping the same way Stewart was clapping. They, too, appeared as if they were plagued by a terminal illness, faces pale and bloodless. When they put their sticklike hands together in that same obnoxious mocking clap, she could hear the *clitter* of their tired bones.

After only a few seconds of listening to that bone-against-bone sound, Avanti attempted to block it out by focusing on the words, *her* words.

But they were still there, those clittering sounds.

As the clapping came in violent waves, Avanti picked out each gaunt, exaggerated clapper from the audience, starting with Storm McBride, whose arms appeared to be moving in slow motion, each one arching outward in synchronization before swinging back inward the same way a bird would flap its wings to display dominance. Storm was graciously wearing "name (fill-in-the-blank)," this custom sleeveless iridescent dress covered in crystal tassels with a silk scarf that matched the color of her dress wrapped tight around her neck to cover a mark or blemish. Avanti knew what exactly she was covering up; however, she was still left baffled from the sight of Storm, who, like Stewart, appeared lifeless. Dead. Yet, here. In the ballroom. Clapping to the equivalent of a stiff soldier's march. She was staring at Avanti with these dark marbled eyes.

The next two to come to her attention were Storm's older brother, Chance, as well as Storm's son, Nicolas—or "Nic"—who were seated at another table across the ballroom. They, too, were clapping. They, too, dead yet *here*.

Throughout the entire audience, Avanti saw many others, all pale and lifeless, their eyes so dark and unnatural; however, of all the causalities who had felt the sharp end of Avanti's "bad side," Chance McBride was the one who stood out the most.

As she had been doing occasionally throughout her speech, Avanti found herself somewhere else other than the ballroom. One second she was standing at the podium. The next, she was sitting at a table stacked with copies of her new memoir in the back of Barley's Bookstore located in the small, predominantly "blue" town of Dire, Pennsylvania.

She was handing a signed copy of her memoir called, Still Intact: The Heartbreaking Journey One Woman Of Color Took In Order To Win Back The Soul Of America, *to a young Reader when the next person in line stepped forward and left Avanti questioning where she had seen his face before.*

After a second study of the man's face, she knew who he was, not a Reader, for sure, but rather a man who had spent hours waiting in line at Barley's Bookstore for other reasons—and they weren't for Avanti Washington's signature. She glanced at her bodyguard, Joel, who, in return, dialed in on the strange man by turning up his already heightened state to a ten. He was two notches away from World War III. The only time he ever came close to twelve was one instance at a trendy roadside diner in Salem called Moe's, which happened to be the same "Moe's" from the cult TV show, Harper's Inn, *when Avanti was abruptly approached by a far-left vamp-sympathizer holding a can of sangria red paint and madly screaming out the governor's previous policy on vamps with a combination of capitalized questions and exclamation marks as she was about to cover Avanti's body in sangria red. With his game face switched on, Joel sprung into action by grabbing the fanatic's wrist before she had time to dump the paint all over Avanti, slamming her to the ground as if she was a bag of top soil, and putting her in one helluva arm bar that'd make The Jam look like an amateur wrestler. Given the cue which either would've come in the form of a simple nod of the head or even the turning of her eyes, Avanti's right-hand man could've ripped the woman's arm clean off—literally! However, considering the sudden uptick in the latest Morron University Polls, Avanti didn't want a passionate yet "misguided" individual to shit all over her parade. Besides, the woman's amplified I'm-going-to-sue-your-ass type of sea lion screech was loud and piercing enough to publicly announce, "Surrender."*

With that same game face switched on, Joel drew his hands down by his side and never took the strange man out of his sight.

As he pulled out his own hardback with a wrinkled dust jacket from behind his back, Joel inched closer to the table, as if, given the cue, he was ready to spring to action. Subtly, Avanti waved off Joel as if she was shooing away a fruit fly. In return, Joel backed away.

The moment the young boy surfaced from the crowd of Readers and potential voters and grabbed hold of his supposed "father's" hand, she realized who the man was based on the stark resemblance in the boy's face.

The sight of the boy's face justified her deepest suspicions. He had her eyes, as well as her nose. However, a part of her wanted to see Stew in his face. Perhaps the boy had his chin or even smile. She looked closer at the boy's face, but he just wasn't there. Her insides coiled up like a snake.

Storm's older brother leaned forward and placed the hardback on the table for Avanti to sign.

As Avanti slowly opened the front cover of the book, a message was written on the first page with a black Sharpie:

I know your secret.

"*Make it out to* Storm McBride," *he whispered and flashed the burner from his jacket pocket.*

As soon as Joel heard that name underneath all the background chatter, he made his move.

Before he could grab Chance by the arm, Avanti held out her hand, resulting in Joel coming to a skidding stop. She never signed the book. Yet, she carefully closed it, handed it back to Chance, and smiled. Trying not to draw too much attention to herself, she waved Joel closer, whispered something in his ear, and then after giving the message, Joel approached Chance and mimicked Avanti by whispering something in his ear.

Before Chance and the boy took off, he looked at Avanti with a heated expression on his face, as if the tears that he held in his eyes were boiling hot. She never forgot that look, even months later.

The memory stopped, so, too, did the clapping.

In the dead silence, Avanti looked around at the audience. Each guest waited in anticipation for Avanti to speak.

Before she could continue, she found herself back inside the memory.

As instructed, Chance waited in a narrow alleyway behind Barley's after the crowds died out. Two silhouettes the size of giants emerged from a cloud of dense smoke spewing from the breathing manholes. Chance stopped pacing around a dumpster and redirected his attention on the two silhouettes, which were shrinking into a more humanly form.

Avanti and Joel eventually made their presences known, leaving Chance in a state of uneasiness.

"*I read your. . . your little book, Governor Washington,*" *Chance started, his words choppy from the pounding in his chest. "I was particularly moved by the chapter where you talk about your daughter and the vivid details surrounding her death. You made it sound so authentic, except for one major hole in your story.*"

Avanti nodded at Joel.

Said his name, "Joel."

First, he pulled out a black wand that looked like a metal detector and waved it around Chance's front side first, then his backside, focusing most of the reading around Chance's chest and upper abdomen region.

"*My friend here is checking you for a wire,*" *Avanti said.*

"*What is this?*" *Chance furrowed his brow in confusion. "I'm not wearing a fucking wire!*"

"*It's only precaution.*"

Joel nodded at Chance's arms.

"*Raise your arms.*"

"*This is ridiculous,*" *Chance murmured, as he raised his arms upward as if he was being crucified.*

Once Joel was finished with his sweep, he patted down Chance's pockets and legs and searched for any weapons. Once complete, he turned to Avanti.

"*He's clean,*" *he said.*

"*The phone?*" *she asked Joel.*

He shook his head.

"No."

"You really think I'd bring my only *leverage to a deal?"*

"How do I know you're not lying?"

"Right before Storm allegedly 'killed' herself," Chance said, "she left a message on my phone."

"And?"

"And she told me enough to know that you're a lying piece of shit."

Avanti nodded at Joel.

"Off you go," she said and ordered Joel to give them space—not too far from sight but well out of reach.

"You sure?"

Once more, she nodded her head.

Joel did as ordered and stood post halfway down the alleyway while Avanti approached Chance.

"Where is the little one?" asked Avanti, who was calm and collected.

"I took him back to the hotel," Chance said with a tremble in his voice.

"Is he alone?"

"I certainly wasn't going to bring him here," he replied, his voice louder and more strained.

Chance threw his head in a nod at the musclehead towering at the end of the alleyway.

Avanti glanced over her shoulder and then, more amused, faced Chance.

She said, "He's harmless—when he wants to be."

Shaking his head in repulsion, Chance let out a noise from his lips, a cross between a snort and a sigh.

"So," Avanti said, holding out her hands, "does he have a name?"

"Why the fuck you care?" Chance said hostilely.

"I'd just like to know the name of his son," she said, remaining cool. "I have a right to know. I was married to—"

"—No," Chance said, ignoring his previous statement, particularly the comment about Stewart's son. "You don't have the right."

"Okay," she said, surprised by his disobedience—and good acting. "So, why am I here? What do you want, Mr. McBride?"

"Two million dollars," he said bluntly.

"Money?" Avanti returned, her coolness wearing off. "You honestly think I didn't have my people following the money Stew secretly sent your sister every month for child support? Tell me, Chance. What exactly did your sister do with all my husband's money? Because I know she didn't spend a penny on that boy."

"Two million dollars," Chance said again, not missing a beat.

"What the hell do I look like to you, an ATM?"

Chance retorted, "Based on all the money you're making off your book deal, it'd be like pocket chance for you."

"Makes sense, now that I think about it, for someone with a rap sheet as long as a fat man's grocery list to lie to police in order to extort me for money." She paused for a moment and looked over the desperate "little" man standing in front of her. Avanti knew better than anyone else never to trust a

man who had nothing to lose. "If it's money you want, Mr. McBride," she said finally, "then so be it. You'll get your money."

"I'll give you the time and the location," he said. "And next time, we meet in public. Somewhere busy. Around people. Not in some sketchy alley where one of your goons can turn me into a hand puppet."

"You really don't trust me, do you, Mr. McBride?"

"Of course, not," he said. "You're a fucking murderer. Why should a trust a fucking murdering politician?"

Avanti took a beat.

"Very well," she said, more calmly. "But promise me that, once you get your money, you're going to disappear. I mean, not a word about what went on here. And if I ever hear from you after *you get your money," she paused for a moment, her eyes darkened, "you're going to wish you never came to me in the first place."*

"And what the fuck does that mean?"

"You're a criminal, Mr. McBride," Avanti said, as she raised her left brow in a sharp letter v. "Use your imagination."

Avanti cleared her throat and for a moment, held her head down in sorrow.

"We must keep the spirit alive," she said, trailing off under the microphone. "We must," she mumbled. Her eyes fell onto to the speech that Bradley had written for her. She noticed a strange discoloration on the paper underneath the front page. It could've passed as a shadow cast from her arm; however, given the circumstances of tonight's event, Avanti soon realized something wasn't quite right.

More intrigued by the dark stain on the paper, she lifted her gummy arm from the piece of paper. The front page of the speech stuck to the underside of her arm, as if she had a strange adhesive attached to her skin.

With no other choice, Avanti held down the paper with her other hand while she peeled away her arm. First, Avanti noticed the blotches of thick blood, which appeared as if they had been pressed onto her skin by a blood-soaked sponge. She followed the blood to the source: a three and a half-inch incision along her wrist. The cut was deep, too, deep enough to draw enough blood to cover one side of the US letter sized piece of paper.

As soon as Avanti laid eyes on the cut and all that blood on her arm, Avanti immediately shut her eyes, as if by doing so, she was shutting out the memory—the only memory she had left of him.

In the darkness behind the curtains, Claire was wearing a look of concern and confusion on her face. She glanced over at poor ole Sonny, who was neither confused nor concerned; in fact, Sonny was wearing a color on his mug that only suggested anger.

"This has gone on for too long," Claire whispered to Sonny, as if she was shooting darts at him with her mouth. "You have to do something—anything!"

"You're right," he said, unfolding his arms. "I'm going to put an end to this goddamn debacle once and for all."

Sonny was rocking back and forth, ready to storm out on stage to pull Avanti from the podium and make an excuse to the audience that Avanti didn't feel well or maybe she had a bad case of the flu—perhaps picked up the kind of food poisoning that made people talk funny.

Claire's eyes lit up. She grabbed Sonny by the arm.

"Wait!"

Avanti embraced a deep sigh and opened her eyes. She ignored the sleeve of blood on her arm.

"Robert—" she started, her voice more clarified, "—Jack was what we originally called him before he rightfully earned the name, Ajax, because he was always getting himself into a heap of trouble when he was little. 'Hey, Jack!' Stew would shout out, as he rushed over to save our curious Robert, who was about to experiment on—or, better yet—test an electrical outlet with a metal fork. If there were two lessons Robert taught us at the very beginning of parenthood, it was to 1.) *Always* childproof a house and 2.) *Never* let him out of your sight. But he was our angel, our *special* angel. It was those mistakes, though, those frequent trips to the ER that made us all stronger. Eventually, 'Hey, Jack!' morphed into the name Ajax. Stew and I shouted out those two words, *hey* and *Jack*, so many times that they blended together. Eventually, the name grew on me,

And so did the young boy behind the name,

Ajax was born on the same day as Echo. Stew and I weren't even expecting twins; however, from the very moment he was born, Stew and I knew he was special, a *gift* that few parents are given. And like most young boys, Ajax was curious about the world and the variety of creatures that lived among it. He was considered what you'd call 'introvert,' and often times, shy. I don't think most of the people who knew Ajax, whether it be from school or camp, saw the side I saw in him: funny, extremely witty, no filter—which, every now and then, got him in trouble—the one in the family who'd always find a way to loosen up the mood. Most people in his class who only saw that quiet, re-served side of Ajax often looked at Ajax's shyness as a weakness, whereas, I looked at it as, not a strength but an invaluable characteristic that very few his age were able to acquire. He was mature beyond his age, an 'old soul' was what my eldest brother called him, who was not only a keen observer con-stantly absorbing life around him, but also a scrupulous listener—which for a parent, who'd occasionally speak out of frustration in wake of a son's bad be-havior or say things that she truly didn't mean, it could've been looked at as a pain in the neck."

The "pain-in-the-neck" comment drew a couple of laughs from the audi-ence, which helped loosen up a reestablished tension inside the ballroom.

"But," Avanti said, more hesitantly, "Ajax was right to call me out, whether it be from recalling what I said or even what I didn't say in the past. And maybe the *greatest* virtue of a scrupulous listener: they are able to show you exactly who you are based on what you say. However, on the downside, they're able to pick up all the terrible things people can say to one another. I understand it has gotten worse over these past couple of years—or so it's made to believe. . . "

Avanti's attention was suddenly drawn to the same waiter as before—the one who looked identical to her son—storming through the back of the ball-room. She noticed that when he pushed open the set of doors and then stormed into the lobby outside he didn't make much of a sound or even noise for that matter, even though his demeanor was hot. Unless the hinges were dripping wet with WD-40 and the door itself was made out of Styrofoam, the waiter would've made quite a disturbance. Strangely, not a single person among the audience turned toward the back of the ballroom.

"Ajax never told me that he was a victim of bullying," she said after a pause. "But, I realize, his actions were telling me a different story. . . "

"I hate that fucking school!" Ajax shouted out at Avanti while she waited for an explanation as to why he pushed Cory Hart from behind and caused the seventeen year old to hit the side of his head on a jagged rock, resulting in a trip to the ER where he received thirteen stitches.

"You've made that clear that you pretty much hate everything, Ajax! You're lucky Cory's parents aren't going to press charges!"

"I'm lucky?" Ajax repeated hotly from the edge of the kitchen. "That bald-headed fuck is lucky I didn't kill him and every single piece of shit like him at New Way. But you don't get it. You never will. All you see is the aftermath—"

"Like most young men, he was afraid to admit that he was the subject of bullying. My involvement in helping the school's administration develop a punishment system for those who partook in bullying had only pushed Ajax farther away from me. But I was only doing my job as a parent. It is our responsibility to get involved. I failed not only Ajax," Avanti said over the chaos roaring inside her head.

"At the end of the day, though, I not only failed Ajax, but I also failed myself. The name-calling. The *shaming*. The incivility. The discourse," she listed. "To say it's *never* been like this, that there hasn't been as much unrest as there is today, would be a straight up lie. We've *always* been like this. It's a sad reality, but it's a 'true' reality. But why do we continue to let it happen? Ever since our Founding Fathers united the Thirteen Colonies and laid the groundwork what would later become the *United* States of America, there have always been," she held up two fingers like a peace symbol, "two parties. Two rivals. If you take a magnifying glass and examine the course of our great country, these two parties have changed names throughout time, even changed policies or positions; nonetheless, two opposing ways of governing yet unified under the same exact message: *Life, Liberty, and the pursuit of Happiness,*

After Stew died, I was forced to take a step back and reevaluate my own life; however, in the process, I failed to acknowledge the pain that my son was enduring on a daily basis. I admit that I was a failure as a parent, for not being there for my son when he needed me the most. All of my time spent as mayor, as well as governor, took its toll on my family, on Ajax. A part of me bears the responsibility of what happened to my son. And I believe a part of any mother should bear the responsibility of her child's future because it is her duty to protect them from the dangers of the world. But there lies the double-edge sword: *If we overprotect our children, then we're smothering them. On the other hand, if we don't protect them at all, then it's up to the world to decide our children's fate,*

And that's where I failed, to find the common ground with Ajax, to meet him halfway, in the middle, to *make* compromises,

My slogan reads: 'Look out, Washington! Here comes a new Washington!' What does that actually mean? For as long as I can remember, we have voted in the same politicians who have waltzed into Washington and have failed to deliver on the promises they've made on the campaign trail. Most—if not, all—of you already know my stances on the current issues this country now faces. You know my stance on healthcare, immigration, gun reform, climate. But who said they're written in stone? I look at them as merely a starting point where *both* parties can find room to work together to propose the best, most reasonable solution. The main problem facing Washington today is that we have too many talkers, not enough listeners."

Parts of the audience started to clap and cheer underneath *Avanti's* words.

"It is now time for Washington to finally take us seriously!" Avanti said, her voicing growing in size. "It is now our time to bring back The Power to where it rightfully belongs, to you—the people!"

Half of the audience erupted in applause. The other half—the money—sat in a state of utter silence. Alexandru, who was seated closest to the stage, glanced at another business magnate next to him and discreetly rolled his eyes from Avanti's speech. The only one at the table who was clapping was Colin, despite the looks of sheer gloom and doom all over the other faces.

Avanti pushed aside all the emotion that she had used throughout the speech and savored the moment before it was lost in the fray.

⊕

UNCOMFORTABLY seated with the bottom of her dress bunched up into her abdomen inside a cramped bathtub in the hotel bathroom, Avanti replayed the previous speech through her head. She pushed through the words, ones she said and didn't say. The words had drawn her eyes to her wrists, both of them not wearing a single drop or smear of blood, uncut. She ran her fingers across her wrist. Only one person had come to mind. She removed her eyes from her wrists, looked around the bathroom, and wondered what it must've been like in those final moments before he sliced open his wrists and spilled his precious blood out into the world that he scorned. As she sat alone, she couldn't help but feel a great sorrow not for being alone but for being imprisoned by her own flesh. She traveled back in time, replaying events that transpired days before his death and all the signs that he was giving her: the hopelessness and despair, heavy drug use and around-the-clock vaping, filling his body with junk food, becoming a parody of the TV commercials and advertisements shoved down his throat, then the raw fascination with death, constantly watching *movies* or reading *comic books* or playing *video games* strictly revolving around death, afterlife, hell, monsters, demons, the devil, Grim Reaper, skulls and skeletons, and all things morose. A part of him, Avanti knew, wanted to be saved, rather than salvaged. He was implicitly crying out to her—to anyone who gave a shit! However, Avanti thought—or at least, imagined—that another part of him, the lighter, softer part that settled just beyond the darkness, couldn't be saved or even spared from a ravenous world that constantly demanded death in order to fertilize the soil which brought forth more life, a vicious cycle on a never-ending feedback loop. He had already made up his mind, so she thought. He wanted to die, so she thought. And in those final days before he decided that he no longer wanted to contribute to a gluttonous world where

328

social hierocracy was distinctly constructed around the perennial binds of currency, Ajax was, in a fiendish way, taunting his mother, proving to her that, in the end, he stood on the shoulders of his own creation and won that Great War.

She reached inside her Bisset rhinestone-covered hand purse and pulled out a folded-up piece of notebook paper. She opened the letter. She only read through the first sentence before she could no longer bear to look at her son's words.

As Avanti wiped a bloody tear from the corner of her eye, she heard a booming *knock* on the door!

Startled, Avanti immediately lifted her heavy head from its dangled-state and snapped her attention toward the door. A shadow of legs appeared below the narrow crack of the doorway. She pushed her body from the empty bathtub and with one hand bracing the side of the tub and the other balling the bottom of her dress against her waist, she stepped out. She placed the hand purse aside, picked up her stilettos from the top of the closed toilet, and holding them like a weapon, inched toward the closed door.

"Hello," she said, listening for a reply but receiving only cold silence.

Avanti readjusted her grip around the toe-sides of the stilettos and made sure that, if there was someone who intended to do her harm at the door, he *or* she would feel the sharp end of her heel first.

As she approached the door, the shadow behind the door remained.

Once more, Avanti called out to whomever—or *whatever*—was waiting behind the door.

No response.

"I'll be right out," Avanti said mysteriously, as if she was trying to catch the knocker off guard. "Give me a minute—"

As soon as she uttered the word *minute*, she swung open the door.

What Avanti thought was the shadow of a person—or *thing*—happened to be the luggage that belonged to one of the aides. The handle was fully erected upright, which, considering her current state, could've passed as a stubby person.

Cautiously, Avanti stepped out of the bathroom, looked around the hotel room, which was vacant, then noticed the hotel door, which was wide open. She walked from the hotel room and like passing a busy intersection, checked each side of the hallway.

On a second pass, Avanti caught a glimpse of that same girl from earlier darting around the corner of a hallway. Every inch of her body stilled. Her eyes were clouded with memory.

A sequence of images came to Avanti, old, yet fond images. *She was chasing after Echo in a game of 'Tag! You're it!' She ran after a cackling Echo who was breathlessly darting around the kitchen island, then around and under the kitchen table, then, once out of the kitchen, around the living room sofa and she'd occasionally stop by a safe area, like behind the corner of the wall or the closet door, to pinpoint the sweaty-toothed, branch-limbed, Cyclops-eyed MONSTER teetering after her.*

With emotion flooding over her, she blocked out the images as quickly as they came to her and focused on tracking down the girl.

After walking down a stretch of desolate hallway, Avanti found the stair-well door slowly closing, as if the girl was leaving behind subtle yet obvious clues for Avanti.

In a heightened state of anxiety, Avanti called out to the girl, but the girl had already taken off. This time, Avanti quickened her pace and as soon as she made it to the stairwell, the girl was already four flights ahead of her. Running over the edge of the landing were wet footprints, which were about the size of a girl who could've been about four years old. She tracked the footprints down the stairs. Curiously, she leaned over the railing and glanced down at a small, dark figure spiraling around the flight of stairs. The girl came to a sudden pause as she made it to the base of the stairs and shot her pallid mien upward at Avanti.

"Echo?" muttered Avanti.

She hadn't seen her baby girl in sixteen years. Yet, Echo looked the same as she last remembered her. She was even wearing that same exact wavy-patterned one-piece bathing suit that she had on when she drowned.

Before Avanti could call out Echo's name, Echo took off down the stairs.

And Avanti chased after her.

☺

YOUNG Echo led Avanti to the lobby where Chopin was playing. She pin-pointed the music to the ballroom. Occasionally glancing over her shoulder to see if her mother was still following her, Echo darted directly toward the closed doors outside the ballroom. Before opening the doors, Echo stopped and once more, turned toward Avanti, who slowed down her pace.

"Echo," she said, catching her breath, "is that you, baby?"

Echo stared at Avanti with a blank, lifeless expression, as if whatever Avanti once knew of her baby girl and the once timeless beam of a smile that harnessed a supernatural power to cleanse even the most damaged of souls or that cackle of a laugh she would—more or less—expel whenever being chased around dangerous corners of the house or the simple yet astute observations she pointed out during times of pause was nevermore. Her baby girl was gone, and all that remained was a shell of a four-year-old girl staring back at her.

Echo turned her shoulder before Avanti had a chance to speak her mind. She pushed open the two doors with a loud grunt, as if they were the massive, arching doors of a castle. Chopin's ever-so delicate *Nocturne op. 9 No.2*, which was playing inside, suddenly became louder and clearer.

Adamant about confronting Echo, Avanti followed her into the ballroom.

When Avanti stepped back into the ballroom after being away for a couple of minutes—it might've been longer—she witnessed some of the guests of the fundraiser slow-dancing on the dance floor next to the dining area. A young, bouncy DJ, who remained tucked in the shadows behind a rat's nest of flashing samplers, turntables, and a laptop of pre-cut jams, was perched on top of a raised booth between two line array speakers, which seemed incredibly odd to Avanti, considering the song playing. Perhaps the DJ was taking requests? Regardless of choice in music, Avanti continued to pursue her daughter—or the body of her daughter—but couldn't find her, or "it," anywhere, which made

330

Avanti question herself whether Echo had led her to where she needed to be, as if the whole speech and everything building up to the big speech was all a brutal façade, including the guests, as well as the donors, which were nothing more than background props, a moving background, and the flaunting and secretions of power, suits and modish dresses, a meek interpretation of "Who Owns Who"; and the real *meat and cheese* of tonight's event had yet to begin. It all became crystal clear to Avanti as soon as she saw herself dancing with Colin on the dance floor. Her head rested against the side of his shoulder. Both of her eyes, closed.

All of a sudden, the ballroom dimmed and then darkened while the spotlight on the stage brightened and brought forth a "new" speaker.

Behind the podium stood Ajax. He was dressed in a holey, wrinkled, oversized *Mobocracy* T-Shirt. His face littered with nose and eyebrow piercings. She hated that shirt, hated that band, and most importantly, hated that look—a "punk band for a punk kid," she'd always say. But Avanti knew it was him, her son, *her* Ajax. He was giving a speech to the audience; however, as soon as Avanti turned toward the dining area, the seats and the tables, she realized the members of the audience all looked the same. Seated at each table was a version of her son, Ajax; unlike the other Ajax on stage, these other Ajax's were wearing suits and ties and even dresses. Avanti took her eyes away from the audience for a moment and as soon as she tried to make sense as to what her eyes were looking at, the audience was no longer present; in fact, the rest of the ballroom was left in pitch black. She turned to the dance floor. The dancers, even herself and Colin included, were no longer there either. Yet, all that remained was pitch black. She brought her attention to Ajax, who was speaking behind the podium—or at least mouthing words. She couldn't hear a word that came out of his mouth. Hoping her son was speaking through a faulty microphone, she stepped closer to the stage for a closer listen. Avanti couldn't hear a word that came out of his mouth. Even though she wasn't a lip reader, she tried to make out her son's words, as if she was deaf yet unable to read or understand sign language and faithfully relied on the translator's over-the-top punctuation or expressive facial gestures. Regardless, Ajax was the kind of kid who was only "punctual" when he needed to be. He often mumbled or spoke under his breath or trailed off in a humming rant. Yet, inside Ajax's dome, he was a master storyteller, respected and at times, adored for such poised eloquence. The only time his words were clear—that is, outside his head—was when he'd yell at her. And, you certainly didn't need a translator for such an event.

As the music softened yet continued to play in the background, Ajax continued to talk not to Avanti, but, more or less, *through* Avanti.

"I can't hear you, Ajax," she said to him. "What are you trying to tell me?"

She asked but, for some reason, she already knew the answer to her question.

While Ajax continued to speak without sound, she inched closer to the front of the stage.

She pleaded and begged for Ajax to speak up, to make sense!

He didn't—at least, to Avanti.

Ajax was having his moment on stage.

Talking.

Reading from a letter, *his* letter.

Frustrated by the lack of sound coming from her son's mouth, she rushed toward the stairs along the edge of the stage and as she was about to climb up the first couple of steps, Ajax pulled himself from the podium and turned to stage-left where his mother had come to a sudden halt.

"Ajax," Avanti said, holding out her arms, "you can talk to me. Please. . . "

Ajax stared back at his mother, as if he wanted to say something but couldn't. He opened his mouth to speak but immediately closed it once the moment passed. Disgusted with Avanti, he shook his head and proceeded through a closed curtain behind the podium.

Determined, Avanti followed Ajax through the curtain. She stopped and saw Ajax walking into the darkness with a strange seven-foot tall creature by his side.

Avanti called out, "Robert!"

Ajax stopped, turned his shoulder, and glanced at his mother.

In the darkness, a scaly clawed hand reached out for Ajax.

Hand-in-hand, Ajax and the upright creature walked away from Avanti until they both faded into the darkness.

Still determined for answers, Avanti followed Ajax into the darkness but only made it a couple of feet before a glass barrier prevented her from passing; in fact, she ended up bumping the top of her forehead so hard against the glass that the sudden impact of the blow forced her backward a few feet.

Stumbling away, Avanti managed to regain her balance. Startled and somewhat shaken up, she eventually recovered from the unexpected blow by taking a moment to find her bearings. Once Avanti was okay to move, she inched closer to the glass. She held her hand out and touched the glass. She walked along the edge of the glass, running the palm of her hand in a wax-on wax-off motion. She cupped both hands around her eyes like goggles, pressed her sore forehead against the glass, and peered through the darkness. She squinted her eyes, as if, by doing so, she was able to tap into a higher range of vision with incredible definition.

In her scan, Avanti *sensed* two figures, her son, Ajax, and another much taller figure with a strong yet a type of magnetic Panglossian-vibe—possibly that same creature from before—walking farther and farther away. Their presence started to dim, leaving behind only a gray film.

Avanti screamed out to Ajax numerous times but didn't receive any response.

Eventually, the figures vanished.

The confusion soon melted away, leaving behind nothing but primal rage.

With her hands curled into fists, she proceeded to BANG on the glass, hoping to break it. She banged until both her fists ached. Then, she banged some more. No matter how hard Avanti banged or pounded, the glass was impenetrable.

Behind the pounding, Avanti heard a man's voice calling out her name; however, she continued to throw her fists against the glass.

"I'm sorry for not being there," she confessed, as that raw emotion started to get the best of her.

As the pounding weakened and slowed, a hand touched her on the shoulder.

Startled, she rotated around, only to find Joel standing behind her. The lighting was less dark.

Baffled, Avanti looked around and wondered how in the world she wound up back in her hotel room.

"Are you okay, Avanti?" asked Joel.

Once more, Avanti faced the glass and found herself standing directly behind a window. The glass was perspired with raindrops. She looked out at the distant cityscape and witnessed the streaks lightning randomly flickering throughout the dark clouds. Then, she moved her eyes downward at the streets below and was left in a state of deeper thought—*Ajax*, he was here, *wasn't he?*

"I was knocking on the door," Joel said, turning toward the general direction of the door—or what was left of the door. Two of the three hinges were dangling on the side of the doorway like loose teeth. Pieces of wooden debris were scattered on the floor. The doorknob looked as if it had been eaten, chewed, spat out, then poorly screwed back into the door. "I heard a noise," Joel said finally, as he caught his breath. "Banging," he said.

"I'm fine," Avanti stuttered, acknowledging Joel's swollenness. "I just. . . " Once more, she faced the window. "I'm fine now."

She looked over Joel's shoulder and saw Colin entering the hotel room. He, too, was flabbergasted by the damage Joel had caused.

Mindful, he tiptoed over shards of door on the floor and tended to Avanti.

"You can go now," Avanti said shortly to Joel as Colin examined her for any injuries on her body.

Joel was hesitant to leave. Eventually, once he saw that Colin had everything under control, he stepped into the hallway outside.

"What happened?" asked Colin, as he consoled Avanti.

Still left in a state of confusion, Avanti's eyes drifted downward as if she was combing through thoughts and straightening out each one.

"I. . . I don't know, Colin," Avanti said unsteadily.

Colin's eyes flicked toward the thumb-sized knot on the top of Avanti's forehead.

"Geez Louise," he said, as he carefully touched the knot. "Did you hit your head on something?"

As soon as his finger grazed the knot, Avanti hissed with pain.

"I must've accidentally hit it on the doorway," she said with a grimace.

Colin walked over to a bucket of ice in the bathroom, placed a handful of ice cubes into a paper towel, and held the cold towel against Avanti's forehead.

"Are you not feeling well?" he asked while recalling what he saw happen with his own eyes as if he was a sports broadcaster breaking down play-by-play coverage. "You left in a hurry, Avanti," he said. "I thought maybe something had happened. Maybe you saw someone you wanted to avoid. An old fling perhaps. . . "

Normally, the comment, albeit innocent, would've been considered a "strike one" for Colin. However, Avanti was more intrigued by the word *left*.

"Left?" Avanti uttered. "Left where?"

"Yes," Colin said, his voice drawn out. He eased his hand from her forehead. "We were dancing, remember?"

"Yes," she said over the mental gap. Then corrected herself, "Of course."

"Here," Colin said and escorted Avanti to the bed. "Have a seat." Avanti did as Colin suggested and sat down on the edge of the bed. Over a comfortable silence, Colin said mindfully, "You're *not* like them, you know that right?"

Avanti let out a sigh.

"I don't know anymore." She rotated her head toward Colin and struggled to find his eyes. "Maybe I am. I'm just good at hiding it."

"Forget about them," Colin said clearer. "The money will come. Just give it time—"

"—I saw him, Colin," Avanti interrupted Colin.

Colin removed the balled-up paper towel of ice from Avanti's forehead. "Saw who?"

"Robert," she said, holding Colin's hand. "I saw him."

"You saw Ajax?"

"Earlier," she nodded, "when I was giving my speech. He was there, Colin. Somehow, I don't know, it's like I can still feel him with me."

Colin held Avanti, who was still tender, closer to his body.

He didn't question her sanity. In all the years he had known her, he knew not to.

As the two embraced one another, another presence made itself known by the doorway: Sonny, who was standing with both his hands planted on his hips like a flamboyant drill sergeant.

Once he collected Avanti's attention, he stormed into the hotel room.

Only a couple of steps in his march, Joel reached out at the last second and said, "I wouldn't do that, if I were you. . . "

Sonny ignored Joel, who shared subtle eye contact with Avanti before easing back into the hallway.

"I hope you feel better," Sonny seethed, as he planted himself a couple of feet away from Avanti and Colin. "Once this whole. . . fiasco is finally over, you can kiss your chances at getting the nomination goodbye."

Colin glanced at Avanti, who, in return, told Colin to give them room. He looked yet again into Avanti's eyes. She had already made up her mind what she was going to do with Sonny. And there was no stopping the hunger.

"Okay," Colin said submissively and let out a heavy sigh. He stood from the bed and touched Sonny on the shoulder. "By the way, I thought it was a wonderful speech."

Avanti said, "Thank you, Colin."

"I bet you did, Colin," Sonny said rudely over Avanti.

Colin turned toward Avanti one last time and gave her a wink.

Then, he exited the room.

Once the room was clear, he began his verbal assault on the governor: "You want to tell me what the hell that was back there? I mean, are you trying to blow the nomination? All you had to do was stick to the fuckin' script. I mean, you honestly think those old fucks out there give a shit about your life story?"

"Some of them seemed to like it," Avanti said coyly.

334

"Some," he said. "Maybe. But *not* the ones we needed to convince. All they needed from you was a two-dimensional candidate, a yes-man able to follow orders, to speak when spoken to, not some. . . " Sonny pointed at Avanti and as he searched for the right word to use, eyed her once over as if she was spoiled meat, ". . . some 'damaged' woman who everyday people could relate to. Whether you like it or not, two-dimensional presidents are what separates leaders, those who are willing and ready to make the tough decisions, from the peons—"

While Sonny was going on a tirade, Avanti peered beyond Sonny, beyond his mouth, beyond his words, and witnessed *the thing* controlling him. These words that Sonny was speaking were not his words but something else's. Somewhere, in a dark room using the dark gift, Avanti saw a glimmer of a pale face speaking the same grating words as her campaign manager was speaking. A narrow beam of artificial light was worn like a mask, bringing forth the shadowy face of tonight's host, Alexandru Adamache.

"*—The American People don't need a friend in the White House. They need a fuckin' leader*," Sonny and Alexandru said simultaneously.

Avanti sorted through Sonny's usage of words.

A half-grin crept onto the corner of her face.

"So," Avanti said suspiciously, "is this Sonny Mims talking? Or, is it Alexandru Adamache?"

Fooled by Avanti's intuitive nature, Sonny thought very carefully about his next words.

"Let's just say he didn't like the speech."

"Too bad."

"Avanti," Sonny said patiently, "you're making a big mistake."

"I'm not a cartoon character, Sonny," Avanti said, her voice trembling as the heat started to rise inside her. "I breathe the same air you breathe."

Once more, he looked over Avanti, but this time with a Witch's brew of feelings etched into his face: confusion, anger, and most importantly, disappointment.

"Forget it," Sonny said loosely over the hot silence and then waved his hand in disgust. "You're on your fuckin' own."

Sonny stormed out of the room, muttering the words *fuck 'n' hopeless*.

Meanwhile, Avanti stood from the bed and turned to Vye, who was stealthily sitting in a chair in the darkest corner of the room. Her face was cold and distant like the dark side of the moon. Her presence alone, unnoticed and yet untouched, as if she was no darker than a midnight's shadow.

More shadows came forward, stretching from the hotel room and *filling up a bustling street in Philadelphia. Daylight blazed. People and cars materialized: a bench made of cast iron, a park, a woman dressed in black, a street, a town car, a face. Action!*

Sitting inside the back of a black town car parked across the Riverwalk Park along the Delaware River, Avanti watched Vye take a seat at the bench under a dense canopy of oak trees hidden from the street cameras.

After a couple of minutes of waiting, Vye spotted Chance wandering around the park. She threw a broad stroke of a nod his way. Acknowledging the gesture, Chance was hesitant to walk over and from his overage insecurity, which was obvious to anyone who noticed, he appeared as if he had two angels, one good and the other bad, waging a war on his shoulders. Privately reveling in Chance's diminishing state, Vye remained seated at one end of the bench while Chance, who appeared more skittish from his fidgety behavior, as well as constantly looking over his shoulder by the time he tottered up, eventually took a seat at the other end of the bench.

"You have the burner?" asked Vye, looking forward and watching two labradoodles sniff each other's butts next to a veteran's memorial.

"Where's Avanti?" asked Chance.

"I'm sure you're aware that she has a busy schedule, Mr. McBride. She told me to tell you that she sends her best wishes."

" The arrangement was for me to meet her," Chance argued, as he started to make a scene. "Not some woman whom I don't even know—"

"—So, the phone?"

"You have the money?" asked Chance, more aggressively.

"First, you show me yours," Vye said, "I'll show you mine. . . "

Chance thought over the perverse comment.

"And," Vye noted, "don't get any ideas."

Eventually, he caved and did as Vye instructed and pulled out the flip-phone from his jacket pocket.

"Hand it over," she said.

"I want to see the money first," Chance said, raising his voice.

Vye grabbed the briefcase next to her knee-high boots, brought it to the middle of the bench, popped it open, and revealed the perfectly organized rows of clean, crisp hundred dollar bills, each perfect stack held together by a mustard yellow currency strap. Chance didn't bother to count the money. All he could see were all those faces of Benjamin Franklin. In all his years of living—or better, yet—scraping from one job to another, he'd never seen so many damn Benjamins. She pinched the corner of one bundle and with one hand, gave it a dealer's dovetail shuffle as if she was giving the poor man a quick tease. Then, not wasting anymore time, she closed the briefcase.

"Nice," Chance said, his eyes wide and filled with what could've been money signs. He handed Vye the flip phone. "Here," he said, as Vye, in return, quickly slid the briefcase toward his body.

Vye looked over the flip phone the same way a dog would look at its master after a strange command.

"This is the only copy?" asked Vye.

"The message is in the voicemail."

"You didn't answer my question, Mr. McBride."

"Yes," Chance said, his voice trembling. "It's the only copy."

Vye made a contemptuous noise with her mouth.

"Ballsy, might I say," she said arrogantly. "But I'll take your word for it."

"Pleasure doing business with you," he said, grabbed his briefcase of money, held close to him like a baby, and stood to his feet.

He had only taken two steps away from the bench before Vye said from behind, "Money's not going to bring back your sister."

Vye's words were cool and sneaky, as if she was slipping a knife between his shoulder blades.

336

Chance stopped, carefully thought over his next few words, and finally faced Vye with tears worn heavy in his eyes.

"Let me ask you one last question before you disappear, Mr. McBride," Vye said nonchalantly. "Do you believe your junkie sister was capable of the crimes she committed?"

"Well, it doesn't really matter what I believe," Chance said, his voice trembling. "My sister is dead, all thanks to you people." Heavy emotion came over Chance, like a flood. He clenched his teeth, curled his fists tight; he even strangled the very handle of the briefcase, as if he was trying to choke out the life from inside. "One day, you people will answer for what you did. And the world will know the truth about what you people are."

"You're one to talk about honesty, Mr. McBride," Vye said, hiding a smile behind her face. The disguised smile was worn carefully for Chance, just barely visible enough for Chance to see the truth behind it. "Besides," she said, holding back the smile before it could grow on her face, "how's that boy doing?"

As soon as Chance witnessed that look on Vye's face, he knew he was in it—neck deep in shit. His skin flushed. Beads of sweat formed on his forehead nearly the size of raindrops.

"Sooner or later," he said, swallowing, "the world will know what you—"

"—And what are we exactly, Mr. McBride?"

Chance paused, held back his words.

"I have nothing else to say to you," he said with tears in his eyes. "The way I look at it. . . you people are already dead to me."

Chance tried yet again to walk away from Vye, but, somehow, she managed to reel him back in with her softly spoken words: "Across the street, there's a donut shop called Sweet Tooth. They have these raspberry puff turnovers that they make once a year, which I've heard are to die for. Perhaps you should try one."

Once more, he stopped and thought about his words, what he could say to put her in her place.

He acknowledged Vye, this time more squarely. She was no longer wearing her sunglasses. Instead, she was staring directly at Chance with hazy, red eyes.

With his brow furrowed in stupidity, he turned back around and walked off.

"Chance," Vye whispered.

Once more, he stopped but didn't turn around.

Once more, he thought about not his words, but this time his actions, what he wanted to do to Vye. A strange sensation came over him, causing him to stagger. He pinched the brim of his nose and shook his head, as if he was shaking away a dizzy spell.

Once more, he turned to Vye, who was no longer sitting on the bench. Instead, he witnessed a familiar man sitting in her place.

He looked closer.

The man was light skinned, thin, yet fairly built, wore clothes that one would only find at a big box store. He had a scar the shape of a lightning bolt running down the side of his face. He was wearing a turtleneck of tattoos.

"Stache?"

The familiar man, whom Chance thought was a man name Stache, stood up from the bench.

"Sup, Chance," he said.

His voice was deep and distinct, Stache's voice. Chance looked over Stache and once he realized that the man was, in fact, Stache, he walked over to him. He hadn't aged a day. The last time he saw Stache was at the Bawkin Correctional Facility in South Carolina where he was finishing up the last stretch of his five-year sentence for assault and battery. Stache, on the other hand, was supposed to be carrying out a twenty-five year sentence for armed robbery—or what he liked to call a "stretch."

"What are you doing here? You're supposed to be. . . "

"Locked up," Stache finished Chance's sentence. "Yeah. I know," he said, approaching Chance. "They let me out earlier on good behavior."

After an awkward silence between the two, they embraced one another. What Chance didn't realize was that he was hugging Vye, not Stache. She gently whispered in his ear, "You can still redeem yourself. Mr. McBride."

Chance leaned back, revealing Stache once more. He looked at Stache, who, in return, flicked his head in a nod at a homeless man hanging out in the shade of a bridge. Chance followed Stache's eyes and noticed the bearded man who was dressed like the street and clinging onto a damp cardboard sign that read, "Help! Hungry, homeless, and hopeless."

Chance didn't say a word to Stache, not even a goodbye or see ya later.

With a vacant expression on his face, he robotically walked over to the homeless man under the bridge and set the briefcase on top of his overstuffed shopping cart that was packed with all of his belongings. Chance didn't utter a single word to the homeless man, who, despite the minor intrusion, couldn't be more thankful once he opened the briefcase and saw all the green faces of Benjamin Franklin inside. Overwhelmed, the homeless man could hardly stand upright for the sight of money nearly caused him to faint; however, Chance didn't care about what the homeless man had to say to him nor did he even acknowledge his reaction. Yet, Chance walked back through the park and spotted the glowing pink sign across the street that read: Sweet Tooth. Even though he had eaten a cheese steak an hour before the meeting with Vye and wasn't at all hungry, he could hear his stomach growling. Driven by the sugary smell of tasty pastries in the air, Chance walked to Sweet Tooth. He didn't even bother to stop for traffic. Yet, he kept on walking through the busy street. He didn't budge or flinch a muscle from the cars swerving around him. His eyes were mesmerized by a display case behind the front window of the bakery. All those beautiful-looking pies and cakes presented to onlookers, walkers, joggers, bikers, drivers, and riders.

"Forgive me, Storm," he said tearfully, as if he was speaking, not to Storm, but the bakery itself.

As Chance crossed the yellow line and proceeded directly toward the bakery, a sudden horn blared out beside him! Before he could even turn his head to acknowledge the horn, as well as the screech of tires skidding to a stop, Chance's blood was decorated all over the truck's windshield, as well as the street. The truck had struck Chance so hard and violently that his blood had even made it to the bakery where it painted the brick walls and window front like graffiti.

From the unlit corner of the hotel room, Vye nodded her head at Avanti, who, in return, flashed a smirk.

As Sonny made his way from room 421, Avanti said from behind, "Let's make it official, shall we?"

Huffing with anger from Avanti's mild "suggestion," Sonny came to halt by the doorway before walking into the hallway and faced Avanti, who was already inches away from him.

"You know," he said, startled from Avanti's presence, "I was rooting for you, Avanti. I thought you had a chance. I really did. Black woman with a bright future in politics. What better time than now for someone like you to come along and reshape the vision of America?" The anger back over him, this time holding him tight like a fist. "Turns out that you're no different from any idealist who has her head stuck so far up her own ass she doesn't even know shit from Shiloh." He leaned in with his teeth barred. "I tell you what, *Avanti*." Sonny spoke her name with a black girl's sass. "Do yourself a favor and come back to reality where the big boys play. Then, maybe, we can talk about the future of your campaign, huh? Until then, you can go right ahead and find yourself another campaign manager to replace me because, frankly, I don't give a shit."

"Is that how you feel?" asked Avanti.

Sonny looked over Avanti with derision.

"I swear, you women," he said, his eyes flicking toward her swollen breasts, "and you're fuckin' feelings. I was a fool to actually think that a woman could be qualified to run this country."

Sonny let out an airy snort from his mouth before storming away. He made it a few feet down the hallway before Avanti called out his name from behind.

Once more, he stopped and faced Avanti.

He had no other choice than to listen—and listen well.

"You want to know where I get my strength from, Sonny?"

"You call that nonsense that I had to listen to for the past two hours you displaying strength? You looked weak. Thankfully, the press corps wasn't allowed inside; otherwise, except for a couple of sympathizers, the entire country would be writing you off right about now."

"Ever since I was a girl, my mother engrained in me a sense of resiliency. It was my mother who raised me to be the woman I am today and if it wasn't for her words, then I probably wouldn't be standing here. She made sure to tell me that I 'could do anything I put (my) mind to.' And 'just remember,' she'd emphasize, 'one man's shit don't smell no different than another. It all stinks the same.' I've used those words throughout my life; in fact, I've learned to embrace those words. Then," she said, as she took a step closer to Sonny, even though he was standing much farther away, "life—or better yet, death—came along and it bit me where I was most vulnerable. When I was in my early twenties," she pointed to the white blotches on her face, "I developed a skin disease. I didn't want it. I knew I could *thrive* without it. Even till this day, people stare. People look at me funny. But I don't—and didn't—let people stop me from being where I need to be—"

"—And where do you need to be, Avanti?"

"Despite what you heard tonight, Stew was a good man," she said, narrowing both her eyes, "a *faithful* man who wouldn't dare harm a single hair on my head. He knew what I was capable of. And, unlike most of the people who have come and gone in my life, Stew was the one man who accepted me for who I was. He embraced me. He held me the way any woman should be held. But most importantly, he understood me," she said, starting to drift off. "When he became sick, I couldn't control the cancer spreading inside him. It was too deep." Avanti drifted in deep reflection, visualizing his skeletal face during those final moments of his life. The thought alone of Stew going out caused her skin to burn. More poised, she said to Sonny, "But overtime, I've realized that every *living* thing dies."

"Huh?" Sonny said sarcastically. "You just now figured that one out." With a sense of superiority, he looked over Avanti as if she was beneath him. "Good luck to you, Avanti."

The words *good luck* were spoken slow and carefully. Yet, they rang out like a symphony triggering a memory.

Disguised among pedestrians, Vye stood across the street from former Vice President Croom's political campaign headquarters that was located in Fairwell, New Hampshire and watched Sonny Mims having a secret conversation with the former veep. After Sonny was finished talking with Croom, the two of them shook hands as if they were making a deal.

Croom winked at Sonny and said, "Good luck."

By any means, Vye wasn't a lip reader, but she didn't have to be. After all, it wasn't hard to read the words good *and* luck.

Once more, Sonny tried to walk away—more like, flee—but couldn't.

Once more, he stopped but never turned around. Couldn't. Yet, he continued to face the other end of the hallway while Joel stood outside the hotel room.

"You underestimate us," Avanti said, as she removed the contact lenses from her eyes. "But maybe that's the whole point," she said while creeping up behind Sonny. "You already have us figured out. Which, to your advantage, makes us predictable. And if there was one trait that voters look for in his or her candidate, it's predictability. Am I right? Or, am I wrong?"

"Save your breath," Sonny said, not turning around. "It's too late—"

"—You're right," Avanti said, standing directly behind Sonny. Her eyes fell onto the pulse on his neck, which was beating like a kick drum. She pulled down the collar around his neck, peeling away the Band-Aid covering the two fresh bite marks directly above his collarbone. Her eyes were different, her irises crimson red, her pupils opening like black holes. "It is too late," Avanti said softly, as she loomed over Sonny. "*For you.*"

Before Sonny could turn his shoulder, Avanti had already sunk her two fangs into his neck. The blood squirted from his neck like a perforated water hose.

Except for a couple of swings of his arms, he didn't put up much of a fight.

Meanwhile, Joel stood guard as Avanti continued to suck the blood from her former campaign manager's neck. Joel kept his attention directed at a painting of Emaneul Leutze's masterpiece, *Washington Crossing the Dela-*

ware, on the wall before him, not even turning his head an inch to acknowledge the violence taking place only feet away from him. By the time Avanti was through with Sonny, she released her fangs from his flesh, which retracted to normal canines. Her mouth, as well as her chin was covered in blood. Sonny fell from Avanti's grip the same way a tired man would fall into a cool, nourishing bed and hit the floor with a soft *thud*. He made a desperate attempt to crawl away from Avanti, but his hands and knees slipped over his own puddle of blood and left him floundering on drenched carpet. Since fleeing was a futile endeavor, Sonny resorted to his last option—his only option—which was plugging the two massive punctures along the side of his neck with his hands; however, like before, it was a futile attempt to salvage whatever life—or what little life—he had left.

As the flow of blood started to slow and Sonny's life started to fade, Avanti loomed over his dying body; and with an air of solemn reverence, she watched his wide, panicked eyes start to glaze over.

She tilted her body into frame for she had one last thing to say to Sonny before he checked out.

As Sonny took his final breaths, Avanti said like a boss: "Consider this your resignation."

⊕

With her feet kicked up on the edge of a desk in a dark office above the Convention Center where she was soon going to hold a rally for thousands of supporters, Avanti pushed the up button on the TV remote to flip the channel from the Phillies baseball game to Channel 9 News where a news reporter was reporting a breaking news story on the sidewalk outside Antonio's Pizzeria in Center City.

"Later this afternoon, workers at this pizzeria behind me discovered the body of a white male in an alleyway. Investigators have yet to identify the body, but they believe he was homeless. As far as the cause of death, investigators are certain the man died from a fatal bite mark on his neck by what they're claiming was a wild animal."

TALORA was making her rounds with a tray of hors d'oeuvres, including cucumber and caviar bites, as well as escargot in garlic butter—which were deliberately positioned at the end of the tray closest to her neck and shoulder and acted as her own repellent for vampires-in-disguise—when she witnessed the red eyes staring at her from behind a congested crowd of well-off socialsuckers in the lobby of St. Gabriel Hotel.

Instantly blindsided by the toll of fear, Talora instantly started to spiral out of control as if she had no clue as to what she was doing, where she was going, and why she was even here. She stopped by the bar and collected her thoughts before she lost control. Talora mentally questioned his presence but could come up with only one reason as to why he chose her.

With more direction, Talora rerouted through the lobby as if by doing so he'd fly off—or phantom jump or whatever they did—and find some other fresh, warm meat to bother. In that moment of climbing suspense, Talora could only imagine what it'd be like to wind up on the national news, her tragic story on the tube, her body covered with a white sheet, another statistic, a "victim;" and surprisingly, it was the thought of her baby brother that had brought on such grim reality. All of those pulses, she thought, beating like a cheap techno song throughout the entire lobby, and if this blood breath was here to party hardy, then he wouldn't have a hard time finding another beat.

Talora shot yet another discreet glance toward his direction. His pale sunken face was drifting in and out of the crowd, those crimson eyes attached to Talora like crosshairs. The man carried a certain hunger in his eyes.

Then again, Talora reminded herself that he was no man.

But something far worse.

A creature spawned from nightmares and forged by daywalkers.

Bloodied and bestowed.

She kept a close eye on the strange creature and with each subtle glimpse of his razor-sharp face, it became clear to her that he most definitely didn't belong at The Governor's Ball—and from the crafty way he tracked her every movement with his blood-soaked eyes, it was even more evident to her that she was his prey. His eyes, magnetic—it was *the gaze*, she realized, the one of an animal, *not man*. His intentions, cold and calculated. That, and the simple fact that not one guest or donor inside the hotel's lobby feared him or, even worse, pegged him as an "outsider," considering the strict dress code and most—if not, all—of the socialsuckers were wearing tuxedos that cost as much as a car opposed to the outsider's informal attire: a raggedy black leather jacket that looked as if it had been handed down by three centuries, a pair of black leather gloves with metal spikes over the knuckles, heavy nose and eyebrow piercings and all that twisted steel on his face, as well as a turtleneck of foreign tattoos along his pallid skin. She figured he was a member of the notorious Vampos gang from those ancient Romanian symbols along his neck and face.

He—or what Talora assumed was an "it"—moved behind one guest the same way a skilled hunter would use a tree or even high grass to conceal its cover from its vulnerable prey. Talora's senses heightened, especially her hearing, as well as her sight. She checked for exits. There was one not too far away. The sight of a glowing green sign that read EXIT in bold lettering showed her the way.

The flash of lightning brought out the two shadowy individuals standing inside a dusty, unlit living room of an abandoned house along the jagged New York coast.

One of the individuals, the taller, wide-shouldered one, a light skinned man with tight cornrows who was wearing a flashy coat that looked as if it was covered in gold glitter, took a drag of a vape pen. He exhaled diabolically. Thick clouds of vapor oozed like smoky snakes from both his mouth and nostrils and trailed around the popped *collar of the Bubblegum Pop-inspired coat.*

Another flash of lightning flickered through the living room in a strobe light-like pattern.

"Promise me," the tall man said, as vapor followed his every syllable, "they won't turn her. . ."

"I can't promise you they'll be nice to her," said the voice of the other individual, a short woman with her dark hair pulled back tight in a ponytail, a smooth operator. "I'm afraid their actions are out of my control." She stepped closer to the partially shattered window, her glossy eyes glowing. "But if you want them to scare her, then, that, you can be sure of."

Talora handed off the tray of hors d'oeuvres to another waitress, who was in the middle of taking a drink order, and shouldered her way through the crowd.

She glanced over her shoulder and saw the creep closing in on her.

His prowl was faster, creepier, deadly.

"I have to ask you, Mr. Japhy," the short woman said, as her pallid face lit up from the flash of lightning, "what exactly did this girl do to you in order for her to receive such. . . horror?"

The tall shadowy man, Mr. Japhy, said quietly over a thoughtful pause, "She stole something that belonged to me. Something I'll never get back."

Three Months Ago

INSIDE a sold-out Madison Square Garden arena, the fueled-up crowd head-banged to the final song, "Recycle Your Pets," by the band Stuffed Animalz.

Riding the choppy, impulsive riffs played by sword-wielding Japanese guitarist, Dexter, aka "T-Rex," real name Akemi Tanaka, lead singer, Japhy Warchild, screeched through his patent pink microphone, *"Razor-Rrection! Razor-Rrection! Razor-Rrection!"*

Concertgoers acted like parishioners hanging onto Japhy's every lyric.

The front of the crowd screamed along with Japhy while these random pockets of mosh pits broke out along the violent tidal wave of flesh like water ripples.

"*Razor-Rrection!*"

"*Razor-Rrection!*"

"*Razor-Rrection!*"

The set ended with a hellish display of pyrotechnics.

After the song finished in a blaze of glory, Japhy caught his breath and took a moment to acknowledge all of his "disciples" shouting out—even chanting—his name. Young teary-eyed women, who were desperate to carry his baby, reached out to him from the very front of the stage.

Japhy couldn't help but laugh at it all.

If they only knew. . .

He pushed the madness aside and thanked the hometown crowd.

Then, he dropped the microphone on the stage.

The lights dimmed.

The entire stage went black.

🕐

"WHAT a way to end the tour, my brutha!" the bassist, Product, said, as he slapped hands with Japhy, who was lounging in the middle of a couch where he was surrounded by at least a dozen of bikini-wearing, apple-bottomed Instagram models.

"I'm ready to hit the road again," Japhy said smoothly.

"Shiiit," Product slurred. "That was probably the longest three months of my life. Here-here!"

Product toasted a Pabst with Japhy, who, in return, took a sip of beer and then secretly spat the mouthful of beer back into the can. Japhy hid his disgust for the taste of beer with a smack of his gums.

While Product chugged the rest of his Pabst, one of the bosomy women who was clinging to Japhy's side, leaned in closer and said to him, "Nice move."

"She talks," he said back.

"She does a lot of things."

Japhy swallowed, but it wasn't the beer.

Instead, it was a lump in his throat.

More seductively, she asked, "If beer's not your poison, then what is?"

The Instagram model brushed her shiny brunette hair from her chest, revealing her fake, perfectly round D-cup breasts. She even gave them a jiggle for Japhy. In return, Japhy's eyes moved at a seizure's pace as he followed her swollen breasts. He wanted to play with them.

He looked around the backstage and couldn't help but acknowledge the other band mates who were flirting with other women. He turned back to the Instagram model and not wasting anytime, touched the strap along her lime-green bikini. He didn't realize—at least not until his eyes fell on his fingers—but his hand started to tremble.

"I can think of a couple of things," Japhy said closely and set his hand down by his side before the Instagram model could notice the tremble.

In the back of his mind, he was wondering the whole time when she'd brandish her phone from wherever she was hiding it—and he couldn't find too many places where she could hide it—and snap a quick selfie or make her own "Me and Japhy" highlight reel.

Phones have literally *ruined everything.*

"You know, for a man who's worshipped like a god, you're pretty shy."

"I like to refer to myself as more introvert—"

The Instagram model giggled from the comment.

"I like shy guys," the model said, as she opened up Japhy's trademarked coat. The glittery gold coat sparkled from the overhead light raining down from above. At times, the coat was bright enough to light up the entire backstage.

Immediately, Japhy grabbed the model's boney wrist.

"*Don't* touch the fuckin' coat," he said all god-like, his voice deepening.

Startled by Japhy's abrupt change in demeanor, the Instagram model leaned back a couple of inches and said timidly, "Okay."

"What's this about shy guys," another much blonder model said as she cozied up to Japhy's other side. "I *luuuv* me some shy-on-the-fly guys." She started to play with the curly hair along his chest. While the two Instagram models primped and pampered Japhy, like a god, he spotted a woman in her early twenties—fully dressed—between the sea of flesh.

Intrigued by her presence, Japhy squinted his eyes and peered closer. One of the bodyguards allowed her, as well as a friend ("Lacey," he concluded) past the gates and through the backstage where they were talking—or better yet, hitting it off with keyboardist/DJ, Pacen, who stage name was DJ Pac-Attack. However, Pacen appeared more interested in the other girl, the one whose name wasn't Lacey.

Pacen was considered the backbone of band, provided leadership for the each member of the group, was known to give strong rally speeches whenever the band mates needed rallying or just a pep talk; also gave their sound that needed "edge." It was fair to say DJ Pac-Attack was Wizard in *Wizard of Oz,* the man behind the curtains.

When Japhy saw Pacen talking to her—of all people, *her! What is she doing here? She hates heavy metal!*—a flash of anger came over him, causing his skin to burn. His eyes went cold, dark. Even the feel of a woman's soft touch felt like knives cutting through his chest.

What made matters even worse: Japhy witnessed Pacen taking her to the tour bus. And he knew exactly what happened on the tour bus.

Lacey stayed behind, found one of the stagehands, and started talking to him.

In a heap of rage, Japhy pushed aide the starfuckers and stood to his feet and despite the complaints coming from all directions, such as "You friggin' jerk!" or "That is no way to treat a woman, asshole!" he kept his eyes on the lucky lady as she walked away with Pacen.

Before they exited backstage, Pacen secretly slipped his hand into hers and the two held hands, as if they were now a hot item.

ONLY two months after the Counting Sheep Tour wrapped in New York City, the band reunited at the drummer, Tommy Bango's lakeside cabin, which was located outside Syracuse.

When lead singer, Japhy, arrived at Bango's rehearsal studio, the band was already there. . . all except for one member, Pacen.

With only three weeks away, the band was scheduled to play for an upcoming festival called Fall Frenzy Festival. Eventually, after much worry and complaint, Pacen finally showed up with, of course, his new fling, Talora. However, to Japhy, the two lovebirds looked as if they were officially "official" from the way they couldn't keep their hands off one another.

As soon as the band geared up, it was clear, not only to Japhy, but also the other band mates, that Pacen didn't want to be there; in fact, Talora was an obvious distraction, making her own little gestures while the band was rehearsing, like winking at Pacen or blowing him kisses. Pacen missed his cues. Couldn't get the beat down correctly. It was like he had other things on his mind and none of them revolved around preparing for the upcoming concert.

Finally, after wasting the entire night rehearsing, Product spoke up and questioned Talora's presence, but did so in a manner that didn't sit well with Pacen.

Product asked something along the lines: *"What the fuck is she doing here?"*

T-Rex interjected: *"My boy here is pussy whipped."*

Defensively, Pacen came back: *"You're one to talk."*

"You, Pussy," T-Rex said under his breath.

Then, Pacen returned wittingly, *"Hey, man. You are what you eat."*

The comment didn't sit well at all with Japhy; in fact, he did everything in his power to keep himself from lashing out at Pacen. Later that next day, when Pacen had gone off with Talora for "a quick hike," which was the excuse he used, Japhy arranged an emergency meeting in the living room to make a vote on the decision whether or not to keep Pacen in the band. Which had made matters worse. The band was split; and those who rebuked the very idea had questioned Japhy's reasoning behind the suggestion. Which created more unwanted tension and division among the band. After all, DJ Pac-Attack was the backbone of Stuffed Animalz!

For Japhy, it felt as if it was the beginning of the end of Stuffed Animalz.

And all fingers pointed at a woman named Talora Katz.

ⓘ

TWO days later after the trip to Lake Oneside, Japhy visited Talora's house, which was located in a small suburban neighborhood in a small town called Ballpointe located in upstate New York. Across the street, Japhy waited inside the passenger seat of his Mustang, while his driver Broot kept the engine warm. The sight alone of Pacen's brand new Escalade parked right next to the burgundy crossover in the driveway pissed him off something awful. *They would never allow it*, he thought. Yet, Pacen and *his silver tongue must've won them over*.

As Japhy opened the passenger door, Broot grabbed him by the arm and said doubtfully, "I wouldn't do that if I was you, Japh."

Simmering with anger, he glared at Broot's chubby, catcher's mitt of a hand touching the sleeve of his coat.

Japhy didn't have to say a word.

His eyes were doing most of the talking.

Broot released his hand from Japhy's coat.

"Think about the consequences. Think about what your parents will do if they find out about you—"

"—Well, Broot," Japhy said over Broot as he hung over the passenger door, "that's the thing. You're *not* me. And you'll *never* know what it's like to be me."

Broot fell witness to a motley crew of emotions shrink-wrapped around Japhy's eyes.

Disappointed by Japhy's actions, Broot ran his finger over the gold W.W.J.D. (*What Would Japhy Do*) wristband around his meaty wrist and then hung his head in despair.

Primed for confrontation, Japhy stepped outside the Mustang and closed the door behind him. He only took one step away from the car before he was greeted by these three neighborhood kids who looked as if they were up to no good. Each one was walking along the sides of their bicycles. Each one leaned in closer for a closer look, as if they were either fans of Japhy or something else—perhaps enemies?

Japhy rolled his eyes once he noticed the three kids, particularly one scrawny kid in the middle, whom his friends called "Lee."

"What do you want now?" asked Japhy, as if he knew the kids.

"What do we want?" Lee returned, as he turned his head to the others. "What are *you* doing here?"

"I can't talk about it right now," he said, the anger coming through his voice.

"Yeah, right. You're too good to talk to us—"

"—It's not like that," Japhy kept an eye on Pacen's SUV, "you know that."

"You know, he's been hanging around here a lot more," another thicker kid boldly said to Japhy.

"Who's been hanging around here?"

The kid nodded at the house across the street.

"Your boy, Pacman—"

"—It's DJ Pac-Attack, you moron."

"Whatever."

More engaged by the comment, Japhy faced the three kids.

"A lot more, how?"

Another more bashful kid said, "Like boyfriend-girlfriend."

"Yeah," Lee said, "like, one day, like in the near future, he's going to be joining the family, if you know what I mean. . . "

"Go fuck yourself, kid."

"Kid?"

"Hey, who do you think you are?"

Lee said over the other kid, "We want Nathan back."

Japhy paused and swallowed his words.

"Nathan's dead," he said to the kids.

Japhy heard the *squeak* of a screen door behind him!

Both Talora and Pacen exited the house, leaving Japhy with no other choice than to react.

Startled by their whereabouts, he ducked behind the Mustang and took cover while, at the same time, the three other kids shooed away Japhy and peddled away on their bikes.

From behind the Mustang, Japhy watched Talora walk Pacen to his Escalade where the two embraced one another. He watched the two kiss before Pacen drove away. Then, he watched her wave Pacen goodbye.

For the first time, Japhy questioned what he was doing back in Ballpointe.

And he didn't the answer.

Not one.

Present Day

As the creature whom Talora thought belonged to the Vampos gang pushed aside a couple of guests, knocking one of them, a frailer man, to the floor, Talora raced through the exit doors and cut through the parking deck.

Not once did she ever look back.

Instead, she ran as if her life depended on it. She knew that if she could make it to her car, then she'd have a chance to survive the night.

However, her chances were slim—considering what she was up against.

Even though Talora's car was parked on Level 3, she didn't bother taking the stairs. The last place she wanted to be, especially if he caught up with her, was in a confined space like a stairwell.

In her escape, the life around her was turned down. The ambience of traffic outside the parking deck was not as prevalent. The chorus of *honking* horns and background chatter, softened. Surprisingly, she never heard the sound of the door opening or closing behind her. Surely, he was right on her tail when she exited the hotel. Which, for a brief moment, made Talora question whether or not he had ended the pursuit.

Running up the incline of the first level, Talora glanced over her shoulder and confirmed that the door was, in fact, closed. And not one person—or thing—had followed her into the parking deck. She was momentarily struck by a glimmer of hope; however, she kept running, never slowing her dash to safety. She ran up the next level and then, the next. From the sharp U-turn, she spotted her white Honda Civic parked at the other side of the parking deck. She ran about halfway toward the car before she slowed in her tracks from the pungent odor of what reeked of a corpse. The odor was like a wall and once Talora walked right through it, she was completely submerged in it. She pinched the tip of her nose and breathed through her mouth. But even then, Talora could taste the smell on her tongue, as if, during each breath, she was taking small nibbles at it. She increased the speed of her run and hurried to her car. Only three strides in, she heard a high pitch sound coming from a car, possibly her car.

She slowed down her run to a loose jog. Which had given her enough time to catch her breath. She listened closer and pinpointed that chalkboard-like scratching of a screech: a sharp claw crookedly running along the side of a car.

But not just any car. . .

Her car!

Stepping out of the warped shadows at the front of her Honda Civic was the mayor of New York City, Mayor Armitage.

"You wanted to see me, Ms. Katz?" said the mayor.

She was struck by a momentary dizziness. She heard of such effects. Once, her friend, Lacey, had told her about a vamp who used the power of seduction on her. She thought they called it a "lure."

For a moment, Talora was convinced it was the mayor.

But then again, they had the ability to shapeshift.

And, why in the hell would the mayor meet her in such a dark place?

Talora stared at the mayor as if she was looking at an autostereogram painting and focused yet unfocused her eyes. She aimed for the center of his face and angled her eyes along the horizon. His true face slowly started to surface like one of 3D image. Behind the mayor's face was the same exact pale face that she was running away from. Talora reminded herself that he was *no* person.

"Nice try," she said.

The creature stepped through the mayor's vanishing body.

As the red-eyed creature stepped forward and revealed himself entirely under the hazy amber light, Talora heard the same screeching sounds all around her.

Out from the shadows around her emerged more of them. She counted six of them; however, she had heard rumors and stories on the news that they traveled in much larger packs—some close to a dozen or even more.

Before the gang could circle around Talora and leave her no room to escape, she turned around and ran back down to the 2nd level where she was greeted by yet more of them emerging from the dark shadows around parked vehicles. She looked for exits. Behind her was an opening in the deck. The drop was two stories. The fall wouldn't kill Talora—that is, if she didn't land directly on her head; however, at the very least, she'd more than likely break a leg. And, Talora knew she wouldn't be any good if she couldn't run on two legs.

She checked her last option, the more doable option, a stairwell behind one of the gang members. Talora had no other choice. She pulled out her car keys from her pocket and as she balled her hand into a fist, she placed each key in the cracks of her fingers—her car key, apartment key, bike lock key.

Make sure to *aim for the eyes,* she told herself.

"Nowhere to run now, bitch," the same creature from before, whom she assumed was their leader, said from Level 3.

As the gang surrounded Talora, the engine of a car suddenly turned on!

The *clah-clah-clunk* of gears switching echoed throughout the parking deck.

Then, the blistering skid of tires!

352

As the supposed leader of the gang exposed the fangs in his mouth and re-vealed himself for not who but *what* he was, a beam of headlights shone upon his pale face. The vampire's attention snapped toward the speeding SUV on his left, putting a new definition to the expression: a "vamp in headlights." Both his red eyes widened, jaw slackened, his entire face stretched out in car-toon-like fashion.

While others jumped out of the way, the alpha remained in the crosshairs of the grill. His body violently rolled along the front hood of the Escalade, his upper body taking the brunt of the hit. He crashed into the front windshield, leaving behind the fractured dent of a body in the glass. His body was flung over the top of the Escalade.

Left in a state of bafflement, it took Talora a couple of tense seconds to rec-ognize the vehicle. Then, as Talora's suspicions came true, the back door be-hind the driver's seat flung open. Pacen waved Talora inside.

"GET IN!" he shouted out.

Talora looked around, as if she was reevaluating her options. The other gang members were standing to their feet. She couldn't find the other one, the leader.

Pacen shouted out again, "GET IN, TALORA!"

Talora quickly leaped into the backseat and closed the door before one of the gang members could grab her leg.

Once Talora was secured inside, Pacen switched the gear in reverse, backed up into another car parked behind him, and lastly, switched the gear back in drive. He floored the SUV around the gang and managed to drive away in one piece.

As Pacen sped from the parking deck and onto a bustling midtown Manhat-tan Street, Talora looked behind the SUV.

She couldn't help but sniff the inside of the vehicle.

That funky smell was back.

Death.

"The other vamp," she said, frantically searching for the one who was struck by Pacen's Escalade, "he's gone. . . "

She heard a *thud* coming from the ceiling.

Her eyes slowly moved upward. . .

She cried out, "Pacen!"

All of a sudden, a hand with claws the size of steak knives burst through the ceiling of the SUV. The claws came inches away from cutting Talora's face.

Thinking of the weapons at hand—except for the one he was driving— Pacen pushed in the car lighter below the dashboard.

Talora ducked and dived and dodged each swipe of the hand. Keeping as low as her body would allow, she crawled toward the passenger seat; and as she was about to slip into the seat, her head suddenly jerked backward. The vampire had grabbed a handful of Talora's hair and was tugging her body to-ward the ceiling. Fighting off the hand by throwing wild punches, Talora cried out for help.

Help arrived in the sound of a *click*.

The car lighter sprung outward. Pacen grabbed the hot lighter from its socket and while steering the vehicle straight with the insides of his legs, he rotated his body around the driver's seat, gripped the vampire's wrist to keep it steady, then pressed the scolding orange coil against the back of the vampire's hand, leaving behind a perfect black circle along his cold flesh.

The vampire released its grip from Talora's hair.

Once she was free, she climbed over the passenger seat.

Pacen told her to fasten her seatbelt.

As soon as she buckled herself in, Pacen slammed on the brakes, flinging the vampire toward the front of the Escalade.

The vampire rolled onto the street; however, from the way he bolted back up on his feet, he looked as if he could do this sort of bat-and-mouse type of thing all day long and not break out in a sweat.

Once more, Pacen floored the vehicle; however, this time, he *em*braced the soon-to-be collision. In a split second, right before Pacen rammed the vampire, a strange smile crept onto the vampire's face.

On impact, the vampire's body suddenly exploded with blood!

Except for the bloody mess, the front of the grill didn't withstand much damage at all; in fact, she was ninety-nine point nine percent sure the vampire's flesh had somehow turned to putty. Not once did the SUV jolt or skid.

Which Talora found was incredibly odd, considering the massive dent he left in the windshield the first time he was struck by Pacen's SUV.

Attempting to wash the blood away from the windshield, Pacen switched on the windshield wipers; however, the dent in the shattered glass was preventing the wipers from properly working. He rolled down the window and poked his head outside for a better look at the street ahead.

"You good over there?" asked Pacen as he continued to drive well beyond the speed limit.

"Apart from some vamp that exploded all over your car," Talora said, trying to relieve the tension. "Yeah," she said shortly. "I'm fine."

"You're welcome," said Pacen.

Talora's mood deflated.

"Thank you," she said finally.

The fact that Talora was riding with Pacen created more unnecessary tension.

"What were you doing at St. Gabriel?" Talora asked over the break.

"I should ask you the same thing, Talora," Pacen returned, his tone bitter. "I could've told you that place was going to be crawling with parasites who'd suck anything with two legs."

"You just always have to turn everything on me, don't you?"

"*Whatever*," he snapped. "What were doing there?"

"I asked you first."

"What you mean?"

"I mean, what were you doing at St. Gabriel?" Talora asked again, her voice keen. "Were you stalking me?"

"I just saved your ass from a ruthless pack of vamps," he said, insulted. "I'd think you'd be a little more appreciative for what I did."

"I am," she said after a moment of pause. "Sorry. I'd just like to know what you were doing there. That's all."

"I know it's weird, Talora," Pacen said. "But trust me, if I wasn't there, then something worse would've happened."

"Worse?" she parroted. "As in what could be worse than getting jumped by a gang of vamps? Pacen, what are you not telling me?"

"It's Japhy," he said.

"Japhy? What the hell does he want?"

"*You*, apparently. I overheard him talking to a high-born. Maybe you don't know it, but you did something to him. And now, he wants you dead. The man's lost his fuckin' mind—"

"—Dead? You're serious?"

"Those animals back there were going to kidnap you, Talora," he said. "And we all know what happens when they get together in packs. So, again," his voice turned more bitter, "you're welcome."

Talora shook her head in disgust.

"I still don't get it, Pace," she said, raising her voice. "What in the hell did I do to that man?"

"I dunno, Talora," he said back. "You ask me."

"I don't know, Pace! You play with him. Surely, you two talk."

"Not anymore," Pacen said depressingly. "He's changed. To be honest, ever since I started hanging out with you, he hasn't been the same."

"What?" Talora argued. "Don't you dare put this on me, Pace. I wasn't the one who got all. . ." Talora searched for the right word to use, a softer word that wouldn't offend Pacen. She could only find the one that had been on her mind for the past couple of days: "*Obsessed*," she said.

"Right," he said resentfully. "Obsessed. That's cruel, Talora."

"Whatever," she said with more attitude. "You, Pace, *you* even said so yourself that you weren't looking for a serious relationship when we first started seeing each other. What exactly did you expect? Why couldn't you just be content with the way our relationship was going? I mean," Talora said, shaking her head, "why would you want to take our relationship to the 'next level' when you and I both know there is—and was—no next level?"

Pacen removed a vape pen from his pocket and took a puff.

"Would you please roll down a window?" she asked, repulsed from the sight of the vape pen. "I don't want to be breathing in that garbage."

"It's mint flavored."

"Exactly."

"Whatever."

Silence built between the two.

Pacen took yet another puff before pocketing the vape pen.

"I quit the band for you," Pacen said finally.

"What?" Talora snapped. "Why?"

"So, we can see each other more," he listed. "So, we can be together—"

"—Did you ever stop and think that maybe I like just hooking up with you?"

"So, that's all I was to you, a fuckin' booty call?"

"Don't be so melodramatic," Talora said, her tone drawn out. "Correct me if I'm wrong, but aren't you musicians the ones banging groupies in every town you play at?"

"You really got the stereotype down pat, don't you?"

"Pacen," Talora said, as if she was saying her *final say*, "I'm not going to be responsible for ruining your career. That's on you, not me!"

"The band was falling apart to begin with," he said dismissively. "It's only a matter of time before we broke up."

"But isn't that what bands do? You breakup and then, you get back together. Then, you breakup yet again. Then, you get back together for a reunion tour some thirty years later."

"You watch too much TV," Pacen said, trying to loosen up the conversation.

"Is that why Japhy wants me dead?" asked Talora.

"What do you mean?"

"*Us*," she said, pointing at Pacen. "For some reason, he's getting back at me because he thinks 'I' sabotaged the band?"

"Talora," Pacen said soberly, "I know this is the last thing you need on your mind right now, especially with what your family has already gone through, but I promise you nothing is going to happen to you."

For the first time during the drive, Talora flashed a smirk.

"You're going to protect me?"

Pacen reached over the center console and opened his palm.

"What other choice do you have?" asked Pacen.

Eventually, over some thought, Talora interlocked her hand with Pacen's.

🕐

THEY headed north of midtown Manhattan toward East Harlem where, after long deliberation, decided to buy a room at a cheap, shady-looking hotel along the Harlem River in Sugar Hill. The hotel was called The Panorama Inn and was known for its picturesque view of Yankee Stadium at night. After Pacen was given a key to his room, he parked the damaged Escalade in an unlit parking lot behind what appeared to be an abandoned building.

"Are you *trying* to get us killed?" Talora said with sarcasm.

"This car sticks out like a sore thumb," he said. "The last thing we need to do right now is draw any attention. Remember what we're dealing with here?"

"Yeah," Talora said, as if the idea of *what* they were dealing with hurt her. "I know, right? It's crazy. I can't believe we're being hunted down by, of all things, vampires. You hear stories about other people, but you never expect it to happen to you." Talora pulled out her smartphone and scrolled through her Twitter feed. "Feels like I'm stuck in a nightmare. But," Talora said, snapping a selfie on herself, "it'd make for a cool story on social media, wouldn't it?"

Pacen grabbed Talora's arm and lowered it down by her side.

"Let's lay off social media crap for right now," he demanded. "We don't want to ring the dinner bell, do we?"

"Sorry," she said and switched off her smartphone. "You're right, I guess."

As soon as they stepped outside the Escalade, it started to downpour. Which, for Pacen, worked in his favor. "Beats taking the car to a car wash."

The rain washed off all the blood from vehicle, including the windshield, making the Escalade less conspicuous.

In a dim, flickering floodlight, Pacen couldn't help but watch the streaks of blood running down the side of the Escalade. The blood was not only thicker than any other blood that he had ever seen before, but it also appeared as if it was moving, not from the falling rain but actually moving on its own, as if, in a vampish sort of way, the blood was alive.

Curious, he followed the trail of blood to the concrete below and with a sense of inevitable doom, watched the blood mix with a stream of rainwater, which was flowing into the storm drain along the curb.

"What is it?" asked Talora, shielding her head with a jacket that she found in the backseat. "I'm getting soaked out here—"

"—Ah," Pacen stuttered, "*the blood*. It was. . . never mind. It's nothing."

Talora looked at Pacen funny.

Pacen nodded toward The Panorama Inn and together, they kept their bodies low and darted toward the overhang.

🕐

AS the rain came down harder, the sides of the streets overflowed.

A stream of rain and blood poured down into a sewer below.

Out of the shadows of the corridor surfaced an emaciated rat that was looking for a drink of water. The rat came across a puddle of the rain-blood mixture along the edge of an overhang.

Drawn to its foul odor, the skittish rat licked from the puddle.

A couple of seconds passed before it reacted to the blood. Its body violently twitched. The muscles in its feeble body started to spasm. The convulsing was so great that its bones broke and shattered. The twitchy rat rolled over onto its side. Jagged bones protruded from its flesh and tangled hide.

As the violence roared in the harsh sounds of *snaps* and *pops* followed by the tearing of flesh, the rat grew into the size of a human; however, it still carried the traits of a rat, although each trait was more exaggerated. During its wicked metamorphosis, a pair of wings suddenly emerged from its back.

Once the rat transformed into its new body, it spread its fleshy wings outward and kneeled downward. The creature launched itself through the narrow opening, its body zipping like a bullet through the grate of the storm drain.

The creature flew away into the night sky.

🕐

ONCE Talora was safe inside the hotel room, Pacen made sure to double-lock the door behind him. Even grabbed a chair and wedged it underneath the door handle as a precaution. Talora walked to the bed and examined the shiny floral patterned comforter. She was extremely skeptical about her skin touching the comforter—after all, it was the shine that gave it away. No fabric was that shiny.

With her head stirring with doubts, she grabbed the other chair from the table and sat down while Pacen fetched two bath towels from the hallway closet. Pacen handed a towel to Talora, who didn't waste any time drying her hair.

357

Out of curiosity, Pacen switched on the TV and flipped through news channels. He came across MTV where Karla Fouler was giving her daily BREAKING NEWS report. In the report, Fouler stated that "Japhy Warchild of Stuffed Animalz was ousted from the band, resulting in the official breakup of Stuffed Animalz. Their manager released a statement earlier tonight, which can be read online. In other news, Teesha Whitehouse was arrested and charged for public intoxication. Rapper, Mo Vega, was shot twice early this morning in what investigators are calling a drive-by and is currently recovering in Burlington Memorial."

"You weren't lying, huh?" Talora turned to Pacen. "If it makes you feel any better, he did need a new look—if you know what I mean."

Pacen switched off the TV and plumped himself on the edge of the bed.

"Not now, Talora," he said, slumped over. "Please. . . " He tried to take his mind off the "BREAKING NEWS" and inspect the shady room. "It's not much, but. . . " Pacen sighed, ". . . it'll make due, I guess."

"Till when?"

"Till we can figure out a plan—"

"—Plan?" Talora placed the damp towel in her lap. "Surely, there has to be someone out there who can help us."

"What? Like the cops?"

"Well," Talora said, thinking, "no. But somebody! What about that cousin of yours. . . Harland?"

"Harland's dealing with enough issues as I speak, and adding two people who are on the run from a gang of killer vamps to that list would be the death of him."

"Okay, so. . . " Talora said, her voice suspended in *dot, dot, dot.*

"So, we hang out here," Pacen said. "Wait it out till sunrise. I've heard they normally don't come out in sunlight. You know with their sensitive skin and all."

"But shouldn't we just keep moving?" She looked around the hotel room. "I feel like I'm just waiting for them to show up—"

"—We will."

"Will what?"

"Keep on moving," he explained. "We have to know where we're going. We can't just drive around. We need a place to go. And," he pointed out, "we can forget about going to the cops. They won't do shit."

"Maybe so, but we can try. Right?"

"It's pointless," he said more decisively. "For all we know, they're expecting us to go to the cops, which very well means that they'll already be influenced—or *lured* or whatever the hell those fuckin' vampnecks call it."

"That's bullshit, you know that right? They do come out in sunlight."

"You've seen them during the day?"

"All the time," she said. "Ever walked down 42nd Street? You can spot them a mile away. Feeding off the rats. Shunned by society."

"All I know is that they're more vulnerable in the sun," Pacen said, checking the clock. "And," he said, reading the time, "it looks like we have at least another six hours until daylight."

Despondent by the lack of options, Talora hung her head in misery. "I've always wondered what it'd be like to be one of them," she said, hanging her head, "to be treated differently. I feel bad for them. In a way, I envy them."

"Envied them? Why?"

Talora shrugged her shoulders.

"I dunno," she said. "Just seems like they've all been stereotyped into something they're not. You only hear about the bad ones, not the good. I mean, there has to be decent vampires out there, right? There has to be good vampires, maybe ones who can help us?"

"Good vampires?" Pacen shook his head the same way her dad would shake his head in disappointment when she was a little girl bringing home a bad grade from school or giving her little brother a bloody nose for acting out of line. "Do you hear yourself, Talora? What world are you living in?" Pacen asked, his nostrils flaring. "They're *savages*. When they find us, they'll kill us in order to survive. And why the whole change of heart? You hate them as much as I do."

"I never said that," she argued. "I hate what they've turned us into."

"Face it, Talora. They've exposed us."

"What makes you any different?"

"What do you mean?"

"How do you survive?"

Pacen didn't have a response for Talora.

"Exactly," she said.

"Talora," Pacen emphasized, "do you know what's going on here? Do you? 'Cuz I really think you don't. We—*you*—have been chosen. You have a price on your head!"

"But why?" Talora cried, waiting for a response from Pacen but only receiving the look of a shrink who was willing and ready to listen to Talora "unburden" herself. "What the hell did I do, Pacen? For once in my life, I finally feel like I could actually have fun again and not worry about all of the bullshit attached to a relationship that is being forced to turn into something that both you and I know it's not. I *liked* seeing you after one of your shows. I *liked* feeling as if I was part of something. I *liked* being. . . adored. I *liked* the way you use to look at me, as if you were carrying this wonderful light in your eyes. Most importantly, I *liked* feeling like I didn't need *more* than I wanted." Once more, she dropped her head in misery. "I guess," she mumbled, as the words began to crumble in the back of her throat, "I dunno. I just—I just thought I met someone who was unselfish. But it turns out, you're just like the rest of them—"

"—You don't feel safe whenever you're around me?"

"I felt," she corrected, "I feel as if I'm being *watched* by you. Like I'm some sort of. . . I dunno, child who eventually started to wander off too far."

"If I ever made you feel uncomfortable, Talora, I'm sorry. Believe me, it was never my intention to push you away from me." He kneeled down in front of Talora, as if he was about to propose to her. He cupped her cold hands in her lap. "I am so sorry, Talora. After all of this is over, I promise you that I will leave you alone if that's what you want—"

"—And what do you want, Pacen?" she asked, sniffling.

"*You*," he said. "I want you."

"But you can't have me," she said.

"I know," he said. "And that's what makes being with you right now so hard, Talora—I'd do anything to win you back. Anything."

Talora wiped away the droplets of rainwater from the side of Pacen's cheek. Her hand slid upward and ran alongside his face until she reached his scalp. She brushed back the wet hair from his eyes. Pacen closed his eyes, savoring Talora's touch as if it was the last time he'd ever feel her again. As soon as Pacen cracked open his eyes, Talora was leaning forward to plant a kiss. Pacen immediately recoiled from Talora's advance, which had caught her by surprise.

"Don't," he said, fighting off that tingling urge to kiss Talora.

"What's a matter?" asked Talora. "Isn't this what you want?"

"No. . . " Pacen stuttered, ". . . I mean, yes. It is. I just—"

"—Just what?"

Pacen thought about all the rights words, yet once they reached the tip of his tongue, they felt like gibberish.

Talora couldn't withstand Pacen's sudden indecisiveness. She stood up from the bed and told Pacen that she was going to hop in the shower.

"Good idea," he said as if the change in subject was a necessary distraction to his epic failure. "To wash away your scent, right?"

"Excuse me," Talora said, her voice laced with frustration.

"They have your scent," he said, "which means you can easily be tracked."

Talora looked over Pacen as if he was speaking a different language.

"Right," she said, furrowing her brow.

Shaking her head from Pacen's strange behavior, she walked off.

Once Talora stepped inside the bathroom, she closed the door behind her but not all the way. She undressed and placed her waitress outfit on the top of the toilet and hoped in a steaming hot shower.

Pacen spent the next couple of minutes pacing around the hotel room, mentally condemning himself in a heated quarrel while, at the same time, going back and forth, back and forth, his good and bad angel replaying all of the lines that he should've or shouldn't have said to Talora. He couldn't take the internal anguish any longer, that seesaw effect of regret, inevitably the "bad" angel getting the best of him. Determined to prove himself worthy, Pacen marched to the bathroom and noticed the door was cracked open.

Which, for Pacen, was nothing more than a glaring invitation.

While washing her hair, Talora heard a *creak* outside the shower. She turned toward the noise and behind the beige shower curtain, witnessed a dark and lanky figure creeping toward her. She suddenly paused in suspense; her heart pounding against her chest from the dark figure whose eerie presence still remained unannounced. . .

Pacen slid open the shower curtain; however, his face was the last part of his body that Talora's eyes had settled on. She took a step backward and made room for Pacen, who, in return, closed the shower curtain behind him.

EIGHT out of the nine members of the Vampos gang made it back to the colony, which was currently residing underneath the Old Delaney Bridge over the Hudson River in a disease-ridden slum called Tent City. The bridge had been shut down for over six years, the cracked road above crawling with vines and an overgrowth of vegetation. Some New Yorkers—particularly those who had a fetish for being "owned," which was a common term used by vampires who leeched onto a host in order to bend a human against his or her will—were fully aware of the danger that surrounded Tent City. Most referred to it as a "breeding ground for bitters."

Inscribed along the concrete columns of the bridge were symbols of the Vampos gang: the dark silhouette of a stick figure-like vampire named Marius Ionescu with thirteen lines protruding outward. The symbol was a child-like depiction of Marius's final moments of sacrifice, the thirteen lines being swords. Each member of the gang had the same symbol along the side of their neck. Over the years, the symbol had been mistaken for a "glowing" man.

While Mihai and another vampire named Andrei fetched themselves, as well as the other vampires, a couple of "drinks" from the main living quarters in Tent City, Fane lead the other six vampires toward their nest, which used to be an old apartment complex; however, after the vampires took over Tent City, converting most of the homeless population, as well as the drug addicts, prostitutes, and bottom feeders into their own personal footstools, the apartment complex turned into a haven for the Vampos gang—"best view in the City," they'd say.

Half-drunk off a couple of ripe frat boys who were riding the haze of last call, five of the six members rode the rickety elevator to the top level of the complex.

As soon as the gang stepped out of the elevator and made their way through the deserted twelfth floor, they were forced into a state of high alert by the sound of shattering glass coming from behind a closed door at the end of the hallway.

They pinpointed the sound to their nest.

Not wasting anytime, the four vampires lead the charge, Fane closely following behind.

As the four vampires swung open the door and stormed into the nest—which could've passed as your typical "vamp cave" (walls covered in the most expensive entertainment system a vampire could steal, including a Playstation, a flat screen TV with surround sound speakers, posters of naked ladies, a billiards table on the other side of the room along with a dart board, a bronze life-sized statue of their messiah, Marius Ionescu, posed in His final moment of being ambushed by thirteen sea monsters, as well as a shrine, and not to mention, limbs, fingers, and random parts of human body scattered around the room like empty beer cans)—they burst out laughing from the sight of the sixth member, Marku, who was crawling his way through shards of broken glass.

He brushed glass from his shoulders and shook off his drunken daze.

"*Holy Marius!*" one of the vampires yelled out with great amusement. "What the hell happened to you, Marku?"

Marku eventually found his bearings and braced himself along the coffee table. Grimacing, he grabbed the side of his head and stood upright.

"Looks like someone missed his landing—"

"—Too much to drink, Marku?"

"Fuck you. . . " Marku said, flashing the bird.

"Cut it out!" Fane snapped. "The both of you!"

"Oh yeah, Marku. Learn how to fly."

"I said, 'Cut it out!'"

Immediately, the laughs tapered off.

The other vampires turned to Fane and froze in silence.

As the tension mounted, Mihai and Andrei returned to the nest with two junkies from Tent City. The vamp slaves were weak and badly emaciated, their forearms riddled with needle marks. Each one of them was swaying back and forth from the heavy drugs in their systems and if it wasn't for the two props alongside them, they'd fall over quicker than a vamp on tainted blood.

Mihai and Andrei walked the junkies into the room and sat them down on the couch where other vampires gathered around as if there were itching for a bite.

Mihai was first to point out the obvious, first the shattered window and then, the tense atmosphere.

⊘

CAMPING inside an unmarked van parked outside the rundown apartment complex was a motley crew of four blood traders known as "The Four Horsemen," as well as Izzy Black, a writer who was tagging along with the Horsemen in order to gain firsthand knowledge on a daily life of a blood trader. Izzy Black was known for his over-the-top journalism and was considered by non-fiction aficionados as the Hunter S. Thompson of his time. With the exception that Izzy Black used different names for The Horsemen, all of the information he gathered was going in a book about the black market, which was tentatively called *Black Caps*. The point of the book—because for Izzy, there was always a point—was to bring more attention to the black market and how easily accessible the black market was to buyers and sellers, including the very same pharmaceutical companies who were taking advantage of those who relied on their so-called "drug."

Believe it or not, The Horsemen used to work "normal" jobs, as in cops, lawyers, drug peddlers who worked for big pharma, even doctors. Truth be told, each and every one had witnessed the dark side of corporate America before their very eyes, the shady "under-the-table" dealings: price gauging, pharmaceutical companies buying straight from black markets; selling counterfeit drugs or "knock offs." The real kicker: drugs that secretly contained VP-23, which was an ingredient genetically modified from white blood cells only found in vampires. Drug companies manufactured drugs containing VP-23 and purposefully marketed them to the expendable youth in stylish ads and trendy hashtags—for example, new cream to "make your skin glow," or even a "hot" new flavor of e-cig extracted from the tit of a thoroughbred that would increase virility and enhance sexual drive, or dried vampire blood known on the streets as "red snow," which was meant to give humans "more than human" abilities, depending on its user—even cures for melanoma and other cancers and ailments, or a broad range of improved impairments, such as better eyesight, all for financial or political gain.

But to get to all of that, of course, the vampire blood had to be extracted.

"No question," said The Pale Rider, also known as P.R, who was seated behind a row of monitors, "we enjoy the rush, but you think we want to do this kind of shit for the rest of our lives?"

"I suppose not," Izzy said.

Next to P.R. crouched Wizzle, who was paying close attention to the monitor of his high-tech camera—or better yet, the camera that he had stolen from MIT.

The super slow motion camera with five hundred sensors that triggered at one trillionth of a second and was able to track the movement of photons—the speed of light—which allowed Wizzle to see around corners of buildings or, in this case, walls. As Wizzle once stated, the applications for the camera were "endless" and could be applied to medical technology, in particularly allowing doctors to be able to see what exactly was going on inside a patient's body. You know, "Top Secret Stuff, Man," which happened to fall into the hands of a blood trader.

Expert hacker, Stuntman, was tapping into a signal from the tracking devices that Mayor Armitage had implanted inside illegal vampires.

"Thank you to the great mayor of New York City—"

"—Eight years of O'vampa will do that to you."

"Any activity?"

"They're just hanging out," P.R. said, checking the vampires hanging from the bottom of the bridge. "Get it! *Hangin'* out!"

"Yeah. Funny guy."

"And the Vampos?"

"I count ten of them altogether," Wizzle said, as he watched each one of the vampires' every movement on the monitor. "Each one is tagged, except for two. Their heat signatures suggest that the two are human. More than likely, groupies. Could be half-breeds, though. But I seriously doubt it." He turned away from the monitor for a second and nodded at Izzy, who was scribbling in a notepad. "Hey, Izzy Man, you know the difference between a full-breed and a half-breed?"

"You can't get turned by a half-breed?"

"No," Wizzle said. "They both suck."

Other Horsemen burst out laughing.

Eventually, Izzy mustered a laugh, which looked like an attempt at fitting in.

"A half-breed's blood is useless—that is, if you want to pick up diseases."

"I'm satisfied with eight," Wizzle said, as he redirected his attention toward the monitor. "Thoroughbreds, they are." He checked another monitor—an infrared. "Looks like they just ate. Their blood is *boiling* hot, I tell you."

"Hotter the better," Stuntman chimed in, as he was *typing* away on his keyboard.

"Is the team suited up?" asked Apache.

363

P.R. heard the two Morose Code-like *clicks* on the radio.

"Suited and in position. They're just waiting for the word."

P.R. knew exactly what Izzy was going to ask before he even asked it.

He leaned in close to Izzy and whispered in his ear, "Remember we're not the only one who's watching—"

"—Wait a sec," Wizzle said, checking a new strange reading. "I just picked up something on the monitor."

P.R. paused what he was doing, pulled out Kevlar neck and cuff from a crate, and handed them to Izzy, who, in return, placed the cuff around his neck, as well as both his wrists.

"They'll protect the vulnerable spots on your body. Think of it like a bulletproof vest against vamps. New age police gear that hadn't hit the market yet."

"Got a new reading," Wizzle shouted out, grabbing the other Horsemen's attention. "It's hard to read on the monitors. Whatever it is, it's fucking *big. . .*"

⏱

MARKU plowed through the roof access door and stumbled his way to the edge of the roof where he proceeded to urinate or as he previously mentioned to his fellow Vampos, "drain his snake."

As he started to relieve himself, he couldn't help but look down at Tent City below and all the junkies and vagabonds and all that tainted meat loitering around drumfires like soon-to-be consumed livestock. He honed in on a slender man who was slouching over a shopping cart and sorting through garbage scraps while nibbling from a peach that he had pocketed from a fruit stand outside Hudson Market earlier that day. Thinking about how sweet his blood was going to taste later tonight, Marku's mouth salivated.

During midstream, Marku felt a sudden gust of wind followed by the *swooping* sound of a vampire directly behind him.

Assured that it was either Andrei or Mihai screwing with him, he shook away the leftover urine, zipped up, and casually spun around as if he was ready to tear a new hole—or holes—into the prankster.

"That's it! I've had enough with your games—"

As soon as Marku laid his eyes on the massive winged creature looming before him, he fell to silence. Other features fell, including his jaw.

He peered closer, recognized the eyes.

"Vasile?" said Marku with surprise. "Is that you?"

The winged creature stepped forward, part of its face revealed in the mounted light above the roof access door.

"It is," Marku said jovially. "Isn't it?"

Marku acknowledged its misshaped head and how it was stupidly tilting from side to side the same way a less evolved species would display "curiosity."

The gesture alone filled Marku with a primitive rage.

Razor sharp claws extended from the tips of his fingers.

Fangs exposed in a display of dominance.

"What the fuck are you?" said Marku, as he puffed out his chest and stepped closer to the winged creature. "You missed Halloween, muthafucka—"

Out of the dark shadows emerged Death-In-Waiting.

⏱

STUFFED Animalz' electronic, gothic-heavy song, "Witch-Hop," an unreleased track which was recorded on a whim while on tour in a makeshift studio outside Atlanta prior to their recent breakup—or "hiatus," as the hardcore fans who were still living in denial called it—was cranking at full volume.

Despite the blaring music, Andrei was still able to hear the *thud* coming from the roof above. He stopped drinking from the junkie's neck and told Mihai to turn down the music.

"What?"

"You hear that?" asked Andrei.

"Hear what?"

As soon as Mihai lowered the volume on the stereo, the door swung open!

Looming at the doorway, the winged creature rolled a severed head into the room as if it was a bowling ball. The blood, veins, and julienne muscle along the base of the head, which conveyed the appearance of a head being pulled, *not cut*, clean off a neck, all whirled around like a vertical boomerang, leaving behind red splotches where it struck the floor. The head didn't roll smoothly, though. Yet, it unsteadily bounced more like a football along the floor until it finally came to rest next to a coffee table.

The junkie, who had two incisions dripping with blood on her neck, pulled herself from Andrei and inspected the round bloody object next to her. Once she realized what it was, she freaked.

The junkie's scream was contagious.

Not too long after, the other junkie screamed out in bloody horror.

Both the junkies fled across the other side of the nest. One ended up tripping a couple of times during her dazed scramble.

Andrei and the other vampires, who weren't as fazed, stood from their seated positions while Fane, as sound as a saint, remained seated on the couch; in fact, he barely reacted from the sight of Marku's head.

Fane nodded at the Rat-Bat-Man creature and asked calmly, "Do you mind?"

"You boys have unfinished biz'ness," the winged creature seethed, his voice like crushed gravel.

Fane immediately noticed the change in his voice; however, underneath all of the grit, phlegm, and anguish, it was *his* voice—

"Vasile?" Fane said, leaning forward. "Is that you underneath all that. . . " he fished for the right word to use. But then again, he wasn't in the business of caring about whether or not he hurt a vampire's feelings. He said, "Grotesquery?"

"Lupu? Really?"

"Yes," Fane said before the winged creature could respond. He appeared delighted to see Vasile. "It's him all right."

"But how?"

"He did what I like to call a lil' 'body swappin','" Fane said from the corner of his mouth, "I used to be able to do it back in the day. But it's been years since the last time I swapped. 'Least you could've chosen someone—*something*—more pleasing to the eye rather than a giant rat."

"It's more like a mutated bat," another vampire suggested.

"What are you fools doing sitting around here when we're still on the clock?" asked the winged Rat-Bat-Man creature formerly known as Vasile Lupu.

"Says who?" Fane said, sharpening his gaze.

"Says me," the winged creature said.

"As you can see, we've already clocked out—"

"—I know where the girl's hiding," the winged creature said to other Vampos before Fane could finish speaking the rest of his excuse.

"Then, why the fuck do you need us? You look like you can handle two meat sticks on your own."

"We haven't finished our end of the deal."

"Deal? Nah. The deal is off, Rat. Besides," Fane said, glancing around the room at the other Vampos, "we don't some high-born bitch giving us orders."

"That high-born bitch made me who I am today. If it weren't for that high-born bitch, then none of you would be here!"

"The money's not worth the time and effort."

"You've lost your vampness, Fane. . ."

Despite the diss, the other Vampos followed along with Fane—clearly, taking their side.

To seal the deal, they inched closer to Fane's side.

"It's official," Fane said, raising his arms. "I'm taking over as alpha."

"Is that so?"

"It appears that way, doesn't it boys?" Fane acknowledged each member of the gang, only to receive what was perceived as unconfident nods of agreement. "Face it: You've broken law, Vasile. A vamp *never* abandons his hunting party, even if that means catching a beat on his prey in order to make a kill."

Fane was speaking church, and the others were now his congregation.

Minus Marku, there were now seven members of the Vampos gang left in the nest—and that didn't include the freakish hybrid that was Vasile Lupu.

The Vampos gang waited in anticipation, all except Fane, who appeared as if he was accepting whatever challenge Vasile was inaudibly proposing. The Vampos didn't know at it—not at first—but they were about to be smack dab in the middle of a battle for dominance and that all-important alpha title, which, in every pack, was held in solidarity. The winged creature, Vasile, temporary alpha himself, was clearly in no mood to hand over his title to, of all vampires, Fane by the way the claws, which were twice the size as they were before, extended outward from his gnarly fingertips.

"In the name of Marius Ionescu, why don't you come over here and take back your title as Head Vamp?" Fane's eyes reddened, his fangs exposed. "As the lil' kiddies say, I double-dog dare—"

Before Fane even had a chance to finish the word *you*, in the blink of an eye the winged creature had already made the first move and was intimately standing over Fane with part of his esophagus gripped in his hand.

Stunned by Vasile's speed, Fane was left without any words; in fact, the only words that dripped from his lips were not words at all but the wet gurgle of defeat trapped inside tiny bubbles of blood.

As other Vampos backed away, the winged creature finished off Fane with a massive chomp to the gaping hole in his throat and slurped enough blood to temporarily whet his never-ending appetite.

"Who's alpha now?" the winged creature said wetly, as he turned to the other vampires.

"You?" said Andrei. "You are, whatever you are."

"I'm still Vasile, you fools."

"Yeah, but you look so. . . "

Vasile stepped in closer.

"So what, Andrei?"

"I was going to say 'different.'"

"Does my appearance frighten you, Andrei?" Vasile asked and stepped even closer, close enough to taste what was left of Fane.

Trembling from the winged creature's presence, Andrei nodded his head.

The blood spoke.

Fear had an uncanny way of stripping lies from a vampire, opposed to a man, who'd lie about anything or everything to save his own ass.

"Would you feel better if I were someone else?" asked Vasile.

Unsure of his response, Andrei shot a glance at the other vampires, who were secretly nodding their heads.

"Yes," he said, as if he had been holding it in.

"And are you speaking for the pack?"

Once more, Andrei glanced at the other vampires, who remained frozen.

"Yes," Andrei said confidently. "We'd feel more comfortable, if—"

"—Very well," Vasile said and turned to one of the junkies.

Andrei followed Vasile's eyes to one particular junkie, a blonde whose blood was like candy.

"How about someone else?" asked Andrei. "I can find you another human."

Vasile suddenly zoomed Andrei; and before he knew what exactly hit him, he was already rising from his feet. Vasile had his hand tightly wrapped around Andrei's neck and he was hoisting him in the air as if he was an action figure.

"You feel uncomfortable taking orders from a woman?"

"No," Andrei uttered, grimacing from the strong grip around his throat. "It's just. . . " the words tightened from the crushing of his larynx, ". . . she belongs to me. I own her."

"You've made her, huh? I'm impressed. And that would be against the rules for a vamp to steal another vamp's property?"

"Pre. . . cisely," hissed Andrei.

"And you will challenge me if I break the rules?"

Andrei's face changed from red to purple. Veins swelled in his forehead.

"No," he choked.

Vasile eventually released Andrei from his grip, which caused Andrei to fall to floor with a heavy thud. Then, he turned his sights on the blonde haired junkie across the room. As soon as she saw Vasile looking at her as if he wanted to eat her, she backpedaled to the bathroom.

"Please," she begged. "Don't do this!"

Vasile followed the junkie into the bathroom. He was polite enough to close the door behind him. A couple of Vampos struggled to listen to the horror inside the bathroom, the screaming, the tearing, and then the sound of splashing.

A dark blood puddle formed underneath the doorway and as soon as the door opened, the blonde haired junkie whore exited the bathroom.

But she was not the blonde haired junkie whore.

At least not on the inside.

One Vampos questioned: "Vasile?"

"In the flesh," the junkie formerly—and presently—known as Vasile said.

🕛

As the Vampos stepped outside, Vasile immediately picked up a familiar smell in the air. He scanned the night sky.

Then, pinpointed the smell coming from the street.

"Keep your eyes peeled, boys," Vasile said. "We have company."

"Yes, sir," Andrei said. "I mean, ma'am."

🕛

WIZZLE tracked the Vampos leaving Tent City.

P.R. returned to coms.

"We're moving," he said. "Keep your distance."

"Roger that."

🕛

THE rainstorm eventually passed.

Dark clouds parted in the night sky.

A sword of moonlight cut across Pacen's face while he nakedly sat in a chair next to the air conditioner and kept a close eye on any activity outside through the slit of the curtain. Occasionally, he flashed quick glances toward Talora, who was sleeping soundlessly in bed. A few rooms down, he could hear a loud couple arguing outside. He couldn't hear exactly what they were arguing about, but whatever it was, it drew enough passion to wake a few nearby guests. Pacen heard another noise, much closer. He listened to bed sheets rustling. He tracked the sound to the stirring in the bed followed by the subtle *squeaks* and *pops* of a loose, faulty bedspring. Talora's shadowy face emerged from the pillow and revealed itself in the hazy moonlit darkness.

"*Hey*, Night Owl," Talora whispered sharply, "Come back to bed, will you?"

"It's going to be daylight soon," he said.

"Even more the reason to sleep," Talora groaned.

He gave one last survey outside the window and saw that it was safe for him to return to bed—at least, for the time being. In his return, he didn't bother to put on any clothes. Yet, he walked as naked as the day he was born back to bed and slipped under the covers, pressing his warm flesh against Talora's.

"I'm just curious," Pacen started, as if he had rehearsed the lines, "What were you doing at St. Gabriel tonight?"

"Ah," Talora said, her voice sleepy, "making money. What do you think?"

"I thought you gave up waitressing."

"I did," she said. "But I needed the money."

"If you needed the money, I could've given it to you."

Talora lifted herself upward onto her elbows as if his question—or inevitable grilling—had disturbed her to the point where the only resolve was a gesture of good night.

"I'm sure you would," she said with a hint of sarcasm in her voice.

She leaned forward and planted a kiss on Pacen's cheek and then dropped her head back into the cooler side of the pillow.

"I would," Pacen drawled.

"Try to get some rest, will you?" she said, her voice muffled.

"But," Pacen said, brooding, "I just don't get it."

"Get what, Pacen?"

The frustration slightly rose in her voice.

"Why drive all the way into The City to work a crap job with very little pay?" Pacen asked, but he didn't receive a quick enough answer from Talora. "It sounds strange, that's all."

"What are you getting at, Pacen?" asked Talora, as she sat upright against the headboard.

"I just feel like you're not being completely honest with me," he said timidly. "Like you're. . . hiding something."

"What are you saying?"

Talora leaned over Pacen and switched on the lamp on the nightstand.

She let out a groan.

"What exactly would I be hiding, Pacen?"

"I dunno," he said, as he folded the pillows behind his back and used them as a backrest. "Is there someone else?"

"Even if there was someone else—which, trust me, there isn't—it's none of your business, Pacen. Remember," she said, her tone stricter, "*technically*, we're broken up. Which means I can see whoever I want to."

"You're right," he said morosely, as he looked her over. "You should. Honestly, I'd be shocked if you weren't. Any man would be grateful to find himself in the presence of a gorgeous woman such as yourself."

"Stop, Pacen," Talora said, pushing away the flattering.

He continued, "I can only imagine what it'd be like to live your life and having to constantly shoo away men, who only saw you on the outside but never had the privilege of knowing the even more gorgeous woman on the inside. And that, in a way, makes me feel lucky." Pacen struggled to look Talora in the eyes. And even when his eyes managed to cross her path, tears formed in his eyes. "Even as I lie next to you at this moment, it makes feel as if I can die and you know what? I wouldn't be bothered by it because I feel nothing but content for having shared a part of my life with a person like you—if only for a moment because, to me, this moment, as well as the moments I shared with you will last a lifetime."

Talora didn't have any words for Pacen; in fact, she had nothing at all but the sting of guilt: *Guilt* that she had left him hanging out to dry in a breakup that was far from mutual; *Guilt* that he had felt so strongly about her, whereas she always felt as if she was living moment-to-moment with Pacen; and especially, *Guilt* that she had just slept with him.

"Excuse me," she said, her face slackened, "I have to use the restroom."

"Yeah," Pacen said. "Sure. Go."

Talora rolled out of bed.

As she opened the bathroom door, Pacen called her back in the room.

"I didn't mean to lay all that on you all at once," he said.

"No," she said, cracking a smile. "Don't be. I thought it was sweet of you."

"You're scared, I can tell."

"I'm not scared of you, Pacen," Talora said. "I'm scared of the vampires out to kill us."

Talora closed the door behind her and as she was relieving herself, she came across a small glass vial containing a red powdery substance inside the left breast pocket of the navy blue flannel shirt that she had borrowed from Pacen. Immediately, she was intrigued by the red substance. She had heard about that substance on the news, through social media. There had been a wave of reports on the news about teenagers—particularly high school students—winding up in hospitals after snorting dried vampire's blood. Apparently, curious students had gotten the idea from vampires, who were known to carry around vials of dried human blood. She heard somewhere that the vampires called it their "cocaine."

Except for more radical states—none of which involved New York—most of the states in the US, had declared the distribution of vampire blood or consuming vampire blood illegal and was punishable by prosecution. It was only fair that she questioned the man who was sleeping next to her as to why exactly he was carrying around a vial of blood, human or vampire. After all, she had explored Pacen's body—more than likely, knew every inch of his body better than he knew himself—and was aware that he didn't have any bite marks on him. The blood wasn't human. That, she knew.

She placed the vial back inside the breast pocket and after some deliberation, figured it was best to save the argument for later.

As soon as she stepped out of the bathroom, Pacen was racing from the window. He threw on his underwear and then grabbed his pants, which he had tossed across the room onto the TV set. He threw them on next. Then scrambled to find his white shirt underneath, which was lying underneath the bed.

"Pacen, what's the matter?" asked Talora.

Pacen snapped his head toward Talora and immediately placed his index finger against his mouth as if he was indicating for her to be quiet.

She mouthed, *What is it?*

Pacen pointed outside.

Talora listened closer to the footsteps outside the hotel room. She tiptoed to the window and witnessed the shadows moving along the balcony outside.

"What do we do?" she whispered to Pacen.

Every second counted, and Pacen made sure not to waste one second.

He raced toward the bathroom, grabbed the single-serving bottles of shampoo and soap, then hurried back to the hotel door. He squirted the remainder of shampoo from the bottle onto the doorway. He did the same with the lavender soap.

"To cover up the scent," he reminded Talora, who was ready to ask the obvious question.

Pacen scanned the room, his eyes landing on each piece of furniture (the bed, the nightstand, the table, the chairs, the dresser, the TV), as well as each piece of item (the clothes hangers in the closet, the iron board, the iron, the ice bucket, the towels, the basket of goodies on the vanity). He knew he couldn't MacGyver his way out of the hotel room. But he knew if he could make it outside without being spotted, then maybe he had a chance to create a distraction.

His eyes scanned the room once more. His eyes landed on light. He pointed at the lamp on the nightstand.

"Cut the lights," he whispered.

Talora did as Pacen demanded and switched off the lamp.

Together, the two rushed to the bathroom and closed the door behind them.

"What's the plan?" asked Talora.

Pacen remained quiet on the outside; however on the inside his thoughts were deafening.

"The rain from earlier should also help mask our smell, but it's only a matter of time before they track us down."

"Why don't we wait till the sun rises?" Talora suggested.

Pacen shook away the suggestion.

"They'll find us before then," he said. "We need wheels. If I can make it to the car, we'll have a chance."

"Okay," Talora said. "Then, we make a run for it."

"No. They'll be on us in no time."

"Then what?"

Pacen became quiet again.

"Pacen?!?"

Talora tugged on Pacen's arm.

"Distraction," he said, thinking out loud. "We need a distraction."

"Okay, what?"

Pacen slipped from the bathroom and searched through the basket of toiletries on the vanity. He came across a bottle of perfume—which, he knew, was highly flammable. *It could work*, he thought. *Just in case his first option failed. Always have a backup, a Plan B.*

Next, he grabbed a hand towel, as well as a pack of matches from the countertop.

Then, a clothes hanger from the closet.

Lastly, an orange cardboard *Panorama Inn* coaster from the table.

371

"What's the perfume for?" asked Talora. "Don't tell me," he corrected. "To cover up your scent."

"Well, yes and no," he said. "I need it for backup just in case I can't find any gasoline."

"*Gasoline*?" Talora said. "Why the hell do you need gasoline?"

Pacen replied, "Distraction, remember. I'm going to make a distraction. . ." he pulled the car keys from his pocket and handed them to Talora, ". . . and once you're given the cue, you're going to run as fast as you can to the car."

"And what exactly is my cue?" asked Talora.

Despite the growing tension, Pacen strangely flashed a smile on his face.

Which, for a moment, had brought comfort to Talora.

"You'll know when you hear it," he said to her.

"How do you know this plan of yours is going to work?"

"Because I saw it once in a movie."

"So you're basing this plan off something you saw in a movie?"

"Got any other suggestions?" asked Pacen.

Except for her plan to wait for sunrise, Talora had nothing.

"This is gonna work, Talora," Pacen said, cupping Talora's face. "You have to trust me. Okay?"

Maintaining her composure, Talora nodded her head in agreement.

Without wasting any more time, Pacen walked to the window and peeked outside. He counted two members of the Vampos gang three rooms down. Both of them were walking in the other direction.

"Now," he said, waving Talora to the door, "now's our chance."

Through the crack of the curtain, he showed Talora the staircase, which was about ten or so feet away from their room; however, to Talora, ten feet hadn't felt so much longer.

"Take the stairs," he whispered, "and remember to stay as low as possible."

"Where are you going?" asked Talora.

"I'm going to be right behind you," he whispered.

Talora reached for the door handle.

Pacen grabbed her by the arm.

"As soon as we reached the parking lot," he emphasized, "I want you to take cover next to the ice machine."

"Ice machine? I don't remember seeing any ice machine."

"It was to the right of the vending machines."

Talora widened her eyes and waited for more explanation.

"Forget about it," he whispered. "I'll take the lead. Just follow me, okay?"

"Okay," she responded.

Pacen took one last peek outside before opening the door. He stepped aside, allowing Talora to exit first. He carefully closed the door behind him and spotted the two Vampos with their backs turned to them.

Staying "low," as he instructed, they both scurried to the staircase.

Sure enough, there was another gang member standing lookout at the base of the stairs. Lucky for Pacen and Talora, his back was turned.

Pacen pointed to an opening along the second floor.

Talora tiptoed up the stairs while Pacen followed closely behind her.

"What now?" she whispered.

"Plan B," he whispered.

Frustrated and, at the same time, furious with Pacen's half thought-out plan, she flexed her hands as if she was tempted to strangle Pacen.

"Follow me," he said and scurried in the opposite direction of the two members of the Vampos gang.

Eventually, they made it to another staircase on the other side of the hotel.

From where he was standing, he had a clear view of the Escalade, which was parked across a back road; however, he spotted two more of those Vampos wandering around the sidewalk outside the hotel. In fact, they happened to be directly in their path. Next to the hotel was a fence that could've been scaled. *But* it was way too risky. They'd easily be spotted.

Back to the original plan, Pacen searched for an area that would allow Talora to hide while he carried out his so-called distraction. He caught the red glow of a vending machine in the corner of his eye. He followed the glow to a recess in the wall. Inside were the vending and ice machine.

"There," he said to Talora and pointed to the ice machine. "Remember, once you hear the cue—"

"—I know, run like hell."

"Now, go. . . "

Talora hurried to the noisy recess and took cover behind the ice machine.

While Talora was hiding, Pacen kept low and snuck into the parking lot in the front of the hotel. He looked for the oldest vehicle. He didn't exactly know why he was looking for an older model. He figured the older, the better, and the more likely they were at igniting.

In his frantic search, he happened to find a camel brown 1979 Pontiac Grand Prix in the parking lot.

Not too far away, three members of the Vampos gang were standing guard at the edge of the parking lot as if they were making sure nobody came in or out.

One of the gang members was distracted by another member who was showing him a mirror selfie of a single vamptress on his smartphone.

Pacen ceased the opportunity and dashed toward the Grand Prix. He made it to the rear of the car without being spotted. He set the clothes hanger aside, then pulled out what he needed from his pockets, including the hand towel first, then the coaster, the perfume—just in case—and last but not least, the pack of matches. He uncoiled the clothes hanger and used the end to pry open the lid.

Once opened, he untwisted the cap. He ripped off a small piece of the hand towel and wrapped it around the end of the clothes hanger.

Carefully, he dipped the end of the clothes hanger into the gas tank and then, once the cloth reached the bottom of the gas tank, he removed the clothes hanger. Based off the smell of gas fumes, as well as the dampness of the cloth, the hand towel was most definitely drenched with gasoline; in fact, when he gave the towel a squeeze, gasoline dripped over the side of the vehicle, as well as the ground below.

Next, he placed the cardboard coaster around the circular opening the tank.

His confidence started to deteriorate.

"What the heck?"

He decided to dump the entire bottle of perfume on the hand towel. The perfume messily splashed on the side of the car, as well as all over the ground.

Pinching the dry end of the gasoline-perfume soaked hand towel, he struck a match with his dry hand and all in one motion, set the hand towel on fire and then placed it against the cardboard coaster.

As he took off running and sought cover behind the rear tire of another car in the parking lot, he didn't realize at the time but, somehow, part of his foot kicked his vape pen that must've fallen out of his pocket while he was removing each of the components he needed to make the fire—the matches, the hand towel, the perfume. The spinning vape pen slid farther underneath the car.

The subtle noises Pacen had made during his escape, such as the metallic *pop* of opening the gas tank or the sole of his shoes scraping along asphalt, caught the attention of the closest vampire. The member of the Vampos gang signaled to the other member to keep watch while he checked out the noises.

The fire suddenly spread along the side of the car and somehow managed to spread to the ground below.

As the fire licked across the pavement, the vape pen came to rest directly below the gas tank. The vape pen ended up catching fire as well.

The member of the Vampos gang spotted a tiny flame burning along the side of the Grand Prix.

With his sense jacked to kill mode, he hurried over to the Grand Prix while, at the end of the parking lot, Pacen nervously watched from underneath a parked car.

Work damn it, Pacen repeated to himself while staring hard at the weakening flame.

After a couple of tense moments, he realized the plan wasn't going to work.

"Fuck the movies," he said to himself.

Curious of the fire, the vampire pressed his clawed hand against the bumper and kneeled down on the ground.

He immediately noticed the vape pen bathing in a mellowing flame.

As he reached for the vape pen, it suddenly exploded in his face. Tiny pieces of shrapnel buried into the side of his burnt face. He fell backward. Both his eyes fell upon the damage underneath the car. He smelled gasoline. And the vape pen was still burning. . .

Before the vampire could run to safety, the Pontiac Grand Prix suddenly exploded into flames!

A massive ball of hell shot up into the night sky, causing hotel guests to poke their heads out of their doors or windows; however, the guests were immediately forced back into their rooms from the sights of Vampos.

"My cue," Talora uttered while bracing herself against the ice machine from the quake of explosion.

Shocked by the intensity of the explosion, Pacen said, "I meant to do that."

While other members of the Vampos raced toward the raging fire in the parking lot, Pacen found his opportunity to escape. He cut through the north wing of the hotel and as soon as he could smell freedom, a young, once-attractive, blonde haired, fair-skinned woman stepped in front of his path.

Pacen recognized that same grin he thought he witnessed before he ran over a vampire who went by the name Vasile Lupu.

"Going somewhere," said Vasile.

"You?"

"Yes," said Vasile. "Me."

Vasile hissed, revealing the sharp fangs in her mouth.

Halfway toward the SUV, Talora heard Pacen screaming from a distance.

She had no other choice than turn around and run back to the hotel. She crept along a fence and found cover behind a dumpster while two other members of the Vampos gang patrolled the area. Once they were gone, Talora walked around the back of the hotel.

She heard—or, at least, thought she heard—the sound of a man struggling.

Remaining stealth-like in her pursuit, she tracked down the choppy, gurgling sounds to a man lying in a puddle of blood in a hallway. As she kept cover behind the corner of the hallway, she took a couple of glances at the man and determined after a third glance that the man was, in fact, Pacen.

And if, somehow, he survived his injuries—primarily, the deep punctures in the shape of a bite mark around his neck—it was only a matter of time before he changed. And the man whom she once knew as Pacen would no longer be Pacen but a dark copy of Pacen. Either way, he was already gone. Dead or alive.

She raced toward Pacen and tried to stop the bleeding around his neck with a towel that she found on a tray of spoiled food resting outside a hotel room.

"Stay with me, Pacen," Talora said, as Pacen's eyes rolled around in the back of his head.

Pacen tried to speak but his words were choked with blood.

While Talora continued to apply more pressure to the bite marks, dark figures surrounded her. She looked up and witnessed four members of the Vampos gang, including Vasile, approaching her. She didn't hear but more so felt them behind her. She turned her shoulder and fell witness to four more members closing in on her, each and every one of them carrying a queer hunger in their eyes; however, it wasn't a hunger—or even a thirst—to satisfy or quench or, in essence, to maintain survival. Yet, the look held the weight of something much more, the bottomless hunger to breed, a sick sort of "welcoming" to her soon-to-be family.

"Stay back!" she screamed at them.

The Vampos continued to close in.

"I said, 'Stay back!'"

Vasile held out her arms the same way a negotiator would approach a homicidal maniac.

"Relax now, Talora," he said calmly. "This can go two ways: Quick and painless or slow and painful. You have a choice, Talora—"

"—How do you know my name?" asked Talora.

"We know a lot about you, Talora," Vasile said, approaching. "We know where you live, where you work, and where you go to have fun. We know what you like to eat and whom you like to eat with," he listed. "We know all of your likes and all of your dislikes. We even know whom you like to fuck," Vasile said snappishly and glanced at Pacen, who was bleeding out. Then, he corrected himself, "Excuse me, *liked* to fuck. Liked, as in past tense. A part of me, that 'hopeful' part of me, was rooting for you two to get back together—"

"—Stay back!" Talora cried out, as Pacen spat out strings of blood from the corners of his mouth.

"But then again," Vasile said, closing in on Talora, "over these past few years I have realized that *hope* rhymes with *nope*."

The other Vampos burst out laughing.

Their laughs were suddenly cut short from the booming voice of a police officer announcing his presence with authority, "Police! Freeze!"

Talora located the voice coming from a police officer with his gun drawn.

Surrounding the officer were at least a dozen other officers and agents, some of them dressed in uniform while others—the rougher, shadier types— dressed in a more casual getup with the letters ICE across the bulletproof vests. Some of the agents were wearing special neck and arm cuffs, as well.

Despite being boxed in, the Vampos prepared for an offensive attack.

With his itchy fangs, Vasile leaped at one of the ICE agents; however, Vasile was immediately shot by a relatively new lasso gun nicknamed The Snake, which discharged an eight-foot Kevlar ® tether around Vasile's torso area, forcing both his arms to his sides. Another agent shot yet another Kevlar ® tether at the lower half of his body. Now, with both of his legs, as well as arms wrapped up like gift-wrap, Vasile stepped forward but ended up falling to the ground.

Even though the Vampos backed off after witnessing one of their own— most importantly, their Head Vamp, their "alpha"—being lassoed to the ground with a Kevlar ® tether as if he was a stray calf, except for the two members of the gang, Andrei and Mihai, Andrei dodging the Kevlar ® tether, then the second, Mihai, being sideswiped by a faulty discharged, the ICE agents used The Snake lasso gun on the remaining Vampos.

Andrei and Mihai slipped past the ICE agents and darted by a group of police officers, who looked more like background props in a movie opposed to a singular body of justice.

An ICE agent drew The Snake on Talora, who, in return, raised both her arms in surrender.

"Human," she declared, her voice trembling.

She couldn't help but turn her eyes to Pacen, who was already dead, and then toward the vampires, who were wiggling around on the ground like worms after a rainstorm.

"Come with us, ma'am," one of the ICE agents instructed Talora to an ambulance, which was parked outside the hotel.

Talora refused to leave Pacen; however, as soon as the ICE agent gave Talora his word that he'd take care of him and then ordered a medic to the scene via his radio, she walked away with another, much younger ICE agent who looked nothing like someone who worked for the ICE organization; in fact, the ICE agent was P.R., the same blood trader who had been tracking the Vampos all night.

Somehow—maybe it was *his mannerisms* that gave it away or the fact that he was awfully fidgety to be working for an organization that demanded precision as well as a steady hand—a part of Talora had a suspicion that the ICE agent wasn't who he claimed he was; in fact, the whole scene felt like a production.

Left in a state of defeat from the latest Vampos encounter, Talora decided to voice what was really on her mind: "You don't look like a cop."

"That's because I'm not a cop," he said robotically, as if he was reading lines from a script. "I work with ICE."

P.R. walked Talora to the ambulance where two other paramedics—Stuntman and Wizzle—were both waiting to tend to any injuries that she might have on her body.

They passed several guests, who were slowly emerging from their rooms and asking questions like "What's going on here?" or "Who died?" or the most important one, "Where the hell is the fire department to put out the damn car fire?" The guests were greeted by a group of police officers, who escorted each guest away from the crime scene and tried to maintain order before the guests stereotypically waddled back into their hotel rooms, brandished the phones, hit the "record" button, and filmed the strange activity from the cozy confines of their dark rooms.

"My name is Agent Rackley," he said, steering Talora's attention away from the police officers.

As before with the ICE agents, Talora knew a thing or two about police protocol after having been around them for so long, both in reality, as well as the fictional world where they were portrayed as either good or bad, a hero or a villain, nevertheless, a clichéd image of a cop that had been worn down like a nub—even worse, having to watch them firsthand in action, either watching them at search parties or even walking around her house, inspecting for clues. She had picked up a sense of who they were and how they acted, how they talked, how they formally conducted themselves. And "these police officers" were much different, dare she say, just as stinky as the ICE agents.

Talora waited for a following up but received nothing. She decided to let her silence bring out his true identity. Talora watched him carefully. He struggled to look her in the eye. Liars never looked a person straight in the eye. Or, someone who had something to hide. . .

"Aren't you going to ask me my name?" asked Talora.

"Of course," he said. "What's your name, miss?"

He is so bad at this, she thought.

Either that, or he was simply a man who turned all mushy whenever he found himself in the company of a woman.

"Talora Katz," she said, eyeing the ICE agent through the corner of her eye.

P.R.'s jaw slackened, his face expressionless.

"By any chance," he said, more thoughtfully, "you're not related to that missing boy, Nathan Katz, are you?"

Of course, she thought. *He* knew the story. Anybody who hadn't been living under a rock for the past year *knows the story*.

"Nathan Katz is my brother," Talora said hesitantly.

"You mean, was?"

"No," she corrected. "He *is* my brother."

"Right."

Despite P.R.'s poor attempt to strike up a conversation with Talora, P.R. regained his confidence and walked Talora to the back of an ambulance, which was parked along the street in the front of the hotel.

Once Talora arrived at the back of the ambulance, she questioned the speediness of the paramedics' arrival. The only reason that she could find through all of tangled wires of thoughts was that someone, possibly a guest or even employee of The Panorama Inn had called 911 and asked the dispatcher to send an ambulance. What other reason would there be an ambulance at an ICE raid? One of the paramedics—Stuntman—was acting extremely coy and for a moment, she thought she saw him holding a syringe behind his back.

"Don't firefighters usually show up before the paramedics?" asked Talora, as the word *fire* in the word *firefighters* forced Talora toward the out-of-control fire that Pacen had started. "Isn't that why they're called first responders? I've never heard of firefighters being *last* responders. What is it that you're not telling me?"

"I can assure you they're on the way, miss."

P.R. paid more attention to Talora, who was displaying all the symptoms of a soon-to-be "problem," including Talora's keen observation of the crime scene and the abundance of strategic inquiries meant to provoke contradictory responses.

With his patience running thin, P.R. placed his hand along Talora's back and nudged her toward the back of the ambulance where the two paramedics were eagerly waiting for her. Talora took the innocent nudge as a push. He was pushing her to the ambulance!

"Excuse me," she snapped. "Get your hands off me!"

P.R. held up his hands as if he didn't want to start a fight.

"They just need to check you for any bite marks," he said.

"But I wasn't bit," Talora argued and pulled down her collar and showed him her bare neck.

"It's just for precaution, Ms. Katz."

P.R. made sure to say her last name with clarity for the other boys.

Wizzle heard that name, *Katz*, and shared a similar reaction to P.R. when he heard the name.

Talora acknowledged the change in expression. Somehow, she knew that they knew that she wouldn't talk. What made Talora so sure? It wasn't what she said. It was what she didn't. It was in her face, her body, even in the way she walked. Most importantly, it was in her eyes. *The eyes never lied.* The eyes never lied.

And Wizzle was reading them like a book.

"Please. . . " P.R. insisted, ". . . it'll only take a minute—"

Wizzle interrupted, "—It's fine. If the woman says that she wasn't bit, then she wasn't bit." He turned his attention to Stuntman and subtly shook his head as if he was giving him a cue to stand-down.

"Are you sure?" P.R. asked Wizzle.

"Positive," he said expressionlessly. "She can go."

"What about Pacen?"

"And who is Pacen?"

"He's the guy back there. He was—he's my boyfriend."

"Right. . . "

Before P.R. could further respond, Wizzle and Stuntman pulled out a gurney from the back of the ambulance and set it on the street. Wizzle assured her that he'd take care of Pacen. Then he and Stuntman wheeled away the gurney and left P.R. alone with Talora, as if she was now his wad of bubblegum to scrape off the bottom of his shoe.

In the awkward silence, Talora's eyes landed on the ICE agent's badge.

The name read: "FERNANDEZ."

It was uncommon for someone who clearly didn't look at all South American to have a South American name. There was a certain irrelevancy about matching a man's name to his looks; however, Talora couldn't help but realize the ethnicity of the man. He was as white as Vanilla Ice.

Talora read his name aloud.

"Fernandez, huh?"

From a distance, she heard the sound of sirens.

P.R. pointed to the sound as if the sound itself was a tangible thing in the air.

"You hear?" he said. "They're on the way. Just as I said."

"Well, maybe you guys can ask the firefighters to give me a lift back home," she lied.

"That's not necessary," he said, as he started to walk away from Talora.

To Talora, it was obvious he was trying to distance himself from her.

Walking away from Talora, he said to her, "You're free to leave."

Talora didn't budge.

Which caused P.R. to pause in his tracks.

"Little advice," he said, more grimly, "If I was you, I'd keep my head down and lay low for a few weeks. Eventually, they'll move onto someone else."

"What makes you so sure they'll stop?" asked Talora.

"Because three years ago I was in the same position you're in. And you want to know how I survived?"

"How?"

"I ran," he said bluntly. "And I never looked back."

"Did you have any family?"

"I did," he said, as the sirens grew louder. "But I had no other choice than to leave them behind, otherwise they would've used them to get to me. Do yourself a favor: *Leave* town while you still have a chance."

"And go where?"

"Anywhere but here."

P.R. walked off.

Then, once more, paused and turned around.

"Think of it as a vacation from your everyday life." He shrugged his shoulders. "Who knows? It could be fun."

After P.R. joined the other ICE agents, Talora walked around the fence along the side of the hotel and checked on Pacen. The members of the Vampos were all gone. Not *one* of them remained. Two coroners were carrying away which she assumed was Pacen's body in the black bag. And all that remained was a puddle of Pacen's blood on the ground. Which, to say the least, was strange. She wondered where the detectives were. She had watched plenty of cop shows in her day to know that they never carried away a body before the detectives arrived or—at least—they'd taken photographs of the body. There was not a damn thing, no protocol, no "What do we have here, Mr. Detective?" It was like they were trying to clean up a crime scene and make it look as if it never happened in the first place.

With the ICE agent's advice at the front of her mind, she rushed to the SUV.

As soon as she arrived at the SUV, a strange feeling came over her. She got inside. Inserted the key into the ignition. Then, she turned the key. Nothing.

Talora reached down below the steering wheel to pop the hood of the car, but the hood was already cracked open.

She stepped outside and opened the hood, only to find a missing battery.

It had been completely ripped out.

"Fucking great," she seethed and slammed the hood.

Left with no other choice than to ride the subway back to her car, which was parked St. Gabriel Hotel, she grabbed a bottle of water and a jacket from the back of Pacen's Escalade and started walking.

As Talora was walking past the front of the hotel, she saw that the ambulance was no longer parked on the street; in fact, she couldn't find the ambulance or the squad cars anywhere on site.

Two fire trucks finally arrived at The Panorama Inn and didn't waste any time extinguishing the car fire.

Which made Talora question what exactly she had just witnessed.

Who the fuck were those people?

Good guys?

Or, bad guys?

🕐

THE thought of having two other vampires out there, still hungry, still on her tail, still ready to strike at any moment, left Talora in a more paranoid state while she was riding the subway back to Manhattan. She made sure to stay extra close to the other riders, maybe too close to their so-called "safe space."

When she arrived at her stop, she heard that distinguishable *swooping* noise coming from the train tunnel. A familiar noise of both warning and dread that she had been hearing throughout the entire night. She made sure to quicken her pace.

They're close.

Eventually, she made it to the street unscathed.

🕐

TALORA was right about the noise.

Once the train had taken off, Andrei and Mihai emerged from the shadows of the tunnel. As they were about to make their way to the platform and follow Talora to the street, a shadowy man stopped them from behind.

Japhy stepped forward, partially revealing himself to the two members of the Vampos gang.

380

Andrei instantly locked eyes on the coat Japhy was sporting; and somehow, he could look beyond its gleam and glitter and recognize its "old country" vibe.

"Where'd you get that fancy coat?" asked Andrei.

"Forget about it," Mihai said to Andrei. "We have other more important issues to deal with—"

"—He's not vamp."

Mihai eyed Japhy.

"He's not human, either." He tapped Andrei on the shoulder. "Let's go."

Andrei couldn't take his eyes off the coat.

Mihai ordered his fellow Vampos to follow him out of the tunnel and eventually, after more convincing, Andrei did.

Not only that, another train was approaching.

"Hold up," Japhy said to the two vampires, "you must roll with the Vampos."

Andrei and Mihai stopped.

"We are Vampos," Andrei said like a boss, as he puffed out his chest. "Can't you see the tats, fool?"

"Yeah," Japhy said, stepping farther into the light. "I see your tats."

"Who da fuck are you?"

Mihai immediately recognized Japhy's face from TV.

"He's that fool from that band—"

"—Yeah," Japhy said with a strange look in his eye. "That fool."

As the train sped by, Japhy suddenly leaped at Andrei and Mihai.

Before they knew what hit them, they were already dead.

In the flicker of the lights, their blood was painted all over the tunnel walls as if Japhy was creating his own masterpiece.

⟨⟩

TALORA made it back to the parking deck where her Honda Civic was parked.

Before entering her car, she noticed the long, winding scratch mark along the side of the driver's side door from where Vasile had run his claw along the paint. She checked the backseat, the trunk, and then, once she felt more comfortable, she entered the car and sped away.

⟨⟩

WITH her nerves still taunt, she crossed over the George Washington Bridge heading west into New Jersey. Then, she got off on Exit 74. She stayed on Palisades Interstate Parkway until she picked up I-87 North and I-90 West to North Ithacan Street in the town, Ballpointe, which was located in the Mohawk Valley region.

During the drive, Talora debated whether or not to keep her smartphone. She wondered about the "supposed" ICE agents and how they were able to track down the Vampos. Or, instead, were these "supposed" ICE agents tracking her through her smartphone? But why would they possibly do such a thing? Talora figured it was best to ditch the phone than to keep it. When the time came to toss her phone from the window, she backed out. She couldn't let go of it.

By the time Talora made it out of New Jersey, the sun was already starting to come up. Depending on the traffic, the drive was roughly a three and a half hours to her parent's house, which gave Talora maybe too much time to spend thinking about the previous night. Any thought of Pacen—or recalling the time she spent with Pacen—had driven her to tears. She turned on the radio, blasted 80's hottest hits to help steer her red thoughts toward a more optimistic road that she was soon going to be traveling on in her not so distant future.

Throughout the entire drive, she was fighting off sleep. Her eyelids were doing pull ups against her eyes, and each blink grew more strenuous and strenuous. The music helped a great deal while driving through the early morning hours—if it weren't for a combination of Flock of Seagulls, Don Henley, Cyndi Lauper, and Johnny Hates Jazz, then more than likely her Honda Civic would've wound up in a ditch somewhere or even Hackensack River.

However, the only thing that wound up in the Hackensack River was Talora's smartphone.

Music from the 1980's had a peculiar way of encouraging those who needed a little nudge of encouragement.

IT was late morning when she arrived at her parent's house in Ballpointe.

From the intersection, she saw both her parents, first her mom, who was picking weeds in the flowerbeds in front of the house, then her dad, who was mowing a strip of grass along the side of the house and working his way toward the back. She knew, once he made it to the back, then she'd lose any chance at successfully sneaking inside the house. He'd most definitely spot her if she drove by the house or snuck in through the back of the house. He was good at spotting things, including "things" that were never there. She knew the only way she'd be able to pull it off was if she took Glenmore Street, which ran parallel to an alleyway, parked her car behind the old beech tree, scaled her neighbor The Compton's nearly unscalable fence, crept through The Compton's yard, then, finally, after digging her way through the branches of dying—and soon-to-be dead—forsythia shrubs lining the side of the house, snuck in through the laundry room window on the opposite side of her mom. And that was exactly what she did, minus the sneaking-in-through-the-laundry-room-window part. In the nick of time, she darted toward the front of the house as her dad moved his way toward the backyard with the lawnmower.

She sneaked in through the front door, which—*phew!*—was unlocked.

With a couple of scratches along her hands and arms from her planned "sneak in," she made it to her bedroom undetected.

She packed a duffle bag of clothing for at least two weeks, consisting of more shirts and sweaters than pants. She emptied out most of her sock, underwear, and bra drawer. She made sure to grab her toothbrush, as well as a tube of toothpaste; and then, she grabbed more personal items, such as face creams, lotions, and tampons, and placed them inside a smaller travel-sized bag.

Once she was all packed, she grabbed a map of the United States—yes, that's right. She was going old school. No phones, obviously. No technology. But, for Talora, that was the whole point. To be completely "untraceable."

Before leaving, she couldn't help but stand by the doorway and take one final look at her bedroom. Most of her attention was drawn to her bed—what she'd do to lay down, sink into those cool sheets, wrap her head around her pillow, and shut her eyes for an hour or two!

But Talora thought about the hunt and being the hunted, not the hunter. *They wouldn't stop coming for me*, she thought, recalling the ICE agent's words about not putting those she loved in harm's way and then the two vampires who escaped from ICE. She knew that they were still out there, ready to seek vengeance. Despite the sad reality, Talora tried her best to look at the bright side of her situation. The road trip! Even as she stood by the bedroom doorway, she didn't know exactly where she was going or what waited ahead of her; however, only one person surfaced in her mind and she just so happened to be someone whom, as of now, she hadn't had more in common with than ever before.

The notion alone of visiting her Aunt Dina had, in a way, made the upcoming trip much more exciting.

Talora's eyes moved past a black and white speckled Composition notebook on her desk. She tore out a blank sheet of notebook paper from inside, grabbed a Zebra pen, and wrote a note the old fashioned way.

> *"Dear Mom and Dad,*
> *First off, don't worry. I assure you that I'm completely fine. The reason—*

Talora scribbled through the note. Crumbled the paper. Threw it in the trash.

Then, she tore out yet another sheet of notebook paper and tried again.

> *"I know things have been difficult lately. And the last thing I would ever want to do is make things even more difficult. It's hard to explain it right now (TRUST ME, ONE DAY I WILL), but there is something much bigger happening to me, and I feel as if it's best for me to make sense of what's happening on my own. That's why I'm leaving. I don't have an exact destination in mind—*

Talora paused. She hated to lie to her parents, especially her mom whom she was closer to. She reminded herself that it was only for the best.

> *But I know the road will take me where I need to be. You may look at my actions as selfish. Maybe I am being selfish. Please don't be mad—*

Again, she stopped writing just for a moment and listened closely to a high-pitched *rustling* sound followed by an out-of-tuned chorus of meows coming from underneath her bed.

P.S. Make sure to feed Bitsy and Bizzy while I'm gone."

— Lora

Once Talora was finished writing, she folded the note in half and addressed it to "Mom and Dad."

In a state of regression, Talora's body buzzed with both eagerness and childish exhilaration from the continuing sounds of two kittens stirring between shoeboxes and old picture frames under her bed. In order to draw the two kittens, she grabbed another sheet of paper from the notebook and crumpled it in her hand.

Talora kneeled down for a closer look.

The *crinkling* sound of paper drew out two small figures from behind a picture frame. Two sets of eyes glowed in the darkness.

Bitsy, who was an orange tabby, and Bizzy, who was black, crawled out from underneath the bed. Their eyes were caked with morning crust and trying to adjust to the brightness of natural light throughout the bedroom. A few months ago, the two wound up on their back porch after their mother, a black longhaired, gave birth to a litter underneath her neighbor's crawlspace. Their neighbor managed to round up at least four of them to give to the cul-de-sac queen herself, Ms. Evans, who had lost her husband three years ago and was in the market for a new pet—or pets.

Talora picked up both kittens, gave them hugs and kisses, and said her goodbyes. She told Bitsy and Bizzy that she'd be back soon. She heard somewhere—maybe on the Internet—that cats forget about their owners after being away from them for a month or even weeks. Talora hoped that she was going to be gone for as long as a month, but she knew her future was uncertain.

And that was the most terrifying part about all of this.

And, at the same time, the most exciting.

⏱

TALORA closed her bedroom door behind her to keep Bitsy and Bizzy from following her downstairs and tiptoed her way into the kitchen.

Centered on the kitchen table was a glass vase of angelic white roses, calla lilies, mums, and daisy poms. The moment she saw her mom receiving the spread of flowers from the deliveryman, who, in return, informed the two about the identity of the sender, Talora wanted to throw them directly in the trash. She figured it was his way of trying to win her back by pulling on her heartstrings. However, after Talora read the note, she learned that they were addressed not to her but to her family, the Katz family. Her mom was a fan of Pacen. "Loved him to death," she'd say.

Becoming more emotional from the sight of the flowers, Talora pulled out the card wedged between a white rose and cally lily and read the quote to herself.

"It is not so much for its beauty that the forest makes a claim upon men's hearts, as for that subtle something, that quality of air, that emanation from old trees, that so wonderfully changes and renews a weary spirit. — Robert Louis Stevenson."

She wiped away her tears and placed the note between the salt and peppershakers on the kitchen table. Her attention was suddenly drawn to her mom, who had now moved toward the front of the house and was picking up weeds from the flowerbeds outside the front living room window. Ever since Nathan went missing, her mom developed quite the green thumb. Her mom's garden, once as small enough to hold in one's arms or placed along the windowsill of a cramped one-bedroom apartment, had grown substantially in size and had turned into a beautiful display of flowers, fruits, and vegetables. Talora knew people grieved in their own way, either subtly or conspicuously. Some people took up golf lessons; self-defense training; or even started their own trendy badminton league on the weekends. Some people started new hobbies, such as finger painting or collecting old coins. Her mom, she gardened.

Her dad made his rounds in the backyard and was nearly finished mowing the lawn. She saw that he only had a couple of strips of grass left!

She scrambled around the kitchen, grabbing snacks and bottles of water. And then, she checked the backyard once more.

Anxiously, she waited for her dad to walk the other way with the lawnmower as he cut the last strip of grass. Once he made the U-turn, Talora managed to escape through the laundry room window. She heard the lawnmower shut off behind her as she stepped between two forsythia shrubs. Her daring escape was much louder than her initial entry.

As Talora gathered the rest of her things that had fallen onto the ground, she heard the footsteps behind her. She darted to the neighbor's fence.

Curious about what he thought was a trespasser, her dad decided to check out the noise; and when he arrived at the side of the house, he followed a noise to his neighbor's backyard where he witnessed a bird feeder swaying back and forth on a tree branch. The bird feeder was swaying so violently that it was dropping birdseed all over the ground. He nonchantly shrugged off his suspicion—because that was all it was, a suspicion—and walked back to the lawnmower to empty out the catcher of grass into a garbage bag.

TALORA was in the clear.

She didn't waste anytime saying goodbye to the ole neighborhood.

In essence, Talora put New York in her rear view mirror and headed toward Soy, Missouri, where her Aunt Dina lived. After all, she had at least a day's worth of driving ahead of her—two, depending on the traffic and how much she stopped to pee, eat, or rest.

🕐

SHE stopped to use the restroom at a rest stop in Lakeland, Pennsylvania.

On numerous occasions, several cars pulled out in front of her and nearly ran her over and caused her to wreck while passing through Cleveland, Ohio. Being a recovering road rager herself, she had little-to-no patience with those who didn't have a clue on how to drive or even had little-to-no grasp on the rules of the road; however, it was in the state of Ohio, of all places, OHIO!, where she discovered some of the worst drivers whom she had ever dealt with on the road—and Talora didn't even carry a single ounce of bias against the driver-state relationship. She figured that maybe it was just a bad day. Boy, did she hope so.

She stopped in a town right outside Columbus to fill up her tank at a gas station called Seven Heaven. She couldn't help but laugh at the irony of the name. She stopped in Indiana to eat a salad and use the restroom. She ate until her belly was modestly full and then she hit the road again. It was when Talora crossed a town named "Perky" that she came close to losing it. The hit song "Cottonmouth" by Stuffed Animalz came on the radio. She couldn't stand to listen to the radio anymore. She fished out a couple of ancient CD's from the glove box and blasted them on repeat. She drove about another hour or two before she decided to call it a day. She was extremely exhausted from not sleeping the night before, and she knew if she kept on keeping on, then she ran the risk of becoming one of those drivers whom she scorned from the confines of her car while driving through OHIO! She ended up spending a rather cold, uncomfortable night in some sleazy hotel in Nowhere, Indiana. The town wasn't called Nowhere; but, in a way, Talora felt as if she was stuck in Nowhere and maybe that was the gist.

That night, she piled up furniture against the window, as well as the doorway, and masked each entry point with perfumes and lotions to hide her scent from the Vampos. There was a window inside the bathroom, which was just big enough to escape through if, somehow, they found her.

During the late hours, Talora sat in the chilly darkness with her nose as cold as an ice cube and listened to each and every sound the night offered. Talora only caught a couple hours of sleep.

The next day, she put all the furniture and whatnot back into its original position in the room and was on the road by first daylight.

While driving, Talora ate from a couple of pastries, including an apple Danish and a cinnamon roll that she had pocketed from the continental breakfast at the Nowhere Hotel. She stopped somewhere in the southern part of Illinois to use the restroom. By lunchtime, she ended up making it to Missouri and decided to stop and eat at Burger Hut outside St. Louis where she ordered, of all things, another salad that tasted as if it was concocted from the remnants of a flood. The lettuce, wilted; the so-called "antibiotic-free" chicken was as tough and rubbery as a tire. She found a dead fly underneath an Iceberg leaf halfway through eating the salad and was tempted to not ask but demand a refund on the salad; however, the notion of possibly drawing a scene in the restaurant had squashed any notion of returning the salad, as well as the french fries, which were cold and tasted as if they sat out all morning. She tossed the rest of the salad, as well as the french fries, in a trashcan and swore to herself that she'd never eat salads—or better yet, never eat at a fast food restaurant again.

Ⓙ

AFTER three more hours of driving on that never-ending road, Talora *finally* made it to Soy, Missouri—or entering "Rhodes Country," as she put it in her own words—where passing a hardheaded redneck driving a noisy truck with a Confederate flag on the bumper wasn't the least uncommon. Despite the "in-your-face" backwardness, the "don't tell me what to do, commie skum" or "how to live" spirit of Soy, Talora never dreaded coming here, even as a little girl. Soy had plenty of country, untouched land that stretched as far as the eye could see, and for a girl who often drove into The City, having a warm slice of countryside at her disposal was nothing short of paradise. She was aware that some of the people of Soy were stuck in their own ways and that some of them, especially the ones who lived in the trailer parks, clung to a bloody past that no longer existed the same way a devout Christian clung to the scripture of a Bible. Of course, Talora didn't agree with any of these people or their beliefs and their ways and the only thing she had in common with them was death itself. In a strange way, she didn't care nor was she the least bothered by them. People came in all *shapes*—Soy had its fair share of shapes—as well as colors. It wasn't like people fell from the sky.

After all, they came from similar institutions that she did.

Talora drove through Main Street and caught up on old times. The last time she had seen her Aunt Dina was about seven years ago and despite the photograph from Talora's college graduation that her mom had mailed to her Aunt Dina, Talora reckoned she wouldn't recognize her today. And vise versa. The only image that Talora had seen of her aunt was from a photo that she posted on her Facebook page six years ago.

Dina's house was a ranch style house located on a sixteen-acre lot, which was passed down to her late husband, Grayson, a millwright who was killed while repairing a faulty conveyor belt, which was used in one of the largest cereal manufacturers in the central part of the United States. After a shoddy investigation into Grayson's death, Amel and Sons, the makers of the popular cereal brands, *Berry Bunch*, were ruled to be blamed for the accident, resulting in a two million dollar settlement. Dina didn't waste a penny with the money from the lawsuit. She ended up giving some of the money to charities and fundraisers, including Research into Alzheimer's—before his untimely death, Grayson always talked about wanting to give money to the organization because his mama, who was as close as a mother to Dina, had died from the disease. The rest of it was spent on one of those stay-at-home colleges where she earned her business degree through online courses, as well as her own clothing store called *La Lueur*, which, in French, meant "glow."

It was late afternoon when Talora arrived at Dina's house, which, except for a new paint job—Talora remembered it being a baby blue color, not lime green—the house looked the exact same as she last saw it. Talora primped her hair in the rear view mirror and made sure she looked presentable for her Aunt Dina.

As soon as Talora exited the car, her stomach fluttered with nerves. *What do I even say?* She mentally rehearsed lines on the slow walk to the front porch; and after the truth revealed itself in each thought with words like *Vampos*, *death*, and *runaway*, slipping through the cracks of her memorized dialogue, Talora decided it was best to lie.

She *rang* the doorbell.

She only waited a couple of seconds for her aunt to answer the door before her mind flooded with the negative—and surprisingly, most realistic—thoughts of bringing Vampos straight to her aunt's front doorstep. Talora could only imagine that doorbell being no different than her ringing a dinner bell. The realization of possibly putting her aunt in harm's way caused her skin to perspire.

Talora tugged herself away, thinking it'd be that moment of doubt when her aunt answered the door. But she didn't. She walked around the house and peeked into the garage. Apparently, Dina wasn't home. Which had given Talora time to think over her unannounced visit. Where would she go? She had Nowhere to go. And, they wouldn't find her here. Talora told herself over and over. If she didn't tell Dina the truth, *they'd never know.* She decided to hang out in her car, which she parked farther into the driveway. She waited about an hour until Dina showed up in a black Mercedes, which looked like a stark upgrade from the hatchback she used to drive.

Once Talora stepped out of the car, Dina followed suit.

It was dark outside and Talora couldn't quite see Dina's face from the bright glow of the headlights masking her face; however, Talora knew it was Dina.

She heard Dina's voice behind the light: "Talora? Is that you?"

Talora stepped forward.

Dina left the car running and walked in an unsteady manner toward Talora.

The sight of Dina's shadowy face revealing itself brought a sense of comfort to Talora. And terror.

"Hey, Dina," she said, her voice trembling.

"Oh my god, Talora!" She stepped forward, her face becoming brighter and clearer to Talora. She looked over Talora's face, then body. Then, she embraced her niece with a hug. "It's so good to see you—"

"—I was going to call, but I didn't have your number."

"It's okay."

"You sure?"

"Of course, I'm sure."

A bit of laughter trickled from her voice.

Dina stepped back and once more, looked over Talora.

"Look at you!" she said with elation. "You're all grown up!"

Talora bashfully responded by not responding.

"Have you eaten?" asked Dina.

"No," Talora said.

Ⓙ

DINA had made an old traditional dish for Talora called "Shakshouka." Her Aunt Dina used to make the dish whenever she would visit as a girl. Served alongside the dish was store-bought pita bread as well as a prepackaged Caesar salad—back in the day, Dina used to make her own pita bread from scratch, as well as her own spin on Caesar salad when Grayson was working, but ever since she started running her own clothing store, she "cheated" a little bit, which, in all fairness, tasted similar to the real deal—almost.

Talora was finishing eating when the doorbell rang.

Immediately, Talora's heart dropped from the *booming* sound of the ring.

Her long face went ghostly pale.

"Oh my god," Dina said in a state of shock. "I totally forgot—"

"—Don't answer it," Talora warned.

"I'm sorry," she said. "I have to. Will you excuse me?"

As Dina broke away from the kitchen table, Talora followed her aunt into the hallway, which Dina interpreted as Talora waving a giant red flag. It started to all make sense to her. She must've had an abusive boyfriend, more than likely, possessive—and, she was running away from him. It was at all true, but Talora could run with it.

Dina stopped at the edge of the living room and turned to Talora.

"Is there something you're not telling me, Talora?" she asked Talora.

"No," she stuttered. "I just—"

"—The City has really taken its toll on you, hasn't it?"

"It's not like that."

"What's it like, Talora?"

"It's hard to explain."

"Relax, okay?"

"But—"

"—Am I allowed to answer my own door?"

The tone in her voice was soft; however, the angle of her eyes was sharp and penetrating.

"Yes," Talora said over a pause. "Of course."

As Dina answered the front door, Talora backpedaled away. She grabbed the poker from the fireplace and was so ready to use it on any member of the Vampos that came barging into the house.

In that moment of great pre-war-like tension, her own prologue to madness, Talora heard another woman's voice coming from outside.

She heard words like *my niece* and then a couple of *sorries*.

Talora poked her head from the living room doorway and saw a woman, who was around the same age as Dina, standing on the front porch with a bottle of red wine in her hand.

"Why don't I call you whenever it's a good time—"

"—No," Talora said from behind. "Please. Join us. There's plenty of food."

Surprised by Talora's interruption, Dina turned to Talora. Then, turned back around to the strange woman outside. She stepped aside and showed her inside.

"After you," Dina said shortly, as if she was hiding her frustration.

Dina introduced Talora to her "new friend" Angie; however, as soon as she picked up the awkwardness between the two, in particular, the way Dina tried her best to justify Angie's untimely appearance by claiming that Angie happened to be in the neighborhood, Talora realized the two were more than just friends.

They had benefits.

⊕

AFTER two glasses of Cabernet Sauvignon, Dina was carrying what Talora would commonly refer to as a drunken sparkle in her eye. In other words, her Dina was a lightweight when it came to drinking. Which, in a way, made Talora envious.

She downed the rest of her third glass of wine, set it down against the outdoor table, and smacked her gums.

"Tell me, Talora," she said, as if she had reached enough drunken confidence to state the obvious, "how's the Big Apple treating you?"

"I'm actually not in The City anymore," she said, taking a bird-like sip from a glass of wine. "I'm staying with my parents Upstate."

"Where? Ballpointe?"

"That's right," she said. "Occasionally, I ride into The City for work."

"What kind of work?" asked Angie.

"Nothing in particular," Talora said. "Pretty much anything I can find. I'm still trying to pay off my student loans."

"Don't you just hate that?" Angie said with annoyance. "It took me ten *years* to finally pay off my student loans. I understand why all these young kids nowadays want free college—"

"—And who exactly is going to pay for it, Angie?" asked Dina, the softness gone from her voice. That diehard Republican coming out of her. Alcohol had a way of mining through a person's "personal" political stance and unearthing it via the spoken tongue. Dina didn't even allow Angie, who couldn't have been more opposite in her politics—in fact, she wasn't even across the aisle, she was hanging out in the corner of the room—a chance to respond or elaborate. "That's right," she said shortly. "People like you and me. These kids nowadays," Dina started to shake her head in what Talora could only acknowledge as a deep-seated disgust, "they are nothing short of rotten. *Spoiled* rotten."

"We're all spoiled rotten at that age. Come on, Dina," Angie said, trying to convince Dina, "you know it's true. Fresh out of college. Professors filling your head with culture and ideology. The 'World Is Your Oyster.' Carpe diem. Seize the day! For once in your life, you start to feel as if Your Voice matters. All that, of course, comes crashing to the ground once we're exposed to the Real World, as in the one outside your phone, and that spoiled attitude tends to go away, and the Real World starts to shape the person you're going to be for the rest of your life."

"Yeah, Angie," Dina argued, "but we didn't have phones when we were Talora's age—"

"—Phones aren't the problem," Angie said, not missing a beat.

"Then, what is?" asked Dina.

"People," Angie said bluntly. "People are the problem. We've lost the ability to talk to one another or, dare I say, possess the willingness to accept any ideas or beliefs that are different from our own or, worse, different from what is considered the norm. We're too focused on what separates us rather than what brings us together."

"I agree," said Talora.

"See." Angie raised her glass toward Talora's direction. "She gets me."

"It's the high-borns who want to keep us separated," Dina said coldly over a moment of silence. "The more separated we are, the more vulnerable we are."

"Here we go again with the high borns," Angie said under her breath and followed with a sigh.

More curious, Talora leaned in closer.

"What do you mean?" asked Talora.

"What I mean is that they're the ones in charge now," Dina said. "They control what we watch and soon, what we say and what we do. Eventually, we'll be living under their thumb. Or, shall I say, claw!"

Dina laughed at her own joke.

Talora wasn't laughing so much.

"You're talking about vampires?" said Talora, more seriously.

"Of course," she said. "Who else do you think I'm talking about?"

Talora didn't have a response. Yet, she thought that maybe her aunt had one too many glasses of wine.

"Those who dictate what news to report to the people, TV producers, founders of certain social media, even our own politicians, all high borns—"

"—Vampires?"

"Yes," Dina said. "*Vampires*. Why is that so hard to believe?"

"Well, I dunno Dina," Talora said, stumbling her words. "It just sounds like some crazy conspiracy theory you heard from the Internet."

"I don't go on the Internet," Dina said flatly.

"Everybody goes on the Internet."

"Not this gal," Dina said, pointing her thumb at herself while making a *clicking* noise from the corner of her mouth.

"How about your business. . . La Lure?"

"It's pronounced La Lueur," she corrected by slurring the words *La Lashhur*. Which relieved the tension in Dina's statement, not theory.

"Surely, you have a website."

"I do," Dina said more superiorly. "I have a guy who runs it. I'm not at all tech savvy. Hey! I'm not ashamed to admit it but I'm what I call tech retarded."

"Dinasaurs!" Talora drawled.

"What?"

Angie said, "You're not supposed to use that word."

"What word?"

"The r-word."

"Oh shut up!"

Dina couldn't help but laugh at what Talora had called her earlier.

391

"You know I haven't been called Dinasaurs in years."

"Old nickname?"

"Way back when, when I wore my heart on my sleeve—"

"—Still do," Angie mumbled from the side of her mouth.

"—Talora used to call me Dinasaurs whenever I'd yell at Grayson. She said I looked like a dinosaur."

"I should've come to his funeral," Talora said out of the blue.

Talora's out-of-the-blue comment created an awkward silence.

Angie excused herself from the back patio by fetching another bottle of wine from the kitchen.

"I wanted to come," she said. "I really did. It's just my dad—"

"—Your dad had his reasons, Talora," Dina said quietly. "It was never a secret to anybody in the family. The relationship between Isaac and I was— how do I say—complicated. He played the overprotective brother who was trying to look after the hard-bitten sister. Over these past few years— especially after Grayson's death—I've learned to accept that. And I'm fine with it. We all play certain parts when we're younger, Talora. Certain roles. You just have to ask yourself: 'What role do I want to play?'"

"Nathan's *still* out there," Talora said, picking up exactly where her aunt was going with the conversation.

"I know he is."

"I even tried to talk to Mayor Armitage—he's the mayor of New York."

"Yeah," Dina said loosely and rolled her eyes. "I've heard about Mr. Touchy Feely."

"I went to the cops," Talora said, keeping serious. "I had no other choice. So I found a fundraiser that he was at. I went there. Tried to confront him."

"And?"

"He was busy."

"Of course, he was."

Talora knew that she was treading a fine line. Knew, if she went further into the story, then the truth would come spewing out like a broken levee.

She left it at that, moved on, and gave no opening for Dina to further question her.

"My mom's already given up," Talora said. "You can see it in her eyes. The defeat."

"Molly is a strong woman, Talora. Stronger than you think. And you take up after her. I mean, look at you, Talora! I never would've had the nerve to confront the mayor of New York City. That takes, pardon my French, balls! And yours, yours are plenty big—"

"—I dunno."

"You might not want to admit it, but you do." In a joking kind of way, Dina sharpened her loosen, drunken gaze on Talora. She touched the bottom of her left eye. "I can *see* it."

Talora hung her head in deep thought.

"What about your dad?"

"I think a part of him wants to believe that Gnat's still out there. But," Talora said, fighting back the tears, "every time I look at him, I *see* Gnat."

Dina scooted her chair closer to Talora's and grabbed her by the hand.

"Everything will work out. It always does—"

Talora didn't want to hear words of reassurance.

She wanted the truth.

Most importantly, she wanted answers.

"What did you say to my dad that drove him away from you?" she asked before Dina could console her.

"It's a long story, Talora," Dina responded, sitting more straight in her chair. "I'd rather not bore you with the details."

Silence crept back into the conversation, the silence forcing Dina to move her eyes elsewhere, such as the kitchen where Angie was standing in reflection by the sink and savoring a new glass of wine all by herself.

Dina sighed, looked over Talora, and witnessed the pain wrapped in her eyes.

"I'm not sure if you were aware, but Grayson wasn't my first husband."

"No," Talora said. "I wasn't aware."

"I was married to a man named Sawyer Hauser. Isaac hated him, in fact, despised him."

"I thought all in-laws despised each other."

"No," Dina said, her voice carrying another sigh. "He *hated* Sawyer, I mean, to the point where he started to get involved in my business."

"Involved? Like how?"

"Like threatening Sawyer behind my back or making up lies about his fidelity. It was not only clear to me, but also Sawyer that Isaac was trying to sabotage our marriage—and frankly, Isaac wasn't too fond of Grayson either." Dina tilted her head to the side in pensiveness. "Now that I think more about it, I don't think he liked any of the men I brought home. Even when I started dating, my brother couldn't stand to see me with another man."

"Why was my dad so protective of you?" asked Talora.

"I really don't have an answer to that question, Talora. I really don't," Dina said, drifting off. "The *resentment*," she snapped back, her voice clearer, "the resentment started to build between me and Isaac after my first marriage. It came to my attention that he was saying all kinds of things about me around the town that weren't true; and *eventually*, those things got back around to Sawyer."

As if she was mimicking Dina, Talora drifted off for a moment as she could hardly make sense of what she was hearing about her own dad.

"What was he saying about you?" Talora finally asked.

"He was telling people that I was being 'unfaithful' to Sawyer."

"Why would he say something like that?"

"He was jealous."

"Jealous of what?"

Dina let out another sigh, as if the truth had a particular way of casting sighs.

"He was jealous because I happened to marry the one man who had a bigger wallet than him."

"You mean Sawyer was rich?"

"*Filthy.*"

"My dad should've been proud of you, right? I mean, you hit the jackpot!"

"He thought I was coasting through life, using Sawyer for his money," Dina said. "After about a year, Sawyer just couldn't deal with my brother any longer—then, Sawyer said he didn't think I was worth the trouble. 'When you get me, you get the brother.' That's how it was and that's how it's always been. High school. College. Sawyer filed for a divorce. I said some things to Isaac that, even till this day, I still deeply regret."

"What did you—"

"—I told him that I never wanted to see him again," Dina said strongly, "and that he was the worst thing that happened to my life, that he'd never live up to our father's reputation. Those were the last words I said to him before I packed my bag and got the hell out of New York."

"I'm so sorry, Dina," Talora said soberly. "I didn't know there was so much bad blood between you and my dad."

"Not bad blood," Dina said. "Just bad memories." She sighed and readjusted her position in the chair. "Let me ask you a question, Talora," Dina said, as if she was waiting for a right moment to change the subject. "And please be honest with me. . . "

"Sure."

Dina asked, "Why don't you want your parents to know you're here? Aren't they going to be worried sick about where you are, especially after everything that they've been through?"

"It's fine," Talora said with hesitation. "I'm fine."

Dina lowered her chin, as well as her voice.

"People who say they're 'fine' aren't really fine."

She didn't respond to Dina, who, in return, took her niece's lack of response as a clear indicated that her niece was *not* fine.

"Talora," she said patiently, "you can stay here as long as you want. You are blood, remember? So, don't you act like a guest. You have a home here. Okay?"

"Yeah," Talora said quietly. "Okay."

With perfect timing, Angie stepped outside onto the back patio. In her hand, she was holding a freshly rolled joint, which happened to be pinkish in color from where her wine-stained saliva had glued the joint together. Angie ran her lighter over and under the joint, which helped dry the saliva.

"How about a cherry on the top?" asked Angie, as she showcased the joint.

"You read my mind," Dina said, more relieved.

"Talora?"

"You like to party?"

Talora finished her glass of wine.

"Yeah," she said loosely. "Sure. Why not?"

🕐

TALORA woke in the middle of the night with a ball of fire in her chest.

The combination of four glasses of Cabernet Sauvignon—maybe five or six, she lost track after three—on top of two helpings of Shakshouka had done a number on her stomach. She figured it was all of that acidic food and drink.

394

She sat up, hoping to ease the burn. When that didn't work, she rolled out of bed and waddled to the guest bathroom in search of any antacids inside the medicine cabinet; however, except for an expired tube of Preparation-H, Dina didn't carry any medicine inside the guest bathroom. Tums was a go-to remedy whenever she had heartburn.

With no other choice, Talora decided to search for other remedies elsewhere, including the kitchen where she scoured through cabinets.

Lastly, she tried the refrigerator.

Dina had a gallon of two-percent milk. In the past, milk helped coat Talora's stomach whenever she experienced heartburn; however, having hopped on the soy milk train three years ago, milk was considered one of her last options to choose from—and since she was in no mood to wake Dina—milk was probably her only option. Trying not to make much noise, she poured herself a glass of milk and did laps around the dark living room while sipping from milk.

Once she finished the glass, the heartburn was somewhat less intense; however, it was still there, like a slow burn.

More awake, Talora left the kitchen, flipped on a lamp next to the couch, and piddled around the living room for a while, mostly checking out all of the knickknacks on the bookshelves and cabinets as though she was browsing through your everyday arts and crafts store.

She came across a shelf of leather bound photo albums tucked underneath a shelf of Mary Higgins Clark novels. She happened to find a photograph of herself after only two flips through the first photo album. The photograph was taken outside near the guesthouse, which Dina had converted into an art studio a few years before Grayson's death. She couldn't tell how old she was in the photograph. If she had to point a number on it, she'd probably say fifteen or sixteen.

In the photo were Talora, who was leaning toward the age of sixteen now that she thought more about it, as well as her younger brother, Nathan, who was about as old as the digits on her hand, her mom, her Aunt Dina, her Uncle Grayson, and, finally, in the middle of the group, was Talora's black cockapoo, Broot, who was a three-week old puppy teething on a toy rabbit. Broot had a specific white patch on his back, very identifiable, in the shape of a heart.

Talora navigated through her memories, specifically recalling her dad and his ill behavior whenever her mom would mention Dina and how he never came with them during the rare visits to Aunt Dina's house and the "off-the-cuff" excuses of having to work that were used commonly whenever any suggestion of driving to Aunt Dina's house for the weekend arose. Pondering over what Dina had told her earlier that night and then examining the photo, the absent father, who, in the case of visiting his own flesh and blood, literally embodied the term "not in the picture anymore," forced Talora to at least try to make sense of the fallout between Dina and her dad.

She skimmed through other photographs for a couple of minutes before walking back upstairs. She passed Dina's bedroom on the way to the guestroom.

With her eyes more adjusted to the darkness, she noticed the door was barely cracked open. She peeked inside and saw two bodies bathing in moonlight. Dina was sleeping next to Angie; in fact, both of their bodies were en-tangled and not in the friend kind of way, but more so like two lovers. She couldn't believe her own eyes. Her Aunt Dina, once a reserved woman who would talk secretly about men, as well as the comfort and ruggedness of men, her Aunt Dina, the one who'd always whisper a comment to her whenever she either saw a handsome—or as she coyly put it, a "hot" or "cute" guy—on TV or even passed one on the street or in public, was now playing on the other team.

One of the women lying soundlessly in bed—she couldn't tell whether it was Dina or Angie—suddenly stirred around while readjusting position. The woman unhooked her leg from another leg and rolled to the edge of the bed, taking more sheets along with her.

The move revealed more clearly the other woman, Angie, who slowly ro-tated her head toward the doorway.

Her glossy moonlit eyes moved toward Talora's direction.

Immediately, Talora stepped from the doorway and tiptoed back to the guestroom as if she was a teenager again sneaking through the night. Each noise, each *creak* of hardwood, each *squeak* of a door, forced her into a mime-like state, as if she was playing red light-green light.

For the first time in a long time, Talora felt, dare she say, happy.

⏰

TALORA concealed her laughter as she made her way back to the guestroom where she fell sight to the open window inside the guestroom.

That tension she experienced back in New York City was back.

She carefully closed the door behind her and crept toward the window where the curtain was weightlessly floating about the room.

As she tried to recall opening the window—maybe she did before she passed out—the sound of nature outside the house rid any doubt in her mind.

A gentle breeze was blowing into the room; however, it wasn't strong enough to blow open the window.

Comforted by the coolness, Talora kneeled down and peered out into the vast countryside before her.

She could no longer hear man or his creations.

She heard the nocturnal life, a familiar yet almost forgotten life that had been masked by street ambience for years. The sounds filled her ears, a sym-phony of a hundreds of species all speaking to her at once.

⏰

THAT night, Talora fought off the burn of an upset stomach and slept well through the morning.

By the time she woke, the bright morning sun was painted all over the en-tire guestroom. She woke rested. She rolled out of bed and walked toward the closed window. Waking up to the sight of a vast countryside opposed to wak-ing up to a neighborhood of cookie-cutter houses or even cityscape brought a sort of Christmas-morning comfort to Talora. She heard the *clinking* of dishes downstairs. She made her way into the kitchen where Dina was washing the dishes from last night. She turned her shoulder, saw her niece through the corner of her eye, and stopped what she was doing.

Talora immediately noticed the Russian blue rubbing against Dina's leg.

"Look who's up," Dina said, drying her hands with a washcloth.

"Mornin'," said Talora.

"Good morning," Dina said and slid out a chair for Talora at the kitchen table.

"And who may this be?" asked Talora, as she kneeled down and pet the cat.

"Vladimir meet Talora," Dina said.

"Vladimir, huh?"

"Apparently, he was hiding last night."

"Doesn't like guests?"

"No," Dina said. "He's pretty skittish. But," she said, admiring Talora's nature with Vladimir, "he looks like he's made a new friend."

"Did you sleep well?"

"So, so, I guess," Talora said honestly. "I woke up in the middle of the night with a wicked case of heartburn."

"You know," Dina said, more reflectively, "I thought I heard someone walking around this morning."

More intrigued, Talora asked, "What time?"

"I dunno," she said. "I believe it was around three or four o'clock. It was not long before I woke up."

She specifically remembered waking up three minutes after midnight; in fact, that time "12:03" was seared in her memory. Talora remembered walking around for a while; she grabbed herself a glass of milk to cool off that wicked heartburn, then nosied through a couple of photo albums. Then, headed back upstairs where she went back to bed. All of that took no longer than twenty minutes or so, which meant Talora fell back to sleep around 12:30—1:00, the latest.

"Why didn't you wake me?" Dina asked, more concerned about Talora's well being than her privacy. "I could've grabbed you some Tums."

Dina's question released Talora from a sudden wave of panic.

"No," Talora said, playing off her previous illness. "Eventually, it passed."

"Well, then, you should probably eat light today—"

"—No. I'm feeling better." She perked up. "What do you have to eat?"

Dina looked around the kitchen counter.

"Well, I can make you some eggs."

Talora passed a box of bagels next to the refrigerator.

"Bagel?"

"Help yourself—" she shooed Talora away and walked her to the kitchen table, "—or actually, why don't you take a seat while I make you breakfast."

"You sure?"

"It's no trouble," she said in a motherly kind of way, "as a matter of fact, it'd be my pleasure."

Talora, who had gotten used to making her own meals over these past couple of years, took advantage of Dina's offer and took a seat at the table.

Dina was watching a famous chef sampling different plates of pork at a barbeque contest on the Food Network.

"You can turn the channel, if you like," Dina suggested.

"It's fine," Talora said. "I don't watch much TV."

"I don't blame you," Dina returned with a concealed resentment underneath her voice. "Nowadays, who can? Everything has gotten too political." *Political,* Talora thought, *right?* "It's sickening to watch. For me," Dina said, "I'm pretty much left with either The Food Channel or Animal Planet. Nothing too political about food or animals."

Talora wasn't in any mood to question the one right Dina had left to exercise, which was her opinion. Her stomach did most of the talking.

"So," Dina said, her voice rising, "how do you want your bagel?" She looked in the refrigerator and listed Talora's options: "I have butter, cream cheese, grape jelly, orange marmalade—"

"—Cream cheese is fine."

"What kind? Strawberry or hazelnut?"

Talora pinched her nose.

"Hazelnut?"

"It's good," Dina said. "Wanna try it?"

"No thanks," Talora said. "I'll go with Strawberry."

"Strawberry it is."

As Dina prepared the bagel with Strawberry cream cheese, Talora grabbed a cat mug from the top cabinet above the dishwasher and poured herself black coffee from the pot.

"You read my mind," Dina said. "Pour me a cup, will you?"

"Sure."

"My cup's in the sink."

Talora walked to the sink and found two mugs lying on top of the dish grate. Both were empty. She didn't know which one to grab—and for some reason, she was hesitant about asking Dina which mug belonged to her. One had one of those inspirational quotes on the side: *Life is short. Drink up!* The other one, newer, less worn, with a smudge of red lipstick along the rim.

Talora grabbed the mug with the message and poured two cups, one for Dina and then another one for herself.

"This will be my third cup." Talora set Dina's coffee next to a box of bagels. "Thank you," Dina said, pulling herself from the bagel to take a sip of coffee.

"Are you hungover from last night?" asked Talora.

"No," she said in a high, untruthful voice. "Well, a little. You?"

"A slight headache, but nothing coffee can't fix."

Talora raised her mug in a one-sided toast.

"Dat a girl."

"I can only drink two cups, though. Three gives me the jitters."

Once the bagel was prepared, Dina placed it on the kitchen table. Then, she poured Talora a glass of orange juice and brought it to the table as well.

Talora sat back down at the table; Dina sat across from Talora and nursed her coffee.

"When did Angie leave?" Talora asked from the one side of her mouth while chewing the bagel on the other.

Dina cleared her throat.

"She left after you dozed off," she said, looking Talora directly in her eye. "I didn't want her to drink and drive."

"She didn't drink that much, did she?"

Dina smirked, then shrugged.

"She's not much of a drinker."

"She's pretty cool," Talora said after washing down the first bite of the bagel with a sip of OJ. "How long has she lived here?"

"She moved down here from St. Louis after an abusive relationship."

"What does she do for a living?" asked Talora.

"She's a stylist," Dina said. "I thought I told you. She does my hair."

"Oh," Talora said stupidly. "That's right! You told me."

"So, what's the plan for today?" Dina asked in a rather hasty manner.

"The plan?" Talora mulled it over. "I was thinking about maybe driving into town. Maybe checking out the new shopping center, ah—"

"—Regalcrest."

"That's the one."

"It's not bad, I guess."

Talora asked, "How about you?"

"I, my dear," Dina said more eloquently, "have to go to work. The bills don't pay themselves." Dina took a sip of coffee. "I'll tell you what. I might be taking a half-day. Why don't you stop by the store later this afternoon? We can maybe grab lunch, if you're up to it. They just put in this new brewery on South Gates Street. I tell you, Talora, they have an arugula-beet salad with crusted, candied pecans topped with their own homemade raspberry vinaigrette that is to die for."

"Yummy." Her eyes widened. She almost purred. Then, she thought more about the name. She furrowed her brow. "Gates Street? I thought Gates Street was located in a bad area."

"It was," Dina said. "It's in one of these new places that was recently, as the kids call it, 'gentrified.' They've completely turned that whole area around. And, believe it or not, it's brought in more money for Soy. It's even brought out all of the hipsters from the woodwork."

"Hipsters in Soy?"

"Apparently so."

Dina raised her mug of coffee in a toast.

FROM the front porch, Talora waved goodbye to Dina.

As Dina drove the car in reverse from the driveway, she stuck her hand out of the window and waved back at Talora. She stuck her head out, as well, and then shouted at Talora, "Call me!"

"Will do," Talora shouted back and watched Dina drive away.

DINA left Talora a number where she could reach her while she was at work. She also left plenty enough food for Vladimir; however, she left a couple of treats for him in the laundry room and told Talora to feed him if he got fussy.

Only an hour since her aunt left the house, Talora was already contemplating giving Dina a call maybe just to talk, maybe just to find out what she was doing at that particular moment, maybe just to ask her a question about whether or not Vladimir liked to be brushed, maybe just to hear a person's voice—a real voice, that is.

Talora had done about everything she could possibly think of doing, including flipping through TV channels but not really finding anything decent to watch on the tube except for a BREAKING NEWS story on a man named Sonny Mims, a campaign manager for the presidential candidate, Governor Avanti Washington, and how his remains were found outside Tent City—investigators believed he was murdered by vamps—or skimming through one glossy fashion magazine after another or washing a pile of dirty laundry, and then, while waiting on her clothes to wash, going through these old boxes of art junk collecting dust in a tiny attic, and then, once the washer finished its cycle, putting the clothes into a dryer, and then, while waiting on her clothes to dry, redoing everything she did after her Aunt Dina left for work, TV, magazines.

While sitting on the couch, she held her finger in the shape of a gun. Placed the barrel that was her index finger to the side of her temple and cocked the hammer that was her thumb and then pulled the trigger.

Boom!

Brains on a wall. . .

What Talora would do to have her phone back?!?

Talora gave the TV another shot and while flipping through channels, landed on the Cartoon Channel where the trendy cartoon, *Japhy and Friends*, was playing.

The sight of the cartoon caused her to switch off the TV and throw the remote across the living room!

After another hour of piddling around Dina's house, Talora decided to take a walk outside and hoped to fight off the boredom with Mother Nature. Talora was surprised by the drop in temperature. Yesterday felt like a crisp fall day, the kind of day which promoted outdoor activities, such as going for a casual stroll through the neighborhood. Yet, today, it was winter. She was only wearing short sleeves and leggings. She decided to power forward and close the door behind her.

With her arms tucked into her chest, she only took seven steps outside before she changed her mind.

As Talora turned back around and proceeded back toward the house to grab more appropriate attire like a sweatshirt or light jacket, she stopped in her tracks.

The back door was wide open!

Huh?

For a moment, that familiar tension gripped her.

Ever since she arrived in Soy, she thought as though she had shed such a feeling. But it was back—or, at least, *trying* to make a comeback.

Talora ignored the feeling, the creeping dread.

She walked back into the house, checked the door as well as the door handle, and made sure to properly close it behind her. She walked upstairs to the guestroom and grabbed an orange BCC sweatshirt from her bag. Once she was dressed in a more comfortable outfit, she walked back downstairs.

Of course, the back door was open—wide open!

"What the hell?" said Talora, as she stepped outside and closed the door with a more forcible tug until the door was completely shut.

She released her hand from the door handle and waited for what she referred to as a hot minute and the whole time during her tense wait, she couldn't help but wonder if the door was going to open as if it had a mind of its own.

It didn't. It was just a door.

And Talora put any doubt to rest.

Weirded out by the back door, Talora walked through the back yard.

Before entering the guesthouse, she came across a worn strip of brown cloth material suspending from a protruded nail on a panel along the doorway. Thinking maybe Dina or whoever had snagged a jacket or even a wool coat on the nail, Talora leaned down and grabbed the strip of clothing from the nail. She couldn't quite tell what kind of material it was, either wool or cotton or something else. It appeared as old as dirt, whatever it was.

Once she rubbed the strange material between both her fingertips, Talora was struck by a momentary dizziness. The feel of the material felt coarse and staticky along her skin, the same feel one would receive while touching the surface of an old analog TV screen. All of a sudden, Talora felt ill. Her fingertips experienced a pinprick sensation.

She dropped the piece of clothing onto the ground. The nausea faded, as if, in an odd way, the material was attached to sickness.

As Talora took a deep breath, she reached for the door handle.

The door opened; however, nobody was on the other side of the door. Talora wasn't able to make contact with the door handle for the door kept moving farther away from her.

"What's up with th doors around here?" asked Talora, as she tried to play off the recent strangeness.

As the door opened entirely, she stood at the doorway of the guesthouse and examined the art studio inside—or what used to be an art studio.

Dusty white sheets were used as coverings throughout the studio and draped over furniture, as well as several easels and unfinished sculptures.

Talora stepped inside the guesthouse and made sure to close the door behind her. It turns out the door wasn't entirely closed to begin with. The door stuck and as with the back door, she had to give it a sturdy tug until it closed all the way.

She wandered around the studio. There were very little curtains covering the windows and natural light poured into the studio, casting out various dust clouds. Talora could only assume that her artwork had been put on hold, especially after starting up her own clothing store. Talora put the suspicions aside and removed a white sheet from one particular easel holding a painting of a

woman—whom she assumed was Angie based on the short, spiky, red hair—
lying nude on the couch. Her body was fully stretched out across the entire
couch. Her right arm holding up her head while her other arm rested along the
side of her hip. Talora wondered if the painting was either driven by the
imagination of a woman who was channeling a lost—even recently discovered—sexuality or Angie, who could've possibly modeled for Dina. Talora
leaned toward the latter.

She placed the white sheet back over the painting and saw a movement in
the corner of her eye. Talora turned toward another white sheet that was
draped over what looked like a sculpture of some kind. She carefully removed
the dusty sheet and before her stood a black cockapoo. The realness of the dog
was uncanny and appeared as if it had been stuffed by a taxidermist.

Intrigued by the so-called sculpture, Talora kneeled down and just as she
was about to touch the side of its face, the old dog let out a bark!

Startled beyond belief, Talora stumbled backward and knocked over an easel. The sudden crash of the easel hitting the floor caused a chain reaction.

Startled by the sound, the dog ran off toward the door but was greeted by a
closed door. Whimpering, the dog pawed at the dog.

Talora caught her breath and regained her composure. She went to let out
the dog, but before she did that, she kneeled down and tried to calm the dog.

Immediately, she recognized the dog.

Confusion flooded her.

"Broot?" said Talora, still and shocked. "Is that you boy?"

⏱

EVEN if the dog wasn't Broot—Talora had a deep suspicion that it was—she
tried to make sense of how the dog ended up in Dina's studio.

Most importantly, *how did he end up in Soy, Missouri?*

That is, if the poor mutt was her old dog, Broot.

Still slightly freaked out, Talora walked Broot to her car and drove to
Dina's clothing store La Lueur. All she could think about was Dina and
whether or not she was being honest with her. If Dina knew about the dog,
then the twenty-five thousand dollar question would be: "Why didn't Dina tell
Talora about the dog?" She gave Dina the benefit of the doubt and went to her
with a clear conscience.

When Talora arrived at La Lueur, Dina was surprised by her appearance.
She handed off the customer to one of the employees, a college girl who was
working part time to pick up extra spending money, and pulled Talora to the
side.

"Nice place," Talora said, looking around.

"You like it?" said Dina. "I've put a lot of work into it—"

"—Listen, Dina," Talora said over Dina's voice, "you wouldn't believe me
if I told you, but. . . " she cleared her throat, ". . . do you know there's a dog at
your house?"

Talora was waiting—in fact, hoping—for her aunt to give her an answer
like "Yeah," or "I know. That's my dog, Donnie." Or, whatever!

She received no such response. Instead, all Talora got was a long, blank face from Dina.

Dina said over the silence, "A dog? What? You're serious?"

"I found it in your studio."

"What the hell was a dog doing in my studio?"

"I dunno," Talora said, thinking of an excuse to tell Dina as to why she was in her studio. "I thought I heard this noise coming from the guesthouse. I went to check it out. Sure enough, I found a dog in there."

"What kind of a dog was it?" asked Dina.

"A cockapoo."

"Cockapoo?" Inherently, the thought turned her into one of the best detectives in Soy. "Didn't you used to have a cockapoo?"

"I did," Talora said. "And that's what's so spooky about it. He went missing the same time Nathan ran away."

"Yeah," Dina trailed off. "Spooky. So, where is it now?"

"In the car," Talora said, pointing over her shoulder.

"And you think it's your dog—"

"—Broot?"

"Yeah."

"I dunno," she said. " Maybe. I mean, it looks just like him. I mean, it can't be a coincidence, can it?"

"Well. . . "

With a pensive look etched on her face, Dina lowered her head for a moment. Her eyes were wrapped in thought. She looked back up at Talora.

". . . I've heard that some animals can travel a great distance to find their way back home. I think it might have to do with the owner's scent or something."

"Are you sure you're not thinking of cats?"

"I'm pretty sure it's dogs. Back in the day, police used bloodhounds to track people—"

"—Yeah, Dina, but this is a cockapoo," Talora said, playing off her frustration. "All it's good at tracking is another dog's butt hole."

Eventually, after a little convincing, Talora dragged Dina outside to her car, which was parked along the curb in front of the neighboring store, Guilty Café.

Talora opened the back door of the car, grabbed the end of a homemade leash that she made from a stretchy blue band she found in Dina's garage, and ordered the dog outside.

"Is that my workout band?" asked Dina.

"Yes." She saw a hint of anger on Dina's face. "It was either this or rope. I didn't want to use rope because I was afraid it might rub against his skin."

"It's fine," Dina said.

She specifically used that word—*fine*.

She trailed off, "I don't use them anymore."

"Good."

Dina kneeled down and examined the dog.

"It looks old." She glanced up at Talora. "Wasn't Broot old as well?"

Talora followed with a closed-mouth yes, which sounded like a *umm-hmm*.

"And you see the white spot on its back?"

Talora pointed out the heart-shaped spot on the dog's back.

"I see it," Dina said, feeling through the dog's matted hair.

"Can't be a coincidence," Talora said.

"This is weird," Dina uttered.

"I know, right?"

"Well," Dina said, standing back upright, "what are you doing now?"

"I just came by to show you the dog."

"While you're here, you want to check out the merch?"

Talora thought over Dina's offer.

She sealed the deal by telling Talora that she can pick out anything she wants.

"My treat," Dina said.

"What about the dog?" asked Talora.

Dina nodded at Guilty Café. Outside hung a "dog friendly" sign. Next to the entrance was a doggie bowl on the ground. A couple was eating lunch with their German Shepard on the patio. Talora spotted other four-legged creatures walking throughout the café. She heard dogs barking over the sound of a crying baby.

"I know the owner, Marisa," Dina said. "She won't mind watching over the dog for a while."

"Why can't I just bring the dog into your store?" asked Talora.

"Because my store is *not* dog-friendly."

Talora was tempted to follow up with a "Why not?" The two words dangled on the tip of her tongue. However, she spent more time thinking about why Dina wouldn't allow the dog into her store. She had put a lot of money, as well as time and effect into the store. Besides Vladimir—or "Vlad," as she called him before leaving the house—who, except for scooping out little, crusted balls of turd from the litter box, required less responsibility and maintenance, Dina didn't have any other pets inside her house—at least none that Talora was aware of. Each room of the house had different smells to match the paintings and colors on the walls, except for the laundry room, which, of course, smelled of cat turds and realistically, should've been painted the color brown. Talora combed her thoughts and specifically remembered the day she brought Broot, who was just a puppy at the time, to Dina's house. Broot wasn't allowed inside the house and he had to stay in a kennel in the garage overnight: Dina's orders. In fact, Talora remembered she was so broken up about her dog— which would later be her brother's dog—sleeping in a cold garage that she grabbed a sleeping bag, her first, then Nathan after he caught his sister fleeing from the air mattress, and they both snuck downstairs while everybody else was sleeping, and the two of them slept next to Broot.

Unless Dina was one of the greatest poker players west of the Hudson, Talora was convinced that the dog wasn't Dina's.

Surprisingly, the question had hit a nerve with Dina.

More promptly, Dina was tempted to follow up by throwing a term at Talora that only the cliché of a soft-celled, swirly-eyed, hypersensitive, so-called "righteous," sham-bot Millennial would commonly use while haranguing on the Internet: Something along the lines of "Am I being '*dog*-phobic?'"

The two held their tongues.

Dina walked the dog inside Guilty Café while Talora, who was less both-ered by not bringing the dog with her, waited outside. A couple of minutes later, Dina returned with a gleeful smile on her face.

"Problem solved," Dina said, holding out her hands.

"She didn't mind?"

"Not at all," Dina said. "Marisa loves dogs more than she does humans. She even has a separate menu for dogs."

"That's cool," Talora said.

"Yeah," Dina said dismissively, "if you're into that sort of thing."

This time, Talora held her tongue.

TALORA spent a good forty-five minutes to an hour trying on various types of outfits and modeling them for not only her number one critic who was Dina, but also for her own reflection in the dressing room mirror.

While Talora was flaunting an autumn squash colored waterfall collar pocket front wrap coat over a nicely fitted black sweater dress, as well as slouchy styling, knee high boots to match the black dress, her eyes crossed the front of the store. She took her eyes off the outfit, then Dina, and witnessed a dark yet, surprisingly, bright figure who was standing on the sidewalk across the street.

Immediately, she stopped modeling for Dina. The childish smile melted from her face. Her demeanor darkened. Both her eyes were pinned on Japhy, who was wearing the same outfit he wore on and off stage, including that same flashy coat, which had a particular way of making everything around it dull and lifeless.

Activity was happening all around him, such as pedestrians walking in close proximity, cars driving by, bicyclists riding by, even a bearded man who was restraining his dog from sniffing Japhy. Yet, despite all of that muted life en-compassing and provoking him, his razor sharp eyes never left her. In that moment, Talora thought Japhy was wearing the look of a man who, yes, wanted to kill her.

Thinking maybe he might've been looking at someone else—but *how could he? The glass was tinted!*—Talora glanced around the store, praying to spot some washed-up groupie whom he had pity-fucked after a show. She turned her shoulder but saw nobody standing behind her. She looked in front of her but saw nobody, who'd warrant such attention. In other words, she had many props around her. But she was the star of the show!

"Talora?" said Dina, her voice giving off concern. "What's wrong?"

Talora snapped from her trance and turned to Dina.

The only word that she mustered from her lips wasn't a word at all but more or less an utterance of what had the potential of being a word.

"Are you okay?" Dina asked again. "You look like you've seen a ghost."

"Yes," Talora said and tried to find Japhy with her eyes.

He was no longer standing on the sidewalk.

Watching her.

In fact, he was nowhere to be found.

Yet, in Talora's mind, he was everywhere.

"I mean," she stuttered, "no. I just thought I saw someone I knew."

"Who?" Dina owled. "Ex-boyfriend stalking you?"

Talora didn't laugh at Dina's innocent joke. She could hardly bring herself to crack a smile.

"I would if I were a guy," Dina followed up as if she was completing a punch line.

As if a light switch had been turned off inside Talora, her confidence was no longer existent. Her posture was more slouched. Both of her arms appeared limp and heavy as they hung along her sides like cured meat. Even her neck started to arch like a turtle.

One minute, she was glowing, a soon-to-be "Maneater," celestial, unstoppable.

The next, decorated trash.

Even though Talora could feel that sense of panic slowly creeping in, Dina's humor helped remove the tension from the air.

More considerate of Talora's feelings, Dina said as Talora ambled back to the dressing room, "You know, Talora, I was thinking, if you're going to be hanging around in Soy for a little bit longer, if you wanted something to do to maybe pass the time."

"What? You mean, like a job?"

"Well, sort of."

"What do you have any mind? As you can see," Talora modeled her clothes once more but did so in a sloppy, amateur manner, "I'm extremely busy."

"Would you be interested in picking up some extra money?"

"Yeah," she said. "Sure."

Talora's voice went up a couple of octaves.

"I'm clearing out the Victorian style house off Colony Street in order to build a new store, which will be a sister store to La Lueur. The store's going to specialize—or better yet—focused more on eveningwear. Plus, I'm gonna add a bar and lounge on the first floor that way shoppers can enjoy a glass of wine while trying on a fun, flirty dress."

"That actually sounds like a good idea," Talora said.

"The place is old, though," Dina said, "and it needs a lot of renovation."

"So, it's an actual house?"

Dina nodded.

"Three stories," she said. "It was once a bed and breakfast before it was partially destroyed by a tornado. I already have a guy on the job. Name's Morrison, and he's great. But he can use a hand."

"Clearing out a house? That sounds like hard work."

"It's not about hard work, Talora. It's about putting a little joy in the work. Come on. What do you say? And, he's kind of cute too."

"Cute?"

"Yeah. Like an old soul kind of cute. And not only that, I'll pay you."

Talora asked, "How much?"

AFTER they decided on eating a more low-key lunch at one of those home cookin' joints, which was within walking distance from Dina's store, Talora picked up the dog from Guilty Café and followed Dina back to the house where she made a bed in the garage for the dog and left him alone with a bowl of tap water and plenty of food to get him through the evening and then some. As her aunt had advised, Talora changed into more appropriate attire, which she wouldn't mind getting dirty. After all, Dina specifically explained to Talora that the job wasn't at all *Pretty in Pink* and definitely "roll-up-your-sleeves" kind of work. Once she was suited up in blue jeans and an older, smaller, more ragged sky blue sweatshirt that she borrowed from Dina, she rode with her aunt to the three-story Victorian style house that used to be the Beatty Fireside Mansion and parked behind an old rust-colored truck that looked as if it was from a time where television was shown in black and white. Dina showed Talora the front of the house, the porch, as well as the space, which would later be a parking lot. She pointed at certain areas along the roof, as well as gutters that had been repaired, while other areas were still marred by past storms, and painted vivid mental images for Talora, such as a gaudy sign, as well as lighting and a Romanesque sculpture on the front lawn.

Before they walked up the front steps of the porch, they passed a pile of discarded wood and scraps, which appeared waterlogged from rain. Next to the pile was a massive dumpster overflowing with what looked like the guts of the house. Dina made sure to tell her that Morrison was going to take the trash to the dump whenever he could get around to it.

"Looks like you have your work cut out for you," Talora said, her eyes crossing another trash pile in the front yard.

Dina told her to watch her step and emphasize nearby dangers, including broken glass and nails.

"Believe it or not," Dina said in defense, "clearing out the tree that had fallen through the roof was the hardest task. Fortunately, we managed to salvage most of the living room, which will be converted into the lounge-slash-bar area. The way I look at it, it's all downhill from here—or uphill?" Dina didn't fully understand the expression nor did she care to use it. She callously waved it off and forgot that she ever used it. "All of the work we have left is mostly cosmetic. Painting. Adding the bar. Well, not entirely cosmetic. We still have to redo the floors. Open up rooms. This, my dear, this is where *you* come in." She walked Talora to the front door. She pointed at the loose beam along the front steps and told Talora to watch her step. "Oh yeah," she whispered, "plus we have to revamp this whole area." This "*area*," Dina said, as in the front porch. "Morrison needs a hand tearing down a wall."

"Tearing down a wall, seriously?"

"Sure," Dina drawled. "I'll give you goggles, gloves, and all of the gear you need. It'll be fun, girl." Acting like her cautious tour guide, Dina escorted Talora farther into the house, which was stripped of flooring. She constantly pointed out other dangers, as well as where to step and where *not* to step. They stepped into the foyer, making their way around a spiraling staircase.

Immediately, Talora had doubts about helping Dina. She didn't know exactly what it was that had turned her off. Maybe it was the piece of plywood in front of the hallway closet with the caution tape marking the floor like a crime scene.

"Right," Dina said, tracking Talora's eyes toward the taped off area. "*That*," she identified. "Don't ask how that happened?"

Talora paused.

Then, teased, "How did *that* happened?"

Dina sighed.

"You want the long story or the short?"

Talora thought it over.

"Short please," she said.

"Morrison was clearing out the guest bathroom on the second floor when all of a sudden the toilet fell through the floor! The toilet ended up putting a massive hole in the floor."

"Really?"

"Yup."

"What's down there?" Talora asked, creeping closer to the caution tape.

"I haven't been down there, but Morrison says it might've been a wine cellar. Trust me. The floors are next on our list; however, our major priorities right now are to clear out all the walls before we can even think about redoing the floors."

"This place sounds like a deathtrap," Talora said.

"Like I said," Dina said, showing Talora the refinished living room, "it's not *Pretty in Pink*."

Dina showed Talora where the bar was going to be. Then, she walked Talora to every room in the house—or as she put it, every "department."

"Basically," she explained, "it's going to be like a mini-department store with a bar. Each room will have different departments: lingerie, gowns, makeup, etc."

"What are going to do with the other store?" asked Talora.

Dina said, "The plan is to run them both."

"Sounds like a lot of work."

"It's going to be," she said, more optimistically. "When I get burned out, I'll probably hand it off to one of my other employees at La Lueur and focus more on this place."

"Curious," Talora said, as she walked inside what used to be the master bedroom, which was now a gutted room, "what's the name of the store going to be?"

"Right now, *Un Verre* By Design," Dina said. "French for 'A Glass.'"

"*Un Verre*," Talora repeated, as she digested the name. "Not bad."

"The store's going to have a common theme: glass. If you think about it, the shape of a woman's body is similar to a glass that we drink out of. Either it be a wine glass, champagne glass, or even a juice glass, *Un Verre* will highlight all of the different shapes of the woman's body."

"Nice," Talora uttered, as she stood next to the window and peered outside at the street below. She turned her attention back to her aunt and said more thoughtfully, "You think you might be misleading the customer, though?"

"How so?" asked Dina.

"Well, you might draw in more drinkers than shoppers."

"No," Dina argued. "The clothes *will be* the focal point. The bar is going to be what separates my store from other stores. In a way, I'd like to think that the store's going to bring some needed sass to Soy. You know, more character."

"You'll have to get a bar license. Which means you may have to serve food as well."

"I'm working with a chef to create a small menu. I'm thinking more of a tapas style menu. I'm also working with a local artist named, get this, Icepick. Not sure if you've heard of him or not. He's all over social media."

"The name doesn't ring a bell."

"Anyway, he's creating all the logos as well as prints. And he's going to help me with the website as well. He's also working with this glass blower in a small town called Circa to create these life-size sculptures of all sorts of shapely women that will be shaped like a drinking glass. It has almost avant-garde feel to it, very 'out of this world'-New York gala."

"Interesting." Then, she added: "Why don't you drop 'By Design' and keep it 'Un Verre.' It has a better ring to it. Less is more. That's what they say in the marketing biz, right?"

"Well, Talora, your feedback is always appreciated and I will take it in consideration."

"Just sayin'."

A loud *thud* coming from upstairs drew Talora's attention upward.

"That must be Morrison," Dina said, as tiny chips of paint came raining down from the ceiling above. "He was supposed to be installing a new window on the third floor. He should be done already. I tell you what. I'll go grab him upstairs; and if he's ready, you two can start working in the kitchen."

Dina ordered Talora to stay put.

"I'll be right back," she said and walked up to the third floor.

When she returned to the second floor, she was walking with a young man—probably a few years older than Talora, maybe even closer to his thirties—whom she assumed he was this guy, Morrison. In fact, after a short introduction, Talora learned that his name wasn't Morrison. His name was actually Leonard Byrd but was called Morrison by mainly her aunt because he happened to share an uncanny resemblance to Jim Morrison, as in "Jim Morrison of the rock band, *The Doors*."

"I forgot," Dina said over Talora's visual confusion, "he's before your time."

Trying to prove her point, Dina pulled out her smartphone and googled Morrison's look-alike and showed Talora the results. She compared the image from the phone to the flesh and bone standing in front of her.

"I see what you mean," Talora said in agreement. "Yeah. I guess everybody has a twin out there."

"You mean like doppelgängers."

"Dopple-what?"

"Doppelgängers," Morrison said. "They're like twins, but they're not related by blood."

"Are you talking about clones?"

"No," Morrison said. "Doppelgängers."

"I literally have no idea what you're talking about."

Talora laughed first, Morrison followed.

"So," Dina interrupted, "lets put this girl to work, shall we?"

Morrison showed them the way.

He said, "After you."

🕐

DOWNSTAIRS in the kitchen, Morrison provided Talora with safety gear, including a pair of goggles to keep debris from hitting her eyes, as well as a pair of gardening gloves, which were the only gloves he could find.

While Dina watched at a safe distance, Morrison ran down the list of do's and don'ts and showed her the ropes on how to properly swing a sledge-hammer. Her first attempt was poor and barely even penetrated the dry wall next to the doorway and Morrison was left with no other choice than to step in behind her and in what Dina perceived as an innocent yet slightly flirtatious attempt at a move, adjusted her grip around the handle of the sledgehammer and told her to hold the handle as if she was holding an egg.

"Don't strangle the damn thing," Morrison specified for her. "The downward momentum will do all the work."

Talora did as she was told and drove the sledgehammer through the wall, resulting in a decent-sized hole. She pulled the hammer away from the wall, tearing away a chunk of drywall.

For about three solid hours of tearing away walls and carrying leftover debris to the dumpster outside whenever the kitchen became too full, Talora and Morrison decided to call it quits. Dina had stepped away for a couple of hours to attend to her other business and returned a few minutes before they finished.

Before Talora parted ways with Morrison, he invited her out for a drink. She immediately declined without putting any thought into the invitation.

Dina said it'd be good for her.

Morrison said he'd show her around town.

Talora told him that she'd think about it, which, in other words, meant "heck no."

🕐

APPARENTLY, while Dina was away, she bought a new leash, one of those extendable leashes that allowed a dog to move around more, and when she pulled into the driveway, Talora noticed the dog was on the front porch. The other end of the leash was strung around the front column. The dog perked up from its sleeping position as soon as Talora stepped out of the car. The sight of the dog responding to her presence convinced her the dog was Broot, even though she didn't have any proof, except for the spot on its back. All she could do was wonder how he ended up all the way out here in a place that rhymed with toy.

A hot shower after an afternoon of backbreaking labor inspired Talora to reconsider Morrison's invitation. Dina's convincing, as well as a constant usage of the word *cute*, was the icing on the cake. He wasn't at all Talora's type; in fact, they couldn't be farther apart in their personality.

Finally, after going over all of the pros and cons of having a drink with a man whom she had just met and, not to mention, a man whom she was possibly going to be working with—that is, if she continued the work—Talora used Dina's phone to call Morrison. Despite his cool composure over the phone, he was glad to hear Talora's voice. He offered to pick her up. She kindly refused and said that she'd rather met him somewhere. He gave her a name of a place called Jaxxx's, which, at first listen, sounded like Jack's. She didn't spend too much time picking out an outfit. She went casual and wore an outfit that would make her blend in.

When Talora arrived at the dive bar, she was turned off by the name. Immediately at first glance, she thought the place was a strip club—because of the three x's. Turns out it was a dive bar. Inside were all things of a clichéd bar. Capitalism at its finest. Glowing beer signs scattered throughout the bar as if Talora was walking through a spam museum. Names like *Miller*, *Bud*, and *Coors* commonly treated like spiritual totems. In the back were two billiard tables, which were being occupied by two groups, the granola types, who looked as if they weren't going anywhere anytime soon. A younger rowdy crowd of redhats was hanging out by a dartboard. Not too far away from the elephants in the room was one of those modern day "smart" jukeboxes where the patrons chose a song from their "smart" devices. Of course, the song "I Killed The Devil" by Stuffed Animalz happened to be playing as soon as Talora made her way through the bar. The owner Jaxxx, who spelled his name with three x's, was sitting at the end of the bar and keeping an close eye on his toadies, who, at any moment, were ready to act out of line or say something that resulted in the boot by a bouncer named Mouse. Surprisingly, the bar was packed for a Tuesday night. Which made Talora wonder if something else was going on tonight—like a special on drinks or karaoke night or whatever. According to Morrison, who had already reserved a seat—or better yet, "spot"—at the end of the bar for Talora, it was a typical Tuesday night at Jaxx's. To say the least, the residents of Soy, Missouri, liked to drink and weren't too particular about what they liked to drink.

Morrison greeted her over loud music and background chatter and spent the next few minutes screaming what her initial thoughts were on the place but only catching snippets of her answer. He waved down some young, perky bartender named Alicia, whom, after acknowledging Morrison's wave, parted ways with a waitress and was waiting at his command as if she was Rin Tin Tin. Talora gathered that the two of them had a relationship outside that seemingly artificial employee-patron bond where *she* was working him for tips and gratitude and *he* was finding the right angle to get inside her pants.

When Alicia arrived, Talora ordered a cranberry and vodka.

Morrison was drinking what looked like whiskey. All she caught was the name "Jack" when she asked him.

After spending the next few minutes trying to talk over the music, Talora decided to seize the opportunity of grabbing a table that had recently opened up.

Once seated, the drink helped take Talora's mind off the song. For the most part, she mainly asked questions. Morrison did most of the talking, and she was fine with hearing what he had to say about the town. "What's there to do around here?" Talora asked while Morrison pointed around the bar as if he was showing off a guilty pleasure. "You're looking at it." Morrison leaned in closer to Talora and came close to that hookup range. However, it was clear to Morrison that he knew exactly where Talora had drawn the line and went straight to it without any hesitation. "I know," he said, "it doesn't have much of a nightlife. I'm sure for a city girl like yourself it must feel like cultural shock."

He backed off, allowing Talora room to talk freely.

She talked about her love for the small town vibe, the quietness of the countryside; however, she was more curious about what Morrison had to say.

Morrison was a single dad of a six year old girl, who, when asked about her whereabouts, was currently staying with Morrison's mother.

Slight judgment came over Talora as Morrison explained his situation, particularly the one involving a "crazy" ex who had herself a "pill problem" and was a "popper" trying to regain "custody over" *his* "baby girl." Her mind drifted from Morrison's words, leaving her vulnerable inside a negative space.

Talora wanted to ask: "So, why aren't you at home raising your daughter like any normal father?"

Instead, she thought, *you're out grabbing a drink.*

Hopefully, the kid will be in bed by the time you get home.

Except for his days off, Morrison never found much time to see his daughter. Which, somehow, made Talora more ashamed than embarrassed for taking him away from spending valuable time with his daughter. Although it was he, Morrison, who invited her out for drinks. He worked two jobs, one as a so-called "contactor," this sort of Renaissance Man who could repair a car, fix any issue inside a house, build a deck, or even cook a three-course meal. His second job was at one of those big shoebox stores as a freighter/forklift driver who worked a graveyard shift. Tonight happened to be one of his nights off.

When asked how or where he met Dina, Morrison said the two met through a new app called *Get Ur Dun*, which was sort of like a redneck version of Angie's List. She needed help with repairing a leak at La Lueur. Morrison had done such a good job with the leak that Dina had kept his contact information and used him frequently with any other issues she had at her store and even at her house. It was fair to say Morrison was the kind of guy who'd you like to keep handy. And Dina had him in her back pocket.

Despite their city girl-country boy differences, after a couple of more drinks, the two hit it off and for the first time in a long time, Talora felt optimistic about a future in Soy.

After her third drink, she excused herself from the table and passed by a payphone next to the restrooms. For a while, she contemplated calling her parents to inform them that they had nothing to worry about and that she was okay.

She went so far to grab the phone and as she was about to insert a coin into the machine, Morrison walked past her. She immediately backed away from the phone.

"Drinking and dialing," he teased, "bad combo."

"You're right," Talora said and walked back to the table while Morrison excused himself.

☉

So far, the night flew by without any hitches.

Before she fell into that stranger-danger zone, she parted ways with Morrison on good terms and one-eyed her way back to Dina's.

By the time Talora pulled the car into the driveway and did so in the manner that would catch the eye of a cop on patrol, it was a quarter past eleven. Dina had left a couple of lights on, including the front porch light. Talora chugged a bottle of lukewarm water that she found underneath the passenger seat of the car before heading inside.

Still riding high on a vodka buzz, she refocused and played her own in-head game of pretending as if she had been recently pulled over by a police officer who suspected her of drinking while under the influence of alcohol, and tried her five-star best to walk a straight line along the edge of the driveway. If Talora had been pulled over and was given a sobriety test, she would've failed miserably.

Talora stumbled two times, one of those times she nearly tripped into a bush. She didn't want Dina to see her like this, especially with her being a guest in her house. But she told herself that Dina wasn't a parent; but, most importantly, not her parent.

When Talora stepped inside the house, she headed to the kitchen and grabbed yet another drink of water. Downed the entire glass all in one breath. Dina, who was watching old reruns of *Shark Tank* in the living room, called out to whom she suspected was Talora and Talora, still feeling loose from the buzz, responded with a Shakespearean-like "Yes."

Dina leaned over the head of the couch and asked, "What are you doing?"

"Nothing," she said, straightening her walk.

Her head wasn't spinning as badly as it was in the car; however, Dina's presence reassured her that everything was going to be fine.

Somehow, the topic of the dog was brought up into a one-sided conversation.

With Broot on her mind, Talora was convinced that the dog was Broot and all of a sudden, had made it a nightly mission to prove to her aunt that the dog in the garage was, in fact, her missing dog, Brooty Boy.

"I'm a ninety-nine point nine, nine, nine percent that it's Broot," she slurred. "You'll see."

"I believe you, Talora," Dina said, as if she was talking to a toddler, who was on the verge of throwing a tantrum, and wasn't at all in any mood to contain such an implosion—and explosion.

"No," Talora snapped. "I want to show you—"

413

She dug out Dina's photo albums from the shelf and as she was about to pull out the photos, Dina eased from the couch in a state of uneasiness.

Talora opened the photo album and flipped to the section where she saw her puppy, Broot.

The entire page was empty.

No photos.

Anxiously, Dina asked, "What happened to all my photos?"

Unable to find the words, Talora opened her mouth in shock.

"Talora? Where did they go?"

"I don't know." She carelessly flipped through the other pages, even bending one of the corners of a photo. "They were right there. I swear!"

"Well," Dina said, "they're not. Where are they?"

She waited to hear an answer from her niece, but all she received was a destroyed young woman who looked as if she was about to melt into tears.

"Talora," Dina said tenderly, "what's going on with you?"

"What d'you mean?"

"I mean, 'What's going on?'" asked Dina.

Again, Talora was unable to find the words.

She set aside the photo albums and told Dina that she needed sleep.

Dina couldn't agree more.

🕐

DRENCHING wet with sweat, Talora woke up at nine minutes after two o' clock.

She checked the time and once she realized what time it was, she felt almost upset. She flipped her pillow to the cool side, shut her eyes, and tried to sleep off the hangover. However, her head was splitting in two, as if she had a valley running through the center of her forehead. She couldn't sleep even if she tried. She decided to search for remedies—as she should. She rolled out of bed. Even moving made the pain in her head much worse. She blindly stumbled her way through the night darkness and made it to the bathroom where she ran cool water over her throbbing face. The feel of cool water pressed against her skin lessened the ache in her head; however, the ache was *still* there, chilling like a movie villain.

When she ambled back into the guestroom, she couldn't help but notice that the window was opened all the way. Not once did Talora ever remember opening the window before passing out. She still had on the same clothes she was wearing the night before. Which undermined the whole reason for opening the window. If Talora was so hot—in fact, she was burning up—then it'd only make sense to remove heavy clothing and changed into a cooler, more comfortable outfit? Why open a window?

Talora knew the answer to that question.

And her answer alone made her that much more terrified.

Cautiously, Talora crept toward the window and as she about to close it, she saw a dark figure standing in the backyard. Talora knew that shape. She knew it was him based on the shape, as well as the glimmer in the passing moonlight.

①

FUELED by questions and yet, at the same time, the alcohol that was still coursing through her veins, Talora marched downstairs and charged through the backdoor. As soon as she stepped outside, she was grabbed by a dark figure. Her first, most basic instinct was one of survival, to get whoever—or whatever—it was who was on her, off her. In one-two combination, she curled both of her arms inward and pushed the figure away and then clawed straight for the eyes. She raked the eyes, her hand falling across heavy clothing covering what felt like a muscular body.

She ran back inside and flipped on the floodlight.

The dark figure, whom she thought was Japhy, was no longer standing on the back patio. He was gone.

Cautiously, she walked to the edge of the back patio and called out his name, "Japhy!" She screamed, "I know you're out here! You coward!"

From behind, she felt yet another presence: Dina.

She turned around and found Dina, half asleep, standing in the doorway.

"Talora," she mumbled, "you know what time it is?"

"I fucking saw him." She checked her arms for marks but couldn't find any. "He grabbed me!" She pointed to the last spot where she saw Japhy last standing. "He was *right* there!"

"Grabbed you! Who?"

"This—this asshole who's been following me."

She raised her voice loud enough for Japhy—or whom she thought was Japhy—to hear her.

"Following you? Talora, are you sure?"

"Yes," she shouted out. "I'm fucking sure."

"Calm down," Dina said, trying to use her hands to calm down Talora. "How concerned do I need to be right now, Talora? Do I need to call the police?"

Talora thought it over.

"Talora, let me call the police—"

"—No," Talora finally said. "That's not necessary."

"Are you sure?"

"Yes." Talora peered out into the night darkness. "He won't come back now that he knows I know what he's up to."

"I'm calling the police—"

"—No," Talora said. "Don't."

Dina looked over Talora and told her to come back inside. She walked Talora back inside the house and closed the door behind her.

①

TALORA woke up to the faintest smell of smoke.

She rolled out of bed, didn't bother checking the time, and tracked down the smell to the bathroom where she discovered the missing photos in the sink. Each and every one of them was curled and burnt. She knew they were the photos for only one image remained clear to her behind the blackened, bubbled print and that was Dina's face. In the photo, she was a younger and more conservative woman, for the most part that is. From the hazy quality of the photo, it appeared as if the photo was taken around the time Talora used to visit her aunt before they stopped talking. Most importantly, the photo was taken around the time Talora brought a puppy named Broot with her everywhere she traveled.

Slightly numb from the hangover, Talora gathered up all of the burnt photographs from the sink and tossed them in the trash. She ran the faucet and washed out the leftover black flakes and smears along the sink.

🕐

MORE composed, Talora walked downstairs. The TV was running in the kitchen; however, Dina was nowhere to be found. She called out Dina's name twice but never receive a response.

As panic started to creep in, Talora started to check each room, including the back of the house. She stepped outside and walked onto the back patio where she found what looked like an old button on the ground. The button was located precisely where she was grabbed. She picked up the button and pocketed it.

When Talora reached the laundry room, which was located in the front of the house, she heard two voices talking outside—one of them, she thought, sounded just like Dina's voice.

She followed the voices to the front porch where she saw her aunt talking to a policeman in the driveway. He was a rather stout man, his face scarred up from a bad case of late adolescent acne. He had a gray mustache looked like as if it was established in 1998. Both his hands were planted on his hips, his thumbs looped over his belt like hooks. She spotted a police car parked in the driveway. Along the side of the car read the word *Sheriff*.

From the casualness of the conversation, she didn't see any reason to panic—at least, not yet. The two appeared as if they knew each other.

Talora decided to crack open the front screen door and eavesdrop on the conversation.

Their voices were muffled. Before the so-called Sheriff parted ways with her aunt, Talora most definitely heard her asking the man if he could keep an eye on things around the house for the next couple of days or so. "Your presence," Dina said, "will scare him away."

Somehow, Dina's words had comforted Talora and a part of her knew that—despite everything that had happened these past couple of days—there was absolutely no reason to get all worked up.

By the time Dina returned, Talora had already jetted back toward the kitchen and fixed herself a Dina's finest brew. Dina wasn't at all surprised to see Talora up so early and considering her inebriated state last night, wearing the same exact clothes that she wore last night. Although, a part of her had an internal bet going on with herself that young gals Talora's age usually turned into pumpkins after a long night out.

Talora asked before Dina could voice the obvious, "What was that all about?"

416

"You saw, huh?"

Talora faced Dina and leaned against the side of the countertop. The coffee was much stronger than the day before. After taking a sip, Talora grimaced from its bitterness.

"Too strong?"

"Nope," Talora said, feeling a bubble of nausea in her stomach. "It's exactly what I need right now. So. . . "

"You had me worried last night, Talora—" she said straightforwardly, as she made her way into the kitchen, "—don't flip. I didn't mention your name."

"Trust me," Talora mumbled. "Not in any mood to be *flipping*."

"All I said was that there was this creep hanging outside my house last night and that I," Dina motioned to Talora, "'we' would feel more comfortable if one of Sheriff's deputies kept an eye out for the next couple of days. That's all. . . "

More relieved, Talora took yet another sip of coffee. She came close to spitting it out. Usually, the first was the worst. The second, better. Then, the third, tolerable. However, it tasted as if the coffee was getting worse by the sip.

"Sheriff Tate is a good man," Dina said, as if she was still trying to convince her niece that she was in the right, *not* the wrong, for calling what her rotten generation commonly referred to as pigs. "*Beloved* by our community," she emphasized. "He looks after all of us, Talora. *All* of us."

"Thanks," Talora said softly. "But you didn't need to do that."

"Well, I don't think you gave me any other choice, Talora. To be honest, you scared the shit out of me last night. So, you want to tell me what's really going on? I mean, who the hell is this guy?"

Talora hung her head.

"You'd never understand," she muttered.

Dina stepped forward and faced Talora.

"Then, help me try to understand."

Talora said again, "You wouldn't understand."

"Is that the real reason why you came here," Dina pursued, "because you're running away from someone? If so, from who, Talora?"

Talora's head was pounding again. Clearly, the coffee was not helping at all, nor was her aunt and her grilling. She pinched the bridge of her nose. Then massaged the ache behind her eyes.

As Talora lifted her head upward, she saw a familiar face on TV.

Pacen's face!

Without drawing too much attention to herself, she shifted her weight to one side of her body and canceled out Dina from her partial view.

"The vehicle of Pacen Selassie, also known as DJ Pac-Attack, member of the popular band Stuffed Animalz, was in an abandoned parking lot next to the Panorama Inn in East Harlem, New York. Mr. Selassie was reported missing last—"

Talora darted around Dina and turned off the TV before Dina could listen to the breaking news report. The last words Talora caught before the TV went black was the *explosion, which was captured by one of the hotel—*

"Too much to drink last night?" asked Dina, as she folded her arms over her chest, stood back, and watched Talora and her strange behavior.

Talora asked, "Can I use your computer?"

"Yeah," Dina said. "Sure. Be my guest."

Talora stormed out of the kitchen.

Dina stopped Talora at the doorway by calling out to her.

"Talora," she said, causing Talora to turn her shoulder, "I'm not your mother. But just know that you can tell me whatever you want, that is when you're ready."

Talora nodded.

"I'm not going to judge you." Dina cracked a smile. "Trust me. I'm the last person who should be judging others."

Insulted by the remark, Talora furrowed her brow.

"And what is it that supposed to mean?"

"It means I'm not perfect," Dina said, "and neither are you."

"Okay," Talora said shortly and walked to the office.

Somehow, the sound of Talora's usage of the word and the way it shot out of her mouth like a dart left Dina feeling small as if, no matter what she said to reassure her niece, she was oblivious to what girls went through nowadays, especially in a technology-driven society. Dina didn't have any children, but she could only imagine what it'd be like to have one.

And a small part of her felt no regret.

Not even a sliver.

🕐

As soon as Talora pulled up the web browser on Dina's outdated iMac, she typed in Pacen's name in the search bar.

Several "shocking" headlines from several untrustworthy news sites came up, most of them being click bait and rabbit holes. So far, according to one news site which seemed to be more consistent to what she briefly heard on the TV, investigators didn't have much evidence or details as to Pacen's whereabouts, other than a shaky cell phone video with someone who could possibly pass as Pacen. Basically, all they had was the SUV. But no Pacen.

Frustrated by the lack of information—and even the information she gathered was either distorted for shock value or taken out of context—Talora decided to go on social media sites, which was the worst decision she could've made. All of the hearsay and garbage spewing from the fingers of Stuffed Animalz haters was only adding to her frustration. She came across bogus stories, rumors, alternate facts, and false allegations—one of them being that Pacen groped a so-called "fan" at a concert and that he was getting exactly what he deserved.

"Burn in hell, white boy," wrote username ScreamQueen@404.

Talora read more hateful comments on the Internet and drew her own conclusion that these people—Russian or Chinese bots or algorithms—were sharing or exposing more about themselves than the actual people or persons whom they were hating on.

Talora even read a theory that Pacen left the band and was living incognito in London under the pseudonym Gaffney Wrinkler.

Dina knocked on the doorway and asked Talora if she wanted an egg or whatever. Her choice. Talora's wasn't hungry; in fact, she was starting to feel sick.

"No," Talora said, rubbing the side of her face. "I can grab something to eat later."

"You sure?"

"Yeah."

Talora checked the time and realized it was almost lunch. Yet, Dina wasn't at work.

"Weren't you supposed to go into work today?" asked Talora.

"I was," she said, "but, you know, I didn't want to leave you here alone."

"What?" Talora exclaimed. "No! I don't want you missing out on work because of me. Dina, if you have to go to work, then go. Please, don't let me hold you back—"

"—Do you want to come with me?" asked Dina. "I'll put you to work. Plus, it'll take your mind off whatever it is you're going through."

"What about Morrison?" asked Talora.

"What about him?"

"Does he need help today?"

Talora regretted asking the question as soon as it left her lips. Although the more she thought about spending the day working up a sweat, the more she realized that maybe it was a good idea. "Sweat out the poison," as Pacen used to say.

"I'm sure he does," Dina said over a pause. "Why? Did you want to help out again?"

"Maybe," Talora said. "Yeah. It'll give me something to do."

"I told you it's fun, didn't I? In a way, it's kind of like a rage room."

"Rage room?"

"You know, they have these rooms where people pay to take out all of their frustration on a TV, furniture, even cars."

"Yeah," Talora said. "I think I've heard of those. I didn't know they were called rage rooms, though."

Dina's phone rang. She excused herself, grabbed her phone from the kitchen table, and walked back to the office.

"Speak of the devil," Dina said, showing Talora the name on the screen.

Talora not only couldn't read the name for the name was too small, but also her eyes still hurt.

"Who is it?" whispered Talora.

"Morrison," Dina mouthed.

She answered the call.

"Hey, Mory," she said jubilantly. "Sup?"

While Dina was listening to Morrison, she turned her attention to Talora and started making strange facial expressions.

"Really?" Dina responded. "Well, let me ask her?"

Dina muzzled the phone over her shoulder and nodded at Talora.

"Morrison," she said softly, "wants to know if you can give him a hand to-day at the new store."

Talora thought it over. The thought alone of losing her mind in Dina's house made her answer easy.

She bobbed her head.

"Yeah," she said, her stomach churning, "why not?"

Talora stood up from the desk while Dina placed the phone up to her face.

"Yes," Dina said over the phone. "She said she can. . ." she nodded over his response. ". . . Sounds great." Then, "She'll see you soon. . . bye."

Dina ended the call.

"How much did you two drink last night?" she asked Talora. "Y'all must've had a good ole time."

"Why?"

"He sounded a little hungover himself."

"Really?" Talora paused. "I don't remember him drinking that much."

She shrugged her shoulders, as if she was shrugging away a dark thought.

TALORA didn't bother to change pants. She threw on another sweatshirt that she borrowed from Dina and left the house with little primping.

On the way to the renovated house, she pulled over on the side of the road to vomit. Afterwards, she felt a hundred times better. Dina told her that, after she finished up at the store, she was going to stop by later that afternoon with a cooler of beverages and sandwiches. Talora was now hungry.

She decided to grab a buttery biscuit at one of those places she swore never to eat at ever again. She managed to hold down the biscuit, as well as the coffee and orange juice.

Once her belly was full, she was looking forward to seeing Morrison again.

When she arrived, Morrison was already there.

Pleased by the sight of Morrison's truck, she carried more pep in her step as she walked up the front porch. Morrison greeted Talora in the foyer. He was acting different, strange. When Talora said "Sup" to him, he mimicked her and said "Sup" back. Talora was bothered by Morrison's demeanor and the words he was using, like following with the word *dog* after sup or using the word *a'ight* or *tight* or *nuttin'* or *chillin'*. These were not Morrison's words, yet they were the words that Talora had grown up hearing. What bothered Talora were his clothes, in particular, that flashy, glittery coat. Talora realized it the same coat that Japhy wore. She knew it wasn't a coincidence. The coat was special, thin and light, stretched all the way down to his ankles, one of its kind. Even Japhy's diehard fans tried to replicate the coat, made their own version of the coat and wore them at Halloween parties, going as their own self-proclaimed "golden god." Even wore that coat at Cosplay events. Morrison didn't strike her as Stuffed Animalz fan.

Talora immediately questioned him.

"What's going on?" she asked. "Why are you wearing that coat?"

With a familiar grin on his face, Morrison reached his hand toward his neck, pinched a handful of flesh underneath his chin, and pulled upward. He

420

kept pulling and pulling and the more he pulled, the more freaked out Talora had become. He ended up pulling off his entire face!

Before Talora, Japhy revealed himself. He held the loose mask of flesh in the air. He even wiggled it around for Talora.

"What the hell did you do to Morrison?" asked Talora, backing away in horror.

"Your buddy, Morrison, is taking a BREAK from work!"

Japhy laughed at the apparent joke.

Talora wasn't laughing at all. Instead, she was looking around the house and searching for nearby weapons and contemplating her next move of attack. To the right of Japhy was a bucket of paint, which could be used as a tool for bludgeoning. In the dining room the sledgehammer was resting against the wall; however, it was too far from her reach and Japhy would be on her before she finished uttering the second syllable of the word *supercalifragilisticexpialidocious*.

With his eyes widened in child-like madness, Japhy yelled out, "Catch!"

He threw the wiggly mask of flesh at Talora, who had no other choice than to catch it.

The flesh was scalier than any normal flesh. She could feel the mask moving in both her hands as if, in a way, the flesh was alive.

She glanced down at the whitish-caramel pattered snake coiling around both of her hands.

Startled by the albino ball python, which was extremely docile by nature despite its fiery red eyes, Talora screamed out in horror!

She dropped the snake to the floor; and, in return, the snake slithered away.

Out of options, she ran away from Japhy, who wasn't so thrilled about chasing after her. Instead, Japhy acted as if he was going to take his time with Talora, as if, in a disturbing way, he was toying with her.

"There's nowhere to hide, Talora!" he yelled out, his voice carrying throughout the entire three-story house.

Talora managed to seek cover behind the wobbly island in the kitchen, which she and Morrison hadn't gotten around to tossing in the trash outside. The minor rest had given Talora enough time to plan her next move—which was to basically keep as much distance from herself and Japhy until she managed to sneak outside and run to her car. Her eyes crossed a body in the next room. . .

Morrison!

Japhy wasn't lying.

With a shard of wood protruding from his side, Morrison was sitting against the wall. He was bleeding badly and was drifting in and out of consciousness. As soon as he laid eyes on Talora, he perked back up. The adrenaline had given him enough alertness to motion to his injuries, in particular his left leg, which looked as if it was bending in a way that any normal leg shouldn't bend.

Seeing Morrison and his current state had changed Talora's plan and she told herself that she wasn't leaving without Morrison.

Japhy's footsteps were closer.

Talora decided to steer Japhy away from Morrison by creeping into the next room, which was the living room.

While Japhy crept his way into the kitchen, Talora took cover behind the living room wall, peeked around the corner, and charted out her next position of hiding, which was the hallway closet.

Japhy left the kitchen.

Talora tiptoed to the hallway closet, sneaked inside, and closed the door behind her. In the tense silence, she waited for Japhy to pass. She watched his dark shadow easing across the beam of light underneath the doorway. Japhy's shadow came and went. Then, it came back again. Talora waited in suspense for Japhy to open up the door and grab her. Strangely, he didn't. He kept on walking. Talora listened closely to his footsteps moving farther and farther away. Yet, the shadow below the doorway still remained!

In the darkest of the closet, Talora heard yet another sound.

However, the sound was coming from inside the closet!

She listened closer to the *rustling* sound. She followed the sound to the floor. Then to the albino ball python, which was now slithering up her left leg. With her body shaking, she held the scream tightly inside her chest and at any second, she was ready to explode. She moved her eyes downward to the bottom of the closet door. The shadow was gone. However, she lost track of Japhy's presence.

The snake made its way up her thigh.

Once it reached her waist, Talora couldn't take it any longer.

All in one motion, she grabbed the snake, threw it to the floor, and ran out of the closet.

Japhy was nowhere to be found; in fact, the entire house was silent.

As Talora listened for Japhy, she heard grunts coming from Morrison.

"Talora," Morrison groaned, "help me please. . . "

Talora didn't budge an inch.

"I think my leg is broken," he said, his voice strained.

Again, Talora didn't make a move.

"Talora!" Morrison shouted out.

She could hear the pain in his voice.

He reassured her by telling her that he's gone and that he exited through the backdoor.

Cautiously, Talora crept back toward the kitchen. She grabbed a screwdriver from the kitchen countertop and was ready to use it if necessary.

As soon as Talora stepped into Morrison's direct line of sight, she peered past the living room doorway and saw Japhy kneeling over Morrison.

Japhy's hand was covering Morrison's mouth.

"Why hello, Talora!" Japhy said in Morrison's voice. "Nice to see you again, Talora!"

Once more, Japhy laughed.

He removed his hand from Morrison's mouth and prowled toward Talora.

Holding out the screwdriver in defense, Talora backpedaled away from Japhy until she reached the foyer. Every now and then, she glanced over her shoulder to see where she was going. Then, when she turned her sights back in front of her, Japhy was three steps closer as if he was able to move triple as fast in blinks.

"Give it up, Talora," Japhy said. "You're mine now—"

"—What the fuck do you want from me?" cried Talora.

Backpedaling away from Japhy, she glanced over her shoulder yet again and saw the caution tape surrounding the sheet of plywood over the floor.

"I want you to suffer until your last breath," Japhy seethed, flexing his hands. His nails extended outward like the talons of a hawk.

"Why?" cried Talora. "What did I ever do to you?"

"What did you do to me?" Japhy repeated hysterically. "You took *every-thing* away from me!"

Talora backed up to the plywood. She placed her right heel against the corner of the plywood. She stopped and held the screwdriver in front of her, as if it was a knife. She had finally reached the point of no return.

Fight or flight.

Talora chose neither because why exactly?

Because neither *fight* nor *flight* was founded by the very essence that irrefutably separated the humans from the animals. And Talora was tired of the games. The hide and seek bullshit. The cat and mouse bullshit. She was sick and tired of all the bullshit. She felt the warm vibration in her pocket. With her free hand, she pulled out the button and held it in her palm and could see the button shaking as if it was an entity far greater than she'd ever know or understand.

"What you got there?" asked Japhy.

Talora balled her hand into a fist and embraced the energy cast from the button. She felt it calling to her, not the button but a life-force attached to the button, coursing through her body and then past her, peeling back worlds beyond her very own, and opening doorways that were opened by the One whose eye, the one and only eye, the Third Eye, remained an interstellar highway of the great universe, a glowing sapphirine light, hollow and eternal.

"You know, *Japhy*," she said calmly, as the whole tearful act started to wear off, "I never told you this but. . . you're a terrible singer."

Overcome with rage, Japhy suddenly charged at Talora.

At the very last second, Talora kicked the plywood away from her, which, in return, caused the plywood to slide over the floor and reveal the massive hole.

As Japhy was about to tackle Talora, she opened her mind.

And like that, she disappeared into the Void.

Japhy tackled empty air, tripped, and fell into the hole. He managed to grab hold of the sides of the jagged flooring.

Talora suddenly reappeared!

Stunned by the move, she found Japhy hanging below her.

The last words he said to her before he lost his grip were "I win."

She dropped the screwdriver from her hand, then button, which ended up falling into the hole.

Once her hands were free, Talora crawled forward and leaned over the hole to grab him but he already fell. She watched him plummet into the darkness. She never saw him land for it was too dark. However, she heard him crashing heavily to the basement floor below.

The sound of the crash filled Talora with relief and caused her to back away from the hole.

As she was about to check on Morrison's condition, she heard what sounded like a *whimper* coming from below.

She listened closer and heard a familiar voice coming from the floor below.

Japhy was alive; however, he sounded hurt.

He sounded younger.

Talora knew it was a trap—*it had to be*, she thought. He was luring her down into the hole where he'd find an opportunity when Talora wasn't looking and then he'd make his move.

She couldn't help but glance at the hole and the torn strip of coat dangling on a jagged piece of wood. The material was different, older, raggedy, brownish, *not* gold.

Suspicious of the voice, Talora found the door to the basement. She'd be lying if the thought of locking the door, even wedging a piece of lumber against the door and keeping it from opening, then covering up that hole in order to keep him down in the basement forever. Leave him there in the darkness and let him think about his actions for the rest of his meaningless existence. The thought came and went.

Out of curiosity, Talora opened the door and a set of stairs leading into a dark basement was revealed. She walked back to the spot where Japhy had fallen and grabbed the screwdriver. Now, with a weapon in hand, Talora walked downstairs and switched on a work light that took a couple of seconds to brighten. She spotted the crash once the light fully brightened and highlighted the chaos; and in that chaos, Japhy—or whom she thought was Japhy—cowering in a dark corner of the basement. Part of his coat was ripped. However, it wasn't that same flashy coat that he wore on and off stage; in fact, it looked more like an old brownish blanket, frayed and covered in dirt. The material itself appeared as if it would disintegrate or even turn to dust at first contact. She couldn't see Japhy in his entirety, only a weakened, shorter man who was curled in a fetal position. Except for crying, she couldn't quite tell what he was doing for that old coat was covering his body.

"Playtime is up," Talora said, as she inched her way toward Japhy. She kept the screwdriver close, ready. "I want you to leave me alone or else—"

"—Fuck you," a young voice of angst said from underneath the raggedy coat.

The voice was *not* Japhy's.

The sound of the voice sent a ripple of shock throughout Talora's body.

With the screwdriver loosening in her hand, Talora stepped through the rumble and debris and pulled the coat from Japhy's smaller body. Even the touch was familiar and had that similar staticky, analog TV screen feel to it.

She released the coat. Her jaw slackened with great surprise from the sight of the teenager. Her eyes, as wide as question marks.

"*Nathan*?" said Talora, her voice curling like a question mark. "What?"

Her younger brother, Nathan, turned his shoulder and for a moment, faced his sister. Tears were running down his face. He could hardly make eye contact with her for the shame was too great.

"Jus' leave me 'lone," he cried out.

Talora pulled the rest of the coat from Nathan's body. The pinprick sensation of the coat's material pressed against her hand caused her to drop the coat.

She waggled her hand.

"What—how did you get here?"

Talora kneeled down in front of Nathan, whose face was cringing with rage. "I said 'Leave me alone!'"

"Nathan," she said, "it's me, your sister."

"Your not my fuckin' sister," he cried, his voice choppy.

"You're telling me this whole time—but how?"

Her eyes fell to that old coat on the floor. She specifically remembered the sensation that she felt when picking up a piece of old, coarse fabric from outside the guesthouse and how it was similar to the sensation that she felt while pulling the coat from her brother's body. She put the clues together, the two memories, three, then four. . .

"You little shit!" Talora barked. "You know the trouble you've gotten yourself into, Nathan?"

"Nice to see you to, *Ta-lora*," Nathan whined.

"Nathan," Talora said, more patiently, "how could you do this to me, to mom and dad?" The disappointment wore off from the very thought of Pacen and was replaced by a greater anger. "And what happened to Pacen, please tell that wasn't you—"

"—Pa' lease," Nathan said with a pout. "That dickhead deserved it. . . "

"Nathan! How can you say that?"

"He's fine."

"Fine? He's dead, Nathan!"

"He's not dead," Nathan drawled. "Well," he paused, a sense of humor coming back to him, "I take that back. He's not alive, either."

"What did you do to Pacen?"

"What did I do?" His body sunk inward, both of his shoulders shrugging in a juvenile "he said-she said" fashion. "I had no control over what those *fang-fuckers* were going to do—"

"—Pacen would still be alive if it wasn't for you!"

Nathan rolled his eyes and downplayed the situation.

"He's not dead-dead, if that's what you're talking about."

"You're telling me he was one of them now?"

"Yeah, well, I helped him escape from those lousy blood traders," he clarified. "You should be thanking me!" Then, he said in a more laidback tone, "FYI, if I were you, Lora, I probably wouldn't take the dude out for spaghetti Bolognese anytime soon. *Fun fact*: the garlic might not sit too well on his stomach."

Tempted to strangle her little brother, Talora said from the side of her mouth, "You're an asshole, you know that?"

Brushing off debris, he stood to his feet in a careless way as any young man recovered from injuries.

"I'm the asshole," Nathan shouted at Talora and pointed at himself. "I'm not the one who stuck her big fat nose into her brother's business."

"What you talking about?" asked Talora.

"*You*," Nathan said, the tears flowing again, the rage, "you're the reason why my band is no longer together. *You* are the one who turned all of them against me and made me look like a fool. *You* are the one who destroyed my dreams, Talora! My dreams!" Nathan screamed. "Not yours! They were mine! Mine! And you, you bitch, you took it all away from me by stealing the one band mate who others looked up to! You could've chosen someone else, anyone, even Product—" Nathan thought more about Product and that couch-modeled body for a moment, the rage on-pause, "well, maybe not Product, but anyone else. But you chose Pacen! And it's all YOUR fault!"

"My fault?" Talora said innocently. "I didn't know it was you who was pretending to be some singer named Japhy—"

"—You knew! I know you did!"

"Nathan," Talora said, her voice riddled with defeat, "I didn't know. And I am sorry that I got in the way. I am. But Nathan, you have to understand that I'm not the one to blame here. I apologize for what happened to your band. But what you did, Nathan, with Pacen, how you've kept Mom and Dad in the dark and had them convinced that something awful happened to you, that's irredeemable. Why would you even want to put them through all that pain? For fuck's sake, *Gnat*," Talora yelled back, "Mom and Dad had your ass buried!"

Even more ashamed from his sister's comment, Nathan looked up at her the same way Broot would look at her after having made a boo-boo.

"They did?" said Nathan.

Talora gave him an exaggerated nod.

"Yes."

"I mean I'm still here. I mean," he said and pointed at the coat, "the coat was disguising me. It's not like I'm dead." Nathan was puzzled by the idea of being buried when he could see his own hands before him. "How'd they bury me?"

"They buried an empty casket with your most valuable things inside," Talora said.

"What things?" asked Nathan.

"Comic books," Talora listed. "Your mp3 player, even your Teddy, food for worms."

"Man," Nathan said depressingly, "now I feel really bad."

"Yeah," Talora said sharply, "you should."

She drew her eyes back to the torn coat, then Nathan, whose eyes were laced with a whole world of awfulness.

"Listen, Nathan," Talora said more seriously, "the time for playing 'dress up' is over. D'you ever stop and think that maybe I like you just the way you are, that annoying little brat?" she teased. "You don't need some special coat to be somebody. You are somebody. You're my little brother, Nathan Katz."

"Shut up," Nathan mumbled.

"You *are* Nathan Katz, not Japhy Warthog," she said deliberately.

"It's Warchild!"

Talora couldn't help but laugh at Nathan's defensiveness of his character. Eventually, the laugh subsided.

Nathan looked in Talora's eyes and spoke the truth.

"I'm sorry, Talora," said Nathan.

Talora hugged Nathan, who broke down in her arms.

"Come on," she said, stroking the back of his head. "Let's go home."

426

BOTH Talora and Nathan, who was dragging the coat behind him the same way he used to drag around his "blanky," walked back upstairs to the first floor. Nathan had a few bruises on his side, but he could walk on his own.

Once they reached the first floor, they immediately checked on Morrison.

Morrison's eyes bolted open from Talora's presence.

"How bad is it?" asked Talora, as she tended to Morrison.

"How bad does it look?" Morrison returned, as he attempted to sit upright to examine his injuries.

Grimacing from the shot of pain, he was forced to lie back against the wall.

"Rest, Morrison," she said and pulled Morrison's flip phone from his pocket. "I'm going to call for an ambulance."

"An ambulance?" Morrison appeared insulted by the remark. "Fuck that! I can't pay for an ambulance!"

"Don't worry about the money?"

While holding his side, Morrison nodded at Nathan, who was standing behind Talora.

"Where the hell did the kid come from?"

"That's my brother, Nathan. You might remember him as Japhy."

"Japhy?" Morrison said heavily. Even talking caused him greater pain. "Am I supposed to know who that is?"

"You know who he is?"

Talora looked into Morrison's eyes.

Morrison had no other choice than to draw his eyes back to Nathan, particularly the coat he was holding in his hand.

In disbelief, he turned to Talora.

"It can't be," he uttered. "But how?"

"It's the coat," she said. "It has this kind of. . . power on people." She turned her shoulder and eyed Nathan. "But it doesn't have the power we share."

Both Talora and Nathan shared eye contact.

The bond, tighter than ever before.

In sudden revelation, she said to Morrison, "You can't tell anyone what happened here. You have to promise me, Morrison. You can't speak a word of this coat, of my brother. You trip and fell into the floor. I found you in the basement. I managed to carry you back upstairs." She opened Morrison's flip phone. "And that's when I called 9-1-1."

She stared into Morrison's eyes and waited for a response.

DINA'S car pulled up in front of the house as soon as the paramedics were pulling out the gurney from the back of the ambulance.

Before Dina could question the two paramedics, Talora was right there to explain everything to Dina. Nearly word-for-word, she told Dina what happened to Morrison, as if she was reading from a script. Dina couldn't have been more devastated by the news. Together, they rushed into the house alongside the paramedics and checked on Morrison while young Nathan watched with melancholy all of the drama unfold from the backseat of Talora's car.

When the paramedics finally arrived at the scene, they asked Morrison what happened. He digested the question and gathered his words. He even shot Talora a look that she'd never forget, one of great indignation and compliance, as if he was guilty yet, at the same time, not guilty, and his injuries, relevant yet irrelevant, were sole contributions of a verse that belonged to a song much greater than anything he had ever heard.

🕐

As the paramedics wheeled out Morrison from the house, he pulled Talora close and whispered in her ear, "You owe me one."

Talora kissed Morrison on the forehead and said back, "How about two?"

For the first time throughout Morrison's suffering, he managed to flash a hint of a smile on his face as if the two had a deeper understanding.

The paramedics loaded Morrison into the ambulance.

As Dina was about to step inside the ambulance with Morrison, Talora pulled her aside at the very last second.

"Thanks for everything, Dina," she said, catching Dina off guard.

With a puzzled expression, Dina tilted her head to the side.

"I'm going to take off now," Talora said again.

"Take off—where? Aren't you going to follow us to the hospital?"

"No," she said. "I'm going back home."

"Are you sure?"

Talora nodded.

Behind Dina, the paramedics were securing the gurney to the floor of the ambulance.

"Oh Talora," Dina said sadly and hugged Talora, "I hate to see you go. Of all times—"

"I'll be back. I promise."

Dina faced Talora.

"When people say they'll come back to Soy usually they're lying."

"No," Talora said, not batting an eyelash. "I'm tired of lying."

"Okay. Well, you have my number, right?"

"Yes."

"Okay, well—"

Once more, Talora hugged Dina and held onto her tightly.

Behind the two, the paramedic called out to Dina.

"A'ight," Talora said. "Go on."

"Bye," Dina said, wiping away the tears from her cheeks.

Talora said, "See ya."

"Hopefully sooner than later," Dina said, stepping into the back of the ambulance.

Talora waved goodbye to Dina as the paramedics shut the doors.

Then, she walked back to her car.

Once she stepped inside, Nathan leaned over the center console and asked his sister, "Was that Aunt Dina?"

"Yeah," Talora said pensively. "Why?"

"She's lost a lot of weight," said Nathan.

"Shut up, You," she said, as she teasingly pushed Nathan's head back, started the ignition, and drove away.

Before leaving Soy, Talora decided to drive back to Dina's house and pick up the old dog. Nathan confirmed that the dog was, in fact, Broot.

In a way, Talora didn't want any explanation as to how her dog, Broot, ended up in Soy.

A part of her had her suspicions.

And all fingers pointed at that little shit stain sitting in the passenger seat.

ON the drive home, Talora decided to take a different, more southern route, which took them directly through Kentucky. After an hour of driving through Kentucky, Talora found a rundown area, which looked like a tetanus paradise, along the side of the highway. Part of the building's structure was collapsed by what looked like a storm and from the look of old and rusty car parts scattered behind the closed-in fence behind the building, Talora could only assume that it used to be some kind of car repair or parts dealership. The place was most definitely deserted and happened to be away from a busy highway. She made an abrupt right turn. The sudden movement caused Nathan to wake up from his much-needed sleep.

She drove down a gravel road until she reached the rundown spot.

"What you doing?" asked Nathan.

Talora parked the car and glanced at the coat lying on the backseat in the rear view mirror.

"Talora?"

Talora moved her eyes to Nathan, who had turned the passenger seat into his own recliner by stretching out his feet onto the dashboard. He looked back at his sister as if she had been smoking something.

"I can't drive anymore until you tell me exactly where you found this coat?" Talora asked.

"I was wondering when you were going to ask me," Nathan said quietly.

"Where'd you find it, Nathan?" asked Talora.

Nathan sat up and straightened the seat.

"You wouldn't believe me if I told you—"

"—Right now, Nathan, you can tell me that the President of the United States is a Martian and the only reason why he's pushing the Mars Initiative on Congress is to bring all of his fellows Martians to Earth where they will inevitably take over the human race and turn us into their own hand puppets and you know what? I'd believe it!"

Nathan looked at Talora strangely.

"Nathan," she said with more urgency, "tell me. I deserve the truth."

"Me, Lee, Tom, and Acorn were messing around Hellerman Mall last fall—"
"

"—Hellerman Mall?" Talora said in a stern manner. "I thought Mom specifically told you not to play there anymore, Nathan! There were two homeless people who murdered there last year! It's only a matter of time before they tear down that place."

"Would you let me finish?"

"Sorry," Talora said, leaning back in her seat.

"Lee was goofing off and throwing rocks at everybody. I tripped over what I thought was a manikin. It was getting dark outside and it was hard to see. I took a closer look and realized it wasn't some manikin."

"What was it?" asked Talora.

"A dead body," he said finally. "But it wasn't human either. Lee handed me a clothing hanger and with the end of the clothing hanger, I pried open its mouth. That's when I saw the fangs. And it looked like it had been dead for some time. I mean, it was old-old. Like some ancient shit. And the smell, Lora, you wouldn't believe the smell?"

"What'd you do with it?"

"Nothing," Nathan said. "We just left it." He turned his shoulder and looked at the coat in the backseat. "I snuck out of the house that night and walked back to Hellerman Mall that night. It was like the coat was drawing me back."

"Well, I think you've proven to me that you're pretty damn good at sneaking around."

"What you mean?"

"Sneaking through the window in Dina's guestroom," Talora said, "trying to scare me."

"What you talking about? I didn't sneak through your window."

"Come on, Gnat," she said. "You did."

"I didn't."

"You're telling me you didn't burn Dina's photographs?"

Nathan glanced at his sister, the growing frustration on her face, and said, "It was me. I did it."

When he spoke, he didn't look her in the eye.

He just didn't.

Talora sighed off her frustration and spotted a gas station not too far away.

"Well," she said, "there's only one thing left to do."

⏲

AFTER the argument was finally settled, Talora drove to the gas station, filled an emergency gas can that she carried in the trunk of her Honda Civic, and bought a pack of matches from the convenient store.

Then, she drove back to the rundown building.

While Broot waited in the backseat, Talora and Nathan got out and walked around. It didn't take them long to find a rusty oil drum that looked like the perfect spot to burn the coat.

Once the coat was stuffed inside the oil drum, Talora dowsed it with gasoline and struck a match.

"Are you sure?" Nathan said before his sister dropped the flaming match into the oil drum.

She held the match in her hand and watched it slowly burn toward the tip of her finger.

"Right before you fell into the hole, I was holding one of the buttons from the coat in my hand," she said, zoning out. "Something happened. Something I can't explain. But I do remember the feeling that I felt. It happened so quickly. In the blink of an eye. And in that split second, I felt this darkness come over me as if, for a moment, I could see Death right before me. It was pulling me in, this darkness, and showing me this power, as if I could be something more than human. I never want anyone to harness that power ever again."

"But, I mean, you can literally be anybody you want. Someone who can be a positive influence on the world. The possibilities are endless!"

"You can be anybody you want and you chose to be some six foot five, funky haired guy who was named after a talking octopus in a cartoon primarily watched by stoners who spend their days getting stoned? I'm not judging or anything like that, but, seriously, little bro, you could've aimed higher." She shrugged, as if she was her drop-da-mike moment. "Jus' saying—"

"—Yeah," said Nathan. "So what?"

Right before the flame reached her fingertips, Talora dropped the match into the oil drum. The coat lit up with flames.

As Talora watched the coat burn, she noticed a piece of the coat was missing; in fact, it was the same area of the coat that had ripped against the flooring.

The flame started to change colors, turning fiery orange to pinkish-purple.

As the blue fire consumed the entire coat, Talora witnessed these gold flakes shedding from the coat as if the fire was igniting the last bit of the coat's energy, which, for a moment, reshaped and changed colors as well.

The coat morphed from a scaly reptilian hide to white silky skin to that same gold coat that Japhy Warchild wore. The coat finally returned back to its original old and raggedy nature. The gold flakes lifted from the blackened burnt coat and became finer, like gold dust floating in the air.

Nathan was left awestruck by the sight of the blue flame, as well as the particles of gold dust floating higher into the air.

Talora was left with even more doubts.

⟨⎮⟩

WEALTHY CEO Charley Schultz of Equinoxx Inc. was talking about the speech in New York City when Avanti started to drift from Schultz's words. He followed by making a joke about her former campaign manager, Sonny Mims, and the mutilated state of his body when it was discovered by a drifter outside Tent City.

"His story had *holes*," was Schultz's punch line.

The table of wealthy businessmen burst out in laughter, including the rest of Avanti's staff.

Surrounded by enough money to own an island, Avanti felt the bind released from her body—at least, most of it. For the first time ever since she was seventeen years old, Avanti could finally breath.

Schultz called out the governor's name.

Before he could finish her name "Washington," Avanti interrupted, "Will you excuse me?"

Avanti excused herself from the table, which didn't sit well with the other fat cats in the room.

🕐

AVANTI ditched the brunch at Connecticut Senator Daemon Batch's mansion and walked back to the town car where Joel was waiting in the driver's seat.

Vye was next to step inside the town car.

"Avanti," she said in confusion, "you want to tell me what that was all about back there?"

"Did I ever tell you the story about the time I was first bit?" asked Avanti in a trance-like state.

"I thought talking about that sort of thing was a no-no," Vye said.

"I was seventeen years old when I met whom I thought was the love of my life. He was everything I had ever dreamed of. Tall, strikingly handsome, charming, intelligent, *wealthy*, and most importantly, considerate. It was too bad I was underage. But, strangely, my age didn't bother him. He was much older than me; in fact, he said he was thirty-seven, which, I knew, even as a seventeen-year-old girl, was a lie."

She pulled her attention toward the window and looked at the mansion.

"Honestly," she said, "I didn't know how old he was. He may have looked as though he was thirty-seven. But, a part of me knew he was *much* older."

Avanti faced Vye.

"As in centuries older," she said blankly, then moved her attention back outside the tinted window. "After I was 'made,' he told me that I would be *his* for all eternity. We would share a bond, even in death. It wasn't until later I found out that he was filling my head with lies. He said that I was 'his one and only love.' I found out that there were others, hundreds, *thousands* of others. I was left with a broken heart. I thought to myself: I'd never find love that would replace the love I had for him. One day, an extremist organization that went by the name *Sons of Man*—a hate group—found out where he was nesting. Sons of Man had beaten him so badly that, eventually, he ended up shutting himself off from the rest of the world. Unable to recovery from his injuries, he simply disappeared. The moment he died, I felt his presence inside me, still there, thriving. A part of me was glad that he was no longer here. *But* another part of me knew the horror had just begun and that he would haunt me for the rest of my days. For many years, I searched for his remains in hopes to rid the awful curse, this 'signature' that he had bewitched on me. I believe someone out there has beaten me to the punch." Avanti's eyes started to water in both sadness and relief. "My own guardian angel. . . ."

"What was his name?" asked Vye. "The vamp who bit you?"

Avanti turned to Vye and said, "His name was Marius Ionescu."

432

AFTER having been on the road with his sister for over ten hours, Nathan reached the point where he was ready to open up. He turned down the volume on the radio and said to Talora, "There's something I need to tell you, Talora. Something I saw when I put on the coat. This, I dunno, this darkness. Like you spoke of."

Talora paid closer attention to her brother.

"Maybe the experience is different," he said. "Maybe it has something to do with the person who's wearing it. But, for me, it was like I was sharing my consciousness with someone who was sharing his consciousness of hundreds of people. I saw all these images. One of them stood out the most. It was this image of this guy, probably a couple of years older than me. I think he needed my help." He turned to his sister. "Did you see him?"

Talora shook her head.

"No," she said. "Like I said, it was only for a second. So, why do you think he needed your help? Help in what exactly?"

"I dunno," Nathan said. "But, in a way, I could see that he was crying out to me through his actions."

"What was he doing? Who was he?"

"His name was Ajax," Nathan said. "Or Jack. I'm not sure. All I do know is that, when I first put on the coat, I saw all whole bunch of images flash before my eyes and in all of those images, I saw another world, Lora, a world much darker than our own. It sounds insane, I know. But it's real. I know it."

"Insane, Gnat! Really!" Talora said hysterically. "You've been disguised as the lead singer of one of the hottest bands out there—or *once* hottest."

"Thanks," Nathan said, taking the comment as a compliment.

"So," Talora said, "who was this Ajax guy?"

"You sure you really want to know?" asked Nathan.

Talora thought about her next response.

⊘

DINA returned to the house after spending a couple of hours at the hospital visiting Morrison.

Mindful of her surroundings, as well as watching her every step, Dina made her way to the hole next to the foyer. She pushed aside the sheet of plywood and examined the dangerous hole in the floor with a flashlight.

Intrigued by her discovery, she shone the flashlight on a piece of cloth hanging from a jagged plank of wood protruding from the hole. Careful not to fall into the hole, she grabbed a measuring tape and extended it outward to about thirty or so inches, then locked it.

With the end of the measuring tape, Dina lifted the piece of old clothing material and as carefully as she could, moved the measuring tape away from the hole in the floor.

Relieved, she retracted the measuring tape and picked up the frayed piece of ancient cloth off the floor. She held the cloth up to her face and couldn't help but think how nice of a scarf it would make for Vladimir.

TALORA and Nathan decided to make a much-needed pit stop at a rest stop once they crossed into New York State.

They both went at the same time and planned to met back in front of the water fountain, Talora heading into the women's restroom while Nathan heading into the men's restroom.

As Talora was finishing up in the last stall, she heard a *swooping* noise coming from the outside. She wiped herself clean, flushed the toilet, and stepped outside the stall with a sense that there was someone—or something—else inside the restroom. A slight draft was blowing into the restroom, yet the air condition was no longer running.

Cautiously, Talora walked to the sink to wash her hands under the faucet. As she was about to run the water, she came across a single white rose lying on the edge of the sink. She picked up the angelic white rose and held it underneath her nose. The smell reminded her of home. Immediately, Talora felt as though, despite the creep-factor, she wasn't alone.

A part of her was *finally* at peace.

And optimistic about the future.

"Those who fear him or hold his name in reverence speak his name as though he was no different than a god. And for those unfortunate to find themselves between the grip of his bite, it's the very last word uttered from a dying breath."

— THE CHRONICLES OF KRILLISH

"New Opening"

A ruthless gang of insects, which, on the streets of Leatherwood, had a rap as being a part of one of the most dangerous crime syndicates called "snatchers," was chasing after a well-known crosser of the High Order who went by the name "Tooth Fairy" when all of a sudden a rare canister made from gold slipped from his furry, stick-like finger grip.

The Tooth Fairy recovered the fumble, picked up the precious container, and checked its condition for any damages; first inspecting for any leaks or breaks along the seal and then, once finding none, the crosser continued his daring escape from the wannabe snatchers, who were closing in on his tail. The Tooth Fairy managed to lose the gang in the Tattered Lands once he left the city.

By the skin of his fangs, the Tooth Fairy made it out of Leatherwood and crossed a crumbly, pothole-ridden highway where a rust-covered, overturned sign read "Welcome to Leatherwood: Your *Last Stop*." The Tooth Fairy cut through a red-washed desert and eventually made it to Hill Falls River, which snaked its way around the mountainscapes surrounding the city, and sought cover inside a drain where he spent a couple of hot minutes catching his breath while three emaciated, alien-framed snatchers were lingering on top of a hill.

Once he caught his breath, the Tooth Fairy made his way through the drain. Having to stop several times to tuck and readjust his broad pointy wings, which were folded underneath the worn cloak, in order to squeeze his body through the tight space, the Tooth Fairy ended up crawling through yet a smaller tunnel, which led to a sewer system.

Finally, the Tooth Fairy emerged from the manhole and found himself on Another Street in Another World.

With his cloak worn more securely, the Tooth Fairy cut through the backyard of an older house and counted each and every single footstep he made.

Making sure to not only conceal his dark scaly face, but also the golden container cradled in his arm, the Tooth Fairy exited from the once country-club type neighborhood and walked through the entire night.

Avoiding cars and all human life, the Tooth Fairy trekked through thick woods and prickly vegetation until he reached a small two-story house with a barn settled along the hump of the postcard-like countryside. He snuck onto the owner's property and stole a pickaxe, as well as a shovel from the barn. He made sure to keep the last number in his mind before his detour, which was four thousand and thirty-two steps, which was approximately two miles of walking.

Then, after he grabbed the tools he needed, the Tooth Fairy walked back to the exact spot where he made his last detour and continued counting once more.

The Tooth Fairy ended up walking an extra two thousand steps, which put him in that three-mile mark.

The Tooth Fairy stopped on the number six thousand and some change.

Repeating that number "six thousand" back to himself, the Tooth Fairy dropped the tools on the ground. There, in the dark woods, the Tooth Fairy began to dig. He dug through the warmer side of midnight. Once he finished digging the hole, the Tooth Fairy placed the special container inside. Then, he filled the hole back up with dirt. Which didn't take as long as digging the hole.

After the container was buried, the Tooth Fairy exited the woods and wandered back through the countryside where he spotted a billboard alongside the highway.

The gaudy billboard was promoting a band, *Stuffed Animalz*, which was performing tonight at Fairway Coliseum in Atlanta. The Tooth Fairy wasn't that far from the coliseum and a part of him knew that he still had time, even though it felt as if he didn't.

Guided by an innate hunger, The Tooth Fairy arrived in Atlanta just as Stuffed Animalz was finishing up their final song in a thirty minute-plus encore. It was on the cooler side of midnight, and the Tooth Fairy found himself on another level of exhaustion; however, the worn and hungry crosser powered through the night in hopes of finding his new host.

Once the Tooth Fairy reached the stadium, the band, Stuffed Animalz, was hanging outside their tour bus.

Sure enough, the Tooth Fairy found the right host—The One.

And he called himself Japhy Warchild, the lead singer of the band.

Japhy happened to be sleeping while the Tooth Fairy snuck onto the bus. There, passed out in a bed in the back of the bus, the Tooth Fairy found Japhy's arm flopped over the side of the bed with an empty bottle of Jack Daniels on the floor. The Tooth Fairy tiptoed toward Japhy and got close enough to Japhy to smell his whiskey-flavored breath. The Tooth Fairy opened up his scaly mouth, releasing a bright red light from inside his mouth. The red beam of light shot into Japhy's mouth, causing him to stir from his inebriated state.

Once the red light was drained from the Tooth Fairy, his body suddenly shriveled up like an old plant.

Two weeks later, when drummer of Stuffed Animalz, Tommy Bango, walked onto the tour bus to catch a nap before the concert, he was struck by one of the god-awful smells inside the bus. Tommy tracked the smell to Japhy's bed where underneath he found a shriveled up bat-like creature about the size of a baby with scaly skin and papery folded up wings, which were so crisp and brittle they looked as if they could crack like dried maple leaves in winter from the slightest bungle.

He kept the dead creature all to himself and once the tour had wrapped for the season, transferred it from an ice cooler to an old pickle jar that he had lying around the kitchen and planned never to tell a soul about it.

Except for his wife, that is, who had recently returned home from visiting her mother and two brothers in Thailand.

She could've walked in on her husband doing worst things.

—

"Within An Inch"

I'm sure you already know my name and the story behind the name.

If you don't, then I advise you to stop reading right now, go outside, and enjoy the weather or something. . . well, a'ight then. Don't say I didn't warn you.

Now that we have all that out of the way, let me tell you what actually happened to me with no chase or filter. I'll do my best to keep it all in present tense, so it's easier not only for everybody to understand, but also for myself included.

As I've come to realize these past few hours while lying in one of the most uncomfortable beds with three broken ribs which makes the air feel sharp, a severed spleen, a bruised kidney, a broken wrist, a black eye that's roughly the size of a grapefruit, and enough stitches along the left side of my face and forehead to run a toy train, life is *way* too short. No question.

One day, you're born into the world.

Then, the very next, you can't wait to get the hell out, as if life has become one never-ending after party and you can't wait to call it a night and crash in your bed—at least one nicer than a hospital bed which makes sleeping on a hardwood floor sound doable.

What I've come to learn is that it's in those fine moments between speaking your first word or taking your first step that life offers the tools to survive even though it's those moments that seem like a haze, some *fragmented* memory stolen from the shattered glass of another person's memory. I've always wondered what it'd be like to travel back in time and relive all those fine moments that I took for granted with a greater transparent knowledge, recognize the most crucial events that shaped me, as well as the people who steered me toward my final destination.

Which can only beg the question: Was this my path all along?

Let's rewind and start where my story—my real one, that is—all began.

The location: A Burger King parking lot outside Downtown Atlanta. That's me standing right there, what boomers would call a 'punk' dressed in an over-sized Raw Dog T-shirt and black jeans that look two sizes too short.

The short-looking guy I'm buying a pound of red rocks from is Ant, my VP-23 dealer; his real name is Anthony—not sure what his last name is, but I think it rhymes with Scalia. Ant is well known for coming off as your every-day pocket-sized gangster who tries to make up for his *small* size with his *big* mouth. I don't trust Ant, never have. For one, Ant never looks me in the eye; and two, he's always wearing way too much cologne. On the real, though, never ever trust a dude who wears a lot of cologne. It means his trying to cover up something.

Today, Ant's hooking me up with a pound of red rocks; claims it came from, of all places, Seattle, where a vamp's blood is richer than Log Cabin syrup, but I know he's just trying to promote what he calls an ill product.

I call Ant out on his lie, pull out the same exact rock I bought from a hush-hush cat at New Way, who happens to be close pals with Ant's supplier.

I name my price, enforce it. He has no other option than to cave, like the little ant he is. The only reason as to why I still keep coming back to Ant is for certain scenarios such as these. Most of the time, I take whatever Ant can sell, then break it off in eighths and gram bags, scatter it around to blood sniffers and VP-23 junkies—on occasion, cut it with my own blood that I keep on ice—sell it cheap, so that way they can depend on me, pocket the profits, then go home A-okay. Every now and then, I exploit Ant, call him out with a low price and a firm hand but more of a firm hand—balance the scales, if you will. It's a push-and-pull type of relationship. I know, with a product such as this, I can turn it around, sell it to uppity greenbacks at Plymouth, and make four times the profit.

Once I part ways with Ant, I hide the pound of red rocks under the owner's manual inside the glove box of my Mercedes. I've never really been the type who shits where he eats. But I'm starving.

At the very last second, I change my mind and decide to drive into Atlanta.

I'm not too far from Café Pearl, which have these bean burritos that, sur-prisingly enough, manage to tame the hunger. I usually buy three of them. Eat one. Then save the other two for whenever the hunger returns.

Once I arrive at Pearl, the place is spilling over with the right kind of crowd, hipsters and every flavor of eco-friendly, earth-conscious college kids whose blood is about as bitter as stomach bile. There's a good reason as to why most vamps don't bother with somebody who'd rather enjoy a kale salad opposed to a greasy hamburger. At the last second, I decide to order four bur-ritos, not three.

As I'm waiting on my food, I get a couple of looks from the lounge area. The same looks coming from the same people who claw their way onto the TV or the Internet to talk about how much they care and all about ones like me. But, when they see one—or at least, think they see one—up close and personal, they turn to jello and all of a sudden, they turn into mutes with serious eye problems. Most of the time, they stare, as if they're getting a rare glimpse at an exotic bird. Others struggle to meet my gaze in fear that they may never return. I'm good at hiding myself; and every now and then, especially when the hunger strikes, my mask starts to slip from my face.

The head cashier calls out my name and does so with a slight tremble in her voice.

I grab my order from her shaky hand. The color drains from her face, leaving it pale and ghostly. I've been coming here for the past couple of months to pick up bean burritos. Yet, every time I pick up food, her look is always the same.

I leave Pearl with the bag of food and walk back to my car when I catch them in the corner of my eye.

I immediately sense the danger before my eyes even cross their path.

In a steady glance, I count five of them altogether, all of who are hanging out around my Mercedes. One is peeking through the passenger's window while another one is keeping lookout like the soldier he is. Clearly, they're after my stash. Maybe junkies or even buddies of Ant's who are trying to rip me off. My initial reaction is to beat my chest and protect what belongs to me.

As I'm about to yell at them, hoping the loudness of my voice will scare them off, a sixth man emerges from around the corner.

Immediately, I recognize the masquerade mask on his face.

Then, I realize they're *not* after my stash.

I do a U-turn and take post in an alleyway next to Café Pearl.

As soon as I walk away, I spot a cruiser with a K-9 unit patrolling the street. Over these past couple of years, there's been an uptick in K-9 units. For one, it's much easier to track red rocks, vamp drops, Holy Bombs, Dracula's Blood, or the gazillion types of drugs on the street with werewolf's third cousin. And two, as of lately, it's hard to find a cop—a human cop, that is—who knows when to turn the other cheek on crime. Nowadays, with cop killings on the rise, you couldn't walk too far without finding a cop who's gunning for vamps. I often wonder if they're any different, a member of Sons of Man and an officer of the law. It's fair to say that nothing is black and white anymore. You're either living or you're not.

I peek around the building and watch the gang scatter from the sight of the cruiser.

I wait for a couple of tense minutes until the cruiser eventually drives past my car.

Knowing that Sons of Man may still be hanging around in the shadows and waiting for the right opportunity to ambush me, I take the alleyway in hopes that they'll be gone by the time I reach my car.

I walk around the block and end up stopping at one of Atlanta's oldest record stores. I kill time browsing through old vinyl. My food's starting to get cold and the hunger grips me like a vise. I can't take my eyes off each person in the record store. The veins in their necks or wrist pulse underneath their flesh, that tiny beat calling out to me and causing my mouth to salivate.

With the hunger intensifying, I walk back to my car and ready the car key.

I take yet another alleyway, which leads directly to my car. I make it halfway through the alleyway until I spot a couple of dark figures emerging from behind a set of stairs and shadowy doorways.

I check my six. Two more emerge from the shadows.

Then, in front of me, two more emerge.

I'm completely surrounded.

I count five of them, like before; however, I don't see the other one until it's already too late.

The blood rushes through my veins as I'm blindsided by a baton. I fall to the ground and recover from the daze.

Before I can stand up, I'm hit yet again from behind. The third blow to my ribs knocks the wind out of me. I fall yet again to the ground, shield my face with my arms, and curl my body into a ball.

Each one hovers over my body and starts kicking me. Throughout the fury of swinging arms, as well as snapshots of oncoming brass knuckled fists and bloody white laces, and sinister faces, I witness the same guy with a masquerade mask from earlier standing at the edge of the alleyway.

As I fade in and out of consciousness, another wannabe gangster kneels over my body, sticks his face in my grill, and flashes that elusive *owl eyes* symbol over his face.

Owls eat bats, brutha!

He backs away while the others beat me within an inch of my life.

—

"Compromises"

Ajax?

Ajax?

You awake?

Brass knuckled fists and bloody white laces grip me like violence.

I block out the violence and follow the voice to the one face that I don't want to see right now. She's sitting by my bedside and has a concerned look etched on her face.

I prepare myself for a soon-to-be lecture by mentally searching for a legitimate excuse as to what I was doing downtown, but knowing her, she's already pried through my thoughts and sorted through them like a sock drawer.

Behind her, a three-man entourage is keeping guard by the doorway.

I recognize Avanti's most loyal of loyalists, Joel, who looks as if he eats babies for breakfast, standing among the entourage.

Joel, give us the room?

Yes, ma'am.

Once Joel and the other security guards are gone, Avanti looks at me the way a cop would look at a suspect; and all of a sudden, that dim fluorescent light behind me becomes hotter along the surface of my skin.

How are you feeling?

I want to lash out at her. Question her for even questioning me: What kind of question is that?

But I'm in no condition.

I just got my ass kicked. What'd you think?

Local PD says it might've been a mugging. When they discovered you, they couldn't find any ID or wallet—

—It wasn't a mugging.

Who were they? Did you get a look at their faces?

Since my left arm is wrapped in a cast, I manage to raise my right arm to my face. I form both my thumb and index finger into a perfect circle and then spread out my other three fingers, making my hand look like the 'okay' symbol. I hold the symbol up to my right eye; however, I'm unable to flip the owl symbol upside down due to the IV attached to the back of my hand. Not like I need to do that anyway. She already knows the symbol before I even show her.

Are you sure it was them?

Yeah. Pretty sure. How'd they know who I was anyway?

Maybe they recognize you from the news. You know, with me trying to win back votes from the community, those who have any affiliation with Sons of Man haven't been my greatest supporters lately—

—Stop!

Stop what?

Stop treating me like I'm one of them, Avanti. You may be able to fool them about who you really are. So, just drop the whole act and speak to me like you're speaking to your son.

She looks around the room, as if she's scanning for ears—and eyes.

I've heard there's a brand new technology making waves on the black market. Apparently, it's a device that's able to pick up these certain heat signatures when unprotected skin is exposed to sunlight.

Serious? That's bullshit.

All right. Enough, Ajax. I'm trying to help you out here. I mean what were you thinking? Were you not wearing any sunscreen?

Sunscreen? Who gives a shit about sunscreen?

Avanti asks me if I saw any of them wearing masks.

One.

By any chance, did you see what color it was?

Color? What does it matter what color he was wearing?

It matters.

Red, I think.

She looks away, her eyes glazed over in thought.

Red's pretty high up for an initiation—

—And that's what you think this was, some initiation?

You may not want to hear this, but they targeted you, Ajax. They know who you are—and *what* you are. You think by dressing like this it's supposed to deter people like that? Every argument she starts always begins and ends with my taste in fashion. I know it's all the piercings that really bother her. She backs off for a moment to gather her thoughts, as if she doesn't want to say or do anything more that she may regret. Most of the lower rank members who monitor initiations are yellows or greens. But *not* red.

And I'm sure you don't want anyone finding out what happened. You know, 'cuz that would make things. . . complicated for you and your constituents.

Why are you doing this, Ajax? You know I have responsibilities. You knew how things were going to be when I first signed up for this job. I'm trying to protect you, Ajax, not hurt you. Now, you're putting me in a position where I'm going to have to lie about what happened—

—Lie? Everything you've said to these people is a lie! If you wanted to protect me, then you'd have those mask-wearing fools off the streets a long time ago. Their time is coming. Believe me.

Oh, yeah! And what? You're going to take them on all by yourself? You're lucky they didn't kill you, Ajax! You have to understand that if you get rid of one of these groups, then another one is going to pop up under a different name, a different look, and then, we're back to square one.

Whose side are you own, Avanti? By *not* standing up to these people, you're basically advocating what they're doing to your kind—

—They're your kind too, Ajax. Don't you forget about that?

You're right. They are my kind all thanks to you. It's all I think about! Yet, I want nothing to do with them? I WANT TO FORGET ABOUT THEM! But as much as I want to, I can't!

I had one of my men search your car, Ajax. He said he found contraband inside. Not only that, he found drugs in your glove compartment. You know what I'm talking about, so don't you dare act like you don't. What in the hell were you doing with red rocks, Ajax?

It wasn't mine. I was holding it for a friend.

A friend?

She nearly laughs from the comment.

How can I lie to someone who's a master at telling lies?

Not only that, someone who can see my every thought?

Have you ever seen a greenback on VP-23? They actually think that they can take me in a fight. It's hilarious, that's what it is.

Beating up on innocent kids at your school isn't challenging enough? Now, you're going after junkies from Plymouth in order to do what exactly, level the playing field? Is that it? I thought you were done with all of this nonsense, Ajax.

I am.

Like I haven't heard that one before. When are you ever going to learn? After what happened with that kid at your school, you said you were done fighting. Don't you see what's going on here? This kind of destructive behavior is going to get you killed—

—*Good.*

It's only a matter of time before you start a fight with the wrong person. You thought Sons of Man were tough. There are people out there who make Sons of Man look like pushovers.

FYI, I didn't pick that fight. I was jumped by cowards—

—I don't care, Ajax! You have to be smarter than this!

I'm tired of living like this! All I have is this evil inside me! My emotions get the best of me and I find myself retracing my words. You know the whole time while they were on top of me all I can think about was the *hunger* and how much I wanted to drain each and every one of them. How do you think that would make you look? Because the last thing I'd ever want to do is mess up your political career!

Based on your actions, I'd say you're almost there—

444

—It's getting worse, you know? These urges to feed. It's gotten to the point where it's all I ever think about.

My confession doesn't sit well with Avanti; however, I can't control the tears anymore. I cry blood.

I just want it to be over. . .

She doesn't even bat an eyelash.

I'm sure you've heard the rumors about me possibly throwing my hat into the 2020 election. The higher-ups have started talking. Word is that they've already given up on next year's election and they're planning on getting behind a younger candidate—me—a supposed dark horse whom they believe will have the best shot at beating Rhodes. That is, if they can't find a way to impeach him from office before the 2020 election.

You're serious? That's five years away!

It's only a matter of time before I start making waves as a potential candidate, Ajax; and you, of all people, know you have to build the momentum sooner than later. And you thought the scrutiny is bad right now. It'll only get worse.

That is, if you choose to run. Right?

Avanti doesn't respond—at least, not with any words.

I find myself mimicking those very self-righteous kids who stare at me from a distance.

Right?

She wipes the tears from my face.

Somehow, I already know what she's going to ask me before it even leaves her mouth.

What if I told you there was a way out of this, a way that would benefit the both of us?

You mean, benefit you.

No.

Her face darkens.

Her eyes sharpen.

The *both* of us. I hate seeing you like this, Ajax. I really do. I can't imagine how it must feel to carry around such a burden. Forgive me, Ajax. Sometimes, I forget that the gene affects you differently. And, if I were given a choice, then I would give you my powers instead of His. But I know, as hard as I try, there are just some wounds I cannot heal.

She touches the crook of my arm just above the cast on my wrist.

The pain slowly vanishes from the bones in my left wrist. I'm able to move around my sweaty wrist inside the cast, as well as the tips of my fingers in my left hand; however, the other pain is *still* there, gnawing at me, throbbing well beyond the bones. I'm able to breath better. I'm even able to see Avanti more clearly out of my left eye, which was once swollen shut.

I catch the tears in the corners of my eyes.

What do I have to do?

Once more, Avanti doesn't even bat an eyelash.

You have to die.

Behind Avanti, I witness a shadow creeping along the side of the wall next to the bathroom. Sitting in the dark corner of the hospital room is Avanti's cryptic aide, Vye. She's wearing all black, a deep black that matches the very shadows that the furniture casts. She removes a pair of sunglasses from her narrow face and leans forward into the pale light, revealing enough of herself for me to identify her. Was she really sitting there this entire time?

What a sneaky bitch.

—

"Slight Fear of Tight Spaces"

One second, it's after dark and I'm *slowly* opening the front door of my house and then, the next, I'm stepping outside into the night darkness. Yet, I'm not walking along the front porch of the house. I'm walking through a dark tunnel in a sewer.

I cover my nose with the wrinkled collar of my shirt to block out the sweaty smells of feces and burnt cabbage. My grip loosens from the sight of a tall, athletic framed-figure walking in front of me, causing the stretched collar to fall from my face. Right then, I don't care about the smell.

With question, I follow the stranger further into the sewers.

Curiosity overwhelms me and forces me to shake my slacked-jaw gape.

After witnessing the reptilian costume, I realize it's a person dressed in a full-body suit of what looks similar to a crocodile or lizard, only it's more slender and humanly designed with not only a short, stubby turtle-like tail opposed to a long tail whipping to and fro, but also two arms that are similar in the shape, as well as size of a human opposed to the small, baby-like arms of a crocodile. Most importantly, the suit is worn as tight as skin. Left in a momentary blip of awe, I can't help but admire how real the costume looks.

Like dreams are known to do, I skip around in time and find myself back in my bedroom sketching a similar creature in my notebook. I can't help but think how eerily familiar the costume looks to that same sketch in my notebook.

I'm back in the dark, smelly sewer.

Walking.

The person glances over his or her shoulder—I'm leaning toward him based on his wide shoulders and toned core. He looks at me with these sharp eyes of a reptile, his head looking more like an iguana rather than a crocodile; his spiky reptilian hair bouncing from side to side in his swivel of a head-turn. The detail alone of the costume and mask is exceptional, especially with that dim, yellowish lighting from the streets above which brings out his sharp cheekbones. The Halloween costume isn't anything close to what you'd find at a Party City, but more so Hollywood-level in its masterful design. Doubts creep in like poison, and I start to believe that it's not a costume or a mask but something else.

My eyes move from the scaly face and move toward a small dark hole at the edge of the tunnel.

All of a sudden, the insides of body churn and everything about me tightens.

"Or was it?"

With my face dripping with beads of sweat, I wake up punching and kicking.

Once I find myself back in my old bed, I try to piece together the dream. But it felt so real, like it *actually* happened. The last images I can remember are the pitch-black darkness spreading over the entire neighborhood street, then a mob of pale, emaciated, rabid people viciously attacking me. The more I think about it, I come to a conclusion that these people, like that man-iguana in the sewer, weren't people—at least not people from my world, that is.

I immediately check both my wrists, particular my right wrist.

Another image comes to me.

I see myself wearing a strange watch made up of a gold band and a glass saucer-shaped ball filled with blood.

I was wearing the watch.

But now, not wearing it.

The sight of not wearing a watch makes me relieved. I don't know why I'm relieved, but I feel more at ease knowing it's no longer attached to my wrist.

I roll out of bed and crack open the blinds.

The warmth of sunlight brings about a comfort, which I haven't felt in a long time, even though, at this very moment, time seems all but irrelevant.

I walk to the closed door and as I'm about to reach for the door handle, I take a step forward as if I'm about to walk directly *through* the door.

My big toe stubs the door before the side of my forehead. I'm not sure if I'm still trying to wake up or what, but I don't think much about where such a radical idea would come from.

I open the door and exit my bedroom where I'm welcomed by a hint of cinnamon raisin toast, as well as coffee in the air.

The smells, like the sun, bring about a cartoon-like comfort.

Before heading downstairs, I walk into the hallway bathroom and relieve myself. As I'm about to flush the toilet, I'm drawn to the bathtub.

Forgetting to flush, I walk to the bathtub and look inside. I kneel down and take a closer look at the inside of the tub. I discover a smudge of dry blood caked onto the edge of the drain.

As with the bedroom door, I don't exactly know why I'm drawn to these certain ideas. All I can think about is that maybe it has something to do with my dream.

As I stand back upright, I come across yet another smudge of dry and crusty blood on the floor. Then another one by the doorway, which doesn't look like a smudge at all but more so a drop. I follow another blood drop on the floor next to the top of the landing.

Searching for more blood, I walk downstairs.

I find yet another one in the foyer.

As I'm about to head outside, I hear Tameron's voice behind me. Tameron's standing with her arms planted on her hips at the edge of the kitchen.

Where've you been? I've been calling your name for the past ten minutes.

Ah. . .

The phlegm grinds in the base of my throat. The words feel lost and broken.

. . . I just woke up. What time is it?

Time for school, that's what time it is. Well, don't just stand there. Come on and grab some breakfast. She waves me into the kitchen. You're already running late as it is.

I follow Tameron into the kitchen where a box of Dragon Puffs is sitting on the kitchen table.

Where's Avanti?

Your mother had to leave early this morning for an important meeting. She has an extremely busy schedule today. You know, she's going to be meeting with the Bulldogs later this afternoon. I told your mother to get me an autograph from one player in particular. Not to mention any names but he happens to be the starting power forward.

Okay. I don't keep up with sports. So, I have absolutely no clue who you're talking about.

Someone woke up on the wrong side of the bed.

No. I just have no interest in talking about basketball.

I thought you liked basketball.

Ignoring Tameron, I grab a bowl from the top cabinet, as well as a carton of soymilk from the refrigerator, and take a sit at the table.

Tameron lets me eat in peace and steps out of the kitchen to finish folding a load of clean clothes in the laundry room.

I pour myself a bowl of Dragon Puffs and as I'm trying to piece together the dream I had last night, I draw my attention toward the kitchen countertop where a TV is playing a wildlife show on the *National Geographic* channel.

On the TV, a crocodile is attacking a wildebeest along the Nile River in Africa. As the crocodile takes a chomp out of the wildebeest, I take a bite of my cereal. The chewing strengthens my train of thought.

Then, it all comes back to me.

Or was it?

—

"Call me Detective Robert Washington"

I only take a couple of bites of my cereal before I lose my appetite.

I rush back upstairs to my bedroom. I close the door behind me and search my bedroom for things, items, and artifacts that will help refresh my memory as to what's going on with me, including drawers and my desk. I search underneath my bed but don't find anything that grabs my eye. I check my bookshelf. I even remove a bunch of books from the shelf and skim through the pages to make sure I didn't leave anything behind, a note or whatever.

Lastly, I check the inside of my closet. A white plastic bag lying on the floor grabs me. Inside are bloody clothes. Two flashes of images come at me.

One, I'm in a sketchy alleyway, getting my ass whooped by an anti-vampire hate group known as Sons of Man.

Two, I'm on the street next to an open manhole, getting attacked by a mob of sickly, spiny creatures.

I block out the second set of images—which happened at night—then focus on the first images, which happened in broad daylight.

As I concentrate on the past events, I'm able to get a clearer, crisper view of what happened.

I was jumped by Sons of Man.

And the clothes in my hands are the same exact clothes I was wearing when I was jumped.

I remember bringing home the clothes in a bag from the hospital.

Avanti asked me if she wanted to wash the clothes.

But I said no.

I wanted to keep them as a reminder.

I hear Tameron calling my name several times from downstairs. I place the clothes back into the bag and then close the closet.

Ajax! You're going to be late!

I exit my bedroom and find Tameron standing at the base of the stairs.

This time, both her arms are folded across her chest. Her weight is shifted to one side of her body, and she has the look of a woman who's three foot taps away from being upset.

You know what? I'm not feeling too well. I. . . I was thinking about staying home today.

Uh-ah. No way, mister. Not on my watch.

But I said I don't feel well.

Tough stuff, Ajax. Your mother specifically told me that you couldn't afford to miss any more days of school.

But Tameron, I'm sick!

Sick my butt. I don't want to hear anything of it. You're going to school today whether you like it or not. Now, get yourself ready. And since you're so sick today, I'll drive you to school.

Brent usually picks me up.

Not today, he *ain't*.

Now, I realize, Tameron's upset with me.

—

"Not Quite Right"

Tameron hardly says a word to me during the entire drive.

It's not until Tameron reaches for the radio that I start to freak out. Her hand is *not* her hand. Her hand isn't even human! Instead, her hand is twice the size of any normal human hand. Not only that, her skin is incredibly smooth and scaly— similar to the creature from a dream—or, *Was it some guy dressed in a costume?*

I look at Tameron, who looks no different than she looked two seconds ago. Then, I look back at her hand and it's look like any other normal hand.

You okay?

I try to make sense as to what I just saw but come up as empty as an old paint bucket that's been left to bake in the sun.

Ajax?

Yeah. I come at Tameron harder than I'd like. I sound snappish. So, I try to mellow my tone. Fine.

Something's bothering you, Ajax. I can sense it.

I'm fine.

The heat rises in me. I just want her to shut up and drive.

You know, you can talk to me, right?

It's nothing. I just have a headache. That's all.

You want an Ibuprofen?

No, Tameron. I don't want an Ibuprofen.

Okay. Jus' trying to help.

I switch off the radio and delve deep back into my thoughts.

Was it?

It had to be.

"New Way"

Tameron drops me off in front of New Way Academy.

As I grab my bookbag from the backseat, she reminds that I need to be on my best behavior and that my mother pulled a lot of strings to reduce my suspension. I completely forgot about the suspension and what I did to Cory.

Since there are no tardy bells, like any typical high school, I take my time and make sure to avoid him—that is, if he shows up. Knowing Cory, he'd show up at school the very second he was released from the AMC. He was probably wearing his stitches proudly, like it was the latest trend, trying to get warm hugs and likes.

Most of the students have left the courtyard and have already made their way to class, although the remaining stragglers who walk past me look at me with the most sour expressions on their faces, as if I embody the traits of tart candy and just looking at me is no different than tasting me. I pass a couple of students who look more timid than disgusted. I admit that I'm used to the looks.

Outside the courtyard, Brent surprises me from behind. Brent's the last face I want to see right now. I keep walking in hopes that he'll walk the other way, considering his first class is located on the other side of the building. He keeps pace and walks with me. The first name out of his mouth is none other than Cory.

Surprised to see you, brutha.

The word *brutha* has me flinching. All I can think about is that bird-looking vampire hater towering over me.

Owls eat bats.

I snap from my trance.

I heard you messed him up good, man! Who's 'woke' now? You know, it's about time someone finally put that little bald-headed drama queen in his place. I heard he got seventeen stitches.

I'm not supposed to talk about it.

Brent waves off my comment, as if nothing I'm saying is registering.

450

You shouldn't be ashamed of what you did, Ajax. You did a lot of people a favor—

—And FYI, it was thirteen stitches, not seventeen.

Whatever, Ajax. I'll take any stitches. I'm just glad you're back. You were acting weird the other day.

Weird?

Again, my comment goes in one ear and out the other.

Man, Ajax! I still can't believe you put that friggin' closet-Nazi in the hospital. I heard while he was at the AMC nurses were spitting in his food.

Where'd you hear that?

Tyrone's older sister works at the AMC. She's a nurse practitioner.

He was only there for like a day, Brent. What's the big deal?

All I know, man: your ass is lucky. I wish my mom were governor. I mean, you can practically get away with murder.

Shut the hell up, Brent.

Whoa! Easy, Ajax. Don't push me, man.

Like you're one to talk, Brent. You'd be expelled if it weren't for your dad being the principal.

Not true. He treats me no differently than any other student.

Yeah. Keep telling yourself that.

I arrive at my classroom.

As Brent and I are about to part ways, Brent points out, of all people, Cory, who's standing outside Forensics. He's no longer wearing thirteen stitches on the side of his face; however, the cut left a noticeable scar.

Cory shoots a glance my way and immediately walks into the classroom.

What a bitch?

Dude. I'm not trying to start shit.

What? You agree he's a bitch, right?

Don't you have somewhere to be right now?

That's right. I completely forgot, man. I'll catch up with you later.

In the reflection of the glass, I witness Brent—or at least, someone who looks like Brent—his face all bloody and cut up, his jaw gone, torn off; his body badly maimed, clothes marked with tire tracks; he appears as if he's gotten run over by a truck. With part of his arm dangling along the threads of cartilage, Brent's reflection dawdles away.

I turn away from the window and glance at Brent, who's taking his good easy time to class. He's neither injured nor maimed, as the reflection shows me.

Pushing away the strange thought, I step into the lab, which is already full of students. I take my seat at an empty computer in the very back of the lab and pull out my screen-printing textbook from my bookbag.

After about thirty-minutes into my design, which is made to look like a kind of cut-and-paste type collage of iconic movie monsters as well as slashers, including Freddy Krueger, Chucky, Jason, Michael Myers, Candyman, *The Thing*, Pinhead and those other three from *Hellraiser*, Brundlefly, the zombie in *Day of the Dead*, the mutated, pink-drenched Dr. Edward Pretorius in *From Beyond*, and then last but not least, the 'Slasher of ALL Slashers,' Don Juan, aka 'The Wolf' from the horror flick, *The Effigy*, I pull my eyes away from the screen, hoping it will rid a sudden dizzy spell.

Then, as I continue to tweak the title 'WITCH-HOP' along the top of my design, the dizzy spell returns and forces me to look elsewhere.

Outside the lab, the same reptilian-like creature is walking down the hall-way. Mr. Steyer, one of the many bad actors who uses his teaching position as a way to conceal his true identity, makes his rounds around the lab. He stops at each computer to give a few pointers to students. He spends the most time at Awny's computer, and it's pretty clear to those who've been paying the least amount of attention that Mr. Steyer appears closer to Awny than the other students, well, some of them. But I know he has his reasons why he tends to be more available to particularly female students. Mr. Steyer is aware that I'm aware he has two phones. Unless you're a drug dealer, who else carries around two phones? Once I caught Mr. Steyer red-handed—no pun intended—scrolling through porn on his phone. And, from the looks, the girls in the photos were clearly *not* of age.

Knowing that Mr. Steyer is more than likely going to spend even more time on Teagan, another one of his favs who's sitting two computers away from Awny, I take my attention off Mr. Steyer and track down the creature once more, only to find him standing behind the door of the lab, peering inside.

Mr. Steyer stops by and asks how the design is coming along. He even gives me advice on making sure to center the words *witch-hop*. Everything around me starts to amplify, the *tapping* of the keyboards, mouse *clicks*, *talking*, even the kid next to me, Orion, who's *sucking* on a cough drop, the hard candy *hitting* his teeth like a hockey stick to a puck. I can't take it any longer, so I excuse myself from the lab and hurry into the hallway.

I look around the hallway but can't find the creature anywhere in sight.

I walk toward the direction where I last saw him going. I make a pit stop inside the bathroom in order to control myself.

Get yourself together, Ajax.

As I look into the mirror, I notice both my eyes are different. I rub them in hopes that it's all in my mind. A good rubbing will help rid the horror. I crack open my eyes, and they look no different than the eyes on the same reptilian creature. I'm drawn away from the mirror by a noise over my shoulder.

Startled, I check out the strange noise coming from the last stall. I cautiously kneel down and look underneath the stall, only to find a pair of scaly legs and feet similar to a crocodile.

More frustrated than frightened, I storm directly to the last stall and kick open the door.

What the fuck do you want from me?

In the last stall some kid is doing lines of red snow on the top of toilet lid. He looks up at me with wide Holy-Shit eyes.

What the hell, dude? Do you mind?

Sorry. I thought you were someone else.

Close the freakin' door!

He doesn't say anything about my eyes, which prompts me to walk back to the mirror. My eyes appear normal. I leave the bathroom and walk back to class.

By the time lunch arrives, I spend most of the time pacing around New Way, trying my best to avoid Brent. I can't eat. I've completely lost my appetite.

—

"In The Eye of The Bulldog"

Once I'm dismissed from the last class, which is Programming, I C++ my way out of the Technology Building and take a minor detour away from the main courtyard where most of the students chill once school is over and have Tameron meet me at the far side of New Way, away from other students.

I hear the one voice that I don't want to hear behind me just as I'm getting in Tameron's car. He's telling me he can drive me home. But apparently, I make a gesture obvious enough for Tameron to understand that I'm in no mood to be letting Brent drive me home. She makes up a lie about us having to be somewhere soon and we're already running late as it is.

If there's one thing about Brent, it's his uncanny ability to be able to sniff out a lie. You know how dogs and cats have a sixth sense about death? Well, Brent has a sixth sense for bullshit. But I don't care whether or not he's offended. Over the past year at New Way, Brent has turned into a puppet who echoes whatever he hears from the Internet, then passes it off as his own. Nobody sees it, except for me. He's been compromised, manipulated, 'owned,' which is a popular word he tends to use. Even when he talks to me now, he sounds like a crowd talking to me, like thousands of voices and they're all echoing the same thing as if he's incapable of any independent thought.

Thanks to Tameron, I'm able to ditch Brent without any problems; and without thinking, I thank her for having my back in my own inaudible way. We don't talk much during the drive home, and Tameron's fine with the silence. I still feel off, as in I recently woke up from a decent nap, when we arrive back at the house. I go straight to my bedroom. From downstairs, Tameron hollers that she has to step out for a while to run her errands. A part of me wants to tag along with Tameron and is begging not to be alone in an empty house. Another part of me wants to get straight to the bottom of the madness and understand why I still feel as though I'm stuck in a dream.

From my bedroom window, I watch Tameron pull out of the driveway. Then I decide to get in my car and drive to Cory's house. I don't know what I'm doing here—or why I'm here. I park on the street and wait for Cory to arrive. After ten minutes of waiting, I decide to leave. I mean, really, what am I doing?

I reach for the push-button.

Cory arrives at his house.

I open the door, thinking maybe I can catch him before he enters the house. I notice he's left the car running and he appears to be in a hurry. I hang back in the car. He's only inside the house for a few minutes. Then he runs back outside and gets back into his car and drives off. I decide to follow him.

After fifteen minutes of tailing Cory, he finally arrives at his destination: Abernathy Medical Center—the AMC. He already had his stitches taken out—even if he was doing some kind of follow up with a doctor, he wouldn't need to go to a hospital for treatment or evaluation—which begs the question what he's doing at the hospital. He parks his car outside a separate wing, a cancer treatment facility, next to the hospital. *The shaved head!* Why didn't I think of that earlier?

Cory grabs the silvery 'Get Well Soon' balloon from the backseat and walks into the cancer treatment facility.

After some deliberation, I decide to follow him inside. Even as soon as I step inside the building, that part of me takes over the other more scared part. Somehow, I feel as though everything makes sense, as if I'm supposed to be here, as if, in an unexplainable way, me being here has already happened.

I search for Cory and locate him entering a Children's Care Unit. Normally, people like Cory would bring a camera crew with him to show the world that he is a good person and whatnot. The flat, smooth surface of his pockets suggests that he left his phone in his car. I follow Cory down another hallway until he reaches a hospital room where a young girl, who's probably no older than nine years old, is lying in bed. I stand just outside the doorway and watch from behind a cleaning cart. The girl perks up as soon as she sees Cory. The first thing that immediately stands out is their haircut. They're both sharing the same haircut.

It's hard to make out what they're saying. I creep closer and eavesdrop. The girl is Cory's younger sister, Hope, and she's receiving treatment for leukemia.

Next to the bed is a photo of Cory. He's a couple of years younger, I can tell. I've only known Cory a couple of years, and ever since I've known him he's been bald, not like he couldn't grow any hair, which he could. I remember seeing stubs on that waxy dome of his one time.

Cory's sister points at me, resulting in Cory to fully rotate around.

Ajax? What are you doing here?

I just wanted to talk.

I have nothing to say to you.

With a smile on her face, Hope waves at me.

Hello.

I wave back.

Hi.

I didn't know you had a sister.

Yeah. This is Hope.

My name's Ajax.

Cory turns his back to me and whispers something in Hope's ear. He stands up and as he starts walking toward me, I notice the bulldog on Hope's red sweatshirt. I don't know why I'm drawn to the sweatshirt. All I can think about is that Avanti was doing some photo-op with the basketball team later this afternoon.

I follow Cory outside and he suddenly changes his demeanor to the Cory I'm used to knowing. For a moment, he looks as if he wants to hit me.

What the hell you doing here, Ajax? You stalking me?

Do I look like the kind of person who stalks people?

Yeah. He gets too close to my grill, close enough to where he's asking for a punch to the face. You do!

All right. Chill. The truth is I was following you. Listen Cory, I know we're not supposed to be talking to one another. But the real reason why I'm here is to say I'm sorry for what happened.

You? You're sorry? Why are you really here?

I'm here to apologize. The words suddenly get lost in the back of my throat. I never thought I'd turn to plasma, especially in front of Cory, of all people, right? The dude who always got involved in other people's business, who acted as if he genuinely cared about people who didn't look like him whenever he was around people, who'd share a heart-to-heart to someone less fortunate while, at the same time, ridicule them behind his or her back, who made sure to be at the forefront of the crowd or whatever trend, who even pegged himself a 'voice' of the people, even though his hair—or lack thereof—suggested a label far more sinister. Cory Hart rolled with the same tribe who'd tell me that my skin was too light, that I had too many freckles or that my hair was too strawberry blood for a black boy, that both my eyes were goofy-looking and ninety-nine percent of the time, warranted a closer inspection. Why was one the color blue and the other green? Most of the girls who hung around Cory's tight knit, supposed 'all-inclusive' crew were more interested in my appearance, than actually getting to know me.

And for me, that was the hardest fact to swallow.

Despite my grudges with Cory, uttering the word, *apologize*, makes me feel lighter.

Is this a joke? Some prank that Brent put you up to?

No. Honestly, I don't know the reasons why I pushed you. I know, though, when I do find out I'll have to take a hard look in the mirror. But I do know why I'm here.

I look Cory in the eye and make it count.

I'm sorry. For sure.

As he looks me over, Cory digests my apology.

He holds out his hand.

I shake his hand, palm-side only, color-to-color.

Then, he pulls me in for a hug.

I point at Cory's head.

You did that for your sister?

Cory runs his hand over his slick scalp.

Yeah, man. I wanted to show her that not having hair wasn't so weird.

That's nice. I didn't know.

Well, I didn't feel the need to explain myself to people. Some things are best left unexplained. We all have our reasons for the things we do, right?

Yeah. I guess so.

You know why I left Bridgemount High to come to New Way?

No.

During my three years at Bridgemount, I was on the honor roll, played three sports: football, basketball, and baseball. Football season ran into basketball. But it didn't matter. I already had a spot on the team. I was *that* good. But the fact is I had no say in the matter. My father was calling all the shots. Then, one day, he got all over me after we lost against our football rival, East Lake. I snapped. I hit him in front of all the other players. I'll never forget the look on each one of their faces. I was their captain. They looked up to me, and I let them all down. Essentially, that tough, hardheaded guy inside me rebelled and tried to convince myself that I was tougher than my old man and that I finally proved to him that I was not going to be bossed around anymore. After I spent the next couple of days thinking about my actions, I realized I wasn't 'tough' for striking my father. I was weak. I let my emotions get the best of me. More importantly, I let my ego get the best of me. A couple of weeks later, I dropped out of Bridgemount.

If you were that good, then why'd you stop playing sports?

I wasn't pursuing my dream. He shrugs his shoulders, as if the gesture alone is attached to his answer. Besides, I'd rather choose a profession that thrives on helping people, opposed to hurting people.

I reach out my hand and shake Cory's yet again. It's a firm handshake, not at all overpowering, but firm as if we're both matching each other's strength.

—

"A telltale bulge of a pen"

I leave the cancer treatment facility feeling way better about confronting Cory and drive back home.

Tameron should've already been back from her errand run. I give her a call, but her phone goes straight to voicemail. I head upstairs to my bedroom and remove items from both my pockets, including my keys and the thirty-three cents of loose change I superstitiously carry whenever I'm out in public, and toss them on my desk. In my other pocket, I come across a strange object: a black pen with the word *Leatherwood* written on the side. I remove the pen from my pocket. I don't remember carrying a pen nor do I remember even owning such a pen—*What the hell is Leatherwood?* I place the pen next to the black and white speckled Composition notebook on my desk. I'm tempted to open the notebook, to look inside, skim through it, but that part of me is telling me to do it later, that it's too soon, save the best for last. So, I listen to that voice and spend the next couple of hours scrolling through RECOMMENDED videos on YouTube. The bizarre, bold, and shocking titles of videos have me backtracking through my lightning-fast scroll and giving each one a second survey. One video is about the TOP TEN animals that crocodiles eat, that particular word *crocodile* grabbing most of my attention.

Other words leave me in a state of surrender, words like *blood, reptiles, lizards, midnight, watch,* or parodies of the current *Toad Prince* of the United States. I give in to the streaming app, watch each and every meaningless video that, after second and even third viewings, has me more confused about the events that have transpired today.

Somewhere between watching a TRAILER for a new show called *Blood and Bones* and a DIY video on *How to Repair a Broken Watch,* I drift for a moment. I wake up from feeling the sudden weight of my head falling into my chest. I snap my head upright and open my eyes. I check the time and two hours have passed! Which is strange because I closed my eyes for what felt like a minute. I turn off the TV and check the driveway for Tameron's car.

She's still not back from running errands, so I try her on her phone once more. Voicemail.

That's weird. She always picks up the phone.

I know I'm only supposed to call Avanti for emergencies but I think Tameron being out well past the time she normally spends running errands justifies a call.

Avanti doesn't pick up.

Instead, it's her aide, Vye, who answers the phone. Her voice is muffled for some reason and I only catch something along the lines of my mother being in an important meeting with the mayor of Atlanta.

The sound of Vye's voice triggers an image inside my mind.

All of a sudden, I find myself in the upstairs bathtub. Of all people, Avanti's aide, Vye, is sitting with her legs crossed in a chair next to the bathtub, and she's instructing me to do something to myself.

I shake away the very thought and hang up the phone. It's starting to get dark outside and Tameron's disappearance is making me worried. What if something happened to her? What if she was in a car wreck?

My mind starts to race with all-thoughts negative.

The best remedy to ease the racing mind. . .

Only one idea comes to me.

Yes.

—

"Rhymes with Bleach"

Only a couple minutes into taking my warm bath, I drift off once more. I'm back in the hospital, nursing the same exact injuries that I sustained after I was jumped by Sons of Man in an alleyway.

Even though I can't see anybody in the room, I can sense a presence close by. I focus on the shadowy corner of the room, particularly the dark figure sitting in a chair.

Sure enough, Vye emerges from the shadows. I can't help but draw my eyes toward her hand and the tiny object that she's holding.

The blade glistens in her hand.

Even though I can feel the metal slicing right through me, I know—because Vye knows—that the oxys help numb the pain.

This is me at my most vulnerable moment.

In her words, *my own Command+Alt+Esc—or better yet, delete.*

Of all the ways I imagined going out, I never thought I'd open myself up like this to the outside elements of the world. I'm an open book, the American Dream gone askew, a walking cliché teetering along the crooked lines of controversy, the representative of a thousand generations reduced to ash and limestone, inevitably torn down and rebuilt over and over again until all that remains of once-was is dust along the shoulder of a tired man who's beating an arthritic hand against the drum of extinction. But it's already done—heavy sigh. She's made the final cut.

My modern delete.

As my eyes fall upon the red highways along my forearms, the world around me starts to spin out of control as if, by opening myself up, I'm letting it all inside me, the air, water, and all of it turning to poison in my veins, and it's too much to bear. I've lost all motor functions. The razor blade slips from my ghost of a grip, strikes the edge of the bathtub, and makes a tiny splash in the bloody water.

Tick-tock.

Tick. . . tock. . . tick. . .

I wake up to the sounds of an old clock.

Expecting to see red, I draw my eyes toward the clear water in the bathtub. A heavy weight is lifted from my chest and finally, I can breathe easier just knowing it was all a dream.

The temperature in the room has dropped to the point where it starts to feel as cold as a meat locker. I examine both my arms and don't find any cuts. The once warm blood running from my entire body is gone. Yet, I can still feel traces of it moving along my skin, resulting in a pinprick sensation along the ends of my extremities. With pinpricks dancing along my skin, this invisible blood is no longer lukewarm. Yet, it's cold, like death, and it sends shivers throughout my body; my chest and arms curl inward, pectoral, abdomen muscles spasm.

My heart flutters from the sound of another more resonate, easier *tock*.

I hear someone knocking on the bathroom door.

Is that you, Death—

Before I can hold the rest of my thought, the door *squeaks* open in the greatest horror-movie like creepiness.

I look twice because, at first glance, I don't believe my eyes.

During my dry swallow, my heart feels as if it's climbing up my throat then, after my final *gah-gulp*, falling deep into my belly where it radiates my bowels.

Towering over the bathtub is a seven-foot tall reptile with the pounding stare of an iguana-faced creature ready to rip right through me.

The creature steps closer to me, my eyes going *blink-blink* as if, by doing so, I'm able to get a clearer picture of what exactly I'm dealing with here. Whatever it is, it's not human even though it stands in a way similar to that of a human; and when it speaks my name, its voice is as soft and sonorous as a voice-over actor.

How'd you know my name?

You called me.

Called you—What?!?

Well, not called per se. Forgive me for my use of vocabulary. Let's just say you. . . you reached out to me. Maybe you don't remember.

From the sound of the creature's deep voice, I can tell it's old, as in centuries old.

The creature takes yet another step closer to the bathtub; and now, it's reaching its scaly, clawed hand toward me in what I can only perceive as a threat.

I find an opportunity to escape.

With the adrenaline pumping through whatever blood I have left in my body, I bolt upright and slip from the bathtub before the creature can grab a hold of me. I race from the bathroom and stumble downstairs, occasionally looking over my shoulder. I'm not being chased, yet somehow, I still feel like I am. I look one last time over my shoulder before I run outside and witness the same creature, which appears much taller than seven feet, probably closer to eight or nine, standing under the doorway, its svelte silhouette dark and ominous behind foggy red light.

I open the front door and dart outside.

As soon as I step outside, I immediately wear the cold like a tight, irritating suit; however, my body is still numb from what I believe to be from oxys. I cover up myself with my hands, as if someone's watching, the neighbor perhaps, whoever.

Trying not to expose myself for the whole neighborhood to see, I run down the porch steps and hurry onto the street, which, after one block, becomes darker. The streetlights lining the neighborhood street provide me with a path forward, as if they're being controlled by a dimmer. Eventually, after a couple of steps onto the street, each one of the streetlights goes dark.

A greater *part* of me knows that I've been here before.

And the horror soon to come.

I'm left standing, cold and afraid, in the middle of a pitch-black street. Each house, each mailbox, each lawn, each driveway darkens to the point of disappearing into complete and utter darkness, as the dark itself spreads closer and closer to the street until it surrounds me. The only house that I can barely make out is my house, and even it appears as if it's, like the streetlights, dimming. Above, a once bright sky is no more. The stars, snuffed out. The moon, nowhere to be found.

As heavy darkness descends upon me, thousands of tormented voices amplify all around me. Screaming at me. Begging for me to come closer to the darkness. They carry a sick desperation in their voice, a hunger: that's the first thing surfacing through my mind. These people—whoever they may be— sound as if they're solely relying on me to provide them with food and shelter.

I look around and there's nobody on the street but me, and that's when I realize they're coming for me. Lifeless, wobbly arms and spaghetti legs emerge from the ring of darkness. Moaning and screaming, the mob of contorted figures totters into the dim light that encompasses me. I'm more frightened of these tormented things than that creature in the bathroom. It's a bottomless hunger driving them. It's noticeable in their wobble, their gibberish, their screams and cries.

As the mob closes in all around me, I have no other choice than to run away. I make it to the house without getting attacked—or eaten—however, I once came close to them in what felt like another life. They did attack me; however, I managed to escape them but not on my own. I had help.

I close the door behind me and immediately feel the same presence from the bathroom coming from a dark living room.

I knew you'd be back, but never so quickly.

Startled, I track the voice to the creature sitting in the LazyBoy recliner in the corner of the room. Its scaly, lizard-like body bathed in darkness.

Talk about making a statement.

I quickly grab a pillow from the couch and cover myself. I search around for a weapon. I find the closest object I can find, which is a poker from the fireplace.

Quite an impressive list you have here.

For some reason, I already know what *list* it's talking about before I can even wrap my head around how it came to learn of the list.

I step forward.

Behind me, the fireplace suddenly lights up with a mellowing flame!

Startled, I turn around and try to understand how the fire lit up all on its own but can find no other reason, except for the creature in the recliner using a remote control. *Do we even have a remote for the fireplace?* Or is the creature *that* good at creeping me out?

Before I can make sense of what's going on with my body, I'm suddenly distracted by the rustling sound of paper.

Getting struck by an oncoming train with wet concrete filled inside my shoes; leaping from the Mallard Bridge onto a blank canvas which will be later shown in an art gallery; robbing the 24-7 with a water pistol, thus resulting in being shot by the heroic clerk named Haibi who carries a shotgun underneath the counter—

—Enough!

It only gets better.

I watch its arm moving across its fossil-colored underbelly; however, I'm still unable to see what's in its hands for it's too dark.

'*For the longest I can remember,*' it reads, '*I've felt as if I've been living in your shadow, trapped by it, unable to move or breathe. All I wanted was to enjoy the pursuits of any normal sixteen year old. But even that was far from possible.*'

Hey! That's private!

Private, huh?

Yet, it's addressed to—

—Who the hell are you?

I hold the poker in front of me and show this bug breath that I'm not afraid to put out a fire.

The question you should be asking is not who I am but *what* I am.

The creature tosses my journal on the coffee table, which lands open on my note. As it extends its hand outward, I notice something—maybe a device— along its wrist. Before I can get a closer look, it pulls its hand back into the darkness of the living room.

The talking caught me off guard. But, now that I realize it can read, I start to wonder where the creature came from and what it wants from me.

Where'd you get that?

In your bedroom.

What the hell were you doing in my bedroom?

Just piddling around until you came back.

What do you want from me?

It's hard to explain in words and even if I did, I believe it would still go over your head. Not that I'm doubting your intelligence. It's just a lot to take in.

The creature leaned forward in the orange glow of firelight. I'm able to get a closer look at its hand, particularly its wrist, as well as a wristband, which is made out of what looks like pearls.

The beating light from the fireplace hits the iridescent wristband, causing it to change colors at different angles.

But since you asked, I don't think what I have to say will convince you. For this, I'm going to have to show you. . . again.

Show me? Show me what?

As the creature stands up, it hit the top of its spiky head along the ceiling fan. It walks back upstairs.

'Show me what,' I said!

The creature walks to the top of the staircase, stops at the landing, and turns around.

Your options.

Options?

The creature nods toward the bathroom.

Believe me when I say this: time is *not* on your side.

Who—what are you?

Name's Creach.

Like creature?

No. Like Creach.

The creature who goes by the name Creach walks to the bathroom.

Halfway toward the bathroom, Creach stops in front of the railing and looks down at me.

What are you waiting on?

———

"The Blood Watch"

Still trying to make sense as to why I've been seeing Creach throughout the day, I decide to follow the seven-foot tall reptile upstairs.

I make it to the bathroom where Creach is standing over the bathtub. Inside the bathtub is my answer. There, I lie in a pool of blood. I appear to be drifting in and out of consciousness.

From the palish tone of my skin, it appears as if I don't have much longer to live before I'm maggot food. The blood runs from my open veins, which prompts me to check out myself, as in the one standing here, Me. I search for the cuts on my arms once more but don't find any.

I look back up and recognize that old chair next to the bathtub. It is made out of cherry maple wood; and over the years, it has withstood more nicks and scratches than one might endure. The chair talked in creaks whenever you sat in it or put the slightest amount of weight against it and sounded as if it was ready to collapse to a dust pile at any moment. Regardless of its age, as well as its sentimental value, the chair was mostly used as a clothing rack for dirty clothes, including soiled socks and sweaty T-shirts.

All I know is someone was sitting in this exact chair while I was carrying out something awful to my body that I had absolutely no control over. That, I'm sure of. This was *not* me. This was *not* my doing or my final farewell, despite having spoken these shameful words in the past, ones that would most definitely warrant more of a roll-of-the-eye than any need for concern. The fact of the matter: I never would've taken my own life!

But it's already done, Ajax.

Who are you?

That is irrelevant at this point.

Have we met before?

Yes.

How many times?

You don't want to know. But you are here now, as we speak. And I have a good feeling this time around.

I walk past the mirror and spot several strange markings on my shoulders, as well as the back of my neck.

Concealing myself with the pillow, I walk closer to the mirror. The markings are scars, old scars, pink and jagged.

I didn't notice these before.

That's because you're changing.

Stumped by Creach's response, I find myself thinking whether or not I spoke the words out loud. Or, was it my interest in these scars that impelled Creach to elaborate on the current condition of my body?

Changing? What do you mean I'm changing?

With the tip of its claw, Creach picks up my pair of dirty boxers lying on the vanity and looks them over with what appears to be a feeling only a human would feel.

This reminds me. You might want to change into some clothes.

I nod at the boxers.

Can you?

Toss them over?

Yes. Whatta you waiting on?

I'm afraid that's soulistically impossible.

Soul-*what*?

You really think that's a pillow you're holding?

I look down at the pillow and find only my hand covering myself.

And that poker I was holding in my hand, nowhere to be found.

I was just. . .

Yes. That's right. You were, Ajax. At least you *thought* you were. In time, as ironically as it sounds, you will come to realize that everything you once knew about life doesn't exist where I'm taking you.

But how come you can touch things and I can't?

Because I exist. Creach points at my other self clinging to life in the bathtub. He exists. Then, Creach points at me. You don't. At least not in physical form.

Am I dead?

Not dead, but almost. Like I said, you don't have much time.

Till what exactly?

I'll explain it all. Right now, time's ah-wasting. So, make it easier on yourself. Where we're going, it's best you put on some clothes. *Trust* me—

—And where are we going exactly?

I'll show you. Just think of something to wear. We have to go.

That's it? Just think of anything—

Yes. The first thing that pops in your mind.

So I have a mind but no body?

Creach thinks over my remark.

Sure.

You don't sound confident.

Yes. You have a mind. Now, let's—

—Then, you're talking about like something out of *Syntronix*.

I'm unaware of this *Syntronix*.

You know, *The Syntronix*. Everybody knows the movie, *The Syntronix*. Was like one of the greatest science-fiction movies of all time. You know, right hand or left hand? Wizard of Oz? Chiromancy? The lines on our palms that pull us toward the inevitability of, you know. . .

I get nothing from Creach, not even a reaction.

What happens in *The Syntronix* can have real-life consequences to your body outside *The Syntronix*, like, for instance, I look around and find the vanity, say if I submerged my head in a sink full of water and drown my—

—No.

No?

I think I know where you're going with this, but no. The answer is no.

But you didn't let me finish—

—We have to get going. Let's go.

I look down at myself and find myself dressed in the same outfit that I wore to the schoolbook pictures: a white *Mobocracy* T-Shirt over a pair of holey black jeans and the Black Edition of Chuck Taylors. Prior to getting inside the bathtub, I remember removing all of my facial piercings.

I touch my face, my nose first and then my eyebrows, and find each ring and stud attached to my face. Along both my wrists are bands and whatnot; although, one band feels different, as if it doesn't belong to me.

On my left wrist is what I believe to be some kind of watch.

I never wore a watch. Never saw the point in letting time control me.

It's not the kind of watch you're thinking of.

I inspect the strange device on my wrist. It has a gold band. In the center—where normally the clock would sit—is a glass circular enclosure filled with what looks like blood; however, it's not entirely full of blood. It appears as if it's three-fourths full. Which makes me wonder where the other one-fourth had gone? Or, has the blood drained that much since I've been wasting my ghost-breath yapping it up with a seven-foot tall reptile named Creach.

I like to call it the Blood Watch.

Blood Watch?

It's pretty simple. The watch indicates how much life force you have left inside your body. Once the blood runs out, the watch will begin to turn black. And once the watch turns completely black, your body dies. I can't stress this enough: Whatever you do, make sure the watch *never* turns black.

What happens then? You know, when my body dies. . .

You only saw a glimpse of what happens outside. And I know you might not want to hear this now, but you're going to wish you hadn't made that final cut.

Cut? I didn't cut myself. It wasn't me!

But it came from your hand.

I draw my eyes toward the wristband on Creach's wrist. It doesn't look like a watch—at least, none that I've seen in my world—but who knows.

How come your *watch* is different than mine?

This is not a watch.

Then, what is it?

This is a Lazarus Cuff, made from old technology used to make the Tunic of Lazarus.

Lazarus? Like Back-From-The-Dead Lazarus?

Where I come from dead isn't dead.

Dead? Dead is dead. And there's no coming back from the dead.

So you think.

So, what? You're here to save me from death? Is that it?

No. Like I said, I'm here to *show* you.

Show me what?

Your story, Ajax.

—

"Careful What You Wish For"

Creach steps out of the bathroom, and I follow.

I stop at the doorway and look back at my other lifeless self lying in the bathtub one last time before exiting. I'm left transfixed in a somewhat religious awe, as if I'm witnessing right before my eyes what former skeptics would call a spiritual enlightenment.

Remember, time's ah—

—Wasting. Got it.

I push aside the glorified moment and follow Creach downstairs.

The creature opens the door and waits for me to catch up. Then, together, we both exit the house.

Once more, I can't help but stop and turn my eyes back to the top of the landing, hoping to find a sign maybe coming from the bathroom, a clue—whatever!—indicating that I'm doing the right thing by following this seven-foot tall reptilian-like creature to wherever it dwells, which, more than likely, is what I consider to be a fiery place that starts with a capital letter H. Raised to be a Catholic—which, I know, is odd, considering that Avanti, the one whom I see whenever she's not in the public eye, doesn't have one Catholic bone in her body—I can't imagine what other place it'd be. I get nothing, though, no signs or clues, no pull, only a bathroom bathing in a red light that appears to be dimming to the color gray.

To paraphrase Creach, time is no longer ticking but dropping. I glance down at the Blood Watch on my wrist. I slosh around the blood inside the glass ball and can't help but wonder where the blood goes once it drains completely.

I face the neighborhood street, and Creach is nowhere in sight.

Not too far away in the center of the street, a manhole has been slid open.

Immediately, I start thinking more about where Creach is leading me—under the street, for sure—but what exactly waits for me when, or if, we get there.

All of a sudden, Creach's lengthy, scaly arm shoots out from the manhole and articulately waves me closer.

A part of me feels as if the creature's luring me into a trap.

Another part of me feels as if I have nothing else to lose.

I remain convinced of the latter—at least, try to.

Vigilantly, I walk down the steps of the front porch and inch my way onto the street.

As I approach the manhole, the darkness starts to fill the street like a storm of darkness approaching me. The surrounding houses darken. The streetlights dim, then, eventually, burn out. In that dark and unruly storm, I hear growing screams laced with greater agony than hunger. The screams continue to build nearly to the point of becoming deafening.

With nowhere else to go, I decide climb down into the manhole.

I slide the cover over the manhole before the darkness overcomes me.

Below, Creach is waiting for me.

I use the ladder to climb down.

Now are you going to explain to me what that is back there?

Not now.

I stand my ground, not moving until I get more answers.

Once Creach becomes aware of my stillness, it stops, turns around, and walks back to me.

Some call it the In-Between—the Eventide, a place where corrupted souls go to live out an eternity searching for those like you to feast upon. And I'm afraid if you don't come with me, then, eventually, you will join them in eternal darkness.

But there were so many of them.

There are more of them. Lots more. They believe that by consuming another tourist it will release them from the darkness that has bound them.

And will it?

No. You see, Ajax, the ones up there, they had second doubts. For the most part, they weren't ready to die. It wasn't their time. Now, they want out. But it's already too late. Their *pneuma* is trapped in that awful place up there in the world you once knew.

Pneuma?

Think of it as the soul, as you see yourself at this very moment.

I look down at myself, my clothes, my 'pneuma.'

My pneuma, huh? Then, why does it feel like I'm still kind of nervous about what's happening?

As long as you're wearing that Blood Watch on your wrist, you still have ties to your body and your world. Remember, Ajax. Only *you* can save yourself.

Creach attempts to walk away, but I reel Creach back in with another question.

465

Can they see you? The people of my world?

Only if they look hard enough. Creach holds up the wristband of pearls along his wrist. The Lazarus Cuff allows me to travel more easily through the shadows.

The shadows? What?!?

Creach was right about all of this nonsense going over my head.

Then, how come I can see you?

You can see me because you're dead, Ajax.

The comment alone sends a ripple of anger through my pneuma.

Not yet.

That's the spirit. Creach waves me along. Now, let's go.

But wait! What happens when you take it off? The Cuff?

Creach hangs its head in what appears to be sadness.

I'm afraid the people of your world aren't ready to find out about me or my kind. Creach brings its attention back to me. Its head jerks right in a directional nod. Let's go. I can answer all the questions you have. But we have to move.

Watching my step along the slick, narrow ledge above a still lane of mystery water, I follow Creach through the sewer tunnel. I only get a few steps in before the questions start flaring inside my mind. I look back up at Creach and suddenly realize that I've been here before. My pneuma tingles, and I'm struck by momentary déjà vu.

Of all the people out there, why me? Not like there's anything special about me.

I take my eyes off the ground for a moment, which is a no-no. Before I can find my footing, my heel slips along a slick spot on slimy concrete. My feet fly out from beneath me. I throw out my arms, trying to grab hold of the wall but all I grab is air.

As I fall backward, Creach's arm shoots outward. It happens to grab me with the same hand wearing the Lazarus Cuff. The cuff itself glows with a faint pinkish-white light. I turn my shoulder and realize that I've come inches away from landing in that disease-infested water, which is probably crawling with super bugs yet to be discovered.

Creach pulls me toward the wall.

Syntronix, right? All in the mind, right?

I ignore the very idea of the mind and soul acting like one and make sure to thank Creach for helping me; however, I'm more interested in its hand.

Creach's hand no longer has the scaly appearance of what I first perceived as a reptilian-like hand. Its claw, now fingernails. Its scaly hide, human flesh.

Even Creach's grip feels soft and feminine. I realize the change in Creach's hand had something to do with touching me, my pneuma.

I immediately point out the change in Creach.

Your hand?

Once I find my balance over the ledge, Creach glances down at its hand.

Creach lets go of my arm and becomes awkwardly quiet and for a second, it even struggles to make eye contact with me. Which, I know, is uncharacteristic. When Creach finally finds my eyes, it looks at me as if, in a strange way, it *knows* me.

The Lazarus Cuff allows me to touch you.

I question why Creach is even telling me. The comment sounds more like an excuse. Tell me something I don't already know.

Another thought comes to mind, a cooler thought.

Can I, like, walk through walls and stuff?

Technically, yes.

But your hand, it was like mine. Only more—Are you a she?

I am female. Yes. Does it make any difference what gender I am?

Ah, no. It doesn't—

—Then, are you ready to continue?

Yeah. Sure.

We make it to an intersection in the sewers. Creach makes a right turn. But then, after second-guessing itself, Creach turns back around and makes a left instead.

You sure?

Yes. I'm sure. It's this way. As much as I've traveled through these tunnels, I never get use to them.

I spend the next few moments racking my brain as to how many times Creach has done this sort of thing. So, I ask him—or her.

Forgive my ignorance. But in your world how many days are there in a year?

Three hundred and sixty-five. Well, not counting a leap year, which is three hundred and sixty-six.

Three hundred and sixty-five. So, I dunno. Take how many days there are in a single year and then multiply that by twelve.

Okay. So a lot, huh? And you've met people like me?

You can say that. Well, they aren't nearly as talkative as you.

Believe it or not, I'm more introverted.

I take the comment as a compliment, sort of.

Does time not exist in your world?

Once, yes. It did. So I've read in the *Book Of.*

Book Of what?

The Book Of.

Yeah. Book of what? Never mind.

After the first explosion, it was written that time slowed down so much that it started to reverse—

—Explosion? What explosion?

The explosion happened the same time a bomb was dropped on the southern coast of the island Honshu—in your world, that is.

I remember researching the bomb on the Internet. I know the answer.

You're talking about Hiroshima, right?

That's the one. Then, there was a second explosion—the 'big one,' as everybody calls it. Happened in 1986—your year, that is—the time of Chernobyl.

Surprisingly, even though it was before my time, I remember researching that one, too. I immediately point out that Creach's facts are all wrong.

But wait! After a contamination, the nuclear power station in Chernobyl was contained. What'r you talking about? There was no explosion!

Not in your world, there wasn't.

You mean—

Creach nodded.

But how?

Whether you believe me or not, Ajax, our worlds are connected and what-ever happens in your world has a greater ripple effect on ours. Forty-one years passed between the two events; however, during that time between explosions everything has been out of whack. Everything. . . evolved. Or, devolved, one would put it.

Devolved how?

The fact I'm talking to a seven-foot tall reptile that has the body of a lizard or crocodile—can't tell which—only much slender and alien in shape, and the facial appearance similar to that of an iguana (and who, by the way, fun fact: happens to be a chick), makes things clearer to understand.

You're talking about mutation! Aren't you?

That's right, including time itself.

What? Time can't mutant. That defines all laws of nature!

Where we're going, Ajax, there are no laws. There is *no* balance.

The comment alone sticks with me and has me reconsidering my options and for one, spending an eternity in darkness seems, suffice to say, tolerable.

Four seconds in your world could be four minutes, four hours, four days, four months, even as long as four years in my world. Where we're going time is nothing like the way you perceive time.

Trippy.

You haven't seen anything yet.

We come to a stop at the end of a tunnel, which, at first glance, appears to be a dead end. I figure we're lost again, although Creach is convinced that we're on the right track. I mimic her movements as she leans forward; and then, she shows me yet another tunnel, a much smaller tunnel, basically a drainage pipe about the size of an escape tunnel which immediately heightens my claustrophobia.

Immediately, I'm bludgeoned by a fury of racing thoughts.

We have. . . to go through. . . there?

I can hardly even finish a thought.

My throat tightens.

Not a fan of tight spaces, are you? Yeah. Who isn't—

—I can't.

Well, I'm afraid you have no other choice, Ajax. The closest entrance is too far away and you don't have time. Trust me on this one. The transitioning takes a while to get used to.

The transitioning? What transitioning? Why are you doing this?

I have a vision of Creach dragging me through that narrow pipe, the Laza-rus Cuff on her wrist glowing a pinkish-white color.

Horrified, I shake away the images.

No!

You have to, Ajax.

I can't do it!

Just think of something positive.

I instantly do the one thing I've always been good at it. I rebel.

In a casual manner, Creach kneels down and readies herself to crawl—or better yet—slither through the pipe. I don't follow suit. Instead, I back away. The very thought of being trapped in a tight space causes the fear to spread throughout my entire body—or my pneuma or whatever the hell Creach calls it! I know it's all in my mind, the fear; however, right now never has a feeling felt so strong.

Gripped by fear, I continue to back pedal away.

Creach only gets half of her body into the pipe before she turns her shoulder and finds me backing away.

Ajax, we don't have time! You must come with me!

I shake my head.

No.

Ajax!

I race back to the manhole cover. I climb up the ladder and barely manage to remove the cover from the manhole.

As soon as I climb my way out onto the neighborhood street, they're already on top of me, a mob of hellish fiends desperate to tear me apart. Their screeches only intensify the fear, as if they can smell the fear emitting from the giant pore of my pneuma. I attempt to flee from the alabaster-skinned mob. One of the fiends grabs me from behind and throws me to the ground. Its long, bony, gnarly hand feels slick along my shoulder, as if it sweats slime. The spastic fiend tosses me to the ground, its jaw chomping and exposing layers and layers of jagged teeth. I hit the side of my head along the street.

In a daze, I shield my face from their attack, curl my body into a fetal position, and hope that Creach was wrong about everything.

I wish someone would just pinch me already.

Hold up. . .

Never mind.

"Wasn't"

Kicking and punching, I fight off the darkness.

Both my hands and feet connect with the carpeted interior of a trunk.

Outside, I can hear familiar voices.

Yelling my name—*Jackie Boy! Hey, Jack off! Afraid of the dark, are we? What a crybaby? Yeah! Cry for us, you lil' crybaby?*

The voices are younger and coming from what sounds like a group of kids.

This is what you get for kissing my cousin! She said your breath stank! Yeah lil' Stinky, buy yourself a Tick-Tack! Oh! I forgot! You ain't getting out! Yea-yeah, boy! That's right! You're stuck in there for the rest of your pathetic life!

I hear a loud and hollow *thud* above me followed by a couple of less intense *thuds* along the bumper of the car.

The kids walk away, laughing.

Their laughs trail off, leaving me trapped in silence.

Eventually, after all of the kicking and punching, I wear myself out.

To my right, a hazy red light brightens, revealing an umbrella and a dirty pair of butters.

My eyes adjust to the darkness. Only a few inches next to my right shoulder a black beetle is overturned on the floor of the trunk. In similar fashion, the beetle squirms and kicks its tiny little legs in the air, as if it's trying to roll over. After a while, the beetle stops kicking and squirming and eventually, gives up.

In that moment of defeat where the beetle accepts its fate, I accept mine. I'm going to die, eventually, like the beetle; however, I'm not going to die today.

Relieved, yet more determined, I flip the still beetle over on its legs. By doing so, the beetle scurries toward the red light, crawls through the crack in the carpet lining, and escapes from the trunk. I peel away the piece of partial carpet covering the light bulb and punch out the brake light with the tip of the umbrella. Natural daylight fills part of the trunk. I peer through the hole in the rear of the car and spot a lady walking past. I yell out to the lady, stick my hand out of the hole where the brake light used to be, and wave her down.

I pull my hand back into the trunk. The lady is coming this way. I tell her to open the trunk.

She struggles at first, but after a couple attempts, the trunk pops open!

The beam of sunlight blinds me, forcing me to shield my face with my hands.

The walker steps in front of the sunlight; however, her figure is darker, taller, inhuman.

I wake up in my old bed with the splash of sun on the side of my face.

As I sit upright, I look around the bedroom and wonder how I ended up back here. Strangely, I'm drawn to my wrist. I touch my wrist and run my hand along my forearm. I remember wearing a watch on my wrist but can't put an image to the memory.

I roll out of bed.

Once more, my eyes are drawn to my wrist, now both of them.

On instinct, I walk toward the blinds to open them; however, they're already open.

I walk to the door and as I'm about to reach for the door handle, I pause for a moment. Then, open the door. I can smell a hint of cinnamon raisin toast, as well as coffee in the air. The smells, like that sunshine, are comforting.

Before heading downstairs, I walk into the hallway bathroom and relieve myself. As I'm about to pull down my sweats, I'm drawn to the bathtub. I hold it in and check out the bathtub instead. I take a knee next to the tub where I discover a smudge of dry blood caked onto the edge of the drain.

As with the bedroom door, I don't exactly know why I'm drawn to these certain ideas. All I can think is that maybe it has something to do with a dream—or a memory.

Standing upright, I come across yet another smudge of dry blood on the floor. Then, during my exit from the bathroom, I come across yet another smudge underneath the doorway, which doesn't look like a smudge at all but more so a. . .

I follow drops of blood to the top of the landing.

Searching for more blood, I walk downstairs.

I find yet another one in the foyer.

As I'm about to head outside, I can feel someone standing behind me. I turn my shoulder and witness Tameron waiting at the edge of the kitchen. She's holding her arms down by her side and staring at me funny.

Tameron?

I was just going to say something, but I lost my train of thought. Oh, yeah. I was going to make you breakfast. She taps herself on the forehead. Silly poor ole me. You hungry?

Yeah. I'm *starving*.

Well, what are you waiting on? Don't just stand there. Let's go. She waves me into the kitchen. You're already running late as it is.

Late?

Yes. Late for school. And don't give me that excuse that you're not feeling well.

I follow Tameron into the kitchen where a box of Snake Eggs is sitting on the kitchen table. I pick up the cereal box. On the cover is a bowl full of s-patterned oats with white marshmallows in the shape of tiny balls—or eggs?

Where's Avanti?

Your mother had to leave early this morning for an important meeting. She has an extremely busy schedule today. You know, she's going to be meeting with the—

—The Bulldogs. Yeah. I remember.

You do? That's right. I forget how much you like basketball.

I used to, I guess.

You know, Avanti told me you were good. Why'd you stop playing?

I dunno.

Well, surely, there has to be a reason.

Ignoring Tameron, I grab a bowl from the top cabinet, as well as a carton of soymilk from the refrigerator, and take a sit at the table.

Tameron lets me eat in peace and steps out of the kitchen to finish folding a load of clean clothes in the laundry room.

I pour myself a bowl of Snake Eggs and as I'm trying to piece everything together, I draw my attention toward the kitchen countertop where a TV is playing a wildlife show on the *Animal Planet* channel.

On the TV, an iguana is hanging out along a tree branch when, all of sudden, the iguana snatches a grasshopper with its long, rubbery tongue while I take a bite of my cereal.

The crunching sound of Tameron eating from a piece of jelly toast pulls me away from the TV.

As she chews, she turns to me. Globs of grape jelly roll down the side of her chin. She licks up the slippery jelly; however, when Tameron does so, her tongue is inhumanly long, more so like a chameleon rather than an iguana, and it nearly stretches down to the base of her chin. Again, Tameron looks at me funny.

What?

Nothing.

I excuse myself from the table and hurry to the hallway bathroom where, this time, I finally relieve myself.

After I flush the toilet, I notice a strange watch on my wrist—a Blood Watch? I try to remove the watch, but it won't come lose. I'm suddenly turned away from the watch by a *banging-sloshing* noise coming from the water. I put my ear to the wall and hear the sound of water flowing through loose, rusty pipes.

Keeping close to the wall, I track the noise outside into the hallway.

The sound leads me toward the basement door. I follow the sound down into the basement, which, halfway down the steep staircase, appears to be a sewer.

Immediately, I rotate around and walk up the stairs. The door is gone and all that remains is a moldy brick wall.

With nowhere else to go, I decide to walk down into the basement. The farther I walk down the stairs, the more and more the basement starts to look like the sewers. The walls have changed. The air is smelly and musty. Even the stairs I walk on are no longer wood, yet they're made of concrete.

As I reach the bottom of the staircase, I find Tameron standing next to a pipe in the base of the brick wall.

You're running out of time, Ajax.

She taps her wrist, as if she's tapping an invisible watch.

I look down at the Blood Watch. Inside the glass ball only half the blood remains.

Remember, once it turns black—

—Yeah. *I don't know how I know this, but, yeah*, I got it.

The sight of Tameron brings back a wave of memories, making amends with Cory, the Bulldog on his sister's red sweatshirt, meeting Creach, seeing myself in a bathtub full of my own precious blood.

Once more, I look down at the Blood Watch and then both my palms.

All your answers lie at the other end.

Tameron points at the pipe below.

Finally, I make a decision.

I walk to Tameron, get down on both my hands and knees, and crawl through the narrow pipe.

While crawling through thick, clumpy sewage, I glance over my shoulder.

Creach, *not* Tameron, is watching me from outside the pipe.

Keep going, Ajax. You're almost there.

I block out the smell by holding my breath.

Surprise, surprise, I end up breaking a world record for the longest someone's ever held his breath. Who would've thought? I actually miss breathing.

—

"Not in Georgia Anymore"

Just as I'm about to give up after crawling for what feels like miles through hella nastiness, a hazy light materializes at the end of the pipe.

The faster I crawl, the brighter and clearer the light becomes.

The light pushes me forward.

Finally, I reach the light and wind up inside an industrial type room. The surrounding walls look like rusted metal. A mesh of steamy pipes everywhere. I look down, give my outfit a once-over, and what should be clothes covered in all sorts of hella nastiness is, surprisingly enough, clean.

Your pneuma, remember?

I look up and Creach is standing in the shadowy corner of the room.

But how? You were just. . . You can't teleport, can you—

—Teleport, huh? I haven't heard that one before.

But how'd you get here before me? You were just—

—Behind you. Yes. I was. And now, I'm not. The question you should be asking yourself, Ajax, is 'How did you get here?'

I just crawled through. . .

I glance behind me and search for the opening in the pipe but can't find it.

Where'd it go?

You've been here for a while now.

But how?

Like most tourists who have a hard time coping with what happened to them, you drifted into a state of repeat after you nearly got devoured by those slimeballs from the Eventide. Your mind was lost and you've simply been drifting through the same day over and over, surrounding yourself with the present; but most importantly, living out the one particular moment where you felt the most regret. I had no other choice than to step in and help guide you to where you needed to be before your mind was lost forever.

Creach shows me the Lazarus Cuff on her wrist.

Using the Lazarus Cuff, I carried—well, more like dragged you here, into my world. However, while you remained in your state of repeat, in order to reconnect with your pneuma, you had to conquer the one thing that most tourists fail to do—

—My fear.

That's right, Ajax. Your fear.

I was ten years old when a group of kids locked me in the back of a trunk. I thought I was going to die. I remember thinking how much I didn't want to die.

I reckon you were not the same after that day.

Images surface inside me, ones of me kicking kids who looked different than me or punching kids who looked at me differently or even beating kids until they bled.

No. I guess you can say I am—was a bully.

But not anymore.

You know, I never liked doing what I did.

You only did what you had to do in order to grow.

I suppose so.

Ajax, you looked fear straight in the eye and told it who's boss. So, how are you feeling?

Better, I guess.

I look down at the Blood Watch on my wrist, which is half-full. I notice several pinkish scars about the size of toothpicks randomly patterned like wallpaper on both of my arms as well, ones that weren't there before.

Now that we've peeled back the layers, are you ready? You still have a long ways to go. Time is—

—Ah-wasting. Yeah. I got that part.

Creach leaves the rusty room and steps into a surveillance room.

Quietly sitting behind a control board is a slender man who goes by the name Sticks. I'm weirded out yet slightly relieved from his presence. He's a human—a plus for me. And except for the somewhat gaunt appearance, he looks completely normal.

Creach waves at Sticks, who bows his head in a careful, robotic nod.

On one of the monitors, another man—who doesn't look human even though he bares the features of a human—is being chased through a junky river by a pack of what looks like wolves; however, they have twice as many legs as wolves. The action alone is dire enough to warrant a closer look from Sticks.

As he turns around and faces his back toward me, I notice the massive crater in the back of his head.

The hole looks as if it has come from a close-range gunshot.

—

"Stranger in a Strange Land"

I step outside the metallic box-like structure Creach refers to as Outpost #36.

Surrounding the remote building is a barren landscape, desert-like in its dustiness, yet the rocky ground has a darker, almost ashy hue to it. Not too far away is a range of hills and small mountains. I immediately notice a murky, trash-littered river running alongside the outpost. I think about the man in the monitor and how he was being chased by strange beasts.

Creach calls out to me and points to our destination past one particular jagged mountain.

Dark Mountain, huh?

While studying the somewhat beautiful yet ominous mountainscapes, I can't help but notice the red sky, not partially red from the setting or rising of a sun, but full on red-red.

Is the sky normally this red in your world?

How do you mean?

I point up at the red sky.

See. Red.

I don't know what you're talking about.

Hard answer to swallow coming from a know-it-all.

What are you, colorblind?

Yes. As a matter of fact I am.

Really? You mean, you can't see the color of the sky?

Creach doesn't respond to my question. In a way, I feel as if, of all the questions I've asked, questioning Creach's eyesight is off limits.

So, where are we going?

Leatherwood.

Leatherwood, huh? So, is that a—

—Yes. It's a city.

So, what's in—

In the corner of my eye, I spot a *squeaky* rodent no larger than an opossum scurrying toward a gap between two boulders. Normally, I wouldn't think much of it. It's just your ordinary animal more than likely evading a predator, which it probably thinks is Creach, although, I'm not too sure what she eats to survive—and I don't plan on asking either. Or, it's chasing after a mouse or insect or whatever's on the menu. I'd rather be thinking of these common everyday essentials, who's eating who or what's eating what. Or, maybe I breathed in a toxic fume while I was crawling through all that hella nastiness and it's caused me to hallucinate—but then again, how can I breath in a toxic fume when I can't even breath to begin with? I wish any of these ideas were on the table, but that's not at all the case.

I don't know if my mind's messing with me, but I swear the animal that just crawled in that hole looked just like Ms. Culler.

Ms. Culler?

She was my third grade Art teacher. She went missing right before I went to New Way. What the hell am I saying? I dismiss even thinking the idea that my fifth grade Language Arts teacher somehow shrunk down to the size of a marsupial and is now living her so-called chalk-free life in this wasteland of a desert. It was probably an opossum, I tell myself.

Were you close to this Ms. Culler?

I dunno. It was a long time ago. Forget I even brought up her name.

———

"Dark Mountain"

After about a mile of trekking through the rugged landscape, we finally arrive at the base of the mountain; however, after I voice a complaint, Creach informs me that we are not going up the mountain but around it. Which causes my pneuma to tingle in what I can only imagine is a new method of releasing a sigh of relief.

Creach, who's remained rather quiet since we left the outpost, stops halfway up the hill and turns to me.

Let me ask you a question, Ajax—

—Ask me a question? You know I thought I was the one who asks questions around here?

Lately, you've been quiet.

Speak for yourself. I've just been thinking. That's all. I point at the barren landscape, as well as the red sky. It's a lot to take in—

—Why don't you fit in?

What?

In your world—

—I fit in.

But you don't.

But I do.

Creach's right, but I'm baffled about how she's right. Somehow, I think it all has to do with what happened in the sewers. The moment Creach grabbed me by the arm everything about her changed; and ever since, she's acted almost as if she's been lugging around a skeleton on her back that seems to be getting heavier and heavier the more we trek.

Which makes me wonder if there's something else she's not telling me, or if it has anything to do with that special cuff on her wrist.

I do what I normally do whenever I feel cornered. I shut off.

Surely, there must be something you enjoy in your world. I noticed you listen to music while drawing characters inside your notebook. Have you ever considered starting your own band?

How would she know these things?

What? How? Have you been watching me?

No.

Then, what makes you think you know so much about me, *Creach*?

Creach holds up her wrinkled palm, as if she's giving me her own version of talk-to-the-hand.

And what's that supposed to mean?

Most shrills would call the ability to see what others cannot a curse. I, on the other hand, consider it, more or less, as a gift.

Shrills?

Me. Shrill. *You*. Human.

So, shrill is a race?

Precisely.

So, you can see what exactly?

I have the ability to see inside anything I can touch. I call it my *sorbere*—a term which was inspired by your world. When I stumbled into your world, I used my *sorbere* to locate you. You may not realize it now but, like I said earlier, you were calling out to me.

I was?

Yes.

And what was I saying to you?

You needed help.

I did?

Yes.

Okay, so, you're talking about telepathy?

Telepathics use the mind. We use our touch.

So when you touched me back in the sewers, you could read my thoughts? Is that it?

Again, Creach gets awkwardly quiet all of a sudden.

Yes. To some degree.

I mean, that's pretty cool. I guess. Avanti, my mom, she has the gift as well. I guess you can say it's kind of like telepathy. Sometimes, it feels as if she knows exactly what I'm thinking, like every now and then, she's poking around up there, trying to understand me. She's not shrill, though. She's what the people of my world call 'vamp,' which is someone you tend to keep your distance from. But, unlike me, she's good at hiding who she really is.

That's the first time I've heard you mention your mother's name—

—A'ight. My turn. So, what's your story? How'd you end up here?

It's a long story, Ajax.

I check the Blood Watch, which appears as if it's below that halfway mark.

I still have enough blood in the watch, which means I'm not dead yet. Right? The least you can do is tell me about yourself. I mean, I'd certainly like to know who's trying to help me.

My name wasn't always Creach. A very long time ago they called me Rapth.

Rapth? Okay. Rapth what?

Just Rapth.

The only response I have is a shrug of my shoulders.

Many centuries ago—which would've been twelve years in your world—this vessel that you're now looking at was dying after being poisoned through Leatherwood's water supply. Tragically, the poisoning killed many of those who lived in Leatherwood, including those of the Rivercry Tribe. The massacre was known as The Great Vanishing.

Rivercry? *Sounds native.*

Who's the Rivercry Tribe?

It is written that they once lived on these sacred lands before The First Migration, which forced them to the Mountains. The leader of the Rivercry, Krillish, is a legend around Leatherwood.

Krillish, huh? Cool name. Who's that?

Krillish is one of the most skilled hunters in Leatherwood, has a bite strong enough to chew through worlds. Even though he doesn't roll with High Order, he is more feared than any member of the High Order. It is written that a member of the High Order whose named was Toofont, was caught deliberately dumping 'corruption' into Leatherwood's main water supply. The corruption was derived from a wicked cocktail of corrupted pneuma, most of those captured from the Eventide. The worst kind of pneuma that has the power to corrode the very life force inside any living thing.

And why'd this Toofont do this?

In the *Chronicles of Krillish*, it is written that the corruption was meant to reduce the overpopulation in Leatherwood. Once High Order found out about this traitor who was working among them, Toofont was stripped of his title in the council and spent the rest of his days in hiding. Like many, I didn't have long before the pneuma of this very body was corrupted and left to perish. As darkness closed in, I was saved by a soul robber named Napone, who stole a pneuma from your world and, in return, sold the pneuma to another shrill, like me, named Pharrow, who then transplanted the pneuma into this vessel—body—you're looking at right now, which, in return, saved me from being swallowed up by the corruption.

So, how did 'Pharrow' transplant a pneuma into your, you know, whatever?

It's not that hard, actually. All you have to do is wait until the pneuma departs its vessel and then grab the pneuma before it wanders away. For instance, in your world, think of it no differently than catching fireflies in a jar.

So, once the pneuma is transplanted into this new body, then what?

The healthy pneuma will rejuvenate the body and mind.

So this Pharrow cat, who's that—

—He was my mate.

And he put someone else's soul into your body?

Yes.

477

Creach makes it sound as if transplanting souls from my world into creatures like Creach in this world is as common as surgery.

So, what? Where is Pharrow now? He die or something? Or, don't tell me, he got mad-jealous because you were showing off your new 'rejuvenated' body to other, much younger shrills—

—He died. But it was many moons ago.

Oh. Sorry to hear.

It was said that Napone killed and stole the Tunic of Lazarus from a member of the High Order to save this very body from death.

I point at Creach's wrist.

So, how'd you get yours?

Those who work for the High Order are connected to Lazarus.

You work for this High Order, huh?

Creach glances down at the Lazarus Cuff.

Sort of.

Well, do you or don't you?

It's a long story. I'm considered what is known as a crosser.

And what's a crosser?

I thought you'd never ask.

So?

A crosser is someone who's able to cross over into the other worlds, including yours.

And what does a crosser do exactly?

A crosser's job is to prevent one's pneuma from being taken by those of the Eventide. Think of a crosser as what your world would call a tour guide, although a crosser's ultimate goal is to guide the pneuma back to his or her rightful body.

And if a crosser 'you' should fail at guiding me back to my body. . .

I never fail.

More confident, are we. So, how exactly does one become a member of this High Order?

In order to become a member, you must save a lot of pneuma.

Curious, how much? If you had to put a number to it. . .

A lot.

So, you *are* a member of the High Order?

That's an even longer story.

Okay, so the High Order? What is that, like another tribe or something?

They are similar to what your world calls men and women of the cloth.

Like priests?

Similar but far more sinister. They are the Kings of the Jungle.

If they're so sinister, then why do you work for them?

I never said I did.

But you said—

—I'm saying it's complicated.

Complicated. I see.

The High Order remains at the top of the food chain and you will soon learn that the closer you are to the top, the safer you'll be.

Doesn't sound any different than my world.

In your world, you are able to pick and chose your leaders. In my world, there is only the High Order, and they are untouchable. They reside in the highest parts of Leatherwood, in a golden palace in the skies called Heaven.

Heaven? You're serious? So, how old are you exactly?

I honestly don't know how old I am, but my body is much older than yours. Yet, deep inside my pneuma, I don't feel as if I'm older than you. For all I know, we could be the same age—if that makes any sense.

No. Not really.

So, a shrill, huh? In my world, *shrill* means something completely different.

Is that right?

Yeah. My mom's housekeeper, Tameron, she's known to have a shrill voice when she starts barking orders at me. Talk about nails on a chalkboard.

According to the ancient text, the shrill race is written to be one of the oldest races in my world. It is written that we're able to survive past three hundred years old. But there are those who've survived much longer. After Pharrow died, I had nowhere else to go. Most of the shrills have migrated out of Leatherwood. Being alone in Leatherwood means you have a target on your head. In order to survive, I clanned up and ended up getting involved with a band of scavengers. We did a lot of terrible things. I was trained to kill those who got in my way. I always said it was effects of the *lingering* corruption still left in this old body. It is not me, though, who I am. On the inside. I have these fragments of memory of another life, the life living in your world. And they're getting more vivid as I age.

What do you see in these memories?

Drowning. Creach drifts off. I *see* myself drowning.

What else can you—

—Whatever the case, Ajax, there is no denying what we are by nature.

And what is that?

Animals. We are animals.

I don't know many animals that can speak like you. You seem more human than animal.

Don't let my appearance fool you, Ajax. I'm nothing like you.

We reach the top of another hill. Down in the valley below a city covered in smog resides.

We're here.

Which still leaves me with more questions than answers.

—

"Leatherwood"

Halfway up on South Hill reads the word '**EAT**' in bold lettering while the other letters, including the L, H, E, R, W, O, O, D, of the word *Leatherwood* are missing from the sign. Some of the letters were eroded by destructive particle storms that Creach says still pop up every now and then while other letters had been torn down and flattened by radical tribes. It's as if residents of Leatherwood are being reminded of their most basic instincts and never has a simple word like *EAT* carried so much weight—and impending doom.

Reminds me of a place I once knew, only way different. I look again. Well, it doesn't seem that much different.

What place is that?

In my world, it's called Hollywood—well, Los Angeles.

Yes. I've read about it. They call it the City of Angels.

Yeah. *And demons*.

Here, we call Leatherwood 'The City That Came Back From The Dead.'

As much information Creach provides me about the city of Leatherwood, as well as all of the bells and whistles of being a crosser, I'm still confused as to how Creach's world, a world literally underneath my nose, has gone completely unnoticed throughout my sixteen years of existence and I hadn't even heard the faintest utterance about it.

A little advice, Ajax: I wouldn't get too comfortable here. Leatherwood happens to be one of the most dangerous cities in my world. You think Los Angeles has its share of demons. Leatherwood makes Los Angeles look like paradise.

So tell me what exactly is this world that you speak of? Does it have a name? Or, you gonna keep calling it My World—

—Midnight World. Creach stops for a moment and holds out her arm. We call it Midnight World.

Midnight World, huh?

I look down at the skyline of Leatherwood below, the sight of the skyscrapers combined looking like the shape of the bottom mandible of a creature with rotten teeth. In the hub of Leatherwood a sturdier, less crooked skyscraper towers into the dark clouds above. The sky appears different from the way it looked back in the desert and has electricity to it, as if a storm is approaching.

—

"Pit Stop"

As we trek down from hills and into the city, we cut through gutted buildings and try to stay out of the public.

Even though we're headed directly toward a long strip of crowded, noisy bars along a desolate street, Creach can't emphasize enough that we, at all costs, avoid being spotted by the self-indulgent ones inside the bars.

We pass by a mutilated statue of a centaur-looking figure called Bucky Leatherwood. Hardly anything remains of the statue's head and the left side of its face is caved in and appears as if it's been melted.

Who's Bucky Leatherwood?

Bucky Leatherwood is the founder of Leatherwood. The city was named after Bucky Leatherwood here, a notorious *junk* collector, former crosser; however, he didn't work for the High Order.

As Creach is explaining the history of Bucky Leatherwood and his obsessions with my world, in particular, 'America' and 'American culture,' I'm pulled away from the statue by a creature slightly taller than me scurrying away into a recess between two dilapidated buildings. I take a closer look at the spryly creature before it disappears in the shadows. I swear the creature had as many legs as a centipede. Yet, it looked more human the animal. I freak out, knowing that Creach is not the only one who looks different in Midnight World.

What the hell is this place?

I told you. This is Leatherwood.

Creach shows me the way.

More on guard, I follow.

As we make are way around a strip of bars, I can't help but notice two particular establishments, one of them appears to be an outer space-themed bar decorated with outer space memorabilia. For example, the round metal panel with the word NASA mounted above a corridor-like entranceway. Perched next to the entrance is an empty suit of a life-sized astronaut holding a black flag.

I peek through one of the tiny windows. Inside the bar are dozens of monkeys; however, these monkeys appear as if they've experienced decades of mutation. I spot a couple of monkey-looking creatures, as tall as your average human, wearing these modified oxygen masks over their faces, while other monkeys have been altered by gravity—or the lack of gravity—making their postures more gangly and hunchback, their limbs longer and leaner. Some of the monkeys are more like the monkeys I'm used to seeing, and those happened to be the ones flinging projectiles across the bar in what I can only describe as an epic dung fight. As far as the other bar. . .

America?

Outside the bar the massive fossil of a Tyrannosaurus Rex suspends from the glowing America bar sign. The American flag, which appears as if it's been torn to shreds, hangs loosely on the front of the door.

Creach holds out her hand, preventing me from stepping forward for a closer look into the bar's window.

I would especially stay away from that place.

Why?

It's a zombie bar.

Zombie bar? What?

I manage to get just a sneak peek inside the bar where hordes of brain-eating zombies are picking apart what Creach calls a Gobile, which is a cross between a goblin and a frog. The zombies appear as if they're trying to consume the light— or pneuma—a popular zombie appetizer.

You don't want to know what they serve up as their main course. The whole 'you are what you eat' expression is all bullshit. You every heard of the 'A zombie walks into a bar' joke?

No. I haven't.

Suddenly, one zombie in particular removes his serrated teeth from gnawing on a Gobile's square-shaped skull and snaps his head toward me, his jaw nearly swinging from his face from the sudden head turn. Several other zombies follow suit and turn toward the window.

I thought you said I could only be seen by those who were wearing the Lazarus thingy, which means I can't be harmed. Right?

You can't.

Can't what? Be seen or be harmed?

As long as you stay close to me, you'll be fine. Now, let's go.

We leave as soon as the zombie pokes his head from the shredded curtain of the flag. Then, he goes back into the bar and continues to eat.

I try to keep up with Creach.

Can you explain to me why we're being so secretive?

Because.

Why do I get the feeling you're not being completely honest with me?

There are those few who can see you without Lazarus, highly skilled predators who can see beyond the walls that imprison us.

Like that Krillish-cat?

Yes. Like Krillish.

And I take it these highly skilled predators are pretty hostile?

Yes. Like I said, as long as you stay close to me, you'll be fine.

We move through the hellish city using the cover of buildings. It's not until I see a ruthless gang tearing apart what used to be a porky-pig looking dude that I realize the imminent danger of Leatherwood. There are no laws here, nor any police to enforce laws. Only some group called High Order, which, from the streets, looks as if they're untouchable.

After a gang of what looks like human-like scorpions finishes eating, Creach sneaks me over to the latest kill—or what's left of the latest kill. All I can recognize is the snout, as well as the tusks on its fleshy face.

Creach reaches down and grabs a loose brick lying on the ground and with the corner of the brick, gives a good whack against the side of the half man-half bore's mouth. Then pries off one of the lower teeth that had been loosened by the brick. Creach pockets the tooth. She kneels back down after second thought and pries off yet another tooth, this time one of the tusks protruding from its shattered jaw. As with the other tooth, Creach pockets the tusk.

You want to explain to me why in the hell you removed its teeth?

I'll need it for later.

Need it for what?

Creach turns to me.

For you.

We leave Downtown Leatherwood, where most of the action is taking place, and arrive at an even rougher yet eerily suspicious part of the city called SOTO, which stands for Soul Town, the district being so quiet and desolate that I wait for tumbleweed to skip by as they do in old Westerns. We stay off the main streets and cut through several alleyways where dark shadows of what looks like empty buildings offer their share of lurking creatures which Creach calls Gigermites, and the reasons we're not currently being consumed— *pneuma* included—is more than likely because the Gigermites have recently feasted on tourists.

With the notion of being consumed by a Gigermite, I make sure to stay even closer to Creach as she takes me to a biker-like bar called Beta.

Looks familiar. So, what are we doing here? I glance down at the watch and noticed the blood just dipped down well past the halfway mark. I'm running low.

This will only take a second.

And what's a second in your world?

It won't take long. Promise.

I follow Creach into Beta, which used to be what looks like a library, and as soon as I step foot inside, the terror hits me and leaves me in a paralyzed state.

Inside is a cesspool of both man and animal, as if genes have been mixed up like a blender, some having more human traits than animal while others more animal. Most of the action comes from the bar, which looks as if it used to be the checkout desk. The rowdiness quiets a bit as soon as Creach makes her presence known. Once hollers and bellows turn to hushed whispers and muzzled laughs. I can't tell whether or not these creatures fear Creach or worse, want her dead.

Whatever you do, try not to interact with other tourists. Like you, they don't have much time.

If they don't much time, then why—

—No questions.

Right.

I don't know what Creach is talking about until I spot a couple of people like me, humans—or better yet, pneumas who have the appearance of your everyday humans. Never have I felt so glad to see somebody who looks like me, who has a nose and chin like me. Who talks without a grunt, gurgle, or hiss. I notice they're sitting next to other creatures, similar to Creach, wearing Lazarus thingamajigs.

Sitting next to a guy who looks no older than twenty years old is a creature with a stubby elegant-like trunk nose dressed in an oily car mechanic's jumpsuit. The name on the nametag reads: 'Demo.' What stands out the most—except for that elephant-baby-like face—is the necklace around its neck, which looks identical to the Lazarus Cuff.

Creach walks me a freelancer named Azzgul, who's sitting at a table near the bar and playing with a Lazarus ring on his ring finger as if it's an oversized wedding band that doesn't belong to him.

Watch Ajax here while I handle some business.

Azzgul, who doesn't at all possess any of the traits of an animal, looks as if his skin is made of putty and someone thought it'd be funny to smash and playfully rearrange the features of his face.

With the lingering fear of being consumed by one of these creatures, I watch Creach walk to a booth in the back of the bar where it's more shadowy. She sits across from a strange man wearing a cloak.

I can't help but overhear one of these so-called freelancers wearing a Lazarus type of earpiece behind me talking about Creach and how she has a price on her head for what she did to Krillish. The name *Krillish* immediately grabs my ghost ear. Then, the name, *Gabriel*, which is apparently the name of a small town outside Leatherwood. I glance over my shoulder and shoot a glance at a root-looking creature with two beady black eyes sitting at a table with two other brutish figures with horns curled around the sides of their heads parked on either side of the creature they timidly refer to as 'Saggelstache.' I make sure not to make any eye contact or worse, stare at these creatures, especially Saggelstache, who looks as if he could be a real thorn in my side.

I'm drawn back to Creach who's sliding underneath the table the tusk he picked off the dead body in that abandoned building. The cloaked man grabs the tusk from Creach's hand.

Creach stands up from the booth. I turn away just as Creach looks in my direction.

If it isn't another Othersider from the Otherwhere. . .

I turn toward the voice of a hairy Sasquatch-type man with a whole bunch of black eyes and eight arms. He points one of his eight arms at Creach.

Be careful with this one.

Is that so?

Before your pal over there was kicked out of Midnight World, he tried to earn his scales by stealing the kill of the one who goes by the name Krillish. If there's one thing you don't do in Leatherwood is get in Krillish's way. Now, she's trying to repay her debt. So, if I was you, I'd keep an eye on her. She's a sneaky one, she is.

Thanks for the advice.

Hey, othersider, you know what the name Creach means?

I dunno. Creature?

Close. It makes a bottom feeder look like an Orderian—

—Don't listen to Data here. He's just jealous Creach has more saves than he'll ever have.

You want to say what you just said in my good ear, Azzgul.

I look around for the Lazarus device on Spiderman's body but can't find one. All I find is a crinkled photograph of a young woman named Chione in one of his many hands. Which makes me remember what Creach said just a while ago about those who were able to see pneumas with the power of Lazarus.

Name's Data, Data Longlegs.

Creach approaches the table.

Let's go.

Nice seeing you, Creach.

Azzgul.

Creach looks at Data Longlegs and doesn't say a word. Yet, the two have a stare off for a moment. Then, Creach walks away. I follow and do so quickly.

We leave Beta without any confrontation, even though the entire time waiting for Creach to do whatever it is she was doing it felt as if fights occurred on a regular basis inside Beta; and Data Longlegs had his eye—or shall I say, eyes—on Creach.

I don't put much thought into what Data Longlegs said to me; however, I'd be lying if I said was thinking about it.

—

"Opportunists"

Where are we going now?

Black Lake. It's an old tar pit located on the outskirts of Leatherwood. It's the place where your story will be revealed.

Are you sure?

Creach stops walking.

Excuse me.

I saw you hand the tusk to Mr. Lord of the Rings back there.

Creach starts walking again.

With danger lurking close, I have no other choice than to follow Creach.

You must understand that in Midnight World it's good to have friends in high places. When we make it Black Lake, you'll understand everything.

So, who was that guy in the cloak?

Let's just say I was buying you protection. You should be thanking me.

My protection? Protection from what?

Creach points at unlit buildings and the same glowing saber-shaped eyes surfacing behind the dark windows.

From that?

The Gigermites.

Listening to their dog-like 'back-off-or-else' growls throughout the darkness of the buildings, I find myself walking even closer to Creach. Close enough that I nearly ride her heels.

Don't worry. They won't bite.

What exactly are they?

Opportunists.

———

"Dinosaur Juice"

We finally arrive at Black Lake without getting eaten by any Gigermites.

Clearly, the name of the lake was derived from its appearance. Which isn't a lake but a tar pit surrounding by jagged hills and boulders the size of buildings. Even the stingy smell of hot tar irritates my ghost nose and naturally has me waving fumes.

I check the Blood Watch and show Creach how much blood is left. The tiny glass ball is about one-fourths full of blood.

I know. Time can be a little glitchy in SOTO.

What happened here?

This is where it all began. Creach points to the center of the tar pit. This is the site of the first explosion. This is where everything changed.

Creach nods at other so-called crossers like her wearing these different Lazarus devices and standing in a trance around Black Lake with other ghosts like me. Some of them are wearing Lazarus bracelets, earrings, piercings, and other accessories.

Other crossers, like me, bring tourists here to Black Lake to show them their truth. It is the final step before the pneuma is reunited with his or her body.

And what happens after people like me see our truth?

You are shown your truth to help you make your decision.

My decision? Which is?

Whether you want to live or die, Ajax.

What about that other place? You know, the. . . the In—

—The In-Between. Think of your transition as stages. You've already made it past the In-Between. Now, it's what your world calls crunch time—however, in our world, it has a different meaning. *Tell me about it.* Anyway, you have to decide whether you want to stay here in Midnight World or go back to your world. However, in order to make your decision, you must first see your truth.

Creach pulls out the same tooth from earlier, the one he pried from the dead man-pig in the abandoned building.

What do I have to do?

Creach holds out her other hand.

For some reason, I hear the words of Data Longlegs flooding my mind. How this one—Creach—is quite a sneaky one. I start to wonder whether or not Creach is using me to earn her so-called scales, as the creature from Beta told me.

In your world, you call it a leap of faith.

I glance down at Creach's hand. Then look back at the tar pit.

With the doubts burning right through me, I decide to grab Creach's hand.

In return, Creach hands me the tooth.

What now?

All you have to do is throw it in.

And what happens next?

Nobody really knows what happens. Only you do.

What about you?

This is *your* story, Ajax. Not mine.

I don't think much about the decision.

I toss the tooth into the tar pit.

Nothing happens, at first.

As the tooth finally submerges into the thick tar, pockets of tar bubble. All of a sudden, the entire lake starts to sink.

What's happening?

I turn to Creach, who's standing motionless. Her eyes are rolled back white.

Creach?

I turn back to the tar pit and watch it slowly drain underneath a floor of rocks and boulders.

Eventually, all of the tar is drained from the lake, leaving behind nothing but a massive crater. In the center of the crater is a dark hole, which looks similar to a triangular doorway.

Without saying a word, Creach raises her other arm and points at the hole.

I release my hand from Creach's hand and climb down the rocks until I reach the bottom of the crater. I duck below a jagged rock overhang and without doubting myself, walk straight into the void.

—

"Ghosts"

From my bedroom window, I'm watching Avanti, her mother, Grandma Washington, and my twin sister, Echo, lounging next to the swimming pool.

Immediately, I'm drawn to the baby blue wallpaper on the wall, as well as the bin brimming with childhood toys and the stuffed animals scattered along the bed, which is covered in a green and pale blue alligator-patterned com-

Dalivia Dlaut

forter. My hand is the first part of my body that sends me into a state of alarm, then, next, my alligator-themed Pj's.

I walk to the closest mirror I can find, and I'm no longer sixteen. I'm a child, no older than four years old.

I walk back to the window and watch Avanti excuse herself from the swimming pool in the backyard.

I leave my bedroom and walk outside where Avanti is making drinks on the patio. I call out to Grandma Washington but she completely ignores me. It's not until she glances over in my general direction in the similar fashion as a blind person tracking down a presence with unsteady eyes that I come to the bitter conclusion that I'm *not* here, my body that is, even though it feels as if I am present.

Underneath the canopy, Avanti discreetly releases one of her fangs and pricks the end of her fingertip. She drops several drops of blood into grandma's virgin piña colada. She brings the tainted drink over to Grandma Washington, who, after a polite thank you, doesn't waste any time sipping from the cool refreshment.

After Grandma Washington has taken several sips of the virgin piña colada, Avanti suggests that she and Echo go swimming.

Grandma Washington agrees and while holding Echo's hand, enters through the shallow end of the swimming pool. Only a couple of steps into the water, she stops for a moment and grabs her chest. She shakes off the slight discomfort and walks Echo farther into the deep end of the swimming pool while Avanti watches from underneath the shade of the umbrella.

All of a sudden, Grandma Washington grabs her chest once more, this time in great agony. She appears to be experiencing what I've always been told to be a heart attack. Echo, who's *not* wearing any floaters, which seems odd, especially for a four-year-old who can't swim at all, slips from her grandma's weak grip and sinks to the bottom of the pool. Grandma Washington struggles to stay afloat as she tries to swim to the edge of the pool. She ends up sinking to the bottom of the pool, as well. Avanti doesn't jump in to rescue Grandma Washington or my twin sister. Yet, she continues to sit in the lounge chair underneath the umbrella as if nothing is happening!

Finally, after Grandma Washington and Echo have already sunk to the bottom, Avanti stands up from the chair and walks to the pool's ledge and leans over. Creeping closer to the pool for a better angle, I first hear the splash of water, then see the water dripping all over the concrete walkway surrounding the pool. I notice a dark shapeless figure lurking in the shadows cast from the giant umbrella. Wet imprints of elongated feet mark the ground. A tall, dark creature, who appears to be cradling what I can only make out as a purplish speck of light *flickering* like a tiny pulse in one of its gnarly yet somewhat blurry arms, is talking to Avanti. I can't make out what the creature is saying to her, but whatever it is, it has a business-like façade of a two-sided understanding. The dark creature turns in my direction. Which doesn't make the least amount of sense because nobody can see me.

Behind the dark shadows, I witness four pairs of grayish marbled eyes tracking down my gaze.

We make eye contact for a moment.

Only for a moment.

Then, the creature slithers back into the pool the same way one of the alligators on my Pj's would hastily enter a body of water.

I hurry to the edge of the swimming pool and look down at the water, only to find the wavy, lifeless bodies of both Grandma Washington and Echo rising to the surface of the water. In their weightless ascent, their bodies collide, resulting in their lifeless bodies floating face down in the water.

And that's the moment I realize they're gone.

The fence opens behind me!

A slender, graceful woman dressed in all black enters the backyard from the side of the house. At first glance, the strange woman wearing cherry red lipstick looks as if she doesn't exist. Like me, she's just a tourist here for the show. After the minor memory lapse, I realize she's Vye. Of course, Avanti's aide. But *what is she doing here?*

Behind Vye is another woman, who I've never seen before. I hear Vye call her Storm. Throughout my entire childhood, I've heard the name before but each time I've heard the name any further questions I had regarding this so-called person behind the name were reduced to the fits or ramblings of a boy's wild imagination. The young woman, Storm, as she's called, appears to be under some kind of mind control—a spell! Her moves are creepily mechanical. Even when Vye instructs Storm to grab the bird's beak knife next to the wedges of lime from the table and then stab Avanti in the abdomen, she does so robotically.

Carefully studying each stab, Vye folds her arms across her chest. One hand erects upright, fingers curling around her chin in her best Thinking-Man pose.

Again! But harder!

Storm rears back and stabs Avanti in the side.

Vye continues to shape each one of Storm's violent attacks, as if she's a film director directing the most seasoned actor.

Now, the leg. We need to make it look authentic.

Gripping her bloody side, Avanti offers up her right leg while Storm searches for a blunt object.

The umbrella will do.

Storm drops the bloody knife, as instructed, and walks over to the table.

Make sure to turn over the umbrella base.

On command, Storm winds up the umbrella until the shade collapses and then removes the umbrella from the table.

Once the umbrella is removed, Storm kicks over the base with her foot.

No! Use your hands, please.

Storm places the umbrella on the table, kneels down, picks up the base, and then stares at Vye, as if she's waiting for further instruction.

Vye points at an area next to Avanti.

There should do.

Storm carries over the base to the edge of the pool and drops it on the ground. She makes her way back to the umbrella, picks it up again, then, without wasting any time, jabs the upper part of Avanti's shin with the umbrella.

Avanti screams out in pain.

Storm hits Avanti yet again.

All right! Enough!

Nursing her leg, Avanti falls to the ground.

At that moment, as a bloody Avanti lays on the ground and clings to her now broken leg, Storm, who can pass as a soulless corpse with her weapon, the umbrella, gripped in hand, stands right beside a crafty Vye, who's carefully picking over each detail of the scene; and then everything pauses.

Both Grandma Washington and Echo stop bobbing in the water, as well. Even the waves and the tiny ripples in the water come to a pause. I'm stuck in a still horrific freeze frame. Yet, I'm the only one who's able to move.

A dark and wavy figure grows in the corner of my eye, sending a series of hot flashes of panic throughout my body.

Thinking that it's the same mysterious creature from earlier, a greater sense of terror overwhelms me and then, strangely, once I lock eyes with Creach, I can feel my body divorcing all terror. I melt with relief.

Creach surfaces.

Dripping wet, Creach gracefully climbs from the pool and walks up to me. I should be freaked out by the sight of Creach, especially in broad daylight, as any four-year-old should be. But I'm not.

Can you please explain to me what's going on? I don't remember any of this happening.

Yes. You do, Ajax. It's buried. Creach points to the side of her temple. In here. You know what happened. For years, you heard the same lie over and over until that lie became the truth. But not *your* truth.

But I wasn't here. I was. . .

In the corner of my eye, I catch my own reflection in the stainless steel charbroil grille and notice that I'm no longer stuck inside my four-year-old body. Yet, I'm still up there, my younger self that is, standing behind the bedroom window, watching the horror below.

The sight of my younger self frozen in a state of trauma leaves me breathless.

But why? Why would she do this to me?

Everybody has a purpose, Ajax. You just don't know what yours is yet. But, in time, you will.

The scene unfreezes: Avanti returns to nursing her broken right leg while, at the same time, applying pressure to her stab wounds; Vye returns to studying the scene but this time doing so with her arms hanging by her side; Storm appears as if she's still frozen—or still on sleep-mode.

I search for Creach, but she's nowhere around.

Make sure you retrieve their bodies.

Give me a second, will you? Avanti pulls away a handful of blood. I think the bitch went too deep.

As Vye walks over to the table to retrieve the phone, her eyes move toward a small figure standing behind the kitchen window of the neighbor's house.

I have a better idea.

Vye extends the cordless phone toward Avanti.

Touch it.

Avanti reaches for the phone with her clean hand.

The left one.

Once more, Avanti reaches for the phone but this time with her bloody hand, leaving behind a bloody handprint. With her hand still wrapped around the upper part of the phone, Vye immediately pulls away the phone and tosses the phone on the lawn.

Vye instructs Storm to stay put while she walks toward the neighbor's house. I can't help but follow Vye to the neighbor's house. Upon arrival, the neighbor, a woman in her sixties, who the neighborhood kids used to call Dog Lady because she was always walking other neighbor's dogs, opens the back-door for Vye. Vye enters. I enter, as well. The neighbor closes the door behind her. Immediately, I notice the phone in the neighbor's other hand.

The neighbor faces Vye.

Slack faced, the neighbor holds the phone against her chest.

Do you have the police on the phone?

In that same robot-like movement, the neighbor nods.

You can speak.

Yes. I have the police on the phone.

And what have you told them so far?

I've told them that I heard screaming coming from the house next door.

Is that it?

The neighbor pauses.

Then, *yes*. That's it.

Very good.

Vye opens the door and as she's about to leave, she faces the neighbor.

You never saw me.

I never saw you.

We never talked.

I'm sorry. Furrowing her brow into a deep crease, the neighbor tilts her head in confusion. Who are you?

I'm nobody.

The neighbor starts blinking her eyelids in a seizure-like pace, as if her brain is somehow erasing Vye from her thoughts. Her face returns to normal, showing more expression.

Then, she places the phone back to her ear and closes the door behind her.

I walk with Vye back to the backyard where Avanti has already removed the two bodies from the swimming pool. She's administering CPR on Echo, which, I know, is all act. Echo is beyond resuscitating.

Vye leaves the scene, Storm follows close behind.

When I arrive at the front of the house, I spot two cars, one is a white hatch-back, which looks like its wheels are about to fall off, then the other one is a black limo. Storm gets behind the wheel of the hatchback while Vye sits in the backseat. Avanti's bodyguard, Joel, who I've known ever since I can remember, steps out of the driver's side door of the limo and opens the passenger door for me.

I don't say a word to Joel.

Yet, I stop and listen to the sounds of police sirens from a distance.

As I get inside the back of the limo, the police show up at the house. I count at least three cruisers, each one cutting the sirens. Each one of the officers exiting the cruisers looks young and trigger-happy. Storm drives away just in the nick of time. Joel follows suit and drives away as well, and keeps a safe distance from Storm's hatchback while the officers hurry toward the backyard.

Where are we going?

Joel rotates his head toward the rear view mirror. His face is different. He's no longer wearing Joel's face. He's not even a he anymore. He is a she, Creach.

What's going on?

I'm afraid this is for your own good, Ajax.

Where are we going?

You'll see soon enough.

Creach drives out of the suburbs to a rougher section on the outskirts of the city. Storm parks the hatchback in front of the apartment building. Vye gets out first, then Storm.

Having not said a word throughout the entire drive, Creach parks the limo across the street and gets out of the car. By the time Creach makes her way to the back of the limo, she is Joel again. Joel—Creach or whoever—waves me out of the limo. I step out. Joel closes the door behind me.

Are you not coming in?

What is about to happen is for your eyes only, Ajax.

As Joel gets back inside the limo, I walk to the apartment building. I walk up a flight of stairs and from the top of the second floor staircase, watch Storm pull out a key from her front pocket and open up the door to apartment 201—which must be her apartment. Storm enters. Then, Vye. I sneak in behind them right before Storm closes the door behind Vye.

In the gloomy apartment, Vye instructs Storm to close the living room blinds. She does. Then, Vye instructs her to grab three things: first, a blank envelope on the kitchen counter, then a Sharpie, which is lying not too far away, then, finally, the knife from the knife holder. After grabbing all of these items, she brings them back to the kitchen table where she takes a sit. Vye stands to the right of her.

Repeat after me—

Dear Stew.

Vye, who looks as if she's trying to mentally fight off Vye but is too weak, struggles to pick up the pen.

With her hand trembling, she writes *Dear Stew,*

Vye leans over Storm and grabs hold of Storm's writing hand, as if by doing so she somehow manages to lessen the tremble.

Storm only gets through two words, *please* and *forgive*, before I zone out.

I already know what she's going to write before she presses pen to paper. It's a letter addressed to Stew, but its primary intention is for the police after they discover Storm's dead body in the kitchen. I don't know the exact moment when it all goes down, nor do I know how it goes down. For the life of me, I don't know any of these events in the final timeline, but I know them to be true. Stew *never* cheated on Avanti with Storm McBride, and despite what I

491

witnessed back at the house, Storm McBride never attacked Avanti—at least, not Storm McBride, who was capable of thinking for herself without anyone else poking around upstairs. Stew's relationship with Storm McBride was completely platonic. The two knew each other from way back when they practically bumped into each other at every public institution made available by the city. They were close, but not close in a way that would suggest anything sexual or worthy of an affair. Stew kept the relationship secret from Avanti—or least, he thought so—and how he attempted to help Storm during a rough patch in her life but ultimately failed.

I snap hard from the heavy trance, as if I'm yanking myself from someone else's own thoughts.

Storm finishes writing the letter and then picks up the knife.

Right before Storm jams the sharp end of the blade into her throat, I zone out once more. This time, I'm not inside Storm's apartment. I'm lying in the bathtub in my bathroom. It's night, not day. Vye is sitting in a chair next to the bathtub, and she's handing me something sharp.

Once more, I snap from my trance.

By the time I realize what has happened, it's already done. Storm is already dead. Even though her suicide may have appeared as if it was carried out by her own hand, I know that it wasn't.

The sight alone of Storm lying in a puddle of her own blood on the floor triggers only what I can make sense of as a memory. I see myself lying in a bathtub full of blood. Vye's sitting right beside the bathtub, and she's pulling the veins in my arms as if they're strings; the ends of my veins are wrapped around the ends of the sick bitch's fingertips and she's controlling my arms like a puppet. Pushing aside the mad dance, I turn toward the bathroom door, which is open, and peer through the darkness; and for a moment, I witness the dark figure of another woman standing in the darkness of the doorway.

All I can think about is whether or not she watched.

I snap from my trance and turn toward Storm's apartment door, which slams close!

In a fit of rage, I grab the bloody knife from the ground and swing at Vye.

I make sure to aim directly at her throat—the death blow.

Right before impact, my body suddenly recoils in a violent flinch as if Vye's not the one I'm stabbing.

More confused, I look around the back of the limo.

Joel is driving me somewhere, but I don't know where.

It appears to be night outside—at least, it appears to be. I soon realize we're riding through a dark tunnel. Bright flickers of headlights run past the backseat of the car like strobe lights. A geometrically shaped beam from a turning headlight stretches along the entire width of the limo's ceiling and runs across my body like a scanner. The light brings out a couple of pinkish scars along my forearms, ones I haven't seen before. Maybe they were there all along, and I simply wasn't looking close enough. I count at least five of them scattered along both my arms in wallpaper-like pattern. Each razor-thin scar is light pink in color, aged and faded like a year-old stain on one of my favorite, go-to shirts that pays a visit to the washer once a month. It's hardly noticeable, if you're not looking for it; even if you have another pair of eyes to look at it,

more than likely you'll receive the same stupid 'What-am-I-looking-for?' expression. But when you look up close and you finally notice it, it's all you see.

As soon as we exit the tunnel, I take my eyes from my arms and marvel at
the vast New York City cityscape before me. The traffic is congested on the
streets, just the way I'd imagine.

What are we doing in New York City?

There's one last thing you must see before we return.

—

"The Governor's Closet"

Joel parks the limo right behind another limo in front of a swanky hotel called
St. Gabriel, which is bustling with mobs of reporters, journalists, and a security
team, which is as tight as a snare drum. Reporters travel in packs. Every now
and then, a lone reporter will pick off what looks like a politician or elected
official wearing a tuxedo that cost more than my entire closet and sock drawer
combined. *Flickers* of camera light shower artificial faces and toothy smiles.

We're here.

Joel steps out of the limo and opens the door for me.

What am I supposed to do?

All you have to do is follow the crowd.

Joel points to the droves of wealthy New Yorkers jamming up into a crowd
of black tuxedos and sparkling white dresses at the entranceway of the hotel.

And what are you going to do?

I'll be around.

I look down at my outfit, the T-shirt and holey jeans.

I'm not dressed for the part.

Well, that's because you're not invited.

Once more, Joel points to the front of the hotel.

I leave Joel and shoulder my way through the crowds until I finally reach
the main lobby where it's more spread out.

From behind, I'm greeted by a sneaky young waitress wearing a pair of
soles as soft as a wrestler.

Excuse me, sir. Would you care for a hors d'oeuvre?

I'm baffled as to how she can see me.

On her shoulder, the waitress is holding a tray of cucumber slices and
crackers covered in tiny black beads, as well as snails, which give off a smell
that burns my eyes.

I wave off the waitress.

No thanks.

She doesn't scram from my comment. Yet, she continues to stand there as
if she's hard of hearing. I give her the cold shoulder.

I insist.

The waitress takes a step closer toward me and extends her hand, which is
no longer her hand but the pale scaly palm of a seven-foot tall reptile named
Creach. In Creach's palm, she's holding a napkin with a live rat with a toothpick speared through its squirming body.

What you doing here?

How about a taste? You might like it. . .
Get that thing away from me!
Your loss.
Creach grabs the squeaky rat by its flabby midsection and bites off its head.
Blood squirts from the opening gap in the rat's severed neck.
Yuck!
You don't know what you're missing out, Veggie Boy.
Veggie Boy? I can eat meat, you know?
Sure you do.
I just choose not to.
Well, I can grab] one for your in case you change your mind.
No thanks.
I've heard that the hotel has a rat problem. Bad for guests. Good for me.
By the way, how'd you keep disguising yourself like that? Is that like one of your other superpowers or something?
I have my ways.
So, you want to tell me what exactly I'm doing at some fundraiser—
Before I can finish my train of thought, three vamps talking to the mayor of New York catch my eye. I know them and their queer vibe. Not only that, I can smell them as strongly as I can smell my own self. They give off a certain funkiness, which is often covered up by dabs of cheap cologne.
What do you want first: the good news or the bad?
Bad.
The bad is this particular *monumental* event happens to take place four years after your death.
You mean, I am dead?
Yes. In an oscillating motion, Creach points out the richest cliques in the lobby as if she's showcasing a future without yours truly. Well, at least you are here now, in this timeline.
I thought time didn't exist in Midnight World.
And is that where you think you are?
I mean—
—How did you get here?
I draw a blank.
With my ghost eyes batting in thought, I turn my shoulder and try to pin-point my point of entrance in the hotel lobby. I was just, you know, in a limo.
Yes. But how did *you* get here, Ajax?
I give up.
I don't remember.
For what's going to happen next, maybe it's best that you don't remember—at least until your story is over.
So, that's it then? There's no going back, is there?
Have you checked your Blood Watch?
I glance down at my wrist.
The Blood Watch is gone—
—Not gone, Ajax. You can't see it because you don't want to see it.
Why?

494

I'm glad you asked. You have others things to see and right now, you don't need the distraction.

What do I have to see?

For starters, how about this? Once more, Creach directs her attention toward the people—and vamps—in the lobby. Close your eyes.

What?

I said, 'Close your eyes.'

Creach places her knobby, scaly hand over my eyes.

Are they closed?

Finally, I close them.

Yes.

Creach removes her hand.

Now, open them.

I do as Creach commands and open my eyelids, which act like curtains peeling back that fine layer of reality in order to reveal a dead man's party. Standing around me are skeletons dressed in tuxedos and designer dresses. Their fangs are sharp and exposed. Even the once golden-laced, ritzy aesthetics embroidering the lobby is dull and disordered and splattered with blood, which has a brown, soiled appearance from where the oxygen choked out its once movie-red color. Among the crowd of skeletons, I witness one particular figure in a light green dress. The dress suggests that she's a woman; however, she's not as skeletal as the others in the crowd, yet the reddish muscle and tissue, even the veins of her nervous system, still remain intact to her partially exposed skeleton. She turns toward my direction. I can only make out the color in her eyes.

Your world is nothing but a filter and it's time you see it for what it truly is.

What is this? What are you doing? What are you showing me?

I'm not showing you anything. This is *all* you.

Me?

You're finally able to see the faces behind the mask.

I can no longer look at all of the death surrounding me. They turn their black eye sockets toward me and stare at me with voids for eyes.

No! Stop it!

In a fluid motion, Creach runs her hand down my range of vision.

The skeletal faces are gone, replaced by the empty, pale stares of New York's wealthiest elitists who wouldn't dare label themselves as a percentage.

I search for that one particular woman who was covered in all that muscle and tissue in the crowd.

With her back turned, she's walking in the other direction.

A part of me knows it's her.

And another part of me now knows exactly what *I'm* doing here.

What did I just see?

You saw a world without a filter. Now for the real reason why you're here in Manhattan. . .

Walking alongside Creach, we enter a ballroom, which, despite the lobby once teeming with vamps galore, appears, at first glance, stark empty. Then, after I take a closer look at the dark and unlit dining area, I witness hundreds of silhouettes motionlessly sitting at round tables covered in white tablecloths.

The silhouettes, as dark as shadows, remain still despite the door abruptly closing behind us, which cancels out all chatter and noise from the lobby. Yet, they just sit there, like film props.

To the left of the dining area, I discover more dark silhouettes dancing on a dim dance floor. The farther I walk into the ballroom, the dimmer the dance floor becomes. Eventually, the dance floor fades to darkness, bringing more light to the stage.

In the center of the stage a single spotlight shines brightly on a podium with a microphone.

Only a few steps in, I notice Creach isn't moving. She, too, remains still and reverent.

Are you not coming?

No. But I won't be far.

Where you going?

I saw a rat near the bar with my name on it.

Nice.

I can't help but glance at the lit podium.

What am I supposed to do?

I'm afraid I can't answer any more questions, Ajax. You already know what to do.

I do—*I think*. But wait a sec!

Creach stops and turns back around.

What do I say?

The faint grayish light dims around Creach until I can no longer see her body standing there.

Creach! What do I say? *Creach*!

Facing the stage, I suddenly feel the heat of the spotlight pressed against my pneuma. The feel alone is familiar. I can actually *feel* the light.

More confident, I walk onto the stage, zigzagging around tables where shadowy figures are sitting still. Each one of them gives off an eerie coldness to them and I can't help but tremble from being so close to their deathly presence.

Finally, after carefully navigating my way through the dimly lit dining area, I arrive at the stage, which is even brighter than before; and when I gaze upon its magnetic lure, my ghost eyes squint from its soft, overpowering glow. I surrender to the bright light and as I approach the podium, I find myself bathing in it.

Once I reach the podium, I catch another dark figure in the corner of my eye. Creach is standing off stage behind the curtain, dipping her head in a nod, as if, in an all-knowing way, she's encouraging me to speak.

I step closer to the podium and as I place both of my ghost hands along the side of the podium, like the spotlight before, I can *feel* the smooth yet bumpiness of the wood on my palms. I direct my eyes forward to the dark audience behind the spotlight and see another figure, this time approaching the front of the stage.

For a moment, I see Avanti's face in the darkness.

I turn to my immediate right.

Speak.

As Avanti darkens to a silhouette, I adjust the mic before me.

The only words that come to me are the last words I wrote in my notebook.

For the longest I can remember, I've felt as if I've been living in your shadow, trapped by it, unable to move or breathe. All I wanted was to enjoy the pursuits of any normal sixteen-year-old. But even that was far from possible.

As much as I want to push the letter to the back of my mind and wish I never wrote it, the spotlight has a peculiar way of fleshing out the words.

So, where am I? I don't know the answer to that question. What I do know is that I did exist—once—during a crucial moment in my life when I wasn't able to form thoughts on my own and my innocence was precious and meant to be cherished, not broken. I had my whole life ahead of me.

I pause and feel the tingle of a new scar surfacing along my skin.

The scar, pink and jagged, forms along the side of my wrist, prompting me to run my finger across it.

Before I can lose myself in the scar, the words force me back to the mic.

I'm in my bedroom writing the words under the hot lamp on my desk.

This is where I've taken myself. To the Dark. To the place of no return. It's not like I had any choice. Right now, it feels as if it's the only choice I have left. Why, you ask. I've tried to put myself out there and show the world what I have to offer. For a moment, I thought I had something inside me, something worth sharing, something that gave me a voice. But the world didn't want to hear my voice. The world wanted absolutely nothing *to do with me.*

I watch Avanti's shadow silhouette moving closer to the front of the stage.

Sure, I could complain about how nobody gave a shit about me. Or, I can cry about how alone I am. Most importantly, I could point at the world and everybody who treated me wrongly and scream to the top of my lungs: IT'S ALL YOUR FAULT!!! YOU COLD, EMPTY WORLD!!! You forced my hand!!!

The truth of the matter. . .

The world didn't give up on me.

I gave up on the world.

I pull myself from the podium; and to the left of me, I find Avanti standing at the bottom of the staircase. She's calling out to me, but her words are going right through me.

I turn the other direction and walk off the stage, the curtains closing right behind me. I walk with Creach into the darkness.

Behind me, a glimmer of light pierces through the darkness.

I hear Avanti screaming out my name.

"Robert!" she cries out.

I can't help but turn toward her voice.

Avanti's standing at the slit of the curtain, half of her face glowing from the beam of the spotlight.

Once she closes the curtain behind her and walks toward me, I lose her in the darkness.

Creach holds out her hand.

Let's go.

I grab Creach's hand, and together we walk into the darkness.

In the darkness, I hear the sound of *banging* over Avanti's voice. The farther we walk, the more her voice lessens. However, the banging intensifies.

Suddenly, I hear two loud, hollower bangs, like a fist pounding on the back of a door.

And like that, a door just so happens to open on its own.

Creach walks me inside a room filled with mirrors.

Where are we?

—

"Mirror, Mirror"

Creach holds out her other hand.

Welcome to the Hall of Mirrors.

Creach guides me toward the center of the room. There, I witness dozens of my own reflections in the mirrors covering the entire room.

I can't help but notice one particular reflection, which looks different than the other reflections.

In the reflection, my entire body is covered in pink scars.

I walk to the reflection while Creach stands back.

I stop in front of the mirror, gaze over all of the scars, then look down at my own self and find scars all over my entire body. Even under my shirt.

I have a sudden flashback of Avanti sitting by my bedside in a hospital room. She's leaning over to touch my arm—*There are just some wounds I cannot heal.*

I pull myself back to the mirror, then to Creach, who's standing behind me.

These scars do not and *will not* define who I am. I know who I am. But, in order to survive, I must first learn how to live with these scars.

Creach opens the door, revealing the darkness.

You have reached the end of your story, Ajax. But just remember, your story doesn't have to end here.

Creach steps into the darkness and closes the door behind her.

Wait! Where you going?

Trapped inside the Hall of Mirrors, I can't help but look around at all of my reflections; and now, each one of them is covered in scars.

Searching for the door, I come across a drop of black liquid bubbling over a tiny chip in one of the mirrors. I run the tip of my finger over the black substance, leaving a black smear along the mirror.

I pull away my hand, look closer at the black smudge of a fingerprint left on the mirror, and realize, in that moment, it's tar.

—*How did you get here?*

I draw a blank.

With my ghost eyes batting in thought, I turn my shoulder and try to pinpoint my point of entrance in the hotel lobby. I was just, you know, in a limo.

Yes, Creach says, *But how did you get here, Ajax?*

I remember standing in front of a tar pit called Black Lake.

Along the top right hand corner of the mirror yet another bubble of black tar oozes from the tiny chip in the glass.

With the bottom of my fist, I strike the glass as hard as I can. More black tar oozes from a larger chip in the glass. I strike the glass yet again and when I pull my fist back, it's covered in black tar. The chip has now turned into a crack that has the potential to spread. I wind back like a pitcher and punch the glass, causing the glass to dent into the shape of a spider web but the glass doesn't break; yet the glass feels thick, almost fibrous when I kiss it with my fist.

As frustration mounts, I remove the shoe from my foot and in a heap of rage, throw the shoe at the mirror.

The mirror suddenly shatters!

A stream of black tar floods into the room, knocking me down to the ground. Before I can find my feet, I'm already swallowed by blackness.

"Exit Poll"

With every muscle in my body tightening, I desperately punch and kick through the thick, gummy blackness until I no longer feel any resistance.

Gasping for air, I propel myself upright.

As I catch my breath, I wipe the tar from my eyes and nose.

Even the eerie, dim light of SOTO seems bright and blinding.

Creach and Azzgul reach their arms out to me. I grab hold of their hands and relief washes over me. They both pull me from the tar pit; and as soon as I feel the weight of coarse ground against my hands and knees, I realize that something has drastically changed. Each one of my senses is back. My entire body is covered in tar. But I can *see* my body with burning eyes. Even when I take in gulps of air, I can actually *taste* the air. Before, I felt as if I couldn't feel anything at all. I was weightlessly floating around like a leaf forever falling from a tree throughout a strange and slightly primitive world that seemed nothing more than a distorted reflection of my very own world.

Frantic, I run my hands over my arms, then my face.

Why do I feel so—what's happening?

I hear sounds of someone coughing to the far left of me. There, another person, like me but much older, is swimming from Black Lake. The man, who's also covered in black tar, is being helped from the pit by a creature wearing a Lazarus Tie. He, too, appears to be without any clothes. Which reminds me. I look down at myself and wonder where my clothes had gone. Fortunately, the sludgy tar is covering up the areas that I wish not to expose to Creach or Azzgul. I think back to the moment I met Creach when she spoke about the powers of the mind, and try to imagine what my pneuma would look like.

I picture myself in clothes, look down, and nothing has changed.

I forget how self-conscious humans can be about their natural appearance.

Creach grabs a soggy strip of a torn TIRESHOP banner draped over the side of the curb and hands it to me. I cover myself with the raggedy banner.

Thanks.

You're welcome.

Not too long after the naked man emerges, another one surfaces, same situation, only this time much slower. His body bounces upright and then sways from side to side like a buoy. The frail man falls facedown in the tar. Yet another creature, this one sporting the Lazarus device over one of its tentacles, pulls the body from Black Lake.

Creach, what's happening to me?

I will explain it later. Now, we must hurry.

Why? What's going on? Tell me what's happening. . .

Creach tracks down the glowing eyes of a Gigermite surfacing from the darkness of a cave.

I look down at the Blood Watch along my wrist. I wipe away the tar from the glass and try to read it. The more I wipe, the harder it is to read.

We have to leave. Now, Ajax. . .

Creach grabs me by my arm. I notice when she touches me the Lazarus Cuff no longer lights up. Yet, it remains dull and lifeless.

I stand to my feet, staggering at first, then toppling over. Creach pulls me up to my feet and helps keep me balanced. My legs feel numb and mushy like noodles cooked well past al dente. The more weight I put on my legs, the tighter and tinglier they feel. I take a step with Creach's assistance. Then I take another step, but this time without Creach's assistance.

There you go. Now, you're getting the hang of it.

What? What's happening—

—Just try to keep up, Ajax. And, by the way, try to stay alive.

Alive?

———

"Give Me Shelter"

After evading Gigermites, we arrive at Azzgul's rundown apartment, which is located directly across the street from Beta.

The apartment looks as if it once belonged to an old lady whose taste in interior decorating hadn't evolved with the times—my time, that is. It slips my mind how such a mysterious place like Midnight World is neither frozen in time nor capable of adjusting to the time, considering time moves so differently here. The walls are decorated in pink floral wallpaper. On each of the maple bookshelves, the shelves are lined with what looks like trash tossed away from my world: three crushed Pepsi cans that have been stretched out like accordions and given metallic arms and legs; broken animal figurines missing limbs; a rare album sleeve of the *Black* album resting inside a display case. I do, however, come across an old radio, which, despite all of the modern collections along the shelves, would match the Roaring Twenties-vibe I'm feeling throughout the apartment. The furniture is covered in plastic to prevent Azzgul and other creatures from clawing the wool of the couch. To make matters worse, the place reeks of rotten cat food.

Why don't you take a shower while I grab you a pair of clothes?

You take showers?

Of course, we do. After all, we were once like you, Ajax.

Right. So, where's this shower?

Creach guides me toward a bedroom while Azzgul, who hasn't spoken a word since we got here, stands guard by the living room window. I walk into a bedroom, which, despite a teenager-like messiness, appears like any normal bedroom.

As I wait by the edge of the bathroom, which, unlike the bedroom, appears as if I'm going to catch malaria by just looking at it, Creach searches for an outfit for me in Azzgul's closet. I block out the brown stains of what I can I only imagine as being blood or feces or both, splattered over the possible disease-riddled bathtub, as well as the walls. I remind myself that the black tar isn't going to come off with a little bit of elbow grease.

Creach returns with an outfit—more or less, a costume. It's not until Creach hands me the folded red suit that I realize I've seen it before.

This is what Michael Jackson wore in the music video, 'Thriller.' Where did you find this?

As I hold the costume closer to my face, a waft of rot hits me in the face.

One man's trash is another man's—in this case—another creature's treasure.

Before Creach can answer, I already know where Azzgul found the costume.

It once belonged to Azzgul's son. He used to wear it when he hung around the Dog Bar. He's a little bit shorter than you. But it should fit.

I see. I weigh my options: either carry around part of a banner to cover up myself, walk around naked, or, the most likely and more suitable option, wear Michael Jackson's 'Thriller' costume that was probably bought at Party City before it was tossed in the trash. Despite the putrid smell, the sight of the costume brings me a sense of comfort knowing that, even though I may feel as though I'm stuck a place worlds away from my own, I am much closer to home than I realize.

So, where's the glove?

I'm sorry. A glove?

Never mind.

I take the costume into the bathroom.

I also put a towel in there.

You did?

I turn toward the bathroom and find a perfectly folded raggedy-looking black polka-doted towel, which looks as if it's used to clean the dirt stains off rims, resting on the top of a crusty phlegm-stained vanity.

Thanks.

I close the door behind me, place the costume on the cleanest spot I can find, and step into the bathtub. I turn on the faucet, which causes the pipes to clink and clank behind the wall before a burst of brownish-red water spits out. The water—if you can even call it that—smells like sulfur and immediately causes my eyes to burn. Eventually, the water loses its color and returns to somewhat normal. I flip on the shower and wash off the black tar from my body. The water is ice-cold, too, and even when I turn the knob to hot, the water feels as if it's getting colder.

As quickly as I can, I scrub and rinse. I can't help but notice my skin. I start to wonder whether or not it's from the tar. My skin feels harder, coarser, scalier. Even the scars along my body have somewhat sunken and connected to one another, leaving behind these deep, grid-like cracks along my arms. Even the hair along my neck feels much hairier.

Lastly, I draw my eyes to the Blood Watch along my wrist. Once I wash the tar from the glass casing, I notice that the gauge is completely black!

I only spend enough time to partially remove the tar. Then, I jump out of the filthy bathtub and rake away the remaining tar from my body with a towel.

I take a moment in front of a murky mirror covered in scratches and caked in what I can only guess as hardened pus. I check my body for any marks. As I rotate around, I point out two swollen areas, which appear like large knots, running alongside my shoulder blades. I reach one arm around my shoulder and touch one of the areas and it feels incredibly sore. I arch one arm out as if I'm about to do a chicken dance while, at the same time, keeping a close eye on my shoulder blade. The shape of the bone looks rounder and foreign.

I change into my new outfit, which, surprisingly, fits like a glove.

Once I step out of the bathroom, I flinch from the sight of Creach standing in the same position I last left her.

Have you been waiting here this whole time?

I wanted to make sure you were okay. Well, are you okay?

Considering the circumstances, yeah. I guess so.

I show Creach the Blood Watch.

The watch. It's black. I thought you said never let the watch turn black.

Correct.

I am dead, aren't I?

Do you feel dead?

I actually think about my next response.

No. I don't. In fact, I feel the opposite.

I roll up the sleeves of my 'Thriller' jacket. Again, I can't help but notice the deeper lines along my scalier skin.

Who were those other people back at Black Lake?

Tourists. People like you, Ajax. People who, you know—

—But I didn't kill myself.

I know you didn't, Ajax.

You know a lot of things, don't you? I'm starting to think maybe you found me for a reason.

And exactly what reason is that?

I dunno yet.

I draw my eyes toward a picture frame on top of a dresser. In the photo I see Azzgul and two other creatures, one, like Azzgul, whose face appears as if a child rearranged the features on his face, and then the other one, a slender and shapely eel-faced creature with purplish-gray skin as slick and shiny as the plastic furniture covers in the living room.

Who's the chick?

That's Azzgul's daughter-in-law, Semi.

I point at the one who looks like Azzgul.

And that's his son, I suppose.

Correct.

So, what's Semi's story?

Semi comes from the shrill race.

The shrill race?

But she looks nothing like you.

I don't look like a shrill because my pneuma is not a shrill.

Your pneuma caused you to look like that?

Over time, this body you're looking at started to *change* after I was saved by Napone. In Midnight World, the air, the water, and all of the resources that your world takes for granted, all of it has a way of tapping deep into your pneuma and fleshing out your true self—

—Mutation.

Apparently, the ancestors of my pneuma had reptile in them. But, like I've said, Ajax, it's not me. Who I am. On the inside.

I glance down at the scars on my scalier arms.

You must realize, Ajax, the stakes are now much more higher than before. In Midnight World, you either survive or you die.

Creach walks toward the window and stares at the glowing Beta sign outside.

The reason why I was so evasive earlier is because there are crossers who'd rather sell a tourist's pneuma to a member of the High Order opposed to earning a position with The Council.

Why?

Survival, Ajax. Just whatever you do, don't die. Azzgul will keep you safe here until the Gigermites lose your scent.

Seriously? So, I'm stuck here?

Not stuck. There is one way you can return to your world—

—I'm all ears.

Become a crosser, get in tight with the High Order. In your world's terms, it won't happen overnight. It may take years.

Years! I can't stay here for years!

It's not like you have any say in the matter, Ajax. It's part of the deal.

Deal? What deal? I never agreed to any deal.

Creach walks out of the bedroom.

Where are you going?

I'm going to sleep, Ajax, as should you.

Sleep? I'll sleep when I'm dead!

Maybe. But I'm cranky when I don't rest. Besides, a 'lady needs her beauty sleep,' am I right? Isn't that what the females say in your world?

I drift off from the sound of the comment. I remember Creach reaching out and grabbing my hand back in the sewers. Her sharp claws were now fingernails. Her scaly hide, human flesh. Even the feel of her grip was soft, feminine. It's not the change in her that I specifically remember. It was the look on her face.

Lost in the comment, I remain speechless as Creach leaves the apartment.

I walk to the window and search for Creach but can't find her.

What feels like only a couple of minutes spent in the 'Thriller' costume and I can already notice the sleeves, as well as the pants and crotch region appear much smaller and tighter, as if, in those couple of minutes or so, it's either the costume that has shrunk several inches or my body is *still* growing. Even those two protrusions along my shoulder blades feel larger and more pointed; and even when I raise my arms over my head, they hurt, not like a sharp, shooting pain, but rather a dull, heavy pain, a growing pain.

My attention is drawn to the bar, Beta, where a flock of business suit-wearing vultures are consuming a weasel-dwarf like creature. One man-vulture in particular is holding a camera and filming the other vultures picking apart the roadkill.

I decide to take Creach's advice and rest in the rickety bed.

I close my eyes.

I can't stop thinking about the comment about Creach being a female.

Then, Creach's expression. . .

—

"Smells Like Chlorine"

I open my eyes!

I roll out of bed and rush to the closet where I dig out a pair of black boots caked with mud. I slip on the boots and exit the bedroom.

Azzgul tries to stop me.

Creach specifically told me to watch over you.

Get out of my way, Azzhole!

I push aside Azzgul, who doesn't put up much of a fight, and hurry outside.

As Creach emphasized earlier, I make sure to stick close to the unlit areas and try not to make myself known.

After scouring the empty streets, I finally spot Creach talking to a disguised figure underneath an amber streetlight. I creep closer and inspect further. I come to the shocking conclusion that the disguised figure is the same cloaked man from Beta; however, he's not any random person who's supposedly giving safe passage for Creach. The man happens to be Avanti's right-hand man.

Joel?

What is he doing here?

As soon as his glossy eyes track mine, Joel pulls the hood back over his head and walks away, leaving Creach alone in the street.

Creach tracks me down.

I'm left with no other choice than to confront Creach.

You lied to me.

I only told you what you needed to hear, Ajax.

I never was leaving, was I?

Creach doesn't answer my question.

Why am I really here, *Creach*?

You made a deal, remember?

I remember. . . Images of lying in a hospital bed flood my thoughts; how-ever, I still can't see the shadowy woman sitting by my bedside, even though I suspect who she might be.

It was all a part of the deal, Ajax. The reason why you can't remember making a deal is because your mother erased it from your mind—or at least, she tried to. But time has a way of exposing the truth. Am I right?

I can remember. Fragments. A flash of anger rushes through my blood. So, what's your deal? What's in it for you, *Creach*? Was I only a job to you? I had a life. Now, it's all gone because of you!

'Two birds, one stone.'

What?

It's an expression from your world.

I know what it is!

My job is to keep you away, Ajax, until the election is over while, at the same time, I'm still trying to buy a ticket back into Midnight World, essentially, redeem myself.

Earn your scales, right? You liar. You never heard me crying for help. You lied to me. *She* sent you. I can't help but think about Creach's so-called 'sorbere' power and wonder if it's all a silly line to make me believe how special she is.

I didn't know who you were at the time.

And what? Now, you do? Besides, why in the hell would you want to come back to this god-forsaken place?

I was reborn here, Ajax. And I will die here.

Then, you belong here.

You're right, Ajax. I do belong here. Leatherwood is my home. This is the only real home I've ever known.

This place is goddamn freak show!

You want to talk about the circus. Your world is too superficial. All you and your fellow members of the human race care about is what you look like or how you act on the outside. Maybe, just maybe one day, when your kind is able to see a living thing for who he or she truly is on the inside, I'll find a way back to your world and hopefully, call it home. But until that time comes, Leatherwood is my home.

So, what? You want to come back to my world because you're scared of what people may think of you. Where I come from, we call that a bullshit ex—

—I'm not scared of what they'll think of me. I'm scared of what they'll do to me if they ever found out who I was. Whether you like or not, Ajax, here, I fit in. At least, I used to. But I'm trying hard to make things right again. Of all people, I'm sure you can understand.

I point at the general direction where I last saw Joel.

And why was Joel here?

He was just checking up on me. Making sure you were safe.

All this time, you betrayed me.

No, Ajax. I saved you. Like it or not, a day will come when you may have to do the same for me.

What did you do that was so bad for such a place like this to cast you out?

Over many moons ago, I got hooked up with scavengers who rolled with this group called Ill-Famy. I was hungry and needed to team up. So, in order to join their nasty tribe, they gave me the specific task of stealing pride of the next civilian who crossed my path. Sure enough, I found a civilian, an easy uprighter wearing heavy disguise, looked suspicious but, if I didn't join up, then I wasn't going to make it alone in Leatherwood. The Ill-Famy hung back while I made a move. The civilian just so happened to be Toofont. Little did I know that Krillish had been stalking Toofont that entire full moon. Unaware that Krillish was about to attack Toofont and avenge those who tragically perished in The Great Vanishing, I jumped in the way and tried to grab hold of Toofont but Toofont ended up escaping into the darkness. Krillish wanted my head for interfering with his business. Krillish figured the worse punishment of all would be to exile me to a world that would enjoy picking me apart. Once the word had gotten out in Leatherwood that it was I who was the one who prevented Krillish from killing the monster behind The Great Vanishing, I could no longer show my face anywhere near Leatherwood. Ever since then, I've been trying to earn my stay.

Creach hangs her head in misery.

Then, she faces me.

Sorry to hear.

There are some wounds that cannot be healed, right?

The words resonant inside me. I start to piece everything together: Avanti, who, surprisingly, hadn't aged a day, standing by the swimming pool and talking to a 'soul robber' that Creach had spoken of while telling me her story about how she managed to survive The Great Vanishing as a result of a soul transplant, essentially, her Great rebirth into the shapely body of an electric eel-looking nymphet known as a shrill; then, I envision myself lying in a hospital bed and sitting at my bedside is Avanti, who's telling me, '*There are just some wounds I cannot heal.*' I can feel her hand touch me on the crook of my arm. Below my cast, the pain slowly vanishes from the bones in my left wrist. I'm able to move around my sweaty wrist inside the cast, as well as the tips of my fingers in my left hand. Despite Avanti's power to heal only on a surface level, the other pain is *still* there, gnawing at me, throbbing well beyond the bones. I'm able to breathe better after suspecting who Creach is and why, of all the living creatures in the world, Avanti chose Creach to watch over me.

For years, she had me convinced that it was all an accident. But deep inside, I knew the truth about what really happened. A part of me didn't want to *know* the truth, my truth, you know what I mean? She helped me block it out.

Well, she's a politician, Ajax. And every good politician has a tragedy story.

There must be another reason as to why Avanti is doing all of this, something she's not telling us.

Take my advice, Ajax. Go back to Azzgul's apartment. Rest.

But I can't rest, knowing everything you just told me—

—You have to try.

Creach makes an attempt to walk away.

I still have to earn my stay. Souls to save, remember?

Well, I don't feel saved! I feel imprisoned!

The only prison, Ajax, is the one you make for yourself.

As Creach walks away into the shadows outside the streetlight, I specifically remember what she told me before entering this chaotic city, about fragments of her memory that, according to Creach, get more vivid as she ages, specifically one event, drowning. My deepest suspicion returns to the forefront of my mind. The name hits me, nearly knocking the wind out of me.

Echo. It is you. . .

Creach suddenly stops from the sound of the name rolling from my lips.

She glances over her pointy shoulder and stares at me. She doesn't speak another word to me. And she doesn't have to. I peer beyond Creach's face and witness an expression, so vague yet so incredibly innocent, pushing through her scaly hide.

Once acknowledging the somewhat religious awe hanging from my face after the epiphany, Creach turns around and disappears in the shadows.

—

"The Lines We Draw/Higher Purpose"

Nathan Katz, who had recently turned seventy years old, was expected to be a grandpa to a baby boy any day now. His daughter, Gila, who was twenty-nine and happened to be a Pisces, like her father, was due by the end of the week, but her OB-GYN told her and her husband, Lekan, that she was entering what she commonly referred to as the "Latent Phase" where Gila's contractions were getting stronger and more regular. Gila's OB-GYN couldn't stress enough that this phase was best experienced at home.

As Nathan did whenever life was about to reveal its certain surprises, he fell into an old habit, which often times turned into a bad habit. Nathan focused on work—and there was plenty of it. Nathan, who had been an architect for over forty years, was currently in the process of building his baby: a new highway called the "You-Way." Privately funded by billionaires across the country, You-Ways were going to be the next big thing in transportation. The ultimate goal was to revitalize the country's infrastructure by eliminating the very roads that had scored the earth and bringing safer, more reliable travel to the skies and reducing the release of carbon emissions.

With a baby boy on his mind, Nathan rescheduled a ten o'clock meeting with Kevin Twine, Director of the Department of Transportation, and decided to step out of the office for a cup of coffee, which would normally be handled by one of his many assistants. However, today, Nathan needed to take the work outside.

🕐

As Nathan was leaving his favorite coffee shop, Black Joe's, he was drawn to a crew of construction workers past the flowing aero pods across the beltway. The construction crew, which mostly consisted of dwellers from Midnight World, was assembling one of the Nathan's gazillion docking posts next to the Empire State building, which would be linked up to the web of You-Ways in the sky. The docking post was inspired by the "tractor beams" used in a broad range of science fiction entertainment, including the television series *Star Trek*. Crazy how some of the greatest inventions on earth originate from reading books or watching TV or movies. However, Nathan's attention was drawn to what was happening next to the docking post.

A young woman, probably no older than Gila, extended her hand to a Dweller who had tripped over a support beam lying on the ground.

The dweller, a warthog-like creature with two dull nubs of tusks who, legally speaking, was currently living in New York City under a worker's permit, acknowledged the woman's hand and eventually, after some patience mostly on the woman's part, grabbed hold of her hand. The woman helped up the dweller, who, in return, thanked the woman, who, in return, started up what appeared to be a pleasant conversation with the dweller.

The sight of man and dweller sharing a moment of connection triggered a sudden memory in his head.

Immediately, Nathan couldn't stop thinking about the number 6,000 and the images attached to it. It *wasn't a dream*. It did happen. He recalled the number of footsteps that he took from the point of origin where he made his daring escape from Midnight World.

🕐

Nathan rode a drone to Atlanta, Georgia, where he visited a once upper class neighborhood that was now rundown. Most of the houses were pending foreclosure and if you listened close enough, you could hear the tweets and chirps of birds among the heavy overgrowth of vegetation. Nathan sat down feet away from the exact location that he last remembered.

Nathan found the *exact* manhole and from there, he started walking.

🕐

Six thousand steps later, he arrived at his destination.

The once wooded area was torn down and turned into an entertainment center called The Epicenter.

Making sure to keep track of the number of steps, he forked out twenty dollars for a ticket into The Epicenter. Once Nathan stepped inside, he continued counting. The sounds and sights of roller coasters tempted him to lose his count. He ignored all the bright lights and flashy signs and sweet smells in the air and powered through the super mall. Finally, his six-thousandth step happened to be directly in front of a movie theatre called *The Twin*.

He couldn't help but laugh at the symbolism.

🕐

Later that night, Nathan called his "go-to" guy named Hoyt, who wrangled up a crew of illegal Dwellers. He couldn't emphasize enough to Hoyt that he needed strong—and *quick*—dwellers, ones who were able to work a job twice as fast as typical hired hands. Hoyt had the right crew for Nathan.

Once The Epicenter was closed for the night, Nathan and crew tranquilized the three security guards, two outside the main gates and one surveying the perimeter, and snuck into The Epicenter. Inside, two half scorpion-half spiders, who happened to be brothers, took out another guard in front of the security monitors. Nathan couldn't stress enough not to tie the guard up in a web. The last thing Nathan wanted was to draw any more negative exposure to dwellers. Nathan wiped the monitors clean while the other dwellers got to work. Among the other dwellers were these two brutish bull-like creatures, who were able to carry jackhammers, a miniature excavator, as well as other bulky digging equipment that weighed nearly a ton on their backs. The rest of the dwellers brought their shovels.

Since they only had a couple of hours to work until the tranquilizer darts wore off, the crew didn't waste anytime. They set up work lights in front of The Twin Theatre, planted shop, and got straight to work.

Only an hour in, the crew reached the special container in the dirt.

Nathan climbed down the hole with the help of one of many cousins of the notorious desert serpents and a highly evolved alien-like stag beetle and picked up the container carrying a twilight lavender light inside, a purplish light that Nathan had memorized by heart and could very well identify from an entire galaxy of lights.

"You did it, boys. You found her."

🕐

Nathan and the rest of the crew managed to leave before the security guards came to.

The crew was handsomely rewarded with ancient currency, which was cash. Lots and lots of cash.

🕐

After Nathan parted ways with the dwellers, it was already dawn. He surprised his daughter, Gila, with a phone call. She and Lekan were still sleeping, since they lived in the itty-bitty town of Colby, New Mexico, and were three hours behind. Gila managed to make it through the night without going into labor, which, for Nathan, was even better.

🕐

Despite having said he was going to visit, Gila was shocked to see her father show up at the house by the time she and Lekan were sitting down for lunch.

🕐

That night, Nathan waited for Gila to fall asleep before sneaking into her bedroom. Prior to sleep, Lekan packed the bags just in case. Nathan knew he was running out of time. With the container in his hand, he crept up to Gila in bed, carefully opened the container, and released the pneuma.

At exactly 4:13 AM, Gila's water broke while she was rolling out of bed to use the bathroom. As soon as she called out to Lekan, they both knew it was time.

🕐

Only a few minutes after Gila and Lekan arrived at Colby Medical Center, Gila was pushing out a baby.

After the baby was delivered at 8:23 AM, not only were Gila and Lekan surprised by the sex of the baby, but also the entire room—well, maybe, except for one person. Later, Gila's OB-GYN had absolutely no explanation other than blaming it on faulty equipment. As far as blood tests that were conducted during Gila's last visit, her OB-GYN claimed that the tests were ninety-nine percent accurate in determining the sex of a fetus. In Gila's case, she fell into that nearly scientifically impossible one percent.

However, Gila knew that having a baby was probably the last great surprise in life. From a cynic's point-of-view, it was something worth relishing. As far as Lekan's current state of mind, he was more upset than Gila even though he never showed it. All Lekan kept thinking about was redecorating the baby's room. He spent all that extra money on pink paint.

🕐

With a weight lifted off his shoulders, Nathan stood in front of the glass outside the hospital's nursery and watched his granddaughter resting comfortably with all the other babies. Lekan moved in beside Nathan.

"Talk about a surprise, huh?" said Lekan, as if he had been thinking of the right line to start up a conversation with his ever-elusive father-in-law.

"Life has a funny way of switching the script, doesn't it?"

"It's weird because, for the past couple of days, I've had his—or her—entire future drawn in my mind. He was going to play basketball like I did when I was younger. Then, after high school, he was going to go to law school. Then, after law school, he would move out of the house, get a job at a decent law firm, and eventually, get married."

"It's only natural for a parent to plan their child's future, Lekan," Nathan said wisely. "I was the same way. As you know, it backfired on me and I'm still left trying to pick up all of the pieces between Gila and I. But as she grows older—your daughter, that is—you will soon realize that the world will open its doors to her and it will show her who she's meant to be in life."

"And what do I do when that happens?" asked Lekan.

Nathan said, "All you have do is close your eyes and hope for the best."

As Nathan touched Lekan's shoulder, he caught a strange woman in the corner of his eye. He moved his eyes away from Lekan and stared at the woman, who was suspiciously dressed in all black. She was wearing a floppy black hat and black sunglasses. For a moment, she turned her head toward Nathan's direction and then walked the other direction. Nathan excused himself and followed the strange woman to the end of the hallway where he lost her around a corner. He searched through a crowd of nurses roaming the hallways. He saw the door to the staircase close but didn't exactly see her enter the staircase. He found the nearest elevator, which wasn't too far from the stairs. In front of the elevator, there was a group of nurses and visitors waiting to ride the elevator. *She wouldn't want to draw any attention to herself*, especially with other people riding the elevator.

Nathan decided to take the stairs.

Once he walked through the door, he leaned over the edge of the railing and peered down through the spiraling staircase. Four flights below him, he saw a dark figure walking down the stairs. He followed, but did so gingerly. He didn't want to aggravate his bum knee.

Nathan lost her once again after he made it to the first floor of the hospital. He searched and eventually found her exiting the hospital.

Once outside, he searched for her and, of course, found her not walking away but sitting on a bench covered in the late-morning shadows towering over the side of the hospital.

In the cool shade, Nathan sat down next to her on the bench. He looked closer at her face, determining her age. What immediately stood out was the heavy makeup worn on her face in order to cover up the spotty skin disease.

"I'm curious," Nathan started, as he turned his eyes toward a younger couple who were passing by, "when they look at you, what do they see?"

"They see the same person you're looking at."

"And is that what you consider yourself, a person?"

"After you lived up to your end of the deal and found a way to destroy the very thing that was keeping the curse alive, the hunger started to settle down two years into my presidency. The curse was—and *still* is—there. But it's fair to say it's not like it once was—"

"—How did you find me?" asked Nathan.

"I can spot your eyes from a mile away, Ajax," she said, removing her sunglasses. The woman was none other than the forty-sixth President of the United States, Avanti Washington.

The comment alone of his mother tracking him through the color of his eyes made him think about the day his eyes started to *change*. He was eighteen years old and about to attend Darmyth when his eyes started to change color; however, neither Nathan nor his ophthalmologist had any explanation whatsoever as to how one eye turned green and the other one blue.

"During my speech at Rosewater Hill, I saw a pair of eyes in the audience. I couldn't help but notice the similarities these particular eyes shared with my son. You know, they say the eyes are the windows of the soul. They are right."

Reflective, Nathan said, "I remember that day like it was yesterday. It was on that day you paved the way for future presidents to come. That was the day you peeled back the curtains and showed the world that we were, in fact, not alone."

I'm standing in a crowd of my peers, wondering what in the hell I'm looking at. To the right of President Washington stands a hairy, short creature who looks as if it's a kid wearing a werewolf costume. But I soon realize it's not a kid.

"You showed the entire world what our past actions have done to our neighbors. And ever since then, people around the entire world have been digging holes in their backyards, trying to locate this 'other' world you mentioned in your speech."

Me and two friends from college buy the last three shovels remaining on the shelves. Nearly every hardware store across the country have sold out of shovels or digging tools. But we manage to find three shovels. While we start digging holes in a soccer field behind the dorm rooms, I stop digging and fall into a deep trance. I can't move at all. I feel paralyzed by the thought of what's waiting on the other side. Alex is asking me what's wrong with me. But I can't speak.

"The speech must've had a powerful impact on you. I see you've made quite a life for yourself. That highway of yours will fail, though. Eventually, man finds a way to destroy what's meant to be good."

Nathan argued, "Given the rise in automobile accidents, I've come to realize how precious life is. Life is worth *living*. That's the sole reason why I wanted to build my highway, to save life, not destroy it. You're wrong about people. People *can* change for the better. I just want to know, Avanti: 'Why'd you kill them?'"

"You know why I did what I did—"

"—I want to hear it coming from your mouth."

"At the time, I needed a tragedy story, Ajax. And believe it or not, it was my tragedy story that landed me in the White House. After the curse started to lift, I realized that it was still there. Those who were close to me noticed and in time, I knew that soon the American people would notice. We all know that a President ages in the White House. So, I aged—or at least, I was made to look as though I aged."

"Violet Odem," Nathan said with hostility, "also known as simply 'Vye.' Yeah. I know all about her. So, what bush is she hiding behind?" Nathan looked around the parking lot. "I have a few words I'd like to say to her."

"You're out of luck. She's no longer with us."

Nathan was at a loss for words.

"One day, we had an argument in the West Wing. Let's just say I came out on top."

"Well, then, I'm glad she got what she deserved."

"It's not merely as bad as what I deserve," Avanti said morosely. "Now, having lived with the idea of what I did to my family, having to wake up every morning to the very thought, that's my hell. Even worse, I get to spend the rest of my existence watching those around me die."

"Such a pity," Nathan said, more cynically. "If I didn't know any better, it almost sounds as if you developed a heart during your time in the oval office."

"Ajax, I never wanted for you to live with this curse. I wanted you to live a fulfilling life and then, at the end, be able to tell the world that you did the best you could, considering the circumstances."

"That's where you're dead wrong, Avanti. I did live a fulfilling life. And the You-Way will be my legacy, *not* yours. It is my gift to the world. Believe it or not, it was Midnight World that showed me my purpose. . . "

After many years of surviving inside Midnight World, I have reverted back to my most primitive existence.

Creach explains to me it's the radiation that is having an effect on my body; however, I'm still convinced it has to do with my bloodline, even though my theory contradicts what Creach said about my pneuma being linked to our ancestors. All insecurity is gone. I no longer worry about what to wear. You know it wasn't long until I out grew that raggedy 'Thriller' costume. At least I'm slightly taller than Creach, which, I believe, is something worth bragging about in front of her. Not to rub it in her face or anything, but, yeah, I also have wings. You dig? She doesn't. I've embraced my new title as 'The Tooth Fairy.' Around Leatherwood, I'm known for being one of the most highly successful members of the High Order with one helluva résumé, including a ninety-nine percent success rate for lives saved. Work hasn't slowed down, but I'm not complaining. The work keeps me busy. Everyday, I find others once like me and show each *flicker*—which, I think, sounds a whole lot better than pneuma—where his or her path went astray in life. It's fair to say I've found a strange pleasure in discovering a flicker's cornerstone. Mostly, I deal with jumpers, shooters, cutters, throwers (those are the ones who throw themselves in front of moving objects like cars or speeding vehicles)—even those who think outside the box when making that final decision to put an end to the suffering. It's the ones who don't think at all that prevent me from sleeping. But I can't help but laugh at the irony and how my entire life I've felt as if I was always late to the party or damned by bad timing, the one who never spoke up at that right moment, yet I held my tongue; and then when it came time to speak, not a single soul was listening.

The only part of my job that helps me sleep easier is knowing that, when the job is done, I saved a flicker from death and reconnected them with the same body they were born in back in the other world. I'd be lying if I said I didn't miss my world, my home, my bed. I wish I was strong enough to fight Vye. Each day, I remind myself that it's the little things, you see, like a bed or clean water or even something you couldn't see, like the smell of an apple pie coming straight out of an oven, that I took for granted during those sixteen years of what I once foolishly called a pathetic life.

But this is my prison now.

And I am bound to it.

"Oh," Avanti said, more casually. "I believe it all right. I've heard a lot about this so-called 'Tooth Fairy.'"

At the peak of my success, Creach becomes one of the many victims from a string of bombs that had gone off throughout Leatherwood. The bomber is said to be another Toofont-fanatic, one who was inspired by The Great Vanishing.

In Creach's final moments, she reveals to me that she is Krillish and that she made up the legend of Krillish in order to give those who lived in Leatherwood a sense of hope. I am left with no other choice than to store Creach's flicker inside the High Chambers in Heaven where the High Order will look after her flicker. However, it is there, during my grievance, that I have another epiphany and realize that the High Order is no different than those corrupted souls from Eventide.

Without members of the High Order watching, I catch them consuming flickers in such a gluttonous manner. Their bottomless need for knowledge of the universe and power has driven them mad. I am no different than a puppet. I'm being used, like Creach was being used, to enrich the very flickers I save, making them brighter and more delectable, in order to later whet the appetite of some fat High Order blowhard who, even if he tried, can't even find his own dick. The flicker is no different than ripe fruit: the riper, the tastier. 'The greater the life the richer the soul': That was once our motto as a crosser. And I've also learned that those 'light baths' the High Order provided to us every full moon are a bunch of bullshit. It's all a production, all lights and camera but not action, all carried out by the letter in order to make us feel more included or 'enlightened,' as they call it. I fear my sister's flicker will soon be consumed by the High Order.

Knowing what is now at stake, I strenuously devise a plan to escape from this awful place. I work a new job: a shooter who shot up a shopping mall during the holiday season when people were buying Christmas gifts. As the cops were closing in to take her down, she turned a gun on herself. Multiple casualties. I do the one thing I said I'd never do: I desert the flicker. But that's the sacrifice. I let one life die in order to save another.

With my plan in full motion, I capture one of the corrupted flickers from the Eventide, bring it back into Midnight World, then release corruption in the High Chambers where all of the flickers are kept in storage. Corruption spreads like a tidal wave to the Walls of Flickers. I locate Creach's flicker just before corruption takes over. Of all the bright colors, her color is easiest to find: *Twilight lavender*. I steal Creach's flicker and I barely escape the Heavens.

"I'm curious, Ajax. What flipped the switch inside you? Was it a memory? Something you experienced?"

Immediately, Nathan went back to the moment he saw a young woman helping up a dweller from the ground.

"It was something an old friend once told me."

Nathan recalled what Creach had said to him a long, *long* time ago.

Maybe, just maybe one day, when your kind is able to see a living thing for who he or she truly is on the inside, I'll find a way back to your world and hopefully, call it home. But until that time comes, Leatherwood is my home.

"That reminds me," Avanti said, pulling out a wrinkled, black and white speckled Composition book from her gator-skinned purse. "I thought you might want your journal. You know, for keepsake."

Avanti handed Nathan Ajax's old journal.

Surprised, Nathan held the journal in his old, papery-skinned hands.

"I completely forgot about this," he said softly.

Nathan flipped to one sketch in particular, a sketch of a seven-foot tall reptile named Creach.

"So," Avanti said expressionlessly, as she pulled Nathan from his trance. "I see you're a grandpa now."

"Yeah," he said, finding Avanti's words. "That's right."

"Impressive."

"To be honest," Nathan said, "I never thought I lived to see the day."

"*So*," Avanti said, her voice rising, "are you going to tell me what they named your granddaughter?"

"I was the one who actually suggested the name."

"So, what did they name her?" asked Avanti.

"Echo," he said, graciously wearing Ajax's smile. "Her name is Echo."

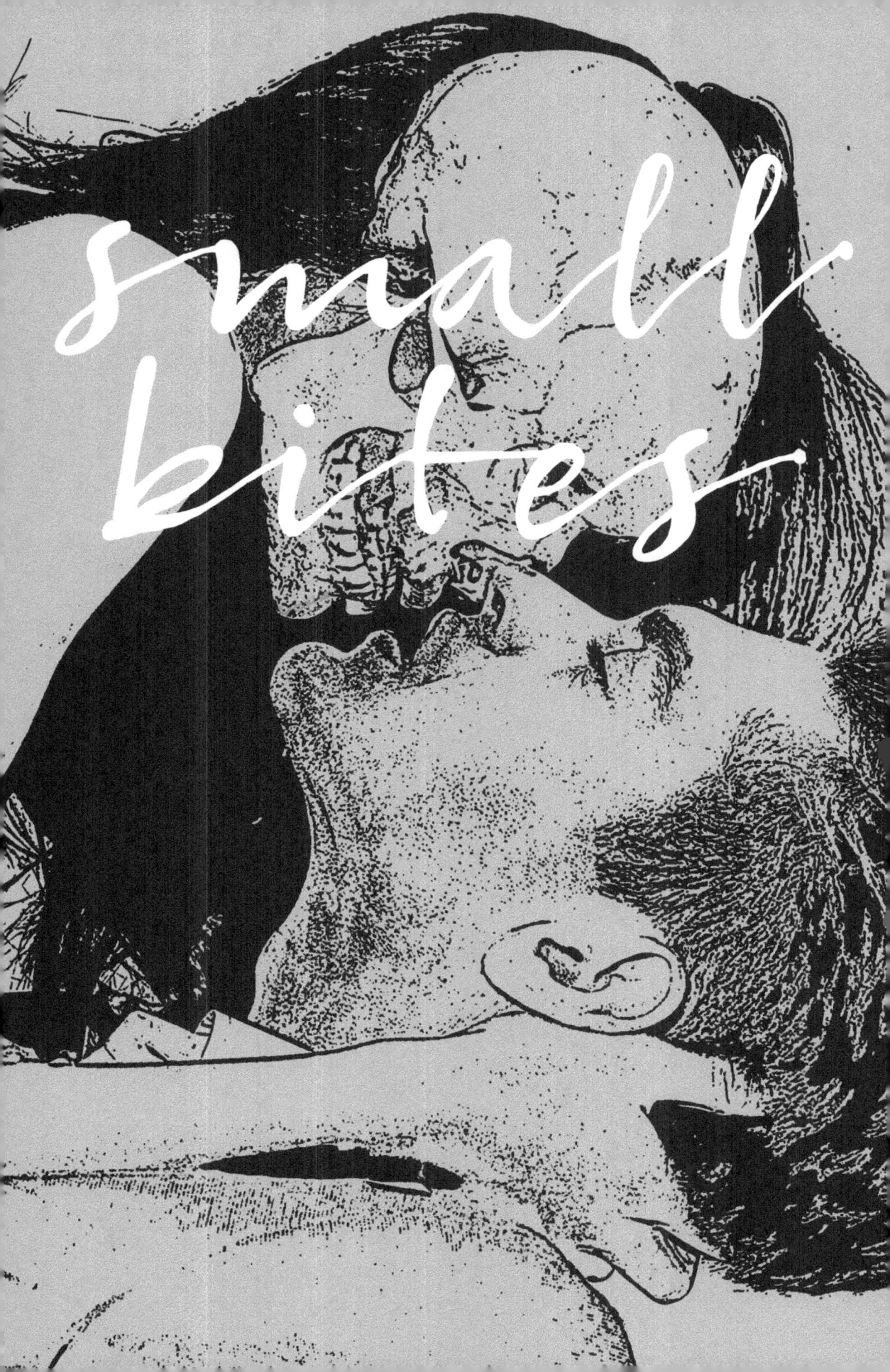

TAKING in gulps of fragrant hotel room air, Sandor let out a grunt as he finished making his fourth and—based on what little he had left to show for the woman—*final* transaction. His shoulders, as well as the upper half of his body, including his head and neck, which were arched upward in the posture of a wolf howling to the moon, deflated. Every muscle in his body, which had been wrought for hours, slackened and swelled.

With sweat dripping down his face, he rolled off Vera's body and plopped to the side of the bed.

Eventually, he caught his breath and turned to Vera, whose cheeks were both clouded with red. The sheets beneath her were soaked with mostly his sweat.

Vera excused herself for a moment while she traipsed to the bathroom where she grabbed a hand towel from the basket of toiletries, held it under the faucet, and soaked it with warm water. She wrung the towel and wiped herself clean, starting with her chest first but doing so briskly as if she was brushing off dust. She spent more time rinsing her private area, giving it a more thorough cleansing.

Afterwards, she tossed the soiled towel into a pile of dirty clothes next to the shower.

With less stumbles and staggers, she strutted back to the bed and as she was about to slip into her black lingerie, which included a sheer lace cup bra with adjustable spaghetti straps, satin bow accents, a hook back closure, as well as a high waist garter belt with metal clips, matching panties with cut-out panels and thong cut back, and thigh high stockings, each and every highly detailed piece of garment draped along the backside of a chair, Sandor patted on *her* side of the bed—he had already claimed his side. The gesture alone caused Vera to pause.

He said bluntly, "That can wait."

"Again?" Vera said, startled by the old man's energy. "You know it's going to cost you extra."

"Whatever," he said, once more patting that wrinkled indentation on the bed.

Vera set aside the panties and eased into bed next to Sandor and began to kiss him on the nape of his neck. However, he didn't show any affection toward Vera; in fact, he placed his phone back on the nightstand and carefully pushed her away before she could kiss him again.

Turned off by Sandor's withdrawal, Vera leaned away and asked naively, "Is there something wrong?"

"Let's just hang out for a while," he said, more seriously, as if he was start-ing the beginning process of a less showy, less *spunky* transaction. "Can we do that?"

"But isn't that what we're doing?" asked Vera.

Sandor didn't answer. Yet, he let out a deeper sigh, one knotted with anger, which made him appear more agitated by the woman's response.

For Vera, it wouldn't be the first time a client wanted to "extend" time with the so-called product. Vera had been with many other clients, more than could be accounted for (in other words, ones destined to be what she called "regu-lars," who were what Vera deemed as more talkers than doers and would say about anything considering their circumstances. Those who were the antithesis of your everyday "Wham bam, thank you, ma'am"-ers. She wasn't a shrink by any means nor was she one to hand out advice; however, she'd listen; and sometimes, despite the heat of the night, listening was all of what the job en-tailed. Because, for Vera, at the end of the day, that was all it was, nothing personal, just a job, bang, bang.

"Yeah," she said shortly. "Okay. Sure. You just want to *hang out*. I can do that."

They rested in silence, Sandor lying flat on his back and Vera, after pushing a pillow against the headboard, lying in an upright position.

Vera pointed at a faded scar running down Sandor's hairy forearm.

"What's the story here?" she asked and gave a tap on the scar as if it was her own subtle way of pounding on emotional floodgates.

Sandor traced the tip of her finger; and for a moment, he needed the woman to further clarify her question.

"This, huh?" He noticed the scar and then, *finally*, the story behind it. "I got it when I was younger."

Despite Sandor's silence, Vera patiently waited to hear the story.

"I was, maybe, I don't know, in my early twenties. Twenty-two maybe," he said, as the AC shut off and gave way to more authentic silence. "A bunch of us used to get together in one of my friend's garages every Saturday night and we'd have these boxing matches. Nothing too serious. You know, just a bunch of guys with high testosterone blowing off steam. We had gloves and everything—even had a couple of girls from the sorority act as the ring girls. They'd hold up signs between each round. To us, it was like Pay-Per-View."

"How many rounds did you guys have?" asked Vera.

"No more than three," Sandor said, intertwining his fingers over the patch of hair along his chest. "Most of us couldn't get past the first round. At least one of us would get knocked out by the end of the night." He held up his arm and once more, looked over the scar, then poked at it. "I got it when I was boxing this one kid named Derrick De Long. We used to call him Rhino, though, because he was born with this defect where his forehead protruded outward like the horn of rhinoceros. So, yeah, Rhino was what we called him. Story goes that during delivery Derrick was, let's say, stubborn and didn't want to come out of his mother's womb, so his father used a plunger to pull him out, resulting in his head looking the way it did. I guess it's because the baby's head is soft—or whatever. Derrick and I weren't at all close. We were once, but ever since I hooked up with his ex girlfriend back when I was a freshman in high school, there had been bad blood between the two of us. In a way, it was *always* there, that resentment. I grew up in East Side, a wealthy part of town. He grew up in Regal Park, which was where most of the crime took place in the city. So, I think, fundamentally, the only reason we were friends was because, one day, we knew we would be enemies. That night, we were beating the dog shit out of one another. I won the first round, but barely. The second round belonged to Derrick. I had him exactly where I wanted him though, if he hadn't thrown a cheap blow. He was a dirty fighter, did anything to win a match. As we were going into the third round, it's anybody's fight. But I know in order to beat him I have to get dirty as well. So, as we tangled up toward the end of the round, Derrick's got me in this headlock while, at the same time, he's throwing these cheap blows to my body. He leaves me with no other choice. So, I pull a Tyson on him."

"A Tyson?"

"You know Mike Tyson," he said, glancing over at Vera, "the famous boxer, probably one of the greatest of his time?" Vera was left expressionless, as if she was waiting for Sandor to give her another description that would piece together a face to the name. "You don't have a clue who I'm talking about, do you?"

"Yeah," she said shortly. "Sure. Mike Tyson. The boxer. I've heard others talk about him."

"Then, I'm sure you're aware of the Holyfield vs. Tyson match."

"*The Bite Fight*," she said, recalling one of her clients in Las Vegas from way back when mentioning that particular fight, as well as the infamous "bite" heard around the world, and doing so with so much hostility. "Yeah," Vera said, using a shorter tone with Sandor. "I have."

Sandor was somewhat taken aback from Vera's knowledge of the fight, considering she must've been no more than six years old at the time of the Bite Fight.

"So, anyway," he said, starting the thought by trailing off, "I pull a Tyson on Derrick. To say Derrick got what he deserved would be an understatement, but if I would've known, you know. . . " he paused, thinking more about what he really wanted to say to Vera, how the bite was going to haunt him later in life and *bite him* right *in the ass*, ". . . certain ramifications, I probably would've never bit Derrick in the first place. But thinking back now, someone really needed to put him in his place. If it wasn't me, eventually, it would've been someone else." Sandor's eyes darkened, as if the thought itself spread directly to both his eyes. "Derrick recoils, touches the side of his head, and pulls away a handful of bright red blood. Then, his face changed, and he was now wearing the face of a man who wanted to kill me. He removes his gloves, charges at me, throws me against the wall, and starts kicking me while I'm down before the others pull him off. Once the chaos dies down, I look at my arm and it's covered with blood. My blood, *not* Derrick's. I follow the blood trail to the floor, then the wall where I find a nail sticking out of the wall. When Derrick threw me against the wall, my arm ran across that nail. The cut wasn't nearly as bad as Derrick's ear. I mean, the poor guy was missing a piece of his ear. Eventually, he had it reattached. He didn't press charges even though he threatened me that he would. As for my cut," he said, raising his arm to glance at the scar as if each time he took a glance at it another new detail came forward, "well, you get the idea."

"Did you get any stitches?" asked Vera.

With his lips hung loosely in a frown, Sandor shook his head.

"No stitches," he said. "A buddy of mine had some superglue. Which made it even worse. The cut got infected. When it finally scabbed over, I remember for weeks I'd pick at it and try to make it worse."

Vera asked, "Why would you do such of thing?"

"At the time, I thought that the longer and uglier the scar you had the tougher you were." Sandor blew out a sigh from his mouth that sounded like a cross between a snort and a sigh. "Talk about the insecurity."

"Who isn't, right? Especially at that age."

Like she would know, he thought. *She's only seven years older than I was at the time* of the scar story.

Sandor rolled his head toward Vera and looked at her as if he wanted her to further explain her response.

"Isn't it natural for a person to feel insecure when he or she is surrounded by other people?"

"Only when you're young," Sandor said coldly, as he rolled his head forward. "Besides, you don't need a scar to prove to others that you're tough. It's all in the past, though. If anything, the only burden leftover from my rebellious days is the appearance of the scar and having to find ways to cover it up."

"You mean, like at work?"

"Yeah," he said hesitantly. "Sure."

As though Sandor had purposefully—or mistakenly—opened the door for yet another topic for conversation, Vera asked, "What do you do for a living?"

"Enough about me," Sandor said, putting aside Vera's question. "How about you? What's your story?"

In a way, Sandor's unwillingness to answer the question or even divulge any information about his work wasn't at all a surprise to Vera; in fact, she didn't expect anything less from a man who was worth so much money.

"I'm afraid my story isn't nearly as interesting as yours," Vera said bashfully.

"Yeah," Sandor said darkly, "but everybody has a story."

"I don't."

"Of course, you do."

"My story may put you to sleep, *really*."

"Start with where you came from," he suggested. "Where were you born?"

"I was born in a small town in Russia called Sviyborsk. I only lived there up until I reached the age of nine. I don't remember much, only that the winters were quite brutal."

"Do you have any siblings?" asked Sandor.

"No," Vera said. "Just me."

"How about your parents? What did they do for a living?"

"My mother cleaned houses for most of her life. We moved around a lot, especially when I was younger. She'd basically find whatever she could find. She ended up finding a sales job when we settled down in London."

"How about your father?" Sandor asked, turning to Vera.

"Daddy lives in the States, like you."

"I take it Mommy and *Daddy* are separated."

"Yes," she said. "They are."

"And let me guess, your Daddy doesn't approve of your profession."

"Actually," she said bluntly, "he does. Believe it or not, ever since I was little, he encouraged me to be whoever I wanted. He felt as if it wasn't his responsibility to get involved in the way I lived my life. No question I definitely take up after him, opposed to my mother."

Sandor asked, "How so?"

"We're both hardheaded."

While she was talking about her father, Sandor carefully watched her, in particular, the expression on her face—or lack thereof. Vera spoke about "Daddy" with a dark stillness, as if, whenever there was any mention of him or the subject of him, whatever followed was delivered with poise and grandeur.

"How's your relationship with him?" asked Sandor, as if he was being more polite.

"Good," Vera said, her voice rose a little from her answer. "Twice a year, I pay him a visit and check on how he's doing."

"And what does 'Daddy' do for a living?"

"He owns a couple of restaurants, one in New York City, the other one in Los Angeles."

Sandor drifted off for a moment. Food—or even the notion of food—had an uncanny way of putting him at ease.

"You know," he said, more loosely, "I've never had Russian food before."

"I don't think Daddy has either, at least not till he moved to the States," Vera said, more laidback as well. "The restaurant in Manhattan is Mongolian. The one in LA specializes in a fusion of North African-Mexican cuisine."

"You'd think one would start a restaurant based on their heritage."

Vera didn't have any response for Sandor. Instead, she turned to him and at the same time, raised both her eyebrows and widened her eyes as if the expression itself was her way of holding back any words.

Losing confidence, Sandor said over the silence, "But what do I know?"

"Well," Vera said, more smoothly, "he looks at the restaurant business as any other business in the service industry: What's the key to success?"

"Supply and demand, of course."

"Let's just say Russian cuisine never quite found its footing in American culture. Can you see the average American eating *borscht*?"

"What's that?"

"It's a sour soup served chilled."

"Who doesn't like cold soup?"

"You?"

"You underestimate us, *Vera*," Sandor said. "We'll eat anything, literally."

"But you've never eaten Russian."

"Well, except for tonight," Sandor teased.

He laughed from the joke; however, Vera barely brought herself to laugh and when she did laugh, it appeared as if it was forced.

Sandor's laugh soon turned to him clearing his throat, which led to a cough.

"You okay over there?"

"Just got something in the back of my throat." He rubbed his neck region as he continued to cough. Eventually, Sandor decided to roll out of bed. He grabbed a pair of silk boxers lying on the floor next to the bed, told Vera that he'd be right back, and walked to the bathroom.

After putting on his boxer shorts, Sandor leaned down into the sink and took a sip of cool water from the faucet, helping ease off the coughing spell a little. He touched his cheeks with both the front and backside of his hand. Then, he felt the top of his forehead. He was incredibly warm to the touch, which didn't cause any need for alarm, considering he had been drinking a wicked combination of alcohol throughout the night, starting off with a couple of glasses of Cabernet Sauvignon, then switching over to shots of hard whiskey chased with brown ale. Sandor didn't think much of his temperature, considering the recent "release," as he was known to call it; however, he felt slightly warmer than he normally did after his nocturnal activities. He splashed his face several times with cold water, which helped cool the warmness in his cheeks; in fact, the feel of cold water was surprisingly soothing to the touch.

As he pulled himself from the sink, he caught an object moving from side to side in the corner of his eye. He glanced into the mirror and witnessed the lower half of a naked man's body swaying back and forth, back and forth like a pendulum, behind the bathroom doorway. Both feet were at least three feet from touching the floor and each one was much darker than the color of the rest of his slender, spotty body; each foot bloated and swollen with blood.

From the ghastly, macabre nature of the man's gentle pendulum-like sway—Sandor thought maybe a draft in the room was causing the body to move like that, even after death—he looked as if he had been dead for quite a while, maybe days, maybe weeks.

In that throbbing silence, he heard the twisty, wringing sound of leather tightening.

Sandor forced himself back to the sink where he splashed his face with cold water. Even shook away the hallucination—because, he knew, it was *only* an image spawned from the darkest recesses of his mind—then he glanced more wearingly into the mirror. The body was gone. The sound of leather replaced with the rushing *shhh* of water.

As the coughing mellowed, he could feel a headache coming on, only a slight pecking of blood along the sides of his forehead yet it had the potential to worsen and completely wreck the rest of his evening. He grabbed two pills from the bottle of Aleve inside a small travel bag along the back of the vanity and washed the pills down with another sip of water. He followed with a sample of peppermint mouthwash inside that complimentary basket of *hotel* brand toiletries. He gargled for about ten seconds, then spat out the mouthwash into the sink.

Once more, Sandor cautiously glanced into the mirror, *not at himself*, but at the doorway.

Holding onto a silver-colored comforter held between her arms while, at the same time, shielding her breasts, Vera was sitting upright against the headboard.

"Should I leave?" she asked as soon as Sandor stepped out of the bathroom.

"Do you want to leave?" asked Sandor, who was approaching the side of the bed.

Vera gave him a child-like shrug.

"It's your money," she said.

"Yes," he returned flatly. "You're right. It is."

He picked up the phone, dialed the front desk, and ordered a bottle of Chardonnay. Before hanging up with the front desk agent—or "receptionist," as Sandor referred to them back in the States—he turned to Vera, who was still hugging the end of the comforter, and asked, "Would you like something to eat?"

Vera declined, said she was fine; however, Sandor insisted she'd eat. "Whatever you like. Let me treat you."

"I'm not hungry," Vera said defensively.

Which came off as, more or less, an insult to Sandor—a *bullshit answer from a bullshitter*, he thought. *She could have* literally *anything she desired* and even if the kitchen staff couldn't make what she wanted, he could have them fetch whatever it is that she wanted: a filet mignon or any cut of meat for that matter, even a stack of pancakes from iHop, which he'd have flown in from across the pond on his own private jet; yet, after spending hours in bed with Sandor, she wasn't at all comfortable enough to share a meal with him.

"Suit yourself," Sandor said to Vera, then ordered a hamburger, cooked "medium-rare," and hung up with the receptionist.

As Sandor sat on the edge of the bed, he checked his business phone. He received two messages on his phone since the last time he checked his phone. He glossed over the messages, then switched his phone from the silent setting to vibrate, then placed the phone back on the nightstand.

Vera asked, "Business?"

Sandor immediately straightened up from the comment. Way more serious in nature, he glanced over his shoulder at Vera with a slanted, narrow eye and said to her, "Yeah. None of your business."

Vera shot her eyes to the time on the large clock hanging on the wall next to the TV set.

"Do you have somewhere you need to be?" asked Sandor, as if he had eyes in the back of his head.

Vera wasn't quick enough to respond.

"I'm starting to think you have become more attracted to that clock than the client whose about to make you a rich woman."

Sandor propped up a pillow against the headboard and sat back in bed.

"It's nothing personal," Vera said quietly. "Bad habit, I guess."

Sandor said thoughtfully, "'*The two most powerful warriors are patience and time.*'"

"Profound."

"You should know," Sandor said. "It's Tolstoy."

"I still have Daddy's copy of *War and Peace*," Vera said, as if she was trying to win back Sandor's trust. "Still haven't read it, though."

"You know your writers, huh?"

"Tolstoy was before my time," Vera said, then threw it back at Sandor. "I'm more of a '*Time is Money*' type of lady."

"Of course," Sandor said. "The First American." With a grin on his face, he glanced over at Vera. "I get it. It's all about the Benjamins."

Sandor slid farther down in the bed and rested more comfortably on his back while Vera attempted to make herself content with the extended time with Sandor by uncoiling her somewhat tight grip around the comforter. Sandor made it easier for Vera as he carefully pulled down the bed cover, drawing her close to his body. She cuddled up to Sandor's side and with her fingers, played with a dark patch of hair along the center of his chest. Vera made certain to keep her hand on his chest and not once did she venture anywhere near areas that might draw arousal, like a nipple, which was known to be an erogenous zone for some men, the loin, or any other sensitive area around his abdomen. After three hours spent with Sandor, she was plenty sore and knew she'd be twice as achy in the morning. The thought of going yet another round with Sandor bored her—and just the notion of him having his way with her, especially after his last mediocre showing, she knew Sandor wouldn't finish until sunrise. Her vigilance was even more fortified, each maneuver of her hand strategic yet retaining its soft sensuality.

While on the subject of time, Sandor found himself falling back into a memory. He said more casually to Vera, "When I was your age all I cared about was money—still do, still nice spending it on beautiful things." Smirking, he glanced over at Vera. The word *thing*, with its usage solely held in the same context as a product, overshadowed the compliment and if the prize wasn't as great as the profession, it might've bothered Vera to the point where it only added more cynicism to her perspective of each one of her clients, in particular, men; and without further explanation, she'd put an end to whatever he thought he was buying and give him a refund. She forced herself to acknowledge Sandor, even though it appeared as if one half of the smile was being pulled by a string. "But it isn't as important to me as it was when I was younger," he said in reflection. "When I was younger, it was my *Holy Grail*. It was everything. Anything else, relationships, my marriage, it simply fell to the wayside."

As though the pale outline of a wedding band wrapped around his ring finger didn't give away the answer, Vera asked anyway, "Are you still married?"

"No," he said despairingly. "After the third, I gave up. What's the point?"

Vera didn't answer; and in a way, Sandor wasn't expecting one.

"When I was younger, I thought, without money, a man was nothing. He was no different than those dirty, sunburned-faced people who use to tap on the passenger side window and ask my father if he could spare some change. I remember he'd yell at them the same way he yelled at me whenever I was doing something I wasn't supposed to be doing, tell them to get a job. All I could think about throughout the entire school day was the rage inside my father. It was so visceral that I felt as if it came from a place that was all but foreign to me. So, whenever I saw one of those people on the side of the road, begging drivers for money, all I could think about was my father and that rage of his. Sure, money may be able to buy a temporary solution to a problem. But it can't fix the damage a man leaves behind in his wake. The ripple effect doesn't waver for anybody—it doesn't care who you are or what you've done—and those affected the most are left with only a tarnished image of the man whose selfish actions were based solely on the curse which he had been given: feeling. *Sadie*, my third wife," Sandor said, a glimmer of reconciliation rising in his face, as well as his voice, which carried a spiritual calmness, "she was the only person in my life who saw me for who I was and who I could've been. She saw the resentment I had for my father, who, when finally confronted, had given me the excuse that he had given me everything." He sighed and scrubbed away the rage that his father had passed down to him by turning all of his thoughts toward his third wife. "*Sadie*," he said more clearly, "she grew up in a home with absolutely nothing; in fact, her father, a welder, who, unlike my father, used to make his living with his hands, was once homeless and living on the streets. When he was younger, he traveled around the world, spent years in India, learning from a guru, then lived in Alaska where he was a deck hand on a fishing vessel. He told me stories about being stuck out at sea, surviving off whatever he had at his disposal. He had a story. In that story, he raised a girl who would later grow up to be my wife, a girl who was surrounded by the unconditional love that every child deserved. So, when I think back, about my father, *that rage*, I wonder if there was something *more* to the rage. For a man who was all about the rules—about order—I often wonder whether or not it was those very principles he lived and died by that internally eroded and eventually, over patience and time, became the foundations of his rage."

"Without order," Vera said wisely, "there is chaos. Life is founded on chaos, both deliberately and accidentally. If it wasn't for chaos, then life would cease to exist."

Sandor nodded his head in subtle agreement. More or less, he was somewhat surprised to hear those words coming from a young woman who was mature beyond her years.

"Honestly, though," Sandor said abruptly, that glimmer back in his face as he nestled his head against the sunken pillow, "I didn't know what in the hell Sadie saw in me. She didn't marry me for my money, if that's what you're wondering."

Having spent more time around people and listening to their deepest, darkest secrets, Vera only partially believed him and his comment about his ex wife, who, clearly, still weighed heavily on his heart.

"If anything," he said, "she showed me the man I had become. And that man scared the living shit out of me. I commend her, though, for trying to clean me up and get me sober. She had recently gotten over a damaged relationship before I met her. Maybe she needed something to fix during that time of her life. Maybe she looked at me as her own personal project. Either way, she recognized who I was and saw who I could've been. *Sadie*," he said, clearing his throat, "she was exceptionally good like that. She could see beyond things that any normal person couldn't see. You could say she had an eye for it. Fully aware, no distractions, in tuned with her surroundings, a constant observer. Which I believe had way more downfalls than perks." He readjusted himself by sitting up more in bed, causing Vera to follow suit. Once Sandor was all situated, Vera rested back down against his side and placed her hand on a bare spot along his left upper pectoral muscle. "There was this one time," he said and coughed a little and then reached down for a deeper breath, "we hired

527

a contractor to build us a swimming pool in our backyard. It was all my choice, not Sadie's; in fact, from the very get go, Sadie didn't like the idea. I went ahead and paid the contractor the money he needed to do the job. After the designs were finished, he said it'd take about two months to complete. Which, I thought, was pretty short for the size of pool I wanted. Sadie told me, the moment after she met him, that he was nothing but trouble. It was almost as if she knew what he was up to before he even started the job. He digs the hole in the ground, makes it look like he and his men are working. Then, a couple of weeks in the job, he or his workers don't show up one day. The next day passes, still they're a no-show. I try to contact him, but the phone number is no longer in service. I try to track him down, but it's like I'm tracking a ghost. One neighbor says he knows the guy, pulled the same shit on him a couple of years back. Then, I hear other stories about the contractor. Each story is the same: starts a job, takes the money, then runs. But Sadie knew the contractor's intentions all along. She saw right through him, like she did with me."

"Did you ever get your swimming pool?" asked Vera.

"No," Sandor said seriously. "And yes," he said, now comically. "Couple of weeks later, we got a terrible storm. Rain flooded the hole. Made an entire mess in the backyard. We had the hole pumped. Then, eventually, we filled the hole back up. No pool."

"Sorry to hear," Vera said but the comment didn't come off the least sincere.

"Nah," he said, waving it off. "It was for the best—"

Sandor paused from the sound of a *knock-knock* on the door.

"Expecting someone?" asked Vera.

"Must be room service," Sandor said.

As soon as Sandor said "room service," a voice behind the door said, "Room service."

"Told you," he said, rolled out of bed, and answered the door.

Sure enough, a room service attendant was standing at the door. Once inside the hotel room, he pushed in a cart carrying a tray with a closed metal lid, as well as a bucket of ice with a chilled bottle of Chardonnay, and rolled it to the front of the room.

"Good evening, Mr. Horvath, I have one hamburger and one bottle of Chardonnay."

The attendant asked if Sandor would like for him to open the bottle; however, Sandor declined, told him to leave the bottle opener, and then slipped him a hundred dollar bill into his breast pocket. The attendant thanked Sandor, left the cart, and then left the room. Sandor placed the "Do Not Disturb" sign on the handle of the door and closed the door behind him. He walked back into the room, first lifting up the lid over the warm plate. He turned to Vera, asked if she'd like part of his burger, which was surprisingly gentlemanly of him. She gave him the same answer she had given him the first time. He constructed the hamburger, removed the slice of onion, then took a bite. He pinched a piece of meat away with his fingers and further inspected the hamburger, which was cooked just the way Sandor had wanted—*Gotta love those goddamn Brits!* And you thought good ole America was the only place where you could find a good burger. He chased the burger with a couple of "chips," or French fries. He had also heard people call them by the name "crisps" during his visit. They weren't as good as the fries he had back home; but they did the job, which was not only to slay that rumbling, pissed-off dragon throwing fits inside his belly, but also help mellow the headache.

He swallowed roughly.

"Damn," Sandor said, clearing his throat, "if I was on death row and about to get executed," he held up the hamburger in his hand as if it was a trophy, "I have 'em call up whoever made this burger before I get the big needle."

"How dark of you," Vera said dryly.

"Just saying," Sandor said, as he took another bite of his hamburger. He said from the corner of his mouth, "Best burger I've ever eaten. You don't know what you're missing out."

Vera listed, "Bad cholesterol, heart disease—"

"—Right," he said callously. "You're one of those people."

While chewing the rest of his food, he inserted the bottle opener by twisting the corkscrew into the cork of the bottle *La Prairie*. He pulled on the lever, releasing the cork with a tiny *popping* sound. He poured two glasses of Chardonnay, one for himself and another for Vera.

Before bringing the glass to Vera, he took a small sip of wine to wash down the remaining food bits inside his mouth. One sip led to a chug. And by the time he lowered the glass, the wine was gone. He coughed, not a full cough but, more or less, another clearing of his throat.

As he was about to pour himself another glass of wine, he glanced into a mirror on the wall and in the reflection, saw Reagan lying where Vera should've been lying. She wasn't at all what he remembered of her. Her body was emaciated, her eyes and cheeks sunken in the sockets of her skull, which was visible underneath a thin layer of skin worn like an oversized body suit. She was reaching out to Sandor, as though for help, to end her suffering, to rescue her from hell itself.

As before, Sandor shook away the image from his head and witnessed Vera, *not* Reagan, waiting for him to join her in bed.

He refocused on Vera, her beautiful, healthy, toned body, and poured himself a glass of wine.

Somewhat satisfied by having a little bit of food inside him, Sandor carried the two glasses over to the bed. When he reached the bed, he realized the bottle opener was still partially gripped in his hand. He placed the bottle opener next to the phone on the nightstand and with his unrestricted hand, handed Vera the glass of wine. Vera, who was sitting juvenile-like on her crossed legs, held up her glass in a toast; and together, they basked in celebration.

"To good health," Sandor said.

Beneath Vera's smile, another smile was forming: a longer, wider, more sinister smile that barely formed along the dimples of her cheeks.

A darker smile under a smile.

"*To good health*," she repeated, as they clinked the sides of their glasses together.

Sandor ignored the strangeness of Vera's look, that sinister smile, and refocused on those calming hazel eyes underneath a curl of golden blonde hair.

Together, they sipped wine.

As Sandor lowered the glass from his lips, he glanced down at the sheets and found a black speck on the corner of the pillow. He picked up the insect by pinching his finger together. Once he realized what was squirming between his fingertips, he smothered it with a massage-like motion and then flicked away its crumbly remains onto the floor below.

"What is it?" asked Vera.

"Bug," Sandor said, glancing at Vera through the corner of his eye.

Sandor reached across his body and placed the glass on the nightstand. The move caused him to cough; however, he made sure to cough away from Vera. He checked his phone for any messages. He had "1" new one from a woman named Tatiana. The message read: "What are you doing?" Which, Sandor knew, was a covert text for "I need money."

More conflicted, he decided to close the phone and tend to the other woman, Vera, who, for some reason—maybe it was the alcohol—carried a glow about her, had these angelic vibes about her, as if she was luring him back into bed and ripe and ready to go another round; however, as much as he wanted to jump her bones, he was growing more tired by the minute. His eyelids were getting heavier, too. He just wanted to lie down.

So, he did.

And Vera made more room by placing the glass of wine on the nightstand on her side of the bed and lying back down as well. He pinched the upper bridge of his nose and rubbed the backside of his eyelids.

"Headache," said Vera.

"Yeah," Sandor said. "A little."

She patted on her stomach.

"Lay down," she demanded.

Sandor slid farther down the bed until his feet were hanging over the edge of the bed and rested the backside of his head against Vera's stomach. In return, she massaged the sides of his temples.

"How does that feel?"

"A lot better," Sandor said.

"It's a little trick Daddy used to do whenever I was feeling under the weather. He'd rub my head, and afterwards any pain that I had simply went away."

"Well, whatever you're doing, it seems be to working."

For a moment during that relentless circular motion of Vera's fingers caressing the sides of his temples, the ends of her fingertips suddenly changed texture. Sandor didn't think anything of it; he thought it was the repetitiveness of rubbing, like, for instance, when you loosened your fingers and lazily shook a pencil back and forth between your fingertips and after a while, the pencil felt as if it was no longer made of wood but rather made of soft rubber. The more he thought about it, the more the panic rose inside him. Her touch started to feel liquidy, as if she was digging further and further into his skin, beneath the epidermis, and swirling around his precious blood.

He cracked open his left eye and witnessed a lengthy leg of not a woman but a black, veiny, thorny leg of a sleek and shiny skinless creature that had the similar shape of a woman's leg. He snapped open both his eyes, lifted his head from her grip, and rotated around to Vera, who was concealing a smile on her face and holding back laughter.

"What?" said Vera in an innocent tone, as she waited for Sandor to respond.

Sandor was left speechless, as though, even if he found the right words to say to her, he didn't know where to begin.

"It's okay," Vera said to a more concerned Sandor. "Lay back down."

"I swear I thought. . . "

What the hell's going on with me?

"Why don't you try to get some rest?" she asked over his trailing thought.

"Yeah," he said, slightly slurring. "Maybe that's a good idea. You mind?"

She shrugged.

"It's your money."

Sandor sighed and rested the back of his head against Vera's stomach. Vera hushed him and stroked what little thinning hair he had left on the top of his head, as he took a moment to glance at her bare leg, which was sticking out of the comforter, then, after feeling the softness of Vera's touch, returning both of his weary eyes to the crown molding along the ceiling above.

"So," Sandor said relaxingly, "what was it like growing up in Sviyborsk?"

"It was cold," Vera said, relaxed as well as she carefully rubbed the sides of his head. "I know, right? Russia? Cold? I don't care who you are. Spending the winter in subzero temperatures isn't easy to get used to."

"No wonder you Russians drink vodka like it's water."

Vera smiled from the comment.

"Yes," she said. "We've been known to drink like fish."

"Well, who can blame you?"

"It's fair to say, for some, it helped get them through the day. I mean, there was absolutely nothing to do in Sviyborsk. For me, I remember being on my own a lot. I didn't have a lot of friends. I was alone but not lonely. I had this Teddy bear that I named Vasilii after a popular Russian fairy tale called *Vasilii the Unlucky*. I took that bear everywhere with me, on my journeys through the countryside. Having spent most of my life living in the city, there's still a part of me that longs for those days where I had nature at my disposal."

"Have you ever thought about going back?" Sandor asked.

"Yes," she said. "Sometimes. I suppose one day I'll go back to see what became of it and if it's the same as I last remembered. To me, I consider Russia like an old friend. One day, when I'm least expecting, I'll somehow find myself there again, in that coldness, in some shape or form, skating along the frozen lakes with the abyss below me. A casual misadventure perhaps."

Or bump in, Sandor thought.

He snorted from the very idea.

Then, shook his head with mild disgust.

The headache eased away as though it receded into his heavy bones.

"A few years back I ran into Derrick De Long—*Rhino*."

"Your friend from college?"

"Yeah," he said, trailing off. "That one. . . he'd changed so much I couldn't even recognize him. He had longer hair. That edge he once had—that look, that fierceness—not entirely gone, more like hidden, domesticated. He looked. . . " he searched his mind for the right word, ". . . *content*. He told me

531

that whatever happened between us in the past was all 'water under the bridge.' He sounded genuine, even though there was still a part of me that thought it might've been a front. So, Derrick and I grab a drink at this local spot not too far away from where I was living at the time. We have a few drinks and play catch up," a faint smile grew on the side of his face, "even joked about all of those boxing matches we had. Derrick did most of the talking. He told me about his business, sort of Mom and Pop-type of vitamin shop. He was successful in his own way. He has a child, too, not a child, actually more like a teenager. Said he got married right after college; in fact, his wife was six-months pregnant when they got married. She gave birth to a baby boy. What was his name?" Sandor paused, thinking of the boy's name. "It was a strange name, I remember—Thrace. The boy's name was Thrace."

With the circular motion of her fingers slowing down over Sandor's temples, Vera narrowed her eyes into sharp slits from the sound of the name.

"He was high school age, I remember. Derrick was proud of him. He played football, had potential to play college. After we catch up, we say good-bye and as we're about to go our separate ways, Derrick invites me to a party. His birthday is next week, and he's invited some old friends from college. I should've told him 'no' and kept on walking. I don't know whether or not it was pity—or something else—but I accept his invitation. Next week, I show up at his party after spending days leading up to it contemplating whether or not I should go. Only a couple of guys show up. Those who said they were going to attend ended up canceling at the last minute due to business and family matters. Derrick is already tipsy when I arrive. I knew I should've left the second I walked into his house. Derrick introduces me to his wife, Reagan. Immediately, there's attraction, this connection, *not* just on my end. Till this day, I don't know what it was she saw in him. I end up talking to Reagan as the party starts to die down. We had been shooting looks at one another across the patio throughout the night. She doesn't love him. She doesn't say it, but I can hear it in her voice whenever she mentions his name. I leave; however, the next day, I call up Derrick. We hang out for a while. We end up rekindling a friendship. In the following weeks, we start to hang out more on a regular basis: fishing trips, basketball games, even a trip to Las Vegas. Derrick started to suspect what was going on when I invited Reagan to Vegas with us. I kept hanging around, but really I just wanted to see her. Derrick knew it, but he couldn't do anything about it. The only reason why they were still together was because of Thrace. In a way, she was stuck with a man whom she didn't love anymore. And I expose the cracks in their relationship. When Derrick was away at a small business conference in San Francisco, I get a call from Reagan. It was the first of many times she'd call me over whenever Derrick wasn't around. Toward the end, we started to take more risks: hotel rooms, the park, parking lots. Do I feel wrong about what I did? Looking back," Sandor thought, then said without any hesitation, "no. I don't. But what I didn't realize was that I was the one who was coming out on bottom."

Keenly invested in the rest of what he had to say, Vera asked Sandor, "What happened?"

"I later found out Reagan was sick," Sandor said, his red eyes filling up with tears. "Bone cancer. Doctors told Reagan numerous times that she only had six months to live. She defied them each time. But I could see—toward the end—that she was getting worse. She refused treatment for the cancer. I ended up writing a check for her treatment. She never deposited it. That's when I realized I was expendable. Some fantasy-fuck. A middle finger to Derrick. Which had me thinking back: Was the time we spent together real? Or, was it one-sided? After she died, I then started to question my own intentions. Was I getting back at Derrick for what he did to me years ago? Had the hatred—that rage—gone dormant and somehow manifested itself the day I bumped into Derrick after years of shoveling him away in my thoughts? Not too long after Reagan died, the son, Thrace, found his father's body when he came back home from his Spring Break. Investigators ruled his death a suicide. A few days later, after Derrick was found dead inside the master bedroom, Thrace was found unresponsive by one of his friends. The friend called the paramedics. But Thrace was already dead. An 'overdose of VP-23' was the official ruling of Thrace's death. A couple of his friends blamed it on a bad batch of *red rocks*. But everybody knew what really happened."

"That's terrible," Vera said, unable to find anything reassuring to Sandor.

"Well, that's not even the worst part," Sandor said more quietly, as he started to drift off. "I have to live knowing that I was responsible for destroying an entire family. My whole life I was the one who was always in control. With Reagan, I had no control. It just. . . " Sandor closed his eyes, ". . . it just happened."

Vera held Sandor in both of her arms while the tears ran down the corners of his eyes. Some of the tears pooled along the inner part of the eye socket and then funneled down the side of his nose.

While stroking Sandor's greasy hair across his forehead, she shushed him to sleep.

The sound of shush trailing like a snake's *hiss*.

Hissing Sandor into a deep black sleep.

Once the *hissing* faded into a heavy silence, a panic rose inside Sandor, gripping him tightly, demanding attention. Under his sun washed eyelids, he charged from the darkness and suddenly bolted upright in bed. His eyes were wide open, as he looked around the hotel room, which was empty. Vera was no longer lying next to him; in fact, the impression she once left on her side of the bed was gone. The sheets were unruffled and strangely pulled tight, organized. And, both lamps on the nightstand were on as well.

Before Sandor could make sense of the last moments leading up to him falling asleep, the bed springs below him twisted and popped!

He sat on his knees, pulled back to the comforter, and closely inspected the bed, which he swore was moving. He leaned closer to the sounds of moaning—a deep, painful kind—coming from underneath the bed.

The moaning sound started to intensify.

As his ear inched closer to the bed, a hand shot up through the mattress and caused Sandor to jerk his head away. The hand, which was veiled by the white bed sheets, reached for Sandor; however, he backed away before the hand could grab hold of him.

He attempted to jump out of bed, but yet another hand shot up from the mattress and prevented him from leaving.

One of the hands grabbed him by the ankle. Another hand grabbed him by the forearm. Another, his wrist.

Once Sandor freed his arm, yet another hand shot up from the mattress. The hands, which were slightly restricted by the bed sheets, managed to pierce through the thin fabric with jagged, gnarly nails.

Sandor fought off each dark, spotty hand; however, by the time he used up all of his energy, there were too many hands—at least two dozen of them—grabbing at him, fondling him, scratching him, and pulling him into the gummy mattress.

The moans, the groans, and screams of torment, became louder and louder as his body began to sink into the mattress with its center caving inward.

In one last desperate attempt, Sandor reached up to the ceiling, hoping to grab something, anything, even it was only air. . .

Reaching deep for a breath, Sandor's eyes snapped open, only to witness a dark figure with glossy reflective eyes staring down at him in the pitch-black.

The strange figure leaned down, the shadows along its face peeled back and revealed. . .

". . . Vera," Sandor said feverishly, as he witnessed the lower half of her pale face in the soft beam of moonlight.

The bed sheets below him were drenched with a pool of sweat underneath his body.

She combed back his soaking wet hair from his sweaty forehead, which was incredibly warm to touch.

"It's just a dream," Vera said tenderly, kissed him on the center of his forehead, and walked away.

Sssleep now, Sssandor, a staticky, hissy-like voice said in the night darkness.

A yellowish beam of warm light speared through the room from where Vera had cracked open the door, the narrow doorway leaving behind a sword shape of light along the patterned carpet.

Sandor wrestled open his eyelids, only to witness Vera's dark, slender figure standing in the lit doorway. She looked over her shoulder at Sandor and then, as quietly as a whisper, closed the door behind her.

In the pitch-blackness of the room, Sandor heard those familiar sounds of anguish rising from the below like an approaching storm.

Ready to shroud him in misery and eventually pull him under to a place that never slept.

🕐

IN the lit hallway outside the hotel room, Vera strutted toward the elevator. Once she pushed on the down arrow, the doors immediately opened. She stepped inside the elevator, pushed the "L" button, and during her descent, pulled out Sandor's belongings from her purse. Vera made sure everything was accounted for before she exited the hotel: *Sandor's smartphone* (since she secretly watched him punch in the password into his phone throughout most of the night, Vera didn't have to worry about entering the wrong password—after all, 1-1-1-1 wasn't a hard one to remember); the business card with the name,

Vera Fedorov, a "companion" for an escort agency called *Loyal Companion*, which, earlier that night, she had handed to Sandor while he was slumped over the bar and enjoying a pint of brown ale at a local pub not too far away from the hotel; Sandor's passport, as well as his wallet, which contained a driver's license, a couple of platinum credit cards, and at least three hundred pounds, consisting of banknotes of £50's and £20's; however, Vera was more interested in Sandor's *keycard*, which granted him access into the main headquarters of Neuvak Corporation.

After she double-checked each one of Sandor's belongings, she arrived at the lobby floor.

She passed the main check-in desk. The doorman held open the door for her as she exited the hotel. She stopped a couple of feet outside the hotel, kneeled down, and closely inspected a lone *Centaurea cyanus*—or "corn-flower," as it was commonly known as—which had absolutely no earthly business being there. The native flower was protruding from the crack in the side-walk. She plucked the bright blue flower from its droopy steam, carefully held it in the center of her palm, then crushed it in her hand and sprinkled the crumpled florets on the sidewalk as she walked away. The doorman, who was standing not too far away, couldn't help but stare at the young woman in a state of bafflement.

Driven by the night, Vera bravely strutted down a grungy alleyway along-side the hotel. She cut through the shadowy London streets until she arrived at a desolate rundown factory building tagged with various landscapes of graffiti and high-fantasy combined with horrific art. She stopped in front of one par-ticular cartoon-like drawing and found herself admiring the piece, yet, at the same time, loathing it: a stereotypical image of a Grim Reaper, albeit with a vulgar spin, spray-painted on the side of the wall. The title above the piece read in a bubbly font: "*Death or Glory.*" Slightly crouching downward with his black cloak animatedly flapping in the gusty wind, the Dark Angel himself was spinning around his bony cock with a cartoon bubble above his mouth reading, "Helicopter!" In one skeletal hand, the Dark Angel was holding his large scythe while, in the other hand, he was holding up the sign of the horns.

"*Psst.*" Vera said amusedly from the side of her mouth, "Humans."

She continued walking through the trashy, rat-infested, disease-infested area. The insides of the building were rather gutted and hollow and appeared to be used mostly as a skate park and a hangout for troubled teens during the day and a shelter for the homeless at night.

Attracting the eyeballs of three homeless men huddled around a small campfire-like flame inside a rusty oil drum, Vera, who was dressed in a skin-tight dress and wearing a pair of black stilettos, strutted straight toward to the three homeless men, who were left gawking at the approaching woman, as well as her expensive yet seductive attire. Each step she made sounded like the *clip-clap, clip-clap* of a horse echoing throughout the grand space.

Vera removed the contacts from her eyes and flicked them on the ground.

"You lost, Love," one of the raggedy-dressed homeless men said to Vera.

"Fuck off," Vera said coldly, as she stepped into the glow of firelight.

Her eyes were all black, demonic.

535

As soon as the three homeless men noticed those eyes—the tone of her voice was deeper, throatier, and rather disturbing as well—the two homeless men hurried away. One of them stayed behind and was left staring at Vera.

"Give me your coat," she said.

The homeless man didn't bother to question Vera's intentions.

He removed the raggedy hooded black coat from his shoulders, placed it on the ground, and then ran off.

Once all three homeless men faded into the night darkness, Vera stood over the fire and began to toss in Sandor's belongings. She threw each artifact into the fire, Sandor's phone, the business card, as well as Sandor's wallet, including everything inside the wallet, except for one particular item: the keycard. She placed the keycard in the pocket of the coat, which was lying on the ground. Then, Vera proceeded to remove her skirt by unzipping the back of it. She kicked the skirt up to her hand, threw the skirt inside the fire, then, next, her top, and then, each piece of lingerie that she was wearing, including her bra and panties.

Stripped naked, Vera removed the final article of her clothing: her skin.

With the tip of her extending needle-like stinger of her index finger, she cut a slit down her face, starting with the top of her forehead and slicing down her nose and mouth, over her chin, and finally, stopping at her trachea.

With both of her hands, she peeled off her face. Then, once the skin was removed from her head, she slid the skin off one shoulder, then the other. Once the skin was removed from her upper torso, she removed the rest of the skin from her body like a sock made of Velcro, revealing nothing but a gummy, thorny blackness underneath. The manikin-like body had neither male or female genitals, nor any breasts for that matter; in fact, it carried no sexual orientation at all.

Finally, the creature tossed the skin suit of Vera Fedorov into the flames, kneeled down, and slipped its arms into the coat first, then, second, placed the frayed hood over its head, then, finally, watched all of the evidence burn, blacken, and melt in the fire.

🕐

THE next morning, one of the staff members of the hotel, who was concerned after Sandor didn't answer the second wake-up call, checked on Sandor; however, the guest wasn't answering the door, either. The attendant opened the door and made sure to announce his presence when entering. He only took several steps into the room before he realized something was terribly wrong. The tray, as well as food on the cart, had been knocked over on the floor. He discovered a body, more than likely, Sandor's body, lying facedown on the bathroom floor. A small puddle of blood was formed into a dark red puddle beside the side of his mouth. The frantic attendant kneeled down next to Sandor and felt for a pulse but couldn't find any.

ONE WEEK LATER

"TWO of our board members have mysteriously died in the past couple of days— one of them now missing—how the hell do you think I feel, Anya?"

Grant's secretary, Anya, stopped walking and stood still with the pointy tip of the stiletto inches away from the narrow, isosceles-shaped streak of sunlight shining a distant mountaintop through the three story-tall window pane covering one side of the massive hallway wall and running across the floor like a starting line. She readjusted a stack of folders from one side of her body to the other and waited for Grant to acknowledge her.

"Mr. Mallory," said Anya, but didn't grab her boss's attention until she spoke his name once more, this time with a tremble underneath her voice, "Are you saying they're *not* coincidental?"

Anya left Grant with no other choice than to stop and acknowledge his secretary's concern.

"It's too soon to tell," he said. "We won't have test results back until tomorrow—"

"—Tomorrow can't wait," Anya said, trying to keep her voice down as other employees walked past them in the hallway. "What does your gut say?"

"My gut says wait until the test results come back before we make any rash decisions." He walked back to Anya, touched her on the shoulder, and said, "Just be mindful of who you interact with. Right now, the only person you can trust is yourself." Another employee walked past them, even eyed them as he walked by. "We'll get through this. Trust me."

"Should I reschedule your lunch with Mr. Silva?" asked Anya.

"Just tell him I'm going to be running a little bit late," he said. "Right now, I could really use a cup of coffee."

"Certainly," Anya said without missing a beat. "Where do you want it—"

"—No," he said abruptly. "I can manage."

"You don't trust me?"

"Of course, I trust you, Anya."

"But I would strongly advise against—"

"—I'll see you back at the office."

Grant started to walk away; however, Anya had so many other questions and concerns to voice after listening in on the board's latest meeting where one of the board members, Salazar, without any proof, boldly suggested that Sandor Horvath and Tomas Zajac were both targeted.

"*But Mr. Mallory. . .*"

Ignoring Anya, Grant kept on walking. He swiped his keycard on the elevator and rode it to the ground floor where a couple of security guards were waiting at a desk. Etched along the marble flooring the golden emblem read: "NEUVAK CORPORATION: PHARMACEUTICALS AND MORE." He walked along the company's trademark emblem as he exited Neuvak Headquarters.

Glancing several times over his shoulder while crossing the street, he made it to a small café called eXpresso. The café sign on the front of the building consisted of a larger, redder, glowing "X" in the word *expresso*, opposed to the other letters, which appeared to fade in the background.

As soon as Grant walked into eXpresso, the barista, a young woman named Lillian, knew exactly what Grant wanted without him even having to say it.

"One regular sized black coffee," she said, as she punched in his order along the touch-screen.

Before Lillian completed his order, Grant eyed a dark chocolate croissant sitting at the front of the pastry case, as if, strangely, of all the times he had bought coffee at eXpresso and skipped on the alluring sweets next to the cash register, the croissant had a spotlight highlighting it. Grant couldn't resist.

"I'll tell you what, Lilly," he said, as Lillian paused midway through tapping her finger against the screen, "add one dark chocolate croissant."

"Feeling adventurous today. Huh, Mr. Mallory?"

"Yes," he said smoothly. "You can say that."

"Will that be all?"

Grant glanced around the café. His eyes found a brunette with greenish-blue eyes dressed in a black cape-like overcoat sitting at the far end of the café.

He couldn't help but notice how long she had been sitting there. Did she follow him inside the café? Or, had she been sitting there this whole time?

After a sudden pause, he turned back around to Lillian, who was smirking by Mr. Mallory's interest in the lone sylphlike woman.

"Yes," he hesitated. Then, smiled back. "For now."

Lillian's smirk rose higher on one side of her face, as her eyes flickered toward the vicinity of the other woman.

Grant held up his smartphone to the scanner and finished the transaction.

As Lillian prepared Grant's order, first by grabbing the dark chocolate croissant from the case with a prong and neatly placing inside a to-go bag, then pouring the coffee from a pot into a cup, Grant waited by the pick-up counter.

During his wait, he shot glances at the greenish-blue eyed woman with long dark hair.

In return, the woman shared a glance or two with him. A rogue strip of hair fell forward over one side of her face, causing her to comb it back over her ear.

First, it was the hair, the primp.

Then came the eyes, both of them looking up from her phone to fully acknowledge Grant.

The eyes were more seductive, pulsing.

"Mr. Mallory. . . " Lillian said from the side. She was standing on the other side of the counter with Grant's order in her hands.

Grant turned to the sound of Lilly's voice.

"Yes, Lilly," he said and grabbed the black coffee and dark chocolate croissant. "Thank you."

Grant found himself at a table next to the window not too far away from the interested woman, sat down, and placed everything on the table, first his phone and then the coffee and the croissant. He first tended to his phone. Before he could scroll through his most recent emails, he saw a dark figure standing over him. He turned his eyes upward and saw that same woman standing at the table.

"Hi," Grant said, surprised by the speediness of her pursuit. He figured that he'd sip from his coffee, check the messages on his phone—or at least act like he was checking messages on his phone—then pull himself away from the device to play a little eye-tag foreplay by occasionally shooting glances at the woman until he finally warmed-up to the inevitable conversation.

"May I join you?" asked the woman.

He loosened the red tie around his neck, pointed at the empty chair, and said, "Please."

She placed her coffee on the table and sat down across from Grant.

As the natural light brought out more details of her face, he couldn't help but stare at her features. He knew her face, had seen it before. It didn't take him long to remember where he had seen her and then the app where he had *swiped* her.

As soon as she spoke her name, "Tatiana Lebedev," Grant realized it was the same woman from his phone. Which, to say the least, was shocking, considering he thought most of those photos were stolen and their real identity happened to be some fat guy dressed in his underwear sitting in front of a computer.

"Grant," he said, maintaining his coolness, "Grant Mallory."

"Pleasure to meet you, Grant Mallory."

He looked around the half-full café, only to find Lilly turning away the moment his eyes crossed hers.

"So," he said plainly, shifting his focus toward Tatiana and nobody else but Tatiana, "you come here a lot?"

"First time," she said villainously.

"Best coffee in the valley," Grant said and took a bird-like sip from hot black coffee.

"Well, I didn't come over her to talk about the coffee."

Grant could feel the blood moving around his body.

"Is that so?"

Tatiana nodded her head.

"You live around here?" asked Grant.

"I have a place up near Rock Creek."

"Nice place," Grant said. "Quiet. Me and a buddy of mine used to take hiking trips up there. One time, we nearly got mauled by a mountain lion, who was looking at us as if we were its next entrée. If we hadn't run into a couple of other hikers, who were more experienced, then you probably wouldn't be talking to me right now."

"How did you defeat it, the mountain lion?" asked Tatiana.

"We didn't," Grant said. "We were told to scream and make loud noises and show dominance. Eventually, it ran away."

"So, why'd you stop?"

"Stop what?"

Tatiana asked more clearly, "Why'd you stop going on hiking trips with your friend? Was it because of the mountain lion?"

Grant blocked out the memory as soon as it came to him.

"He passed away," he said politely.

"Sorry to hear," she said.

"It's okay," Grant said. The last angle he wanted right now was a sad angle, even worse play the sympathy card. But then again, at this point, he had no angle, no card. She was, more or less, the aggressor. Which meant he already had her in his pocket—or, the other way around. He straightened his shoulders, reaffirming his superiority.

Tatiana pointed at Grant's phone and said, "May I?"

Without thinking, Grant unlocked his phone, then handed it to Tatiana, whose hand deliberately and flirtatiously grazed the side of Grant's hand during the exchange. She entered her information into Grant's contacts and then slid the phone back to Grant.

"I have to run," she said. "But if you want to hang out later—perhaps tonight if you're not too busy—or, we can just talk. It's up to you. Either way, you have my number. Don't be afraid to call it."

He scrolled to her name under the letter "T" in his contact list, clicked on it, and found her phone number.

"I won't," he said and checked out Tatiana's backside as she exited from the café.

He couldn't help but shake his head in amusement.

Too easy.

⊕

LATER that same night, Grant kissed his wife, Nadia, goodbye, as well as his three children, two who were still young enough to embrace bear hugs from their father, and one, technically not a child, who had reached an age where an electronic device and the alternate world inside it received way more attention; and the only form of affection Grant had to look forward to was an involuntary nod of the head coming from a person, who, each semester, was slowly turning into a stranger.

With his travel bag packed for the supposed business trip, Grant felt nothing but relief as soon as he pulled out of the driveway.

Once Grant reached the hotel, which wasn't too far away from the airport, he checked in. He made sure not to draw any unwanted attention by checking in under a different name.

On the way to his room, he received a text from Tatiana, saying that she'd be at the hotel in "ten minutes."

Which left Grant some time to get comfortable inside the room, mainly making sure that he was presentable and looking and smelling his finest by brushing and flossing his teeth, gargling mouthwash, trimming any unwanted nose and ear hair, as well as doing some last minute manscaping.

As soon as he finished in the bathroom, he stepped back into the room where he received a text message on his phone. The text read: "I'm outside."

Shortly after reading Tatiana's text, he heard a *knock* on the door.

As Grant arrived at the door, his heart started to race. Through the tiny peephole, he witnessed the dark figure standing behind the door, waiting for Grant to open the door. He followed a tip his yoga instructor had given him and breathed in deeply through his nose and exhaled through his mouth. He was already past the point of no return. Yet, Grant no longer carried any rational thought inside his head nor, at this time, did he ever welcome such reason. Instead, his actions were solely driven by a primordial force. She was there, waiting for him. And he was there, standing with only a door separating himself from her.

Grant reached for the door handle, and as he was about to open the door, his hand started to tremble.

Quidãguin

County Diet

ROUGHLY seven thousand feet below a sun-baked boulder field along the southernmost rim of Snake Spine Canyon located in Crimson, Arizona, which, after geologist, Mel Dewing, discovered chalcocite containing rich copper deposits inside sulfite veins extracted deep within the earth, was home of one of the largest copper ore bodies in the world—estimated to be as large as Crimson Mountain—known as a "porphyry copper deposit," water droplets seeping from rock like a wrung-out sponge rained down into manmade tunnels like hot showers and sauna-like steam, which miners commonly referred to as "Lucifer's Hand," poured from deep pockets of the earth as though the devil was reaching out to touch those who had braved such a dark and unforgiving place where the only source of light came from the one glimmering from within the human psyche.

Chip Long, mine superintendent at New Frontier Mine, once told his men and women who made it his or her livelihood to descend into darkness, "When you're a mile below the earth's surface, anything could happen. And it wasn't a question of *if* it was going to happen, but rather a question of *when* it was going to happen. Down here, nobody could hear you scream—that is, except for the devil himself."

One of Chip's men, Xavier Chávez, son of a miner, knew the risks; his father had lost a good friend of his named Peru in the mines after a tunnel caved in on him, leaving rescuers to toil for weeks on end. After two weeks passed, it was no longer a rescue mission, but, more or less, a mission to salvage the remains of the trapped miners. Eventually, seventeen of the thirty-four miners were discovered. Peru was one of the seventeen bodies. As for the others, till this day, their bodies still remained missing. Every now and then, Xavier would think about those who came before him, like his father and his friend, Peru, who tragically perished, and tell his wife that he was ready—and most certainly, willing—to explore other career options and pursue a less dangerous path that would make him more "economically viable."

But a part of Xavier liked doing what he did.

It was in his blood, his namesake.

And he'd have it no other way.

XAVIER, who was geared up in his hardhat, diggers, boots, and the safety harness that he wore each and every day on the job, placed a sign-in card on a board inside the office—which was mandatory for every person who entered the mine just in case the "inevitable" thing happened—rode an elevator-like cage down a narrow, nearly pitch-black shaft with two other miners, one of them being Chip, to a new tunnel, which, earlier, had been blasted from the method called block caving, which allowed gravity to naturally push manageable fragments of the deposit into a funnel inside the tunnel underneath that rich copper deposit.

With each shift lasting only three hours due to the extreme conditions, Xavier ran into a bit of trouble with the automated extractor right before he was about to take his break. He hollered at one of his colleagues, Terry Bannon, told him that he'd be right back, then checked out the problem.

When he arrived at the extractor, the teeth of the shovel were wedged underneath a massive boulder protruding from the ground.

Xavier closely inspected the boulder and realized he'd have to manually release the shovel from its stuck position.

As he tugged on the shovel, he witnessed a crack stretching between his feet.

Before he could even react, the ground below him suddenly collapsed into a dark pocket in the earth. The extractor was first to fall into the hole, then Xavier; however, fortunately for Xavier, the fall was no more than twenty feet.

He landed lightly, the pressure of the impact causing his bright orange hardhat to spring from the top of his head like a cork.

As the dust cleared away, Xavier inspected the damages, first, the extractor, which was overturned on its side and came inches from rolling over and squashing him, then, his injuries, only one of them, his right ankle, which he had twisted during the landing.

Xavier tried to stand to his feet, but he could barely apply any pressure to his ankle.

He shouted out to Terry, who, eventually, arrived at the hole.

"Xavier," he said from above, "are you hurt?"

"No," he lied. "I'm good."

He couldn't help but laugh at the fact that he had just faced death and dodged it by the skin of his teeth.

All he could think about was "Sweet Jesus" looking after him. The one—and only—savior came to his rescue yet again.

He motioned the cross over his head, chest, and shoulders, and pointed up at the gaping hole above as if Jesus Himself was looking down on him.

"Gracias."

Soon after Terry discovered his injured colleague below, a team of other men was quick to check on Xavier; however, they were extremely cautious to maintain a safe distance from the hole to keep it from further collapsing.

As Terry went to fetch a rope, Xavier inspected the inside of the dark cave-like hole.

Waving away dust and smoke, he limped around the extractor and shined the light along the jagged walls. Xavier could compare it to a large room, a din. The floor was covered in rock dust, which had the consistency of—sand? Even the air was somewhat dry, which was odd as well.

While scanning the rest of the cave with the flashlight, he caught a glint in the beam of the light. He redirected the flashlight back to the glint, inched closer to it, and mindful of his surroundings, picked up the hardhat from the ground.

He put the hardhat back on and made his way to the tiny flicker of light.

"Terry," Xavier shouted out, "I think I found something down here. . . "

Chip had now taken Terry's place and was monitoring Xavier.

"Try not to move around, Xavier—"

"—Chip, there's something down here!"

"What is it?" Chip asked while carefully leaning over the hole and shining a flashlight down below.

"I dunno," Xavier mumbled, as he arrived at the glinting object.

He kneeled down and shined the flashlight on a silver charm bracelet. As he pulled the bracelet from the ground, a misshaped skull rose from the rock dust and forced a frantic Xavier to backpedal away.

"Xavier," Chip shouted from above, "what'd you find?"

"It's a body," he said, trailing off.

He gathered the courage and closely inspected the skull, which was about the size of a baby's skull. He touched it with his own hand. The bone was incredibly soft, almost spongy. It was somewhat human. Yet, it was disproportionate. The forehead was much larger than any normal forehead, the chin much more shorter and narrower than any other human skull. Even one of the arms—the right one—was much larger, adult-like, opposed to the other arm, the left, which appeared half the size as the other one. He placed the flashlight on the ground.

With a handkerchief, Xavier dusted away the rest of the skeleton, which was the size of a young girl. As with the skull, the bones of her skeletal structure were soft and spongy. Xavier discovered a knife-like shard of black crystallized rock, similar to dark graphite, gripped in the skeleton's hand.

Using more force yet, at the same time, mindful not to break it, Xavier pried the black crystal from the hand of the skeleton and closely examined it.

He picked up the flashlight from the ground and carefully ran the beam along the black crystal.

"Holy Shit," he uttered, as he fell witness to an entire universe in the palm of his hands.

FOUR YEARS AGO

FROM the edge of the worn couch which, over the past couple of months, had become an exciting new game where checking underneath the cushions once a week was filled with more surprises than a daytime soap opera, Pan was watching controversial candidate, now president-elect, Richard R. Rhodes, aka the real-life "X-Man," who was constantly teased for his said-to-be supernatural power to hypnotize over half of the country—in particular, those voters who lived in and around the Rust Belt, as well as states who typically leaned blue—along the trail with his outrageous "sound bites" and constant "wall-to-wall" news coverage, giving his victory speech to an estimated crowd of two-hundred and fifty thousand red hat-wearing supporters at Cherry Hill in his home state of Tennessee when Brob suddenly blurted out from the other end of the couch, "This is some fucking bullshit! You really stepped in it now, 'Merica!"

"*Yeah*," someone mumbled from the corner of the room, "*we're neck-deep in it now, aren't we?*"

Brob was wearing a special helmet that he only wore wherever he wasn't in the public eye. He worked at one of those big box stores. One day, a pallet fell on his head, cracking open his skull. Brob sued the company, got millions from the lawsuit; however, most of that money had gone straight to pixie dust.

Sitting in a recliner chair next to Brob was Skinny Gee—or just "Gee"—who was resting his head against his hand while, at the same time, shaking his head in a trendy theme of disgust. Gee here, a former user of dipping tobacco, as well as a "two-pack-a-day" smoker, lost his jaw after years of heavy tobacco use.

Replacing the old, rickety eclectic shaver of a electrolarynx, which was used underneath his metal mandible implant, for a portable handheld talk box stocked with over three million words, including the latest slang that was downloaded in a weekly update, Gee sounded off: "*Bollocks.*"

Which, he knew, sounded much better than "Gee golly."

The voice of talk box had a British accent and came with a "wide" variety of British lingo; however, at the time he upgraded to the talk box, due to a shortage in supply, the only other option was a talk box with a Wisconsin accent; and there was no way in hell he'd go for that.

On the TV, Taylor Swipe, whose song "A Christian Eagle" had become sort of an anthem—or rally cry—on The Trail, introduced Rhodes: "Now, ladies and gentlemen, without further ado, it is my honor to introduce to you the next president of the United States. . . ."

"—Not my president," Brob chimed in.

". . . Richard R. Rhodes!"

"Know what the R stands for?"

"What 'Redneck'?"

"No," Skinny Gee said. "Remington."

"I wonder where he got that name?"

Skinny Gee said, "Certainly not from the painter."

In a sea of *red*, white, and blue—red, being the most predominant color—the crowd roared and waved their red hats, as well as their miniature American flags as Richard Rhodes and his wife, Karen, as well as their two children, J.R., five, and R.J., seven, who were both dressed in matching tailored suits and red clip-on ties, walked out onto stage.

"Wow," Whiskers said aloofly from the corner of her puffy mouth, "if it isn't the two future serial killers. Soon, they'll have their own reality TV shows."

Whiskers, who had spent her entire life's savings on plastic surgery to make herself look like a cat—literally, as in the eyes, nose, cheeks, ears, teeth, even the whisker implants, all resembling the features of the common household feline—held up a bowl of milk (soy, of course) with both her hands, which were balled up into fists, or in Whiskers' case, her kitty paws, and licked up the soy milk with her normal human tongue. Or, at least she tried to. Considering a cat's tongue had a rougher texture, often compared to sandpaper, and was way more flexible, unlike a human's tongue, Whiskers was getting brown and spotty milk with tiny bits of cereal all over the armrest of the couch.

Pan found herself staring at Whiskers, more so out of amusement rather than repulsion. For Pan, watching not only her roommate, but also one of her fellow addicts from her recovery meetings lick up soy milk, which, for Whiskers, was as ordinary to her as a human sipping from an environmental-friendly straw, never got old. *Never* a dull moment around this bunch. However, a part of Pan couldn't help but hold in a laugh at how serious Whiskers was taking this whole "cat business." Who could blame her, though? For Pan, there was something incredibly special about being in the company of those who shared the same addictions that truly brought out a deep rawness in each addict's story.

According to Gwynne Banks's story, she was struck by a car while crossing the street after receiving a "WALK" signal. As her contorted, mutilated body lay in a puddle of blood in the middle of the intersection, Gwynne began to slip away; technically, her heart stopped beating for exactly one minute and thirty-three seconds before the emotional driver, who had been aggressively performing CPR on Gwynne, slapped her across the face in hopes to wake her up from death. When Gwynne came to, she actually believed, as devoutly as a Christian to Christ, that she was a tortoiseshell trapped inside the body of a twenty-four year old female named Gwynne Banks.

Pan often wondered if it wasn't getting hit by a car but rather pixie dust re-arranging her brain, rewiring it, if you will, then, just for kicks, removing screws, adding new ones that didn't quite fit. After all, she drank catnip tea as an alternative to dust and in her own words, said it made her more "phlegmatic." However, Pan knew the tea had more of a placebo effect on her. She had done her research.

Whiskers pulled her face from the bowl and stared back at Pan with her wide cat eyes, "What?"

Pan rapidly shook her head.

"Nuttin'," she said and concentrated on the TV.

"I can't believe for the next four fuckin' years we're going to have to listen to this clown. I mean, how can these people," Whiskers pointed at the supporters in the crowd waving flags, "be so gullible? They have absolutely no clue what he's going to do to this country."

Jay, the most handsome one of the bunch, said from the corner of the room, "Let me guess: your *third eye*, huh?"

"You don't need a third eye to see who this man is—or isn't."

"Screw it, man," Brob said. "I'm moving to another country. Anybody with me?"

Brob combed his stringy black hair from his face and looked around the living room for any takers.

"You're just saying that, Brobby," Pan said.

"Canada? Who's down?"

"Well," Pan said and gripped the TV remote and just as Rhodes was about to address the nation, she flipped the channel to Cartoon Network, "you know you're right, Whiskers—"

"—Why'd you do that?" Jay whined. "I wanted to hear what he has to say?"

"Yeah," Brob said. "Turn it back."

"Why? You already know what he's gonna say, Brobby," she said. "Plus, all it's gonna do is make you upset, then, for the next hour, you're gonna continue on this 'moving out of the country' talk until you're blue in the face; but the fact is, Brobby, you're not gonna move out of the country. So, please, do us all a favor: Don't be that person. It's unbecoming."

"What person?"

A "sore loser" was what Pan wanted to say, but she wasn't at all in the mood to hurt Brob's feeling. As she could see, Brob was already hurting. *What was the point adding more hurt?*

Next to Jay was Ogre, who was looking at Pan as if he was disappointed by her unwillingness to listen.

Silence grew between the group as *Animal Jack* was barking on the TV.

"Fine," Pan said and flipped it back to the speech where Rhodes was talking about "unifying" a nation after he had spent an entire campaign trying his best to rip it apart down the middle with his insensitive, xenophobic rhetoric for the sake of igniting enough passion out of voters in order to bring them to the polls.

If there was one thing she'd give Rhodes, it was his way of drawing out the best in people—and the worst.

But that time had come and past and absolutely nothing remained forgotten, especially the divisive words Rhodes used while running for the highest office of the country.

As tempers flared, Pan tossed the remote on the glass coffee table, which was littered with food crumbs and candy wrappers and empty potato chip bags.

She stood up from the couch and gave Brob the "screw you" eye on the way from the living room.

Inside the master bedroom, which she shared with Whiskers—Pan taking one side of the room while Whiskers taking the other side, her rather sparse side consisting of only a queen size mattress and a bin of kitty toys—Pan wiggled loose a small stash of pixie dust that she hid between the rough, crumpled pages of a raggedy-looking pocket sized book inside a compartment underneath the lamp on the nightstand. The book was old, obviously. At least centuries old from the ruggedness of the texture. She ran her fingers over the bumpy surface of a circular *sun*-like symbol engraved in the cover. In her other hand, she held up the baggie to the light. There wasn't enough to get high. She knew that the only way she'd be able to obtain a true high, the flying kind, she had to "re up" her drug supply; and if there was one thing she dreaded the most, it was paying an announced visit to her dealer.

The thought alone of having to visit that man—or whatever the hell he was—made Pan want to use even more. She licked the tip of her index finger as if she was using her spit as adhesive and picked up whatever glittery pinkish pixie dust was left in the very bottom of the bag and spread it along the top of her gums.

With the glow of the TV flickering the living room behind him, Jay stood at the edge of the bedroom doorway.

"What you think you're doing?" asked Jay.

The sound of Jay's voice caused her to flinch. She immediately crumbled the plastic bag in her hand and brushed away whatever dust was left on her finger.

"What does it look like I'm doing?" Pan asked more bitterly, as she struggled to look Jay in the eyes.

"I'll tell you what, Pan," Jay said, "we'll play a little game. Every time Rhodes says the word *train* you can punch Ogre in the face. It'll be fun."

"No thank you, Jay," Pan said while placing the book back into the compartment and closing it.

"Pan," Jay said seriously, "what about the past two weeks? It will all be for nothing. Please, Pan. Don't do this—"

"—I just want a little bump. That's all."

"A little bump? Right. A little bump turns into a big bump. Then, next thing you know, you're off flying in the clouds for the next three days."

"I can control myself, Jay."

"Pan—"

"—Jason," Pan said over Jay. "It's my life, not yours."

"You're so right," Jay said and held up his hands. "You are."

As the tension grew and Pan redirected her attention toward finding money, a voice said from behind: "*I'll call David.*"

More irritable, Pan stopped, turned, and faced Jay.

"Oh yeah?"

Her cheeks were full of blood, eyes pulsing, breath shorter.

"Please don't make me, Pan."

"You call David and we're done. For good."

"You said that last time."

"This time, I mean it," Pan said, her expression dead-serious.

"If I was feeling like the way you're feeling right now, then I'd expect you to do the same."

"And how am I feeling, Jason?"

"I can't say exactly how you're feeling. Only *you* can," Jay said. "But I sure as hell can imagine you're feeling like you got something inside you trying to get out and the only way you can stop it is by going back to the vice that stopped it before. The one that nearly killed you, Pan. Listen, I understand you saw some things after the wreck—these other 'worlds,' as you've said. Shit that everyday people wouldn't want to see even if they didn't have a choice. You've been there. But, face it," Jay said and turned back to the group and pointed at each person—or animal—in the living room, "we *all* have."

Holding back a cocktail of emotions, Pan seethed, "You don't know what I went through."

"I'm not trying to argue with you," Jay said. "Let's watch some TV. If you want, I can rent a movie on-demand—"

"—A friend wouldn't call her sponsor behind her back," she said over Jay.

"Sure they would."

"What? Because you care?"

"Of course, I care. This is not you, Pan. This is the fuckin' brain candy talking. You know that, right?"

Pan didn't answer. In a way, she was done talking.

Jay stepped aside and went back to the living room to watch Rhodes's speech while Pan scrounged up whatever money she had stashed around the bedroom, as well as the rest of her apartment, including the seat cushions, for a gram of pixie dust. In the kitchen, she came across a check lying on the countertop. The check, which expired in two days, was from her insurance company, Omni Health, which had sent her the amount of money that they were going to pay for the hospital bill. The banks were already closed, obviously; however, she'd be lying if she said the thought didn't run past her mind. *What's the worse that could happen? People skip out on bills all the time.* Besides, *eating was so overrated. Worse case scenario: I could always bum some of those protein shakes from Gee. The guy has a large enough stockpile to last him through two Armageddons.* She put aside the thought for the time being, placed the check inside the drawer, and after Brob was enabling enough to chip in a couple of bones at the very last second—which had drawn even more outrage from Jay—Pan barely had enough money to buy a gram of pixie dust.

As she was about to head out, she grabbed her phone on the coffee table. The phone only had three percent power left and more than likely, it'd probably die on the way to Apple Bottoms. She grabbed the phone charger lying next to several owner manuals, as well as a stack of DEV, Pro-Tips, and *Software Development For Dummies* books, which were scattered on top of her computer desk.

She plugged the phone into the charger and switched off the light to her bedroom and told the others that she was going on a "quick" dust run; however, once again, Jay urged the rest of the group not to condone Pan's actions.

In Pan's defense, Brob, the enabler that he was, argued that the dust was just for one night. "Considering the circumstances," he said directly to Jay, "we could use it to take off the edge from, you know. . . "

He pointed at Rhodes, who had shifted his speech toward illegal immigration.

Pan searched the strongest person in the room. Clearly, it was Jay, mentally that is; however, she needed someone with more brute strength.

"Say, Ogre," Pan said, as she threw on a light jacket, "wanna grab some fresh air with me?"

Ogre shrugged, then nodded.

"Are you sure you want to do this?" asked Ogre.

"Is that a *yes* or *no*?"

The six foot seven inch tall Ogre stood to his feet and followed Pan outside.

"I won't be long," she said to the others.

Before Pan shut the front door behind her, Gee said through his talk box, "Be careful, darling."

"Always am," Pan said quietly, as the small hit of pixie dust suddenly sent a rush of euphoria through her body. The whites of her eyes brightened. She threw her head in a nod at Whiskers and said with a smirk, "If you use the toilet Whisky Poo, make sure to raise the seat."

Whiskers did her best to ignore Pan by focusing in on the snake oil salesman on TV. She knew it wasn't Pan talking but rather the dust.

"Better yet," Brob teased, pointing to the hallway with his thumb, "the crazy lady next door has a litter box. I'm sure she wouldn't mind if you used it—"

Whiskers opened her mouth, revealing her fangs. With both her pupils black and swollen, she hissed at Brob, who, in return, held up his hands in surrender for the sake of not getting scratched.

As Whiskers redirected her attention to the TV screen, she crossed her arms over her chest and then glared at Pan as she exited the apartment with Ogre.

On the way downstairs, the two bumped into Pan's landlord as he was taking out a bag of trash. She already knew what he was going to ask her before he even opened his mouth.

"I know, Frank," Pan said and held up her hand as if it was an impenetrable brick wall. "I'll have the money for you tomorrow. Promise."

"You said that last week, Pandora. Now, if you're not going to—"

"—Tomorrow," Pan said finally over Frank, who was killing her high.

The tone in her voice caused Ogre to step forward in defense. His presence alone caused "Mr. Buzzkill" to back away.

"If I don't have the rent money by tomorrow, you're out of here."

Pan left the apartment. Frank's comments had only made Pan's temptation to use again much worse. Not only that, of all the people to run into right now: Dexter the "Texter" Martinez, who was dressed in all black, no labels—in fact, whatever labels he had on his attire were either torn off or blacked out with a bold Sharpie—was hanging out on the street corner with a couple of his so-called "righteous" goons who were bored out of their brains and looking to "fuck up *shit*," shit as in like a monument of a historical figure or a museum or a passerby wearing an article of clothing that blatantly screamed to the Heavens, "Appropriation!"

Dexter shouted out at Pan, but she did her best to ignore him by continuing to walk.

"Where's your *pussy* cat?" asked Dexter, putting an emphasis on his favorite word in the English language.

Pan slowed down her walk, Ogre tempting to step in.

"Hey," Dexter continued, "why don't you tell that *pussy* cat to come outside. I have a little treat I want to give her."

"I'm sure it is *little*," Pan retorted, making sure to put an emphasis on a word that was destined to do more harm than good for her, especially on a night where she was jonesing for dust.

Dexter's goons snickered at her remark, which only made him more fired up.

"Why don't you come over here for a taste?" Dexter's confidence crumbled. He finished by mumbling under his breath, "*Bitch*."

Pan rotated around, tightly squeezed her crotch, and seethed at him, "Pet this, Sticky Fingers!"

While Dexter and his friends were "*oh*-ing" and "*ah*-ing," she held back from Ogre from turning the teens into his human-pretzels.

After digesting what was intended to be an insult by Pan, several of Dexter's friends turned to Dexter and asked what Pan meant by the name; however, based on a certain "sticky" discovery last week inside a trashcan in Dexter's bathroom by one of his friends, it didn't take them long to figure out what Pan was insinuating, more like revealing.

"Forget about 'em," Pan said and continued walking on the sidewalk.

"So, where we going?" asked Ogre.

"Apple Bottoms," Pan said.

"Hold up," said Ogre. "You talking about the strip club?"

More laidback, Pan nodded.

Ogre, who was slightly terrified, replied, "What the hell are we gonna do at a strip club?"

"That's where Lil' Beelze is."

"Lil' Beelze? Who in the hell is Lil' Beelze?"

"He's one of the part-owners of the club. He also happens to be my dealer."

"You're getting dust from some guy who owns a strip club?" said Ogre, as if, by verbally running it back to Pan, she might reconsider using the money on the essentials, like food or having a roof over her head. "Sounds pretty sketchy—"

"—Aren't you the same guy who doesn't even do dust, yet he got Jay hooked on dust? The same spoiled guy whose rich father owns a chain of car dealerships across the entire East Coast?" Ogre didn't retort from Pan's comments. "So, now what? This guy's going to hand out advice to me?"

"You don't know me," Ogre said darkly.

"Let me ask you, Ogre," Pan said and stopped walking on the sidewalk. "Did Jason ever tell you why he got hooked on dust?"

Ogre shook his head.

"Nah," he said coolly.

As the north wind started to pick up from a cold front pushing in, Pan curled her hair around her ears and said to Ogre, "Two years ago, Jay's brother was accidentally shot twice in the chest during a Fourth of July celebration. Jay held his brother in his arms and had to watch him die while everybody else around them were celebrating. Till this day, they still don't know who shot him. Before the judge ordered Jay to take a recovery class to help curb the addiction, he was one of the brightest basketball players in the entire country. He always said basketball was an easy sport, *simple*; you put the ball in the basket, but for Jay, after he became a dust junkie, trying to kick the addiction was tougher than any sport he had ever played. So, the next time, before you open your mouth to criticize or speak about something you don't entirely understand, you might want to save it for your diary."

More impressed by Pan's fierceness, Ogre said calmly, "I can see why you're so close to him. You know, because of what happened to your—"

"—Don't," Pan snapped before Ogre could finish his sentence.

Pan glared at Ogre as if she was looking straight through him.

In the corner of her eye, Pan suddenly witnessed her sister's face in the passenger seat of a passing car on the street. She blinked away the face. The woman looked similar to her but was *not* her.

"Sorry," Ogre said more compassionately. "Everybody has their plights. For me, it's getting punched in the face. Like I have any room to talk."

"By the way," Pan said and shifted the focus away from her sister, "what do you get out of all of that?"

"For some," he said, "the pain is no different than a drug."

Pan accepted Ogre's comment for what it was.

Then, they proceeded to Apple Bottoms, which was only a couple of blocks from the apartment complex.

THEY arrived at Apple Bottoms where there was a line of people—mostly men— wrapped around the building. Pan went straight up to Flattop, who was one of the two bouncers standing at the front entranceway.

Flattop acknowledged Pan, who possessed a sort of local status from her immediate connection with the two bouncers. Without hesitating, Flattop unclipped the velvet rope along the stanchion and let Pan inside the club.

As Ogre was about to follow Pan into the club, Flattop closed the barrier and held out his hand. Pan tapped Flattop on the arm and said, "He's with me."

Flattop paused and carefully thought about whether or not he should let Ogre inside.

Eventually, after receiving a nod from the other bouncer, he let Ogre inside.

Together, Pan and Ogre walked into Apple Bottoms. First, Pan was greeted by a chubby, scraggly-bearded man named Rico who was overseeing the inside of the club from a booth above the cash register.

"Hey, hey, Pandora," Rico said jubilantly.

"Sup, Rico."

Without having to state her business, he flicked his head in a nod toward the back of the club and said, "He's in the back."

Once Pan was through talking with Rico, her palms became sweaty. She felt a bubble of nausea inside her belly and stepped outside her head for a moment in order to rid the thought of puking on the floor. *Once I do a little bump everything will be chill.* The more Pan concentrated on all that flesh surrounding her—an ass shake here, a titty jiggle there—the more her thoughts spiraled out of control. All she could think about was the dust, as though she couldn't walk through this place or even function properly for that matter, unless she had more dust in her system.

Pan and Ogre made their way through the club, passing several strippers who were working the pole and gathering tips, two others who were having a twerking contest to see who could make their butt cheeks clap the loudest, others giving lap dances in the darker recesses of the club. Others said hello and looked at her as if they were running into an old friend and followed with the curl of a smile.

Considering most of the club was rather dark, the only light came in sudden bursts from a flickering strobe light along the ceiling.

"Stay close to me," Pan said to Ogre, who was unable to hear Pan due to the blaring industrial-like synth wave music, which was intensifying that dark, steamy vibe. Ogre leaned in closer as Pan repeated herself once more.

With their sense heightened, the two cautiously shouldered their way through a crowd of rowdy college kids, who were burning away whatever brain cells they had left with an endless carousel of Fireball shots.

Still clinging to boyish attire with their baseball caps spun around backwards, several of the guys were throwing handfuls of dollar bills at the voluptuous stripper, Ms. Queen Apple Bottom herself, Serena, who put a new definition in having "too much junk in the trunk" with an ass so plump and holy that it was easily mistaken for implants. However, the boys in brands certainly weren't complaining; in fact, each one was left gawking as Serena twerked her ass through a rainstorm of crisp, coke-powdered bills. When Serena made it clap, it thundered.

Pan braced for any remarks but only received one, a soft and drawn out "Hey, gurl." Eventually, the two made it through the testosterone-driven chaos without drawing too much attention and located Lil' Beelze and his motley crew seated in a booth in front of a mirrored wall.

"*If it isn't Tinker Bell herself,*" a voice rose from underneath the mountain of flesh.

Lil' Beelze's face emerged from the bodies of two strippers. The top, as well as the top part of his scalp was covered in a tattoo of gnarly horns curling around the sides of his forehead. He wore an earring of an upside cross on his right ear. His clothing attire was minimal: black jeans that were so tight that looked painted on, which matched the black leather biker jacket with a set of metal spikes on the shoulder pads. The jacket was worn open, revealing his chest that had thousands of tattoos; however, each one consisted mostly of names, which, whenever asked, Lil' Beelze touted that they were the names of his "followers."

Pan stepped forward while Lil' Beelze rudely pushed aside the two strippers, as if they were objects.

"Long time no see, Pandora," he said, grinning.

Lil' Beelze noticed Pan's somewhat fidgety state.

"You should've taken my advice."

"And what advice was that?" Pan asked bitterly.

"*Once you have a taste of the dust, your soul starts to rust.* Didn't I tell you that before you came to me, Tinker Bell?" Eyeing Pan from head to toe, Lil' Beelze gave Pan a once-over. "You, my dear, look as rusty as a junkyard."

More paranoid, Pan said with her voice trembling, "I'm just here for a gram."

"Just a gram, huh?"

"Yeah."

Lil' Beelze leaned back in the booth. "The last time we saw each other, you said you were gonna quit the dust, Pandora, but I remember I specifically told you that you'd be back and now, here you are."

"I am," Pan said, as she started to lose patience with Lil' Beelze. "Just cutting back, you know?"

"Right." Lil' Beelze devilishly smirked. "And the only way to fix a broken record player that keeps skipping is to smash it with a baseball bat."

"Just a gram, Beelze."

"I would love to, Pandora, but I'm afraid I can't help you out. I'm only pushing pounds these days. I'm sure you can understand." He carried a dark twinkle in his eye when he said, "Cut out the middleman. It's nothing personal. It's just business. Of all people, you know my product is the best in the city, no additives, pure as a virgin, manufactured straight from '*The MW,*' unlike that purple knock-off *narwhal* tusk you call dust that my competitors be hustlin' on the other side of town."

Pan looked around the strip club and grew more fidgety. Lil' Beelze was first to acknowledge her fragile, shaking state.

"I'll tell you what, Pan. . . "

As soon as Pan directed her attention back to Lil' Beelze and saw that concealed darkness in his face, she knew exactly what he was going to ask of her because he had that same look when he asked her the last time she saw him.

". . . You work for me tonight and I'll give you your gram of pixie dust."

Pan's stomach turned to knots from the very thought.

Lil' Beelze said, as if he was trying to entice her, "We'll make it a new theme for tonight: '*Opening up Pandora's Box.*' And you'll be our main attraction. Just imagine for a second the star you will become. I'll get wardrobe to create the perfect look for you. Cute and innocent and yet, deep down inside, hiding a dark secret. You have the look, Pan. Cleopatra had the look as well."

Pan's skin started to burn from the sound of Lil' Beelze bringing up the subject of her sister.

"She knew it, too," Lil' Beelze said.

Pan finally responded, "My sister wouldn't have been caught dead in a place like this."

"Maybe not," he said, shrugging. "She was more headstrong than you. As I've said before, I've always had a certain 'thing' for your sister. More than some crush. When we were in school—"

"—I know," Pan interrupted, as Lil' Beelze drifted off into reflection and did so with glossy dark eyes. "You told me you used to shoot spitballs at her from the back of the classroom."

"In a way, I guess I was always searching for her to show me that look. *But you,*" he said and shook away the memory, "it's there. You may not believe you have it. I've been around plenty women and I know the look when I put eyes on it. You got it all right, Pandora. And believe me, once everybody finds out about you, you'll be the new sensation around town. Men, even women, will be shouting your name, begging you for more. You'll have them on their knees, Pandora, asking for your hand in marriage. I can make you famous. After all, what's every person's wet dream?"

Pan didn't answer the question.

Instead, Lil' Beelze answered for her.

"It's turning a broken angel, like yourself, into their own personal devil."

"I'm not broken," Pan said, as her chest tightened.

Revealing the two golden canines—his "bling"—underneath his wicked grin, Lil' Beelze shook his head.

"I like you, Panny. Maybe not entirely broken," he said and paused. "I'd say more like 'out of order.'" Another one of those wicked grins found its way onto his face once again. "So let's get you working again, Pandora. What'd you say?"

Darkness spread over Pan's face.

"Every time I come in this shithole, you're trying to get me to work for you," she said darkly. "Each time I give you the same answer. What makes you think my answer will be any different this time?"

"Like I said," he said with a glint in his keen eye, "you have the look."

As Pan thought about Lil' Beelze's proposal, Ogre touched her on the shoulder and said, "Come on, Pan. Let's get outta here."

Ogre was only thinking about the others who were waiting for her return with a gram of dust back at her apartment, which was a safe space where she could use and at the same time, be monitored by her peers.

Strangely, Pan was putting way more thought into what Lil' Beelze said than she'd ever thought she would. Ogre knew it was the small amount of pixie dust in her system doing most of the tinkering for her.

🕐

AFTER Pan gave Lil' Beelze her answer—which wasn't exactly a yes but wasn't a no either—she excused herself to the bathroom while Ogre hung back and pulled out the gram of pixie dust that Lil' Beelze had given her free of charge from his own personal stash. She poured a couple of pinches worth of dust over the flattest part of the vanity, cut it into two fine lines with an old gift card from Café Cloud, dug out a crumbled Stop N' Shop receipt for two *Dark Cavern*™ bars and a 22-ounce can of Tree Sap from inside her pocket, straightened out the receipt by unfolding it first and then running it along the edge of the counter, rolled it up, and snorted each line of dust through the rolled-up receipt. She jerked back her head while, at the same time, pinched her nose, as the pixie dust hit the very back of her throat, causing it to burn. Eventually, that burning mellowed to a cool, throbbing sensation. The drip hit her next, causing her to clear her throat and spit up a glitter-covered loogie covered in the sink. Soon after the dust settled, parts of her face went incredibly numb.

All of a sudden the left side of her body started to twitch. The muscles on her left arm, mostly her bicep, pumped like a spasm. She squeezed her arm and massaged the muscles until the spasms stopped.

Pan glanced at herself in the mirror and studied the dust coursing through the veins in her face, each one lit up like a 120-volt light bulb. She traced the lit veins past her eyes, which were much brighter. As the dust settled, each line of her face smoothed out as though the dust was shaving off years from her face, which was slowly fading into the hazy vanity light overhead. She was now wearing the face of an intruder, beautiful and deadly; and that manipulative intruder was starting to consume her body. She peered past the smooth, glowing flesh, past each contour of that pretty white skull, and stared into the void. In the darkness, she witnessed the dust underneath flashing like an electrical storm inside her brain.

Just as she was about to lose herself in the light, she readjusted her eyes and wiped away any dust she had on her nose. She took a deep breath. Then, exited the bathroom.

Once she made it back to Lil' Beelze, she noticed Ogre was gone; in fact, he was nowhere to be found inside the club.

"So," Lil' Beelze said, "have you made up your mind, Pandora?"

From the untrustworthy expression on his face, Lil' Beelze looked as if, in a way, he already knew Pan's answer before she even opened her mouth to speak.

"Where's Ogre?" asked Pan, as she continued to scan the club.

She caught a glimmer in the corner of her eye. She looked down and found a necklace on the floor. She kneeled down and picked up the necklace—which she knew was Ogre's necklace; however, when she stared at it, she couldn't help but notice the similarities in the necklace. She peered closer and realized it wasn't his necklace. It was her bracelet, the same charm bracelet she lost during the wreck. Each charm was accounted for, such charms including the "*compass*" charm, the "*unicorn*" charm, the computer "*mouse*" charm, the "*two hearts*" charm, the "*paw print*" charm, the "*letter P*" charm, the "*elephant*" charm, the "*tooth*" charm.

In a state of disbelief, Pan studied each charm along the bracelet.

But *how could this be?*

She was starting to feel the dust working its way through her veins; however, there was a tinglier feeling inside her body, as if the dust was laced with another drug. She closed her eyes, shook her head, and rubbed the backside of her eyelids as though she was rebooting herself. When she opened her eyes again, she witnessed Ogre's necklace in her hand, *not* her bracelet.

"What'd you did with Ogre?" Pan asked, clearly upset.

A voice among the noisy music said that Ogre had left, but Pan knew it was a lie.

She felt a darker presence looming over her. She looked up and saw Lil' Beelze standing in front of her. Slowly, the tattoos of those two horns on his head started to protrude from his flesh. The two horns were no longer tattoos but actual horns extending from Lil' Beelze's head. And massive horns, they were!

As a pendulum of fear and anger gripped her, she narrowed her eyes.

She stood to her feet; however, her body didn't stop moving upward.

She kept rising, as both of her feet started to lift from the floor.

🕐

PAN woke up on a leather couch with one helluva splitting headache.

She didn't own a leather couch nor did she know anybody who had a leather couch. Jay maybe, since he once commented that he liked the feel of leather.

As she rubbed away the blur from her red eyes, she didn't even recognize the environment. Even after a thorough study, the sticky couch she was lying on was foreign to her.

She carefully sat upright, which caused the pain in her head to intensify to the point where the living room started to spin. She closed her eyes, breathed deeply, and then opened her eyes. The spinning lessened and gave Pan a moment to make sense of where she was, how she came to be in a stranger's apartment, even what she was wearing, which was a white XXL T-shirt that ran down to her thighs.

In a sudden frenzied state, she searched for clothes, including her underwear, but didn't find any clothes scattered around the living room. She heard a noise in the other room. She checked it out. There, she found a strange man and a woman sleeping in the bed. She located her clothes on the floor next to the bed.

Trying not to wake the strange people, she grabbed her clothes, as well as her underwear from the floor and tiptoed out of the bedroom.

Suddenly, she heard a *creak* of a bedspring behind her.

She turned her shoulder, only to find that the man was repositioning himself on the bed.

As Pan slipped on her clothes and exited from the apartment, she still had no idea as to how she wound up on a couch in someone's apartment. Maybe she had met him at Apple Bottoms. She tried to attach the man's face to a memory but, as before, she found nothing.

Only pain.

⊕

GROWING more anxious about not be able to remember the night before, Pan used the hand railing to walk down three flights of stairs.

When she made it to the front of the apartments called Village Square, which she knew were located on the *other* side of town, as in at least a good twenty minutes from where she lived, she couldn't help but notice the sunshine.

The sight of the bright blue sky and the crispness of the air triggered a memory.

It was overcast on the night she went to Apple Bottoms, and she remembered the forecast for the week and how her favorite, most trustworthy meteorologist on Channel 9—Bryan Showers, yes, that was his actual name— predicted that for the next two days it was going to be cloudy with an eighty percent chance of rain.

Has it been that long?

Pan forced herself to think and whenever she did, her head started to pound.

She soon confirmed what day it was with one of the residents, who, after telling her that it was Friday, stared at her as if she was from another planet.

Once Pan was made aware of the day, she immediately thought about what she was supposed to do on Wednesday, two days ago.

The only words that came out of Pan's mouth: "I'm fucked."

⊕

AFTER bumming enough money from a nice man to catch a ride on a bus back to her apartment, Pan could feel the dread creeping through her body.

She sprinted from the bus as soon as the doors opened and hurried toward her apartment complex. She finally arrived at her apartment, only to be greeted by an eviction notice on her door. She walked to Frank's apartment and knocked on his door. He opened the door but only as far as the lock chain would reach. Through the crack of the door, he said what he needed to say, which was a short "sorry, it's too late," then closed the door before Pan had a chance to beg him that she'd have the rent money in his hands in the next hour.

Pan had no other option than to find a way into her apartment. With the help of a dumpster, she climbed up the fire ladder until she made it to her window.

Since the window was locked, she was left with no other choice than to kick a brick from the corner of the wall with her heel and use it to break the window.

Mindful of the jagged glass, she carefully snuck into her apartment.

She went straight to the check in the drawer. It had already expired, but she had to at least try and cash it. Her only hope was that the bank teller was in a forgiving mood. While she was inside, she grabbed a glass of water. Of course, that jerk, Frank, even cut off the water.

In a burst of rage, Pan threw the glass against the kitchen wall, causing shards of sharp glass to fly everywhere.

Among a whirlwind of thoughts, only one came forward and seized her attention.

Pan raced to her bedroom and snatched the phone from the charger.

The phone was dead.

"What?"

Pan rushed to the light switch and flipped it.

No light came on.

Then, she checked the time on the wall clock, which read "3:33."

The time sent another wave of rage thought Pan's body. She checked all the other lights in the apartment, but none of them came on.

Not only did he shut off the water, but he also cut her power.

"Goddamn it," Pan seethed.

Once she left the apartment with her dead phone and charger, she heard the sound of police sirens getting louder and heading toward her direction.

She ducked in an alleyway and from a distance, watched the two police officers enter through the front of the apartment. In her mind, Pan wasn't exactly breaking and entering since her belongings were still inside the apartment. With a little bit of wishful thinking, she assumed they were here for someone else. Although, in the back of her mind, she knew a certain someone—not to name any names—had called the cops on her.

She just knew.

At this point in time, she couldn't even utter his name.

All Pan could think about was his face and putting a hole directly through it.

🕐

BY the time Pan arrived at the bank, she felt like death. She hadn't eaten anything all morning and she just wanted to lie down and close her eyes for an hour or two; however, she knew that if she didn't cash the check, then she'd be sleeping on the streets tonight.

There were only two bank tellers, both were occupied; however, one was being slowed down from having to converse amicably with a sweet old lady whose voice was raised to a near shout as she wanted to know the bank teller's life story.

While waiting behind six other people, Pan started to become unhinged.

All she could hear was that old, senile lady who kept repeating herself over and over, asking the same questions over and over in a vicious loop as though she was broadcasting it to seven continents via voice transmission.

The bank teller answered each one, loudly too, for the old lady was also hard of hearing. She even stopped counting money a couple of times to answer a question about her son, his age, and what her son did for a living as if it was her right to know his business. Apparently, the teller's son, whose name was Bret, worked as a construction manager; in fact, he was currently overseeing a new "E-Spand" project in Market Square. Not like Pan cared at all about the bank teller's son or anything, she fell into Bret's story, his life, and if he had any children. If so, was he a good father? Was he married, divorced, or separated? She had it stuck in her head—a sort of preconceived notion—that somehow this "Bret character" was an abusive father, in fact, a monster who ate worlds and on the side, treated his more than likely nonexistent wife and nonexistent children the same way he treated the very land that he was in charge of raping. Pan didn't know where such darkness had originated, how it had taken a man whom she knew nothing about, except for one) his profession and two) his mother working as a teller at Asset Bank, spun his life into what she only perceived to be true, then turned him into someone—or something—he was possibly, more than likely, not. All she could think about was Bret, "Bret the Rapist," as those close to him called him, the spawn of by a bank teller who had spent her entire career behind a pane of glass as if she was no different than a zoo animal handling bills covered in pixie dust and feces. *Bret, you toxic waste of the synthetic world, you shit stain, you "little" puppet whose will was bent by his corporate masters, who was being paid vast sums of money to tear down the natural earth, smear it with cancer, and drive it straight into the darkness in order to build some brand new "one-size-fits-all" e-Mall for glutinous consumers who unwittingly lived up to the very name they had been branded, putting the *consume* in consumer.

As Pan's thoughts spiraled out of control, she witnessed two other guys ahead of her in line.

One of them turned his shoulder, looked once at Pan, moved his eyes somewhere else, then looked back at her as if he had seen her before.

Immediately, Pan recognized the guy's face from Apple Bottoms.

While she mentally saw herself aimlessly flying around on stage—or *was it a dream?*—she witnessed his face in a dark crowd behind splashes of pink and blue lights. He was seated with these two other guys and they were all pointing at Pan and laughing at her.

The guy tapped his buddy or partner—she couldn't tell whether or not he was straight or gay—on the shoulder. The other guy turned his shoulder and glanced around the bank before shooting a quick eye toward Pan's direction.

Then, their heads dropped to the phone below.

They were watching a video on their phone and covering their mouths as they laughed.

Pan could hear the giggles and snickers.

Their whispers were like needles against her skin.

As her world started to spin out of control, Pan closed her eyes and breathed deeply. Which had helped before. But this time, it seemed to be making matters worse.

By the time she opened her eyes, a third bank teller, who had stepped from a closed room in the back of the bank, took her post and called out to Pan.

Relieved, Pan walked up to the bank teller and handed her the check through the narrow opening under the glass.

"I need this cashed please," Pan said, her voice slightly trembling.

"Absolutely," the bank teller said professionally.

As she looked over the check, Pan's heart started to beat faster.

Then, the bank teller moved her eyes upward at Pan and gave her a closed lip frown.

"Sorry," she said. "I can't cash this check. It's expired."

She held up the check and showed her an area below a date that read, "NOT NEGOTIABLE AFTER 90 DAYS."

Technically, it had been 91 days since she received the check.

"Please," Pan begged, "I was sick for the last two days—"

"—My only advice is that you contact your insurance company and *maybe*," she emphasized, "they can send you another check."

Pan rotated around and saw more people waiting in line. The line had tripled since she stepped forward.

"They're just going to give me the runaround," she said to the teller, who appeared as if she wasn't wavering from her initial position. "I'm begging you," she glanced down at the woman's name on the nametag, "Helen," she said, "if I don't cash this check, then I have nowhere to stay tonight. Is that what you want?"

"I'm sorry," the bank teller, Helen, said. "That's not my problem."

"It is your problem," Pan said, her voice growing louder. "All you have to do is cash the check and it will no longer be your problem."

The bank teller crossed her arms over her chest and remained stern.

"Please, Helen," Pan begged, lowering her voice. "Don't you recognize me? I was all over the news a few months ago. The woman who drove off the bridge? Ring any bells? Please. . . "

The bank teller's eyes flicked toward her right.

Before Pan could follow her eyes, a security guard approached Pan. He gently grabbed Pan's right arm; however, to her, she felt as though he was tugging at her arm.

She cried out, "Let me go!"

The security guard's hand tightened over Pan's arm; however, Pan suddenly jerked her arm away.

Calm and collected, the security guard pointed toward the front door.

"I'm going to have to ask you to leave, ma'am."

Pan resisted.

"This cunt won't cash my check," Pan said to the security guard and then she turned to the bank teller, "Why won't you cash my check, *Helen*? You cunt!"

Pan slammed the palm of her hand against the top of the counter in front of the bank teller, which caused the security guard to use force. He subdued Pan by grabbing both of her arms and manhandled her toward the front of the bank.

"If you don't stop, I'm going to call the cops. Understood?"

Pan finally surrendered.

Then, a thought came to her, a more strategic thought.

If I keep up, he'll call the cops, as he stated. *Which means I'll have a place to stay for the night.*

She wasn't at all thinking about money or how much it was going to cost for a bail or any of the legal charges she was about to face if she assaulted the security guard.

All she thought about was having a bed to sleep in.

She reacted and elbowed the security guard in the stomach, which caused him to pin Pan to the floor.

As the security guard secured Pan's arms behind her back and straddled both of his legs around her body, a flood of memories came back to her.

There, in those flashes of rough sex and violence and utter brutality, she saw other men, *not the security guard*, but many others, who were all undressed or in the middle of undressing and circling her, and several of them were pinning down her body to a bed in the back of Apple Bottoms. One had a shiny object in his hand, which was about the size of an average arm. She fell deeper into the memory and realized it was a golf club in his hand and they were performing sexual acts to her body, as well as inserting objects inside her, including that golf club. Among rising clouds of dust Lil' Beelze was sitting on a throne in the darkest part of the room while watching these men take advantage of Pan. The last images she had before she blacked out were a scaly tail slithering over her shoulder and moving down her chest and abdomen, then the faces. She looked up and tried to trace the origin of the tail; however, when she drew her eyes up at the faces above her, these men were no longer men. They barred their fangs at her. The drool dripped from their mouths and showered her face.

A bead of sweat rolled off the tip of the security guard's nose and dropped onto the side of Pan's face.

She flipped out from the feel of his sweat against her skin.

Pan cried out in horror, trying to squirm her way free from the monster; however, the security guard, some thirty-something who couldn't make it as a police officer, wasn't letting her go from his grip.

"Get off me," Pan said, as her chest started to tighten.

She pleaded for the security guard to let her go; however, the words became harder and harder to speak through her labored breath.

As the security guard—knowing or unknowingly—continued to smother Pan, the world around her started to spin out of control once more.

As a couple of other men in line broke through barriers and rushed to Pan's defense, her eyes rolled back in her head.

The world, as she once knew it, slowly turned black.

PAN woke up to a bright overhead light.

One of the nurses, who was checking Pan's vitals, fetched the doctor from the hallway.

The doctor placed a clipboard under his armpit and approached Pan.

"Where am I?" Pan asked the tall smooth-faced man, who she assumed was a doctor based on his clothing attire.

Pan stirred around and suddenly felt a restriction against her arms. She took a glance downward and witnessed the restraints on her wrists.

"What is this?" asked Pan. "What are you doing to me?"

"Take it easy, Ms. Nikopoulos," the man, who called himself Doctor Cherkis, said to Pan. She was starting to get uneasy from his shady presence. "You had a panic attack, which caused you to lose consciousness."

"*Panic attack?*" The doctor's words alone infuriated her. A minor scare was what he really wanted to say; and if anybody knew that what Pan was experiencing, it was Pan herself. *Panic attack*, she thought to herself. *What a total bunch of bullshit?* "First," she said, as the anger rose inside her despite the sedatives she had been given through a drip feed, "I'm going to sue the bank. Then, I'm going to get that piece of shit fired."

"Are you referring to the security guard who restrained you?" asked the doctor, whom Pan thought came off as a smartass.

She ignored the doctor and looked around the emergency room. Everybody was going about his or her business in the ER as if her being restrained to a hospital bed was considered customary, dare she say, "normal."

Once more, she pulled at the restraints; however, it was useless trying to free herself. The restraints were on good and tight.

The doctor nodded at the nurse, who, in return, closed the curtain behind him.

Immediately, the doctor's cold mannerisms struck Pan the wrong way and for a moment, she questioned herself whether or not he was actually a doctor with a medical degree.

Once more, Pan tried to free her hands.

"Take it easy, Pan," the doctor said more calmly, as he stood at her bedside. He placed the clipboard on the tray next to the bed, pulled out a flashlight from the breast pocket of the white coat, and attempted to shine the light in Pan's eyes. At first, she flinched, then turned her head away; but after the doctor displayed the flashlight to her and specifically told her that he just wanted to "look" at her eyes, she moved the back of her head on the center of the pillow.

The doctor shined the flashlight in her left eye first, then pulled it away, then shined it back into the left eye and studied the reaction of the pupil. He moved to the right eye, did the same movement as he did with the left eye. Both of her pupils were still slightly dilated; however, the left one especially appeared to have two pupils, as though one pupil was starting to grow out of the other one.

Letting out a sigh, the doctor holstered his flashlight and overlapped one hand over the other and loosely held his arms along his waist in the shape of a letter v.

"With your permission, Ms. Nikopoulos, we'd like to run some blood work on you, but I'm ninety-nine percent certain as to what I might find," he said with a sense of glum coming over him.

"—What the hell does that mean?" Pan said abruptly but was cut short by the doctor's hand.

"Please, if you would, let me finish," he said sternly. "I'm not here to lecture you, Ms. Nikopoulos, *but* if I had to guess, that dust was laced with Renatafill and whoever gave it to you doesn't seem to care about your well-being." He lowered his head and looked closer at Pan. "Trust me. You're not the first person to wind up in the ER after coming off a dust binge."

How would some doctor, whom she had never met before, *know these things?*

Pan looked at him strangely.

"You're extremely lucky to be alive," he said directly to Pan, as if he could read her thoughts. "One of the police officers at the bank talked to several witnesses, who claimed they saw you snorting lines of 'pixie dust' at a nightclub last night—"

"—What? That's bullshit!"

"We contacted your mother, who was listed under your emergency contacts. We told her what happened—"

"—Where is she?"

"Where is who?"

"Who do you think? My mom."

"She said that she was tied up with work but she would be here as soon as she could."

"Of course."

"Your mother did us a favor by contacting a few people, including your sponsor, David Flores, as well as the people who you might've been hanging out with the night before your disappearance. They confirmed that you were relapsing and experiencing common 'drug-seeking' behavior—"

"Who said that?" Pan asked, sitting upright. "Was is Jason? Or, as it Brob?"

The doctor held out his hand, as if he was signaling for Pan to *stop* before she worked herself up again.

"That's irrelevant at this juncture," he said. "All that's important now is that we get you clean again. With that said," he grabbed the clipboard and unclipped a purple brochure, "I'm going to give you three options, Ms. Nikopoulos." First, he showed her the brochure of a treatment facility in Arizona called Golden Springs Rehabilitation Center. "The first one: Golden Springs. You've probably heard of it through your meetings. If you haven't, I should tell you that it's quite an amazing establishment." Pan briefly glanced over the brochure before she placed it aside. "The other option is putting you on a drug called 'Quidaquin.'"

Pan had heard of that name, *Quidaquin*, but didn't know where.

"Right," Pan said, more dismissive. "Another drug. Makes total sense." Her voice was climbing with sarcasm. "You people make up some ridiculous disorder and put me on one drug. I stop taking that drug, which ultimately leads to my addiction. Then, *now*, you want to put me on yet another drug?"

"It's a fairly new drug on the market; however, based on all of the feedback, it's been known to show great results to those who have to be on it; in fact, the over day, I just recently saw a young man whom I treated last year. He's about your age. I asked him how everything was going. He told me he's been clean ever since I got him on the Q."

"So what? You want me to be a guinea pig? Is that it?"

"Well, Ms. Nikopoulos, the way I look at it, you only have these two options. The third and final option: You walk straight out the door and I'd say, in the next two to three weeks—but based on your recent behavior, I'd give you a couple of days—before you wind up back here. I go over this whole spiel with you again. We do this back and forth rigmarole for the next few months or so until, one day, you wind up back here," the doctor turned to the nurse behind him, pointed at her face, then his own face, "and these are the last faces you'll ever see. The fact of the matter, Ms. Nikopoulos: If you don't stop using, you're going to die. Simple as that. I see it all the time. Way too many times, if you ask me."

Pan thought about her options. Even though there was a force driving her out West, there was another force keeping her on the East Coast.

She looked up at the doctor and asked, "What was the second option again?"

PRESENT DAY

EVER since Pan started using the drug Quidaquin, she started to put on weight.

After the first year while taking Quidaquin, Pan went from a size 8 to a size 16 and did so without paying much attention in the mirror.

The second year she started to see the difference in her shape, as well as her stamina, especially when none of the clothes in her closet fit her anymore. Once she started shopping for a size 18 on retail store websites that she had never been on before, in particular, a website for plus-size women where all of the models, in regards to their physical shape, looked similar to her, she saw the changes in her body and wondered how she hadn't seen them before. For the rest of the year, she found a way to be content within her own skin; however, underneath, Pan didn't feel quite like herself and it felt as though someone had high jacked her mind.

The third year on Quidaquin was when everything went straight downhill for Pan. Not only did she decline physically, but also mentally. Doctors had warned her that weight gain was a side effect of Quidaquin. Once Pan kept putting on the weight—not just a few extra pounds that were manageable through self-discipline and diet but weight that was increasing dramatically every week—it had become apparent that something other than diet was going on with Pan.

By the end of the third year on Quidaquin, Pan couldn't even reach her folds when she bathed. Her whole body ached, especially her back. Food had become her new "go to" drug, which was triggered by mostly boredom or depression or both. Thinking about those blurry nights that she had spent at Apple Bottom sent her even farther down the rabbit hole. After a while, food was her *only* comfort. What added even more grief was the one time during a rare

567

outing she bumped into one of her former dust addict friends on the street. Jay didn't even recognize Pan; worse, when he locked eyes with Pan, he displayed a look of utter disgust on his face. Later that day, after bawling for hours, she turned to her comfort. When she started to spiral out of control, she also turned to the Internet and became what was widely known as a "catfish," harvesting multiple fake profiles on social media websites, one of them going by the name of "Aerial," who was in a steady relationship with a twenty-something named Guy who lived in Washington. Aerial had shoulder-length dirty blonde hair— Pan making sure to put an emphasis on the *dirty* part—blue eyes, and weighed a buck twenty. Aerial was a librarian during the day, bartender at night. Or so Guy thought. Like a sexy villain in a movie. A "sexillain," as Aerial referred to herself. Guy had a pretty wild imagination.

By year four, she was up to seven hundred pounds and was continuing to gain weight, despite having cut out a lot of high-calorie foods from her diet. She used a walker at times, as well as a customized wheelchair to get around whenever she was out in public; however, leaving the house had become a rare and each time was nothing short of an "event." Even rolling out of bed or standing up from the futon was an issue for Pan. She put on an additional thirty pounds in a matter of two weeks. It wasn't until one night when she had a terrible nightmare where, in the not so distant future, she weighed over a thousand pounds. She was nearly the size of one of those heavy-duty trucks, like the ones she would see on those smash-mouth TV commercials during Sunday football, and the only way she was able to get around was via forklift. She woke up sweating profusely and feeling as if she had the rear tire of a truck spinning over her chest, as if the tire was stuck in a pile of flesh and it kept spinning and spinning and spinning until she could no catch her breath.

Pan's mother, Vivian, had no other choice than to intervene. She paid out of pocket for an aide to help her daughter with whatever she needed, including errands such as groceries, necessities, even helping Pan with everyday functions.

It had gotten *that* bad.

🕐

VIVIAN showed up three and half hours late from the time she said she was originally going to arrive, which was eleven o'clock.

From the intensity of the car door slamming outside, Pan could not only see, but also hear obvious changes in Vivian's behavior and how visiting her daughter had turned into what she thought was a household chore. The sound of Vivian's footsteps were shorter and quicker as if all of her movements and actions once she found herself in the range of her daughter and her stellar ears were premeditated. Pan knew that one of the many reasons as to why her mom avoided meal times, such as eight o'clock, *eleven o'clock*, or seven o'clock, and how once she showed up, she'd only stay for no more than an hour, was that she couldn't stand to watch her daughter eat. Having been raised by a father, a "functioning" alcoholic—as in he needed a drink in the morning in order to function properly—who reminded her of the Zeus character she read about in books, it was no different than watching a person with a drinking problem, like her father, pounding down beers, one after another, only, instead of booze, it was a spread of platters, endless sides, and happy meals of food, as if somewhere beyond the flesh, he or she was bearing a black hole, an endless void.

As Pan's mother stepped inside the house, she displayed a fixed stiffness in her brow as if she had been primed to fight ever since she rolled out of bed—or in Pan's case, arrived.

Vivian checked on Pan, who was lying on the special bed in the corner of the bedroom, and asked how she was doing today and did so with a hostile tone.

Hardly able to look her mom in the eyes, Pan pouted and answered miserably, "Fine." Vivian knew the answer was clearly a cover-up to how her daughter was really feeling and had been feeling for the past four years.

With her arms planted over her hips, she stood over Pan and waited for her to give her something more, a follow up to the word that would explain how she was really feeling, but all she received was "Fine." All she ever received was a word that was anything but its true meaning.

"Okay," Vivian said shortly, grabbed the two paper bags of groceries from the living room, and stormed into the kitchen.

The crinkling sound of paper piqued Pan's interest, but only for a moment.

First, Vivian placed the bags on the kitchen counter and opened the fridge.

Pan knew what her reaction was going to be before she even let the expletives fly. The next sounds Pan heard were the *rustling* of bags followed by *thuds* of her mom throwing bags of frozen ice cream bars, as well as other junk food on the counter.

Finally, she heard her slam the fridge door, the *clinking* of glass bottles rattling around the shelves inside. She carried a frozen TV dinner of country-fried steak smothered in sausage and gravy into the bedroom and showed Pan the box.

"*What*—what the hell is this?" asked Vivian.

Pan shrugged.

"Food."

Vivian widened her eyes.

"Food?" she parroted. "This is *not* food, Pandora. Did Cary-Anne buy this for you?" Pan wasn't quick to respond. "I asked you a question. Did Cary-Anne buy this—"

"—Why does it matter who bought it for me?" Pan said, as her eyes watered.

"Pandora," Vivian barked and for a moment, couldn't even stand the sight of her morbidly obsessed daughter, who looked like nothing more than a stranger to her. She gathered herself by taking a deep breath, which only momentarily ridded the animosity that she had bubbling deep down inside her. The sight alone of her daughter and her confinement caused her to lose it once and for all, "You are on a very strict diet! You cannot be eating this *shit* anymore. Do you not know what it's doing to your heart? Do you want to die, Pandora? Because if you keep eating this garbage you'll be dead before you even reach the age of thirty. I mean, is that what you want? Do you want to die, Pandora?"

"Stop it," Pan said, more wounded from her mom's words.

"Believe me, Pan," Vivian said, trying to soften her tone. "I hate being the bitch around here. But I've about had it. I'm going to have a little talk with Cary-Anne when she gets here and if she continues to feed you this garbage, I'm going to find another aide." Vivian checked her watch, as she had been doing ever since she entered the house. "By the way," she said, her voice growing louder, "where is she? She should've been her by now."

"It's not her fault," Pan said, sniffling. "I made her buy me that."

"Quit defending her," she said shortly. "You're always defending her.'"

"It's not her fault!"

"Well," Vivian said, taking back by her daughter's behavior, "she knows better. That's all I have to say."

Vivian paused and looked over her daughter and her current state. She let out a sigh, a deep one that she had been holding onto for quite some time.

"Pan," she said, trying to chose her words wisely for they might come back to haunt her, "I'm sorry for lashing out at you. I just. . . *I want my daughter back*. That's all." Vivian took a couple of deep breaths, which calmed her down; however, beyond each feature of her face, like the center of her brow or the corner of her eyes, which had been pumped with Botox, Pan could see the frustration in her mom's face, the same frustration she witnessed during Cleo's funeral where Pan and Vivian filled her empty casket with Cleo's shoes, her favorite magazines and posters, and all sorts of memorabilia that was six feet deep in the cold earth. Everything that made Cleo "Cleo," all except for an actual body. "Listen, Pan, I have a friend who lives in Portland. She's a herbalist—"

"—You mean, your hippy friend?"

"She used to work at Golden Springs," Vivian said, referring to the rehab facility in Arizona. "Now, she works independently. I think she can help you, Pan. Can you give her a try? Please. For me."

"I don't want to," Pan uttered.

"Right now, it doesn't matter what you want, Pan. You need—"

"—Don't tell me what I need!"

Fed up, Vivian threw up her hands as if she wasn't even about to have a conversation with her daughter. Which, in most—if not all—cases, would end up in a heated agreement driven by fire and fury where eventually Vivian exited stage right from the house feeling way more stressed out than before she arrived. She'd later thank the Academy in the car for her speculator performance.

Vivian stormed back into the kitchen where she restocked the fridge with the food that she had bought from the grocery store. Most of the food was fresh, not frozen. Fruits, including oranges, kiwi and avocados, as well as vegetables such as broccoli, spinach, carrots, cauliflower, and an assortment of leafy greens: all of which she placed inside the fridge. The only boxed food Vivian bought was several boxes of wild and brown rice. She placed them inside the pantry, which was heavily stocked with soda and other carbonated canned drinks to get Pan through the End of Days. Vivian poured out the soda in the sink and threw the empty bottles in the trash. The only drink she wanted her daughter to be drinking was water.

LATER that night, Cary-Anne wheeled Pan into the living room and made sure she was positioned in front of the TV. She had already stayed an hour past her shift; however, she didn't like leaving until Pan was situated and taken care of.

As always, Cary-Anne listed everything Pan needed, which was within arm's reach, including the TV remote, phone, and bedpan—just in case.

"Call me if you need anything," Cary-Anne said, as she left Pan.

Pan didn't even say goodbye to Cary-Anne as she opened the front door. She was still upset by her mom's visit earlier that day.

"Pan," she said, thinking, "one day at a time. Remember?"

Pan could barely bring herself to nod.

Cary-Anne dropped her belongings onto the floor in the foyer before heading out and walked over to Pan, who was crying.

"What's the matter, Pan?" asked Cary-Anne.

"This is no way to live, Cary-Anne," Pan said, crying. "*Everything* hurts. It feels like I got something growing inside me, a cancer, and I can *feel* it spreading all over my body."

"Do you want me to take you to the hospital—"

"—I'm tired of living like this!"

Cary-Anne rubbed the top of Pan's hand.

"It's okay, Sweetie," she said. "I can stay, if you want—"

"—No. Just go. I'm tired of being a burden to everyone."

"What? Whoever said you were a burden?"

"My mom thinks I'm a burden."

"I'm sure she didn't mean it."

"She didn't actually say it, but I can sense it."

"Don't think that way, Pan. You're just tired."

"I know this all started ever since they put me on Quidaquin," Pan whined.

"Well," Cary-Anne said, "I'll get you a doctor's appointment first thing in the morning. How does that sound?"

Pan wiped away her tears and barely nodded.

"Pandora," Cary-Anne said more somberly, "can I ask you a question?"

Once more, Pan barely nodded her head.

"Did you take your medication today?" asked Cary-Anne. Before Pan could respond, Cary-Anne said sternly, "Don't lie to me."

Pan shook her head.

"No," she mumbled, then whined, "I don't like the way it makes me feel."

"I tell you what?" Cary-Anne said and paused. "How about I make you a cup of tea before I go? You'd be amazed what a warm cup of tea can do?"

"But I don't like tea," Pan said.

"*But* you haven't had my tea."

"What's the difference?"

"I make mine with love, darling," Cary-Anne said with a smirk.

"M'kay."

Cary-Anne excused herself.

In the kitchen, she put a pot of water on the stove and while she brought the water to a boil, she grabbed a cup from the cabinet, as well as a teabag of chamomile from the pantry.

As the water came to a rolling boil, she poked her head from the kitchen; and as soon as she noticed Pan distracted by flipping through the channels on TV, she tiptoed into the hallway bathroom. She crept behind Pan and grabbed the bottle of Quidaquin from the medicine cabinet. She removed one capsule from the bottle and crept back into the kitchen where she twisted open the capsule and poured the powdery medicine into the cup. To say the least, she was glad Pan chose capsules instead of tablets that way she didn't have to be sneakier than she desired to be when crushing the pill into a napkin with the butt of a saltshaker. The capsules were harder to swallow, too, even Pan often said so herself whenever she gagged while downing a capsule, which was followed with an extra sip of water; however, the doctor specifically recommended capsule-form because, in the past, patients were known to break the tablets in half and only take a half-dose when he or she should've been taking the "whole" dose.

The Quidaquin slowly sank into the warm water; then, she carefully stirred it around, trying her best not to make any *clinking* noises from the spoon hitting the sides of the teacup; however, she noticed that the medicine was still visible in the tea and left a dark ring on the bottom of the teacup. She raised the cup to her nose and breathed in the steam. She picked up a slight odor. She decided to add a little bit of milk, as well as a dollop of honey to help mask the taste of medicine.

Then, once the tea was prepared, she set the floral-patterned teacup on a saucer, let the tea steep for three minutes or so, which gave Cary-Anne plenty of time to side-chat with Pan from the kitchen, first asking Pan what was on the tube tonight, then Pan responding by running through a list of TV shows, including *Big Brother Redux* and *Luv Island*, then Cary-Anne following up as if she was oblivious and had never heard of such TV shows.

After four minutes had passed, Cary-Anne brought the tea to Pan.

"Here you go," she said and handed Pan the teacup and saucer. "Be careful," she warned, "it's a little hot."

Pan, who smelled everything she tasted, took a whiff of the tea.

"Not bad," she said and sipped from the warm tea.

She nodded her head as if it was her silent way of approval.

"Drink up," Cary-Anne said. "By the time you finished that cup, all of your troubles will melt away."

"'Kay," Pan said depressingly.

Cary-Anne checked her watched.

"Well," she said with a sigh, "I'm going to go now. Call me if you need anything."

Cary-Anne collected all of her belongings, said good night to Pan for the second time, and locked the door behind her with her own copy of the house key.

As the headlights on the car in the driveway cut across the living room wall, Pan took yet another sip of the tea. Her face turned sour from the taste of the tea. She spat it back into the cup and placed it on the saucer and set it aside on the tray right bedside the futon.

With the end of her tie-dyed T-shirt, Pan wiped her tongue as if she couldn't get rid of the taste quick enough.

She turned her attention back to the TV and flipped through all of the channels. She wound up on Channel 3, MWC, which, every Thursday night, aired old interviews by authors, musicians, actors, as well as forward thinkers.

Tonight's program was airing an interview with Doctor Riley, who, from the stretch of '94 through '95, had run a circuit of interviews on TV to promote a new book called, *World Next Door*. She was well known for her theory on the "Multiverse."

Pan listened to Doctor Riley talk for a few minutes—Pan was more drawn to those three long, jagged scars running along the left side of Doctor Riley's face—and for a moment, was tempted to turn the channel until the doctor referred to the very first time she experienced the so-called "Multiverse" after having choked on a piece of food. She talked about the experience as if she had lost her virginity. In the most articulate way possible, she explained it as falling *not* to the floor but "through" the floor. The inside of restaurant lowered, "like an elevator," and then she found herself in another world, as real as the one before her eyes, not inside her head, but real. The second experience happened when she was mauled by a wild Bengal tiger during a visit to India as her so-called "awakening."

Doctor Riley interrupted the interviewer before he could bring "science" into the conversation and provoked a question of her own: "*What if there was another world beneath our very own—another realm, if you will—one where its inhabitants gazed up at us the same way we gazed with awe at all of the stars among the Heavens? Ever since I was a little girl, the unbridled power of 'what if' had consumed my thoughts, as if the two words alone were part of a phenomenon as volatile as loose papers whirling in a windstorm that presented no origin, yet a sequence of events that shared an inevitable outcome based on how the material world had shaped my expanding mind. I always wondered about that 'what if' world and its 'what if' life forms: What would they think of us? Would they see us as their gods? Their saviors? Or were they canny enough to tap into our filtered armor and see us for who we truly were—their corrupters?*"

"*So,*" the interviewer followed, resting the side of his chin along the sides of his fingers, "*you're saying humans are to blame for the corruption in the world.*"

"*I'm not saying that humans are to blame per se,*" Doctor Riley replied. "*I'm saying human nature is to blame. Human nature and its vile interference with the natural world. From the dawn of mankind, we have been driven by a primordial force to connect and understand our surroundings and the nature all around us and in doing so we've managed to pass the torch. Overtime, however, as population of humans increased, so too did our need for understanding, which, inevitably, led to our willingness to reign. Now, we live in a society where flesh is king. Instead of rebalancing the scales by snuffing out corruption, we've tied our own nooses around our necks and reattached them to the fingertips of our sponsors. Imagine buying a bag of seeds and when you open the bag, every seed is bad, rotten. Do you eat them? Or, do you throw them away? Imagine a society where good or bad no longer exists; yet the lines separating good and bad are too blurry to distinguish. Eventually, every-thing that's good turns bad, and everything that's bad turns good. Who are we to say what's good and what's bad? We've become more concerned with our image and what we do to enhance that image instead of genuinely supporting a world where* every human *thrives. No question, ever since we discovered that we were not alone in this world, we've lived in the* 'Age of the Alpha,' *a soci-ety where social dominance has exploited our need for connection. To say, though, that we've never been this way would be ingenuous. We seek. We conquer, whether we like it or not. And eventually, given time and energy, we destroy. That's* the real *human nature. If anything, my second near-death ex-perience only reinforced human's role in this world."*

"Which is?"

"We are a disease," Doctor Riley said coldly. *"And how exactly do you stop a disease?"*

"With a cure, of course."

"And you ask what cure that may be?"

"You tell me."

Doctor Riley tapped on the side of her temple.

"Self-awareness", she said, *"knowing that one day we're going to die and our actions will leave behind a mark for generations to come. We are nothing more than pebbles being thrown by those we yearn to become into a tranquil lake that bridges our world to the next. Based on our 'spin,' how hard we fall, or how far we travel, we ultimately create a ripple effect that resonates into the next world. The question: How big of a splash do you want to make?"*

"Let's backtrack," the interviewer said, shifting his weight, *"can you ex-plain more about the incident in Boston at The Wicked Dish? How long would you say you 'blacked' out?"*

"My boyfriend at the time said I blacked out for at least twenty-seconds," she said, *"however, to me, it was more like twenty hours. I went somewhere else. Somewhere that shared the same similarities as our world, only one thing remained disparate: humans. They had reverted back to their most primitive form. That's when I knew 'what if' was only a conduit to the truth. Brand it. Advertise it. Slap it on a slogan. One thing remains certain: 'The end is not* end. Yet, it's only the beginning. And we are not alone.'"

Pan zoned out and thought about Doctor Riley's comments about this "other" world.

A shadow caught the corner of her eye.

She turned toward the dark kitchen and in the doorway, witnessed a dark figure lurching forward. Her pale face was barely visible from the bright glow of the TV flickering in the darkness; nonetheless, Pan knew each feature on her face; she knew each contour, each birthmark, each freckle, each blemish, each scar, in particularly, the inch-long scar on the top of her forehead. When she was nine years old, she had gotten that scar after using the living room couch as her own version of a vault. Her knee buckled in mid-jump along the arm-rest, causing her to flip over the couch and hit the top of her head on the edge of the brick fireplace. Pan, a proud tag-along who was six years old, remembered that day as if it was yesterday. In those months following the 2000 Summer Olympics in Sydney, Australia, which were considered a difficult time for a parent who was raising a daughter, many young girls wanted to become world class gymnasts, not because their parents pushed them toward gymnastics but because of US Olympian Tiffany Kibbler, who won the gold medal that year. Of all the Olympians, "Tiff" had a way of attracting the youth through cartoons, cereal commercials, and clothing advertisements on TV. Pan wasn't a Tiffany Kibbler fan; in fact, Pan wasn't at all interested in athletics or the country's obsession with athletes. The only person she looked up to was her older sister. She was basically her sister's shadow.

"Cleo?" said Pan. "Is that you?"

"Hello, Pan," she said from the dark kitchen.

"What are you doing here?"

"Is that some way to greet your sister?"

Pan frowned.

"Hey," she said, more glum.

"Hey," Cleo responded.

"Am I dreaming?"

"Does it feel like you're dreaming?"

Pan shook her head.

"No," she said.

"Well," Cleo said, smirking, "then I guess you're not."

The tears brimmed underneath Pan's eyelids.

The haze from Quidaquin started to wear off, bringing Cleo's face closer to the light. Pan picked up a strange vibe from Cleo. She'd be lying if she said that the thought didn't cross her mind, but she questioned whether or not this person she was talking to was, in fact, her older sister. After all, why would she cling to the darkness of the room?

With her voice trembling, Pan asked, "What you want from me?"

"What do you want from yourself?" she turned the question back toward Pan. "Isn't that the reason why you stopped taking the medication, because you were curious about what would happen?"

Pan didn't respond.

"As hard as you try, Pan, you cannot erase me. I am here to stay—"

"—You're *not* my sister," Pan cried.

"What makes you so sure I'm not?" asked Cleo.

"My sister was afraid of the dark," Pan said clearly.

The glow of the TV glistened in Cleo's dark, maddening eyes.

As Cleo—or the imposter who was pretending to be Cleo—stepped back into the darkness of the kitchen, that pale glow of the TV changed color and warmth.

Pan heard the words *don't ssstare at it* hissing in the darkness.

With the warmth pressing against the side of her face, Pan turned toward the TV and no longer witnessed a TV. Instead, she fell witness to a large campfire.

The beat of the orange flames replaced that flickering glow of the TV.

Circling around the fire were strange, disfigured faces, young faces she could tell.

"What happened next?" one of those faces repeated.

Pan snapped from her trance.

"Where was I?" asked Pan.

"You were talking about the song on the radio, the one you heard right before the accident."

"Yes," Pan said, shaking off the daze. "I was singing the song 'Me Too' by Meghan Trainor—"

"**—You mean, *we* were singing the song 'Me Too' by Meghan Trainor.**" She heard Cleo saying next to her.

Startled by the sound of her sister's voice, Pan corrected, "Right. We were both singing the song when all of a sudden a car veered across the center lane and forced me to swerve off the road—"

"**—Probably some effing moron texting and driving**," Cleo said.

"The car plowed straight through the guardrail, I remember. The next thing I know, we're headed straight toward a river below. The drop must've been at least twenty stories. At least."

"**Hold up a sec**," Cleo said over Pan. "**We must have two completely different versions because that's not how I remember it. We were clearly hanging from the bridge for quite some time before the car tipped over.**"

"We were?" Pan uttered, as she tried to visualize the moments leading up to the fall.

Turned off by her sister's resilience, Cleo copped an attitude with Pan and in the most exaggerated way possible, rolled her eyes and then smacked her gums as if she was a cartoon.

"Yeah," she said, her voice drawn out. "**Don't you remember?**"

That tone. Pan didn't hate much. Seldom did she ever use the word. But she hated the tone her sister would often use whenever she was feeling like the Queen of All Bitches. The king's bitch. The bitch of state. Her Bitchesty.

She puts the itch *in bitch.*

Cleo always had a way of throwing the ball back onto Pan's court after making her feel so little and stupid. Pan couldn't help but wonder how much Cleopatra sounded like Mom, who was notoriously known for her innate ability to display the same condescending behavior to both her daughters, mainly Pan; however, very rarely did Vivian ever press the tip of her stiletto against Cleo. It's like that old saying: "If you step on a snake, don't expect it not to bite."

"I remember the wreck," Pan said finally, "*then* falling like I was in slow motion, *then* everything got chaotic once the car hit the water."

"**Well**," she said more superiorly, "**it happened. How about this?**" she suggested, as she moistened her lips. "**Why don't we rewind for a sec, go farther back in the story, start with *why* we're driving clear across the country to being with.**"

As always, Pan protested with her silence.

Here we go again, Pan thought.

CLEO'S VERSION

We were driving to Reno to reunite with our biological father whom we met on Ancestry.com. *Actually, it was me who came up with the idea.* **His name was Kirk, but our mom referred to him mostly as 'Jerk. She hardly talked about him, but whenever the subject of 'Kirk came up, she'd try her best to avoid that convo. I don't know all of the details. But what I know for certain is that only a couple of months after Pan was born, the man ran out on our mom. She said that he was going through issues. He was a drinker. He couldn't handle the responsibilities of raising a child, let alone two of them. Since our mom had grown up around a father, who was also a drinker himself—What is it about some men who just can't get enough alcohol? She told me she gave him an ultimatum. Clearly, he chose Jim and Jack over our own mother. A couple of years after Kirk ran off, our mom met a man named Truman. He said he was named after the writer, not the president. To me, I never looked at him as a stepfather or a man who was trying to fill someone else's shoes. To me, Truman was my father.** *Maybe to you, he was. You weren't around him in the afternoons when you were too busy hanging out with your friends, trying to retain your perfect image.* **So, one day, Pan decided to go on Ancestry.com. I heard some of my friends doing it for shits and giggles. So, immediately, it sounded intriguing. We filled out the form and whatnot. A couple of weeks later** *we* **found him, our long lost father, Captain Kirk. So, we said, 'What the hell?' Right. Well, let's backtrack, I had to do a little convincing, considering Bubble Girl over here hardly left the crib.** I leave the house. **Okay. Sure you do.** *Like you would know what I do when you're not around, Bitchosaurus.* **So, it was official. Pan and I were finally going to go on that road trip we had always been talking about.** *You mean, that road trip you've always been talking about. You just want to drag me along because none of your friends would go with you since most of them are either getting married or have jobs and families.* **To say I was excited about the trip would be an understatement. Pan was excited as well.** I was. Strangely. **So, we told ourselves, 'Reno, here we come!' The first two days went by so fast. We stopped in front of the road signs at each state line and took a selfie. FYI, Selfie 101: Always take a selfie in front of the light; if you're outside, the best light is going to be the *sun*light.** Thanks for that pro tip.' Now, can you do us all a favor and speed it up a little? I don't think they're interested in advice on how to take a proper selfie. **Hey, it's my story too!**

PAN'S VERSION

Your story is missing several key details, Cleopatra. **I hate it when you call me that.** First off, we didn't stop to take selfies. *You* stopped to take selfies while I waited in the car. Which makes me start to wonder your real intentions as to why you wanted to go on this road trip so badly in the first place. The whole time it was as if you were planning each stop in order to take a photo of yourself and post it on your Insti.' Let's face it, *Cleopatra.* The whole trip was about you—you always make it all about you—when, in fact, the trip really should've been about reconnecting with Kirk. **That's not fair.** Not fair? Secondly, the first two days didn't go fast—maybe for you—but not for me. You were complaining the whole time. You wouldn't listen to a word I had to say and whenever I tried to actually talk' to you, you changed the subject to whatever made *you* more comfortable. I don't like talking about what's currently fashionable. I don't like talking about all of the crap on the Internet, who said what to whoever, or who fucked who, or did this or that. **Complaining? Excuse me. You were the one who was complaining, Ms. 'My stomach hurts-I'm hungry. Now, if you don't mind, I would like to finish my story please before you ruin it like you always do.** *Bitch.* **After Day Two on our journey out West, we had ourselves a breakthrough. Sure. At times, we were at each other's throats but I think we started to bond after we nearly got kidnapped by some psycho road rager who was literally the dude from *Hitchhiker*. If it weren't for your impressive driving skills—thanks—then both of our heads would probably be mounted on the wall somewhere like hunting trophies.** What was it exactly you said to that guy to tick him off? **It was what you said, not. . .** Me? **Ah yes. Don't you remember? You complimented the guy's trench coat, but apparently he wasn't too fond of your sarcasm.** *She said that, not me. While I was at a pump filling up the tank, she stuck her head out the passenger window and said, 'Nice coat, Draven.' The name was obviously a jab at the stranger. Since Cleo was a woman who constantly referenced scenes from movies or recited popular movie quotes—when she wasn't off Columbusing around the world, she watched a lot of movies on a portable DVD player in her downtime—the comment clearly came from her mouth, not mine.* **All he needed was clown face paint and he'd fit the part. About a mile down the road I saw the same car that the man was driving in the side-view mirror. He was closing in. . . and fast! It was like a car chase out of the movies. He pulled up beside us, inches, and shouted through the passenger window, 'Is that gasoline I smell?' which, now that I think about it, was a line straight out of the movie, *The Crow*. I knew we were both in big trouble. You nodded at the fuel gauge on the speedometer and noticed the needle dropping from F to E. You glanced in the rear view mirror and saw the trail of gasoline.** He must've punctured the gas tank when we both went to use the restrooms behind the convenient store. **Like I said, if you hadn't been quick to react, that psycho's face would've been the last face we'd see before he turned us into wall decorations. It was like you knew *exactly* what the dude was going to do before he even did it. He suddenly turned that POS he was driving toward us and tried to ram us off the road. If I was driving, I would've swerved and more than likely, we'd hit that telephone pole head on and we'd be roadkill. Instead, you hit the brakes. His car fishtailed right in front of us. He swerved out of the way of the pole, but the car ended up barreling over into a ditch on the side of the road. Good thing for us there was a repair shop two exits away. The mechanic was nice enough to fix the leak in just a couple of hours. And that wasn't even the most insane part of the day. The mechanic's name was Eric. And, not only that, the guy was totally into you. You saw the way he was looking at you.** *But you, Cleo, you managed to screw up my chances to meet a decent* *guy. As always, you find a way to shatter my confidence by pointing at my flaws and giving me pointers on how I should wear my hair, only to steal the spotlight as soon as Eric handed me the car keys. You know my buttons and no coincidence there, know the right moments when to push them.* **But, of course, you were too chickenshit to talk to him.** I can't believe that you actually started to open up to me during those couple hours of waiting. Some guy, who was clearly in the wrong for what he did—even though what *you* said to him was uncalled for—**you mean, what you said**—whatever. We go through a traumatic event. You finally share to me the reason why you dropped out of Creston last year, which lead to a meaningful conversation about our trust issues, then, once Mr. Nice Hair reenters the picture and it's so obvious he's way more interested in me than he is you, you go straight back to your usual annoying self. By the way, I thought we were still on my version of the story where—get ready for it—while you were grabbing yourself a *Dark Cavern*™ bar and Slam energy drink inside the convenient store, I cut myself a deal with *Road Warrior* to chase our asses all around the state of Texas, which, in return, would help us reconnect. What better way to get closer to someone than sharing a near-death experience? Don't act like you didn't know. You saw us talking when you stepped out of the convenient store. That's when you made the comment because, straight up, you jelly.

Cleo's face slackened into a blank expression.
"Run that by me again. You did what? You mean. . . "
Pan suddenly burst out laughing.
Eventually, after falling for the joke, Cleo laughed as well.
"Not funny," she said. **"Not funny at all."**
"Admit it. I had you going for a moment."
"Okay. You got me. Now, can I continue?"
Again, Pan's silence was her protest.

CLEO'S VERSION

Like I was saying before *Joker* over here tried to dim my shine, Pan had her chance with a cute, very smart guy who was very 'hands on, but blew it because she's just a big normie. Okay. I'm a normie? Says the one who basically mimics everything Danielle does. That's not true. Danielle takes a trip to Belize with her rich boyfriend who has so much money he doesn't even know what to do with it. Then, what do you know? Three weeks later, you're in Belize. **I booked that trip long before her.** Danielle goes hiking in Flagstaff. A month later you go hiking in Flagstaff. Danielle spends an entire week in Italy. Sure enough, after draining nearly all your money from your savings, three months later, you're taking selfies along the canals in Venice with some Italian dude you probably just met. **Least I'm not a hermit like you.** That's your only comeback? ***Day Three*, I arrived into New Mexico. I stopped at a hole-in-the-wall taco stand called Julio's. Every time I pass through New Mexico, I have to grab the tacos al pastor. Julio's are out of this world. He marinates the pork in tequila. Adds just enough pineapple. To die for. *Straight up.*** I see what you're doing. So, I'm no longer part of your journey.' Is that it? *Go ahead. Continue to ignore me. Why don't you tell these nice folks what happened while you were scarfing down your 'famous' tacos al pastor? She doesn't. And I know she won't because the way she treats my medical condition is reprehensible. First, I was diagnosed with acid reflux, which I managed on my own through years of meditation and change in diet. Then, after the first year of college, when I was feeling super stressed out, I went through this stage where I had a hard time swallowing my food halfway through eating a meal. It felt as if the food would get stuck directly in my chest. Doctors called it a 'hiatal hernia.' It's where the stomach literally pushes up into the diaphragm. They always have a label for something, but to me, I called it 'hell' and it was all brought on by people like Cleo and how, after she inhaled her food, she'd rush me, causing me to eat faster than I should, thus sending me straight to a world of regurgitation. Try swallowing your food, only to have your stomach reject it as if it doesn't want it despite how hungry you may feel. She's fully aware of my poor stomach; knows exactly what closes me up. Yet, anytime she's feeling like watching a show, she'll pull the same shit my mom used to pull when I was younger. She'll hover and linger and wait for me to take the one bite that will stick to the bottom of my esophagus and for the next hour or so, cause all kinds of havoc and sap all of the energy from my body. I remember this one time I wasn't eating the way all the other young girls were eating, so she stopped at McDonalds, drove through the drive thru, bought me a Big Mac, and then she wouldn't pull out of the parking lot until I downed the entire burger. I know, later, it will cause my problems—more mental than anything, just the thought of getting married to a man who's a faster eater than me and having him find out the hard way that his wife has a tendency to regurgitate her food like a fly gives me chills and makes me want to never get married to another life form. Cleo's so insensitive. Only those who lack understanding of issues are forged by a cruel world where dominance is the only motto to living. She thinks it's fun to rush me while I'm eating. Sometimes, I'd like to shove my foot right down her throat and watch her squirm and gag. Then, maybe, she'll know what it's like to feel completely powerless.* **So, after I left Julio's, I decided to pay a visit to the White Sands. I've always wanted to see what all the fuss was about. It's. . . it's not at all what I expected.** *Your typical Cleo. Ms. Center of Attention who, after the first smell of blood, wears her heart on her sleeve. The emotion is extra heavy on her face. She knows what she did to me. So, she does what she always does: She turns it against me.* Sorry about what I said about Danielle, all right?

In the heavy silence, Cleo started to tear-up.

"It was wrong for me to bring up her name," Pan said sympathetically. "The truth is I'm the one who's jelly. I've never had a close friend like you had with Danielle. Once, maybe I did, but that was so long ago that I can't even remember. In a way, I was always destined to be alone. You, on the other hand, are the opposite. I'm not saying it's your weakness—"

"—**See,**" Cleo blurted out, "**that's the difference between you and me, Pan. You think by me wanting to be with someone else is a weakness,** whereas I think it's what makes us human. **Humans need connections as much as they need air to breath.**"

Pan said with slight annoyance, "I said I'm sorry. Geez."

Cleo sobbed for a while before she used a similar tactic Pan used to protest.

PAN'S VERSION

Despite all of the drama, it was fair to say *we* were having a good time whether or not a certain someone didn't want to admit it. I believe it was those few hours we spent at the Grand Canyon that brought us closer. Then, of course, once we left the Grand Canyon, I somehow got lost. I never get lost. **Hey, I always say it's the best way to travel. The best way to get where you need to be is not knowing where you need to be.** We went so far out of the way. That's what I get for relying on my phone. Of course, for some reason, my shitty GPS stopped working and it kept rerouting me somewhere else. I can't even remember the last time I used an actual map, you know, one made out of paper. The guy who sold it to us was a creep, wasn't he? **Yeah. I know how much you like those creepers.** It's like they're attracted to me. **You can say that.** After we crossed into Colorado, we decided to stop at Sharptooth Mountain Park to stretch our legs. Do you remember how loud it was? **You mean nature? It was loud, wasn't it?** Like nature was having itself a giant orgy. We wandered through a couple of trails and ended up at a gorge. We stood over the edge of a cliff and watched the river running below. The sound of the water was loud as well, yet, it was so tranquil. So, that brings us to how we wound up here. We left the park and continued on our journey to unite—and reunite—with our biological father, Kirk. Throughout the entire trip, we saw all these Richard Rhodes signs either on the side of the highway or in people's front yard or on the billboards. Then, once that Approved Advertisement' came on the radio, I nearly flipped my shit. The guy couldn't get the clue. He didn't give a fuck-all about people. Yet, he wouldn't go away. He was like a ghost haunting America. Every time I saw his face, I couldn't help but go on these long-winded rants until I was *blue* in the face. Fortunately, your song came on afterwards, which rid any thought of Richard Rhodes. As we were driving over a bridge, we were both singing along to the song 'Me Too' and getting our swerve on when, all of a sudden, some *dog ran out into the road.* It all happened so fast. One second, we were having so much fun, then the next thing, we were falling to our deaths. Everything was hazy when we hit the water. Both of my shoulders were completely yanked out of socket. Never have I experienced so much pain when I swam to the surface. I could literally feel my shoulder rubbing against bone. It's a good thing that you rolled down the windows right before we crossed the bridge. **Always do.** I know how you are and all of your superstitions. Once we surfaced, the river carried us downstream. The water became rough. I tried to swim toward you, but you were too far from reach. As I struggled to stay afloat, I sank underneath the water for a moment. Once I resurfaced, you were nowhere to be found. Then, the sound of water became louder as I was being carried down the river. All I could think about was *waterfall.* I was heading straight to a waterfall—a big one, too, based on how loud it was. I hoped that you somehow managed to swim to the shore. At that point in time, all I was thinking about was survival. My arms were heavy. I couldn't reach the shore in time. That's when I basically gave up and let the water carry me wherever it was going to take me. Once I reach the edge of the waterfall, everything slowed down again, like the moments when we were falling from the bridge. Before me was a vast valley. The clouds above were as massive as mountains from the storm that had recently passed. They were parting ways, revealing the blue sky and the sunbeam shooting down. I fell for at least ten stories. Once I hit the water—yet again— the impact knocked me out. When I cracked open my eyes, I was blinded by this bright light shining down on me. *But* it wasn't the sunlight. It was this Lazarus' light coming from a large, bulky device in the back of a truck—Light of Lazarus,' as I've heard it being called several times since I've been here. *Oops. Here it comes.*

Beyond the firelight, the dark, shadowy faces in the night darkness shouted, "The Light of Lazarus! The one true light! The light of. . . "

. . . all life, Pan thought. *Yes. I get it already.* She couldn't help but stop and acknowledge those Gabrielites for a moment, as well as their commitment to the special light every time the three specific words *Light of Lazarus* were mentioned.

She delved back into the story as to how she wound up in such a strange town called Gabriel. *I woke up on the shore like a beached whale. Two people were standing over me, one of them a young girl named Kazlauskas Inc. and the other, a rather short stocky man named Cupid. The dark-faced man asked the girl,* "Any crossers with her?" *She replied,* "No. Not that I'm aware of." *As soon as I found the strength to stand on my feet, I realized that I was some-where else. Cleo was nowhere to be found. Or, was she?*

"I was extremely worried about Cleo," Pan said. Then, "Kazlauskas Inc. here informed me that she was abducted by some clan called. . . well, I don't. . . "

All of a sudden, the name of the clan slipped her mind.

Pan's eyes drifted in thought. The more she thought about the name, the more it fell deeper into the blackness of her thoughts.

"I wasn't taken by The 1999 Star Cruisers," said Cleo, as she rolled both her eyes. **"Where in the hell would you come up with such a ridiculous idea?"**

Not my idea, Cleo. Your idea.

All of a sudden, a darker thought crept into her thoughts as if somehow it was starting to consume her.

Although I know for certain that little freak show stole my charm brace-let—you mean, my charm bracelet—I was the one who bought it for you, didn't I? She found the bracelet on the riverbank after they shined that light on us. It slipped from your wrist and the little freak show snatched it when you weren't looking.

As Pan turned her eyes toward Kazlauskas Inc., who was sitting on the other side of the fire, Pan drifted deeper in thought and remembered young Kazlauskas Inc., *not* the one Cleo had described, telling her about this so-called clan and how they were known to kidnap or at times, wrangle up "strays," referring to Cleo and Pan or any others who crossed over to the other side, then sell them to a ruthless organization who went by the name the "High Order" in order to obtain a higher knowledge, or "enlightenment," as Cupid simply put it.

Cleo capped off the gesture by smacking her gums.

"**Whatever.**"

CLEO'S VERSION

Not too long after the incredible expandable water toy who happened to be named after the makers of a popular candy bar and fairy boy found you on the shore, they found me farther down the river. *Kazlauskas Inc. and Cupid's disfigured appearance isn't what I'd call photogenic, more of a carnival act, neither is the rest of the townspeople for that matter. However, the notion that Cupid was actually named after the god of love was somewhat comical. That is, if Cupid aged thirty years, put on a beer belly that protruded under his undersized T-shirt, shaved once a week, became a heavy smoker, and developed, in any god's terms, a winged dysfunction. According to Kazlauskas Inc.'s explanation, the real reasons as to why Cupid cut off his wings, leaving only two small nubs where two wings used to be, was that they no longer worked and they hung from his back like wet blankets and after a while, Cupid was sick and tired of looking at those limp things. Talk about a hopeless romantic. I've heard rumors about small, sleepy towns located in the middle of Bum Hole, Nowhere, such as Gabriel, getting involved in incest and all kinds of icky stuff, like rituals and sacrifices. The fact they worship three children called the Underlings as their gods was one of the first of many red flags. Maybe that's why they look like they way they do, the features on their faces disproportionate, their abilities mutant. Cleo's tells them 'everything leading up to that was a blur. That being swept away by a raging river. There's one thing I can relate to Cleo: Ever since I arrived here it seems like everything has been a blur.* **All I remember was thrashing around the water, then I hit the shoulder on a boulder in the bottom of the river after I fell from the waterfall, then I was sucked into a black hole at the bottom of the surface, like a funnel of some sorts, then I remember floating around a cold, thick blackness. Only instead of waking up on the shore, I'm clinging to a rock in the middle of the river. The water was much different, too, murkier, heavy, like sludge. After I found what little strength I had left, I manage to swim to the shore. That was when I saw** *these* **two characters coming to my rescue. They told me that they found you and that you were okay.** *They did?* **Yes. For the trillionth time, Pan,** *they* **did.** *But there was someone else. A man. He was injured. He couldn't walk on his own.* **Once I was able to walk on my own, they collected their fishing stuff and I hopped in the back of their rusty truck and we rode down a foggy dirt road through the woods where every tree was stripped bare by what looked like a fire and the only life forms came in warped shadows.** *I won't forget what she said to Cupid: Where's your halo? I hadn't felt so humiliated in my entire life. And* **I won't forget the sounds all around me. There were no sounds, not a single bird chirping, no insects, no animals. Nothing. Everything was silent. When we made it to the highway, the sky was different as well. Dark**

red and eerie, like the morning of a bad storm. Strangely, though, I knew it wasn't going to storm. A part of me knew the storm had already passed. I thought maybe we wound up all the way back in New Mexico, or maybe Utah or even somewhere in the Midwest. I soon realized we weren't in any of those places. We were somewhere else, something strange. . .

Pan lost herself in her sister's words, her "version" of the story, and given the situations that had occured, started to believe her.

What if my version was all wrong?

What if I was *confusing it with a dream?*

Or, what if *Cleo's version was the only version?*

But what about the one man who was injured? Pan could see the man's face as if she was looking at him in real-time. He was a cave diver from Arkansas, had an accent so thick it sounded foreign, also had a rugged handsomeness to him as if he could've played a lead role in any American Western. He said—or claimed—that he was taking photographs of an underwater cave which he referred to as the "Devil's Throat" when all of a sudden he felt a force tugging him into a crevice. He compared the pull to a rip current. Pan, too, had felt a similar force twice as the man described: once when she was driving over the bridge, then another time once she hit the water after plummeting from the waterfall. The name was what seized her attention the most: "Devil's Throat." She had heard of the name before in the news. She read it in the headlines but, among the cross-chatter of her thoughts, couldn't quite put a story to the name. Then, as she was about to lend the man a hand, a great silence rushed through the woods, she remembered. When we were about to help him to his feet, the fisherman—Cupid—started acting fidgety and he insisted that we leave him alone. Before Pan could even question him, the cave diver was pulled into a narrow opening underneath a boulder. He struggled for a bit, but he was sucked into the hole as though he was being sucked into a vacuum. *His entire body violently folded inward like a lawn chair.* His head, hands, and legs were the last parts of his body to be sucked into the hole and when they did so, they ballooned outward as if, any moment, they were ready to pop.

Pan fell deeper and deeper into "Cleo's version" until finally she was reliving the story as if it was her very own.

"As you said earlier, this place doesn't share the same rules as the world we come from," Cleo said. **"This place is special."**

🕐

THE fisherman with two worn down nubs protruding from the back of his shoulder blades asked them for their names.

Cleo was first to speak: "I'm Cleopatra," she said and pointed at Pan, "this is my little sister, Pandora."

"Pandora What?"

"Excuse me," Pan uttered, speaking over Cleo.

"You have a last name, don't you?"

"Pandora Nikopoulos," Cleo said for Pan.

"How you spell that?"

More upset from the way her sister was speaking for her as if she was a mute, Pan said louder, "N-i-k-o-p-o-u-l-o-s. Nikopoulos. What's your name?"

"Cupid," he said.

"Cupid *What*?"

"Well," he said blandly. "Just Cupid." He pointed at the young girl who was throwing pebbles into the sludgy river. "That there is Kazlauskas Inc."

Normally, such a tongue twister of a name would've drawn way more attention than a name like Cupid; however, Pan was somewhat disturbed as to why this stranger "Cupid" wanted to know her last name and even weirder, how to spell it.

She retorted, "What kind of name is Cupid?"

"Easy, Pan," Cleo said and walked to the back of the truck.

"Come on, Kaz," Cupid waved at the young girl and said that they were now leaving.

To the left of Pan, she heard what sounded like a man groaning in the woods.

🕐

AFTER riding for a few miles down a desolate highway through a flat country-side, which had the similarities of Indiana yet slightly similar to New Mexico with jagged mountains underneath dark, stormy clouds at a distance, they passed several cars, mostly older models, ones she hadn't seen since she was a child.

Pan shot weary glances at each driver inside each passing car and was completely stumped by their inhuman appearance.

As Pan redirected her attention forward, she saw Cupid and Kazlauskas Inc. leaning forward and looking up at the sky through the windshield.

Cupid pulled the truck underneath an overpass and from the sliding window, instructed Pan and Cleo to get out.

As Cupid parked the truck, Kazlauskas Inc. stepped outside and hurried to the tailgate where she waved Pan and Cleo toward a recess underneath the bridge.

In the corner of her eye, Pan witnessed the shadow speeding across the road. She heard the sound of what she thought was a drone; however, it was way higher in pitch, like an amplified beehive.

Nursing her injured shoulder, Cleo gingerly stepped out of the truck.

The noise coming from above grew louder and louder, nearly deafening, and forced Pan to help Cleo up the ramp while Cupid and Kazlauskas Inc. closely followed behind.

"What are we running from?" asked Cleo.

Cupid immediately shushed Cleo and pushed the two up the ramp.

Together, the four hunkered underneath the bridge while more of those same shadows zipped across the road, as well as the open field.

"*They* can sense us," said Cupid, as he escorted Cleo and Pan farther into the recess.

585

Pan turned to Kazlauskas Inc., who had shrunk down to the size of a toddler in the very back of the dark, dusty recess. She couldn't help but notice Kazlauskas Inc. and her sudden change in size. She had gone from the average size of a teenager to the size of a girl who looked as if she could barely walk on her own. Even those raggedy clothes still remained the same size and were loosely hanging from her body.

"How the hell is she able to do that?" Pan asked Cupid, who, in return, placed his index finger over his mouth, signaling for Pan to be absolutely quiet.

Once more, Pan glanced at Kazlauskas Inc., who was trembling in fear.

"Wait till *they* pass," Cupid whispered to Pan.

"They?"

Before she could further question the seemingly dire situation, Cupid pressed his index finger against his lips once more, but this time exercising more urgency.

It was easy enough to see the fear in Kazlauskas Inc. considering her age, but to see it in Cupid's eyes was something else entirely for Pan.

The sky above darkened like a cloud, thus causing the area under the bridge to darken as well.

As the buzzing sound intensified past the overpass, Pan felt a cold, staticky gust of wind hit the side of her face. In the corner of her eye, she caught a massive creature, which was about the size of a human, swooping down and landing behind Cupid's truck. The creature looked similar—if not, identical—to a mosquito. Of course, considering its size, it clearly was *not* a mosquito or at least not like any mosquito Pan or Cleo had ever seen. Its proboscis was nearly the size of Pan's arm. When fully stretched out, its wings could cover twice the height of her body. It hunched over the tailgate and ran the end of its proboscis along the bedding; then, after a speedy inspection, it flew away.

Soon afterwards, that harsh buzzing sound lessened.

The light brightened slightly. Eventually, those sounds faded away.

"All clear," Cupid said, breathing a sigh of relief.

"Now, can you explain what those things were?" asked Pan.

"They are carriers of a virus that has recently plagued our town. Other towns within our county have been hit hard, Finnegans and Fielding, Castaneda, Huxley, Mann, Outpost 13, all of them are now hot spots. It's only a matter of time before it spreads to the city of Leatherwood—"

"—You're talking about mosquitoes?" said Cleo.

"The *Culexx* with two x's," he said. "Mosquitoes on steroids."

"What about you?" Pan said, nodding at Kazlauskas Inc., who was starting to return to her normal size. "How are you able to shrink like that?"

Kazlauskas Inc. bashfully shrugged her shoulders.

"I dunno," she mumbled.

"You don't know? Seriously?"

"You have to realize," Cupid said before Pan lost her cool, "in this world, we don't have any rules, not like in your world."

Finally, Cleo asked the inevitable question: "Where are we?"

"Gabriel," Cupid then corrected, "well, technically we're still on the outskirts of Outpost #7."

"Are we in another country?" Pan followed.

"No," Cupid said bluntly. "More like another world."

"What do you mean 'another world'?"

"I promise I can answer any question you want," Cupid said. "Right now, we need to move. They'll be back. And next time, they'll be in a greater numbers."

"The mosquitoes?"

Cupid hesitated.

"If that's what you want to call them, then, yes. The mosquitoes."

Pan and Cleo inched down the ramp; Kazlauskas Inc. shouldered by the two and hopped into the passenger seat. Lastly, Pan and Cleo used the tailgate to step in the back of the truck. Then, as soon as they were seated, Cupid drove away.

🕐

ONLY a few miles of riding through the flat countryside, they drove past what appeared to be a cornfield, which gave off the odor of a corpse. The crops were rotten and infested with what looked like disease. Behind the dead, rotten stalks Pan witnessed three tentacles flailing around in the air. She tapped Cleo on the shoulder and pointed to the cornfield, but the tentacles were no longer visible.

Cleo shrugged off her sister's paranoia for she was more concerned about the town they were approaching.

They passed the sign for "GABRIEL," which was constructed of a mound of painted black rocks. Seven of the rocks were painted white with the letters G, A, B, R, I, E, L painted in red.

Pan couldn't help but pick out each and every detail of her surroundings. She had driven through towns such as Gabriel; in fact, she had driven through similar countrysides. However, each detail wasn't quite right, yet slightly. . . off, as if it was a poor imitation of "her" world, as if those who had built these roads or threw up these buildings had done so without any blueprint, but rather solely based on a memory. Even the road they had been driving on for the past few miles looked as if a child haphazardly poured asphalt through the rough terrain, didn't even bother to smooth out the surface or the edges of asphalt before it dried, painted a couple of red lines, *not yellow*, in the middle of the road. The same went for the buildings, which sat crookedly along their foundations: each building was very similar to everyday buildings that she saw everyday in her world, but, on the other hand, weren't. The only way Pan could put it was that they, like the roads, the bridges, or even the signs, were *off*.

For Cleo, however, Pan knew the easiest way to explain what they were experiencing was with a movie. This one being *Beetlejuice*. Cleo mentioned to Pan how much it reminded her of that movie. Cleo only shared this with Pan because Pan knew it was how Cleo tried to make sense of situations, especially ones that were all but foreign to her, by comparing it to a movie. She felt that, like those two characters who were portrayed by Alec Baldwin and Geena Davis, they were stuck between worlds, living and dead.

Pan teased, "I don't see any sand worms yet."

Cleo wasn't at all amused by Pan's humor.

Curious, yet at the same time, skeptical, Pan drew her attention to the cooler-like container next to the wheel well. She cracked open the lid and took a peek at Cupid's so-called "catch of the day." She immediately gagged and covered the bottom half of her face from the horrendous stench, which reeked of a warm turd baking in the sun. Most—if not all—of the ice was melted inside the cooler. The surface of the water was rather oily and left a swirling array of bright colors, including pinks, purples, and blues, along Cupid's "catch," which appeared as if it was scraped off the road instead of being fished out of the river. The texture of the mollusk-like creature reminded Pan of a jellyfish, only it was bumpier, like gooseflesh. It had a lot of tentacles; however, Pan couldn't quite count how many since most of them were either bundled up or knotted. What struck her the most was its eye, as well as its vaginal similarities. It had only one, like the eye of a cyclops, swollen, rather elongated, and protruding along the center of a vulva-shaped head, which rested underneath a cap-like hood—or *was it a fin?*

A part of Pan sure hoped it was a fin.

Repulsed, yet more so intrigued by the sight of what she assumed was a creature fished out of the river, Pan gently elbowed Cleo in the arm, nodded her head at the cooler, and whispered to her to take a look inside.

Startled by Pan's interest, Cleo didn't bother to question her sister. Instead, she did as Pan asked, looked inside the cooler, and then, following a similar reaction as Pan, immediately pinched her nose and recoiled from the sight of the slippery, smelly creature inside the cooler.

"What is that?" mouthed Cleo.

"Look at the head," Pan said. "Doesn't it look kind of like ah. . . "

"A what?"

"You know?"

Cupid glanced in the rear view mirror, causing Pan to close the lid.

As Cupid turned his attention back to the road, Pan turned to Cleo with what could only look like a guilty expression on her face.

She had no words, and even if she did, she didn't even know where to start.

As they rode past several houses, Pan and Cleo witnessed the pale, disfigured faces behind the windows: faces creeping past the edge of curtains while others gawking at the two sisters with wide glassy eyes. Neither Pan nor Cleo saw anybody outside, no children playing, no adults doing any yard work or repairs to the shoddy-looking houses. Each Gabrielite appeared quarantined inside their homes.

Pan glanced inside the cab of the truck and saw Cupid checking a wristwatch that was pulsing with a soft white light.

Thinking it might've been one of those digital watches, Pan peered closer at the watch; however, she saw no time, no numbers, no minute or hour hand either, just a light pulsing like a heartbeat.

Cupid tapped Kazlauskas Inc. on the shoulder and showed her the wristwatch thingamajig. Then, turned to Pan and Cleo and cracked open the back window.

"We have to make a pit stop," he said over his shoulder.

"Sounds good to me," Cleo said, turning his sights to several houses where, strangely, that same pulsing white light on Cupid's watch was pulsing behind the windows of each house.

The light, Cleo noticed, was also coming from the inside of buildings. It was a white, bluish light, angelic, like the soft glow filter she had seen being used in the 1970's movies during a flashback scene. It reminded her of a time when she was young and how she and Pan would go to the pool during those hot and humid summers. Pan used to wear goggles; however, Cleo always lost hers and thought they were distracting and a burden to carry around, especially when she was having so much fun in the sun. She'd swim with her eyes open, even while under the water, and when she'd surface, her vision was blurry, especially when she looked at the light.

Pan followed Cleo's eyes and she, too, recognized the light.

"When I woke up next to the river," she said quietly to Cleo, "they were shining that same light down on me."

Cleo read the name engraved along the side of the device next to her.

"*Lazarus*," she whispered, then turned to Pan, "What do you think it means?"

"I dunno."

They drove past a church-like building that was missing a cross; however, in its place was a wooden circular symbol with three lines positioned upward. Pan thought it looked like a sun rising—or setting—along a horizon with the lines being sunrays shooting into the sky. In the very front of the building, she saw three bronze statues of what looked like children.

As they made it to the Main Street of Gabriel, Pan saw the *same* symbol on a bumper sticker on the back of a parked car, looking exactly the same way she saw it on top of that building, with a circle and three lines, the first line slightly slanted left in a sixty degree angle, the second line straight, the third line slightly slanted right in the same sixty degree angle.

Immediately, Pan began to worry while Cleo became unusually quiet.

Usually, she'd be talking her head off, throwing out movie quotes and jokes about Gabriel.

Not a peep from her.

🕐

THEY arrived at Gulps.

Cupid and Kazlauskas Inc. were first to exit the truck, then Pan, who helped her sister out of the truck. Cupid suggested that they come inside and wait, if they liked, since it wasn't entirely safe to be outside because of, you know, the "giant mosquitoes." Pan and Cleo tagged along and followed Cupid and Kazlauskas Inc. inside Gulps, which, surprisingly, had the traits of a convenient store. They had aisles of snacks and refreshments. Pan felt at home.

"Watch your step," Cupid said, pointing at a couple of beige colored circles of what looked like the spill of a milkshake on the floor. Next to the spill was a yellow "Caution" sign indicating a wet floor.

Cupid mentioned to them that he had to pick up a few supplies before heading back home, including a bag of ice. Which, in a spur of the moment,

589

prompted Pan to bring up that "strange smell" in the back of the truck. Not to point any fingers. But the crusty turd muffin coming from the cooler.

"Yeah," Cleo said bluntly. "It smells like a fart." Then, mumbled under her voice, "Or better yet, a queef."

Wearing her best mean face, Pan elbowed Cleo.

"Queefs don't smell," she whispered.

She couldn't even believe she was saying the word *queef*.

"Some do," Cleo said.

Immediately, Pan shushed her, trying to put an end to the topic of smell.

Pan's veiled attempt at asking Cupid what that creature was inside the cooler didn't go over so well.

"Must be coming from the plant," Cupid said plainly and made his way to the front of the store where a featureless-looking clerk escorted him to a secret room.

While Cupid was off doing who-knows-what, Pan and Cleo moseyed around the store, checking out a shelf of candy bars called LiverSticks. She read the ingredients on the back and sure enough, it was actual liver. Pan dropped the candy bar in disgust and made her way to the back where she found a refrigerator full of Type A Negative bottles.

From behind, Cleo asked, "Is that what I think it is?"

"Blood," Pan murmured.

"What the hell is this place?" asked Cleo.

The clerk, whom she heard Kazlauskas Inc. refer to as "Wax," returned to the front counter with Cupid, as well as the supplies that he needed: a bag of ice and a Mason jar filled with a white cream said to be a special ointment extracted from a rare hepa-pod, which was on the verge of extinction.

Listening to the sound of Wax's gravelly *phlegmy* voice from across the store seized Pan's attention; in fact, she couldn't ignore his voice. She inched closer to the front of the store. Cleo followed closely behind. As soon as Pan stepped past a shelf of more organ-flavored snacks and laid eyes on Wax's face underneath the bill of the cap, she covered the gasp with her hands. He wasn't at all human—his face, that is. He had the body shape of any average man; however, underneath the raggedy jumpsuit and burgundy baseball cap, his gooey skin was moving.

She moved her eyes from his face and inspected his hands, which were gooey as well. The cuffs around his sleeves were stained with his own dripping skin.

Wax removed the rag from the breast pocket of the jumpsuit and wiped away that loose skin falling from his brow and then pocketed the soggy rag. Strangely enough, the skin kept oozing, then falling like sweat beads, then once it hit a surface, for instance, the countertop, the skin started to mold and harden.

Hence why they called him "Wax."

Made sense.

But *not really*, Pan thought.

She realized where that wet spill from earlier had originated.

590

"The hot weather does this to me every time," he said, as if he was explaining himself for Cupid and Kazlauskas Inc., who were well-aware of his "condition"—if that was what you called it.

"We're most definitely not in Colorado anymore," Pan uttered to Cleo.

Kazlauskas Inc. voluntarily expanded in size in order to touch the shard of a chalky black crystal inside a squared glass case next to the cash register while, at the same time, sneakily grabbed an air freshener in the shape of a mushroom from a clip of "magical" fresheners on a wing stack in front of the checkout counter.

Once Kazlauskas Inc. slipped the air freshener inside her back pocket of her sweatpants, which were starting to rip down the rear seam from the change in her size, Pan knew the move was what she observed as a distraction.

Without realizing what Kazlauskas Inc. had done, Wax slapped her hand and told her no touching. The slap left behind a smudge of his thick, gooey skin along the top of Kazlauskas Inc.'s hand.

"Sorreee," she uttered, as she shrunk back to her normal size.

Cupid placed the bag of ice next to that jar of cream on the counter. The bag of ice split open, causing a couple of ice cubes to spill out onto the counter.

Wax attempted to gather the rest of the ice cubes, but Cupid stopped him.

"Not so fast, Wax," he said, holding out his hand. "I got it."

One of the ice cubes slid from the counter and landed next to Pan's foot.

Pan picked up the ice cube.

At first, it looked and felt like any other ice cube; however, the sensation on the edge of her fingertips intensified. The ice cube was no longer cold, yet it was sharp and prickly. Pan held the ice cube to her face and saw hundreds of parasitic creatures squirming around inside the ice cube.

As the ice starting to melt into that same colorful rainbow-like water that she saw inside the cooler along her fingertips, her skin started to become more translucent.

Pan immediately handed Cupid the ice cube and dried her fingers along the side of her pant leg. The outer layer of her skin peeled away like an open blister; nonetheless, her skin did return to normal.

Must've been some kind of reaction to the water.

"Thanks," Cupid said. Then, introduced Pan and Cleo to Wax, "Found them by Raven's Gullet."

"Pan," she said to Wax. "My sister, Cleo."

Cleo said hello; however, Wax hardly acknowledged her.

"Tourists, huh? Passing through or just passing away?"

Wax laughed by himself, whereas Cupid and Kazlauskas Inc. remained dead serious—no pun intended.

Pan had an inkling as to what Wax meant by the comment.

Over the awkward silence, Cupid gathered the rest of the ice cubes and paid Wax with a handful of teeth, varying in size and shape. Among the teeth, human as well as animal, Pan spotted what looked like the fang of a snake.

Once Cupid paid for the bag of ice and that "special" ointment, he pinched Kazlauskas Inc. on the arm and told her to put back the air freshener.

Over his shoulder, he said to Pan, "Please excuse Kaz here. She has a knack for taking things that don't belong to her."

Pan felt as though her attention was being physically—and mentally—pulled back to the black crystal with the same force surrounding a magnetic field; however, she fought through the attraction and couldn't help but notice the product on the wall behind Wax. After all, it was "pixie dust," or at least, that was what the label had read.

Pixie dust?

No joke.

Cupid recognized Pan's interest in the dust.

"Like what you see?" Wax said to Pan but didn't expect any reply from her. "Grounded down from the horn of a unicorn. It works too," he said to Pan before she could follow up, "in case you're wondering."

"What do you mean 'it works'?"

"Well," he said, "pixie dust worked before the virus." He nodded at the fully stocked shelves of pixie dust on the wall. "Now I wouldn't really call them a best seller. Before the ZOMBA virus, pixie dust allowed us to fly. Yes. Like in those movies you watch. But now, *they* own the skies."

"The mosquitoes?"

"Yes," he said and shot a glance at Wax, "the mosquitoes."

"In a way, though, the virus has been for our own good. It has grounded us, made us more appreciative to what we have in front of us instead of what's below us."

Pan nodded at the black crystal and asked, "So what's that?"

"That there is a piece of resin leftover from the gods, which was pulled from *your* world," Cupid said.

"My world?"

"It is said to have the power to foresee the future of those who come in contact with it. Which, ultimately, allows those who come in contact with it a chance at immortality. I know. Pixie dust. Gigantic mosquitoes. Deadly virus. A tiny sacred *rock* that can see your future. It's a lot to take in. Me," Cupid said, pointing at himself, "I don't personally believe in some of the stuff I hear around here." He flicked his eyes toward Wax behind the counter and winked his left eye; however, to Pan, it came off more as if his eye was twitching and he had an eyelash or grain of dirt stuck behind an eyelid and he was trying to flick it out. "Not to mention any names, but I think there are some corrupted folks who find any opportunity to take advantage of the more weak-minded."

"—Like you have any room to talk, Limp Wing," Wax said abruptly, as part of his mouth broke apart and dripped along the collar of his jumpsuit. "How can you criticize something that you've never tried?"

In an instance, the part of his mouth that had fallen from his mouth regenerated and reformed along his lips, as well as the one side of his chin, as if he had an endless supply of skin—or wax?

Cupid shook off the insult and swallowed what, to Pan, appeared to be a dark shade of despondency behind his face.

"Before the virus, you'd have folks lined up around this entire building, waiting to buy dust. Now, as you can tell, it's like a ghost town around here. Everybody has sort of given up on hope."

Hope?

Cupid said, more soberly, "Whether the resin works or not, in a way, it made folks more. . . "

Pan waited for Cupid to finish the sentence.

Cleo said, "More what?"

"More present," he said thoughtfully.

Wax grinned at Pan.

"Why don't you give it a try, *Pan*?" he said. "I'll cut you a discount. What'd you say?"

"You know she doesn't have any loot."

"Hey, some of us still have to make a living around here."

"Maybe next time," Cupid said and made his way from the store. "Be seeing you around, Wax." He waved at Kazlauskas Inc. "Come on, Kaz."

Cleo eventually left with Cupid and Kazlauskas Inc.; however, Pan wasn't so quick to follow. Instead, she crept over to the shard of black crystal mounted like a museum piece inside the glass case and once more found herself being "pulled" into the black crystal. In that trance, Pan envisioned herself lying on the floor of a dark living room with the glow of a television screen flashing on her face; however, she couldn't even recognize herself, mainly her body. In her right hand, she was holding a knife and staring at a stranger inside the refection of the blade. Just as she was about to use the blade on herself, she bolted upright.

🕓

PAN suddenly yanked herself from the vivid memories, as though she was actually experiencing them outside the threshold of her mind.

Was it really the Quidaquin that was suppressing these memories?

As the memories grew stronger and more brighter and vivid and forced Pan to reconcile her time spent in Gabriel with an image here of a car ride from Gulps to Cupid's house or an image there of Cupid removing that smelly river creature from an ice cooler, Pan couldn't take it any longer. Her thoughts were spinning. *Her world* was spinning. She so desperately wanted them out, the memories—if that's what they were and not something else entirely. She just wanted to go back to the way it was before, when she didn't remember.

Using every single muscle in her body, she reached for the TV remote, which had fallen on the floor. Once she was able to reach the remote, she turned up the volume to drown out voices from the beyond, only to hear a much gentler voice, a soft-spoken one from one of those depressing commercials about abused and mistreated dogs that aired mostly during Christmas time direly pleading for her help and, of course, money.

"For just a dollar a day you could help Charlie find a home!"

It got every time. But, she told herself, not tonight.

Once the sickly images zapped away in a bright flash and the TV screen went dark, the reflection in the screen displayed not only herself but also someone else, a scruffy-looking man with a belly so large and round that he looked pregnant.

Startled by the reflection, she turned to her immediate left and without thinking, uttered the name, "Cupid?"

593

Nobody was standing in the corner of the living room. She turned back to the reflection in the TV. He was gone.

Once more, she turned to the same spot where he was standing. Nothing.

Pan was more confused by the name, where she had heard the man, why she even uttered the name. Her thoughts raced. Once more, she found herself in spin city.

Unable to think straight, Pan maneuvered herself from the futon and managed to stand on her own. Just standing up was taxing enough for Pan. Her breath, labored. She only had twelve steps to the bathroom where she saw the Quidaquin bottle lying on the vanity. At this point, twelve steps was like twelve miles.

Exerting all of her strength, Pan made her way to the bathroom.

Halfway to the bathroom, she had to stop by the dresser to catch her breath. She used the dresser to lean against.

"You can do this, Pan," she told herself.

She continued to move forward.

Only five steps left.

Four.

Three.

Two.

By the time she made it the bathroom, she was completely gassed. She could hardly stand on her own two feet. She worked up quite a sweat, too. The thought alone of that strange-looking guy from the convenient store and his dripping skin made Pan more uncomfortable. Not only was she sweating from exerting herself, but she was also sweating from the anxiety. She leaned up against the side of the vanity and took a moment to catch her breath and relax. She turned on the faucet, ran warm water over both of her hands, which helped calm her breathing.

Then, she switched over the water to cool, placed a washcloth underneath the faucet, and soaked it with water.

She placed the cool, damp washcloth on the areas of her body where she was sweating the most, including her forehead, her cheeks, the back of her neck, then her armpits, her folds.

Once she was able move again, she grabbed the bottle of Quidaquin from the vanity. She opened the bottle, took out one capsule, and placed it in the center of her palm; however, she never popped it or swallowed it. Yet, she just stared at it.

After debating whether or not to take the Q-capsule, Pan threw it against the mirror and cried out in great agony.

As the pain settled, she listened to the wind over her labored breath.

To her right, a curtain was blowing around like a mane of lush hair from the wind blowing through the open window.

Once more, she drifted off into a trance, but this time, she was back in a small town called Gabriel.

FOUR YEARS AGO

PAN wondered to herself if these Gabrielites were the real monsters instead of the monsters they were hiding from.

Where would such an idea originate?

A voice pulled her from her thoughts.

"Pan?"

Pan pulled herself from the open window of the living room and turned to the voice.

"You sure you're not hungry?" asked Cupid.

At the kitchen doorway, Cupid was holding a plate of bunkfish, which didn't smell nearly as pungent as it did in the ice cooler; in fact, it smelled like any other fish that was well seasoned.

As though its smell was imprinted inside her nasal cavity, all she could think about was the bunkfish prior to being charred over an open flame and how there was absolutely no chance in hell she was going to eat something that smelled as if it was scooped out of a toilet.

Pan held up her hand.

"I'm good," she said and looked around the dark living room where the only means of light came from an old lantern.

Cupid cut the bunkfish in half and brought one half to his son, Enoon, who was lying in a bed in one of the bedrooms next to the living room. According to Cupid's story, Enoon, who, at times, was lucid while other times he would blather away and not make any sense, had recently been bitten by the "Culexx."

When Pan had pressed him, he also referred to the Culexx as an "experiment" gone wrong. "I know. Let the madness begin, right?" There was no truth behind Cupid's statements, yet they were merely conspiracy theories.

Pan couldn't help but overhear Enoon in the other room. She swore that she heard two voices, not just Enoon's but someone else in the room as well.

Disturbed by the two different voices, she decided to occupy her mind by focusing on the visuals. As though it came natural, Pan roamed around the living room, snooping through whatever she could find. Which, first, happened to be a closet. She cracked open the closet and found various coats, which were raggedy and covered in a red dust. One coat in particular stood out the most. It was translucent, as if it was made out of plastic. She reached out to touch the texture and as soon as her fingertip grazed the sleeve of the coat, it suddenly flickered like an old bulb; however, the light was similar to that light she saw back on the river, as well as the light behind the windows of the other houses.

The sudden burst of light caused Pan to remove her hand from the coat, thus causing the coat to dim and return back to its normal translucency.

She heard the floor *creaking* behind the door. She closed the closet door and saw Cupid standing right next to her. She flinched from Cupid's presence.

"Didn't meant to scare you," he said.

"No," Pan said, searching for reasons as to why she was snooping around his closet. "I thought I heard someone in the closet."

"You heard someone in the closet?"

"Okay," Pan said, surrendering. "You caught me. I was just being nosy."

"I know you were. I get it. You're still freaked out a little."

"It's that obvious, huh?"

Cupid pointed to a chair.

Pan followed Cupid back into the living room. She didn't take a seat, though. Instead, she walked to the window where she saw more flickering light, this time coming from a fire. She peeked outside where Kazlauskas Inc. was sitting alone in front of a fire pit. The glow of the flame flickered over her face. Feeling Pan's dim presence, she looked up and locked eyes with Pan.

"Don't worry about her," Cupid said from behind. "She's much tougher than she looks."

Pan asked Cupid if his son Enoon had any brothers or sisters.

He didn't.

Which prompted Pan to follow up by asking Cupid if he had any friends over. Again, he didn't.

It was just him and Cupid and, of course, Kazlauskas Inc.

Cupid walked up to Pan and stood next to her and together, they watched the fire burning in the backyard.

"The fire repels them, you know, the mosquitoes, that is."

"Your world doesn't seem so different than mine."

"It had its similarities," he said. "Yes. Of course."

She nodded at Kazlauskas Inc. "What's her story?"

"Kaz?"

Pan nodded.

"Right," he said. "You noticed, huh?" Referring to Kazlauskas Inc.'s interest in Pan. "Let's just say she's not used to strays. She might not look like it, but like the others, she's extremely curious about your world."

"What happened to her?"

"I found her out there, in the woods, all alone, no home. She had no family, no friends, no one. So, I took her in. Gave her a home. She helps out around the house."

"How is she able to change her body like that?" Pan asked.

"That's a good question," he said. "You should ask her, but I wouldn't guarantee you that she'd give you an answer that will make any sense."

Struck by a sudden state of confusion, Pan looked around the room.

Cleo was nowhere around.

Cupid said that she stepped outside for a minute to clear her head. Pan didn't remember her sister saying anything about stepping outside and even if Cleo did, Pan would certainly join her.

No way I'd leave her alone, she thought, *with those monsters out there.*

"Where's your bathroom?" asked Pan.

From the corner of her eye, she caught Cupid reaching for a small object, thin and pencil-like, from a drawer. The move was rather quick and if she blinked, she would've missed it.

Once she turned her eyes toward Cupid, he straightened up and placed a hand behind his back as if he was hiding something from Pan.

Looking at Pan suspiciously, Cupid told Pan it was just down the hallway, to the left. He specifically told Pan, in fact, he couldn't emphasize enough that the restroom was on the "left."

With her legs stiff and heavy as though she had been sitting for hours without stretching, Pan exited the living room. Not only was it nerve-racking to be inside a stranger's house, but it was also enthralling to be caught in the middle of a situation, possibly dangerous, where she had no idea what was going to happen next. Her mother, Vivian, was a strict parent of conservative background, an untrusting, cynical woman who had often warned her daughters of situations such as these.

Feeling Cupid's lingering presence behind her, Pan waited till she was halfway down the hallway before she shot a quick, innocent glance over her shoulder. Cupid was gone from her line of sight.

To the left was the restroom, a poorly managed one at best and looked as if it hadn't been cleaned since the fallout that Cupid often spoke of. To her right was a normal-looking boy's bedroom with juvenile furniture and posters of swimsuit models hanging on the wall. At the very last second, Pan hooked a right into the bedroom and saw what she assumed was Cupid's son, Enoon, lying on a bed in the corner of the room. His head was rolling back and forth along the pillow, as if he was having a nightmare. His face appeared emaciated, cheeks sunken in, eye sockets dark and hollow, and his forehead dripping wet with sweat.

Pan could hear two voices, one of them coming from Enoon, who was groaning in agony, then another coming from underneath a tattered comforter, a weaselly, voice snickering and whispering in tongues.

More curious to uncover what was wrong with Enoon, Pan inched farther into the bedroom. She noticed the same cream that Cupid had bought at Gulps on the side of Enoon's neck and upper chest.

Suddenly, Enoon cracked open his eyes and turned to Pan.

His breath became rapid, his chest pumping up and down, up and down like a piston.

"Who'ah you?" Enoon asked feverishly, his beady eyes riddled with panic. "Wh'ah you want from me?"

"My name is Pan," she said softly. "I'm not going to hurt you."

"Why you here?" Enoon said, his voice louder.

Pan couldn't take her eyes off Enoon's left side, which was slightly moving. She thought maybe it was his elbow underneath the comforter; as she looked even closer, she realized it was a protrusion.

"Are you okay?"

Enoon, who must've been around the age of eight years old, had both of his frail hands tightly gripped on the ends of the comforter as if he was holding onto the handlebars of a rollercoaster.

As she stepped closer, she heard a whispering voice coming from underneath the comforter. She studied Enoon's lips, which weren't moving.

Once she realized that Enoon wasn't alone, she saw a third hand, a redder and rawer hand emerge from underneath the comforter, crawl up the side of Enoon's neck, then grab hold of the nape of his neck as though it was trying to pull Enoon underneath the comforter.

597

A hand grabbed Pan by the shoulder, startling Pan.

"*What you doing in here?*" a voice said from behind.

Pan rotated around and saw Cupid standing with both of his hands planted on his hips. The center of his brow was curled inward, showcasing two deep, narrow trenches across the lower half of his forehead.

"I was just. . . "

Pan pointed at Enoon, then his hands, two hands, *not* three.

"You were just leaving," Cupid finished.

"I must've gotten turned around."

"What part of bathroom on the left do you not understand?" Cupid asked, as he escorted Pan from the bedroom. He showed her the bathroom across the hallway.

Pan stepped into the bathroom and just as she was about to close the door behind her, she noticed Cupid wasn't leaving until she closed the door.

"You gonna watch me pee too?" asked Pan.

Disgusted by Pan's tone, Cupid shook his head.

"Just make sure you flush twice," he said. "I've been having trouble with the piping as of lately."

"Got it," Pan said shortly and closed the door behind her.

She was immediately hit by a god-awful smell. It wasn't like any bathroom she had ever smelled before. Most shit smelled about the same. This, however, it had the smell of death, like the human body had been turned inside out. Along a filthy vanity, she found a couple of imported toiletries, including a bottle of hand lotion, which was spotted with dark stains and streaks that closely resembled dark mud—Pan hoped it was only mud—and a bar of soap covered in pubic hairs.

Too repulsed, Pan didn't bother using the toilet or any of the imported toiletries. She waited a couple of seconds before she flushed the brown-colored water.

Then, as she stepped out of the bathroom, she heard a noise coming from the outside. She walked to the door at the end of the hallway and tried not to make a sound as she carefully opened the door.

The noise was coming from the back of the garage.

She crept inside the garage and closed the door behind her the same way she had opened it.

Yet again, she heard the same noise and pinpointed it to a shelf of rusty tools and hardware.

As she inched closer to the shelf along the wall, she couldn't help but notice an old blanket covered in dark spots on the ground.

Distracted by the blanket, she changed course and checked it out. She peeled back the blanket, which was folded in half. Inside the blanket she witnessed what looked like a severed arm in a pool of brownish colored blood. The smell nearly knocked her over. She covered her nose and examined the insect-like arm, which, after a thorough study, she concluded to be the same arm that belonged to one of those gigantic mosquitoes.

Startled by more of that same racket coming from the shelf, Pan drew her attention away from the bloody blanket.

To her left, Cupid was standing by the doorway.

"Pan," he said, surprisingly more cautious than angry, "come back inside. It's not safe."

"Is there something you're not telling me?"

"I don't know what you're talking about."

"What's one of these creatures doing in your garage?"

Cupid immediately noticed the blanket, which was open.

"*Pan*," he whispered with urgency, "*come back inside. Now!*"

"What are you hiding, Cupid?" asked Pan.

"I'll explain later," he said and followed by waving Pan inside the house, "for now, just please come back inside."

Pan was startled by yet another racket, this time louder and more violent and coming from a black coffin-like crate perched against the other side of the wall.

Overwhelmed with curiosity, Pan decided to check out the noise while, at the same time, Cupid urged her to come back inside the house.

Expecting a Culexx to suddenly pop out and give her one helluva jump-scare, Pan opened the crate without thinking twice. She braced herself. No Culexx. No scare. The crate was empty.

More relieved, she closed the crate, only to find a dark figure looming before her.

The mosquito-looking creature, which was missing one of its arms, pounced on Pan! She defensively threw up her arms to shield her face from its assault. Its power was doubled her own. The impact had forced her backward, causing her to land on her back. Pan grabbed whatever she could find within her reach, which was a jerrybuilt shovel and swung at the creature. The creature wasn't at all fazed by each baseball-like crack at its body. One of its wings, however, appeared crippled and badly injured while the other one, which was torn down the middle, fluttered around and prevented it from flying.

Once more, the creature attacked Pan and chased her around the garage until it leaped from behind a shelf and planted the end of its proboscis directly into her neck like a vampire sucking her dry. It managed to drain at least an ounce or two of her blood before she saw yet another dark figure in the corner of her eye.

An incredible large figure!

Before Pan could turn to see who—or what exactly—it was, the creature was suddenly flung in the air. The spear penetrated the center of its thorax, the velocity of the spear sending the creature against the farthest wall where it was pinned up like a crucified exhibit.

While grabbing hold of the area of her neck that was turning red and starting to swell, Pan noticed Kazlauskas Inc., standing in front of Cupid on the other side of the garage. Her right arm was incredibly veiny and muscular and was the size of a brutish bodybuilder. The arm was so thick and massive that it was nearly the size of her entire body. Eventually, the arm shrunk and returned to normal size.

Cupid brushed past Kazlauskas Inc. and rushed toward Pan to check on her condition.

"I feel dizzy," she said, staggering.

Cupid caught Pan before she collapsed and eased her limp body to the ground where she sat lazily with one hand holding her upper body upright while the other one constantly rubbing the edge of her brow as if she was trying to massage away a dizzy spell. He kneeled next to her and waited to catch her if—or when—she should pass out.

She said unsteadily, "What the hell just happened?"

"You were bit," Cupid said.

"*What.* . . what was that thing?"

Cupid said hesitantly, "It was same one that bit Enoon. I thought I killed it. I guess I was wrong."

Initially, the next follow up question for Pan would've been "Why didn't you bury it or dispose of it? *Why save it*?!?"

Instead, she turned more outwardly and focused on the throb along her neck.

"What's happening to me?" she asked Cupid.

Her breath was labored; everything about her was frail and panicky.

"Just relax." He turned his shoulder and told Kazlauskas Inc., who was still standing in a state of disbelief, to grab a blanket and that special "cream" that he used to treat Enoon.

Cupid was well aware of Pan's breathing. Once he had seen it before with a stray whom he found wandering through Gabriel: a gunshot victim named Treble who couldn't quite understand his situation and had trouble understanding that he was no longer in a world where such faculties existed. Over a full moon Cupid watched that gunshot wound on Treble's head grow wider and wider throughout his brief time with Treble, first starting out as a tiny red speck in the middle of his forehead, then as night fell, that speck growing redder and bloodier until it was a gaping gunshot wound.

"I'm having trouble. . . catching my breath," she said shortly.

"This is going to be difficult to understand, Pan," Cupid said somberly, as he let out a deep sigh, "but it's all in *your* head. The breathing part, that is. There's no easy way of putting this. Your being, your soul," he struggled to even utter the words but when he did so it brought him great relief, "your *new-me*, as we call it, it's reacting to the parasite."

Kazlauskas Inc. returned with a blanket. She handed it to Cupid, who, in return, unfolded it and carefully placed it over Pan's shoulders.

"My what?"

"New-me," he said. "Soul. The you in what makes you. . . *you.*"

I knew it, she thought. *I am dead.*

"Not dead," Cupid said with clarity as if, oddly enough, he could read Pan's thought. "You're just stuck."

"I told you you shouldn't have used Lazarus on her," Kazlauskas Inc. griped over Cupid's shoulder. "Didn't I?"

"Zip it, Kazy!"

Pan somewhat gained more control over her breathing—or lack of breathing. *The device in the back of Cupid's truck*, she thought, *the Lazarus Light*. She retraced her footsteps back to the moments she wound up on the riverbank. Cupid was shining a pale bluish light on her. But what exactly were his intentions?

"What is she talking about?" she asked Cupid.

Her feverish body was shaky. Her face more flush, the bite more swollen.

"To put it as plainly as I can," Cupid said, struggling to find the right words, "the Light allows you to. . . "

"To what?"

"It allows you to interact with us. We feel more comfortable if you're like us opposed to, you know, walking through walls, closed doors, or worse," he tapped on his head, "getting inside our minds."

Bemused by his comment, Pan insisted that he further explain himself. She asked him for the "no bullshit" version.

"Once," Cupid said methodically, "we decided not to use Lazarus on this one stray who wandered into Gabriel. Miles was his name. *Miles Straum.* I'll never forget that name. So sneaky," he said in reflection. "Anyway, apparently, he had himself a crosser—"

"—Crosser," Pan said feverishly. "What's that?"

"Think of it as a companion, a sort of 'tour guide,' if you will. The crosser can be your best friend or worst enemy. Most of the strays who come here without crossers end up staying here. Just the way it is. Miles ventured away from his crosser and *apparently*, thought it'd be fun to get inside the locals' heads and start screwing with their minds. He had an agenda all right."

"Which was?"

"The same agenda that all frustrated young men have on their minds, which is to undermine everything they don't agree with. Fortunately for him, his crosser found him, brought him back to his world. If there's anything we took away from the incident, it's awareness. Being more aware of who comes into Gabriel. So," he let out a sigh, "does that answer your question?"

"No," Pan said, lacking the energy to retort. "Not really." She remoistened her lips and cleared her throat. She started to see two Cupids before her. Then, three. She drunkenly dropped to her elbows before she rested on the ground.

Cupid bunched up the blanket underneath her, preventing her head from lying on the ground.

Pan asked more dizzily, "How can we get back to our world?"

Cupid paused, thinking more about Pan's usage in wording, in particular, the word *we*. After Enoon was bit, Cupid heard his son using that one particular word every now and then.

"I know this one crosser," Cupid said and for the time being, pushed aside the one question, which was on his mind. "Goes by the name Creach. I can't promise you that she'll get you where you need to be, but she'll try."

"Creach?" Pan said, as she started to fade. Her eyes bobbed around like pinballs against the sockets of her skull. "What kind of name is Creach. . . "

Pan's eyes suddenly rolled in the back of her head. She fainted. Cupid was there to grab her head before it hit the ground. In doing so, an object fell from his back pocket and hit the ground with a *clinking* sound. A burst of life shot through Pan's body, causing her to power through the gray haze. She concentrated on that clinking sound, then pinpointing it. Her eyes drunkenly followed Cupid picking up the object from the ground. It wasn't a pencil. It was a syringe filled with that same brownish liquid she found pooled over the blanket.

Once more, her eyes rolled in the back of her head.

Everything went dark, as if she had internally flipped off a light switch.

Cupid nodded at Kazlauskas Inc. and told her to grab Pan's legs.

Together, they carried Pan back inside the house.

PRESENT

PAN woke up to the squeak of Cary-Anne opening the front door.

She checked the time on the clock on the nightstand and saw that it was seven o'clock on the dot. Cary-Anne was literally like clockwork.

After shaking away the thought of what happened to her fours years ago, Pan attempted to roll out of bed. Cary-Anne dropped her belongings and rushed to her aide. Pan brushed her away.

"I need to do this on my own for once," Pan said, as she struggled to sit upright.

She tried several times to roll out of bed. Eventually, after much frustration, Pan managed to sit upright on her own. She took a moment to catch her breath.

"How'd you sleep last night?" asked Cary-Anne.

Pan shrugged.

"Not good," she said and grimaced and grabbed her left side.

"Is it still bothering you?"

Once more, Pan shrugged.

Then, over the silence, nodded.

"I can call the doctor if you want," Cary-Anne said, which was met with Pan shaking her head.

"If it's not better by tomorrow," Pan said, "then I'll go."

"You sure? You said that last time, Pandora."

"Yeah," Pan said straightforwardly. "Promise."

🕐

ABOUT an hour before lunch, which normally started around eleven o'clock since most of the restaurants closest to her house didn't serve lunch until ten-thirty, Pan was binge watching the entire third season of her favorite dramedy *4 Reelz* on the streaming service, Shh! The show was centered around four family members of the Reale Family: *the father*, Emilio Reale, a wealthy movie producer who spent most of his time away from the camera in a million-dollar beach house in Malibu with the girlfriend-of-the-week and throwing what were known as the most epic parties that'd make a carnival look like an appetizer, if compared a three-course meal; *the mother*, Esther Reale, an inmate of San Anita who already put in six years of a twenty-five year stretch for third-degree murder; *the* hundred and one year old *grandmother*, Mamma Chiara, a well-admired chef who immigrated from Italy to New York City when she was seven years old and made her living from a popular cooking show called *Cooking With Chiara;* the stepsister, Kennedy, a real estate agent who was the daughter of Emilio's second wife; and finally, *the star of the show*, Emilio's rebellious *daughter*, Gigi Reale, a struggling film projectionist who, unlike Kennedy and her humbled background, grew up privileged, yet, after three years in high school, rejected her comfortable life in order to make it on her own as a screenwriter. After Kennedy moved back home from No-where, Texas, to Los Angeles, Gigi moved in with her stepsister in a cramped apartment in Beverly Hills. Most of the show revolved around Gigi's life and her frustrations with the movie industry, as well as her job at a less-than-perfect movie theatre struggling to survive during a constantly evolving society where widespread streaming services were slowly, in Gigi's own words, "mur-dering" movie theatres. The two sisters argued a lot about various issues, ei-ther old ones or recent, trendier ones on the news; however, at the end of each show, somehow the two managed to find common ground, despite their stark differences in opinion. After many headlines surfaced from one of the cast members making some off-the-cuff comments about upcoming governor, Avanti Washington, the show was cancelled halfway through filming the fourth season due to what studio execs called "creative differences."

Pan had seen episode three, which was called "Peanut Butter and Jelly." The New Pan, who had been taking a Q-capsule everyday for the past four years, wouldn't have thought anything of the scene when she came across it. If anything, the New Pan would've found it more comical than relatable.

In the episode "Peanut Butter and Jelly," as Gigi, who was scheduled to work on the opening day of the new blockbuster, *Cybersaurus,* which had been sold out ever since its first trailer debuted back in spring, and Kennedy, who was holding an important open house that she had been planning for the past week and a half, were about to head out to work, the two happened to rush out of the living room at the same exact time, thus causing them to get stuck be-tween the doorway. As hard as the two tried to force themselves free, their attempts were unsuccessful. Kennedy would try wiggling herself free—of course, being the drama queen she was, she'd make several insidious jabs at Gigi while doing so—and then Gigi, the quirky anti-social character whose morbid sense of humor drew stocked laughs from a so-called audience, would try kicking herself free—of course, it wouldn't be Gigi without her own share of more personal attacks at her stepsister. Eventually, they gave up and ac-cepted their fate. They were both stuck. Like that rare moment when a bas-ketball got stuck between the rim and backboard. As *4 Realz* had a tendency to do—which was an unearthing comedy from the most serious situations—the two sisters were left to duke it out until they reached the very cornerstone of their personal, yet, at times, trivial gripes.

Most of the episode took place with the two sisters stuck in the doorway, trying to work out their issues. The one issue weighing heavily on Gigi's mind was the fact that Kennedy wouldn't dare let Gigi ask out one of her guy friends, Clark. Kennedy was extremely protective of Clark and knowing Gigi's wild history with men, would find any opportunity to steer Clark away from Gigi by making up the worst traits, like for example, she never used nail clippers to trim her toe nails—which was a lie, Gigi used garden shears (audi-ence laughter)—yet, instead, Gigi chewed them off. Her attempts had an op-posite effect and Clark ended up liking Gigi even more based on how uncon-ventional Kennedy had made Gigi out to be.

Toward the end of the episode, Gigi and Kennedy worked through their trust issues. Kennedy gave Gigi her blessing to ask out Clark. Still stuck between that doorway, one of Kennedy's friends, Shay, who was stopping by the apartment to drop off a DVD, found the two sitting on the foyer floor, shoulder-to-shoulder, stuck between the doorway like a human wedge. As Shay reached out her hand to pull Kennedy, Gigi slipped out on her own. Realizing that Gigi could free herself at any time, Kennedy was absolutely furious, as in that "fire and fury" kind. The show always ended with a freeze frame. What better way to end the episode with a freeze frame of Kennedy snarling at Gigi as she leaped at her with both hands curled like hooks, ready to choke the life out of Gigi.

Audience laughter.

Roll credits.

Fade to black.

By the time Pan finished watching the episode, she found herself drifting off into a memory where Vivian was making a comment about the wide doorways in the house. She said it about a year or so ago while she was helping Pan clean out old clothes and accessories from Pan's bedroom. She was carrying an oversized box of childhood stuffed animals packed inside a cardboard box from the bedroom. She couldn't help but mention the doorways throughout the house and how they were built much wider than any traditional-sized doorways.

"Thank God that whoever built this house," she said with her breath labored, *"had an appreciation for wide doorways."*

As Cary-Anne stepped into the living room and asked Pan if she had any suggestions for lunch, Pan knew she was going to push her mom's "menu" on her whether she liked it or not. As soon as Pan asked for fried chicken, Cary-Anne, in her own subtle way, suggested grilled chicken. The two went back and forth, Pan suggesting one food while Cary-Anne returning with another.

Eventually, Pan broke down Cary-Anne with her unwillingness to eat any of the more healthier food that her mom had bought her yesterday and convinced her to pick her up some Eddie Macs.

Cary-Anne suggested a couple of places close by.

On the verge of temper-tantrum, Pan demanded Eddie Macs.

"I'll start eating better tomorrow," Pan said, pouting.

"No more after today," Cary-Anne said dourly. "Okay?"

"Yes," Pan said. "Okay."

WHILE Cary-Anne left to pick up fast food at Eddie Macs, which happened to be located on the other side of town, Pan took the opportunity to search the house. She looked under things, electronic devices, appliances, and whatnot. Even tore apart items, including ripping the feathers out of the couch cushions.

By the time Pan went through every nook and cranny of the house, she could hardly stand, even with the help of the walker. She knew that if she sat down she probably wouldn't be able to get back up again.

Completely wiped from the physical excursion, she sat herself down against the overturned couch and decided to rest for what she told herself would only be a moment.

As she leaned her head back against the corner of the couch, she noticed the ceiling fan above. She peered closer at the light fixture underneath the fan and couldn't help but notice a wire protruding next to the frosty glass covering.

After some struggling, she managed to stand to her feet. She grabbed a stepladder from the closet and positioned it underneath the fan. She removed the fixture and yanked on the wire, which revealed a camera inside the ceiling fan. The lens of the camera was mounted between a small, narrow opening in the fan. Pan remembered an electrician stopping by not too long ago to repair the ceiling fan. She specially remembered that whenever she flipped the ceiling fan on it'd trigger the breaker and cause the power to cut off inside the living room. Most importantly, she remembered how strange the electrician was. He was not only staring at her, which wasn't at all uncommon, but he was also watching her. He'd frequently mention his parents whenever he talked, as if, in a way, they had control over him and what he said.

Doctor Cherkis, Pan thought. She remembered the conversation she had with him after he prescribed her Quidaquin. It was Doctor Cherkis who referenced Pan to that non-profit organization, RESET, who, essentially, provided Pan with a new custom-built house. Ever since Pan moved into the house, everything went straight downhill for her.

As though she was right on cue, Cary-Anne arrived with Pan's food.

Which was cold.

Cary-Anne dropped the bag of Eddie Macs on the floor from the sight of the destruction inside the living room.

Her mouth was open, but she had no words.

Which, Pan knew, was all an act.

FOUR YEARS AGO

BEYOND the flames, the hazy reflection of Cary-Anne's gawking expression faded in the living room window and was replaced with a blurry face that appeared featureless, as though the face was moving back and forth at a breakneck speed while a photographer was snapping a photograph and the resulting image had what was known as a ghosting effect. The individual—Pan knew he or she was young based on lack of confidence, insecurity, and fidgetiness— was standing over her shivering body on a thick comforter next to the living room window and staring down at her with shaky black eyes. Pan refocused away from Kazlauskas Inc., who was sitting with other shadowy-faced Gabrielites by the fire and redirected her attention toward the stranger danger standing behind her.

In the hallway outside the living room, Pan heard Cupid talking to one of the locals, who had a voice as deep as a well. Among those words, she heard Cupid telling the local that *the reaction was quick*; then he heard *quicker than Enoon*.

"She's still a traveler, Que," the local said.

She heard other words—at least, she thought she heard—words like *narcissist* and *crossing over*.

The two voices turned softer.

Next, she heard footsteps.

Then, the *thap, thap, thap* of snapping fingers at the other end of the room!

"Shim," Cupid whispered. "Out! Now!"

Pan watched the young stranger's reflection dart away from the room, leaving only a fuzzy, fading silhouette in the mirror.

She tried to remember how she wound up here, in the living room, but it felt as if she was hungover and couldn't find a legit timeline, only bits and pieces, like an image of Cupid's son, Enoon, lying in bed.

As Cupid entered the living room and Shim exited left, Pan rolled over to her side until she was facing the hallway. She grimaced slightly from the soreness on her side. It felt as if the left side of her body had been hit by a truck and her entire side pulsed with a heavy pain. Cupid approached Pan.

"He wasn't bothering you, was he?" asked Cupid.

Pan acted as if she didn't know what Cupid was talking about.

"No," she said dumbly.

"Well, if he was, I apologize. Shim's never seen a stray before."

"Why do you keep calling me that?" asked Pan.

"What? *Stray*? Don't take offense. It's just a term we use around here. It's nothing personal."

Pan rolled back on her other side where there was less pain and looked outside. There had to be at least a dozen locals and each one of them was whispering and skittishly shooting worried glances toward the living room window.

"Forgive me for the audience," Cupid said from behind and closed the curtain on the window. "As you can tell, word travels fast around here whenever there's a stray in town. Don't you worry about 'em. They're just curious. That's all."

"Who are they?"

"Mostly locals," he said shortly. "Residents of Gabriel. A few from the town over, Castaneda, who are just passing through. "

He kneeled down to Pan's level and asked how she was doing.

"I'm burning up," she uttered, as she glanced at the Mason jar of cream in his right hand. "What happened to me?"

"You were bit by a Culexx."

"I was?"

"Yes."

Once more, Pan glanced at the Mason jar. She noticed the difference in the color, which was much lighter in tone than the other cream he bought at Gulps, as well as the texture of the cream, which was much smoother, less clumpy, like lotion.

"It's the fever," Cupid said.

"So, what the hell does that stuff really do?" she asked.

"It helps slow the spread of the virus," he said and held up the jar for Pan. "If I can slow the spread, then I can bring down the fever. May I?"

She lifted her hand and attempted to feel the red, swollen area along the left side of her neck, which was partially covered with a blanket, but Cupid redirected her hand and told her not to touch it.

"Is it a rash or something?" asked Pan.

Cupid opened the jar.

Immediately, Pan noticed the hint of sweetness while sniffing the cream.

"Not exactly," he said and placed the lid aside. "More like a growth."

"A growth? You mean like what? A tumor?"

Cupid was hesitant to answer.

"Sort of," he said unsurely.

This time, Pan tried to sit up and look at the "growth." Cupid grabbed Pan by her good shoulder and told her to relax. Pan was too weak and exhausted to fight Cupid, who followed by scooping out a dab of so-called "hepa-pod cream" with a tongue depressor and showcasing it to Pan.

"It's for your own good, Pan," he said with untrusting eyes.

Pan allowed him to spread the cream along the side of her neck. Not like he was giving her any choice. At first, the cream was surprisingly cool on her skin.

"It may burn just a bit."

Which it did.

Pan did her best to ignore the burn. Eventually, the burn subsided and the left side of her body felt somewhat numb.

As Pan lay down on her back, she started to relax. She didn't know whether or not it was the cream. But she did feel somewhat more relaxed than she did before Cupid applied that hepa-pod shit.

"Tell me, Cupid," Pan said thoughtfully, "you part of a cult?"

Cupid laughed.

"How you mean?"

"When I was in Enoon's room, I saw a symbol of a sun on his wall. I saw the same symbol a couple other times while we were riding through town."

"You mean The Trinity."

"What's their deal?"

"Many of those in Gabriel worship The Trinity as gods and consider them as the holders of The Light."

"And I take it you don't believe in this Trinity?"

"Once," Cupid said sorrowfully, "maybe. Eventually, though," he said more bluntly, "I came to my senses."

Cupid stood up, walked to a drawer along the wall, reached inside the bottom drawer, and pulled out a raggedy-looking book. He handed Pan a book that bore that same symbol of a sun with three lines projecting outward. Cupid called the book the *First Light*. Pan cracked open the dusty *First Light* book and after skimming the first couples of pages, realized that it wasn't at all different than a book she had once read when she was a young girl. That book had many versions, but she simply called it *The Bible*. And those lines, which she thought were sunrays, were children, three underlings called "The Trinity."

The so-called Genesis of the story started out similar to the Bible's Genesis, albeit with a slight twist. She flipped halfway through the book and being the fast reader she was, skimmed over the filler and managed to catch only the juicy parts: "*The white coats scoured the site of explosion that had paralyzed Maven,*" and "*collected a shard left behind from The Darkness,*" only to later use it in a secret government project called "*Project Third Eye.*" The "*white coats found ways to release that ancient Darkness,*" first "*experimenting it on rats, curing*" rats from all "*ailments.*" One day, a "*white coat became obsessed with the black shard*" and "*used it on his ailing wife*" without anybody knowing. *"The wife survived."* After recovering from ovarian cancer, *"she (the wife) gave birth to triplets called 'underlings,'"* which would later be known as *'The Trinity.'"*

"Interesting read," Pan said and handed the book back to Cupid.

"Keep it," he said. "Maybe it'll come to use one day."

"You sure?"

"Positive—yes."

"Thanks," she said softly, as she ran her finger along the rough texture of the book.

Over the quietness, her eyes lit up with surprise and the thought alone of her sister nearly stole her breath away.

"Cleo?" she uttered. "Where's Cleo?"

She turned toward Cupid, causing the cream to rub off on the blanket.

"Try to keep still," he said, using his hands like a guardrail to keep Pan from sitting up. "You have to let the cream dry."

"Where's my sister, Cleo?"

"I'm sorry," Cupid said. "Who?"

"Cleo," she said louder. "My sister!"

"I don't know what you're talking about, Pan—"

"—What don't you mean? Where is Cleo?"

Cupid scooped more cream onto the tongue depressor, which, after a second and more thorough study, Pan realized was the severed scaly toe of what appeared to be a reptilian creature—possibly an alligator—attached to the end of a wooden stick like a popsicle. As Cupid was about to apply more cream to the areas that Pan had rubbed off, his face slackened. For a moment, he actually flinched from the sight of Pan's shoulder.

Pan immediately recognized the shock rippling through Cupid's face.

"What?" she said while filling up with panic. "What is it?"

Cupid was hesitant to respond.

"Cupid?"

In return, Cupid shook his head with mild disgust and discreetly leaned away from Pan.

"It's nothing," he said. "Just let the hepa-pod cream do its magic."

"No," Pan protested. "I want to see it."

Cupid cleared his throat.

"I'm afraid that's a bad idea. It's in your best interest not to—"

"—I want to see!"

Her voice overpowered Cupid and left him with no other option but to show Pan the site of the bite.

Cupid rushed to the bathroom where he grabbed a grimy, cracked handheld mirror and brought it into the living room. He was cautious to hand Pan the mirror and before he committed himself, he warned Pan about what she was about to see and that she must keep calm; otherwise, it would only make her condition much worse.

Pan didn't even give a second's thought to Cupid's advice as she snatched the mirror from his hand, arched her head away from the bite, and aimed the mirror at the area between her neck and shoulder. Pan gasped in horror from the reflection of an ear—or many ears, due to the cracks in the mirror.

"What the hell is that?" asked Pan, as she searched for the best angle by tilting and turning the mirror.

Cupid didn't respond.

While keeping her eyes on one particular piece in the mirror, which happened to be the largest section, a triangular piece that gave her the most detail, she lowered the mirror closer to her neck until she had a clear view of the ear. She picked at the ear with her other hand, even played with it a little by flicking the tip of the ear up and down, up and down.

Surprisingly calm by the discovery, Pan asked, "Is that what I think it is?"

"Please, Pan," Cupid said carefully. "Don't freak out."

"I'm not," Pan said, trailing off.

All of a sudden, the thought hit her—again!

"Just try to relax, Pan."

Pan puckered her face as if she was trying to hold back the emotion.

"Where's Cleo?"

"Like I said, Cleo is not here," Cupid said more patiently. "This may be difficult to understand, but you are now a host and the parasite inside you is trying to manipulate your thoughts, showing you things that aren't there—"

"—But Cleo was with me."

"Maybe she was," Cupid said and touched the side of his temple, "but in your mind. It was just *you*. Your new-me. No one else."

"New-what?" Pan uttered. "I don't understand."

Cupid consoled Pan and suggested that she step outside and meet the locals—he was tempted to tell her, "grab some fresh air to clear your head," but he caught himself.

As Pan delved deeper into herself, her legs grew incredibly numb as if, for a moment, they no longer belonged to her.

🕐

As Pan told her version of the story, she could *feel* Cleo rolling her eyes as if Cleo was ultimately showcasing disapproval to the rest of the locals who were gathered around the fire.

Pan dismissed Cleo's gesture and searched for what she was going to say.

"A few days before you went missing," she said finally and recalled the past events, "I was sitting on the edge of the pool with my feet dangling in the water when my phone rang. I looked down at the phone, and I saw your number on the screen. I contemplated whether or not I should answer. I almost didn't. I knew you weren't the type of person to call me because you wanted to talk. You hardly ever called me—"

"—**Not true.**"

"And whenever you did," Pan said over Cleo, "you usually called to ask if I wanted to go on a trip with you because the truth is that you had nobody else to go with you."

Not only that, you think you're better than me; you use me, deep down inside though, you don't care about me, only calls whenever you have no one else to talk to. The truth is I always came second to you.

So not true.

I killed you hundreds of times in my mind. Electrocuted in a bathtub—you always had a way of singing while bathing. You said the acoustics of a bathroom made you sound like Mariah Carey.

They did.

The list goes on and on: burned by the blow dryer; strangled by an electrical cord; pushed off a water slide; choked to death by gramma's famous falafel; run over by an eighteen wheeler while riding *my* Big Wheel that you always hogged; gauged by a Barbie Doll; bludgeoned in the back of the head with a croquet ball; trampled by Staley High Bulldogs during a Friday night football game.

Countless times, I sent you to the grave. Yet, each time the phone rang and I saw your number, it was like you kept rising from the dead.

Again, Pan could *feel* her eyes rolling.

"The more the phone kept ringing, the more I kept wondering where Danielle went this time. What excursion prompted you to plan your next getaway: Back to Belize? The Ozarks? Sharkman's Cove? Orange Hill? I was even tempted to go on Danielle's phony InstiGarbage page and scroll through her most recent posts of her latest 'vacay.' It was an hour before lunch and there was nobody hanging out at the pool, except for Nurse Ratched who was sunbathing on the other side of the pool and shooting daggers at me while deliberately mouthing every insult in the book under her breath. Vegas from Apartment 213 hadn't showed up yet for his weekly dip and I was still searching for the right starter that would open up our overdue conversation. So, I picked up the phone. Sure enough, I was right."

I wondered why, of all people, you would want to invite me. *What was your real agenda?* You felt as if I always ruined all the fun for you, that I never had a good time, was a party pooper, always complaining, always finding some excuse to be miserable: "that" person. I heard once from Mom about Kirk and his behavior toward her, how he always complained. Yet, behind Mom's back, he'd go off with his drinking buddies and have the time of his life. *Yet*, he'd never allow her to have any fun. So, *immediately*, I was skeptical.

"'The last one for a while,' you said. This time, you were asking to go white water rafting in Colorado. You said how much fun it'd be even though you knew that I wasn't much of a good swimmer and how I *hated* getting into any body of water that wasn't super chlorinated. The last time we talked, I told you about a story involving someone I knew from my junior year and how water went up her nose when she was rafting and a couple of days later, she was hospitalized due to a brain-eating bacteria. You know how much that story freaked me out. Yet, you asked me anyway. Either you did it out of spite or you forgot, like you always do, like everything I say goes through one ear and out the other. You never listen."

"I do to."

"You tried to convince me that it'd be for my own good," Pan said over Cleo as if she wasn't allowing Cleo to respond and whenever Cleo did manage to retort, it was no more than three words. "The thing is you hated water, too. Worst than me."

"**You lie—**"

"—Yet, after I declined your adventurous getaway, you still ended up going. You were going to go regardless of what decision I made; in fact, you didn't even want me to go with you. You knew what my answer was going to be. Yet, you went ahead and asked me anyway as if you were looking for someone to fight with that day because you were sick and tired of fighting with yourself. I won't forget what you said to me right before you hung up on me." Pan paused, thought carefully about that time leaning over the pool and listening to her sister throw all kinds of expletives at her, most of them beginning or ending with the word *bitch*. Then, finally, once Pan was left bleeding out from insults, Cleo went for the final kill. Those four words resonated inside Pan as she stared at the wavy reflection of herself in the water. *"You're dead to me."*

You're one to talk. "**Bull! What a bunch of bull! I never said that—**"

"—But you did. And that was the last time I talked to you. Face it, sis. We never got along. You were bubbly, outspoken, the sociable one who craved attention and would dominate a conversation by only talking about herself. I was the introverted one who'd rather spend an evening curled up with a book opposed to hanging out at parties. But *you*, you just couldn't accept that. Could you? I was never good enough for you. You wanted me to be more like you. But the fact: I wasn't you. And I was just fine with that."

Cleo made an airy noise with her mouth, as if she was dry-spitting.

"**Are you still talking?**"

You're just like her, Pan wondered, especially the part where she completely blotted out everything post-first sentence.

In those final moments, Pan ran through the timeline of the story as to "how" she wound up in Gabriel. Cupid had discovered her alone on the riverbank. Cleo was not there; in fact, she never was. Riding through the countryside, stopping at Gulps, or driving into Gabriel in the back of Cupid's truck: Cleo was a mirage of a thought, a figment, a conjuring inside her head. Whatever Cleo had said either at Gulps or in the back of the truck, Pan had either said or thought. Cleo's actions were instead Pan's actions.

Pan visualized herself entering Gulps with both Cupid and Kazlauskas Inc., then, after momentarily losing herself inside the grip of the black crystal, exiting with Cupid and Kazlauskas Inc.

"You're not my sister," Pan said darkly.

"**Whatever, Two Face,**" Cleo said, smirking.

As Pan fought through the heavy restraint of the parasitic passenger weighing on the left side of her body, she moved her eyes downward toward her feet. The imitation that was Cleopatra attempted to take back control over Pan by forcing her eyes upward at the fire. Pan overpowered Cleo. Her entire body was drenching wet, her hair stringy, her face dripping with murky river water.

To Pan's right, Cupid was telling her to come back inside the house. He advised her to get some rest.

Pan ignored Cupid and focused on her feet, which were submerging in thick mud. Pockets of water bubbled to the surface. Her feet continued to sink until the water reached her shins. She felt a sudden pressure pressed against her body as if even the air itself was pushing against her. Her breath was shorter;

the ends of her fingers became tinglier. The tingle rushed up her arms, shoulders, then down her chest.

As Pan sank deeper and deeper into the wet mud until she was neck deep, she felt a balled up fist beating against her chest like a hammer. Her body convulsed, then jolted upward. She was met by a burst of sunlight first, then the worried face of a man in his mid-sixties. He was wearing a yellow helmet, as well as a matching life vest. Behind him was a red kayak rested along the riverbank.

The kayaker sat Pan upright and rubbed the center of her back.

"That's it," he said reassuringly. "You're okay. Just breathe."

Pan did as the kayaker said and breathed in through the nose, out through the mouth. Her lips were blue and bloodless. Blood streaming down the sides of her face.

Once Pan caught her breath, she gathered the rest of her surroundings. From the sound of the rushing water next to her, to the birds chirping in the trees, to the blue skies above her, it looked and *sounded* like home again.

The kayaker shook Pan on the shoulder.

"For a sec," he said, smiling, "I thought I lost you."

Pan combed back the stringy, bloody, soaking wet hair from her face.

"Where am I?"

Then, said, "Sharptooth River."

"What world?"

The kayaker puckered his face in a "huh" expression.

"Earth?"

PRESENT

WHILE Cary-Anne was going number two—or so Pan thought, based on a) Cary-Anne's more than usual coffee consumption due to oversleeping, which led to b) Cary-Anne's breakfast, which consisted of fast-food, more than likely Dempsey's, Burger Inn, or Sandwich Shack, which brought on c) Cary-Anne rubbing her belly throughout most of the morning, which, finally, inspired d) Cary-Anne "quickly" excusing herself to use the bathroom—Pan took advantage of what little time she had left and rummaged through Cary-Anne's purse.

As soon as Cary-Anne flushed the toilet—Pan knew she had at least another flush left—Pan dug out a company card inside the inner pocket.

The card read "Neuvak Corporation."

As predicted, Cary-Anne flushed once more.

Pan put the card back in the purse and walked back to the futon where she sat down and watched the rest of episode nine of *4 Reelz*.

🕐

MOST of the day was a complete haze for Pan.

Apart from spending most of the day keeping a close eye on her aide, who, without Pan's consent, scheduled an appointment with Doctor Cherkis tomorrow after she witnessed Pan making a grimace, she put together the missing pieces of what happened four years ago. She couldn't believe it had been that long. *Four* flipping *years*. Where did the time fly? Pan tried her best to hide the pain in front of Cary-Anne. She thought it was best not to argue with Cary-Anne. She thought it'd only make it harder to do what she needed to do.

Instead, Pan complied and went along with Cary-Anne.

Once night fell and Cary-Anne ended her shift, Pan hobbled past the "Doctor Apt." reminder on the fridge. She fixed herself what she thought was going to be her last supper: a plate of leftover fried chicken, which she heated up in a microwave, steaming hot collared greens and baked sweet potatoes with a side of hot glazed donuts that she had stashed away late last night. She even planned to peel and eat the skin off the chicken. There was nothing tastier than eating the skin of fried chicken. The food did not require a knife, but Pan grabbed the sharpest one she could find in the holder. She placed the food on a tray and took her food back to the living room, ate, and savored each bite.

Once she was finished with her dinner, she sat in silence. Not once did she ever turn on the TV or even contemplate watching TV. She turned to that knife, which was lying on the table. She picked up the knife and ran her fingertip along the edge of the blade to feel its sharpness. She pulled up her T-shirt over both her saggy breasts.

Pan could still feel it moving around inside her as if it was slowly growing on its time, not Pan's, stealing every precious moment of her day, manipulating her, and at times, resisting each move Pan made by sending waves of stabbing pains throughout the left side of her abdomen. It was either slithering around underneath her folds or beating its pointy fingers along her ribcage like a xylophone or tugging at her nerves, bunching them up like spaghetti, or gnawing at her bones or pushing and reshuffling her vital organs around as though it was playing a wicked game with Pan.

Once and for all, Pan turned the tip of the blade to herself and aimed directly at the protrusion along her loin.

As she was about to thrust the blade into her flesh, Pan pulled up the image of Cleo's face in her mind as if she could now easily access it at any time.

Then, Pan cut away.

🕐

IN the darkness, Pan heard birds *chirping* and *tweeting*.

The chirps and tweets synchronized to the repetitive sounds of beeping.

Pan cracked open her eyes and followed the sounds to a heart monitor next to her bed.

The number on the machine skipped a couple of points, shooting up from 78 to 85. The beeping sound increased slightly.

"Where am I?" she mumbled.

Her mouth was parched, the words like sandpaper rubbing against her throat.

"What happened?" she asked the dark, blurry figure standing at the doorway.

The lanky dark figure stared at Pan and just as Pan's eyes started to focus, it stepped out of the room.

"Who are you?" Pan asked groggily.

The words became harder and harder to deliver. Each one was heavy, sluggish, and brought on a stabbing, choking-like pain.

Moments later, another figure stepped into the room.

Pan realized it was a hospital room; however, everything appeared somewhat larger in size. The heart monitor was the first indication, then the TV mounted in the corner of the room, then that uncomfortable bed, then the mesh of cords and tubes attached to her body, then, finally, the nurse.

"Welcome back to the land of the living," she said, holding Pan's hand.

"What. . ." The words were so dry that she couldn't even spit them out.

The nurse grabbed a Styrofoam cup with one of those twisty straws.

"Here," she said, as she held the cup to Pan's face, "a little sip of aqua."

Pan didn't question what was in the cup. The nurse helped nudge Pan's head forward, as she maneuvered the end of the straw into Pan's mouth. Pan took a sip of the "aqua." The sip, like the words, was heavy. She could feel the liquid sliding down her throat and entering her stomach. Nonetheless, the words came out more fluidly.

"What happened?" asked Pan, as she cleared her throat.

"Lucky for you," the nurse said, as she placed the cup on the tray and stood by Pan's bedside, "you have a guardian angel looking after you. A good Samaritan found you wandering around on the side of the road. You were pretty banged up. You had several lacerations on both your arms and lower abdomen. You had a laceration just above your right eye. It was deep enough to require some stitches. He thought maybe you were struck by a car, maybe a hit-and-run."

Pan raised her arm, which was attached to an IV, and ran her fingers over the area above her right eye. She felt a bandage first. Then, she ran her finger along the cheekbone of her skull, which was still tender.

"Give it time to heal," the nurse said.

As Pan drew her attention back to her arm, a rush of panic suddenly flooded her body. The size of her arm and hand was much different. Her breathing was different as well; and each time she spoke, she felt as if she was no longer carrying around a load. Her eyes moved down her body. The panic was tight now. All up inside her. In her chest. Her throat. Her head. To her left, all of those machines were getting louder, that *beeping* sound faster.

The nurse looked closer at the heart monitor.

"Pandora," she said, reading Pan's BPM, "I need you to relax." She leaned closer to Pan and asked motherly, "Can you tell me what's bothering you?"

Pan was touching and studying every inch of her body as if she was somehow trapped inside a suit of flesh that did not belong to her.

"What happened to me?" asked Pan, as her heart rate increased. "What world is it?"

"World?"

Pan continued to study her body, her arms. They no longer had flab hanging underneath her biceps. She pulled off the blanket and lifted up her gown. Her abs were flat. She no longer had burdensome folds of flesh.

"As I've said, Pandora, you were found injured on the side of the road," the nurse said patiently, "a man brought you here to Peach Street Memorial."

"Mirror," Pan said, holding out her hand, "do you have a mirror?"

"Please, Pandora," the nurse said and deliberately let out a sigh, "I need you to relax."

With her voice raised, Pan asked once more as if she wasn't going to ask it again, "Where's a mirror?"

The nurse reached into her pocket, pulled out a compact mirror, and handed it to Pan. Pan immediately opened the mirror and looked at her face in the reflection. She was her old self again, as in she looked the same way she did four years ago. Except for one minor discrepancy.

"My eye," Pan said. "Why is my left eye brown?"

Her once green eyes were always the two features of her body where she felt the most confidence. She was the most proud to have those three letters GRN on her driver's license. She received many compliments on her eyes. She believed that the only thing she and her mom had in common were their eyes. Cleo, on the other hand, had gotten her eyes from their biological father, Kirkland, whose eyes proudly matched the color of his skin.

"Right," the nurse said and hung her head for a moment. "I assure you Doctor Berzins will explain everything."

"I don't understand," Pan said, the mirror lowering from her face.

"Pan, can you remember anything?"

Pan combed her thoughts and searched for answers. She had nothing, only a flickering image of herself sitting in front of what looked like a campfire.

She made an attempt to answer the question, but her words turned to mush.

"Give it time," the nurse said. During the pause, she pointed at her nametag and read her name to Pan, "Name's Maya. Doctor Berzins will be in here shortly. For the time being, is there anything you need that I can get you?"

Pan drifted off for a moment.

"No," she said and started messing with the IV along the top of her hand.

Maya separated Pan's hand and told her to leave the IV alone.

"You were severely dehydrated," she said and held Pan's hand. "I know how irritating it can be, but it's for your own good, okay."

As Maya was about to walk away, she was sidetracked by a thought.

"Oh yeah," she said, rotating around. "Your mother was here earlier, but you were out of it. She told me to call her as soon as you woke up. Is there anything you want me to tell her?"

"No," Pan said again.

Maya walked back to the bed and showed Pan the nurse's button on a corded remote dangling over the handrail.

"If you need *anything*, just hit that button. Okay?"

"Yeah," Pan said, trailing off.

Maya smiled and left the room.

🕐

PAN heard a *knock* on the door but was too exhausted to open her eyes.

She drifted off for what felt like a few hours; however, by the time she finally woke up, Vivian was staring down at her.

Startled by her mom's presence, Pan wondered how long she had been standing by her bedside.

615

Wearing the look of a woman who appeared more frightened than comforted by her daughter, Vivian held Pan's hand and asked her how she was doing.

Pan broke down and told her that she didn't know where she could even begin to answer that question.

"Pan," Vivian said, as the disappointment appeared in her face, "I talked to a detective earlier today. He wants to talk to you whenever you're able. He said he has a few questions he'd like to ask you."

"Detective?" Pan furrowed her brow. *The blood*, she thought, as she noticed only a couple of cuts along her arms and legs. *Was it mine?* Or, someone else's? "Why does a detective want to talk to me?"

"There was some damage to a bus stop," she said to Pan. "They found some blood on the shattered glass. They're still trying to find footage. The reason why they're so interested in talking to you is because you were found not too far from the scene."

"I remember crashing through glass," Pan uttered, as she searched deeper into her thoughts. "Everything is foggy before and after that."

Pan suddenly heard yet another *knock* on the door.

Vivian awkwardly removed her hand from Pan's and clutched the hand railing alongside the bed.

The doctor first nodded at Vivian, as if they had already spoken to one another.

Pan pointed out the white coat that he was wearing. She couldn't stop staring at that white coat.

"Sorry. I didn't meant to disturb you, Pandora," he said, drawing his attention to Pan. "My name is Doctor Berzins. How are you feeling today—"

"—What happened to me?"

"As Maya had already explained to you, you were found on the side of the—"

Pan said more fiercely, "It still doesn't explain how I lost over six hundred pounds in one day."

Vivian rubbed Pan's forearm.

"Honey," she said, "six hundred pounds? What are you talking about?"

"Just the other day I weighed around seven hundred and fifty pounds. Maybe even more than that. Now, I'm back to the same size I was four years ago. Please explain to me how that is even possible? Not to mention, my eyes are a different color."

"Pandora," Doctor Berzins said mildly, "what I'm about to tell you may very well come as a shock to you, but you probably came as close to death as anybody would in your condition."

The word alone *condition* infuriated Pan.

"Condition? What's my condition?"

"What I do know for certain, Pandora, is that you ingested a cocktail of over-the-counter sleeping pills that could've easily killed you and if we hadn't found you when we did, then you wouldn't be here talking to us. That's the hard truth. To be blunt, the only explanation I can give you is that you had a mental breakdown."

For someone who was in a line of work that thrived off long, complex words attached to words like *syndrome* or *disease*, his vague usage of words, like mental breakdown, sounded as if the doctor didn't have a clue how to diagnose Pan or her condition.

"What about my weight?"

"What about it?" the doctor said in a snarky tone, as he overlapped his hands over one another. "When you arrived here, you were the same weight as you are now."

Pan had absolutely no words; in fact, even her thoughts were sparse. Just the thought alone of losing all of that weight in such a short period of time sent waves of heat flashing through her body.

"What about my eye?" asked Pan.

"It is extremely rare, but the iris is known to change color whenever the nerve pathway from the brain to the eye has become disrupted from blunt force trauma and in your case, a possible fall." Then, *how does that explain both eyes, smarty pants?* "Unfortunately," he said, carefully delivering his words, "the damage may be permanent."

"What does that mean?" Vivian asked over Pan. "Will her eye color eventually return to normal?"

"Most cases," he said grimly, "it's unlikely. I can refer you to an ophthalmologist. For the time being, he or she may recommend wearing contacts."

"I'm not wearing contacts," Pan said.

The doctor had no response for Pan. He gave her more of a "you're shit out of luck" type of shrug paired with a facial expression that Pan was almost tempted to open-hand slap.

🕐

AFTER a series of survey-style questions and satisfactory ratings and formalities, which were all a part of the tedious process of being discharged from Peach Street Memorial, Pan was super-relieved once the orderly stepped into the room with a wheelchair.

Pan said that she could walk, but Vivian insisted on having the orderly wheel her out.

Speaking through the corner of her mouth, she teased, "Who would pass up the offer to be carried out like the queen consort?"

He was *kind of cute*, Pan thought. She admitted to herself that the notion of being wheeled around, if only for a short while, intrigued her.

The orderly, whose name was Kyle, helped Pan into the wheelchair; and once she signed her signature on the discharge form, she was a free woman.

Kyle wheeled Pan from the hospital room.

On the way out, Doctor Cherkis was talking to a nurse at the other end of the hallway. Pan had seen the doctor's face before but couldn't quite pinpoint when or where, even though that *where* part was a no brainer.

The doctor keenly turned his eyes toward Pan, kept them there in a cold gaze, then walked the other way.

Pan jarred the many questions she had bouncing around her head and focused on her surroundings.

Vivian excused herself for a moment.

"Geez Mom," Pan whined, as she fiendishly bounced her leg against the foot rest, "you act like you enjoy being here."

As one of her many nervous ticks, like chewing her nails or cracking her jaw and knuckles, Cleo used to bounce her leg a lot. Pan didn't understand why, all of a sudden, she was bouncing her leg.

Vivian told the two that she'd meet them in the lobby.

"You can't stand it here, can you?" Kyle said, as he wheeled Pan to the elevators.

"You're very perceptive," Pan said moodily.

"I'm not a fan of this place either."

As Kyle wheeled Pan down the hallway, Pan couldn't help but notice all of the dark and empty hospitals rooms. They passed one room, which was occupied with a couple of janitors. One of them was pulling the blood-soaked sheets from a hospital bed while the other one was mopping up a puddle of blood.

"Frankly," Kyle said over Pan's trance, "it gives me the creeps."

Pan only caught that one word *creeps*.

"Then why you work here?" she asked, looking forward.

"Well, every now and then, you get to meet beautiful women like yourself."

"Wow," Pan said, unimpressed. "Is that a line?"

"Not a line," he said shortly with a smirk on his face. "Just an observation." Kyle received nothing from Pan, who couldn't even remember the last time a guy had given her a compliment on her appearance. Somewhere behind her blank expression, the corners of her lips were rising into her cheeks in what appeared to be a smile.

They arrived at the elevators.

Kyle was first to push the down arrow.

As they both waited for the elevators to arrive, Pan picked out her mom from behind a crowd of nurses. She was talking to two men, one being Doctor Berzins and the other one a tall man who was dressed in an all black suit. The top button of his shirt was unbuttoned. Pan thought he looked like a more refined version of a minister, one of those televangelist types who flew around in expensive jets paid for by his flock and profited from selling God. He was wearing Wayfarers, which Pan thought was unusual since they were indoors. He had a round gray spot about the size a quarter, which appeared to be a birthmark, in his finely trimmed beard.

The *ding* of the elevator pulled Pan's attention forward. Before her the elevators doors were opening.

Pan redirected her attention back the strange man talking to Vivian at the end of the hallway. Several nurses were obstructing her line of sight.

As Kyle wheeled Pan into the empty elevator, she noticed a sign on the wall, displaying the different floors.

The name of Floor 13, which was the floor she was currently on, was crossed out with a piece of tape.

The words *Under Construction* were written in a black Sharpie.

Kyle pressed the L button.

Which she assumed was Lobby.

She closely inspected the other numbers along the panel. There weren't any. None. Only two buttons, the L button and then a blank button that had a lock next to it. The only way it appeared to work was through a key.

As Kyle talked about a book with the name *March* in the title, Pan zoned out. She slightly rotated her head to the right. In the reflection of the metal wall, she spotted the ring of keys attached to a string hanging from a clip on Kyle's waistband. *Why would you need a key to access that floor?*

As soon as the question reached the tip of her tongue, she was startled by yet another *ding*.

The doors opened to a narrow hallway.

Pan didn't recognize the area until they rounded a hallway and arrived at the lobby.

"Just a short cut," Kyle said, as if he could predict what Pan was going to say before she even said it.

The sight of the lobby triggered a memory. She spent two weeks in the hospital, mostly coming and going after her grandmother went in for a simple procedure called an upper gastrointestinal endoscopy and wound up on life support due to a bacterial infection that nearly killed her. The more she thought about it, the more she started to question her own memory. Wondering whether or not it was a dream. Or, if it really did happen.

As Pan kept to herself in front of the receptionist desk, Vivian finally arrived.

"Who were you talking to back there?" asked Pan.

"I had a couple of questions for Doctor Berzins."

"No," Pan said. "Not him. The other guy. Who was he?"

Caught off guard by the question, Vivian said hesitantly, "What other guy?"

"The black one," Pan said bluntly, as if her mom only identified by color.

"Right," she said, as if, for a moment, she had what she'd call a human moment. "That's the hospital administrator. He's a nice man. He just wanted to ask me how your stay went and if there was anything he could do for us—"

"—And what'd you say?"

"What do you think I said, Pan?" Vivian asked more strictly. "I said everything went well."

"*Well*," Pan said, thinking, "why didn't he ask me? I mean, wouldn't it make more sense to ask me?"

Trying not to make an outburst in front of Kyle from Pan's persistent grilling, Vivian clenched her teeth. She said sharply, "It wasn't like I was planning to talk to him, Pandora. He was just trying to be nice. That's all."

"Okay," Pan said, trailing off.

Kyle wheeled out Pan from the front of the hospital and the two waited by the curb while Vivian fetched the car.

She should've felt a weight lifting from her shoulders as soon as that fumy air hit her face.

Surprisingly, the weight felt heavier.

🕐

AFTER a few minutes of riding in silence, Pan lazily rested her head on the passenger door and stared at herself through the side view mirror. She was more fascinated with the color of her eyes and how one of the irises was brown.

"What happened to my father?" asked Pan.

Surprised by the question, Vivian knew she was referring to Kirkland instead of Callum. Ever since Vivian and Callum were married, Pan never ever referred to Callum as "father" or "dad." He was just Callum, the man who was present.

"Your father, Kirkland," Vivian said, gaining more confidence, "he died last year. Liver cancer. I'm sure you were aware he was a drinker. I guess his drinking days caught up with him." The comment didn't draw any reaction from Pan. Which caused Vivian to look over at Pan several times to make sure she was all right. Pan continued to stare at the ghost in the mirror. "Pan," Vivian said more directly, "I was going to tell you—eventually. Before the car accident I knew you were trying to reach out to him. *But*," she said, sighing, "after your accident, you never spoke a word of his name. I hoped maybe you made your peace and moved on with your life." Once more, she took her eyes off the road and shot a longer glance at Pan. "So why are you asking me about your father, Pan?"

Pan sat up more straightly and shrugged.

"I dunno," she said. "I was just thinking about him."

"I'm sorry I didn't tell you about him sooner, Pan," Vivian said while glancing back and forth from the road to Pan.

"You hated him that much, didn't you?"

"No," Vivian said, as sorrow came over her. "I didn't hate him. I just. . . "

"What?"

"I gave up on him."

🕐

THE rest of the ride home was quiet.

As soon as Vivian pulled the car into the driveway in front of Pan's house, Pan perked up from the sight of the house.

"I live here?"

"Four years ago, a generous individual anonymously paid for the house, had it furnished, you didn't have to make a single house payment. The word *lucky* is an understatement. You were blessed."

"I don't feel blessed," Pan said depressingly. "Why in the world would some stranger buy a house for me?"

"There are decent people out there, Pan," Vivian said, as she studied the confusion on Pan's face. "People who want to help out others without the publicity. Personally," she said from the corner of her mouth, "those who help out others in front of the camera are doing it for *other* reasons."

"It just doesn't make any sense. That's all."

"It doesn't have to make any sense." Vivian placed her hand over Pan's and said more friendly than motherly, "Doctor Berzins told me it'll take some time for your memory to come back."

"Who are you again?"

Silence formed inside the car.

Vivian glared at Pan, who was holding back the laughter.

"That's not funny," she said seriously.

"It is, a little," Pan said, as Vivian cut the engine.

She walked around the car, opened the passenger door, and as she was about to assist Pan from the car, Pan waved her away and said, "Not like I'm crippled."

Vivian stood back, watched and waited for Pan to stand on her own, and then, once Pan was able to walk on her own, she led the way. She opened the door for Pan. Pan stepped inside the house and surveyed the living room. Like the exterior of the house, the interior was similarly, if not, more foreign to her.

WHILE Pan and Vivian were eating garden salads for lunch at the kitchen table—Pan mostly picking at hers—Vivian's purse chirped. She stopped eating, reached into her purse, and pulled out an iPad.

"That's must be Allen."

"Who? Your slimy lawyer friend who I talked to at the hospital?"

"Don't talk about Allen like that," Vivian said, her tone bitter. "Believe it or not, but it's my lawyer friend who's working his butt off trying to get your butt off the hook. If worse comes to worst: you may have to pay for the damages."

"That's the most butts I've ever heard you say in one sentence."

"I thought you couldn't remember anything."

Pan shrugged and pushed around the grape tomatoes inside the bowl of iceberg lettuce.

Vivian opened her iPad and clicked on the email Allen had sent her.

"It's the surveillance video from the corner of 3rd and Harkam," Vivian said, as she opened the link and watched the video clip.

Pan moved her eyes from the salad and carefully watched her mom watch the video.

"So?"

"You wanna watch it?" asked Vivian.

"Should I?"

Vivian sighed.

"Yes," she said, placing the iPad on the table. "You should."

Pan reached over and grabbed the iPad. She played the video clip, which was thirty-seven seconds.

In the video, she was stumbling over the sidewalk along a fairly quiet intersection.

"I don't remember any of this," she said while watching. "I look like a baby taking her first steps."

"Keep watching," Vivian said, as she, too, carefully watched Pan and her reactions to the video.

In the video, she staggered and tripped over her own feet and crashed directly into a glass pane of the bus stop.

Pan cringed from the sight of the fall.

"Luckily, there was nobody waiting for a bus," Vivian said, "otherwise, you could've been looking at a lawsuit."

Pan stopped the video and slid the iPad toward Vivian.

"Yeah," she mumbled and hung her head. A dark, devilish grin flashed along her face. She said sardonically, "**We sure are glad that didn't happen.**"

Unaware of the grin, Vivian immediately noticed the change in Pan's behavior and how she had gone from depressed to super-depressed.

"Are you okay?" asked Vivian.

Pan thought carefully about the question.

Then, responded: "Even when I try to remember what happened on the day, I only get these flashes, certain tastes and smells. And it all feels like the past four years of my life have been one on-going nightmare that I can't wake up from even if I try." With tears brimming in her eyes, she turned to Vivian and asked, "Why can't I remember what happened to me?"

Vivian reached across the table and grabbed Pan's hand.

"It'll come back to you," she said, tightening her grip. "Just give it time."

PAN walked Vivian to the front door and said her goodbyes.

Vivian said she'd stop by tomorrow and check on how Pan was doing.

After Pan watched Vivian drive away, she walked back into the house.

As she was making her way into the kitchen, she stepped on a sharp object in the carpet. A sudden pain shot up her big toe, causing her to recoil. Pan lifted up her foot and pulled out a tiny shard of glass, which was embedded in the carpet.

She held the squared piece of glass close to her face and closely inspected it. Then, she kneeled down to the carpet and found yet another piece of glass below the coffee table, which was made out of oak; however, she was more intrigued by the smell of the carpet. She leaned down for a closer whiff. The carpet had a fragranced smell, as though it had recently been cleaned.

As she sat upright, she also noticed the sales tag hanging from the bottom of the futon. She yanked off the tag, which appeared brand new. She ran both hands over the fabric covering the futon and strangely, it appeared new. She moved toward the fold of the futon. Normally, she should've found crumbs or coins, anything that had fallen in the gritty wrinkles of the fabric. She didn't find anything. She stood up and studied the other furniture in the living room.

For some reason, Pan thought the furniture looked larger in size, as if she was the only feature of the living room that didn't quite fit.

LATER that afternoon, when Pan was using the restroom, she came across yet another item that made her question what had really happened to her.

As she reached for a square of toilet paper, she noticed the capsule behind the toilet in the warped reflection of the toilet paper holder. She finished her business and did so in a rush, then flushed the toilet, then slipped her pants back on.

She squatted down in a tight space next to the toilet and used the end of the plunger like a hockey stick to slapshot out the capsule.

Once the capsule was within reach, she picked up the capsule, which had the letter "Q" on it.

Instead of flushing the capsule down the toilet, she decided to pocket it.

RIGHT before Pan was about to fix herself a healthy TV dinner that Vivian bought for her earlier that morning, she found herself wandering from the kitchen to the bedroom for no apparent reason. She stepped into the bedroom and found herself looking around. She completely forgot what she was doing in the bedroom. She pulled her attention to the bedroom doorway, in particular, the width, and found herself studying it.

She walked over to the doorway and closely examined it.

"I don't remember these doorways being so wide," she said to herself.

Over the sound of the running air condition, she heard Vivian's words inside her head: *I just want my daughter back.*

Pan froze.

Was it a dream?

Or was it the other?

She leaned toward "the other."

THE strange man in black, whom Pan had witnessed talking to her mom and Doctor Berzins at Peach Street Memorial, exited from a parallelogram-shaped building numbered "36" inside a heavily-guarded business park occupied by a crew of heavily armed security guards attired with orange and burgundy uniforms that had the letters "NC" written on a badge worn over the sleeve.

With a small blue ice cooler in his hand, he made his way through a parking lot until he finally reached a black Crown Vic.

Once he stepped inside the car, which was as hot as an oven from the Arizona heat, he placed the ice cooler in the passenger seat and cracked open the windows to air out the car. He removed the black shades from his cloudy grayish eyes and wiped the sweat from the top of his brow with a handkerchief.

He paused mid-wipe and felt a chilly presence in the backside of the car.

All of a sudden, a burst of Lazarus Light shined throughout the inside of the car.

Once the brilliant light dimmed to a soft, computer monitor-like glow, Cupid, who was wearing the Lazarus coat, revealed himself in the backseat.

"What's in the cooler?" a voice asked from behind.

"If it isn't my favorite crosser—"

"—Ex-crosser," he said and nodded his head at the strange bearded man sitting in the driver's seat. "Hello, *Narcissus*. So, what's in the cooler?"

The strange man, Narcissus, used one of his strongest senses to pinpoint Cupid's exact location.

His nostrils flared.

"None of your damn business," Narcissus said. "That's what."

"Very well," said Cupid, as he stared at the storm clouds in Narcissus's eyes. "So, how'd you know it was me?"

"I can smell you from a mile away, Lover boy."

"Amazing," he said cynically, "even a blind man can detect me. You know, I really thought I could maneuver my way around your world without getting spotted. Was I wrong? Lately, it's been slightly more challenging considering people now all have a camera in their possession and would jump at any opportunity to capture something, let's say, foreign to your world."

"Right," Narcissus said. "Big Brother. Who can blame them?"

"I see you're still doing all of Neuvak's dirty work. When you finally gonna realize those people don't care about you? Never have."

"Unlike you, Cupid," Narcissus said, "I don't let my personal feelings get in the way of an impersonal job."

"Yeah," Cupid said more arrogantly. "That's because you're not human."

"You don't know what's going on, do you?"

"Should I?"

"Someone," he corrected himself, "*something* is picking off members of the Board of Directors. Five now just in the last month. Last week, one of the board member was sent home after complaining of a sore throat. Out of precaution, he took the afternoon off; and a few hours later, his body was discovered about two miles from his house by a delivery truck driver. He dropped dead on the street, no warning at all. Just a sore throat, as he said. His wife mentioned that he went out for a jog around the neighborhood to help sweat out the sickness. Now, I have to contain the situation before it gets out of hand."

"Well, it shouldn't be a problem for you."

Narcissus didn't respond to Cupid's comment.

Then, in the wake of the silence, Cupid decided to make up his own theories, sort of fill in all those blanks: "Sounds like a disgruntled employee getting back at those in charge."

"Hardly," Narcissus said, as he was in no mood to hear Cupid and his soapbox lecture. There was something about the summers in Arizona that made him as irritable as a toothache. He'd cringe at those who flippantly disregarded it as a dry heat. "So you're here to collect, am I right?"

"That's right," Cupid said. "So, you got it or what?"

"Yeah," Narcissus drawled, reached into the glove compartment, and pulled out a small jar carrying a toxioplexus. "I got it."

Narcissus handed the jar to Cupid.

"I can't believe it survived in the heat."

"*This*? It'll survive in any condition."

"You really think it works?" Cupid said, looking over the toxioplexus.

"The snake worm will absorb the parasite," Narcissus said. "*But*," he emphasized for Cupid, "make sure you remove it after the infection is gone."

"How will I know?"

"You'll know."

Once more, Cupid looked over the toxioplexus.

"I'll take your word for it."

"By the way, how's he doing?"

"Not good," Cupid said grimly. "It's spreading faster. How about the girl?"

"Which one?"

"Pandora."

"So far, so good."

"Does she remember anything?" asked Cupid.

"I thought you didn't care."

"I don't," he said callously.

Narcissus flexed his right ear. "You know, you're not any good at lying, Cupid. I know you've been checking up on her? Don't bother," he said before Cupid could return. "I can't hear the lie in your voice."

"I just—she seemed different from the others."

Narcissus backtracked to Cupid's original question.

"As far as we know," he said, "no. Not that much. For all she knows, it was all a bad dream. But I'm sure, you already know that."

Cupid said more casually, "If my memory serves me correct about your world—or, at least what I remember of my time spent in your world—a bad dream lasting four years isn't a bad dream. That's hell."

"And that place you now call home isn't any different?"

Ignoring the comment from Narcissus, Cupid said, "So, that's it. The project was considered a success?"

"According to Berzins, he thinks so. Say," Narcissus said, as if the idea just sprung to mind, "I might have another job for you, a big one, if you're interested."

"No chance in hell." Cupid smirked. The Lazarus Light suddenly brightened and shot like a knife-like glare through the car. "See you around, Narcissus."

"Yeah" Narcissus said, as he moved his cloudy grayish eyes to the rear view mirror as if he was undisturbed by the blinding light. "See ya."

Cupid faded away inside the glare, which could've past as the sun reflecting off a metallic surface. Eventually, like Cupid, the glare faded.

To the naked eye, the back door appeared to open and close on its own.

Narcissus placed the black shades back on his face, started the ignition, and drove away.

JACK anxiously waited inside the stolen minivan with a Virginia license plate that appeared as if it had been recently—and suffice to say, poorly—screwed-in based on the wear and indentations along the corners of the plate, as well as fresh circular-shaped etching around the holes from where the bolts that secured the plate to the bumper had been stripped and replaced with brand new ones.

The parallel parking appeared rushed or done by a driver who wasn't familiar with the city or all of the above. The minivan was parked with the front left end slightly protruding outward into the street. On the other side of the minivan next to the sidewalk was an old, rundown twelve-story building that consisted mostly of small businesses, one of them being a heavily-trafficked jewelry store run by "Billy Bling," his real name William Steinman, whose clients included A-list celebrities, elites, and top tier athletes.

As the windshield wipers sloshed back and forth, Jack stared at the handful of customers who were waiting on line. Some with umbrellas while others braving the downpour by doing the whole popped-collar jaded gumshoe gesture with their heads sunken between their shoulders like a frightened turtle. They were standing in front of *Sal's* Bagels, a popular bagel shop that had its roots firmly embedded in New York. Sal's had been around since The Great Depression. Several investors tried multiple times to persuade, even, at times, coerce Sal into franchise by tempting Sal to start up his own chains across the country or expanding his brand by offering him a spot for his famous bagels in the bread aisle of every grocery store. Sal had five shops, one for each borough. Except for the one in Brooklyn, which shared space with a laundromat simply called "The Mat," each shop had its own building.

The sound of shouting made Jack more alert.

Appalled yet, at the same time, incredibly frightened by the bombastic chatter on the sidewalks, both in front of the building and the other across the street, between the two heated New Yorkers who were about to swap bullets, Jack rolled up the window to drown out the noise.

"*Are you ready*?" a phlegmy voice said from behind Jack.

"After driving clear across the country, I think I deserve an explanation as to what's really going on here," Jack not only said, but demanded. "What is it that you're not telling me?"

Jack turned his eyes toward the rear view mirror and shot a glance at the dark slender figure sitting in the back of the minivan. The grayish, wrinkled face was covered in the shadows of a hoody. Which, for Jack, had only made the situation worse, especially after having seen her face, then having to witness it in a darker, moodier light.

"In time, I promise I'll tell you everything—"

"—Star," he said, tightening his fists over the steering wheel, "I'm losing my patience here. You have to give me something. Anything. . . "

Star, the dark damsel in disguise, remained quiet. Both of her beady black eyes—which were much farther apart on her face and nearly touching the sides of her temples—lit up a hazy gray color from the headlights of a passing car.

"Listen, Star," Jack said, his voice calmer, "I know a lot of plastic surgeons, good ones, who can take a look at you."

"Are you going to help me or not, Jack?"

"I wouldn't have driven this far if I wasn't. This Billy guy," Jack said, trying to block out the noise outside, "he knows I'm coming, right?"

"He does."

The shouting across the street intensified.

One of the men had his hand behind his back, as if he was about to brandish a gat.

"We're running out of time, Jack," Star said to Jack, who turned his bloodshot eyes from the man on the sidewalk to the rear view mirror.

"All right," Jack said, giving up. "You sure you don't want to come in with me?"

"No can do," Star said. "Warrick has eyes everywhere."

"He's that dangerous, huh?"

"I wouldn't exactly refer to Warrick as a he." Jack managed to get out one word from his mouth, which wasn't a word at all but more so an incoherent utterance, before Star cut him off, "Even though Warrick may be wearing the body of a human, trust me, Jack, Warrick is anything but human. But if it makes you feel more comfortable referring to Warrick as your own kind, then so be it."

"You mean, *our* kind," Jack said sharply.

Star ignored Jack, especially his passion.

"Take the most dangerous entity in the world and multiply it by ten. That's what I'm up against."

"What *we're* up against," Jack said, less sharp, more doubtfully.

"Right."

"So what the hell does he," Jack paused and corrected, "Warrick want?"

"What every asshole who can't handle their own shit wants," Star said more upfront. "*Control.* He could've just stopped by sacrificing that poor girl for his little experiment, got his magic medicine, and been done with it." She shakes her head from the very thought of his plan. "That wasn't good enough for him, nothing ever is. He wants complete control over people, to bring people back into a world where they lack free will. Does that remind you of anybody, Jack?" Star asked but didn't expect an answer from Jack. "Just imagine an entire world under one. . . " Star paused in a similar fashion to Jack and thought extra carefully about her next usage of words to explain this tyrannical-type of character whom she was so tempted to refer to as, not a thing, but something far less relative than an inanimate object, ". . . *man's* control. Worse case scenario, if that was to happen, 'if,' that's not a civilization anymore, Jack. That's a puppet show."

"Then, we can't let that happen. Can we?"

"The world doesn't belong to Warrick, Jack," she said. "It *never* will. This world, this land, it doesn't belong to anyone. Never has. I'd like to think that we were put here to take care of the world, not destroy it."

"In an ideal world, yes," Jack said unsurely. "I'd like to think so too."

Star said solemnly, "The world doesn't have to be ideal, Jack. The world was never intended to be ideal. But if it's a fraction of ideal, I'll take that any day of the week." Under the brim of the hoody, she moved her beady eyes up at Jack. "Of all people, especially one who makes a living repairing the human heart, you should know this better than anyone."

With heavy eyes, Jack glanced through the rear view mirror and didn't even follow up on what Star was telling him. He already made up his mind about Star, already had ever since she snatched him while he was on the way to the hospital and forced him inside a car with her what felt like a millennia ago.

"Before I do this," Jack said, as if he wasn't leaving until Star gave him a tidbit as to why Star looked the way she did, "I need to know. Is it true about what happened to you? The news said—"

"—You actually believe the news? What are you really trying to ask me?"

"Star," he said confidently, "did you die?"

"I'm here talking to you, aren't I?"

"After Mandy's death," Jack started, as he took a moment to drift off in reflection.

Buried within that reflection was a bottomless rage, which had made the lines along his brow run longer and deeper.

The thought alone of Mandy, the savagery of her brutal passing, and how that opportunistic jackass in the White House had completely smeared the memory of her with a serious of tweets, all to benefit his own prejudice against "fangs," caused the emotion to simmer inside Jack.

"It's weird," he said, "but part of me felt as if she wasn't dead, yet she was somewhere else; and at times," Jack paused and laughed at the images in his head, "she'd stop by the house just to fuck with me either it be switching on a TV or tilting a picture frame or reorganizing the fridge or even, writing me messages in a steamy window. She was never going to forgive me for what I did to her, for what we did."

"That sure doesn't sound like the Doctor Jack I know."

Jack's eyes filled with tears.

"We had a good thing between us, you and I did. Was it real?"

"Of course, it was real."

"I'm sorry I wasn't there for you before, you know—"

"—Before I lost my shit."

"I should've been there."

"You were," Star said. "In a way."

Jack inhaled deeply through his nose, as he wiped away a tear from the corner of his eye. He cracked open the door.

"Are you forgetting something?" asked Star.

Jack closed the door.

"He'll only accept cash," Star said, as he pulled out the briefcase from underneath the seat and handed it to Jack.

Jack asked, "How much is in here?"

"Trust me," Star said. "You don't want to know."

While holding the briefcase against his body, he reached for the door handle. Just as he was about to pull on the handle, he paused and turned to Star.

"Why me?" he asked.

Star said bluntly, "You're the only one I can trust, Jack."

JACK ran through the rain until he reached the door next to Sal's. He walked inside and rode the grimy elevator to the seventh floor.

Keeping a tight grip over the briefcase, he made his way to Room 710.

Outside, two well-built security guards were standing in front of the door.

One guard ran a metal detector over Jack's clothes while the other one patted him down for any weapons.

Once Jack was cleared, they escorted him inside the jewelry store.

There, Jack met Billy Bling, who was standing behind a case full of diamond rings and necklaces.

"You must be Doctor Jack Sender," Billy said and shook Jack's hand.

Without wasting anytime, Jack asked Billy, "Where is it?"

"Right," Billy said. Then, sarcastically, "The *magic crystal*. Right this way."

Jack followed Billy back into a dimly lit private room where he had the black crystal sitting on top of a display case.

"Here she is," Billy said, as he picked up the shard of black crystal and held it up in the light.

Jack placed the briefcase on the countertop.

Being the businessman he was, Billy didn't waste anytime either. He opened the briefcase, revealing all of those Benjamins inside. There had to be at least two mill inside. At least.

"That's a lot of money," Jack said, clearing his throat.

Billy laughed and said to Jack, "You're telling me. Saving the world has its price, my friend."

DOCTOR Berzins stopped by his office to make a couple of calls before calling it a day.

As he stepped inside his office, he was greeted by Vivian, who was standing with her arms crossed in front of a window overlooking the city of Atlanta.

"Ms. Nikopoulos," he said, surprised, "how did you get in here?"

Vivian snapped, "Why does one side of her look more like Cleopatra? What did you do to her?"

The doctor hung his head from the question and after collecting his thoughts, closed the door behind him,

"I thought we had an agreement, Ms. Nikopoulos," he said, as he cautiously approached his desk. "I told you it wasn't going to be easy. Didn't I?"

Vivian didn't respond.

"Eventually, she'll come around. And so will you—"

Scowling, Vivian faced Doctor Berzins, "She's not my daughter, is she?"

The doctor held out his hands.

"I'm aware it might be a lot to take in right now, considering what you had to endure for the past four years," he said. "But I assure you she is *your* daughter."

THE pizza guy happened to arrive as soon as Pan stepped out of the shower. She didn't even know where the time had gone. One minute, she was jumping in the shower to rinse off after a jog around the neighborhood. The next, she drifted off and found herself inside another place, talking to a man with bulky shoulders. He called himself "Cupid."

As Pan rushed out of the shower and threw on some clothes, she called out to the pizza guy and told him that she'd be out in one minute.

On her way out of the living room, she bumped into the dresser, knocking the lamp to the floor.

During the impact, the bottom of the fixture broke apart, revealing the tiny compartment underneath the lamp. The corner of a book was protruding from the bottom part of the fixture. Pan kneeled down and pried a raggedy-looking book from the lamp.

The front of the book had a symbol of a sun with three lines projecting outward. Pan had seen the book before, but she couldn't quite tell where.

AFTER spending the last three weeks living a hermit-like life, Pan decided enough was enough. She packed extra light and managed to fit four to five outfits inside a travel bag—six or seven if she mixed and matched. Then she hit the road like a warrior, first by making an impromptu visit at a tourist site in Louisiana called the Swamp Park where she spent an afternoon riding in a boat full of tourists and picking out alligators along Louisiana's bayous; then after exhausting herself by soaking up the wild life, she headed West. She stopped multiple times: local family-owned restaurants—"dives"—where she tasted local cuisine; rest stops to relieve herself; convenient stores to refuel. She spent the night in a hotel three times during the trip, once in Mississippi, then another night in Texas, then another night in New Mexico. Her memory started to come back to her when she drove through the Land of Enchantment. She stopped at a hole-in-the-wall gas station to fill up both her tank and her belly. It was there, at Zed's Supplies, when she was taking the last bite of a *Dark Cavern*™ bar and as she was about to toss the wrapper in the trash, she noticed the maker of the popular candy bar below the ingredients. If it were any other day of the week, she wouldn't have looked twice at that name, Kazlauskas Inc.; however, the sight of the name triggered a memory, buried miles deep inside her and locked away by the chains of time.

When Pan crossed into Colorado, each and every detail of the road, the surroundings, including road signs and businesses along the highway, were familiar. She had been here before. In a way, Pan felt as though she was chasing after her own ghost.

Once she reached a steep bridge that towered over Sharptooth River, the very same river where her sister, Cleo, had gone missing, she knew—at least, a part of her did—that her sister wasn't missing.

On the contrary, a part of Cleo was found.

And still alive!

Guided by a lost memory, Pan turned the car around and drove to Sharp-tooth Mountain Park, which was empty that day, not a single car in the parking lot. She told herself that the rest of her journey would be traveled by foot. So, she did.

Carrying only the book that Cupid had given her, she took her time exploring the vast wilderness, marveling at the life pulsing throughout its lushness, basking in its wave of comfort, and trekking through unbeaten trails until she wound up in a familiar spot underneath the waterfall where the water was calm. She walked to the edge of a rock and peered into the water below where she witnessed a reflection of a dark figure standing directly behind her.

Not frightened, instead, rapt by the presence, Pan kneeled down for a closer look at the reflection and realized it was her sister, Cleo.

In a state of euphoria, Pan was swift to rotate her shoulder as she scanned the woods behind her. Cleo wasn't there. Pan wasn't expecting to see her sister, but part of her wasn't entirely convinced.

Pan turned back around and watched the reflection slowly fade into the water. As she sat back upright, she saw the water rippling in the middle of the pool.

A pale arm inched its way to the surface. Graceful in manner, the hand of the arm meticulously waved Pan into the water.

Pan found herself laughing at the sight of the hand.

It can't be real, can it?

She carelessly shrugged her shoulders.

With the book *First Light* gripped in hand, she placed her foot into the water and while doing so, the hand slowly submerged.

"I can't believe I'm doing this," Pan said to herself.

She placed the book on the top part of a rock, which was dry, and walked farther into the water. Each step became heavier and heavier the farther she walked into the water.

By the time the water reached her waist, she was trudging forward.

She wasn't even thinking straight. She wasn't even thinking at all. She was merely seizing a moment, one where its outcome remained in uncertainty.

As she moved farther and deeper into the water, the questions would eventually resurface. A part of her knew that she would discover the answers in a place called Quidaquin County.

The Tragedy of the Five Fistfuls

KEY waits for a response as he watches Nevaeh dress.

In spite of his attempts at convincing her to stay home for the night, the girl's already made up her mind.

Who can blame her?

As Key points out, she takes up after her momma.

"It's final, Key," she says more harshly to Key, who's lying in bed. "I'm going out whether you like it or not. And believe me. . . " she stops midway through dressing, squares up to the bottom corner of the bed, does this cute gesture where she shifts all her weight to one side of her body, her hips tilted upward like a seesaw, which really has Key turned on, and as his Baby's been known to do whenever the mood strikes her, uses both of her hands like a magician to convey—or conceal—her emotion, "we can bicker for an hour or so, distract Alexa from doing homework, but it sure as hell ain't gonna get us anywhere, is it?"

"You underestimate her," Key says, moving his eyes to the ceiling. "Alexa's got the focus of a samurai. The way she wields that pencil like a katana."

Emotion builds to the point where it floods over Nevaeh, which, surprisingly, makes Key harder.

Nevaeh eyes the growing bulge in Key's pants and rolls her eyes.

"You and I both know that what's going on out there is much bigger than the both of us, Key," she says, forcing Key's eyes elsewhere.

With both hands intertwined behind his head, Key arches his upper body forward and rests against his elbows as he glances at a small VHS/TV set perched on Nevaeh's dresser.

On the grainy screen, the cable news is replaying the footage from earlier that afternoon in the small town of Conoma, La Verite Valley, where four of eight police officers, who were charged last year and had been awaiting trial for the beating of a Los Angeles resident, Antwain Chaquille Grady, who is best known by his peers as "Straight A," are exiting with an entourage from the courthouse. The verdict is in: "*Not guilty* on all counts." Outside the rowdy courthouse, the mobs are standing shoulder-to-shoulder in full force, one lining the sidewalk, the other lining the street, both sides expressing how he or she truly feels about those four police officers, now considered "free men." The sides are split down the middle. One side is "pro-cop" and more or less, condones the brutality inflicted on Antwain Grady, who was left with several broken ribs, a shattered eye socket, which led to the loss of vision in his left eye, fractured arm, many cuts and bruises, flesh along his chest seared, beaten. The other side is outraged as it should be, and feels as if justice did not prevail, never was going to prevail based on a stacked jury and a broken system and everything in between; and the end result was, indeed, not only a miscarriage of justice, but also a prime example of how poorly American citizens, in particular, young black men, regardless of their background, were being treated in a country where a word like *equality* didn't exist; in fact, those who are in favor of the conviction by the fullest extent of the law, believe Antwain Grady was nothing more than a subject who was playing a role in part of a greater, more malicious pattern that had been going on for decades, even centuries.

"Nothing's ever gonna change," Key mumbles to himself. "Soon they'll find themselves another race to pick on. They always do." He switches off the television and moves his eyes back to Nevaeh, who's leaning in close to a standing mirror and picking out an eyelash from the corner of her eye. She finds the eyelash, blows it away, and finishes dressing. He loses himself yet again as she maneuvers her hips into a pair of blue jeans. He reaches out and grabs Nevaeh by the wrist, trying to pull her back to bed. "Come on," Key begs. "I have a bad feeling about this, Baby. I tell you what. Tomorrow, we can take Alexa to the lake."

"The lake sounds good and all, Key, but it ain't gonna change my mind from going out tonight—"

"—Baby," Key says, sitting more upright, "I'll stand by you in whatever you choose to do, but to say I'm cool with you going out with, of all people, Jada on a night like tonight, I'd be lying to myself."

"What's wrong with Jada?" asks Nevaeh, her tone shifting.

"Don't give me that, Nevaeh," Key says more defensively. "You know how she gets when she's around other people. Not to mention her long-standing history with cops. She's like a magnet for trouble."

"I dunno why you ain't sticking up for her. You've had your run-ins with the police."

"Of course I have, but she's known to blow up, Nev. You know it—"

"—Don't even start," Nevaeh says, as she throws on her last article of clothing, a black windbreaker worn underneath a purple and yellow LA Lakers T-shirt. "You can go somewhere else with all of that bullshit. Jada be like my sister to me and her name won't be talked about negatively in my house."

"Then, who's gonna watch Alexa?"

Nevaeh says over her shoulder, "I can always drop her off at my parents'."

"You can't be turning them into your own personal babysitters, Nev. Besides, your Pops has his hands full as it is."

"He don't mind," she says, primping. "Anyway I think he likes having Alexa around while he works. But. . . ." she glances at the reflection of Key in the mirror, ". . . she likes being with you more."

"She does, doesn't she?" he says, drifting off.

"She practically talks about you all the time. You're good for her, Key."

Silence forms between the two.

Key rolls out of bed and holds Nevaeh from behind while she does some last second primping in the mirror. He breathes in Nevaeh's scent and licks his lips.

"I can't lose you, Nev," he says, kissing the side of her neck.

"Whoever said you was."

"I can't lose Alexa."

"You ain't."

She feels the bulge pressed up against her backside.

"You really are something tonight," Nevaeh says, impressed. "Whatchu been feeding that creature?"

"Come on, Nev," Key begs. "Alexa needs her momma tonight."

"Oh please!" Nevaeh says, rolling her eyes in a well-demonstrated exaggeration. "I think someone else needs *this* her momma tonight."

"Maybe so," Key says, more quietly.

"She listens more to you, than me. You know?"

Key moves his hand underneath her arm and reaches for her breast.

"You know I need some, " he sings the words of Marvin Gaye, "*Sexual Healing*, Baby."

"Nice try, *MI6*," Nevaeh says, grabs hold of his hand, and redirects it somewhere else. Her eyes flick downward at Key's crotch-region below and says with contempt, "I'm afraid you gonna have to unload that weapon somewhere else tonight, Mr. Machine Gun, cuz there *Ain't No Mountain High Enough* to keep me from going out tonight."

"So it's like that, huh?"

Key smacks his gums and leans away from Nevaeh.

"Don't give me that. . . "

Nevaeh mimics Key's gum-smack.

Waving off Nevaeh, Key leaves the bedroom and walks into the living room where the TV is airing the same news footage from earlier that afternoon. Those four cops who were charged but not convicted walking out of the courthouse with mass chaos following their every step. Chants of "*No Justice, No Peace*" or "*Justice For Straight A*" simmer underneath commentary like background noise. The cries and screams all share a common theme, which has been heard too often over the years. Those who stand with law enforcement and solely believe the opposition is the doings of a mob provide their own personal opinions to news reporters, who strategically seek out those who would only inflame the situation.

Sitting at the kitchen table that bleeds into the edge of the living room, Alexa, undistracted by the TV noise, is drawing a picture with a crayon.

The sight alone of Alexa intrigues Key and how, despite what's going on in the city, she maintains a keen warrior-like focus on the drawing before her.

As Key checks on Alexa, he stops halfway into the living room. A headlight in the corner of his eye pulls him toward the front door where he sees a car pulling up in front of the house. There, he notices Jada's red Oldsmobile Cutlass Supreme parked outside.

With all of her windows rolled down, she's blasting the song "Disco Inferno" by the 1960's soulful, super group known as The Trammps. From her exuberant, pre-party-like glow to her singing along "Burn baby burn!" Jada appears unfazed by the powder keg-like situation in the city.

Dressed for a night out, Nevaeh exits from the bedroom and kisses Alexa before she leaves the house.

"She's not coming in?" asks Key.

"What?" Nevaeh returns. "So you can try to talk her out of it?"

"Why you doing this, Nev?" asks Key, growing more agitated.

"I told you, Key, I ain't doing this right now," Nevaeh says, as she heads to the front screen door.

Jada sticks her body out of the driver side window and shouts at Nevaeh, telling her to get moving and that "What you waitin' on, Nevaeh? We got ourselves a city to burn!"

"Nevaeh," Key says more fatherly, "you're gonna get yourself killed. Is that what you want?"

"Jada is just being Jada," she says reassuringly. Then, lowers voice so Alexa can't hear. "You know she ain't gonna do shit."

"So that's it, huh?" Key says, losing his stance. "So, there's nothing I can do that'll change your mind?"

"Quit be so dramatic, will you?" she says, grabbing Key by the hand. "I'm only going out for a couple of hours—"

"—You don't need to do this," Key says with defeat in his face.

Nevaeh places her hand along the upper part of Key's chest and rubs a small starfish-shaped scar left behind from a gunshot wound, which is partially exposed underneath the white tank top.

"I do, but I understand why you don't want me to go. And that's okay." She kisses Key, but Key doesn't kiss her back. "I promise we'll go to the lake tomorrow morning cuz I know how much you love going to the lake to feed them Mallard ducks." Smiling, she shakes Key's arms, as if she's trying to shake—more or less—cast the drama out of his body. "A'ight, *Malle*," Nevaeh says. "When we get back from the lake, I'll drop Alexa off at Pop's studio. You can drop off that book that he's been bugging you about for months." From the corner of Nevaeh's mouth, she says in side-thought, "—You know how he be about his books. After that, Alexa can hang out with her Paw-Paw while me and you take care of some beeswax." Her eyes trail downward and stay pinned to Key's nether regions before finding there way back to his eyes. "It'd be worth the wait. Promise."

"A'ight," Key drawls and finally, returns a kiss on Nevaeh's lips.

Nevaeh says her goodbyes to Alexa firstly, kissing her two peace-loving fingers and blowing a kiss to Alexa, Key secondly, only giving him a wave goodbye. She exits from the house and greets Jada with a hug outside the idling Cutlass Supreme. All the while Key watches the two ride away into the fading daylight, that soulful jam "Disco Inferno" shaking the very concrete of the street.

Once Nevaeh is gone from view, he walks back into the house and grabs the paperback, *New Harlem At Sunrise*, from the edge of the coffee table. He brings the book into the kitchen where she checks on Alexa and that drawing.

Key asks her, "What do you got there?"

"A drawing," Alexa says shortly.

"Yeah," Key says, grinning. "I know it's a drawing, but what is it a drawing of?"

"It's the Nowhere Land," Alexa says and with her purple crayon, shades in a lanky figure standing on top of an orange-colored hill.

"*Nowhere Land*, huh?" Key points at the figure on the top of hill. Alexa has gone through nearly the entire set of crayons to fill in his tie-dye like attire. "And who is this person here?"

"That is Lollipop Man," she says. "He is a protector of all people. Today, he is going to help Don Juan find his way back to his family. Paw-Paw said that he's going to create Lollipop for me."

"Did he now?"

Key studies the drawing of the countryside with rolling orange hills. Standing in front of a green two-story house is yet another figure, this "Don Juan" character who is wearing much darker attire and appears no brighter than a shadow. Above the figure are swarms of flying creatures, which look like black birds.

"Lollipop Man," he says out loud while studying Alexa's colorful character on top of the hill, as well as the upside down rainbow that he casts from his bright smile. "So, you come with that idea on your own?"

"I'm drawing it, aren't I?"

"You sure are." Key decides to take a seat next to Alexa at the kitchen table. "Not bad for ah. . . How old are you again?"

"Six."

"Six? What? That can't be right. Swear I thought you were much older than that."

"How old did you think I was?"

"I was thinking more like, I dunno, ten or eleven."

"No," she says, her voice drawn out.

Key studies Alexa and that cool, calm, and collected aura about her when she focuses her mind on one thing, such as a drawing. He moves his eyes toward her neck and can't help but study those deep, wrinkled-like marks around her neck from where she was nearly strangled to death by the umbilical cord when she escaped Shelly's polluted womb and entered the world, only to, many years later, be gazed upon by yet another. Key notices Alexa watching him through the corner of her eye while she continues to draw, moves his attention away from Alexa, and turns his focus back toward the drawing. He points at all of those dark, winged, scribbly creatures flying above the shadowy man—or "Don Juan."

"So are these supposed to be birds or something?" he asks Alexa.

"These are Lollipop Man's helpers called 'Swooshers,'" Alexa says, pulling her eyes from Lollipop Man. "They're going to help carry Don Juan up the hill because Don Juan is having trouble reaching Lollipop Man."

"And why's that?"

"He's sick, well, more like broken."

"Broken, huh? Broken how?"

Alexa innocently shrugs her shoulders.

"So let me get this straight," Key says directly to Alexa, "we're talking 'bout the same Don Juan from the movie your Paw-Paw be working on?"

Alexa nods her head.

"*The Effigy: The Curse of Don Juan*." Her round face lights up. She chirps, "You've seen it yet?"

639

"Me, you know I don't do horror movies," Key says closely, glancing at the living room TV where a Breaking News story flashes across the screen.

"Why not?" asks Alexa.

On the TV, a shaky overhead shot from a helicopter is filming protests on the streets of Los Angeles. Violent riots are forming among the streets outside businesses and shopping malls. Protestors using rocks and Molotov cocktails to vandalize parked cars and property. Abandoned police cruisers are being set ablaze. Along a strip mall, a mob of looters are shattering shop windows with bricks and street signs, storming through barricades, tearing through fencing and metal gates, and breaking into small family owned businesses. Major retail stores completely gutted of merchandise. In a busy intersection, swarms of mobs are pulling drivers out of vehicles and beating them senseless. One of the victims—a truck driver—is beaten to death and left to die on the streets. While the man dies, two protestors cover the man's face and body with black spray paint.

Staring at the violent images, Key finally answers the six-year-old's question: "Reality is filled with enough horror as it is."

Key faces Alexa, who, in return, follows his eyes toward the TV; however, Key pulls Alexa's attention back to the conversation at hand. "Besides," he says directly to Alexa, as those images on the TV intensify and become more graphic in nature, "aren't you too young to be watching horror movies like *The Effigy*?"

"I don't watch them," she says. "I'm not allowed to. Plus, they're too scary for me."

"Yeah," Key says, laughing. "*And* your momma would kill your Paw-Paw if she found out he was sneaking you on set without her permission."

"How come you never talk to Paw-Paw?"

"I talk to him."

Alexa immediately detects the lie and displays her disapproval on her face.

"Can you keep a secret?" Key says, guilty.

Alexa nods again, this time more vigorously.

"Between you and me," he says, "your Paw-Paw and I don't exactly see eye-to-eye, meaning we're not as close as, say, the way me and your momma are."

"Are you saying you don't like Paw-Paw?"

"It's not like I don't like him. It's just we often have a difference of opinion. There's nothing wrong with having differences; in fact, it's those differences that make us closer."

"That means you should be closer to Paw-Paw, right?"

"Sure," he says, backtracking. "It's just, at times, your Paw-Paw has a way of saying things that would get most people in trouble."

"Trouble how?"

"Trouble like something bad happening to him," Key says more coldly. "But we wouldn't want that, would we?"

With exaggeration, Alexa shakes her head and indicates a clear "No!"

Key's comment finally settles, causing Alexa to stop drawing. She hangs her head.

"You know, when Ralph's not playing The Wolf, he's not that scary."

"I'm sure he isn't," Key says. "There's a reason why they call it acting. It's all make-believe."

"I know," Alexa returns.

"From what I heard, he and Paw-Paw are pretty close."

"Well, Ralph's always cracking jokes and Paw-Paw gets a real kick out of his jokes," Alexa says briskly as if she's trying to say it all in one breath. "There was this one time I was doing my homework in the trailer while Paw-Paw was putting on Ralph's mask—which took like, hours, because Paw-Paw had to mold Ralph's face before he could paint the mask—and Ralph cracked this joke about Imani's butt. Paw-Paw was laughing so hard that he started to cry and I asked him why he was crying and he said he wasn't and that not all people cry when they're sad."

"Yeah. That's true," Key says, amazed by the girl's energy. "Your momma told me how much you like movies. That's must be cool, right? Spending time hanging around actors and all kinds of celebrities?"

"Well, I don't look at Ralph as a celebrity. To me, he's no different than you or Paw-Paw."

Leaning over the table, Key nods at the drawing.

"So, he put that in your head, huh?"

"Well, no."

"Then, who did?"

"Jacob says I have a wild imagination."

"Who's Jacob?"

"He works with Paw-Paw. He's a set designer."

"Well, Jacob is spot-on about your imagination."

"I know," Alexa says and returns to her drawing.

In the corner of his eye, Key sees yet another more graphic scene on TV. A liquor store on the street corner—but not just any liquor store, he looks closer and realizes it's Terrell's store—is burning while protestors gather in front of the store and bask in the fiery blaze. Palls of black smoke pour into the sky and, at times, block out the overhead shot from the helicopter hovering above. Terrell, an older man whom Key had gotten to know over the past couple of years, is standing outside, trying to push protestors away while his business burns down to the ground.

But there's nothing Terrell can do to stop the fire.

"RAT RACE"
(PRESENT DAY)

ON one side of the alley, you have "Stat," whose attire consists of a brown leather vest worn over a tight white Tee with a Snakebreath logo, black jeans that, similar to his shirt, appear two sizes too tight, a pair of checkered Vans that match the red logo on his shirt. Red, being a common theme sprinkled throughout Stat's getup, is the color of a band to hold his dreads in a bun. His accessories include twenty-four wrist bracelets that his daughter, Deja, made for him. Each bracelet, according to Deja, represents each year of her poppa's existence, each one varying from rubberbands to multi-colored beads, pearls, or faux jewels to twine, including nylon and hemp.

On the other side, Key, who, more or less, given his capitalist-like nature and willingness to devour any and *all* competition, self-branded himself the nickname "M16," a cross between a less punkish Eel-Baby and a more vitriolic MoVega, minus the villainous bleached blonde bowl-cut wig and Youngblood Priest sideburns. Contrary to Stat, Key's attire is consistent to what you'd see in a rap video from the mid to late Nineties: each article of clothing oversized, including a New York Knicks basketball jersey numbered 00 with the sales tag uncut and hanging from the bottom seam, as well as Nautica blue jeans which he wears sagging well below his waist. Like the baggy jersey, the jeans appear untouched and unaltered, the long size sticker, XL, still attached to the back of the pant leg. The Yankees hat with the flat, stiff bill was cocked to the side in an angle. His footwear: a pair of wheat-colored Timberland boots, unspoiled and unlaced, despite scattered rain showers. His accessories: an 18k gold plated chain, as well as an off-brand gold watch that he bought half of what you'd normally pay at a retail store from a hustler on the street.

Hugging the edge of the sidewalk while taking cover from a passing shower, Key and Stat are chilling against the side of two adjacent buildings, one being a law firm, Willhouse and Maylay, while the other, a rundown apartment complex, which is in the middle of a renovation project, albeit temporarily on hold due to the weather.

To their right, a bunch of news reporters, as well as protesters gather and conform along the blocked off street in front of the New York City Court House.

As droplets of rain splash on the back of his shoulders, Stat slightly hunches over with both hands in his pockets. Key remains in a fixed position, "posted up," his lower half shaped like a reverse letter four with one foot pressed against brick, the other one planted on the slick asphalt. Key's interest is directed more at pedestrians walking along the sidewalk instead of those forming crowds.

With the thought weighing heavy on his mind, Key points out the passerbys to his eager prodigy, Stat.

"Take a good look them," Key says to Stat, as he flicks his head in a nod at the pedestrians shielding themselves with umbrellas. "What do you see?"

"Well," Stat says, sighs, and pays closer attention to the passerbys, "Besides the small worlds that keep 'em occupied, either it be the hot-blooded text from a fling that expires in two weeks, maybe three, depending how imaginative she can be, or the misleading headlines that bait her in for clicks in order to profit from her gullible character or NSFW photos from that fine-ass pawg who is everything his average wife ain't or the group email of a plotted coup, using all sorts of code words to throw off whistleblowers who are anything but righteous in their pursuits, or a rigged game that helps ease anxiety of a stressed-out homey from being in public, besides all of that, shit," Stat shrugs, "I see opportunity."

"What else?" Key says with a blank expression.

"What else?" Stat repeats, his mind wrapped in thought. Then says thoughtfully, "*Pasts*." Stat focuses on one particular woman who's scrolling through the texts on her phone while trying to stay dry underneath the black umbrella. "They all have pasts, whether or not they like to admit it. Everybody's either running to or from something. *The past or the future.* How else can you get where you need to be? Then, there are those who prefer to walk, and I guess that's a'ight by me. Just get out of my way, you feel me?" Stat chuckles but squelches the laughter after receiving another icy stare from Key. "But then," Stat says, more seriously, "you got those who ain't even moving at all, who just sitting as if they waiting for something awful to happen."

"And once they remove their eyes from the self-serving worlds that bind them to their masters, what do you see then?"

"Hard to see through so many layers without making contact, but I guess I'd see people who just want purpose."

"You guess?"

"People want a purpose, Key," Stat says, more confidently. "No doubt."

"You want purpose, right?"

Stat shrugs.

"Of course," he says shortly. "Why not?"

Key says, "You said earlier that you felt as if there was something 'missing' from your life, but you didn't know what exactly."

Once more, Stat shrugs.

"Yeah," he says. "That's right. The blur. But that's the trade off, yeah?"

"It can be," Key says. "Every gift has a curse, and every curse has a gift."

"Lately, it's felt more like a curse," Stat says. "Just a curse."

"Well, of course, we got an election coming up soon, Stat. Emotions are particularly amped up around this time of year. There are some who choose to capitalize on those emotions while others simply ignore them."

Stat says from the corner of his mouth, "*Man*, it's hard to ignore this shit."

"Let me ask you something personal, Stat, if you don't mind."

"Shoot."

"How do you feel about your family?" Key ask, then adds: "And try to push past the blur, if you can."

"Family?" Stat says, as if the repeating of the word opens up more space for brain chatter. "There ain't a blur there when I think of my family. My whole life I felt like I never had one. My dad was never there. He spent most of his life in and out of prison. Briefly worked as a loader before he bit the bitter end of a bullet. My moms did the best she could raising me and my sisters. But, eventually, when I was twelve years old, it had gotten so hard on her that she decided she was done with us. She dropped us off at my grandparents' crib and was gone for good from my life. By the time my grandparents passed, I dropped out of high school. They left the house to me and my sisters, but, eventually, they let the house go to shit by turning it into a hotel for broke-ass, wannabe gangstas who took full advantage over both my sisters. Like a bunch of vultures with bottomless appetites, always lingering around, picking up the scraps. As hard as I tried to put down my foot, act like man of the house—no matter what I did—I was still that younger brother who didn't even know how to change a light bulb. It don't take a gift to realize when one ain't wanted. I was done with it. With *all* of it. So, yeah, family, for me, that shit don't exist. Never has."

More thoughtfully, Key asks, "You ever hear about the cat Andre St. Croix, who was locked up for murder a while back?"

Stat half-frowns.

"Name sounds familiar."

"Changed his name to Drenelle."

"Drenelle, right," Stat says, the frown moving into a grin. "The she-male."

"Just a *she* now," Key says, as he keeps a tight hold over his blood.

"Right," Stat says, more dismissively. "Whatever."

"Before Drenelle's transition, she spent years alone, trying to figure out who he was. Like yourself."

"You comparing me to some prissy, eye-collectin' ass clown who can't even figure out his own sex?"

"So, you *have* heard the stories about the eyes?" asks Key.

"Now that you mention it," he says, more heated, "*yeah*. Who hasn't? If you trying to make a point or something, why don't you just give me a Cliff Note Version."

"Well, my point is, Stat: When Drenelle looked at herself in the mirror, she didn't like the person looking back at her. The body she was in, it wasn't her on the inside, you feel me?"

On the verge of saying "No," Stat hesitates.

"In a way," Key says before Stat can give him an answer, "she felt as though it didn't belong to her. So she rejected that person, *that body*, then started to alter it to the way she looked on the inside. Before the transition, Drenelle lived in fear for most of her young adult life, always wondering when his mother, Shakira, or any of her extended family members, would figure her out—if they hadn't already but just kept it secret, like the same way she was keeping how she really felt secret from those who surrounded her. After she hit puberty and her 'male' body started to change, she got hooked up with a crew of older people—mentors, you could say—in charge of running this small theatre on the ass-end of town called *Common Theme* Theatre. They were once misfits, like her, lone wolves who were trying to break the mold and most importantly, fit in before they created their own thing. Once she joined Common Crew, she started seeing and *feeling* things differently, like she had this image of herself deep inside her the whole time, locked away, protected, and then once she put herself with the right people, all of these feelings started flooding out of her. Everything *clicked*. The transition was a long process, but it was one she was willing to take. One day, she had reached the end of the road and had gone as far as the Common Theme would take her. She decided to leave the Crew, went off and did her own thing. She went 'mainstream,' if you will. Leaving Common Crew would eventually be Drenelle's greatest mistake; however, it later would set forth a Series of Unfortunate Events that would lead us to the inevitable Now. After Drenelle started up her own brand and became a success in her own right," Key carefully thinks of his next word of choice, "an '*event*' happened, one that nobody could explain—even if they tried. She was no longer Drenelle, even though she looked and acted like Drenelle. She changed into something else, something she had absolutely no control over, something beyond visceral, deadly, something that only thrived in the dark. And the world saw her for what she became and it came running for her with torches and pitchforks; now, she's back in that prison, the same one she was in when she was a boy trying to figure out who the hell he was. Only this time, it's a prison with bars and four walls."

Stat tilts his head to the side and narrows his left eye.

"Key," he says, thinking hard, "why you telling me this?"

Staying unperturbed at his post, Key directly calls out Stat and the talent that he has been given. "It's yours and yours only to bear," he says. "If you lose control over it, the world will change you into something you're not. You must recognize your talent for what it is, as well as the power it possesses. If not, you will wind up like Drenelle St. Croix. The street is an unforgiving place, and it's too crowded for talented people like yourself. You have a purpose. We *all* do. You may not be sure of what that is right now. But if you let me, I can show you."

Across the street, the crowd starts to buzz with rage.

Commotion builds higher, forcing the two to pay attention.

A security team exits first from the courthouse, which causes the angry mob, as well as a swarm of news reporters and cameramen to rush to the barricades that have been set up by the NYPD.

Surrounding himself with an entourage, disgraced journalist, Miles Straum, is next to exit from the courthouse. He walks down the front steps of the courthouse while one member of his security detail shields his face with a jacket. The other members circle Miles and protect him from the ensuing chaos before him.

"What goes around comes around," Key says to Stat. "It doesn't matter who you are and what you look like. If you're against them, they will do everything in their power to destroy you—"

"—He didn't do It," Stat says, referring to the Big "It."

Key glances at Stat through the corner of his eye.

"They don't care whether or not he killed that young girl," he says. "They've already chosen their man. But it doesn't matter anymore, does it?"

Key and Stat watch the growing crowd surround Miles, as one of his bodyguards blocks a projectile from hitting Miles with his shoulder.

Underneath his blank stare, Key clenches his teeth and tries to hold back his anger from the sight alone of the scoundrel who tried to steal, copy, and profit off his "world" by peddling it off as an animated TV show, which, ultimately, would, as he put it mildly in a podcast, "Make Miles Great" again.

"One thing's for sure," Key says mindfully while watching the news reporters bombard Miles, "you're either on the top or on the bottom. If you're on top, those on the bottom will do anything to erode the foundations that made you reach the top. They'll try to tear you down by delegitimizing you and eventually, breaking you. Miles Straum was *never* on top, even though throughout his career he thought he was. He created a lie to the world, and the world bought it. But it didn't stop the world from wanting more. The world enjoys watching people like Miles Straum squirm. Even after Miles was exposed for what he was, which was a sham, *they*," he nods at "they," the news reporters who, according to Miles post-controversy, constantly "feed and sicken" the world with the disease of misinformation and extreme bias, "still give him coverage and will continue to do so until there's nothing left of him but bones. Their goal is to make you feel less threatening because they believe that anybody who's on top will always be the threat when, ironically, it's the top that they strive for. Then," Key says while carrying a dark light in his eyes, "you have those who are on top but nobody has the slightest clue they're on top." He looks Stat directly in his eyes and asks, "You're not scared of heights, are you?"

AFTER suggesting hailing a taxi opposed to riding the subway from Manhattan to Brooklyn, Stat agrees to take the subway. Plus, Key says it'll be quicker, which is fine by Stat, especially with the circus in town.

By the time they reach the subway, the rain eases down to a drizzle. Part of the sun peeks through the dark clouds and is destined to create a rainbow over the steamy skyline of Manhattan.

"Back in the late Sixties, early Seventies, when I worked briefly at a loading dock in Newbay," Key says while stepping onto the train with Stat, "the honkies I used to work for called me Midnight."

"Honkies?"

"You know, it's a term used for white people," Key says. "Forgot. Way before your time."

"So, the Sixties, huh? How da fuck old is you?"

"I told you 'I'm ancient.'"

Key takes a seat next to the door.

While chuckling to himself, Stat sits down next to him

"For realz," Stat says, smirking. "Fuckin' vamp over here."

"Listen, Stat, it doesn't matter how old am I. Sure. I may look like your age. Check this out here. Lesson Number 1: *See with your ears.*"

"See with my ears? How da hell am I suppose to see with my ears?"

"Exactly. How you supposed to see with your ears? It's physically impossible, right?"

Stat shrugs.

"Guess so."

"How do you see with your eyes?"

"Is this a trick question?"

"Just answer the question," Key says.

"*Focus,*" Stat mentions. He confirms his answer by saying more clearly, "By focusing."

"Now close your eyes and apply that focusing part to your ears. What do you hear?"

"For realz?"

"Yes."

"A'ight."

Stat closes his eyes and listens closely to his intimate surroundings, from the back and forth chatter of two overzealous guys breaking down each track of a latest Eel-Baby and The Cuts album to the rustling of a finger-heavy hand reaching into a bag of potato chips followed by the crunching of the same person chomping down on a mouthful of potato chips to the digital chirping of a sudden notification on someone's smartphone to the rapid clicking of someone texting to the booming "ha" of laughter to the raspy whisperings of a trip-hop jam scolding from a pair of headphones to the crinkling of someone flipping a page in a magazine to the shuffling of a bookbag to the phlegm-logged sniffle of a running nose.

Stat cracks open his eyes and says to Key, "Life."

Key appears amused by Stat's answer.

"You know what I hear?"

"What?"

"Noise."

"Maybe so," Stat says, "but there life behind that noise. Don't you agree?"

Key doesn't answer Stat's question. Yet, he remains quiet and amused.

Stat nods at Key.

"So, Key," Stat says, his tone sharper, "why those honkies you work with call you Midnight? Hold up. Lemme guess. Your dark complexion?"

"You'd think being black certainly had something to do with why they called me Midnight—" Key says, "—I mean we talking 'bout the Sixties here. The way I see it, though: People looking for an excuse can easily find one. Your skin tone, your color, whatever it may be: Of all the excuses out there, it's the easiest ones to find. But, *for real*," Key says, emphasizing the very words Stat is known to use, only without a common letter that normally indicated sleep, "whether they like to admit it or not, most people are considered visual-creatures, meaning they rely on visuals: appearances, colors, shapes, and sizes. To these certain people, it's much easier to understand something, for instance, a person, they can see with their own eyes. However," Key says, pausing, "the color of my skin had nothing to do with the reason why they called me Midnight, even though most liked to think it did."

"Then why did they?"

"I always worked late in the night, mostly till midnight, even well past midnight, hence the name Midnight. The guy working the next shift was the one who actually came up with the name. After a while, it sort of stuck."

"Busy bee, huh?"

"I didn't mind working late," Key says casually. "I get all my best ideas late at night. You see it gave me a sense of comfort knowing that, while people were sleeping, I was blueprinting worlds inside my head."

"I can't go a day without sleep," Stat says, easing farther into the seat. "If I don't get at least eight hours in me, I'm one cranky bitch-ass nigga the next day."

"People, like yourself, Stat," Key says, "sleep is like fuel for your talent."

"Yeah," Stat says. "If you want to look at it like that. Sure."

They ride in silence for a while until Key comes up with an idea—a "test," if you will, to pass the time.

Key searches the train and spots a lonely woman sitting just a few seats away. Her hair is held in a ponytail by a black scrunchie. Her attire, which consists of a black, thigh-high skirt, as well as a silk buttoned down blouse underneath a metallic-colored lapel, long sleeve blazer that stretches past her thighs, is professional and business-like, yet it accommodates the warm weather. Both of her sleeves are rolled up to her forearms. The only piece of the woman's outfit that seems out of place is a black silk scarf worn loosely around her neck. In one hand, she's holding a worn paperback in front of her and using her thumb to keep the pages spread open while, in the other, she's massaging a tiny object. Her head is planted in the book; however, most of her interest appears to be solely directed at that object in her other hand.

"A'ight, *Thermostat*. "Let's see your magic," Key says, nodding at the sister without a mister. "How about the bookworm over there?"

"What about her?" asks Stat.

"You tell me," Key says. "Go on," he urges. "Do what you do."

Stat accepts Key's challenge, which, for Stat, isn't much of a challenge at all. Based on the slack expression, the woman is distressed; however, broken-hearted may be a more accurate description. Stat guesses, no, corrects himself, tells Key that she's somewhere between the age of thirty-three and thirty-five, even though the woman looks much younger, say, early twenties. The woman takes, not good care, but great care of her body, works out four times a week, alternate days from free weights to cardio, eats foods that don't have two or four legs, never indulges, uses facial creams and moisturizers to combat wrinkles and blemishes.

With his male gaze sharpening, Stat closely studies the woman, starting with her gestures and moving toward each one of her possessions. The woman's story unfolds right before his eyes.

"She's upset, obviously," he says right off bat. His eyes narrow. "She's not one to hide her emotions, even though she considers to lean on a more introverted side. She prefers to find comfort in a cat. A white long-haired that sheds a lot."

"You can tell she has a cat just by looking at her?"

"She has cat hairs on the bottom of her pant leg," Stat says. "She has one of those sticky roller thingamajigs. Considering she was in a rush today, she missed a few hairs on the bottom of her pan leg."

"You can see the cat hair on her pants?" Key says in doubt. Then, raises his brows in astonishment. "Not bad," he says.

"Well, it's there if you look hard enough; however, a cat can't give her solace on a day like today. The objects in her hands will, first starting with the book in her left hand." The **Braggadocio** font on the spine, as well as the front cover makes it trickier to read from where he's sitting. Stat leans forward to get a closer look at the book. "*New Harlem. . .*" he reads, leaning more without making himself seem too suspicious. "*New Harlem At Sunrise*, I think."

Key says, "It's a story that follows a young couple whose love is put to the test after the girlfriend and protagonist, Raven, learns about her boyfriend's dark past."

"So you've read it?"

"A few times, yes."

"Whatever, man."

Key replies with a question of his own for Stat, "When you've been known to work till midnight, what else you suppose to do with your free time?"

"I ain't judging." Stat says jokingly, "You don't strike me as a brother who reads romance novels."

"It may sound like a romance novel," Key says, his tone shifting darker, "but it's not."

"Then, what is it?"

"It's a horror story."

"Okay," Stat says, more interested in the book.

"Regardless of the contents of the book, from the worn condition of the cover and those faded pages, the book has been touched by many hands. The dog-ears on the corner of the pages are significant as well. Same goes for the writing along the pages and the highlighted paragraphs, *key* excerpts. The person who gave her the book did so with guidance and good intentions."

"How do you know it was given to her?" asks Key.

Stat notices the top half of the eReader tablet protruding from floral patterned purse.

"Normally, she reads her books on her tablet," he says. "The person could've shared the book with her through the tablet or bought the ebook version as a gift. This person is old school, though. This person is not her father but, more or less, an important figure in her life who had given the book to her before he passed to let her know that everybody has a past, even the person who looks back at you in the mirror, which brings me to the item in her other hand. It's a special pendant." Being the keen observer he is, he points out the jagged yet smooth volcanic glass-like rock held inside an interwoven swirling silver pendant attached to the collar necklace made out of a black leather cord. With the underside of her thumb, the lonely woman pets the pendant as if she's releasing energy trapped inside it. Each stroke radiates throughout Stat's body. "From what I can sense, it's sentimental, *not to her*," Stat emphasizes, as he shoots a glance at Key, "but to the person who gave it to her. Like the book, the *contents* inside the pendant carry a tremendous weight. They're irreplaceable, priceless; and based on how carefully she holds it in her hand, it belonged to a very special woman, one who was adored by many." Again, Stat finds himself glancing over at Key as though Key chose that particular woman for a reason. "However," Stat says, redirecting his attention back at the woman, "the thing is she's not entirely sad. She's actually relieved."

"Relieved?" Key says. "Relieved from what?"

Stat studies her closely, gestures and mannerisms, even the way she looks up at the passengers seated in front of her when she turns a page.

"Ever since she was in her early twenties, she lost her trust in guys. She went through a spell of bad relationships that ended up in disaster. Over time, she became more cynical. She lost confidence in herself. Relationships got shorter and shorter until any love life at all was reduced to a casual weekend hookup. It all started when she was around seventeen. She was in love—or at least, thought she was in love. Ever since that moment she first felt love, she spent years searching for that feeling again but nobody lived up to him and the way she felt for him. He was much older and meant everything to her. One day, she caught him cheating on her with one of her friends and she never forgave him for it. What he had done to her hung over their relationship up until the very end; planted doubts inside her head about *all* guys, especially one whom she thought she loved." Stat moves his eyes back to that pendant in particular. The stroking stops. She reads more aggressively. "Eventually," Stat says, "the relationship ran its course. Now, years later, she finds herself in love again. She's sad that, of all the women out there to choose from, he chose her to give her that special pendant because she knows that in the end the relationship will, like the previous ones, run its course. She enjoys her freedom, yet she enjoys his company even more. He's good to her. He never raises his voice at her. He treats her right. He's strong, too, and makes her want to be better in everything she do. He's nothing like the man who she once looked to as a father, the one who both her grandparents talked about with such hostility; in fact, it was her grandfather who had given her that book. However, she *feels* like her grandparents, especially her grandfather, whom she adored growing up, might've gotten this father figure all wrong, and a distant part of her feels like he was a good man, despite all the stories she heard about him over the years and just that feeling alone reminds her of the special person who gave her the pendant and that feeling alone, it brings her great ease. But that's not the only reason why she's so relieved. Throughout all her struggles, she finally found someone who she could struggle with."

Key digests Stat's rundown of the woman.

"You got all that just from looking at her?" Key asks.

"Yeah," Stat says and shrugs. "It just comes to me like a feeling. But it's not just any feeling. It's *her* feelings."

As though on cue, the train slows down while approaching their stop.

The two stand up as soon as the train comes to a stop.

The doors slide open.

Key taps Stat on the arm.

"What do you know?" he says and nods at the woman, who slips the crinkled paperback back into her purse, and readies to exit the train. "It's her stop too."

🕐

"WHO those cats I saw you hanging out with the other day?" Key asks Stat, as the two exit from the subway tunnel.

"The skinny fool is named Deadwave," Stat says. "The loudmouth is this cat from Queens named 'Stream. The big fellow is Big Magma. The sketchy muthafucka is N17."

"N17?" Key repeats. "You shitting me?"

"Shit you not, Key."

"Well I dunno know who that fool thinks he is," Key says, his tone rather bitter, "but if he doesn't change his name, I'm going to have to make him change it myself. Make sure you pass along that message for me next time you see N17."

As they make their way to the sidewalk, he grabs the Coffin Nail tucked over his ear, as well as a lighter from his pocket. He lights the cigarette as soon as they approach the bagel shop, Sal's. Key looks toward the minivan with the Virginia license plates parked along the side of the street. He hones in on the hooded passenger sitting in the back seat of the minivan.

The door next to Sal's bagels swings open.

Key drags from the cigarette and blows out a cloud of smoke as soon as Jack steps outside the building.

In the smoky cloud, a pair of dark slits for eyes takes shape, then two nostrils to form a nose, then a gaping mouth, wicked like a V, extending well-past the two eyes. The wavy, demonic face materializes and lingers in front of Jack's face before it funnels into his nose and mouth, causing him to cough.

With his hand firmly pressed against the inner pocket of his jacket, Jack uses his other hand to wave away the cloud of cigarette smoke.

As he walks past, Jack gives Key a look of detest on his face; however, from his rushed manner and the valuable possession that he holds inside his jacket pocket, he appears in absolutely no mood to confront Key or his friend. Not only that, based on a recent confrontation that he witnessed between two hot-blooded New Yorkers who were about to swap bullets on this very street a few moments ago, Jack realizes that breathing in someone else's secondhand smoke isn't at all worth dying over. He doesn't know whether or not Key is packing any heat, but he has a pretty good idea.

Or, does he?

As Jack proceeds toward the minivan, he slows down to a near-amble. Eventually, he stops in his tracks. His face slackens, as he rotates around toward Key and stares at him before walking away. He passes the minivan, causing Star, that hooded passenger, to slide open the door. She extends her head outward and calls out to Jack; however, Jack ignores Star and keeps walking by.

Key and Stat wait at the edge of the alleyway. As before, Stat observes other pedestrians before him and takes mental notes of each and every one of them as if he's readying himself for another one of Key's off-the-cuff tests.

Keeping to himself, Key carefully watches Jack and tracks his every move.

Once more, Star calls out to Jack.

"Where are you going?" she asks.

As before, Jack doesn't respond; in fact, Jack acts as if he doesn't even know Star, as he walks toward a construction site.

TWO construction workers, first, Peter, forty-six years old, a husband and father of two children, Liam and Mateo, and second, Paul, twenty-seven, a proud parent of a chocolate brown Labrador named after one of his all-time favorite video games called *Goliathon*, dig into both their lunches on a scaffold along the thirty-seventh story of a partially constructed high-rise, which, except for buildings like the Empire State Building, Peter calls "*Second best seat in the City.*"

Peter takes a bite of a classic Reuben sandwich from Louie's Deli and Shakes and says from the other side of his mouth, "This country's going straight down da tubes. You know that, right?"

"Oh yeah?" Paul replies, peeling the rest of his orange. He says with a mock-innocence, "What tubes?"

"You know, the fuckin' tubes."

"Haven't heard that one before."

"Quit being such a smartass, will ya?"

Peter wipes the juices from the warm corn beef and sauerkraut dripping down the side of his chin with a napkin.

"I never understand that expression and why so many people from *your* generation use it all the freakin' time," Paul says and breaks off a wedge from the orange. "I mean, where these tubes go? Huh, Pete? Underneath the streets? In the sewers? These are important questions you should be askin' yourself."

"How the hell am I supposed to know, Parrot?"

"Then, why you say it, Peter Peter Reuben Eater?"

"Hey, it's an expression, knucklehead," Peter says, voice loud, face even redder.

"Well, you and your generation might wanna think about updating your expressions because, frankly, Pete, they don't make any sense."

"Yeah, yeah, yeah," Peter says, trailing off. He takes yet another bite of the Reuben and waves off Paul and his comments. "Mr. Wise Guy here," he says upfront, "I tell you what: It's all of this commie bullshit that you hear about lately on the Fake News Network."

"Settle down, McCarthy," Paul says to Peter, as if he's unofficially taking a neutral stance.

"What the hell you know about McCarthy?" Peter asks Paul. "You were still swimming around your daddy's balls."

Paul shrugs.

"The Internet."

"Get outta here," Peter says, waving off Paul. "Just another way for you kids to get brainwashed by your YouTubes and Twitters. You can't fuckin' escape it, all of the nonsense out there, especially with the election coming up. It's everywhere you turn the gaddamn channel."

"Sure," Paul says, as Peter's passion starts to wear off on him, "the headlines, the anchors reading the headlines, the rage-reporting with an *obvious* slant against Rhodes—Not like I'm a fan of his but come on! Doesn't take some 'wise guy' to figure out the media's bias toward him—all of that is probably tweaked, some of it, sure, as fake as your wife's tits."

Peter puts down his sandwich and points at Paul.

"Hey! Watch it, Parrot—"

"—But you agree. The images ain't fake."

Peter fired back, "How you know Washington and her goon squad don't have a director out there, directing people to act a certain way for the camera? It's all staged. You know that, right? Washington's practically got the media wrapped around that claw of hers. They did that same exact shit in Vietnam, reporters directing soldiers to burn down villages, all to fit their narrative. Besides, they can manipulate images on that Photo-Thingy. . . "

"Photoshop?"

"That's the one."

"I guess, anything's fair game these days," Paul says, losing confidence in his stance.

"Now, what? You think 'Avanti Washington' is gonna swoop down here and save the day? It doesn't take a miner to dig up her past." Peter takes another bite, laughs. "The woman should run under the fuckin' Halloween Party."

Paul shakes his head from the insult, as if he wants to laugh but doesn't want to contribute or further invoke Peter's prejudices.

"Get this," Peter says, slapping Paul on the arm, "she could appoint all of her goons to her Cabinet. The Wolfman as her Secretary of Defense. The Mummy as Secretary of the Treasury. Frankenstein as Secretary of Energy—"

"—Dracula as Secretary of Transportation?" Paul joined in.

Peter bursts out laughing, Paul not so much.

"What a world we live in," Peter says to himself. Then more directly to Paul, "This ain't the first time this county has gone through a rough patch. You should know, Computer Boy. What people don't realize is that this country was founded on rough patches and it's up to us folks to help smooth them out."

"Gee," Paul says sarcastically, "that's something, Pete. You should make it one of your 'Quotes of the Day.'"

"Get outta here," Peter says bitterly. "Wake up and smell the manure, Parrot. We've gotten soft, and if you let all of these little snowflakes, who want us to live in a gaddamn utopia, continue to run around these streets and destroy the property of hardworkin' folks, we won't have a country anymore. I tell ya just the thought of that piece of shit torching Bucky's Place really chaps my ass. That spoiled rotten fuck. Inbreeds like him telling me what I can or can't say. Like you can't say 'this' or you can't do 'that' cuz you might offend somebody. Last time I checked the First Amendment of the United States Constitution still exists. *And*," he says, his voice growing louder, "by the way, who in the hell are these little shitheads to judge with their purity tests and moral fuckin' authority and all their mommy and daddy issues when these shit-for-brains can't even hold a gaddamn job? You stop one of these morons on the street and they don't have a fuckin' clue what they're talkin' about. You ask 'em to explain what communism is and then grab yourself some fuckin' popcorn."

"Man," Paul says, casual yet, at the same time, entertained by Peter's passion, "these kids are really getting to you, huh? You were young once, weren't you?"

"Yeah," Peter says, "I was young. I did the whole peace, love, and war bullspit until I realized that holding each other's hand and singing Kumba-fuckin'-ya around a campfire ain't gonna pay the gaddamn bills. Hey, you know what these people remind me of?"

Paul shrugs and says while chewing his orange, "You got me."

"A bunch of two-year-olds throwing temper tantrums whenever things don't go their way," Peter says. "Maybe they should start calling their little organization 'The Terrible Twos.' See how far that takes 'em?"

"If you go so far left, you end up all the way on the other side. A full circle, you know?"

"Right," Peter mumbles. "The circle of fuckin' life. It don't take a gaddamn genius to see what they're doing to our country. Think about it, will ya? They're literally becoming the very thing they stand against. First, they want you to conform and build their mob of drones who can't even hold a thought, let alone think for their gaddamn selves. If you don't obey, then they destroy you. Look at what they did over in Europe after World War I. Who's to say they won't do it here?"

"You talkin' about Cancel Culture, aren't you?"

"Fuckin' Cancel Culture," Peter repeats in agreement.

"Last time I checked, though," Paul says, "these so-called socialists ain't killing other people."

"You mean, commies?"

"What did I say?"

"You said 'socialists.'"

"I thought we were talking about socialism."

"Hey, Cheech, how much weed did you smoke last night?"

"What?" Paul says sourly. "You my father now?"

"Listen, Parrot," Peter says. "I don't know what in the hell you smoking, but to say these little shitheads ain't a threat to our democracy then you, my friend, as the kids say these days, are 'out of touch.'"

"Me? Out of touch?" Paul says quietly. "A'ight, McCarthy."

"You serious? What about that one guy who got gunned down during a protest the other day? The guy was minding his own fuckin' business!"

"I mean, sure, Pete, some people are gonna get hurt, even die, when you got a whole bunch of people boiling over with emotion and protesting a whole bunch of different stuff, but you agree, the world is in a better place than it was sixty-some years ago. Pete, I mean, come on. We live in a country where you can say whatever you want without having to worry about waking up in the middle of the night with a black bag thrown over her head and being rushed outta your house into an unmarked van."

"They've already started canceling the movies we watch," Peter says, staying firm in his stance. "Even the *books* we read. Wait till they start burning books."

"Wait a sec," Paul says seriously. "You know how to read?"

"Speaking of comedians, you and your kind are next on the chopping block. Imagine that, will ya? A world where we can't even laugh at ourselves."

"You're one to talk."

"Hey, Parrot," Peter says, the passion holding tightly in his voice. "I ain't no saint, you neither. But I ain't gonna live in no world where I can't even laugh at a joke. I mean, you know that's how it all starts, right? They start changing around things, what we see, what we read, then eventually, they start erasing things. *Peter Peter Pumpkin Eater?*" Peter says, letting out a cross between a hiccup and a sigh. His eyes light up in a eureka-like moment. "Bet you didn't know this, but that nursery rhyme wasn't originally about Peter learning 'how to read' or spell or loving his wife very well. Peter was a murdering son of a bitch before they soften him up. Peter, the Peter I read about before they changed him, he killed his whore of a wife after he caught her sleeping around with other guys, then hid her corpse in a pumpkin. Huh? There's even another version where he threw his wife down a chimney. But still, you get my point."

"What's that?" Paul says, the passion bubbling up. "You rather read the version of Peter being a murderer to some poor kid who's about to go nite-

nite? Talk about giving a kid nightmares. That kid's gonna be so messed up in the head that every time he looks at his old man, he's gonna be thinking: 'So, when's Dada going throw my mommy down a chimney?'"

Peter removes the white hardhat for a moment to comb back his sweaty hair. He places the hardhat back on his head, but this time wears it more loosely.

"My point is, Parrot," Peter says and pulls out a fruit smoothie from a brown bag, "you can't just go around changing things for the sake of changing things in order to cater to what's fashionably acceptable. Okay. Sure," he says, less confrontationally. "You can make things better. I'm all for making things better, but a nursery rhyme, give the fuck outta here. If these know-it-alls don't like it, then they can make up their own fuckin' nursery rhyme. But, no, that'd be too difficult to create something. For these fuck-holes, it's much easier to destroy."

"Man, Pete, you're on a roll today."

Paul places the rest of the corkscrew-shaped orange peel back in the Tupperware and closes the lid.

With his appetite ruined from the latest rant, Peter picks up the fruit smoothie and struggles to open the cap.

"Eating healthier today, are we?"

"At least I'm not the one eating fruit and nuts for lunch, you fuckin' rabbit."

"Sounds like you got ya animals mixed up."

"Why don't you eat some real food?" Paul says. "Look at you. You're nothing but skin and bones."

"Why?" Peter snaps back. "So, I can to make your ass feel better about your weight? Not my fault that you're so damn insecure about your 'weight problem' that you have to tell other people to eat more so they can look as pathetic as you."

"Whatever," Paul says dismissively. "Can't take a man away from his meat."

"You're disgusting, you know that?"

"Hey, I'm only doing this for the wife. It helps balance out the corn beef."

"That's not how it works, you know?"

"Well, it does for me."

"Sure."

"The wife's trying to get me on this special diet. Ever since my blood work came back last week, she's been up my ass about me taking better care of myself. My cholesterol was through the roof. The bad kind, not the good."

"I didn't know there was such thing as good cholesterol."

"Well, look it up on your *Internet* toy," Peter says sarcastically.

"Maybe you should throw your wife down a chimney, huh?"

"Not my Sally," he says softly. "Don't know where I'd be without her."

Once more, he uses more arm strength to twist open the cap. The cap doesn't budge at all.

"Who the fuck they expect to open these things—Superman?" Peter nods at the adjustable wrench on Paul's tool belt. "I got an idea," he says, holding out his hand. "Here. Hand me your wrench."

"And get your greasy fingers all over my shit? Hell no?"

"Come on," Peter pleads. "I left my tools with José."

"That ain't my problem."

"Are you gonna hand me the fuckin' wrench or what?"

"Fine," Paul says and pulls out the wrench from the holster. Right before he hands it to Peter, he playfully recoils, causing Peter to grab air.

"Quit jerkin' off, will ya? You tryin' to kill someone?"

Peter makes it much easier for Paul to hand over the wrench by casually wiping the grease off his palms and fingers with a napkin.

Eventually, Paul hands the wrench to Peter, who uses it to open up the fruit smoothie.

Once he twists open the cap, Peter hands the wrench back to Paul.

"There," he says. "Was that so fuckin' hard?"

"You can be pushy, you know that?"

"Yeah, yeah, yeah." Peter waves off the comment. "So, how's your lunch so far, Rabbit?"

"You know what you need, Pete?"

"What's that?"

". . ."

Fed up with Peter's insults, Paul rotates his hips around until he can see the empty holster along the tool belt. As he insets part of the wrench into the holster, the wrench suddenly slips from his hand!

In a desperate attempt, Paul reaches out his hand, trying to grab the wrench before it falls below. He comes up empty. The wrench hits the side of the scaffold and pinballs around the metal beams before plummeting thirty-seven stories to the ground.

As both Peter and Paul lean over, they both fall witness to what appears to be an accident. On the sidewalk below, a man's laying face first on the ground and a red puddle of what looks like blood forming below his head.

A couple of construction workers, one of who is responsible for keeping pedestrians from the work site, gather around the motionless man.

With his long face slackened and pale-white from the shock, Paul watches a hooded woman hurry over to the lifeless, unresponsive man. She kneels over his body, reaches inside his inner jacket pocket, removes an item—maybe a wallet— and then darts away.

🕐

BELOW, a couple of construction workers rush to Jack, who remains still, lifeless.

Other construction workers are screaming and pointing at Star, who is fleeing from the scene.

In her hand, she's holding a small pouch, *not* a wallet.

🕐

FROM above, Paul watches Star run into an alleyway where she escapes through a manhole.

Peter sits up from the overturned bucket and steps closer to Paul, who is still ghost white. Growing even more concerned by what had just happened, he asks Paul, "Did that girl just take that guy's wallet?"

🕐

KEY and Stat observe a growing crowd, consisted of mostly construction workers and passerbys, circling around Jack's body.

Some of those pedestrians, giddy and gluttonous, all brandishing their phones and anticipating a "viral-worthy" moment in which they're about to capture, rush past Key and Stat.

In a studious manner, Stat carefully watches the people passing by him. His eyes light up with deep thought, as he identifies the very lifeless source that compels each one and them.

"Amazing how things come together in the Eleventh Hour," Key says to Stat, but more so himself.

"What you mean, Key?" asks Stat.

Key continues to watch the crowd, which gets larger by the second. Among the crowd, each spectator is clinging to their phones, either capturing Jack's final moments of life or filming themselves capturing those moments with their own selfie-like shot followed with commentary. Only one person, a young man in his early twenties, shoulders his way through the crowd, rips off his shirt, and tries to stop the massive hemorrhaging. But his attempts appear to be too late. In one last attempt to save Jack, the young man cries out for someone to call "9-1-1!" But all he receives in return are the lens-side of over a dozens smartphones beating down at him, as if he has unwillingly found himself in a horror movie that he so desperately wants to end, and God willing, never see the light of day.

Stat nods at the crowd and asks Key, "What the hell's going on over there?"

Key doesn't respond. Yet, he remains still, observant.

Stat steps next to Key for a closer look.

"Key," he says, "you okay?"

Once more, Key doesn't answer. He watches the people and the smartphone that controls them, as if, in a way, it has become a part of their very fabric, not an extension but, more or less, a replacement, a master to his or her slave.

"Yo, Key," Stat says, leaning into Key's range of vision, "you good?"

Key turns his head toward Stat.

"Couldn't be any better," he says distantly.

He's already *seen* enough.

🕐

As Star climbs down the ladder and enters the sewer system, she takes a moment to find her bearings by scanning both directions of the tunnels, all of which appear to trail off into darkness. She wonders which way will lead her back to what she scathingly calls that "other world." However, Star doesn't put too much decision into which path; yet, she simply follows the strongest stench.

The stench leads her to an intersection of tunnels.

Four dark tunnels wait before her, each one dark and smelly, the air thick and soupy.

Unable to detect the strongest since the stench is everywhere, Star pulls out the small pouch from the hoody pocket. She removes the black crystal from the pouch and holds it in her hand. She breaks down and cries.

While sobbing, a shadow darts along the tunnel wall.

The water splashes behind her, seizing her attention.

Immediately, Star stops crying and remains vigilant.

"Who's there?" asks Star, as she looks down each tunnel.

She stops at one tunnel in particular. In the middle of the tunnel stands an old and raggedy dressed figure, which Star first assumes is a homeless man.

"Hello."

A strange voice rises from the darkness.

"You too, huh?"

The stranger's bony shoulders bob up and down, up and down from what is supposed to be a laugh but comes off like a fiendish snicker, which sounds like a soaked rag being wrung.

Underneath a wall of shadows, the movement reveals an inverted cork-screw-shaped mouth layered with sharp, jagged teeth.

Star immediately recognizes that mouth for she had spent days, even weeks, during her transformation trying to make sense of the mouth while staring, picking, and dissecting it in the mirror.

"Who would've thought?" the gravelly, hissing voice says.

"Who are you?"

"An old friend," the voice says.

To Star, the voice has a certain *click* to it as if there's a certain name attached to it; in fact, she recognizes it, that click, that voice—at least, pieces of his voice.

"Myko?" she says suddenly. "Is that you?"

"I'm afraid Myko's dead," the voice says, as the raggedy-dressed man steps closer into the ray of dim, steam-covered light. "The Myko you once knew. All that remains of him are the memories we share."

"Who are you?" asks Star.

"The real question you should be asking: Who are we?"

"I know who I am," Star says, louder and more ticked off while rejecting the very thing that she has become.

The must, as well as the mugginess, wears on her.

"Who the fuck are you and what do you want?" Star asks, lowering her right gray hand along her waist. Each elongated finger slowly stretches downward and hangs by her side like unwinding spools of rope, revealing these tiny faces similar to her very own face on each fingertip.

"Easy there," he says and points at Star's hand-weapon. "You sure you know how to use that thing?"

"I don't have fucking time for this," Star seethed. "Who are you?"

"I'm Harry," he says.

"What'd you do with Myko?"

Harry holds out his hands.

"*He who wearsss the Crown shall rule the Town.*"

"What the hell does that even mean?"

"Myko was weak, unworthy of the Crown," Harry says. "I can say the same about you, that is before you *crosssed* over, but everybody knows that vamp poison turns you into something you're not."

"You don't have the slightest clue of who I am," Star rebukes.

"Maybe not entirely, but I do know: What doesn't kill woman only makes her stronger. Most of us wouldn't dare brave this world, let alone try to take back the life we once had."

Losing her patience, she asks the parasitic creature formerly known as Myko, "Why are you following me?"

"You haven't changed one bit, Star Walker," Harry says, stepping closer into the light, "well," he corrects teasingly, "despite your new. . . *look*. When are you ever going to learn that the world doesn't revolve around you? Funny, though, us bumping into each other in the bowels which binds us from this world. . . " Harry points at the streets, his beady gray eyes faintly glowing from the streaks of light pouring through a rusty grate along a busy sidewalk above, ". . . to the next. Perhaps it's a sign from the *Catsss*."

Fearful of her safety, Star carefully takes a step back.

"Ever since our last candidate, who couldn't handle the pressure of wearing the Crown," Harry says to a more timid Star, "we've been searching for the One to rightfully wear the Crown and represent our cause."

"Your cause?"

Approaching Star, Harry says, "A New Age of Disinformation is upon us and it's gaining momentum." Between the raggedy and ratty raised collars of his coat, Harry reveals part of his ill-colored face, like Star's, wrinkled and in-human. "For decades, the world has become more sterilized. Now, it has reached an era where it must be ridden of its cleanliness and artificiality. The chemicals, disinfectants, sanitizers, all of it must come to an end once and for all." He steps closer to Star, revealing more parts of his face in the dim light. "The Dirty One who *wearsss the Crown* will bring back order and balance to the natural world. Those who oppose us will be baptized in the Righteous Filth in which they loathe."

"Yeah," Star says slowly. "Good luck with that. Now, if you would excuse me. . . "

Tempting to deviate from her planned route, which is straight through Harry, Star turns toward the tunnel on her right, which appears safe.

Left at a crossroads, Star's choice becomes clearer to her as she hears a series of laughter, higher in pitch and witch-like, coming from the end of the tunnel directly behind her.

Underneath the chorus of haunting sounds, she picks up at least a dozen footsteps splashing through the sludgy water and heading directly her way. The footsteps grow louder and louder to the point where they demand Star's full attention.

Those clownish and witch-like giggles resonant throughout the maze of sewers, creating a siren-effect. She rotates around and finally acknowledges the disturbance. There, at a distance, she witnesses beams of flashlights cutting through the darkness of the tunnel.

"The *Catsss* have spoken," Harry says grandly. "You are the chosen One."

"Cut the shit," Star says, growing more panicked. "What's going on here?"

"From the smell in the air, I detect Cutas."

"Cutas?"

"Part of the CROCUTA Clan. And hungry too, I may say."

"You mean, as in. . . "

Star can barely muster the words from her mouth as if, by speaking them, she will be hexed by one of their spells.

"Yes," Harry says. "*That* CROCUTA Clan."

"I've heard rumors about them."

"And more than likely, they're all true," Harry says, his tone remaining calm. "What your friend, Myko, would call 'fiercer than his ex mother-in-law.' An elite group of heavily-armed mercenaries with only one objective. Sure, they may not sound like much, but these group of gals, when in numbers, are a force to be reckoned with. I can smell at least eight of them, maybe more."

"And what's their objective, these Cutas?"

"Seek and devour, of course."

"Great," Star says, as the sharp laughing sound grows louder and louder. "So can you help me or not?"

"I can hold them off, but you must leave now before it's too late."

Star starts making her way to the tunnel on the right.

"This way," Harry says, pointing toward the other tunnel on the left. "If you follow this tunnel toward the end, you can take drainage pipe and wind up in California in just a few minutes. I know," he says before she has a chance to respond, "not so bad, huh? These tunnels can come in handy."

"I'm not trying to get back to California," Star says. "I'm trying to get back to the other world."

"*That world*, huh? Why didn't you say so?" As though he's in no rush at all considering the possible danger quickly approaching, he steps aside and points at the tunnel directly behind him. "Take this tunnel here to the first intersection," he directs. "Once you reach the intersection, take a right and count twenty steps, no more, no less, until you find a crack on the right side of the wall. It's going to be a tight fit," he looks over Star's slender body, "but you'll fit. We *alwaysss* fits."

"I'm not like you," Star says with indignation.

"Don't be ashamed of what you've become, Star Walker."

Star hears yet another sound, much deeper yet, at the same time, much higher in pitch than the laughing hyenas.

"What's that sound?"

"Just a few friends of mine," Harry says calmly.

To Star's right, she witnesses a growing wave of what looks like thick brown floodwater charging through the tunnel. She peers closer and realizes that it's not a wave but a wall of scurrying rats, each and every one of them moving directly at Star whether it be rolling or toppling over one another, nonetheless, a mad dash to the present danger.

Suddenly, Star hears gunfire coming from the other end of the tunnel, forcing her to stay low.

Bullets buzz over her head and strike the walls around her.

Once she spots the shooter—or multiple shooters—she's left stunned by what she's actually seeing with her own eyes.

In a highly trained, tactical stealth-like manner, the clan of half-woman half-hyena mercs storm through the tunnels. Each one is dressed in dark tactical clothing, bulletproofs vests, heavily armed, assault rifles drawn and aimed directly at Star. Their shoulders are much wider, their posture slightly more hunched over.

In a quick glimpse, Star acknowledges their facial appearance, which appears more animal than woman: their wide eyes are black and sinister, their coarse skin spotted with brownish spots and birthmark-like patterns, their hairdo worn in Mohawk-fashion. The flashlights bring out their manes, creating a disturbing silhouette. The only feature of their face that appears the most human is the mouth and nose region. Instead of a snout, their nose is smaller and slightly darker in color.

Each one is quite vocal too, with their giggles and growls.

Right before Star takes off, she leaves with a snapshot of one image in particular in her mind: a heavily-armed mercenary gawking at her, eyes black, sweat like slime dripping down the sides of her face. Of all the Cutas—eight of them, as Harry indicated—based on the unique patterns along her skin, she appears different than the other Cutas. She has dark stripes, *not* spots.

While the highly dangerous clan closes in, the wall of rats barrels past Harry and acts like a shield against the barrage of gunfire.

Among the chaos unfolding behind her, the Cutas still remain the most vocal by whooping and whining or grunting and groaning; however, the one sound that stands out the most is the giggling.

Star barely manages to escape without getting struck. Harry stands back as if he has an unspoken bond with the rats—in a way, he's like a maestro conducting his great symphony, his rats being his orchestra hitting each note, whether it be an aggressive attack on one mercenary or a sudden formation of a barricade to prevent bullets from striking him. A mischief of at least a hundred rats swarms several mercenaries, nibbling at their paw-like hands and pulling the rifles from their grips and smothering them.

As Harry "holds off" the mercenaries with his backup of rats, Star manages to barely escape from the chaos.

She makes it to the first intersection where she is given three pathways. She does as Harry said and takes a right. She counts out each and every footstep until she reaches the number twenty. There, she locates a crack in the wall. She kneels down and peeks through the narrow opening. "It's tight," as Harry said; however, Star understands that she has no other way out of here.

As Star's about to kneel down, a shadow appears in the corner o her eye. The dim light becomes dimmer.

With the tension building, she hears that familiar laugh next to her. She turns her head upward and finds one of those mercenaries, the one with stripes, bearing down on her.

The mercenary uses the butt of the assault rifle to strike Star in the forehead.

Dazed by the blow, Star is forced to the ground. She struggles to gain control over the mercenary's weapon; however, the hyena-looking woman is stronger and much more aggressive. For her, she doesn't need her clan. She is a hunter, not a scavenger; however, what the mercenary doesn't realize is that Star has a weapon of her own.

As the mercenary overpowers Star for the assault rifle, Star rears back her fist and using all the strength in her body, punches the mercenary directly in her gapping, drooling mouth right before the mercenary open fires. Star's hand—better yet, most of her arm—rams down the mercenary's throat, causing her to choke.

Squealing and, at the same time, laughing, the mercenary pulls the trigger but wildly misses her target. A string of gunfire runs across the tunnel ceiling above in an oscillated sprinkler-like motion.

With her snake-like fingers crawling deeper down the mercenary's throat, the mercenary drops to one knee. Hundreds of those pervasive snake worms are visible underneath the mercenary's skin, slithering around her brain, strangling vital organs, clotting certain vessels.

Once the mercenary flops over dead, Star retracts her hand from the mercenary's throat. Her hand and forearm covered with salvia and chunks of vomit.

"Yuck," Star says, wiping her hand along the hoody.

She directs her attention back to the narrow opening in the wall.

Now, where were we?

☉

STAT glances down at a manhole in the parking lot and can *feel* the tension rising from below.

Key nods at Stat and tells him to wait a minute while he handles some business inside the dilapidated, decaying structure tagged with graffiti and gang signs, which was once a pump house before it was abandoned in the early 1960's. Over the years, kids have branded the building "Stickman," due to the shape of massive steel beams constructed along the rusty pipes that crisscross the interior walls. If you stand at a certain angle, the beams look just like a stickman.

While Stat waits outside, Key enters the pump house. The floors caked with mounds of dust and leftover bits of coal and old gutted out cars, which was said to be the remnants of a chop shop that was once in operation years after Stickman's House was abandoned.

As Key stands before the Stickman, five of the surviving Cutas of the CROCUTA Clan emerge from the shadows.

"Where's the rest of the group?" asks Key.

Heloisa steps forward and assumes her role as the alpha of the Clan. Among the Cutas, Heloisa's injuries are minimal. She has a couple of cuts and bruises on her face and arms, unlike the other four Cutas whose injuries vary from torn, nibbled off flesh to severed fingers, even arms, to deep, war-like wounds. Each one limping or clutching their injuries.

"We were outnumbered, sir," Heloisa reports. "She knew we were following her."

"You tellin' me she was responsible for the way you look?"

"She wasn't alone," Heloisa says, struggling to look Key in the eyes. "She had help."

Key surveys the other four Cutas behind Heloisa.

"Where's Taytu?"

Knowing how close Key was to Taytu, Eshe, who is considered the mouthy one of the Clan, answers timidly, "She didn't make it. It was the girl. She is responsible for Taytu's death."

"The girl is responsible," Key says, as a heavily concealed anger floods over him. "Right."

Key asks for Heloisa's assault rifle. Willingly, she hands it over. Key looks over the weapon.

"Did I ever tell you how I earned the name, M16?" asks Key.

Heloisa responds with a shake of her head.

"The year was 1984," Key says, "just two years before I rescued Taytu from those savage witch lords in Addis Ababa. Peak of summer," he says, as he paces around Heloisa. "The heat has a way of bringing out the best in people—and the worst. One hot afternoon, these two cats wearing whiteface stormed into a small Mom and Pop shop on the street corner and robbed them blind. They took all the money from the cash registers. Both armed. Both desperate. The two didn't stop with the registers, though. You see the Pop in 'Mom and Pop' goes by the name, Clint. Clint keeps his life savings inside a safe in the back of the store. The obvious question is 'So how'd these cats know about a safe to begin with?'" Key asks but doesn't expect Heloisa to answer. "Well, one of the cats happens to be Clint's nephew, Bobo. I couldn't recognize Bobo's face because of the white paint on his face; but anybody who knew Bobo, knew that nervous tick he made in the corner of his face. He lived on my street, but I never spoke to him. I didn't particularly care much for Bobo's gang and their so-called 'mission.' Two days later, police busted them based on an anonymous tip they received. So, initially, I was the first person on their radar. Me, and of course, Uncle Clinton. I didn't give a shit about the crimes those two fools committed. But I knew they had already made up their minds. First, it was Mom and Pop who caught a bullet—the thing about the bullet is that the bullet has a way of bringing out the truth in any man. Turns out Uncle Clinton would do about anything to save his own skin, even if it meant making up some bullshit about the snitch who he made me out to be. On the next night after they came for Mom and Pop, Bobo's boys waited till I left work and followed me back home. Before I had a chance to turn to the car creeping up behind me, it was already done. They turned my ass into Swiss cheese. Bullets bounced around my insides like pinballs. Over the years I've been hit countless times before. I mean, after all, how many battles have we fought?"

"Too many," Heloisa responds, her head lowered in a dog-like shame.

"Never knew that I'd be named after the very thing that almost destroyed me. After awhile, the name sort of grew on me."

Key walks up to Eshe, who's clutching her side, and without hesitation, aims the M16 assault rifle at Eshe's lower half and pulls the trigger. Holding the rifle with only one hand, the recoil causes Key's arm to swing upward, bullets plugging Eshe's body from her lower abdomen and up.

After Key finishes off Eshe, he hands the rifle back to Heloisa. He turns his sinister gaze toward the others, Makda, Jazarah, and finally, Nuru, who is missing part of her arm.

"Find her and bring her to me," Key says to Heloisa and then emphasizes, "I want her *alive*. You understand?"

"Yes, sir," Heloisa says and as she's about to exit Stickman's House, glances at Eshe's dead body with a sense of melancholy in her black eyes.

"THE CURIOUS CASE OF BIFF CRALEY"

"YOU guys ever seen that one movie where he played a bank robber?" asks one of the head surgeons, Doctor Harcourt, who makes another deep incision through a second layer of tissue along the side of the patient's lower left abdominal area.

"*Stolen Heart*?" one of the nurses says.

Doctor Harcourt pauses mid-slice, looks up through the oversized spectacles.

Unsure of the name, he asks, "Was that the name of it?"

"Pretty sure," the nurse says in a monotone voice.

"I swear I thought it was something else, like, I dunno, forget it—" Doctor Harcourt says from the corner of his mouth, shakes off the thought, and proceeds to cut, "—move the light two inches to the right, will you?"

Another nurse moves the overhead light, as directed, two inches to the right, revealing what looks like an ear protruding from the bloody cavity.

"Thank you kindly, Teresha," Doctor Harcourt says and continues to cut until the full head of a man is revealed underneath all that flesh and bone. With a tube, the nurse, Teresha, cleans and sucks out the blood from the cavity, revealing more the side of a face, Biff's face. "Anyway, Karen and I didn't have anything going on last Saturday night so we decided to do a little dinner and a movie. We hadn't done one in quite some time, especially with the kids trying out these new virtual classes. I remember our last dinner and a movie Karen cooked while I picked out the movie, which was one of those shoot-'em up movies—*Maneater*. Seen it?"

The nurse's cheeks lift underneath the mask. "Nia forced me to watch it last week. It was. . . " she shrugs her left shoulder, ". . . meh."

"Just meh?" The nurse doesn't respond to Doctor Harcourt. "Who doesn't like watching a strong female protagonist take the law into her own hands?"

"Apparently, Teresha doesn't."

"I'm more of a rom-com type of gal."

"Well, anyway. . . " Doctor Harcourt says and hands off the bloody scalpel to the nurse while he adjusts a massive retractor system over the patient's morbidly obese body, ". . . this time I was in charge of the cooking while Karen picked out the movie."

"What'd you make?" asks one nurse from behind.

"Filet mignons sautéed in butter, two baked Russet potatoes, and then, a side of asparagus topped with Parmesan cheese, all local, of course. For dessert, Karen and I shared a slice of cheesecake dusted with flakes of white chocolate and drizzled with a raspberry sauce, which was to die for. I tell you it was the highlight of the night."

"Stop it, Richard," the nurse says, "you're making me hungry."

Doctor Harcourt inserted the retractor along the sides of the opening.

"So, I take it you didn't care much for *Stolen Heart*?"

"To tell the truth," he says, "no. Not really." He looks down at the covered patient on the operation table. "Sorry to break the news to you, Biff, buddy, but you should stick to the old Westerns."

"Really?" Teresha says. "I actually thought his acting improved when he left spaghetti Westerns."

"You sound just like Karen," the doctor says and maneuvers the bloody head from the opening in the patient's body. "If I didn't know any better, I'd say Karen has a crush on Biff here."

"Fun fact," one of the other nurses says from the darkness of the room, "you know Biff's not even his real name. It's his stage name."

"Huh? I didn't know that."

"Want to know his real name?"

"Absolutely—"

"—Sparrow Watcher."

"Sparrow, huh?"

Doctor Harcourt laughs following a string of nurse laughter. He jokes, "I can see why he changed his name to a manly name like," he quotes with the flicker of his brow, "'Biff Craley.'"

"Another fun fact: Craley is the name of the town he was born in."

"Well, *I did not know that*," Doctor Harcourt says teasingly in his worst attempt at a Johnny Caron impersonation. "Okay," he finds a grip around the sides of the head, "I think our new friend here is ready to enter the world."

Another nurse steps into the dark operation room and says from the doorway, "Narcissus has arrived, Doctor Harcourt."

"Great," he says, struggling to wiggle free the head, "tell him I'm in the middle of an extraction and I'll be with him shortly."

"Yes, sir," the nurse says, exiting the room.

As Doctor Harcourt pulls the body from the vessel, two other nurses step in and give him a hand.

"On the count of three, I'm going to ease the specimen down on the other table," he says, gently removing the so-called "specimen."

The team eases the bloody naked body onto a smaller table while the pulse of the other body, the obese one covered in a greenish blue sheet, begins to fade.

"Okay," Doctor Harcourt says to the nurse. "Finish him."

The nurse injects the "finish-all" drug into the IV, causing an immediate flatline.

The doctor snaps the face of a newly born Biff.

The newest version of Biff slowly cracks open his eyes.

Doctor Harcourt removes the surgical mask from his face and says kindly to him, "Welcome back."

○

AFTER scrubbing down, Doctor Harcourt meets Narcissus in a waiting room outside the operation room.

"Narcissus," he says professionally and shakes Narcissus's hand.

"Richard," Narcissus says.

"How's Mickey?"

"Busy."

"I bet," Doctor Harcourt says.

"How are the elephants doing?"

"As a matter of fact," the doctor says, "they couldn't be better."

"And the vaccine," Narcissus says. "How's it coming along?"

"Well, we've just finished the first test on the rats and already started the next trial," Doctor Harcourt says. "We won't know much until results come back. But so far, knock on wood. . . " he says and searches for a piece of wood to knock on, finds a coffee table, *knocks* on it, ". . . everything's going according to plan."

"Key will be pleased to know."

"So, what's Mickey up to these days? Still trying to take over the world?"

"He's preparing a trip to Heaven where he's going to wrap up some last minute business. Tie up loose ends."

Carrying a small portable ice cooler, the nurse enters the waiting room.

"The package, sir," she says and hands the cooler to Doctor Harcourt, who, in return, thanks the nurse, Melissa, and hands the cooler to Narcissus.

Narcissus opens the cooler and grabs the bag of two recently severed eyeballs sitting on a couple of ice packs.

"I assume these are the right ones."

"As Mickey requested."

Narcissus closes the cooler.

Doctor Harcourt holds out his hand.

"While you're here, would you like to take a quick tour of the complex? I'd like to show you around the housing units. We have a new—"

"—Can't," Narcissus interrupts. "Gotta long drive ahead of me."

Even though Doctor Harcourt realizes Narcissus can't see his expression, yet he only senses it mainly with his ears and nose, which are rumored to be stronger than both a bloodhound and wax moth combined—in fact, rumor has it that these two senses are so strong they're able to sense the dead—he smiles anyway and in a friendly manner, gives Narcissus a gentle touch on the shoulder. Finally, the doctor says to Narcissus, "Some other time, then."

○

DRIVING in a white unmarked van along a narrow two-lane road, Teresha makes her way through the pitch-black desert until she finally reaches the hazy, unnatural lights radiating from the Red Rocks along the outskirts of Sedona, Arizona.

Passing through mountainscapes, she drives down a rugged valley that opens up to even more desert. The source of light comes from the main headquarters of Neuvak Corporation, the entire property covering roughly seven thousand acres.

Once she reaches the massive state-of-the-art complex, she stops at the first security post where she's greeted by a security guard named Elliot.

"Back again, are we?" says Elliot.

"I forgot a couple of my belongings."

"If you want, I can have one of the guys bring them to you."

"That won't be necessary," she says. "I promise I'll be in and out."

Instead of using the implant, Teresha swipes her keycard along the scanner.

Once Elliot authorizes Teresha to enter, he nods at yet another security guard who is camped inside the station. The guard hits a red button, which opens up the heavy steel gate.

"Have a good night, Ms. Dolby," Elliot says, nodding goodbye.

Upon entry, Teresha arrives at yet another security post where another security guard opens another much smaller gate without any question. Teresha drives through the town-like complex with numerous buildings until she reaches a parallelogram-shaped building numbered "36." She parks the van behind the building where yet another security guard, younger and scrawnier looking, named Bautista, exits from the backdoor.

"About time," he says, surveying the back lot in paranoia.

Teresha exits from the van and opens the backdoor while Bautista disappears inside for a moment and reappears with a bagged body tied to a wheeled stretcher.

Trying not to tear or rip the bag by hitting the sides of the doorway, Bautista struggles to wheel the corpse to the back of the white van and with Teresha's assistance, slides it off the stretcher and places it inside with a loud grunt.

Teresha unzips the bag and peeks inside. Among the pile of flesh stuffed inside the bag, she locates Biff Craley's head. She immediately notices that both of the eyes are missing.

"What happened here?" asks Teresha, nodding at the hollowed out eye sockets.

"The hell if I know," Bautista says. "I did my part. Now, it's time for you to live up to your end of the deal."

"Very well," Teresha says, zipping up the bag.

She closes the doors behind her.

Nodding to the front of the van, she first removes and loosens the tucked shirt from the waistband, then unbuttons the top button of the shirt.

"Let's make this quick," she says, walking toward the driver's side.

Teresha opens the door and steps inside.

Licking his lips, Bautista follows suit and walks to the passenger side.

✧

AFTER Teresha drives off with Biff's corpse, Bautista casually makes his way into Building "36" and stops at the men's restroom to take a piss before heading back to the surveillance room. Once finished, he stops by the sink to, not only wash his hands, but also wash other areas of his body. Using a paper towel, he vigorously washes his genitals, making sure to scrub away every inch of Teresha.

Afterwards, he returns to the surveillance room.

While skimming the monitors, another security guard, Harrison, glances over his shoulder at Bautista, who, strangely, develops a cough after returning from the restroom.

"Nice work, *Don Juan*?" Harrison asks, kicks up both legs, crosses them, and rests the backside of his heels against the edge of the table. "You finally get that bug outta your system?"

"Shut up," Bautista says, fighting off the sudden cough.

"Hey," Harrison says, "I know how long you've being trying to hit that. I'm surprised you're not doing flips right now."

"Whatever," Bautista says, powering through the words. "Least," cough, "I can," cough, "get," cough, "some action, unlike you," cough, "miserable prick."

"I got ninety-nine problems and hooking up with a coworker ain't one."

Bautista coughs more, his face reddening, veins in his forehead swelling.

"You okay over there, Don Juan?" asks Harrison.

Annoyed by Harrison, Bautista waves off the security guard.

"Good," he says, gaining control over the cough.

✧

NARCISSUS parks the car in front of Forest City Penitentiary, a maximum-security prison located in North Ridge, California.

He pulls out the small case tucked away in a breast pocket and carefully removes the contact lens with his index finger. He tilts back his head and with his other hand, pries open his left eye and inserts the first contact lens. Following the same method, Narcissus inserts the other contact lens into the other eye. Once the contacts are in, he blinks both of his brown eyes, as if, by doing so, he's straightening the lens. The last thing he'd want to do is walk in there with one eye looking one way and another eye looking the other way, like a wall-eye, and having the guards guessing, even asking unnecessary questions.

Adjusting to the contacts, he reaches over the center console, grabs the cooler from the passenger seat, and cracks it open, revealing that bag of eye-balls resting on several ice packs.

✧

STROLLING along Cell-Block 6, a prison guard named Ray stops at one particular cell and slips a pack of *Gypsy Wides* through the food slot.

Ray leans down next to the opening and says, "It looks like you got yourself a secret admirer, Pretty Boy."

Sitting behind a desk along the cell wall, Drenelle, who's sketching an outfit with a shrapnel of graphite, glances over the purple-framed reading glasses at that wider than usual cigarette pack lying on the floor.

"You know I don't smoke," she says sassily at Ray.

"Sure," Ray says shortly, closes the slot, and walks away.

Drenelle drops the graphite along the messy desk, which is covered in various sketches of outfits and new clothing designs, and runs her hands over her shaved head.

With a sigh, Drenelle slides the chair out from under the desk, stands up from the seat, walks over to the door, and picks up the pack of cigarettes. Immediately, she notices two slight bulges along the surface of the pack, as well as the weight, which seems inconsistent. She takes the pack back to her desk and while bracing herself, cracks it open. On the underside of the lid are a couple of streaks of dark blood. Carefully, she pulls out the two eyeballs from inside the cigarette pack and sets them along the edge of the desk.

FIGHTING against strong gusts of wind created by the rotary blades, Ruby stands firmly at a safe distance as the helicopter descends onto the helipad, which sits on top of one of the tallest buildings in Downtown Los Angeles.

After the helicopter sticks the landing, Key, who's sporting a white suit, exits from the cabin and meets up Ruby.

"Any word from Narcissus?" Key asks over the sound of the helicopter behind him.

Holding the hair from her face, Ruby leans in closer and says, "I'm sorry."

"Narcissus," Key says, louder. "Any word?"

"Not yet, sir," Ruby says, as she escorts Key to the seventy-third floor where, along the side of the entranceway, those letters of the logo "U.S. BANK," which were once displayed on the crown of the tower, remain stacked against the wall.

"Something's not right," Key says, passing the famous logo. "He should've called by now."

Another item catches his eye.

Perched next to the logo are two large cardboard boxes, which have recently been delivered to the building formerly known as U.S. Bank Tower.

Key cracks open both boxes, first starting with one box. He digs through the popcorn padding until he reaches the massive letter "M," which will replace the former logo on the crown of the tower. He checks the other box and discovers the other letter, "W," buried underneath all that Styrofoam popcorn.

"I was meaning to tell you," Ruby says, walking ahead, "the new logo came in."

"Looks nice," Key says, leans down, and runs his hand along the giant letter "W."

"Also," Ruby says, recalling the recent phone call with the copyright holders of the movie franchise, *The Effigy*, as she makes her way to the bar. "We also secured the rights to *The Effigy*."

"Good," Key says plainly and leaves the sign. He walks into the penthouse-like room overlooking Downtown Los Angeles while Ruby waits by the bar and does some last second primping, as well as adjusting her black blazer and matching skirt.

Her phone rings. She checks the number.

"Speak of the devil," she says.

"Is it him?" asks Key, as he removes the white well-tailored sports coat and tosses it on the back of a sofa.

"Unknown number," she says. "Must be."

"Answer it."

Ruby does.

Turns out Ruby is right.

"Narcissus," she says, walks over to Key, and hands him the phone.

"Give me good news, Narcissus."

"She'll do it," Narcissus says. "It took a little convincing, but she's in."

"How was she?"

"Well, she's making the best of her time. She mainly focuses on her work. It keeps her sane. Every now and then, the guards give her a hard time. She won't have to worry about them anymore. Other than that, I believe she's ready."

"Good," Key says. "Well done, Narcissus. I'll see you soon."

Key hangs up and hands the phone back to Ruby.

"So, it's on?" Ruby says, her voice dragging out like a question.

"It's on," Key says and walks to the window overlooking the downtown. "I would like you to be there, Ruby."

"Sure," she says plainly.

As Key gazes at the city before, he says to Ruby, "I bet you didn't get views like this when you were prancing around New York."

"I can't say I did."

An awkward silence forms between the two.

Ruby does what she does best and kills the silence with questions.

"So, how was your business trip?" asks Ruby.

"Terrible as always," Key says with disdain. "Never seen so many repulsive creatures throughout my entire existence. Those gluttonous fools call themselves the High Order, yet there's absolutely nothing 'high' about them. If they were so goddamn enlightened, they would possess the intuition to see what's coming their way." More disgusted by the recent business trip to Heaven, he shakes his head. "Not like anything I have to say to those gassy blowhards would make any difference. Their days are numbered," he trails off and moves his attention toward the exterior structure of the building. "You know what they used to call this building?"

"No, sir," Ruby says.

"The Library Tower."

"Why'd they call it that?"

"Never thought you ask." Key turns his deep study from the structure to the fading sun along the hazy horizon. "Before this property was leased back in 2003 to U.S. Bancorp, whose parent company happens to be U.S. Bank, the tower was originally constructed following the two fires at the nearby library in 1986 as part of a one billion dollar Los Angeles Central Library redevelopment area. The City of Los Angeles ended up selling air rights to the project's developers to pay for the reconstruction of the library, hence naming the tower the Library Tower."

"I learn something new from you everyday," Ruby says, standing anxiously next to the bar.

"I know sometimes you feel like you might've made a mistake leaving your cozy job working at that failing magazine to work for someone whom you know very little about," Key says, facing Ruby. "Not to come off as. . ." Key pauses, searching for the right word, ". . . What's the word? Right. *Pretentious.* I assure you, Ruby, that what I'm doing here will change the world forever."

Ruby's cheeks fill with red. She shakes her head.

"You don't have to stress importance of what you're doing, Mickey. Otherwise, I would've never accepted the job."

"Right," Key says, grinning. "Of course."

Key walks closer to Ruby, who, in return, becomes more fidgety by his presence.

"But *still*, you have doubts, as you should. You must realize that you have a role here, Ruby. And it's not just assisting me. You play an intricate part in shaping how the story plays out."

"Yes," Ruby says, finding the strength within to display confidence. "And I want to thank you for the opportunity."

"It's normal to feel uneasy, Ruby," Key says, standing before Ruby. "After all, it's not everyday you get to work for a god."

Despite the unusually "big" magic trick he pulled the other day with making a real-life dragon appear slumped over directly the iconic *Hollywood* sign situated on Mount Lee in the Hollywood Hills of the Santa Monica Mountains, she nearly loses it from what she perceives as his male ego. Sure, he's good at getting inside people's heads. But an actual god is stretching it, Ruby tells herself.

Maintaining her best straight face, Ruby says sharply, "Right."

Her eyes trail downward, head following, which causes a rogue bang of hair to loosen from the ponytail and fall alongside her face.

Key uses his fingers to curl the bang of hair around her ear, securing the hair in place.

"Thanks," she says, as she remains unflustered by Key's closeness.

"Say," Key says, drifting off in mild reflection, "did I ever tell you the story behind the High Five?"

"No, sir," Ruby says, shaking her head. "You didn't."

"Except for the name, which, as I speak, is still a work-in-progress—"

"—Yes," Ruby interrupts, "well, according to the latest update on the roster, they came up with a new name for the show."

"Really?"

"Want to hear it?"

"Absolutely."

"The. . . " Ruby stops for a moment to compose herself.

"The?"

"The Fuck-It-All Five, sir."

A thick, tense silence forms between the two.

Surprisingly, Key laughs, his booming laughter cutting through the silence.

"The Fuck-It-All Five," he repeats, trailing off with laughter and disbelief. "I like the name. I do. *But* I'm afraid they're going to have to come up with something else."

More relieved by Key's amusement in the new name, Ruby says in good spirits, "You should've heard the other two names the girls were work-shopping before they landed on Fuck-It-All Five."

"I'm listening."

"Five Spice was the first one," Ruby lists, pauses, and thinks about the second one.

Unimpressed, Key makes a face.

"And what was the other one?" Ruby asks herself; however, she doesn't have to think too hard about the name. "Right," she says. "Fist Fuck Five."

"Blunt yet, strangely, catchy," Key says with a grin on his face, "maybe too on the nose, though. Those girls know we can't use the word *fuck* on cable TV. I know, right? We can televise a werewolf snake tearing apart a pig, yet we can't even use the word *fuck*. It's too bad we couldn't cut a deal with HBO. But, then again, not everybody has HBO."

"That's what I told them, sir."

"Don't worry. I'll handle it. Now, where was I?" He stops Ruby before she has a chance to answer, "Right." His face lights up as he repeats the name, "The Fuck-It-All Five!"

"THE ACT"
(THE WITCHING HOURS)

PAST the firelight, a tall, lanky silhouette appears along the dark, reddish horizon, following the dribbling sound of jagged pebbles rolling down the mountainside.

"I told you so," a voice says from the darkness outside the fire.

A cloaked figure returns to a circular platform right below the steep summit of Dark Mountain where the other four members of the group formerly known as the "High Five" gather around a small fire inside a rock pit.

All five of them are dressed in matching costumes: a frayed, oversized cardinal red cloak that stretches to the ground. The hoods help keep their faces lost in the shadows. Except for those trademark personalities (which haven't changed one bit!), it's hard to distinguish who is who based on the similarities in their appearance; however, one of the members of the group, who was once known in another life as Rhonda Abbott—or as her "kids" referred to her as simply "Ms. Abbott"— stands slightly hunched over.

"Told you she'd say 'I told you so,'" Carmen says to Rhonda.

Fay approaches the fire pit and takes her position next to Star, who has stayed relatively quiet ever since her return from the Big Apple.

"They want us to change the name," Fay says boringly.

Carmen says in an uproar, "You're kidding me?"

Fay sighs.

"I shit you not."

"After we spent what felt like years trying to come up with the perfect name."

"FYI, Carmen," Rhonda says, "two years, to be precise. It took us two years to come up with that name."

"Two years?" Fay says questionably. "You mean two months."

"No," Rhonda says, more steadily. "Two years."

"How you know? Have you been crossing over without telling us?"

"Fay, I know it's difficult to get used to, but you must come to terms with the change in time—"

With a stern, almost dark, composure, Mandy says over Rhonda, "—So back to the drawing board."

"We're cutting it kind of close, don't you think? I'd say we go with our second choice."

"What? Five-O?"

"No," Fay says. "Five Spice."

"Seriously?"

"What's wrong with Five Spice?"

"It's super lame. That's what. Can you imagine having to explain what the five spices are in an interview? You didn't think we could name ourselves Five Spice without identifying ourselves as five different spices, did you?"

"Well, it's more collective, you know, like a blend of spices—"

"—More like tribal. We are still individuals, aren't we?"

"I got dibs on Cayenne Pepper," Fay says abruptly. Then tosses in a joke on the side, "Cuz you know I'm come with a little kick. "

"Is Cayenne Pepper even considered a spice? It's grounded from dried chili peppers."

"I know it's grounded from dried chili peppers. But thanks for informing me, Ms. Abbott." Fay mocks Rhonda using a whiny voice, "I'm so sorry for not being a good girl and not raising my hand. Please! Oh please don't punish me!"

"How about ginger?" Mandy says to Fay. "You do come off as some-what—you know—*gingery*."

Fay looks around the circle.

"Is she calling me what I think she is?"

"Face it, Fay. You have turned into a klutz every since, you know. . . "

"Don't even go there, Carmen."

"Oh! I went there."

"Watch it, Carmen. I'm warning you—"

"—Would you two chill the fuck out," Star says over the two, the sudden interruption bringing about a wave of silence and stares.

"What's up with you, Dark Star?" asks Carmen.

"Obviously, nobody is satisfied with Five Spice. That's why it was our second choice. So, let's just come up with another name. It can't be that hard."

"I'm totally fine with that," Mandy says.

"So, what? I can't be Cayenne Pepper."

"You can still be Cayenne Pepper, Fay," Star says, lifting Fay's crushed spirits, "but we're not using the name Five Spice. Period."

"So, Fuck-It-All is too offensive. So, what then?"

"Ruby said that it wasn't exactly offensive. She just said we couldn't use the word *fuck*."

"Can anybody remember any of the other names we had?" asks Mandy.

"Well," Fay lists, "there was Five Hole, Five Fingers, Top Five—which was, personally, my favorite. Five Below—"

"—Five Below has a ring to it, don't you think?"

"Yeah, I get the whole double entendre. Five Below actually means the five of us below the ground. But face it. Most people are going to associate that name with temperature. So what? Are we going to show up on stage wearing fur coats, toboggans, and snow boots?"

"And have PETA come up with their own campaign in order to cancel us because we're wearing fur? No thank you."

"Any publicity, good or bad, is the best publicity."

"We can always wear faux fur—"

"—That's not the point. Five Below goes to the Slush Pile."

"Not the Slush Pile," Fay whines.

"Bye-bye Five Below."

"I wish we still had High Five. High Five was us. That was our thang, was it not?"

"The name's already been taken, Fay."

"We should sue that nerdy piece of shit for taking our name."

"Technically, he used it before us—well, publicly that is."

"Yeah, but we've been using that name for years."

"I know we have—and yes, High Five was who we were until somebody else used it—but if we use it on the show, then it'll look like we stole it."

"I heard a saying once," Fay says, thinking, "not sure where I heard it, but it went something like this: 'A good artist borrows. A great artist steals.' Or something like that."

"I think it was a good artist replicates, not borrows."

"You sure?"

"I'm pretty sure."

"I got it!" Carmen blurts out. "How about Five Stars?"

"I like it," Rhonda says, nodding. "Or, how about Five Star Review?"

"Five Star Review," Star repeats. "I don't know about that."

"What? Come on! Five-Star Review. Get it? When you review a meal or a book or movie or whatever, you rate it from one star to five stars. There are five of us. Five stars. Get it?"

"Yeah," Star says, her voice drawn out. "We get it. But, Carmen, just think about what doors we're opening with that name. Critics are going to use the name as their own pun."

"Star's right," Fay says. "If we have a bad showing, then we're basically giving people the opportunity to ridicule the name or use it toward their advantage."

"People—critics especially—are always going to take advantage of a name or idea in whatever they're reviewing."

"Five-Star Review is a little *too* confident, don't you think?"

"Fine," Carmen says. "You're the creative one here, Fay. Let's hear it."

"How about we drop the adjectives, cut all the bullshit, and just simply name ourselves The Five?"

"Lame!" Rhonda says after Fay. "Not only lame, but also *super*-lame."

"Really," Carmen says. "Come on, Fay. You disappoint me. The Five? The Five-What? The Five Parasite-Looking Bitches Whose Sole Act Involves French-Kissing Some Poor Schmuck. . . " Carmen rotates around and points to the "poor schmuck," who happens to be a frail naked man lying on the ground with his right ankle chained to an oblong-shaped boulder and a gag tied to his mouth, ". . . Who, Eventually, Will Turn Into Some Parasite-Looking Bitch? Or, should we be a little more concise?"

"How about The Scaly Five?" Mandy suggests while peeling a piece of dead gray skin from the side of her cheek.

"Being a giant snake worm has its advantages like smelling things from miles away or being able to squeeze into tight places. It reminds me of the time I was a girl crawling my way through tight spaces, like under the bed or inside a closet or inside this cubbyhole underneath the staircase. It was probably the one cool thing about being a kid, crawling into places that most adults couldn't."

"Well, now you can, Fay?"

"Yeah," Mandy says over Carmen, "but its disadvantages do outweigh its advantages, like dry, scaly skin."

Mandy flicks away the piece of skin.

"Does your skin ever get dry and scaly?" Fay asks Star.

"Yes," she says. "At times. Why wouldn't it?"

"Well, you know, black don't crack."

"If I may, let me ask you a question, Fay."

"Be my guest."

"Do I look black to you?"

Fay looks around at the others until, finally, she rests her beady black eyes on Star.

"No, but you were—"

"—I was, but not anymore. *Clearly*." Star composes herself. "It looks like I'm no different than you now, Fay, only a little less two-dimensional and a little less racist."

"Damn," Many utters. "She said the r-word."

"Ouchhh," Carmen hisses, as if she's slowly rubbing in the diss like salt to an open wound.

"Does that offend you, Fay? That we're now the same color? You, no longer 'white' and me, no longer 'black.' Or, hold up. Didn't you describe yourself as 'light orange,' was it?"

"Oatmeal-brown, to be exact."

"Right," Star says sarcastically. "Oatmeal-brown. How did I forget?"

The other three, Carmen, Rhonda, and Mandy, burst out laughing at both Star and Fay picking at each other's former skin tone.

"Are you through, Star?" asks Fay.

"How would you describe this tone?" asks Star, as she holds up her hand.

"Looks like gray to me," Carmen says before Fay can answer.

"Well, technically, it's cerulean frost."

"Cerulean frost? Get outta here!"

"I dunno, Fay," Mandy says, studying yet another dried flake of skin between her flat, wrinkled fingertips. "Looks more like manatee gray."

This time, all five, including Fay, laugh.

"But seriously, guys—

"—Where we go again."

"What?"

"You offended the pronoun police."

"You know we're not allowed to use the word *guys* anymore."

"Says who?"

"Says, you know, them."

"Them who, Fay?"

"Now, what's wrong with the word *guys*?" asks Rhonda, as Fay thinks more about who these mysterious "them" are. "I've been using 'guys' for years. None of my students had a problem with it back then. So, what gives?"

"It's sexist."

"Sexist? How is it sexist when the plural word 'guys' refers to either male or female? What are they going to complain about next: the word *human*? Does the 'man' part in human offend them? Or, how about *mankind*?"

"Well, Rhonda, take a good look in the mirror," Mandy says grimly. "I don't think this argument involves us?"

"Whatever," Rhonda mutters. "Let's just start referring to ourselves as letters in the alphabet in order to identify our sexual orientation."

"Pop quiz, Rhon-Rhon," Fay says, "but you're, like, I dunno, two generations late to the party."

Rhonda shoots a glance at Fay and says with a patronizing tone, "No offense, darling. But this is how it all starts. People get offended by words we use, even if it's as innocent and trivial as the word 'guys,' which inevitably leads to those who we vote into power to ban certain words; then, those who use these certain words will be severely punished. What's even worse is when they 'soften' the words for our ever-so precious children, who need to be coddled and told that everything is going to be okay. They've been doing this shit for years; and then, when banning words isn't good enough, because nothing ever is, what do you know? They start eradicating speech altogether—"

"—Are you through, Rhonda?"

"You haven't changed one bit, *Ms.* Abbott," Fay says, emphasizing the "Ms." in Ms. Abbott. "As one of those letters you were referring to, I take great offense toward your blatant insensitivity—"

"—First of all, Rhonda is clearly upset and doesn't mean what she's saying," Carmen says over Fay and aims those menacing black eyes at Rhonda. "And secondly, when's the last time you looked underneath your cloak?"

"You're right, but still," Fay says sadly, "words do hurt. Not all the time, but sometimes."

"Sorry, Fay," Rhonda says, more sincerely.

With her head lowered in the long shadows of the hood, Fay struggles to look at Rhonda.

"As I was saying before you two interrupted me," Carmen says, as she rotates around and points to the gagged man chained to the boulder, "we have our debut coming up. We have *no* name. No only that, not a single one of us has mastered, you know, 'that,' whatever you want to call it."

The rest of the group waits in an awkward and rather uncomfortable silence.

Finally, Mandy is first to speak.

"Star has," she says bluntly.

Star chimes in, "Star has what?"

"You know. . . "

"No," Star says over Mandy, "I don't know, Mandy. You're going to have to be more specific."

"I thought you knew how to *do* 'that.'"

Star doesn't reply, not at first. Instead, she contemplates her next response.

"Is Mandy telling the truth, Star?" asks Carmen.

"Of course, I'm telling the truth. I've seen her do *that*."

"Oh yeah," Star retorts. "When?"

Mandy says to the others, "I followed her into Leatherwood. She was doing 'that' to some bar fly—*literally!*—a six-foot tall walking-talking horse fly dressed in a trench coat. She followed the fly from the zombie bar and grabbed him in the alleyway."

"How'd you know it was a male?" asks Rhonda.

"What?"

"You said 'him.'"

"Him, her, it," Mandy rants, "whatever it was Star did the thing on the fly and it worked. Not too long after Star walked out of the alley, I saw that fly crawling behind her. Its coat was frayed and tattered. Part of its wing was missing. It was no longer a fly."

To say that Star isn't relieved by Mandy's statement is an understatement.

"Mandy's right," Star says, holding her head downward. "I know how to do it."

"You do?"

"Yeah," she says. "I do."

"Why didn't you tell us?"

"I wanted you guys to figure it out on your own."

"You said 'guys.'"

"I did, Fay," Star says, reserved in manner. "Just because we might look different on the outside doesn't mean we're not the same person underneath."

"Well," Carmen says, growing excited, "are you going to show us or what?"

"Okay," Star says finally. "Just one of you. Afterwards, the rest of you have to learn how to do 'the act' on your own." Star turns to Fay, who's still wounded from Rhonda's previous remarks. "What do you say, Fay?"

"I dunno," she says. "Can't we like spin a bottle or something?"

"Come on," Star says with encouragement. "It'll be fun."

"Fun?" Indicating disgust, Fay's round mouth curls inward in an hourglass-like shape. "Seriously? What's so fun about regurgitating your insides into another *man*?"

"You might enjoy it."

"What's to enjoy?"

Star nudges Fay.

"It's like learning how to ride a bicycle."

"I dunno, Star."

"Quit being such a drag."

"I'm not being a drag."

"Yes," Star says. "You are—"

"—All right!" Fay seethes. "I'll do it."

Together, Star and Fay tend to the man lying in a fetal position on the ground. She kneels down and removes the gag from his mouth.

"Please," he begs, "whatever it is that you're about to do, don't do it—"

"—Sorry, pal," Star says. "It's nothing personal. You drew the short end of the straw."

"Technically, Star, the 'drawing the short end of the straw' is irrelevant, considering the usage of straws are banned throughout most of the country."

Star glares at Fay.

The man cries out, "Please!"

With Fay gripping next to her, Star places the gag back in his mouth when, at times, she'd like to place the gag in Fay's mouth.

"Why are people always so whiny before the shit hits the fan?" Star whispers to herself.

"They don't want to get covered in shit," Fay says simply with a shrug.

"Also," Carmen says, as she and the others gather around Star and Fay, "who in their right mind want to clean a room afterwards. Can you imagine trying to remove shit from the wall, let alone the carpet? More than likely, you'd probably have to repaint the wall and if you couldn't remove the stains with carpet cleaner, more than likely, you'd have to replace the entire carpet. I can remember whenever Charlie went number two it was like prepping for surgery. I'd deck myself out in PPE equipment. I'm talking facemask, goggles, gloves; then, afterwards, I'd burn everything in an empty oil drum in the back-yard, as if I was burning evidence."

Both wearing a look of concern on their faces, Star and Fay look over their shoulders at Carmen.

"Thanks for the visual trip there, Carmen San Diego."

"What?" Carmen says, shrugging. "My memory's coming back."

"Is that a good or a bad thing?" Fay says to Star.

"Okay," Star says straightforwardly and reels in Fay's attention back to what appears to be nothing more than their guinea pig. "It's not like swapping spit with another person. That's too easy, right?"

"Well, to be honest, I can't even remember the last time I kissed a man."

"Don't worry," Star says. "It's not like that. Take your hand, for example."

Star holds up her hand, Fay mimics.

"Got it," she says. "Now what?"

"The concept is precisely the same," Star says to Fay. "Once you're able to do it with your hand, then you can do it with your mouth or any part of your body for that matter."

"What do you mean 'any' part?" asks Fay.

"I mean *any* part."

"So, for instance, if I wanted to do it with, say, my nipple, I could?"

Fay's face twitches.

"Don't," Star says before Fay bursts out laughing.

"Got it," Fay says, collecting herself. "Any part."

"I know. It sounds insane, right?"

"Yeah."

"Once you unlock the potential of what you're capable of, the options are endless, Fay."

"Tell me more, Professor Walker," Fay says jubilantly.

Star raises her hand again.

"The hand," she says.

"Why not start with my elbow?" Fay asks, as she bends her elbow inward as if she's striking the air. "I feel more comfortable using my elbow—"

"—*The hand*," Star says over Fay.

Fay listens.

Following suit, Fay holds up her hand.

"M'kay," she says.

"First off," Star says clearly, "you have to forget about everything you once were. Believe it or not, you can do things with this new body that your old body wasn't capable of doing; however, you must understand that the way of doing the most basic things is not much different from the way your old body once operated. I mean, how long does it take a baby to walk?"

"A year, maybe more."

"So, think of this as walking."

"Easy for you to say."

"Once you've mastered it, Fay," Star says, honing in on the hand before her, "it will come natural to you."

"I'm confused, Star."

"Let me show you," she says, her hand slightly trembling.

All of a sudden, a tiny slit along each one of her fingertips opens up, releasing several snake worms from the openings. The snake worms squirm and wiggle freely in the air. With her other hand, Star pulls one of the snake worms from her hand and holds it in the air. Once exposed to the elements, the snake worm slithers down her palm and into another pore-like opening along her forearm.

"How'd you do that?" asks Fay.

"I like to think of it as—how do I make it simple for you understand? I think of it as peeing when you don't have to pee."

"Peeing?"

"Yes," Star says, narrowing her eyes as if she's bracing for a verbal assault of harsh criticism. "That's right," she says with a burdensome sigh. "Peeing."

"How would I know what it's like to pee when I don't have to pee? Whenever I had to pee—that is, in my other body—I just went. I never like forced myself to pee. That would be absurd."

"I never really thought about it like that," Carmen says to Rhonda.

"Yeah but Fay. . . " Star says, stumbling around her words as she tries to clarify herself, ". . . have you ever felt like you were being pressured to pee like when someone was waiting for you outside a bathroom stall or maybe a time when you were outside, maybe camping, and there were no bathrooms in sight, except for, of course, nature, and you were around other people, maybe some guys, as in the male kind, and you didn't really have to pee, but you were about to do something really fun or whatever, and you knew that this was the only time you could pop a squat so you did and you somewhat forced yourself to pee."

Fay thinks over Star's comments.

"No," she says blankly.

All of a sudden, a snake worm slithers out of what used to be Fay's middle finger.

"Whoa!" Carmen shouts out. "How'd you do that?"

Fay shrugs and says, "I was just thinking how much I'd for this moment to be over with."

"Well," Star says, "that's just like peeing, am I right? We all just want it to be over with. I mean, who looks forward to peeing?"

"Bet you can't do it again, Fay," Rhonda says from behind.

On command, Fay concentrated on her hand. More snake worms slither from the tips of her fingers.

"Wow!" Fay says. "Now, I know what it feels like to be a man shooting his load."

"Fay! Gross!"

"What?"

"You're ready," Star says, as she removes the gag from the man's mouth and holds his arms behind his back. "Now, I want you to do the same thing with your hand, but this time use your tongue."

"I'm not going to kill him, am I?"

"No," Star teases, "but he's gonna wake up wondering why the hell he looks like Some Parasite-Looking Bitch."

Except for Fay, who remains more nervous from the upcoming performance, the remark draws a couple of laughs from the group.

As Fay anxiously prepares to stick her snake worm-riddled tongue down the man's throat, Carmen sets the mood by singing the song "Let Me Kiss You" from Morrissey's album, *You are the Quarry.*

"Eat your heart out, Morrissey," Mandy says, impressed by Carmen's voice.

Fay kneels down to the man's level.

The man struggles with Star; however, he's too weak to overpower her.

As Fay leans in closer, the man turns his head to the right and holds it firmly in place with his chin pressed against his shoulder as though by doing so he's trying to shield his mouth from Fay's. Star wraps part of the chain around the man's wrist and uses her hands to keep the man's head steady.

"Go on, Fay," Star says, maneuvering both of her arms into a headlock. The man wildly swings around his arms, landing several blows and slaps to the side of Star's head, which forces her to tighten her grip. Eventually, the man's arms lose velocity. He's too pooped to fight. Even when Star forces him to open his mouth by pinching his nose he barely has enough pneuma to resist and uprise.

With a sinister grin growing on one side of her wrinkly face, Mandy whispers to both Rhonda, "He actually believes that's air he's breathing."

Intrigued by what happens next, Carmen stops singing.

The moment the man opens his mouth gasping for what he perceives to be a breath Fay realigns her mouth with his and leans in for a kiss. She uses that same tactic she used earlier, that "think of waterfalls" and "get it over with" type purge, which, considering the circumstances, works even better this time around, especially with all those beady black eyes pounding down on her.

Fay sticks her tongue into the man's mouth, causing his eyes to balloon outward in a state of sheer panic. The panic ripples throughout his face in a domino effect, spreading from his eyes to his brows, which rise into the trench-like lines of his forehead. Fay's tongue presses against his. Her tongue suddenly multiples, doubling at first, then tripling, quadrupling. In similar fashion as his eyes, both of his cheeks balloon outward as dozens of those vicious snake worms slither and fill into his mouth.

Before he can clamp down on her tongue, Fay suddenly pulls her head away in the nick of time. Star moves her hand from his nose to his mouth and covers it completely, not giving him any chances to spit out what Fay had given him.

The snake worms slither down his throat and enter his body, allowing Star to remove her hand.

As the man starts convulsing on the ground, both Star and Fay back away and give him space while the snake worms, in essence, work their so-called "magic."

"How long does the transformation take?" Carmen asks Star.

"It varies," Star says. "Considering his current fragile state, I'd say not long; however, it takes much longer in our world."

Star ignores the tongue-slip and hopes that none of the girls call her out on it.

"Could affect the timing of our act."

"I don't think Mickey would want to cut to a commercial," Rhonda says. "I mean, wouldn't that ruin the whole trick?"

"It won't take that long," Star says, confident. "If we can keep the act within our allotted time, then it should be fine."

"We can totally toss out the whole introduction then."

"If we have to, then we will," Star says. "Besides, you really think the viewers care about who we are. All they want to see is what we can do."

The group doesn't have to wait long at all.

Gradually, the man's skin texture becomes rougher, the tone much paler. His once white eyes start to rot away, turning black and gooey.

"I got it," Fay says over the man's whimpers. "The Tongue Twister."

The other members of the group don't respond to the name.

"Not the name of the group but the name of the trick," Fay says. "Let's call it 'The Tongue Twister.'"

"Hey, not bad," Rhonda says. "I kind of like it."

While the name of their trick is debated, the transformation process suddenly intensifies, causing the man to scream out in bloody horror.

"I'm okay with the name," Mandy says calmly over the man's screams.

"What'd you say?"

"I said 'I'm okay' with the name," Mandy says louder.

"Sure," Star says in final agreement. "Tongue Twister it is."

Rhonda turns to Fay and says, "At least we can agree on one thing."

Repulsed by the man's reaction to the snake worms, Mandy points at the man squirming around on the ground and asks, "Does he have to be so fucking loud?"

"I say we put him out of his misery," Fay says.

"Thank Cats," Mandy says and grabs the Blade of Axlar from the top of a flat rock. She walks over to the man, kneels down, and puts an end to his suffering by slitting his throat.

"Wait!" Star hollers out, as Mandy runs the blade across the man's throat.

The man's screams come to a gurgling silence.

Mandy rids the dead body by rolling it from the platform. The body tumbles down the side of the mountain, the bolts of the lightning flickering in the distant dark clouds. Mandy glares at Star and says, "Circle of life."

"Hold up," Carmen says more thoughtfully, as she directs her attention back to Star. *Too late.* "You said 'our' world? What'd you mean by that?"

Star's too shocked by what she had just witnessed to digest Carmen's comment.

Mandy says before she can answer, "Star didn't tell you, did she?" Any relief Star has about Mandy and whether or not she knows about what she was doing—or better yet, planning—back in "our world" dissolves. "She's been making secret trips back to our world with second-rate crossers."

"Have not," Star says, her response strategic despite the shock to her body.

Mandy comes back at Star and says, "Have to, you skank."

"Okay," Star says hysterically, "since we're doing this right now, Lady *Justice,* who'd do about anything to catch a lift even if meant cutting deals with filthy dredgers, you want to tell them about what you were doing back in our world?"

"I don't know what you're talking about," Mandy asks innocently.

"Don't give me that bullshit!"

"I seriously don't know where she's getting her information—"

"—Jack told me you've been paying him visits."

"Jack said that?"

"Yes," Star says. "Jack did."

"Why are you talking to Jack, Star?"

"I wanted to see how he was doing," she says, as the internal wounds left behind by the recent events start to open. "That's all." She contemplates whether or not she should tell Mandy about Jack's fate and how Mickey was the one responsible for him receiving a swift visit from the Eventide. She nearly breaks down in front of the group. She collects both her thoughts and composure. "I know you don't want to hear this right now," she says, gaining more confidence, "but he's not doing good." She makes sure not to slip her tongue again by speaking of Jack in the present tense, *not past*, since past tense would raise one too many red flags. "He blames himself for what he did to you."

"Good!" Mandy cries out.

"Jack loved you, Mandy, *not* me. I was just a. . . a toy to him."

"Aw! You need a tissue, Star?" Mandy asks with scorn. "No," she answers for Star. "Good! 'Cuz you're not getting one! You ruined our relationship!"

"I didn't ruin your relationship, Mandy," Star says. "Jack needed someone to talk to, and let's face it, you weren't there."

"You're a heartless bitch," Mandy says, struggling to look at Star.

Speak for yourself.

"Sure," Star says, as she pushes aside the insult, which, she knows, is more of a reflection of Mandy herself than the recipient of her verbal lashings. "I can take it," Star says, but she really can't. "Now, you want to explain to everyone why you've been going back to our world to haunt Jack?"

"Seriously, Mandy," Carmen says, disappointed.

"Like you have any room to talk, Dust Buster," Mandy fires back at Carmen. "I know about you and your addiction to dust. You've been cutting it with Lazarus light to sneak away on your own little private vacays." She looks at the others in disbelief. "You all actually believed her when she said she was making trips to Leatherwood—"

"—That's total BS, Mandy."

"You know it's true."

"This isn't about Carmen, Mandy," Star says over Mandy.

"I don't have to explain myself to you, *Skank*."

"You know, Mandy, I heard those dredgers carry a plethora of diseases," Star says with a concealed, deep-seated anger. Her beady black eyes flick downward at her waistside. "I wondered where that strange smell was coming from. Now, I know."

"You're an evil bitch—"

"—Right back at you, Sweetheart."

"Enough," Fay shouts over Mandy. "Would you two stop fighting? It's getting old, you know?"

Even though Mandy still wears that same lopsided expression on her face, the one where she looks as if she's hiding important information from the group, she has said what she needed to say and will gladly wait for her turn to speak again.

"Real talk," Star says, ready to unburden herself, "I ran into Myko."

"Myko?"

Right, Mandy wanted to say. *Your partner in crime.*

"I've been looking for him for a while now," Star says, diverting the conversation from the real reason as to why she went back to our world. "I just wanted to tell him how sorry I was for dragging him into all of this mess."

"So, what's Ol' Myko been up to these days?"

"Well, let's just say he's made a lot of new friends." Star pauses and contemplates whether or not she should tell the group about her plans. "Fuck it," she says to herself. "I'm not coming with you all to the show."

"What?" Fay says. "Why not?"

"Last time I checked the Fuck-It-All Five requires all five members."

"We still haven't come up with other names."

"You will," Star says. "It will have the word five in it. I found someone who can replace me."

"What?"

"Who?"

"She lives in Leatherwood."

"Why are you telling us now, Star?"

"I was going to tell you sooner, but I had to be sure that you all know how to perform the trick without me."

"Star, we're not going to do this without you."

"Well, you're going to have to," Star says. "I would love to join all four of you, including you, Mandy—"

"—Gee," Mandy says darkly. "Thanks."

"But I have some personal business to attend to."

"Personal business?" Fay says, more heated. "Where is all this coming from, Star? You can't just back out at the last second—"

"—But I am, Fay."

"What is it that you're not telling us, Star?" asks Rhonda.

"You know something, don't you?"

"Let me ask you something, Fay: Do you remember anything about how you got here?"

"Of course," she says, turning to the spiral set of stairs right below the summit. "I took the stairs."

"No, Fay," Star clarifies, "here. How did you wind up here, in this world?"

Fay stumbles with her response, forcing Star to look at the confusion on the other members' faces.

"None of you know," she says.

"Know what, Star?"

"Warrick didn't save you."

"Of course he did," Carmen says in defense.

"Why exactly are you sticking up for him, Carmen, especially what he did to you?"

"But he saved my life. We wouldn't be here if it wasn't for Mickey. . . "

"He didn't save you, Carmen, like he said or whatever he planted inside your head," Star says.

"You're saying he's lying to us?"

"He killed you," Star says candidly and looks around at the other three members. "He killed *all* of you."

"Mickey didn't kill me," Fay says. "Some distracted little piece of fucking shit who was yapping on his phone while driving killed me."

"I'm sorry, Fay, but some distracted little piece of fucking shit who was yapping on his phone while driving did hit you, but he didn't kill you."

"What are you talking about?"

"Think about it, Fay," Star says convincingly. "You were fed a lie by a very deranged individual who doesn't have your best interest at heart."

"But I was. . . " Fay trails off, her head wheels spinning those final moments before she crossed the great divide.

She specifically remembered that day as if it was yesterday. She was driving home from picking up lunch at an Indian restaurant called Tandoori Takeout. Her go-to dish whenever she was feeling down was the famous red curry chicken, which, as most customers described, was better than sex. She had just pulled out of the parking lot and was making a right turn onto the highway when the song "One of Us" by Joan Osborne came on satellite radio. Fay used to own the album, Relish, when she was younger; however, like most of her CDs, she lost it during the move after college. Now, it was mp3s that sounded like hammered shit or random jams from 90's Craze on satellite radio or the small collection of expensive vinyl, which, when played, was like listening to liquid gold slowly ooze from the speakers. Halfway through singing the song—in fact, it was right after the lyric "God is good"—Fay was droning the words "Yeah, Yeah," when she caught a large dark object in the corner of her eye. Before she even had a chance to turn to see what the object was crossing the intersection, this large dark object, a forest green Rav-4, plowed directly into the side of her Prius, T-boning her. Her Prius violently spun like a coin. The back half of the car was crushed like a soda can. All four windows, as well as the back windshield, shattered. Pebbles of glass in her hair, her eyes, her mouth, and scattered all over the seats, the floors, as well as the street outside. As the driver, who was texting when he sped through the red light, lay unconscious with the side of her bloody face pressed against the air bag inside his totaled Rav-4, Fay managed to crawl her way out of all that chewed-up metal. Fay collapsed onto the glass-covered street. A smelly, hooded homeless man leaned over her dying body and inserted a snake worm into Fay's mouth. He placed his gloved hand over Fay's mouth. He didn't have to worry about plugging her nose for it was broken and shifted to the side like a page that had been dog-eared. Fay struggled a bit, but she was fading too fast to make any attempt at prying his hand from her face.

"Someone was there with me," Fay says softly, "in the end."

"It was him, Fay," Star says. "It was Warrick."

As she falls deeper into the memory, she recalls the sound of a man *whistling*, which triggers an image of a homeless man skipping away from the wreckage as he twirls his raggedy rainbow umbrella and whistles the song "One of Us."

"I dunno," Fay says. "Maybe. Everything was so blurry."

Star nods at Rhonda.

"Same goes for you, Rhonda."

"What? No way."

"Yes way."

"It was an accident," Rhonda claims.

"Are you sure?"

Mentally grasping at the fuzzy images beyond the ball of snake worms swirling inside her head, Rhonda finds herself traveling to that one particular day, her Death Day. Like Fay, Rhonda easily accesses that day she crossed over; however, as she delves farther, her memories become clearer in detail than Fay's.

According to Rhonda's recollection, she just returned home from her teaching at Red Valley High School. She was behind in grading and had promised her "kids" that she'd have those grades for their quizzes finished by tomorrow, which only added more stress to what was, in Rhonda's case, a beautiful day. On top of that, she was exhausted from spending the previous days off not as eleventh grade English teacher, Ms. Abbott, but "Ron," the fearless weekend warrior who could drink any man underneath the table. The aftermath of two days of heavy drinking left her with a three-day hangover that was best remedied with uninterrupted sleep and a strict liquid diet consisting of Gatorade and chicken noodle soup. She was tempted to call out sick, both days, Monday and Tuesday, but she was saving her sick days for a getaway to Belize. She dropped her belongings on the kitchen table, removed a handful of quizzes from her first and second period, poured herself a tall glass of Zinfandel, locally grown and bottled, and went straight to the bathroom where she stripped down to her undies and turned on the hot water and prepared to take a nice warm bath to help melt away the frustrations of the day. Despite their misdirection, she loved her students, her "kids," as she called them, but something was in the air that day and they were extra-wild. She ended up having to throw a couple of them out of class for misbehaving. One of them called her a "Lonely-Ass Bitch Who Had A Dick Stuck So Far Up Her Ass That She Needed A Shrink To Pull It Out" as he was being escorted from the classroom. The student's comment had eaten away at Rhonda like a tick for the remainder of the period and well through the school day. As water filled the tub, she decided to skip the bath. She turned off the water, threw on her jammies, which was an old No-Cal shirt and a pair of loose, holey sweats, and took her pity party outside. With a glass half full of Zinfandel in one hand and quizzes in the other, she hung out on the hammock, which was secured to two cypresses in the backyard. The temperature was more than ideal, low seventies, low humidity, a nice—and rewarding—break from the heat wave last week that left her longing for cooler fall weather. As she kicked back on the hammock, sipping wine and grading quizzes with a red pen, she was struck by a hit of euphoria. After working her way through yet another glass of wine and knocking out the first period quizzes in no time, she suddenly became flushed, then lightheaded. She set the glass of wine on the ground and did so heavily, causing the glass to topple over. The trees above her started to spin, branches and leaves multiplying and becoming one intertwined mess. In the chaos, she witnessed a dark, shadowy face materialize among the rays of sunlight pouring through the openings of the treetops. As the world shrunk all around her, she fell from the hammock, trying to stand to her feet. Even a simple task such as standing felt impossible. She crawled toward the bottle of Zinfandel, pulled off the cork, and smelled the inside of the bottle. She couldn't detect anything out of the ordinary. She inspected the cork next. Next to the jagged hole where she inserted the corkscrew, she saw what she perceived to be a much smaller, finer hole. Immediately, she realized that the wine had been tainted. Before she could reach for her phone, the world tightened. She struggled to catch her breath. She fell to her back where she witnessed a creature moving toward her feet, leaving behind a serpentine-pattern track in the grass. She couldn't even move. She felt paralyzed, even when the snake worm started to slither up her leg.

"Rhonda?"

Rhonda searches for the words but can't find any.

"I think Star might be onto to something here," Carmen says, remembering. "The day before I wound here," she pinches each side of her red cloak, extending it outward as if she's displaying a dress, "looking like a monster straight out of a Creature Feature, I was at home preparing a lovely dinner for Maxime. It was our seventh year anniversary. I picked up some steaks from the butcher at the grocery store. While I was cooking, I heard a story on the news about a famous actor, Biff Craley, who had been reported missing for two years. After two years of searching for Biff, his wife, Ivanna, decided to end the search and finally, lay her husband to rest. I smelled. . . smoke coming from the kitchen. The steaks, I remembered. I checked on the steaks and nearly overcooked them. I know how much Max liked his steak rare in the middle, so I wasn't looking forward to breaking the news to Max. When Max returned home from work, I noticed that he was acting incredibly odd. It had nothing to do with the overcooked steak. It had nothing to do with me. When I looked into his eyes, I saw someone—*something*—else. The man standing before me wasn't the man I married."

Carmen remembered Maxime walking straight through the front door, dropping his bags in the foyer, and not saying a word to her when she asked about the "important thing" that he had earlier that day. He had spent the night before in his office, making last-minute tweaks to his "big" presentation. All Carmen received in return was a foreign stare coming from an entity that had stolen the body of her husband.

"It happened so fast," Carmen says, skimming through the images of violence inside her head. "Before I could make a run for it, he was already on top of me."

Maxime hit Carmen over the head with her old violin that she had displayed in the dining room. Bloody and dazed, she floundered on the hardwood floor.

"The man who killed me wasn't my Maxime," Carmen says without a doubt.

With the violin string, Maxime strangles Carmen from behind until she's blue in the face.

Somewhere among the violence, Carmen saw herself stepping out of her own dead body and witnessing a strange man casually strolling from the dining room. The power flickered throughout the house. The man turned down the switch on a dimmer. The lights *not only* darkened, but the man's skin also *darkened*, as if he was dimming the tone of his skin. He removed several features, including a nose as well as a cheek and brow that appeared glued onto his face and dropped them on the floor. Next, he removed the contact lenses from both his eyes. Finally, the stranger looked toward the staircase where a young boy stood clinging to the banister. He glanced at the terrified boy, then rotated around, and faced Carmen. Before she could recognize of the stranger's face, the lights suddenly went out.

"I can't believe you're actually believing her," Mandy says, pointing at Star. "You all know she went nuts, right? She was admitted to Stillwater."

"After everything that happened to you," Star says in return, not at all rattled by Mandy's comments, "you're still going to take that monster's side." Star turns to the others. "None of you know how she crossed over, do you?"

The other members shake their heads.

"She's never told us—"

"—Don't force her, Star. She'll tell us when she's ready."

"Now's a perfect time," Star says over Rhonda, who, despite her favoritism, tends to sticks up for Mandy whenever situations get heated between her and Star. "Why don't you tell them what happened to you, Mandy?"

"What happened to me is irrelevant," Mandy says coldly.

Star retorts, "Irrelevant, huh? You're in denial, Mandy."

Mandy waves off Star and her comment.

Star seethes, "You think getting gangbanged by a bunch of fuckin' vamps is irrelevant?"

Stunned by the accusation, Fay says more seriously, "Is that true, Mandy?"

"No," Mandy says hesitantly. "Of course it's not true. Who are you going to believe? Me? Or, some full-on nutcase who did a swan dive from thirteen stories off Stillwater *Mental Institution* because she was one-hundred convinced that one of the orderlies slipped snake worms in her body and she was going to cut them out if they didn't take her seriously?"

"But that part sounds pretty accurate, Mandy," Carmen says over the silence. "I mean, take a look at us."

"After they took their turns on her," Star says, as Mandy's black eyes start to water, "they tossed her body in the lake as if she was trash. Warrick was behind it all. That monster orchestrated the whole thing. And what makes it worse is Rhodes used Mandy's story for his own political gain. Mandy became nothing more than a pawn in a chess match for power."

"I don't get it," Rhonda says soberly, "why us? If what you say is true, Star, then what does Mickey want with us? What makes us so special?"

"It's not like Warrick just drew our names out of a hat," she says. "Who the hell knows? Maybe he did. What I know for sure is that he chose us because he knows he can manipulate us by sending us to Dark Mountain to. . . " she points at the spot where the man once laid,". . . to master some ridiculous act for his ridiculous TV show."

"How do you know all of this?" asks Carmen.

"Yeah, Star," Mandy says, the anger coming through her voice, "how do you know all of this?"

"I know his type," she says.

From the reaction of the other three members, Star realizes her response isn't adequate enough to put the topic to bed.

Lastly, she turns to Mandy, witnesses that sinister look on her face—in fact, the same exact one she gave her the moment she found out about Star and Jack—and right then and there, she realizes that Mandy knows the reasons as to why Star went back to our world.

A hunched-over silhouette appears behind Mandy.

Star experiences what she can only describe as a sinking feeling.

Another silhouette appears behind Rhonda, then Carmen, then, finally, Fay.

A series of clownish high-pitch giggles pierce through the darkness.

Startled, the other members turn to the sounds, except for one member in particular: Mandy.

She doesn't even flinch.

Instead, she stares directly at Star, as if she's burning a hole right through her, condemning her.

"*And what type is that?*" Mandy finally speaks.

Star has no reply.

"What the hell is going on here?" asks Carmen, as Nuru, one of the members of the CROCUTA Clan, holds a Beretta Cheetah against the backside of her head while, at the same time, nurses her other ghost hand.

Jazarah appears behind Rhonda, Makda behind Fay, Jazarah aiming an M16 while Makda aiming a Colt AR-15.

Lastly, Heloisa walks around Mandy and makes her presence known behind Star, who, in return, holds up her hands in surrender.

"Don't do this, Mandy," Star says directly at Mandy.

Heloisa giggles at Mandy.

"You're not allowed to speak to me anymore, Star," Mandy says. "You gave up that privilege as soon as you betrayed us."

"I wasn't going to betray you, Mandy," Star says.

Heloisa glances down at the back of Star's cloak and notices the large snake worm slithering up the side of her back.

"Don't even think about it," Heloisa says, as she sticks the barrel of the assault rifle along the back of Star's neck.

The snake worm recedes back into Star's body.

"You win, Mandy," Star says, surrendering.

"What the fuck is going on, Mandy?" asks Fay, her voice shaking.

"They're here for Star," she says. "That's it."

"Why?"

"She stole a valuable object that doesn't belong to her."

"What object?"

"Doesn't matter, Fay," Star says.

"All right, Ms. Walker," Heloisa says, tapping Star with the barrel of the assault rifle, "you're coming with us."

As Heloisa holds the assault rifle on Star, Nuru handcuffs Star and escorts her from the platform.

The rest of the CROCUTA Clan slowly eases away in the darkness.

Star walks past Mandy. She stops walking and says to her, "Whatever happens to me, just remember: Death is the only thing we'll *ever* have in common."

"Enough chit-chat," Heloisa says, tugging on Star's arm.

As the Clan walks Star down a flight of stairs made from stone, a well-known crosser, who goes by the name Saggelstache, appears along the side of the mountain, ready to accompany Star and the Clan back to our world.

"Where are they taking her, Mandy?" asks Rhonda.

Mandy doesn't answer.

"Mandy?"

"I'm afraid it's out of our hands," she says finally. "Star made her decision."

"That's fucked up, Mandy, and you know that," Carmen says, raging. "You
could've told us. We could've *all* talked it over. Instead, you'd rather throw
her to the wolves?"

"Hyenas," Fay corrects.

"Whatever!"

"Mandy, you can't do this—"

"—It's already done, Carmen," Mandy says and glances over her shoulder
at Star, who shares one final stare down with Mandy before she's walked back
down Dark Mountain.

🕐

THE two heavily-armed Cutas, Heloisa and Nuru, escort Star into Chop Soy
while the remaining members of the CROCUTA Clan wait outside.

All of the lights are off inside the restaurant. The only sources of light
come from the amber-colored floodlights outside. Beams of light pour in
through windows and cast monstrous-looking shadows along the walls and
floors. Among the shadows, Star witnesses a dark figure sitting at the end of a
table near the back of the restaurant. His dark face is momentarily brought out
by the orangish glow of a cigarette. A cloud of smoke rises from his face.
Heloisa guides Star to the mysterious man while Nuru stands guard at the front
door.

Once Star reaches the table, she recognizes Key's face.

He takes yet another drag of the Coffin Nail.

As he blows the smoke from his mouth, a wicked-looking face appears in
the cloud of smoke. The face gracefully moves toward Star's face. Immediately, she waves the smoke from the face and says, "Sorry but that little magic
trick of yours won't work on me."

Key points at a chair at the other end of the table.

"Thank you, Heloisa," Key says. "I'll take care of her from here."

Heloisa leaves Key and both she and Nuru exit Chop Soy while Star timidly
takes a seat at the table. Her eyes move away from Key and trail downward to
a juice glass that has been turned upside down on the tabletop. She can't make
out the creature for it remains lost in the shadows—possibly a spider, she assumes—however, whatever the creature is, it appears trapped inside the glass.

"What's the special occasion?" Star asks, as she draws her attention back to
Key's white suit.

"What? This?" He grabs his white sports coat and says casually, "I just got
back from crashing a dead man's party."

Completely flustered by Key's comment, Star surveys the dining room. As
her eyes adjust to the darkness, she maps out an exit strategy. She knows that
she can rule out the front entrance. More than likely, the Cutas are hanging
outside, waiting to pick her off if she should make a run for it. The only exit is
the one in the kitchen; but, of course, Key is sitting directly in the path of the
kitchen.

Discreetly, she redirects her attention back to Key, who's staring at her.

690

"Did I say something?" asks Star.

"No," he says. "It's just, you remind me of her—I mean, the you before your five-star makeover."

"Let me guess," Star says, studying Key. "She broke your little ole heart."

"Not exactly," he says, pausing. "She was taken from me."

"Sorry to hear," Star says and for a moment, feels saddened by Key's heartbreak. She turns inward and acknowledges her own heartbreak. The sadness dissolves and all that's left is anger. "What does this have to do with me?"

"Nothing."

"Right," Star says, the emotion building inside me. She feels almost depleted by the feeling. "Nothing."

"Her name was Nevaeh," Key says, as he drags from the cigarette. "She was struck in the head by a stray bullet during the infamous 1992 Los Angeles Riots. While she lay dying on the sidewalk, rioters were walking all around her. Half of them didn't even know she was dying until a couple of hours later when her girlfriend stumbled across her body. By then, Nevaeh was already dead." Key takes another drag from the cigarette, savors it, then blows out the smoke, a sad-looking face appears in the cloud of smoke. "The next night after her death I hunted down the man who shot her. I brought Neveah's girlfriend Jada along with me because, in a way, she was also responsible for Nevaeh's death by leaving her behind when she should've been looking after her. What I did to them would result in me being branded in a name that still lingers over the streets of LA?"

"Let me guess," Star says cynically, "you shot them with a *M16*."

"No," he says, glaring at Star. "That would be too easy. After that night, the word spread on the street. People were whispering the name 'M80' with a quiver in their voice. Now, granted, M16 sounds much cooler than M80—my opinion."

"Am I getting my numbers mixed up here?"

"Not the gun, Star."

"I give up," she says. "Why were people calling you M80?"

"Like I said," Key says, "I found the man who shot Nevaeh. I tied both him and Jada to a chair. I placed a M80, the firework—" *That M80* "—inside Jada's mouth and Nevaeh's shooter's mouths, lit the M80s, and duct taped their mouths closed. Nevaeh's shooter received a special touch. I decided to duct tape both his hands to his mouth." With a cigarette still in hand, Key animatedly demonstrates with his hands placed flat against the sides of his gaping mouth in an "uh-oh" type of expression. "The explosion didn't kill both of them—not at first. Jada later died in the hospital. Which wasn't part of the plan; but every now and then, when you're trying to get your point across, sometimes the point triggers another point. Nonetheless, Nevaeh's shooter survived, which was *the point*. Killing him would be too easy. I wanted him to wake up every single day and be reminded of what he did whenever he looked at himself in the mirror."

"You know I've witnessed this scene play out a million times in my head and even if I try doing something differently, each scenario ends the same."

"The power of the crystal has its limits," Key says, "especially to those who are *limited*; although if the crystal should wind up in the hands, its power can be endless."

"You can't change the course of the future," Star says, as if she's accepting her fate. "Everything that's going to happen will happen. It's inevitable."

"Curious, Dark Star," he says sarcastically. "Why do you care so much about this place?"

"I care because. . . " Star says without thinking, ". . . it's still home to me."

"Right," he says softly and cracks a smile.

"After listening to your little story, I can tell it was once your home too."

The smile melts from Key's face as he takes a puff of his cigarette. He lifts up the glass just enough to blow smoke underneath the glass with that small creature trapped inside. Once the glass fills up with smoke, Key closes the glass and leans back in his chair. He says vacantly to Star, "Looks like it's time for you to face The Inevitable."

Star carefully watches the smoky glass, as well as the small creature squirming around inside.

All of a sudden, the glass shifts a couple of inches along the table.

Despite having already witnessed the same exact scenario play out by gazing into the future with the black crystal, Star accepts her fate and waits for the great beast to tear her to shreds. The creature grows in size, causing the glass to crack. The tiny fracture zigzags up the glass in the shape of a lightning bolt.

As more cracks spread, the creature continues to grow until it can no longer fit inside the glass.

Eventually, the entire glass shatters all over the table.

The small creature isn't so small anymore. It grows into the size of a fist and from there, it continues to grow and grow.

From a fist to the size of a basketball, the creature's tentacles stretch outward and crawl over the edge of the table. The creature ends up becoming so large and heavy that its weight causes one of the legs of the table to snap in half, resulting in the table to collapse. The chair overturns. Star falls backward, as foreseen. The blob-like creature, now as wide as a walrus, wraps one of its many slimy tentacles around Star's ankle. Star tries to kick away the tentacle, as foreseen; however, her attempts at breaking free are pointless.

Star searches for a weapon—anything! She finds a shard of glass on the floor and stabs the side of the creature's body as it makes its way up her leg. The creature's hide is so thick and leathery that the glass breaks in her hand as soon as it makes contact. The glass cuts the inside of her palm.

In one last desperate attempt, she tries to crawl away. Again, her attempts are pointless. Once the creature sits on the lower half of her body, she can't move at all. Hoping to scare it away, she punches and elbows at it. Each blow has little to no effect on the creature. Star lands a blow directly in its spiraled shaped maw.

The pain bolts up her arm and radiates throughout her entire body.

As she pulls away her arm, she realizes that her arm is gone.

The creature had completely bit it off!

Screaming and bleeding for help, Star continues to strike the creature, but this time using her other arm. The creature's tentacle strikes back. The tentacle enters Star's mouth and slithers down her throat, causing her to choke.

Key stands from the chair and walks up to Star as her eyes start to roll in the back of her head.

His face—that face—is the last thing she witnesses before she blacks out.

In the flash of blackness, Star springs upward in a burst of life!

She opens her eyes and before her sits Key at the other end of the table. That creature, which was once choking her, is back to its normal size and resting comfortably in Key's palm.

"For a moment, I thought I lost you there," says Key.

Out of breath, Star takes a moment to find her bearings.

"What. . . " she says, catching her breath, ". . . what the hell just happened?"

"What just happened is that you just died," Key says. "In your head, that is." He pets the small creature in his hand. "Something, ain't it?"

"What did you do to me?" asks Star, as she surveys the dark dining room.

"Not me," he says and showcases the creature for Star, "That was lil' Genette here. She takes up after her old man, only her telepathic abilities are much greater than his. My opinion."

"But how?"

"How what?"

"How was it able to get inside my head?"

"What part of telepathic don't you understand?" Key asks but doesn't expect Star to answer. "Forget it," he waves off Star and stands up from the seat. "You see, Star, like lil' Genette here, I can do whatever the hell I want." Approaching Star, he asks, "You know why?"

Again, Star doesn't answer and even so, he doesn't give her any opportunity to answer.

Key stands next to Star, leans in closer, and whispers in her ear, "This is *My* Fuckin' *World*. That's why."

As Key stands back upright, he holds out his other hand.

Confused, Star looks up at Key and doesn't know what he wants from her—at least, not until she feels the black crystal climbing up her throat. Star gags and tries to prevent herself from vomiting. Maybe it has something to do with that lil' creature in Key's hand. Maybe it's Key's presence alone. Or, perhaps the cigarette smoke that he's been blowing in the air. Whatever the case may be, Star feels extremely nauseous. The gag turns into a cough. The cough then turns into a violent hawk. She vomits up the black crystal into Key's palm. He wiggles the phlegm-soaked black crystal in the air before he dries it off inside a napkin.

"Good girl," he says, as Star recovers from the exhausting purge.

"Can't believe you actually swallowed the damn thing," Key says, looking over the black crystal.

Key holds it in his hand and closes his eyes as he embraces its power.

He opens his eyes, glances over the black crystal in surprise, and says, "Huh? So, that's what's going to happen." He shrugs. "We'll see about that."

Without wasting anymore time, he closes his hand until it forms a fist. After he crushes the black crystal in his hand, there's nothing left of it but black pepper-like dust. He blows away the black dust onto the floor and wipes his hand on another napkin.

"Are you going to kill me or not?" asks Star, as she hangs her head.

"Kill you?" Key repeats. "Why would I kill one of the 'Stars' of my show?" He pauses, waiting for Star to laugh at the comment. "Get it," he says. "Stars of my show. Cuz your name is Star." He waves off a poor attempt at comical relief. "Never mind." He nods to the front door where Heloisa and Nuru are waiting for Star. "Let's get you back to your friends. Shall we?" Key holds out his arm and shows Star to the exit. "By the way," he says, as Star hesitantly stands to her feet, "you *guys* ever come up with a group name yet?"

"AN OLD FOE"

EXCEPT for the California license plate, not Arizona, the same exact van that Teresha was driving pulls into the parking lot of a small dive bar called, of all names, Dive. Like the name of the bar, everything about the bar is simple and straight to the point, nothing too fancy. The building itself, shaped like a soggy, worn down shoebox, is painted off-white. Displayed on the front windows are pink and green glowy signs that read several "Domestic" beer brands. Wrapped around the structure is a sidewalk littered with smothered cigarette butts as well as earthquake-like cracks where weeds sprout through the concrete.

The driver—a woman—turns off the ignition of the van and places what appears to be an ancient-looking wooden case inside the glove compartment before she steps outside. She is dressed "comfortably," red plaid sweat pants and a navy blue hoody jacket with the word *pink* written in PRINCETOWN font. Definitely not Teresha; however, the woman has the same weight, same height, and a similar profile as Teresha, and can probably pass as a distant cousin or sibling. Even one of her eyes, her left eye, is the same color green; however, her other eye, her right one, is the color brown.

The young woman, called Polly, which rhymed with her favorite Saturday night drug, and would often get dirt from the boys, who'd ask her if she wanted a "cracker," walks around the back of the van. She opens the back doors, revealing the body bag holding Biff Craley's corpse lying over a fresh bed of ice, as well as one other addition being a black heavy-duty garbage bag stuffed to the brim. The bag, too, is surrounded by ice cubes; however, a couple of ice cubes are starting to melt, causing sludgy water to leak onto the parking lot. Polly rips open the last bag of ice that she bought at the convenient store and pours the ice cubes over Biff's corpse. One at a time, Polly closes the doors and heads toward the front of Dive.

The interior of Dive, like the exterior, is very Plain Jane. They pretty much have one of everything, a billiards table, a dartboard, a TV, even one of those machines where one could play nudy games. Polly counts only five people inside, a couple sitting in a booth, two men hanging out at the bar, one of the men wearing dark shades, then, finally, the burly bartender, who's having a conversation about the Dodgers with the one shade-less hombre at the bar. Polly has her eyes on the man with the dark shades, Narcissus, who's sipping from a glass of aged whiskey while listening to the Local News at the other end of the bar.

The bartender gives Polly a subtle yet tentative nod of hello. Polly nods back at the bartender and makes her way to the far end of the bar where she approaches Narcissus. She passes the couple at the booth. The two are sharing a nacho platter and are so engrossed in each other's company that a violent riot could be raging outside, straight up the making of fire and brimstone, and neither one of them would give what any riot or rioters so urgently crave.

Polly finally arrives at the other end of the bar.

"You mind?" she asks, as she points to the bar stool next to Narcissus.

Speaking of attention, Narcissus doesn't even acknowledge the young "comfortably-dressed" woman standing next to him, doesn't need to; instead, he takes a whiff of the air, as if his nose is doing the looking for him. He can't tell whether it's the rot or just a bad laundry day. Either way, he shrugs it off.

With his senses slightly dull from the liquor, he says, "Be my guest."

Polly slides out the bar stool and takes a seat next to Narcissus.

Chewing on the toothpick, the bartender walks up to Polly.

"What will it be, miss?" he asks, throwing the damp rag over his shoulder in all its stereotypical glory.

"I'll have a beer," she says.

The bartender, who not only looks, but also acts as if he was pulled directly from a movie set, grabs her a domestic beer from the cooler, cracks open the bottle by pounding the serrated lip of the cap along the edge of the counter-top—here, bottle openers are for amateurs—and slides it in front of Polly.

"Two-fifty," he says, as the foamy head of the beer slowly oozes from the top and slides down the neck of the bottle.

Polly plays a game of pocket-pool in her pocket before she pulls out a crinkled five-dollar bill. She hands the bartender the money and tells him to keep the change.

"Thank ya, ma'am," the bartender says, springs open the cash register, places the five inside, removes two dollars and fifty cents from the cash register and then places the leftover change inside a weaved basket labeled, "Tips," the messy writing on the label sharing the qualities of a third-grader.

He walks back over and asks "Stevie Wonder" if he'd like another double.

Narcissus says, "Sure thing, Father."

"That's strange," Polly says, as the bartender pours Narcissus another whiskey. "You two don't look related."

"We're not," Narcissus says loosely.

Polly still wears that scribbled-on confusion on her face.

Narcissus makes it clear for her.

"When Father Dawson isn't plying his patrons with alcohol," he slurs, as he downs the last sip of whiskey, "you can find his ass down at Saint Patrick's reading scripture to his congregation."

"By the way, Narcissus," the bartender, Father Dawson, says, as he brings the glass of Pillars aged whiskey to Narcissus, "what's it gonna take for *me* to get *you* to join *my* flock?"

"You couldn't pay me enough to listen to you ramble on for hours."

Father Dawson laughs as he sets the Pillars in front of Narcissus.

"One day," he says, grinning.

"We'll see about that," Narcissus says.

"We will see, won't we?" Father Dawson says mysteriously as he makes his way to the other end of the bar where he reignites a controversial topic about the star left fielder simply known as "Mando," who is currently leading the league in most hit home-runs. The scrappy patron believes the rumors are true and that the big slugger might be on "the juice"—hence why, in the past year, his physical appearance has significantly altered: he put on at least thirty pounds of lean muscle; his head has gotten slightly bigger, whereas his balls have shrunken down to a couple of *Raisinets*—Not like the patron was "looking" or anything and even so, he'd never say so—not to mention, Mando's temper has been reduced to a three year old throwing fits on the field. In the past year alone, Mando has gone through an average of three bats a day—you don't want to see what the man does to one after he strikes out. According to the patron, these are the top three indicators (thirty pounds of muscle, big head and small, shrinking balls—which he pairs together—and the uptick of temper tantrums) that the man is clearly juicing.

Narcissus removes the shades from his face and rubs the backside of his eyelids.

"Long day?" asks Polly.

"I've had longer—" he says.

He nearly stops midway through his sentence as he picks up a more pungent smell in the air.

On the Local News, a sudden news report flashes over the TV. Polly draws her eyes to the screen. The TV shows a camera crew from Local News positioned outside a rundown convenient store next to a gas station called Gas and Go, which sits along the border of Arizona and California. A heavy police presence is seen in most—if not, all of the shots. One of the shots includes a pair of detectives lingering near a white tent, which has been used to shield the human remains behind Gas and Go.

A reporter appears on the TV. Next to him stands a clerk named Emmanuel Pierre. The reporter asks Emmanuel about the suspect—or "person of interest." Emmanuel states that he saw her walking away with the bathroom key and that he stopped her right before she was about to drive off. He went on a rant about the key and how it had stayed in the store for the twenty-one years that he had worked at Gas and Go, "always returned," Emmanuel emphasized for the reporter. When he approached the woman, she was searching around the floor of the vehicle and he thought maybe she had dropped a key, not his key, but the car key, between the seats and somehow, it had gotten lost underneath the floor mats and stuck in that tight space next to the seat. He knocked on the window and when she looked up at him, she was squinting one of her eyes. The clerk made sure to demonstrate to those late-night viewers out there who were watching Local News what a squint of an eye looked like. His thinking was that maybe she had something caught in her eye, like an eyelash or piece of debris or dirt—the winds have been known to kick around dust from the desert. Nonetheless, the woman reached in her pocket and handed

him the key and said that she was sorry, that she "forgot." What struck Emmanuel as "odd" was that she arrived in a "blue sedan," came inside for the
bathroom key, used the restroom out back, left the restroom, walked through
the parking lot, got inside her vehicle, although *not* a blue sedan, as he witnessed her driving when she pulled up to Gas and Go, but a "white van"—that
is where he stopped her and was given back his priceless key attached to the
round head of a gear shift—then drove away into the night.

When pressed about why he didn't stop her, knowing that this "person of
interest" was leaving his store in a different vehicle, Emmanuel shrugs and
says to the reporter, "It didn't occur to me at the time."

"You're getting sloppy," Narcissus says to Polly, as a weather report flashes
across the screen.

"Did you know a rat is no different than a human when it comes to peer
pressure?" asks Polly.

"No," Narcissus says quietly. "I did not. . . "

He takes another sip of the Pillars, this time a gulp.

Looking forward at the vibrant shelf of liquor, Polly says, "The desire to
feel accepted among its peers is so great among the rat community that one
single rat would literally eat shit if it was in the company of other rats who
were eating shit. If that's not conformity, then I don't know what is. The urge
to feel accepted can be man's greatest strength and weakness." She faces Narcissus and says directly, "I'd say it's no different than gaining control over another man's free will."

"Free will, yeah, sure," Narcissus says, inwardly laughing at Polly's remark. "People don't have a choice when they hang around you. I'd say you
do a pretty good job at deciding who lives and who dies. Free will," Narcissus
says, taking yet another gulp, "free will gets thrown out the window."

"How's Melanthius holding up?" asks Polly.

Narcissus responds, "I haven't heard anyone use that name in quite some
time, and believe me, I've been around the block for a minute."

"Your boss is interfering with my business," she says and leans dangerously
close to Narcissus.

"Don't even try it," Narcissus says with a scowl, as he turns and faces
Polly. "I'm immune to fleas like you."

"I know," she says, still leaning in close to Narcissus. "You are indeed a
rare specimen, Narcissus. Forged by the hands of a god, only to be later exiled
by his own creator. Enlighten me, Narcissus: What's the world look like
through those eyes of yours?"

Narcissus thinks carefully about his next response.

With a smirk, Polly waits patiently.

"*Dark*," he says glumly. "It looks dark."

Polly leans back and takes a sip of beer. She glances around the bar, first at
the couple, who are both oblivious to their surroundings, and then Father Dawson and the other patron, who are arguing about Mando's cup size.

As Narcissus slides on his pair of shades and faces forward, Polly removes
a knife from her sleeve, the same one that she had stolen from the table while
those two lovebirds were stuffing their mouths with pulled pork nachos and
strumming their heart strings with the melody of sweet murmurings.

In the blink of an eye, she makes one swift jab across Narcissus's neck, precisely nicking his carotid artery, which is one of the major blood vessels that supply blood to the brain. She drops the knife handle-side down into the slit of Narcissus's coat pocket, grabs his other arm, and settles the crook of his elbow along the side of his face while the gash starts to squirt blood. Finally, once Polly positions Narcissus's upper body against the bar, she holds him in place as he bleeds out in a matter of minutes. Narcissus doesn't struggle. He doesn't even call out for help. Yet, he accepts his fate.

As Narcissus loses consciousness, Polly takes another sip of beer and leaves the bar. She nods goodbye to Father Dawson, who wishes Polly a good night.

He wraps up his conversation with the patron and checks on Narcissus, who, from Father Dawson's perspective, appears to be taking a nap against the bar.

Amused, Father Dawson says teasingly, "Calling it a night already. Are we, Mr. Wonder?"

It's not until Father Dawson stands in front of Narcissus and witnesses a puddle of blood forming on the bar that he realizes the severity of the situation.

By the time he races out of the bar, Polly has already driven away in a white van.

🕐

DETECTIVE Prentiss digs through the trash strewn all over the ground while Detective Moriarty still remains in a state of disbelief from the sight of the Jane Doe.

"What kind of individual would do such a thing to a person?" asks Moriarty, as she closely examines for any entry wounds along the bloody corpse.

"Could be the cartel," suggests Prentiss, as he holds up a used condom on the tip of his pen. "They've been known to make an example of their victims. . . " the detective trails off and flings away the condom. "Yuck," he says, making a face.

"What example is that, Mike? We're looking at a young woman, probably in her twenties. Not one single mark on her body. This was done by a professional, possibly someone who knows his or her way around the blade."

"Hey," one coroner says from behind, "it could be like one of those creatures from that one movie. Skins its victims, hangs them from trees. You know which one I'm talking about—"

"—Cut the crap already, will ya?" Moriarty says, as she stands up and glares at the coroner, who's taking a break from photographing the crime scene.

The coroner holds up his hands and backs away from the detective.

Detective Prentiss joins his partner at the other end of the tent where both of them gaze out into the heavy rainstorm.

"We have a young woman who's been skinned alive, body possibly dumped here," Prentiss says, as if thinking out loud is his way of gathering a motive. "Car without plates. Owner of the car, a woman named Polly Krakauer, a college student, bags in the backseat suggest she's driving back to her parent's

698

house in New Mexico. Possibly freaks out after coming across the corpse. Speeds away in another vehicle—"

"—Which doesn't make any sense at all."

"She could've been driving away for another reason," says Moriarty.

"Your gut?"

"My gut's in knots, Mike," Moriarty says bluntly, as she draws her eyes to a surveillance camera on the corner of the gas station.

THE dark entity stands in front of a furnace and burns the flesh of what used to be Polly Krakauer when, from a distance, an old, dusty payphone rings underneath a pile of rubble.

The entity leaves the fire and answers the call.

The payphone isn't even hooked up to a line; yet, the phone appears as if it hasn't been used in over three decades. And yet, somehow, the phone manages to still work.

The entity holds the phone to its shadowy slender face.

On the other line is a crumbly voice, which sounds like broken-up static.

The Void speaks, and the entity known as "Black Death" listens.

"NUTS AND BOLTS"

TWO prison guards escort the now former prisoner, Drenelle St. Croix aka the artist formerly known as the one and only Poochy Queen, who's rocking a tangerine orange Adidas tracksuit and "faux" rabbit fur boots with an emphasis on the *faux* in order to put that loyal fan base of hers, or her "lil Poochies," from trolling the Internet—one faction of her tribe tearing her to shreds and calling for her cancellation while the other defending her choice in attire until their fingers fall off—from the front gates of Forest City Penitentiary.

Both local and national news networks from around the country are gathered outside. A cloud of smoke lingers in the air like a thin blanket of fog.

With their microphones and digital tape recorders ready, starry-eyed reporters anxiously await Drenelle's release. The cameras are running. "We're live at Forest City Penitentiary!" Of course, it wouldn't be Poochy without its fair share of controversy.

As the guards release Drenelle into the sweaty arms of a private bodyguard of Samoan decent named Mahi, who escorts the former inmate of Forest City Penitentiary toward a black town car parked along the curb, an aggressive "pissed off" reporter manages to stick a recorder into Drenelle's face and shout out a question over the hoopla, *How does it feel to be a free woman?*"

Drenelle stops in her tracks, causing the crowd noise to ease down a bit. She eyes the reporter up and down while she puckers her lips in the most exaggerated way. She suddenly lets out a high pitch *paa-kaw*, which sounds like a screech of a bird. More exaggeratedly, Drenelle rolls her eyes at the reporter, who, any other day of the week, she'd call out as your typical soy boy who read too many *Hardy Boys* books growing up in a privileged household where you could pee with the toilet seat down without being punished.

Mahi makes a hole through the crowd as he walks Drenelle to the town car.

The back window of the car is cracked about two inches and a cloud of what smells like to Drenelle as cigarette smoke is pouring out.

As Drenelle approaches the car, he peers through the bodies surrounding him and spots two men, who, from outside the car, appear to be Arendt and Zwicker, two high profile lawyers, or "celebrity lawyers," sitting in the back-seat.

Mahi carefully pushes aside a couple of reporters from the car without breaking one of their limbs, even though breaking one of their limbs seems like a more suitable option, and opens the back door for Drenelle.

Becoming more and more agitated—but making damn well sure not to show it—by the growing hysteria from the mob, Drenelle steps into the vehicle without much thought. Before her are seated Key and Stat, not those two law-yers, Arendt and Zwicker, as she first observed from outside the car.

"I assume I should be thanking you two for getting me out," Drenelle says, cautiously studying the two strangers.

"You assumed right, Drenelle," Key says while Stat remains silent. "I had to pull a lot of strings to get you out, Drenelle, but you don't have to worry anymore. It's done. Based on 'new' evidence, you are no longer part of the system."

Mahi is next to enter the town car. He takes a seat in the passenger seat while the driver pulls away from Forest City.

"Well," Drenelle says as she does what she always does in situations that she can't explain and "runs" with the story, "what should I call you two?"

"This is my colleague, Stat," Key says, introducing Stat to Drenelle.

Stat doesn't say much at all; instead, he gives Drenelle a nod of, more or less, acknowledgment.

"Stat?" Making a frown, Drenelle shrugs and says sassily to Stat as both of her loose, flappy hands do most of the talking, "Okay. So what? I take it you're like *Robin* and he's your *Batman*. After all, you do look like a sidekick. No offense, Boo."

"Not exactly," Key says patiently before Stat has a chance to respond to that "sidekick" claim.

"So," Drenelle says, crossing one leg over the other, "what'd they call you?"

Drenelle waits for a response from the man who calls himself "Key," but it's nothing close to what she ever expected.

🕐

AT the base of Dark Mountain Star is greeted by Fay while Heloisa and the rest of CROCUTA Clan wait till Star is safe and secure within her group before leaving.

Star and Fay join the group.

Each one of the members embraces Star and welcomes her back to the group, except for Mandy, who, as of now, feels as if she's become a "fifth wheel."

REACHING the halfway mark of the tour through Neuvak Corporation & Pharmaceuticals, Doctor Harcourt walks American investor Rakesh Sorbet, philanthropist and CEO of Sherman Faulkner, to a secured door in front of a massive corridor.

The doctor places the underside of his wrist against a sensor next to the door. The red light remains red.

Doctor Harcourt gives Rakesh a crooked smile and says, "We've been having some issues with the implants." He reaches in his pocket. "No need to worry," he pulls out a card and shows the card to Rakesh. "Fail safe," he says and places the card against the sensor.

The door lights up green, opens.

Doctor Harcourt guides Rakesh toward one of the latest attractions.

"The housing units," he says, reaching a narrow hallway that stretches as far as the human eye can see. "Each one of our units is specifically furnished based on a subject's interest."

The doctor shows Rakesh the first unit where, inside, one of these "subjects" is sitting in a recliner chair and watching TV inside an average, homey, cozy living room.

"Each housing unit, which is roughly the size of a one-bedroom apartment, comes with a kitchen, a bathroom, one bedroom, and as you can see here, a living quarters."

The two occasionally stop and look through a monitor outside the unit, which displays the subject inside.

Rakesh points out the weight of each subject.

"Are they normally this, you know. . . "

"Fat?"

Rakesh nods, glancing inside the housing unit once more to observe the thousand pound man lying on the bed, hooked up to an IV.

"Yes," Doctor Harcourt says and finds himself backtracking, "well, not at the beginning stages. Thanks to your generous contribution, Mr. Sorbet, we found a way to speed up the process of growth from four to now two years through a new procedure known as 'dripping.' During the first trial runs, we would set up a location for our subjects outside the compounds, but after a while we realized how extremely difficult it was going to be to safely monitor the subjects without drawing any *unwanted* attention. Not only that, we soon learned that administering the Quidaquin through a drip feed increases the growth, opposed to the capsule form. So," he points at the housing units and showcases them as if they're works of art inside a gallery, "we decided it was best manageable to create these special housing units behind Neuvak." Doctor Harcourt goes on to say that eventually, he and his crew would like to expedite the process with such sufficiency and speediness that, once they *obtain* the subject—which Rakesh knows is just another word for kidnap—it will seem like a "quick swap."

The doctor says directly, "Nobody will ever know they went missing."

"Do the subjects ever interact with other subjects?" asks Rakesh.

"No," the doctor says. "Each subject is separated from other subjects—"

"—And how's that any different than a prison?"

"Well," the doctor says, not missing a beat, "we have a team of highly trained caretakers from all around the globe. Each one of our first-rate caretakers is specifically tasked to forge an unbreakable bond with our subjects in order to give the subjects a sense of belonging, as well as companionship." He turns his eyes back to a section of housing units before him. "This particular wing right here houses subjects who are at the final stages of their transition— or as we like to call around here, their 'awakening.'" He cracks a smile, leans in closer to Rakesh, and utters from the corner of his mouth, "Hence why they look like beached whales."

Rakesh doesn't find much amusement from the doctor's joke; in fact, he can barely bring himself to react to the comment.

"Anyway," the doctor says, continuing the tour, "we've already started Phase Two of the expansion of the housing units, which are scheduled to be complete by late fall."

Finally, the tour stops at one particular section, which Doctor Harcourt calls the "recovery room." Behind the glass window, Biff Craley is being instructed to recite from a script that has been given to him. On the table lays a folder named "PROJECT SLEEPING ELEPHANT."

"So," Rakesh says, stating the obvious, "how exactly are you going to explain Mr. Craley's disappearance to the public? If the press ever found out—"

"—The press isn't going to find out," the doctor says, more seriously. "And, as far as I see, the press will *never* find out. Our team of writers is now working on a story regarding Mr. Craley's disappearance. Next time you stop by, I would like to introduce them to you. Let's just say they're quite an imaginative bunch. Having said that, I have faith that they'll come up with something truly inspiring."

Both Doctor Harcourt and Rakesh pay closer attention to the commands Biff is given by one of Neuvak's staff members.

"And now, without further ado, it is my honor—"

"No, no, no," the frustrated script supervisor says, "he wants an emphasis on punctuation. Not 'And now,'" she says sluggishly, "'without further do.' Instead, it should to be 'And now!'" she cries out, her voice more booming, "'without further ado, it is my honor to introduce the talented, the haunting Five Fistfuls!'"

Rakesh turns to Doctor Harcourt and asks, "Five Fistfuls?"

"It's a group that's going to be part of the big Telethon next Saturday night," he says. "Originally, they called themselves Fuck-It-All Five, but they ended up changing the name because they're not allowed to use the word *fuck* on TV. So, the girls changed their name to 'Fistful Five.' Grammatically, the word *fistful* is considered a noun so they thought it would be in poor taste to use a noun before a number so one of the girls, Rhonda, suggested that they just switch the two words around—"

"—You know what. . . " Rakesh says over the doctor and returns his focus to Biff inside the glassed-in room, ". . . forget I asked."

The script supervisor places the script aside on the table and tells Biff to recall the movie, *The Runaway*. She explains that, in the movie, Biff played a confused young man who, after the death of his father, ran away and completely shut off society. She wants Biff to channel the character, Spud, particularly, the one scene where Spud got upset at his mother and yelled at her in his best imitation of his father, who was a car salesman; and using his father's game show-like personality, Spud vociferated his fears of turning into his father after years and years of loathing him.

"Remember that one line," the script supervisor says to Biff, "*I have one helluva a Beamer. She's quite the screamer. . .* "

"*Come on down,*" Biff recites the line with the script supervisor, both their voices punctuating each word, "*give her a spin,*" his voice gets louder, his manner more animate, "*Fully loaded with AC, radio, and adjustable seating. . .* " he rambles on and on about the features of the automobile until, eventually, Biff stands from the seat to read those lines from the script, "*And now, without further ado, it is my honor to introduce the talented, the haunting Five Fistfuls!*"

"That's it, my man," the script supervisor says, more than pleased by the performance. "Now, you got it!"

"I can't believe it," Rakesh says in awe. "The man actually sounds and looks just like Biff Craley. The resemblance. . . it's uncanny."

"Amazing, huh?" Doctor Harcourt says. "But don't be mistaken, Mr. Sorbet. The subject is still Biff Craley, only now he's *our* Biff Craley."

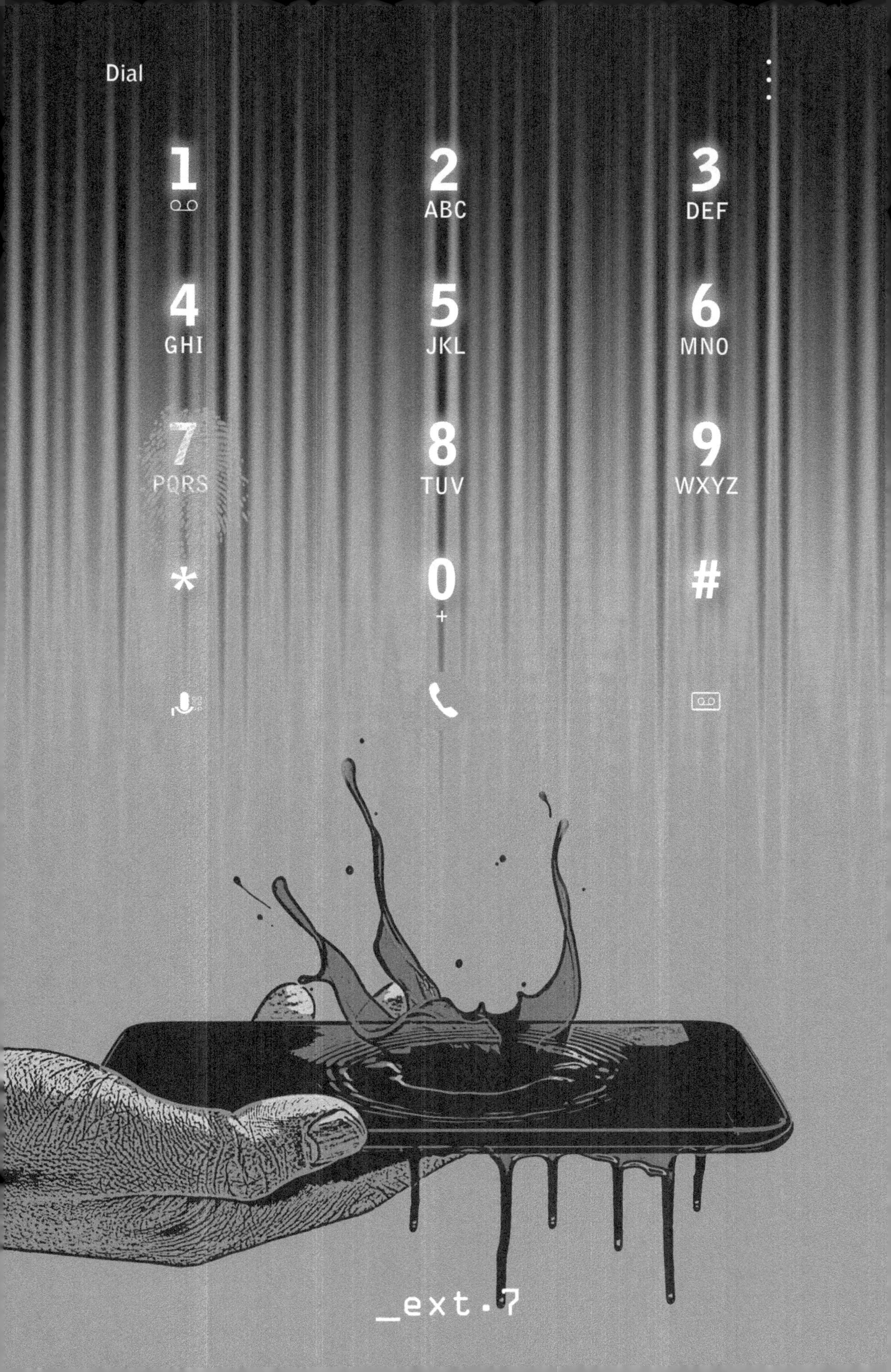
Dial
1
2
ABC
3
DEF
4
GHI
5
JKL
6
MNO
7
PQRS
8
TUV
9
WXYZ
*
0
+
#
_ext.7

STANDING tall in his all black Mao suit, Key was beginning to lose his patience.

Behind Key sat his own personal "mood ring," Stat, who was slouched over a microphone on a desk tucked away in the darkest corner of the room.

In front of Key was a large one-way mirror, which was most commonly used for interrogation rooms.

In the other brighter, much larger room behind the one-way mirror were precisely ten chairs, each one placed next to one another in a perfect line. Ten volunteers of various ethnicities, as well as varying in weight, height, and size, sat like guinea pigs in each one of the ten chairs. In front of each one of these volunteers was a tray holding a smartphone.

Extremely cool in demeanor despite the screaming match of a million angry voices inside his head, Key embraced the sound of the door *opening* to his left.

"She's here," Ruby said, poking her head into the dark room.

"Thank you, Ruby," Key said with relief as his attention remained focused on the ten volunteers. "Let her in."

Only a few seconds after leaving the room, Ruby fully opened the door and revealed a team of doctors, who were gathered around in the hallway. She reentered with presidential candidate, Avanti Washington, as well as two secret service agents.

Avanti told the two agents to wait outside while she conducted her business.

Key glanced at Ruby, who, in return, was waiting for Key's permission.

"It's okay," he said calmly. "Leave us."

Following commands, Ruby escorted the two agents from the room.

In the corner of her eye, Avanti witnessed the volunteers.

"Don't worry," Key said to Avanti. "They can't see us."

Stat sat upright from Avanti's presence.

Acknowledging Stat, Avanti nodded her head with a "hello."

"This is my advisor, Stat," Key said, pointing at Stat.

"Nice to meet you, Ms. Washington," Stat said with a tremble in his voice.

"Yes," she said, her eyes keen on Stat. "Likewise." She walked up to Key, who greeted the candidate with a handshake. "If it isn't the Master of Macabre," she said, shaking Key's hand. "Hello, Mr. Warrick. It's a pleasure."

"Trust me," he said, maintaining his composure. "The pleasure is all mine."

"I have to say Mr. Sorbet was quite impressed with what you've managed to pull off," Avanti said, referring to the wealthy investor, Rakesh Sorbet, or better yet, Neuvak's knight in shining armor who, not only came to the pharmaceutical company's rescue after their stock was hit hard after the recent outbreak, but also one of Avanti's major contributors to her campaign.

"Well, it's fair to say an artist does his greatest work when faced with a deadline."

"If you can give me the votes to beat Rhodes, Mr. Warrick, then I'd say you created yourself one of the greatest tools money can buy. I'd go as far to call it a masterpiece."

"Oh," Key said confidently and at the same time, flattered by Avanti's comment, "I'll get you the voters you need to win the election. You just have to live up to your end of the deal."

"A deal's a deal," she said. "And as far as I see it, you're providing a service to this country."

"Well," Key said, cracking a smile, "like Bob Dylan said, 'The times are ah-changing.'"

"Indeed they are."

"Tell me, Governor," Key said, "if voters knew who you really were, do you think they would still vote for you?"

"People only criticize what they don't understand, right?" Avanti said. "Inherently, people are frightened of what they don't understand. For most of them, regardless of who they might think I am, they look at me as a threat to their perfect world."

"The age of decadence is coming to an end once and for all, Governor," Key said, turning his attention back to the volunteers. "It's an *awakening*. The people who occupy this world are finally realizing that they've been sold a lie."

"And isn't that what you're doing? You're essentially selling them immortality while promising them prosperity. Which we both know is a lie."I'm giving them a way out from the madness."

"Funding your own death doesn't exactly strike me as way of the American Spirit, Mr. Warrick."

"If it makes you feel comfortable," Key said sarcastically, "the Great Merger will be, let's just say, more 'inclusive.'"

"You underestimate their kind," Avanti said to Key. "They're survivors. It's in their nature."

"Save the talking points, Governor."

"Well," Avanti said, holding out her hands, "let's see it then. . . "

With his arms held behind his back, Key turned his shoulder and nodded at Stat, who, through an intercom, instructed the ten volunteers to pick up the smartphones in front of them. Then, he told the first five volunteers to TEXT "7" at the number 32756377 while the other remaining five volunteers were told to dial the phone number "1-800-DARKNES, ext. 7."

"The signal is activated," Stat said, flipping a switch on a controller.

Somewhere in a dark corridor inside an unknown location hidden deep in the mountains, the lights on a wall of towering servers, which were covered in slimy roots, changed over from a beating purplish-blue to the color blood red.

As the volunteers texted, as well as called these specific numbers and eagerly placed the phone's receiver up to their ears, a piercing "bleep"-like sound blared out from the receiver, penetrating into their eardrums and deep into their brains.

All of a sudden, nine out of the ten callers and texters grabbed hold of their chests. Their hearts instantly stopped beating, resulting in some of the volunteers to fall forward over the trays while others to fall back in their chairs and collapse to the floor. The tenth volunteer—one of the five callers—wasn't clutching his chest, but rather standing up in a state of bewilderment. He staggered around and grabbed his head.

As the confusion turned to utter panic, the veiny red-faced volunteer cried out in bloody horror, "What the fuck is happening to me?"

As he screamed out, parts of his head bulged outward.

He suddenly darted toward the mirror on the wall and slammed the top of his forehead against the glass, partially shattering it.

Before the volunteer could ram his head into the mirror once more, his head exploded in the popping sound of a water balloon!

Blood splattered all over the mirror. Pieces of brain matter dripped down the glass.

The volunteer's body flopped to the ground.

A team of doctors and handlers entered the other room and carried out nine out of the ten volunteers on a gurney.

"Doesn't exactly count as a potential voter," Avanti said with a dark sense of humor.

"Well, it wouldn't be the first time a dead man's cast a ballot. Would it?"

"How about the others?" Avanti asked, referring to the other nine volunteers. "We need actual bodies to show up at the polls, not the Headless Horseman."

"As I'm sure Sorbet has already explained, each volunteer's pneuma will be injected with a special parasite by *our* folks on the Other Side. When the volunteer's pneuma returns to this world, his or her body will act as a host for the parasite. Within twenty-four hours, the growth will be removed from the body, which will be incinerated, and you, Governor Avanti Washington, will have yourself a voter. They'll be back at home before they were even missed."

"And what about the ones that won't make it?" asked Avanti, as she directed her attention back toward the headless corpse.

"Comes with the price of winning," Key said callously and watched the body handlers carry out one of the "temporarily dead" volunteers from the other room.

Avanti provoked the most obvious question: "And this so-called 'parasite,' it'll do whatever you tell it to do?"

Key nodded.

"If we wanted to, Ms. Washington," he said, "we can train it to roll over and play dead."

"CALLER BEWARE"
(THE DAY OF)

WITH Key's "*Midnight World!*" Telethon only hours away from airing "LIVE" on national television, Key was backstage going over the final design for the packaging of the "*Midnight World* Bundles" with controversial artist, Cleft Lip.

Key was dressed in a stiff yet showy oversized bright purple suit with shoulders pads twice the size of a football player. Lightning bolts in the shape of "Ms" and "Ws" were trimmed into the sides of his tight fade.

"Each donor will 'supposedly' receive a bundle containing various products," Cleft Lip listed, as he cracked open the MW box of goodies on the table, "Poisonous Flower perfume for the ladies," he said, pulling out all the MERCH, "or Dog Breath cologne for the fellas." Then, "trading cards, *Midnight World* T-shirts and shorts, vamp hoodies, and other swag. . ." he held up a black coffee mug with the political slogan "Vote 4 Washington or Die" written in bold red, white, and blue Arial font, as well as other swag, including "Vote" pins and buttons, the capital V shaped like the tooth of a vampire, ". . . books, including origin stories, as well as *The Chronicles of Krillish* and several Best-Selling paperbacks by the author Neil Reddy, a free one-year subscription to the *Midnight World* channel with *The Five-Minute History of Midnight World*, movies, posters and figurines signed by spin-celebrity Ericka Barnes, the replica scissors used by The Snipper, Mr. Moonlight glow-in-the-dark sunglasses, a 1,000 piece puzzle 'The Last Jam' featuring former professional wrestler Blaine Toussaint, a key chain with the good luck charm of a werewolf snake's claw, a Dr. Love stress-relieving plush toy, then," Cleft Lip stopped to catch his breath, as he pulled out one last item, the black matte-finished bottle with a skull and crossbones design embedded on the side, "finally, a bottle of Immortality."

With a look of surprise on his face, Key said straightforwardly, "Impressive."

"Thank you, Key," Cleft Lip said, all jittery. "It's a honor coming from you."

"Very nice work," Key said, lifting up the bottle of Immortality.

"Thank you," Cleft Lip, more relieved by Key's approval.

Key opened the bottle of Immortality.

The bottle was empty.

"It's a prop, of course," Cleft Lip said before Key could question the product. "They're all props."

Key picked up the book, *The Chronicles of Krillish*, and opened it.

The pages inside were blank white.

"You know, you almost had me convinced," Key said and nodded at a mound of *Midnight World* Bundles stacked on the pallet waiting to be transported to the display wheel behind the curtains. "How about the other boxes?"

"Props," Cleft Lip said and turned his focus back to the table. "This box here will be on display for the audience."

Cleft Lip waited in suspense for Key's *final* approval on his work.

Over a tense pause, he placed the book on the table and held out his hand for Cleft Lip to shake.

More stoked, Cleft Lip shook Key's hand while, at the same time, letting out a sigh of relief.

With perfect timing, Ruby shouldered her way past several lighting guys and riggers, who were hauling in equipment from the back of a truck parked in a loading dock, and approached Key from behind.

"Excuse me, sir," she said, pulling Key away from Cleft Lip, "you're needed in Marketing. Eleventh hour is approaching, and we need your feedback."

"Sure thing," he said, checking the time on his wristwatch. He left Cleft Lip and walked with Ruby to the "Bot Farm" room. "Let's make this fast, Ruby. I've got to check on Craley and make sure he's fully prepped. Last time I checked on him he was acting a little glitchy, if you know what I mean."

"Could be last-minute nerves?" Ruby suggested.

"They weren't trained to be nervous, Ruby."

On the way to Marketing, Key walked past a monitor displaying a video of a segment, which was going to be aired during the Telethon. The video showed a caller who appeared down in the dumps while sitting on a couch in a dark living room with the glow of the TV pressed against his face. Somewhat skeptical, he picked up the phone from the coffee table and dialed a number. Once the dejected man started to talk to the operator on the other line, his mood began to change and surprisingly, his spirits were suddenly uplifted.

While walking, Key said to Ruby, "Tell the Video Department to bring up the lighting in the promo shots. We want the callers to actually see each actor's reactions, not be left in the dark."

"You got it," Ruby said, typing in a MEMO on her eTablet. "Anything else?"

"Maybe add some music in the background."

Ruby typed in "Add music" to her MEMO.

Passing by several more staff members, Key and Ruby finally arrived at the Marketing room. The sign outside the room said, "BOT FARM."

Bracing herself for the unexpected, Ruby cautiously opened the door for Key, who immediately wrinkled his nose due to the foul, pungent smell emitting from each one of the zombie-like creatures that were standing in slouched over postures inches apart from one another inside a humid and dimly lit room. The creatures' faces were slack and droopy and hung like oversized masks, each orifice on their face hollowed out. On the back of each creature suspended fleshy umbilical cord-like tubes attached to the callused nipples of a subterranean Hog Maggot, which was bathing in fresh manure.

Undistracted by Key's presence, the zombie-like creatures, these "Bots," had a smartphone in their hands. Their heads were hanging downward and planted in the devices as they mindlessly typed away a hundred tweets per minute.

"What's the problem, Ruby?" asked Key.

"It's nothing big," she said and at times, held her breath from the awful smell. "Well, it's just some of their tweets are suspicious in nature."

Ruby showed several "flagged" tweets on her eTablet device.

One read from **John Smith @IAMJOHNSMITH**:

@MidnightWorldOfficial The whole damn thing is a scam!!! **#MidnightWorld** #Tele-not

Another from **Claude Barnshed ☠☠☠ @ClaudesKitchen**:

Don't believe whateva they be tellin u. **Midnight World** is not real. #MidnightGate

Then, another:

Melissa Kyle @BatshitCrazyBitch All u mouthbreathers r being played by these fools in charge of #FakeWorld. The telethon 2nite is the END OF THE F'N WORLD as we no it. You can all kiss ur ass goodbye ✆ ✋

More timid than cautious, Ruby hesitantly escorted Key to three of the zombie-creatures who were mis-tweeting. They were tweeting at a much more lethargic pace, Key noticed. He looked around the farm, saw the half-full water bottle in Ruby's hand, and asked for it. She handed over the water bottle to Key, who, in return, squeezed the bottle in the zombie-creature's face, dowsing it with water.

Key ordered Ruby to pull up John Smith's latest tweets. The zombie-creature was typing faster and doing so with more liveliness.

John Smith @IAMJOHNSMITH: So looking forward to **@MidnightWorldOfficial** Telethon tonight. Can't wait to see Zip Drive live in action!!! Going to be off the hook!!! **#MidnightWorld**

"There you go," Key said, handing the eTablet back to Ruby. "Get one of the interns in here. Make sure you tell them to keep the Bots hydrated."

"Will do, sir," Ruby said, following Key from the Bot Farm.

On the way out, Key's massive shoulders hit the sides of the doorway, forcing him to exit sideways from the room.

"DRENELLE'S GUEST"

As Ruby parted ways with Key, she ran into Drenelle, who was standing next to a line array speaker.

Dressed in orange tights underneath a tracksuit jacket, she was holding what looked like a script in her hand. Next to her was the scriptwriter, Calyx, who had written the speech for Drenelle.

Clearly, while rehearsing lines, Drenelle wasn't at all comfortable with parts of the speech.

She pointed at one line in particular: "How are people going to sympathize with. . . *being raised in a mental institution*? People have a nose for sniffing out bullshit. Besides, all my followers know I spent most of my adolescence raised in the city. It ain't me—"

Drenelle paused from the sight of Ruby, who flashed him a smile.

Speechless, Drenelle couldn't help but lose herself in Ruby's familiar face as she passed by.

Deep down inside, a part of Drenelle knew Ruby; strangely enough, in what felt like another life, she was, once, acquainted with Ruby and she'd go so far to call her a "friend" or even more than a friend.

"Drenelle?"

Calyx was chirping in Drenelle's ear.

Both Drenelle and Ruby shared eye contact. Ruby was skittish from the sight of Drenelle, being that she was in the presence of a notorious murderer known as The Snipper. Drenelle, on the other hand, found—if anything—great comfort in Ruby's presence.

Drenelle snapped from her trance and pulled her eyes away from Ruby's familiar face and while doing so, noticed a pig with a leash being walked down the hallway by the pig's caretaker, a stout man dressed like the countryside.

She wondered what a pig was doing here.

Maybe it was part of the show.

A prop perhaps?

Nonetheless, Drenelle couldn't take her eyes off the domestic pig.

Overwhelmed with nostalgia, she handed the script to Calyx, who insisted that Drenelle finish rehearsing the rest of her speech.

Annoyed by Calyx, Drenelle excused herself and followed the man, who was walking the pig down the hallway.

She was more interested in the pig than the man.

"MANDATORY"

STAR, as well as the four other members of Five Fistfuls, or what advertisers were advertising as a "Not Your Everyday Coven," shuffled through the line in front of the spread of the most succulent food. On a silver tray sat a roasted pig with an apple in its mouth. Rhonda helped herself to a part of pig butt, which drew a look of disgust from Fay, who immediately recoiled and said, "I think I'm gonna puke."

"What's the matter, Fay?" Rhonda said innocently while placing a generous helping of sautéed green beans on her plate.

She kept the line moving by shuffling her way to a dish of sweet yams and helped herself to not one scoop but two scoops of yams.

"So, what? You a vegetarian again, Fay?" asked Carmen.

"You're one to talk, Carmen," Fay said sickly. "Self-proclaimed vegetarian who promotes herself as a 'vegetarian' one week while, the next, you're secretly stuffing your gullet with fucking meermaarms."

"So what's wrong with meermaarms?" asked Carmen, holding up the line for Star, who was waiting in the back of the line. "They're rich in protein."

"But they're so hard to catch—"

"—Not if you're doing it right."

"Gotta take whatever you can find, Fay," Mandy said in defense of Carmen's dietary indecisiveness. "After all, we're kind of limited in the desert."

"Quit your bellyaching, Fay," Rhonda said, piling on a slice of cheesecake with raspberry sauce on her already packed plate of food. "You need to eat something or else we're not going to perform to our best abilities." Rhonda's temper became more heated with every word she spoke. She grabbed a couple of glazed donuts and piled them onto the plate, as if the anger itself was driving the snake worms' enormous appetite. "There's a reason why we're called *The*

Five Fistfuls. Five Fistfuls, meaning it takes all five of us to contribute to the act!"

"Yeah," Carmen said mildly. "Rhonda's right. You're being selfish, Fay. If you have to, force yourself to eat. You need your strength."

Fay turned to Star, who remained quiet in the back.

"Thanks for coming to my rescue, Star," Fay said, turning her attention back to the endless spread of food stacked on top of the table, which stretched across an entire room that was curtained off from the rest of production.

"Just shut up and eat something, Fay," Star said without a care in the world.

"Easy for you to say," Fay said, grabbing two vegetable spring rolls from the tray and doing so with disgust.

"If we blow it tonight," Mandy said, ignoring Fay's childish behavior, "millions of people are going to rip *The Five Fistfuls* to shreds on Tweeter. We don't need that kind of bad publicity."

"We?" Fay said under her snake worm breath. "You mean 'you.'"

"Besides, what does eating have to do with our act?" asked Fay.

"It has everything to do with our act, Fay," Mandy said, losing her cool with Fay. "You need to feed those little puppies inside you."

As of lately, Mandy referred to the snake worms as "puppies."

Which only made Fay sicker to her stomach.

As Fay was about to rush behind the curtains, Drenelle entered the room.

Standing in a frozen posture as if she got caught in the act of doing something she wasn't supposed to be doing—or better yet, sticking her nose in a place that was considered off limits—Drenelle's presence alone forced *The Five Fistfuls* to acknowledge her and, let's just say, her "unwanted" presence.

"Sorry to interrupt whatever it is you're doing, but. . . " Drenelle said, trying to make sense as to what exactly these five red-cloaked snake worms were doing, which, to Drenelle, went well-beyond just your average eating, ". . . have any of you seen this man walking a pig?"

Over the tense silence, Carmen said, "Excuse me?"

"A man," Drenelle reiterated for the members of *The Five Fistfuls*, "who was walking a pig on a leash, did he come through here recently?"

More tension built.

Misplacing sass for sarcasm, Mandy said to Drenelle, "No. But we got ourselves a pig right *her*."

The comment provoked laughter from the other members, except Star.

Over the laughter, Star said in a more serious tone to Drenelle, "No. We haven't seen him."

"Thanks," Drenelle said to Star, who replied, "No problem."

As Drenelle exited through the curtains, Mandy turned to Carmen, saying without any shame, "Weirdo."

"I know, right?" Carmen returned. "Can't believe that creep's going to be the main attraction."

"She's the creep?" said Star, releasing the pent-up frustration.

"Yeah," she said. "*She* is—"

"—When's the last time you looked at yourself in the mirror?" asked Star. "Like you're any different?"

Feeling more at ease with the others' discomfort by Drenelle's presence, Fay said, "Face it, Carm. You're just jealous because you're not the main attraction."

"Whatever," Carmen said to herself.

From a distance, Drenelle could hear those "things" arguing behind the curtains. Normally, she'd be amazed how her presence alone created such contention among both sexes—but snake worms?

Who would've ever thought?

Drenelle picked up the pig's scent coming from down another hallway, which led her to cage where a werewolf snake was being held. From the rattling of the cage's bars, it was clear to Drenelle that the werewolf snake appeared agitated.

As Drenelle peeked behind the wall, she soon realized why it was so agitated.

There, only feet away from the cage, stood the pig's caretaker, who was teasing the werewolf snake with the pig.

The caretaker, who was anything but a caretaker, picked up the squealing pig and held it up to the cage, only inches away from the werewolf snake's reach.

As the werewolf snake swiped at the pig with its massive claws, the caretaker retracted the pig.

"Here, *Zippy Zippy*," the caretaker said more cruelly.

The werewolf snake reared back in a defensive position and made a low, guttural noise, which sounded like a cross between a hiss and a growl.

"Looks like someone's going to be supper tonight," the caretaker said to the squealing pig, who was trying to kick itself free from his arms.

Drenelle had no other choice than to act. She searched around backstage for a tool, anything sharp. She found an open toolbox next to a rig. She dug around the tools but couldn't find any scissors; however, she found a screwdriver.

She told herself that it would have to make do.

"A PING—OR LACK THEREOF"

WHILE Key was talking about the album *Flaming Skyline* with Eel-Baby from the band Eel-Baby and The Cuts, he heard a disturbance behind Eel-Baby. Key was in mid-sentence when he leaned past Eel-Baby, only to witness Stat rushing to the bathroom.

Key excused himself and checked on Stat, who appeared extremely fatigued as he exited from the stall. He went straight to the faucet to wash his mouth.

As Stat looked up at the mirror, he witnessed Key standing behind his reflection.

"Sup, Key?"

"Sup with you, Stat?" Key asked, as if his question was more appropriate.

"I ain't feeling too well," he said honestly.

"Well," Key said, "you know I need you for the show, right?"

"Yeah," Stat said, drying the corners of his mouth with a paper towel. "It's just. . ." he waved his hand, ". . . Never mind."

"Out with it."

"It's just strange. That's all."

"What's strange?" asked Key.

"I was making my rounds through the building when, all of a sudden, I had this feeling come over me. It came out of nowhere—"

"—What kind of feeling?"

"It's hard to explain," Stat said, thinking. "It's like I felt. . . nothing. Like an emptiness, you know?"

"I see," Key said and drifted off for a moment.

"What's going on, Key?" asked Stat.

Lightning flashes lit up the dark skies in Key's mind.

The sound of Stat's voice forced Key to snap from his trance. He told Stat to stay close; and together, the two exited from the bathroom.

"COLD FEET"

IN the dressing room, Biff Craley was closely watching old videos of himself—or his former self—on the monitor.

The footage displayed on the monitor was a scene from the flick, *The Shallowing*, where ole Biff played a savvy marine biologist named Mark Riddlehouse, who was studying the reasons as to why the ocean waters were drastically receding across the entire East Coast.

He'd carefully study TV-Biff's body gestures, facial expressions, and movements. Then, while looking back and forth from the vanity mirror to the monitor, he'd mimic TV-Biff, starting with a smile, which looked as though the corners of his lips were being pulled by strings.

Frustrated, Biff turned off the TV with a remote and snatched the script from the vanity and looked over his speaking parts but could only get through a couple of lines of the opening monologue before giving up.

Saved by the *knock*, Biff turned to the door where Key was poking his head inside the dressing room.

"Just checking in," Key said, carefully studying Biff. Standing next to Key, away from Biff's range of sight, was Stat. Without Biff noticing, Stat was listening in on the conversation in order to detect any irregularities in Biff's voice. Key asked Biff, "How's everything going?"

"I don't know if I can do this, Mr. Warrick," Biff said unsurely.

Clearly, based on his insecurities, he wasn't like the debonair actor but rather a far cry from the man who once possessed a supernatural-like charm, which had ladies from across the entire world swooning while moaning his name with a faint tremble in their voice.

"Sure you can, ole buddy," Key said, stepping into the dressing room. Key placed his hands over Biff's shoulders and began to massage them. "Just remember your training and you'll be fine." Biff appeared more disheartened by Key's reinsurance. He slapped Biff on the back. "Smile, Biff. This is your comeback."

Distracted by the sound of *knocking*, Key pulled his eyes from Biff's reflection in the mirror and turned to the door where Paige, one of the PAs, was muffling the speaker along her headset.

"What is it now, Paige?" asked Key.

"It's Drenelle," she said, pulling down the headset.

"What about her?"

"She's missing," Paige said, bracing herself for Key's wrath.

Key asked, "Have you checked the other dressing rooms?"

"Yes," Paige said. "I can't find her anywhere. Also. . ."

Key found himself clenching his teeth from that word *also*.

"There's one more thing. . ." Paige said, as she struggled to finish the rest of her sentence.

"CUT, PASTE, COPY"

PAIGE escorted Key and Stat to the werewolf snake's cage.

Immediately, Key knew something was terribly wrong when he saw the puddle of blood outside the cage, as well as inside the cage where the werewolf snake was curled up like a coil. Extremely protective of its kill, the werewolf snake was obviously in the middle of consuming its meal, and all that remained of the caretaker was one of his tennis shoes.

Stat picked up the bloodstained shoe, which was lying outside the cage.

Key called out to Stat, "Help Paige look for Drenelle."

"Where are you going to be?" asked Stat.

"I'll be in my office," he said.

"WHO REPLACES THE REPLACEABLES?"

BIFF returned to the script and was enthusiastically reciting his lines for to-night's telethon, "*And now, without further ado, it is my honor to introduce the talented, the haunting—*", when he was caught off guard by the *squeak* of a closet door behind him.

Biff set the script down on the vanity and checked out the noise.

As he reached the closet, which was partially cracked open, a black rat about the size of Biff's foot, suddenly darted out of the closet!

The black rat scurried underneath Biff's feet, causing him to dance around a bit.

Startled by the pesky rodent, he followed the black rat back to the vanity but ended up losing it underneath the table.

As he stood up, he noticed someone standing behind him.

In the reflection, he witnessed another reflection staring directly back at him. The reflection looked identical to himself; in fact, it was a mirror image, the only difference being that this man—this stranger—was dressed in more casual attire, opposed to a suit and tie.

Biff rotated around until he was face-to-face with the look-alike.

Stupefied, Biff asked, "Who are you?"

"Death," the look-alike said and before Biff could respond or even make any attempt to flee from this darker, sinister presence before him, a stinger withdrew from the tip of the look-alike's finger.

Once Biff spoke, it was all over.

The look-alike already had the stinger jammed directly in Biff's ear.

Biff's eyes swelled outward, mouth gaping, screaming.

His screams were soon cut short as the stinger violently thrust its way farther into Biff's head.

By the time Ollie, one of the several makeup artists who was helping out the Wardrobe Department, entered the dressing room, the talent, Mr. Craley, was sitting in his chair, casually rehearsing lines.

Ollie picked up the tie off the floor and placed it on a clothes hanger.

As she tended to Biff by first making sure his face was properly powdered before he appeared on camera, she stopped what she was doing and further examined the piece of loose skin on the back of his neck. A couple drops of blood ran down the strange-looking cut—or burn, Ollie couldn't tell which. Ollie excused herself from the dressing room, grabbed a first aid kit from another room, and by the time she returned to Biff's dressing room with a band-aid, as well as gauze, the loose piece of skin was no longer there; in fact, all that remained was a couple of drops of blood that had stained part of Biff's white collar. Ollie was stumped, but she didn't think anything of it.

Right now, she'd take any break she could find.

"A CONVERSATION"

BOUNCING his leg up and down along the floor in a state of anxiety from the domino effect of mishaps, Key was sitting in a high back leather chair inside his office when the door unexpectedly opened.

With the back of his chair facing the doorway, he didn't bother spinning the chair around to acknowledge or even make eye contact with the visitor; yet, somehow, based on Stat's "feeling" or his "*lack of*" feeling earlier that night, Key had a pretty good idea who was creeping up behind him.

"Have a seat," he said and spun the chair around until he was facing the desk. There, sitting stiffly in the chair on the other side of the desk was none other than his host of the tonight's telethon: Biff Craley.

"What can I do for you, Biff?" asked Key, who was pretending that the handsomely rugged yet debonair man sitting in front of him was, in fact, Biff Craley.

"What can you do for me. . . " Biff responded, his voice somewhat raspy as if he had a glob of phlegm stuck in the bottom of his throat. He momentarily paused to massage away the grittiness. He used his hand to straighten out the vocal cords, as if, in a way, he was tuning them. As Biff's voice returned to normal, he finished saying, ". . . there is one thing you can do for me."

"Oh yeah," Key said, sitting upright.

Biff kept a surprisingly fidgety Key waiting as if he received pleasure in watching his boss squirm and wiggle in his seat.

Just as Biff was about to respond to Key, he said, "I saw what's her name? Is it Drenelle?"

Key barely nodded.

"I saw Drenelle storming from the studio," Biff finished. "Now that she's no longer part of your show, who's going to replace your final act?"

"I don't know, Biff," Key said, going along with Biff's game. "You tell me, since, clearly, you know more than I do."

"It sucks, doesn't it? When things don't go your way—"

"—We'll find a replacement," Key said, bleeding internally.

"I'm sure you will." Biff turned his head in thought. "Your whole plan was to 'humanize' a man, now woman, for the viewers who were going to tune-in into tonight's show, am I right? As the talking heads call it, play the 'sympathy card.' It's not a bad strategy, though. What better way to gain more viewers than to exploit the media and how *they* tried to ruin and destroy a human being's life? 'Call 'em out,' as they say. All for what? Ratings? Most people, who won't be tuning in, are well aware of Drenelle's past crimes. But it doesn't matter, does it? It's all about the clicks. More clicks means more revenue. More revenue means more advertising. More advertising means more revenue. Round and round we go," he moved his hand in a circle, "the money keeps pouring in. Did you ever think that you, Melanthius, the son of the great Drómia, has a story worth telling?"

"I haven't been called that name in," Key said finally, not thinking about his story but rather his last encounter with the dark, manipulative entity sitting before him, "I dunno," he uttered, "seems like centuries."

"Hello, Thius," Biff said, confirming Key's suspicions.

Key pulled himself from the office and mentally found himself back on Dark Mountain, confronting Black Death. *Lightning flickered all around them. The air was electric and it felt as if something incredibly wicked was about to happen—a sort of calm before the storm. Right before Black Death was about to pounce on Key, that wickedness, the storm, was upon them; however, it wasn't like any other storm that neither one of them ever expected. A warm bright light flashed in the corner of Key's eye, forcing him to shield his face. The once dark sky lit up with an array of orange, red, and purple colors. The flickers of lightning muted from a distant explosion. Directly above Key, the great beast, the serpent known as Sheik disrupted the dark sky, coiling the very clouds that protected them from the other, more hostile worlds. Coiling and slithering in and around the swollen clouds, Sheik wrung out the rain, which provided the nutrients to the life below. As the radioactive rain turned to an all out downpour, each and every life form below started to change and mutate. Key readied himself to attack Black Death when it was the most vulnerable; however, before doing so, Black Death had already fled from the summit of the mountain, leaving Key with no other choice than to seek refuge back in the neighboring world.*

"What did you say to Drenelle?" asked Key.

"I didn't say anything," Biff said innocently. "She left on her own *free will*." Biff studied Key and the contours of disappointment forming underneath his face. "No matter how hard you try, Thius, you can't control people."

"And you can?" said Key.

"No," Biff said, narrowing his eyes. "I have no interest in controlling them, Key. I'd rather kill each and every last one of them. But I agreed to live up to my end of the deal. . . "

"Deal?" said Key. "What deal?"

Key was well aware the entity that sat before him, the one that wore the face of a man named Biff Craley, the one who was the former advisor to Drómia, the one that innately spat on Deals of Man, would strut to the edge of oblivion in order to stop the manufacturing of Neuvak's new "soul-controlling, award-winning" drug, Quidaquin, or Q, for it felt as if its greatest competitor was gaining the upper hand.

Biff said to Key, "You thought she was just going to stay out of your way as soon as you got her the votes she needed to win the White House? All you are to her is a failsafe. A woman like Avanti Washington would risk wiping out half of humanity, if it gave her a greater lead in the polls, which, by the way, are sliding the wrong direction despite the death of her son, whom, by the way, I've heard is making quite a name for himself. You, of all the travelers, should know that there can only be one cook in the kitchen."

"You think I didn't know she'd try to take me out after she got elected president?" Key asked but didn't expect Biff to answer. "Surely, I thought she would at least send some low-grade assassin after me: Lil' Grim or the Darker Angel, the Russian Bot, even the so-called 'Cosmic Vigilante,' the balancer of good and evil. Hell! The fuckin' Corrector. You and I both know that genocidal maniac is always looking for work; *but*, the fact she sent you after me shows me how desperate she really is."

"What can I say, Thius?" Biff said arrogantly, displaying a crooked smile. "I am good at what I do." The smile grew wider and wider into the side of his face. "Ask Narcissus," he said, evoking a reaction from Key.

"Curious," Key said, as he attempted to put the remark about his loyal right-hand man behind him, "What do you get out of this so-called 'deal' anyway?"

"Every few years or so I get to unleash a disease onto the world without wiping out humanity in its entirety."

"Thought your ass worked alone."

Biff held up both of his hands while holding his shoulders in a shrug. He said foolishly, "Gotta make ends meant somehow."

"She obviously doesn't know what she's up against, hiring a piece of shit like you who piggybacks off fleas."

Biff shrugged.

"I'll take that as a compliment," he said, smirking.

"You might want to consider updating your name from Black Death to something a little more modern, don't you think? I mean," Key said and paused as he dug through an entire list of names that Black Death had used throughout the past millenniums, "you can always go back to *Creode*. That name suited you well."

The sound of the name "Creode" wiped the smirk right off Biff's face.

For Black Death "Creode," Key learned over the millennia, it was its button. The creature, as powerful as it was, despised the name for it bore so many stereotypes. Throughout print, the name was associated with insignificant hearsay, lies and conjectures, conjured as a drawing of a slender-looking silhouette which possessed no gender, an advisory being completely void of the "be" in *being*, a stick figure that lacked any detail whatsoever, no background, no origin story, nothing more than an ink stain standing in the shadows of legends. Yet, the imposter sitting before Key happened to be one of the deadliest creatures to ever share the same air as him.

Biff shrugged off the comment and said freely, "I'm open for suggestions."

Not at all interested in giving Black Death any suggestions, Key watched Biff closely and waited for the perfect opportunity to make his final move.

"However," Biff said, "this story isn't about me, Thius, nor is it about Drenelle. Don't you think people would like to know what's it like living the shadow of such powerful entities? Me, personally, I'd think people were more inclined to hear your Mommy and *Daddy* issues than opposed to—you know—the misguided host of a nuclear kid in embryo."

Biff was right to the fullest extent, Key understood. Drenelle's story was one worth telling—like the real Biff, it was a comeback story, more or less. However, he was weighed down by insecurity, as well as the notion that human beings—the modern human being that is—as artificial as they might sound on paper or appear at times with their techno-crafted judgments and hacked brains, wouldn't find any relevance or similarities in the story of an Individual who was forged by the hand of a blood god. Even though his flesh was no different than their flesh, his blood was not of this world.

Key envisioned himself pulling back those curtains and walking on stage and telling his story to that world beyond the lens of the camera.

What would they think of me?

Biff said over Key's thought, "It's just too bad you skipped the one gene that would've ultimately saved you from your own demise."

"And what's that?" asked Key.

"Immunity," Biff said.

Not at all shocked by the comment, he glanced down at his hand on the armrest and witnessed a couple of fleas biting at his flesh.

"Wrong again," Key said with a checkmate-type victory. "You think I didn't know your ass would show up here? Little do you know we now have a vaccine to stop the spread of your disease. It looks like we both wound up on the wrong side of the deal. . . ."

Key moved his eyes upward at Biff, who was sitting across from him. Millions of fleas were pouring from each one of Biff's orifices on his face, most of those fleas coming from his gaping mouth, as well as the piece of torn flesh peeling along the side of his neck, revealing the veiny, plated blackness underneath.

Key nodded at the place on Biff's neck.

"Check yourself, *Creode*," he said. "You peeling, boy."

While Biff was adjusting himself, Key reached below the desk and hit a dime sized "Red Button" located underneath the table.

Once Key pressed the button, a bookshelf along the side of the wall slid open, revealing a dark chamber.

Out of the darkness, a werewolf snake darted from the room and charged directly at Biff.

With its mouth open and its dripping-wet fangs ready to dig into Biff's body, the werewolf snake leaped at Biff. At the last second, Biff threw up his arm and held it as straight and stiff as a sword and while the werewolf snake was in midair, stabbed the werewolf snake in the head with the stinger protruding from his index finger. With its slack mouth hanging open, the werewolf snake slid from the stinger and dropped dead to the floor.

Biff turned to Key and asked, "Anymore tricks up your sleeve?"

The sight of the dead werewolf snake caused Key to tremble with rage. The walls all around him started to drip with blood. Blood seeped from the molding, past the corners of the ceiling, down all four walls, soaking them with blood.

As the blood flooded into the office, the beads of sweat along his skin turned to blood. Like the walls, eventually, Key's entire body was covered in thick, rich blood.

In return, Biff used the sharp stinger to slit open the skin along his forehead. He ran the stinger down his entire face and peeled away the skin suit that Black Death was wearing.

As the two squared off against one another, Key pulled yet another trick out of his sleeve. He summoned the great serpent. Sheik burst through the floor below, causing Key's desk to explode with tiny fragments of wood.

With its fangs exposed, the massive serpent let out a sharp hiss right before it struck at Black Death. . .

"BREAK A LEG"

THE chaos lasted for only a few seconds before falling to silence.

The door swung open.

Key exited from the office as victor.

He gathered himself by adjusting the oversized shoulder pads of his suit and made sure he looked presentable for the show. He stopped next to a reflection on a massive clock, which read "11:53 PM." Using the reflection, he wiped a couple of smears of blood from the corners of his face. He resorted to licking his fingers and using the saliva to wipe away tougher spots where the blood was caked on his skin. He checked the ticker at the end of the hallway, which read the time counting down to the airing of the show. The time read "6" minutes and "37" seconds.

As Key made his way toward the main stage, many of the crewmembers were scurrying around backstage. Among the crew was a disturbed Stat, who immediately tracked down Key.

"Did you just feel that?" asked Key, who was calmer than Stat expected him to look after the recent rumble.

"No," Key said nonchalantly.

"It must've been an earthquake."

"Well," Key said, grabbing Stat by the shoulder, "it's nothing we haven't experienced before, am I right?"

"Are you okay?"

"Do I not look okay?"

"Nobody can track down Biff. . . " Stat paused, ". . . did Ruby not tell you?"

"Of course," Key said. "There's been a slight change in plans. I'm going to be taking over for Biff."

"You are? When did you decide this?"

"Just now," he said, again remaining nonchalant despite having only six minutes, going on five, to prepare before the show began.

Stat looked into Key's eyes and saw nothing behind them.

As the fear crept in, Stat backpedaled from Key and trailed off, "I'll catch up with you later."

Key left Stat and made his way to the curtains but was stopped by Ruby, who appeared way more uptight than Stat.

"I can't find Biff anywhere—"

"—Don't worry, Ruby," Key said over Ruby, as he adjusted the jacket's collar. "I'm going to take Biff's spot—"

"—But what about the promo—"

"—The show must go on, Ruby," Key said, putting Ruby in her place.

Ruby stared at Key's face, studying it.

Key acknowledged the strange expression on her face.

"Is there a problem?" asked Key.

With her eyes widening, Ruby reached forward and grabbed a black speck of what she assumed was an insect on the side of Key's chin.

"There," she said, smothering the tiny insect between her fingertips. "Got it."

"What was it?"

"A flea, I think."

"Thanks," Key said and made his way to the curtains.

Ruby said from behind, "Break a leg."

"THE DENOUEMENT/ 'GET DOWN WITH THE DARKNESS!'"

KEY pulled out a pack of Coffin Nails from the breast pocket of the jacket. He lit one up; and as he was passing a crewmember, who happened to be a middle-aged man from the Lighting Department, he took a drag and blew a cloud a smoke in the man's direction. He walked right through the cloud of smoke, breathed in the smoke, and took a couple of steps forward before stopping dead in his tracks. He rotated around and faced Key, who, like Ruby before, was studying his face. All of a sudden, the middle-aged man barked.

Then, as though his brain was on autopilot, the man walked away.

Amazed, Key glanced down at the cigarette in his hand.

"Nice trick, Thius," he said and continued walking toward the main stage.

He arrived at the red curtains surrounding the stage; and just as he was about to step through the slit in the curtains, he heard the sound of a *squeak* below him. A rat crawled between his feet, causing him to take a step back. The rat acknowledged Key's interest. What stood out were the eyes of the rat. They were cloudy and gray, familiar.

Without hesitating, Key lifted up his foot and stomped on the rat, causing the rat to let out a high-pitch *screech*. He removed his foot from the bloody squashed rat, whose entrails were lying on the floor, took yet another drag from the Coffin Nail, and dropped it to the floor.

He meticulously smothered the butt with the sole of his purple wing-capped shoe and more energetically walked through the curtains. He took his position at the center stage. To his left suspended a countdown ticker, which read "10" seconds to airtime. To his right dozens of actors and actresses were seated in a raised booth, waiting to take the upcoming calls from viewers, as well as listeners from around the country.

During those final remaining seconds, a couple of makeup artists patted down Key's face with cotton pads, preparing his face for the camera.

The cameraman held up five fingers, representing one second for each finger. By the time he was down to three fingers, the overhead lights came on and shined down on Key.

Two fingers.

One finger. . .

"GOD SAVE(D) THE PIG(S)"
(FOUR DAYS LATER)

DRENELLE lost count of the number of "Mystery" billboards that she passed about forty-something miles after she crossed the state line of Arizona. Each one of the billboards, as enticing as they were whenever they rode past them along stretches of vast, empty desert, had a hoax-like vibe to them based on the goofy font, the S in the word *Mystery* spelled in the serpentine-pattern of a snake. Each one would provoke certain enticements like "You have to sssee it to the believe it!" or "Find out the myssstery behind The Mystery!" or "What is The Mystery?" She pointed out the upcoming sign on the side of the highway to the rescued pig named Runt, who was sitting in the passenger seat of the beat-up powder blue Grand Caravan.

After what was perhaps the sixth or seventh billboard, Drenelle was left with no other choice than to fall for the possible gimmick and make the detour to Interstate 10 where the great "Mystery" would be revealed to weary travelers. Feeling the hype of The Mystery, Drenelle spent the past thirty minutes of the detour making guesses as to what they were about to witness. Runt sat there and listened to Drenelle rattle off guesses, each one sharing a common theme of extraterrestrial life forms. For sure, she thought it was an alien or some kind of alien artifact. After all, the so-called Mystery was located in the small desolate town of Sopalm, Arizona; and once she made her way into the town, which was known as "Da Palms" by locals, her deepest suspicious started to come true. Main Street, or "Mystery Way," as the mock street sign read, was literally about the length of two blocks. Drenelle spotted only few businesses, one being a small 1960's style diner called Annie's, a bar called The Watering Hole where outside perched three cartoon-like blow-up dolls of bright green colored aliens, as well as silver saucer-shaped toys of UFOs hanging from the windows, a corner building with the sign "Kross Real Estate," which, to Drenelle, was strange considering the population of the town of Sopalm must've been under a hundred, then, a boutique-sized town hall which shared the same building as the police and mayor.

Driving more cautiously, Drenelle passed more signs with large arrows pointing her the way to the great Mystery.

"I have to say, Runt," she said, more doubtfully, "I'm a little nervous."

Finally, Drenelle and Runt arrived at a gift shop, as well as a museum, where a large yellow sign with red lettering read "Mystery Inside!"

Drenelle pulled up to the roadside attraction. The sight of the parking lot being half-full relieved Drenelle.

After parking, Drenelle used a leash to walk Runt to the front of the gift shop. The sign on the door read, "No dogs allowed."

"I think we good, Runt," she said to Drenelle. "You ain't a dog, is you?"

Drenelle and Runt walked into the gift shop. Behind the counter was a slack jawed man who was wearing glasses and had what Drenelle referred to the classic "eye problem." Drenelle immediately recognized the purple "Washington 2020" T-shirt with the sticker "I Voted." On the TV above the counter displayed the results of yesterday's election, which Avanti Washington won by a landslide. The clip showed last night's highlights of Washington's victory speech.

In the back of the shop hung the sign "The Mystery is Here!" along the top of the black curtains. Giant arrows were pointing to the curtains. On the way to the attraction, Drenelle couldn't help but look around the shop. She didn't notice one single shopper in the vicinity. Except for that strange clerk sitting behind the front checkout counter, she didn't see anybody for that matter. No shoppers. No *weary* travelers. She told herself that maybe they, too, wanted to see what the mystery was about and that they were already inside the attraction, taking selfies and posting and doing whatever trend people did these days. Honestly, she didn't know what to think of the atmosphere for it felt as if she was in a different reality and everything around her was nothing more than props. More mindful of her surroundings, she reached the front of the black glittered covered curtains where yet another man was standing behind a podium. As with the clerk, he was wearing a purple "Washington" T-shirt. The features on his face appeared like abstract art. His bird-like nose didn't fit properly and was way too big for his face; one eye was bigger than the other; his eyes long and saggy and hung like damp towels along the side of his shrunken head. The man, whose name was Braille, glanced down at the pig on the leash.

Lethargically, he looked back up at Drenelle.

"Five dollars," he said in a child-like voice.

"You take credit cards?"

The man, Braille, looked confused by Drenelle's question as if, somehow, he didn't how to respond to the question.

Drenelle awkwardly smiled and dug her hand into the red leather fanny pack worn around her waist. She pulled out a crinkly five-dollar bill and handed it to Braille, who, in return, handed Drenelle a ticket, which looked more like a bookmark with the words "*Mysterious World*."

"Enjoy the mystery," Braille said to Drenelle.

After giving a nod of thanks to Braille, Drenelle stepped through the curtains and entered a dark and narrow corridor, which was covered in neon-colored snake tracks along the walls and ceiling.

She walked to a sign that explained the discovery of "The Mystery." Benjamin Winslow Nahum had discovered "The Mystery" inside an abandoned mineshaft. Locals who knew Benjamin called him "Cannon," because he was said to have an "explosive personality." Legend said that Cannon went mad and wound up in a mental institution and blamed his mental decline on spending years trying to solve the origins of The Mystery.

Intrigued to uncover the mystery surrounding The Mystery, Drenelle and her pig, Runt, continued down the corridor until they reached an exhibit hall basking with black lights. Inside the hall were artifacts that were collected from a place called the "Nether Realm."

The artifacts included misshaped skulls caused by mutation, shrunken heads, a special sparkling log of driftwood, which was taken from Resurrection River, as well as volcanic glass-like rock known to foresee one's fate.

Drenelle and Runt left the hall and walked down yet another corridor covered in snake tracks. Not once seeing another visitor or traveler in sight, they followed the dimly lit corridor, which zigzagged into the main attraction, "The Mystery of the Mysterious World." Those snake tracks led up to the unveiling of The Mystery, which was lit up by a bright yellow spotlight.

Displayed inside a glass enclosure was the great "Sheik," which was a giant mummified snake. The snake was three times the size of an anaconda and said to have been a great "king" who had slithered its way from "The Void." According to the engraved description along a gold plate, the serpent, Sheik, was discovered by the artist, Benjamin Winslow Nahum, inside a mineshaft. The artist, Cannon, also discovered over a dozen of hatched eggs, each broken, cracked, and chipped shells being roughly the size of footballs, which were displayed on a bed of wheat straw in a glass case next to Sheik. After reading up on this "Sheik" character and how this so called "Cannon" fellow believed it had escaped from the Nether Realm, Drenelle drew the conclusion that all of it was smoke and mirrors. One giant hoax.

A big fat waste of time. Simply fake. And the money she spent to see such bogus nonsense!

She was, in fact, duped. For a moment, she actually contemplated storming through the curtains, confronting Braille, and demanding her five dollars back.

Drenelle smacked her gums and glanced down at Runt.

"Come on, Runt," Drenelle said, putting aside her disappointment. "Let's get outta here. . . "

Once Drenelle left the gift shop with a bookmark as proof that she had braved the journey and finally, after miles of passing one enticing billboard after another, could say that she unveiled the great mystery along Interstate 10, she walked back to the van and laughed off the recent experience. She helped Runt into the passenger seat; and then, once Runt was all buckled up, she walked around the front of the Caravan and took her seat behind the steering wheel. First, she buckled her seatbelt, making sure she was secured in the driver's seat. Next, she rerouted the GPS along the dashboard to her final destination, which was mapped for Loganson, West Virginia. She wasn't entirely certain of what that next chapter of her life was going to look like, even though she carried around images in her head of the dangers—and adventures—that awaited her. Those images were only images, Drenelle knew, and dare she say, it was useless trying to understand the origin of their inception. And maybe, just maybe, that was the best part of life: not knowing how things came to be or where she was going to end up; and in essence, traveling into the dark without a flashlight. What better way to discover the light?

www.ingramcontent.com/pod-product-compliance
Lightning Source LLC
Chambersburg PA
CBHW081353050726
47504CB00015B/1896